FIRST AMONG EQUALS
&
CAT O' NINE TALES

Jeffrey Archer, whose novels and short stories include *Not a Penny More, Not a Penny Less*, *Kane and Abel* and *A Twist in the Tale*, has topped the bestseller lists around the world, with sales of over 250 million copies.

He is the only author ever to have been a number-one bestseller in fiction (fourteen times), short stories (four times) and non-fiction (*The Prison Diaries*).

The author is married with two sons, and lives in London and Cambridge.

www.jeffreyarcher.com

ALSO BY JEFFREY ARCHER

NOVELS

Not a Penny More, Not a Penny Less

Shall We Tell the President?   Kane and Abel

The Prodigal Daughter   A Matter of Honour

As the Crow Flies   Honour Among Thieves

The Fourth Estate   The Eleventh Commandment

Sons of Fortune   False Impression

The Gospel According to Judas
(with the assistance of Professor Francis J. Moloney)

A Prisoner of Birth   Paths of Glory

Only Time Will Tell

SHORT STORIES

A Quiver Full of Arrows   A Twist in the Tale

Twelve Red Herrings   The Collected Short Stories

To Cut a Long Story Short   And Thereby Hangs a Tale

PLAYS

Beyond Reasonable Doubt   Exclusive   The Accused

PRISON DIARIES

Volume One – Belmarsh: Hell

Volume Two – Wayland: Purgatory

Volume Three – North Sea Camp: Heaven

SCREENPLAYS

Mallory: Walking Off the Map   False Impression

JEFFREY ARCHER

FIRST AMONG EQUALS
&
CAT O' NINE TALES

PAN BOOKS

First Among Equals first published 1984 by Hodder and Stoughton
First published by Pan Books 2003
Cat O' Nine Tales first published 2007 by Macmillan
First published by Pan Books 2007

This omnibus first published 2011 by Pan Books
an imprint of Pan Macmillan, a division of Macmillan Publishers Limited
Pan Macmillan, 20 New Wharf Road, London N1 9RR
Basingstoke and Oxford
Associated companies throughout the world
www.panmacmillan.com

ISBN 978-0-330-54536-5

3 5 7 9 8 6 4 2

A CIP catalogue record for this book is available from
the British Library.

Printed and bound by CPI Group (UK) Ltd, Croydon, CR0 4YY

FIRST AMONG EQUALS

TO ALAN AND EDDIE

Raymond Gould

Simon Kerslake

Charles Seymour

Andrew Fraser

PROLOGUE

WEDNESDAY 10 APRIL 1931

If Charles Gurney Seymour had been born nine minutes earlier he would have become an earl, inherited a castle in Scotland, 22,000 acres in Somerset, and a thriving merchant bank in the City of London.

It was to be several years before young Charles worked out the full significance of coming second in life's first race.

His twin brother, Rupert, only just came through the ordeal, and in the years that followed contracted not only the usual childhood illnesses but managed to add scarlet fever, diphtheria and meningitis, causing his mother, Lady Seymour, to fear for his survival.

Charles, on the other hand, *was* a survivor, and had inherited enough Seymour ambition for both his brother and himself. Only a few years passed before those who came into contact with the brothers for the first time mistakenly assumed Charles was the heir to the earldom.

As the years passed Charles's father tried desperately to discover something at which Rupert might triumph over his brother – and failed. When they were eight the two boys were sent away to Summer Fields where generations of Seymours had been prepared for the rigours of Eton. During his first month at the Oxford prep school Charles was voted form captain and no one hindered his advance *en route* to becoming head boy at the age of twelve, by which time Rupert was looked upon as Seymour Minor. Both boys proceeded to Eton, where in their first half Charles beat

Rupert at every subject in the classroom, outrowed him on the river and nearly killed him in the boxing ring.

When in 1947 their grandfather, the thirteenth Earl of Bridgwater, finally expired, the sixteen-year-old Rupert became Viscount Seymour while Charles inherited a meaningless prefix.

The Hon Charles Seymour felt angry every time he heard his brother deferentially addressed by strangers as 'My Lord'.

At Eton, Charles continued to excel and ended his schooldays as President of Pop before being offered a place at Christ Church, Oxford, to read History. Rupert covered the same years without over-burdening the examiners, internal or external. At the age of eighteen the young viscount returned to the family estate in Somerset to pass the rest of his days as a landowner. No one destined to inherit 22,000 acres could be described as a farmer.

At Oxford, Charles, free of Rupert's shadow, progressed with the air of a man who found the university something of an anticlimax. He would spend his weekdays reading the history of his relations and the weekends at house parties or riding to hounds. As no one had suggested for one moment that Rupert should enter the world of high finance, it was assumed once Charles had left Oxford that he would succeed his father at Seymour's Bank: first as a director and then in time as its chairman: although it would be Rupert who would eventually inherit the family shareholding.

This 'best laid plan' changed, however, when one evening the Hon Charles Seymour was dragged off to the Oxford Union by a nubile undergraduate from Somerville, who demanded he should listen to the Eights Week motion, 'I would rather be a commoner than a lord'. The President of the Union had achieved the unique coup of having the motion proposed by the Prime Minister, Sir Winston Churchill.

Charles sat at the back of a hall packed with eager students mesmerised by the elder statesman's performance. Never once did he take his eyes off the great war leader during his witty and powerful speech, although what kept flashing across his mind was the realisation that, but for an accident of birth, Churchill would have been the ninth Duke of Marlborough. Here was a man who had dominated the world stage for three decades and then turned down every hereditary honour a grateful nation could offer, including the title of Duke of London.

From that moment Charles never allowed himself to be referred to as 'the Hon' again: his ultimate ambition was now above mere titles.

Another undergraduate who listened to Churchill that night was also considering his future. But he did not view proceedings crammed between his fellow students at the back of the crowded hall. The tall young man dressed in white tie and tails sat alone in a large chair on a raised platform, for such was his right as President of the Oxford Union.

Although Simon Kerslake *was* the first-born, he had otherwise few of Charles Seymour's advantages. The only son of a family solicitor, he had come to appreciate how much his father had denied himself to ensure that his son should remain at the local public school. Simon's father had died during his son's last year at Lancing College, leaving his widow a small annuity and a magnificent MacKinley grandfather clock. Simon's mother sold the clock a week after the funeral in order that her son could complete his final year with all the 'extras' the other boys took for granted. She also hoped that it would give Simon a better chance of going on to university.

From the first day he could walk Simon had always wanted to outdistance his rivals. The Americans would have described him as 'an achiever', while many of his contemporaries thought of him as pushy, or even arrogant, according to their aptitude for jealousy. During his last term at Lancing Simon was passed over for head of school and he still found himself unable to forgive the headmaster his lack of foresight. Later that year, some weeks after he had completed his S-levels and been interviewed by Magdalen, a circular letter informed him that he would not be offered a place at Oxford; it was a decision Simon was unwilling to accept.

In the same mail Durham University offered him a scholarship, which he rejected by return of post. "Future Prime Ministers aren't educated at Durham," he informed his mother.

"How about Cambridge?" she enquired, continuing to wipe the dishes.

"No political tradition," replied Simon.

"But if there is no chance of being offered a place at Oxford, surely –?"

"That's not what I said, Mother," replied the young man. "I shall be an undergraduate at Oxford by the first day of term."

After eighteen years of forty-yard goals Mrs Kerslake had learned to stop asking her son, "How will you manage that?"

Some fourteen days before the start of the Michaelmas Term at Oxford Simon booked himself into a small guest house just off the Iffley Road. On a trestle table in the corner of lodgings he intended to make permanent he wrote out a list of all the colleges, then divided them into five columns, planning to visit three each morning and three each afternoon until his question had been answered positively by a resident Tutor for Admissions: "Have you accepted any freshmen for this year who are now unable to take up their places?"

It was on the fourth afternoon, just as doubt was beginning to set in and Simon was wondering if after all he would have to travel to Cambridge the following week, that he received the first affirmative reply.

The Tutor for Admissions at Worcester College removed the glasses from the end of his nose and stared at the tall young man with a mop of dark hair falling over his forehead. Alan Brown was the twenty-second don Kerslake had visited in four days.

"Yes," he replied. "It so happens that a young man from Nottingham High School, who had been offered a place here, was tragically killed in a motor cycle accident last month."

"What course – what subject was he going to read?" Simon's words were unusually faltering. He prayed it wasn't Chemistry, Anthropology or Classics. Alan Brown flicked through a rotary index on his desk, obviously enjoying the little cross-examination. He peered at the card in front of him. "History," he announced.

Simon's heartbeat reached 120. "I just missed a place at Magdalen to read Politics, Philosophy and Economics," he said. "Would you consider me for the vacancy?"

The older man was unable to hide a smile. He had never in twenty-four years come across such a request.

"Full name?" he said, replacing his glasses as if the serious business of the meeting had now begun.

"Simon John Kerslake."

Dr Brown picked up the telephone by his side and dialled a number. "Nigel?" he said. "It's Alan Brown here. Did you ever consider offering a man called Kerslake a place at Magdalen?"

Mrs Kerslake was not surprised when her son went on to be President of the Oxford Union. After all, she teased, wasn't it just another stepping stone on the path to Prime Minister – Gladstone, Asquith . . . Kerslake?

Ray Gould was born in a tiny, windowless room above his father's butcher's shop in Leeds. For the first nine years of his life he shared that room with his ailing grandmother until she died at the age of sixty-one.

Ray's close proximity to the old woman who had lost her husband in the Great War at first appeared romantic to him. He would listen enraptured as she told him stories of her hero husband in his smart khaki uniform – a uniform now folded neatly in her bottom drawer, but still displayed in the fading sepia photograph at the side of her bed. Soon, however, his grandmother's stories filled Ray with sadness, as he became aware that she had been a widow for nearly thirty years. Finally she seemed a tragic figure as he realised how little she had experienced of the world beyond that cramped room in which she was surrounded by all her possessions and a yellowed envelope containing 500 irredeemable war bonds.

There had been no purpose in Ray's grandmother making a will, for all he inherited was the room. Overnight it became his study – full of ever-changing library and school books, the former often returned late, using up Ray's meagre pocket money in fines. But as each school report was brought home it became increasingly apparent to Ray's father that he would not be extending the sign above the butcher's shop to proclaim 'Gould and Son'.

Shortly after his eleventh birthday Ray won the top scholarship to Roundhay School. Wearing his first pair of long trousers – turned up several inches by his mother – and hornrimmed spectacles that didn't quite fit, he set off for the opening day at his new school. Ray's mother hoped there were other boys as thin and spotty as her son, and that his wavy red hair would not cause him to be continually teased.

By the end of his first term Ray was surprised to find he was far ahead of his classmates, so far in fact that the headmaster considered it prudent to put him up a form – "to stretch the lad a little", as he explained to Ray's parents.

By the end of that year, one spent mainly in the classroom, Ray managed to come third in the form, and top in Latin and English. Only when it came to selecting teams for any sport did Ray find he came bottom in anything. However brilliant his mind might have been, it never seemed to co-ordinate with his body. His single greatest academic achievement during the year, though, was to be the youngest winner of the prize essay competition in the school's history.

Each year the winner of the essay was required to read his entry to the assembled pupils and parents on Speech Day. Even before he handed in his entry Ray rehearsed his efforts out loud several times in the privacy of his study-bedroom, fearing he would not be properly prepared if he waited until the winner was announced.

Ray's form master had told all his pupils that the subject of the essay could be of their own choosing, but that they should try to recall some experience that had been unique to them. Thirty-seven entries arrived on his desk by nine o'clock on the closing date six weeks later. After reading Ray's account of his grandmother's life in the little room above the butcher's shop the form master had no inclination to pick up another script. When he had dutifully struggled through the remainder he did not hesitate in recommending Gould's essay for the prize. The only reservation, he admitted to its author, was the choice of title. Ray thanked him for the advice but the title remained intact.

On the morning of Speech Day the school hall was packed with 700 pupils and their parents. After the headmaster had delivered his speech and the applause had died down, he announced, "I shall now call upon the winner of the prize essay competition to deliver his entry: Ray Gould."

Ray left his place in the hall and marched confidently up on to the stage. He stared down at the 2,000 expectant faces but showed no sign of apprehension, partly because he found it difficult to see beyond the third row. When he announced the title of his essay some of the younger children began to snigger, causing Ray to stumble through his first few lines. But by the time he had reached the last page the packed hall was still, and after he had completed the final paragraph he received the first standing ovation of his career.

Twelve-year-old Ray Gould left the stage to rejoin his parents in the body of the hall. His mother's head was bowed but he could still see tears trickling down her cheeks. His father was trying not to look too proud. Even when Ray was seated the applause continued, so he too lowered his head to stare at the title of his prize-winning essay: 'The first changes I will make when I become Prime Minister'.

Andrew Fraser attended his first political meeting in a pram. True, he was left in the corridor while his parents sat on the stage inside another draughty hall, but he quickly learned that applause signalled his mother would soon be returning. What Andrew did not know was that his father, who had made his name as Scotland's finest scrum-half since the Great War, had delivered yet another speech to the citizens of Edinburgh Carlton in his efforts to capture a marginal seat on the City Council. At that time few believed Duncan Fraser was more than a rugby hero, and consequently he failed to win the seat for the Conservatives, if only by a few hundred votes. Three years later Andrew, a sturdy four-year-old, was allowed to sit at the back of several sparsely filled halls as once again he and his mother trailed round the city to support their candidate. This time Duncan Fraser's speeches were almost as impressive as his long pass, and he won his place on the City Council by 207 votes.

Hard work and consistent results on behalf of his constituents ensured that the marginal seat remained in the hands of Councillor Fraser for the next nine years. By the age of thirteen, Andrew, a stocky wee lad with straight black hair and a grin that no one seemed to be able to remove from his face, had learned enough about local politics to help his father organise a fifth campaign, by which time neither party considered Edinburgh Carlton a marginal seat.

At the Edinburgh Academy it came as no surprise to his fellow pupils that Andrew was chosen to captain the school debating society; however, they were impressed when under his leadership the team went on to win the Scottish Schools debating trophy. Although Andrew was destined to be no taller than five-foot-nine it was also widely accepted that he was the most complete scrum-half the Academy had produced since his father had captained the school side in 1919.

On matriculating from the Academy Andrew took up a place at Edinburgh University to read Politics, and by his third year he had been elected President of the Union and captain of rugby.

When Duncan Fraser became Lord Provost of Edinburgh he made one of his rare visits to London, to receive a knighthood from the Queen. Andrew had just completed his final exams and, along with his mother, attended the investiture at Buckingham Palace. After the ceremony Sir Duncan travelled on to the House of Commons to fulfil an engagement with his local member, Ainslie Munro. Over lunch Munro informed Sir Duncan that he had contested the Edinburgh Carlton seat for the last time, so they had better start looking for a new candidate. Sir Duncan's eyes lit up as he savoured the thought of his son succeeding Munro as his Member of Parliament.

After Andrew had been awarded an honours degree at Edinburgh, he remained at the university to complete a thesis entitled 'The history of the Conservative party in Scotland'. He planned to wait for his father to complete the statutory three years as Lord Provost before he informed him of the most significant outcome the research for his doctorate had produced. But when Ainslie Munro announced officially that he would not be contesting the next election Andrew knew he could no longer hide his true feelings if he wanted to be considered for the seat.

'Like father, like son,' read the headline in the centre-page of the *Edinburgh Evening News*, who considered that Andrew Fraser was the obvious candidate if the Conservatives hoped to hold on to the marginal seat. Sir Duncan, fearing the local burghers would consider Andrew too young, reminded them at the first selection meeting that eight Scots had been Prime Ministers and every one had been in the House before the age of thirty. He was pleased to find members nodding their agreement. When Sir Duncan returned home that night he phoned his son and suggested that they should have lunch at the New Club the following day to discuss a plan of campaign.

"Think of it," said Sir Duncan, after he had ordered a second whisky. "Father and son representing the same constituency. It will be a great day for the Edinburgh Conservative party."

"Not to mention the Labour party," said Andrew, looking his father in the eye.

"I am not sure I take your meaning," said the Lord Provost.

"Precisely that, Father. I do not intend to contest the seat as a Conservative. I hope to be selected as the Labour candidate – if they'll adopt me."

Sir Duncan looked disbelieving. "But you've been a Conservative all your life," he declared, his voice rising with every word.

"No, Father," replied Andrew quietly. "It's you who have been a Conservative all my life."

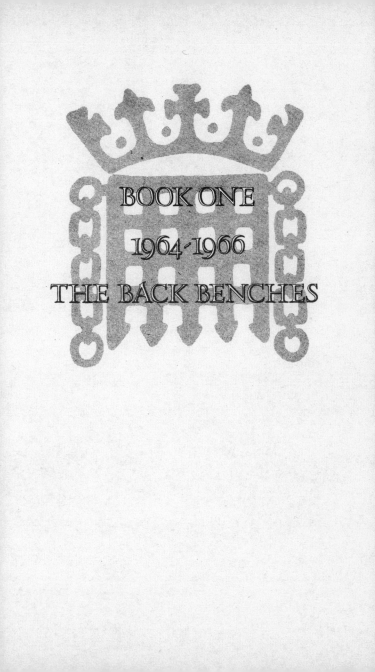

BOOK ONE

1964-1966

THE BACK BENCHES

CHAPTER ONE

THURSDAY 10 DECEMBER 1964

Mr Speaker rose and surveyed the Commons. He tugged at his long black silk gown, then nervously tweaked the full-bottomed wig that covered his balding head. The House had almost got out of control during a particularly rowdy session of Prime Minister's questions, and he was delighted to see the clock reach three-thirty. Time to pass on to the next business of the day.

He stood shifting from foot to foot waiting for the 500-odd members present to settle down before he intoned solemnly, "Members desiring to take the oath." The packed assembly switched its gaze from the Speaker to the far end of the Chamber, like a crowd watching a tennis match. There, standing at the bar of the Commons, was the victor of the first by-election since the Labour party had taken office some two months before.

The new member, flanked by his proposer and seconder, took four paces forward. Like well-drilled guardsmen, they stopped and bowed. The stranger stood at six-foot-four. He looked like a man born with the Tory party in mind, his patrician head set on an aristocratic frame, a mane of fair hair combed meticulously into place. Dressed in a dark grey, double-breasted suit and wearing a Guards' tie of maroon and blue, he advanced once again towards the long table that stood in front of the Speaker's chair between the two front benches which faced each other a mere sword's length apart.

Leaving his sponsors in his wake, he passed down the Government side, stepping over the legs of the Prime

Minister and Foreign Secretary before being handed the oath by the Clerk of the House.

He held the little card in his right hand and pronounced the words as firmly as if they had been his marriage vows.

"I, Charles Seymour, do swear that I will be faithful, and bear true allegiance to Her Majesty Queen Elizabeth, her heirs and successors according to law, so help me God."

"Hear, hear," rose from his colleagues on the benches opposite as the new MP leaned over to subscribe the Test Roll, a parchment folded into book-shape. Charles was introduced to the Speaker by the Clerk. The new member then proceeded towards the chair where he stopped and bowed.

"Welcome to the House, Mr Seymour," said the Speaker, shaking his hand. "I hope you will serve this place for many years to come."

"Thank you, Mr Speaker," said Charles, and bowed for a final time before continuing on behind the Speaker's chair. He had carried out the little ceremony exactly as the Tory Chief Whip had rehearsed it with him in the long corridor outside his office.

Waiting for him behind the Speaker's chair and out of sight of the other members was the leader of the Opposition, Sir Alec Douglas-Home, who also shook him warmly by the hand.

"Congratulations on your splendid victory, Charles. I know you have a great deal to offer to our party and indeed your country."

"Thank you," replied the new MP, who after waiting for Sir Alec to return to take his place on the Opposition front bench made his way up the steps of the side gangway to find a place in the back row of the long green benches.

For the next two hours Charles Seymour followed the proceedings of the House with a mixture of awe and excitement. For the first time in his life he had found something that wasn't his by right or by effortless conquest. Glancing up at the Strangers' Gallery he saw his wife Fiona, his father the fourteenth Earl of Bridgwater and his brother, the Viscount Seymour, peering down at him with pride. Charles settled back on the first rung of the ladder. He smiled to himself: only six weeks ago he had feared it would be many more years before he could hope to take a seat in the House of Commons.

At the general election a mere two months before, Charles had contested a South Wales mining seat with an impregnable Labour majority. "Good for the experience, not to mention the soul," the vice-chairman in charge of candidates at Conservative Central Office had assured him. He had proved to be right on both counts, for Charles had relished the contest and brought the Labour majority down from 22,300 to 20,100. His wife had aptly described it as a 'dent', but it had turned out to be enough of a dent for the party to put Charles's name forward for the Sussex Downs seat when Sir Eric Koops had died of a heart attack only a few days after Parliament had assembled. Six weeks later Charles Seymour sat in the Commons with a 20,000 majority of his own.

Charles listened to one more speech before leaving the Chamber. He stood alone in the Members' Lobby not quite certain where to begin. Another young member strode purposefully towards him. "Allow me to introduce myself," the stranger said, sounding to Charles every bit like a fellow Conservative. "My name is Andrew Fraser. I'm the Labour member for Edinburgh Carlton and I was hoping you hadn't yet found yourself a pair." Charles admitted that so far he hadn't found much more than the Chamber. The Tory Chief Whip had already explained to him that most members paired with someone from the opposite party for voting purposes, and that it would be wise for him to select someone of his own age. When there was a debate on less crucial issues a two-line whip came into operation: pairing made it possible for members to miss the vote and return home to their wife and family before midnight. However, no member was allowed to miss the vote when there was a three-line whip.

"I'd be delighted to pair with you," continued Charles. "Am I expected to do anything official?"

"No," said Andrew, looking up at him. "I'll just drop you a line confirming the arrangement. If you'd be kind enough to reply letting me have all the phone numbers where you can be contacted we'll just take it from there. Any time you need to miss a vote just let me know."

"Sounds a sensible arrangement to me," said Charles as a rotund figure wearing a light grey three-piece suit, blue shirt and a pink-spotted bow tie trundled over towards them.

"Welcome to the club, Charles," said Alec Pimkin. "Care to join me for a drink in the smoking room and I'll brief you on how this bloody place works."

"Thank you," said Charles, relieved to see someone he knew. Andrew smiled when he heard Pimkin add, "It's just like being back at school, old chum," as the two Tories retreated in the direction of the smoking room. Andrew suspected that it wouldn't be long before Charles Seymour was showing his 'old school chum' just how the bloody place really worked.

Andrew also left the Members' Lobby but not in search of a drink. He had to attend a meeting of the Parliamentary Labour party at which the following week's business was due to be discussed. He hurried away.

Andrew had been duly selected as the Labour candidate for Edinburgh Carlton and had gone on to capture the seat from the Conservatives by a majority of 3,419 votes. Sir Duncan, having completed his term as Lord Provost, continued to represent the same seat on the City Council. In six weeks Andrew – the baby of the House – had quickly made a name for himself and many of the older members found it hard to believe that it was his first Parliament.

When Andrew arrived at the party meeting on the second floor of the Commons he found an empty seat near the back of the large committee room and settled down to listen to the Government Chief Whip go over the business for the following week. Once again it seemed to consist of nothing but three-line whips. He glanced down at the piece of paper in front of him. The debates scheduled for Tuesday, Wednesday and Thursday all had three thick lines drawn under them: only Monday and Friday had two-liners which at least after his agreement with Charles Seymour he could arrange to miss. The Labour party might have returned to power after thirteen years but, with a majority of only four and a full legislative programme, it was proving almost impossible for members to get to bed much before midnight during the week.

As the Chief Whip sat down the first person to jump to his feet was Tom Carson, the new member for Liverpool Dockside. He launched into a tirade of abuse against the Government, complaining that they were looking more like Tories every day. The under-the-breath remarks and coughing that continued during his speech showed how little support there was for his views. Tom Carson had also made a name for himself in a very short time, for he had openly attacked his own party from the first day he had arrived.

"Enfant terrible," muttered the man sitting on the right of Andrew.

"Those aren't the words I'd use to describe him," muttered Andrew. "Altogether too many letters." The man with wavy red hair smiled as they listened to Carson ranting on.

If Raymond Gould had acquired any reputation during those first six weeks it was as one of the party's intellectuals, and for that reason older members were immediately suspicious of him, although few doubted he would be among the first from the new intake to be promoted to the front bench. Not many of them had really got to know Raymond as the north-countryman appeared remarkably reserved for someone who had chosen a career in public life. But with a majority of over 10,000 in his Leeds constituency he looked destined for a long career.

Leeds North had chosen Raymond to be their candidate from a field of thirty-seven, when he showed himself to be so much better informed than a local trade-union official whom the press had tipped as favourite for the seat. Yorkshire folk like people who stay at home and Raymond had been quick to point out to the selection committee – in an exaggerated Yorkshire accent – that he had been educated at Roundhay School on the fringes of the constituency. But what really tipped the vote in his favour had been Raymond's refusal of an open scholarship to Cambridge. He had preferred to continue his education at Leeds University, he explained.

Raymond took a first-class honours degree in Law at

Leeds before moving to London to complete his studies for
the bar at Lincoln's Inn. At the end of his two-year course
Raymond joined a fashionable London chambers to become
a much sought-after junior counsel. From that moment he
rarely mentioned his family background to his carefully
cultivated circle of Home Counties friends, and those comrades who addressed him as Ray received a sharp 'Raymond'
for their familiarity.

When the last question had been asked, the party meeting
broke up, and Raymond and Andrew made their way out of
the committee room – Andrew for his tiny office on the
second floor to finish off the day's mail, Raymond to return to
the Chamber as he hoped to deliver his maiden speech that
day. He had waited patiently for the right moment to express
his views to the House on the subject of widows' pensions and
the redemption of war bonds, and the debate in progress on
the economy was an obvious opportunity. The Speaker had
dropped Raymond a note earlier in the day saying he
expected to call him some time that evening.

Raymond had spent many hours in the Chamber, carefully studying the techniques demanded by the House and
noting how they differed from those of the law courts. F. E.
Smith had been right in his assessment of his colleagues when
he had described the Commons as nothing more than a noisy
courtroom with over 600 jurors and absolutely no sign of a
judge. Raymond was dreading the ordeal of his maiden
speech; the dispassionate logic of his arguments had always
proved more appealing to judges than to juries.

As he approached the Chamber an attendant handed him
a note from his wife Joyce. She had just arrived at the
Commons and had been found a seat in the Strangers'
Gallery so that she could be present for his speech. After only
a cursory glance Raymond scrunched up the note, dropped it
into the nearest waste-paper basket and hurried on towards
the Chamber.

The door was held open for him by a Conservative member who was on his way out.

"Thank you," said Raymond. Simon Kerslake smiled
back, trying in vain to recall the man's name. Once Simon

was in the Members' Lobby he checked the message board to see if the light under his name was lit up. It wasn't, so he continued on through the swing doors to the right of the lobby on his way down past the cloisters to the Members' Car Park. Once he had found his car he headed off in the direction of St Mary's, Paddington, to pick up his wife. They had seen little of each other during Simon's first six weeks in Parliament which made the thought of tonight even more enjoyable. Simon couldn't see any easing of the pressure until there was another general election and one party had gained a sensible working majority. But what he feared most – having won his seat by the slimmest of margins – was that such a working majority would not include him and he might end up with one of the shortest political careers on record. After such a prolonged stretch of Tory rule the new Labour Government was looking fresh, idealistic and certain to increase their numbers whenever the Prime Minister chose to go to the country.

Once Simon had reached Hyde Park Corner he headed on up towards Marble Arch thinking back over how he had become a member. On leaving Oxford he had completed two years' national service with the Sussex Yeomanry, finishing his military days as a second lieutenant. After a short holiday he had joined the BBC as a general trainee. He spent five years moving from drama, to sport, to current affairs before being appointed a producer on 'Panorama'. During those early days in London he had rented a small flat in Earl's Court and continued his interest in politics by becoming a member of the Tory Bow Group. When he became the Group's secretary he helped to organise meetings, and had then progressed to writing pamphlets and speaking at weekend conferences before being invited to work at Central Office as personal assistant to the chairman during the 1959 election campaign.

Two years later Simon met Elizabeth Drummond when 'Panorama' carried out an investigation into the National Health Service and she had been invited to be a participant. Over drinks before the programme Elizabeth made it perfectly clear to Simon that she distrusted media men and detested politicians. They were married a year later. Elizabeth had since given birth to two sons, and with only a small break on each occasion she had continued her career as a doctor.

Simon had left the BBC somewhat abruptly when, in the summer of 1964, he had been offered the chance to defend the marginal constituency of Coventry Central. He held on to the seat at the general election by a majority of 918.

Simon drove up to the gates of St Mary's and checked his watch. He was a few minutes early. He pushed back the mop of brown hair from his forehead and thought about the evening ahead. He was taking Elizabeth out to celebrate their fourth wedding anniversary, and had prepared one or two surprises for her. Dinner at Mario & Franco, followed by dancing at the Establishment Club, and then home together for the first time in weeks.

"Um," he said, savouring the thought.

"Hi, stranger," said the lady who jumped in beside him and gave him a kiss. Simon stared at the woman with a perfect smile and long fair hair that turned up at the shoulder. He had stared at her when she had first arrived at the 'Panorama' studio that night nearly five years before and he had hardly stopped staring since.

He switched on the ignition. "Want to hear some good news?" he asked, and answered his own question before she could reply. "I'm paired for tonight. That means dinner at Mario & Franco, dancing at the Establishment, home and . . .'

"Do you want to hear the bad news?" asked Elizabeth, also not waiting for a reply. "There's a shortage of staff because of the flu epidemic. I have to be back on duty by ten o'clock."

Simon switched off the ignition. "Well, which would you prefer?" he asked. "Dinner, dancing or straight home?"

Elizabeth laughed. "We've got three hours," she said. "So we might even find time for dinner."

CHAPTER
TWO

Raymond Gould stared down at the invitation. He had never seen the inside of No. 10 Downing Street. During the last thirteen years few Socialists had. He passed the embossed card across the breakfast table to his wife.

"Should I accept or refuse, Ray?" she asked in her broad Yorkshire accent.

She was the only person who still called him Ray, and even her attempts at humour now annoyed him. The Greek tragedians had based their drama on 'the fatal flaw', and he had no doubt what his had been.

He had met Joyce at a dance given by the nurses of Leeds General Infirmary. He hadn't wanted to go but a second-year undergraduate friend from Roundhay convinced him it would make an amusing break. At school he had shown little interest in girls as his mother kept reminding him that there would be occasion enough for that sort of thing once he had taken his degree. By the time he graduated he felt certain that he was the only virgin left at the university.

He had ended up sitting on his own in the corner of a room decorated with wilting balloons and Day-glo orange crêpe paper. He sucked disconsolately at a shandy through a bent straw. Whenever his school friend turned round from the dance floor – each time with a different partner – Raymond would smile broadly back. With his National Health spectacles tucked away in an inside pocket, he couldn't always be certain he was smiling at the right person. He began contemplating at what hour he could possibly leave without having to admit the evening had been a total disaster. He wouldn't even have answered her question if it hadn't been for that familiar accent.

"You at the university as well?"

"As well as what?" he asked, without looking directly at her.

"As well as your friend," she said.

"Yes," he replied, looking up at a girl he guessed was about his age.

"I'm from Bradford."

"I'm from Leeds," he admitted, aware he was going redder by the second.

"My name is Joyce," she volunteered.

"Mine's Ray – Raymond," he said.

"Like to dance?"

He wanted to tell her that he had rarely been on a dance floor before in his life but he didn't have the courage. Like a puppet he found himself standing up and being guided by her towards the jivers. So much for his assumption that he was one of nature's leaders.

Once they were on the dance floor he looked at her properly for the first time. She wasn't half bad, any normal Yorkshire boy might have admitted. She was about five-foot-seven, and her auburn hair was tied up in a pony-tail, matching the dark brown eyes that had a little too much make-up round them. She wore pink lipstick, the same colour as her short skirt from which emerged two very attractive legs. They looked even more attractive when she twirled to the music of the four-piece student band. Raymond discovered that if he twirled Joyce very fast he could see the tops of her stockings, and he remained on the dance floor for longer than he would ever have thought possible. After the quartet had put their instruments away Joyce kissed him goodnight. He walked slowly back to his small room above the butcher's shop.

The following Sunday, in an attempt to gain the upper hand, he took Joyce rowing on the Aire, but his performance was no better than his dancing, and everything on the river overtook him including a hardy swimmer. He watched out of the side of his eyes for a mocking laugh but Joyce only smiled and chatted about missing Bradford and wanting to return home to nurse. After only a few weeks at university Raymond knew he wanted to get away from Leeds, but he didn't admit it to anyone. When he eventually returned the boat Joyce invited him back to her digs for tea. He went scarlet as they passed her landlady. Joyce hustled him up the worn stone staircase to her room.

Raymond sat on the end of the narrow bed while Joyce made two milkless mugs of tea. After they had both pretended to drink she sat beside him, her hands in her lap. He found himself listening intently to an ambulance siren as it faded away in the distance. She leaned over and kissed him, taking one of his hands and placing it on her knee.

She parted his lips and their tongues touched: he found it a peculiar sensation, an arousing one; his eyes remained closed as she gently led him through each new experience, until he was unable to stop himself committing what he felt sure his mother had once described as a mortal sin.

"It will be easier next time," she said shyly, manoeuvring herself from the narrow bed to sort out the crumpled clothes spread across the floor. She was right: he wanted her again in less than an hour, and this time his eyes remained wide open.

It was another six months before Joyce talked about their future and by then Raymond was bored with her and had his sights set on a bright little mathematician in her final year. The mathematician hailed from Surrey.

Just at the time Raymond was summoning up enough courage to let her know the affair was over Joyce told him she was pregnant. His father would have taken a meat axe to him had he suggested an illegal abortion. His mother was only relieved that she was a Yorkshire girl; like the county cricket selection committee, Mrs Gould did not approve of outsiders.

Raymond and Joyce were married at St Mary's in Bradford during the long vacation. When the wedding photos were developed Raymond looked so distressed and Joyce so happy they resembled father and daughter rather than husband and wife. After a reception given at the church hall the newly-married couple travelled down to Dover to catch the night ferry. Their first night as Mr and Mrs Gould was a disaster. Raymond turned out to be a particularly bad sailor. Joyce only hoped that Paris would prove to be memorable – and it was. She had a miscarriage on the second night of their honeymoon.

"Probably caused by all the excitement," his mother said on their return. "Still, you can always have another, can't you? And this time folk won't be able to call it a little . . ." She checked herself.

Raymond showed no interest in having another. Ten years had passed since that memorable honeymoon; he had escaped to London and become a barrister, but had long since accepted that he was tethered to her for life. Although Joyce was only thirty-two she already needed to cover those once-slim legs that had first so attracted him. How could he be so punished for such a pathetic mistake? Raymond wanted to ask the gods. How mature he had thought he was: how immature he had turned out to be. Divorce made sense, but it would have meant the end of his political ambitions: Yorkshire folk would not have considered selecting a divorced man. To be fair, it hadn't all been a disaster: he had to admit that the locals adored her, and his parents seemed every bit as proud of Joyce as they did of their son. She mixed with the trade unionists and their frightful wives far better than he ever managed. He also had to acknowledge that Joyce had been a major factor in his winning the seat by over 10,000 votes. He wondered how she could sound so sincere the whole time: it never occurred to him that it was natural.

"Why don't you buy yourself a new dress for Downing Street?" Raymond said as they rose from the breakfast table. She smiled: he had not volunteered such a suggestion for as long as she could remember. Joyce had been left with no illusions about her husband and his feelings for her, but hoped that eventually he would realise she could help him achieve his unspoken ambition.

On the night of the reception at Downing Street Joyce made every effort to look her best. She had spent the morning at

Harvey Nichols searching for an outfit appropriate for the occasion, finally returning to a suit she had liked the moment she had walked in to the store. It was not the perfect fit but the sales assistant assured Joyce that "Modom looked quite sensational in it". She only hoped that Raymond's remarks would be half as flattering. By the time she reached home she realised she had nothing to match the unusual colour.

Raymond was late returning from the Commons and was pleased to find Joyce ready when he leaped out of the bath. He bit back a remark about the incongruity of her shoes and new suit. As they drove towards Westminster he rehearsed the names of every member of the Cabinet with her, making Joyce repeat them as if she were a child.

The air was cool and crisp that night so Raymond parked his Sunbeam in New Palace Yard and they strolled across Whitehall together to No. 10. A solitary policeman stood guard at the door. Seeing Raymond approach, the officer banged the brass knocker once and the door was opened for the young member and his wife.

Raymond and Joyce stood awkwardly in the hall as if they were waiting outside a headmaster's study. Eventually they were directed to the first floor. They walked slowly up the staircase, which turned out to be less grand than Raymond had anticipated, passing photographs of former Prime Ministers. "Too many Tories," muttered Raymond as he passed Chamberlain, Churchill, Eden, Macmillan and Home, with Attlee the only framed compensation.

At the top of the stairs stood Harold Wilson, pipe in mouth, waiting to welcome his guests. Raymond was about to introduce his wife when the Prime Minister said, "How are you, Joyce? I'm so glad you could make it."

"Make it? I've been looking forward to the occasion all week." Her frankness made Raymond wince; he failed to notice that it made Wilson chuckle.

Raymond chatted to the Prime Minister's wife about the difficulty of getting poetry published until she turned away to greet the next guest. He then moved off into the drawing-room and was soon talking to Cabinet ministers, trade union leaders and their wives, always keeping a wary eye on Joyce, who seemed engrossed in conversation with the General Secretary of the Trades Union Congress.

Raymond moved on to the American Ambassador, who was telling Andrew Fraser how much he had enjoyed the Edinburgh Festival that summer. Raymond envied Fraser his relaxed clubbable manner and had already worked out that the Scotsman would be a formidable rival among his contemporaries.

"Good evening, Raymond," said Andrew. "Do you know David Bruce?" he asked, as if they were old friends.

"No," Raymond replied, rubbing his palm on his trousers before shaking hands. "Good evening, Your Excellency," he said, glad to see Andrew slipping away. "I was interested to read Johnson's latest communiqué on Vietnam and I must confess the escalation . . ."

Andrew had spotted the Minister of State for Scotland arriving and went over to chat to him.

"How are you, Andrew?" Hugh McKenzie asked.

"Never better."

"And your father?"

"In great form."

"I'm sorry to hear that," said the minister, grinning. "He's giving me a lot of trouble over the Highlands and Islands Development Board."

"He's a sound chap basically," said Andrew, "even if his views are a little misguided." They both laughed as a slight, attractive woman with long brown hair came up to the minister's side. She wore a white silk blouse and a McKenzie tartan skirt.

"Do you know my daughter Alison?"

"No," Andrew said, holding out his hand. "I've not had that pleasure."

"I know who you are," she said, in a slight lowland accent, her eyes flashing. "Andrew Fraser, the man who makes Campbells look trustworthy. The Tories' secret mole."

"It can't be much of a secret if the Scottish Office know about it," said Andrew.

A waiter, wearing the smartest dinner-jacket in the room,

approached them carrying a silver tray of thinly-cut sand-wiches.

"Would you care for a smoked salmon sandwich?" Alison asked mockingly.

"No, thank you. I gave them up with my Tory back-ground. But beware – if you eat too many you won't appreci-ate your dinner tonight."

"I wasn't thinking of having dinner."

"Oh, I thought you might enjoy a bite at Sigie's," teased Andrew.

Alison hesitated, then said, "It'll be the first time anyone's picked me up at No. 10."

"I hate to break with tradition," said Andrew. "But why don't I book a table for eight?"

"Is Sigie's one of your aristocratic haunts?"

"Good heavens no, it's far too good for that lot. Why don't we leave in about fifteen minutes? I must have a word with one or two people first."

"I'll bet." She grinned as she watched Fraser comb the room. His years as a Tory party fellow-traveller had taught Andrew all he needed to know about how to make the best use of a cocktail party. His trade union colleagues would never understand that it was not in pursuit of endless smoked salmon sandwiches drowned by whisky. When he arrived back at Alison McKenzie's side she was chatting to Raymond Gould about Johnson's landslide victory at the polls.

"Are you trying to pick up my date?" asked Andrew.

Raymond laughed nervously and pushed his spectacles back up his nose. A moment later Andrew was guiding Alison towards the door to say their farewells, and Raymond watching them, wondered if he would ever learn to be that relaxed. He looked around for Joyce: it might be wise not to be the last to leave.

Andrew was ushered discreetly to a corner table at Sigie's Club and it became quickly evident to Alison that he had been there several times before. The waiters ran around him as if he were a Tory Cabinet minister, and she had to admit to herself that she enjoyed the experience. After an excellent dinner of roast beef that wasn't burnt and a *crème brûlée* that was they strolled over to Annabel's where they danced until the early morning. Andrew drove Alison back to her Chelsea flat a little after two a.m.

"Care for a nightcap?" she asked casually.

"Daren't," he replied. "I'm making my maiden speech tomorrow."

"So this maiden is to be rejected," she said to his retreating back.

The House of Commons was well attended at five o'clock the following afternoon when Andrew rose to address his fellow members. The Speaker had allowed him to follow the front-bench contributions, an honour Andrew would not be granted again for some considerable time. His father and mother looked down over the railings from the Strangers' Gallery as he informed the commoners that the Lord Provost of Edinburgh had spent a lifetime teaching him all he knew about the constituency he was now proud to represent. The Labour party chuckled at the Opposition's obvious discomfort, but they abided by tradition and made no interruption during a maiden speech.

Andrew had chosen as his subject the question of whether Scotland should remain part of the United Kingdom despite the recent oil discoveries. He delivered a well-argued case, assuring members that he saw no future for his country as a tiny independent state. His rhetoric, and his relaxed turn of phrase, had members laughing on both sides of the House. When he came to the end of his argument, never having once referred to a note, he sat down to loud cheers from his own benches and generous acknowledgement from the Tory side. In his moment of glory he glanced up towards the Strangers' Gallery. His father was leaning forward, following every word. To his surprise sitting in front of his mother on the benches reserved for distinguished visitors was Alison McKenzie, her arms folded on the balcony. He smiled.

Andrew's success was considerably enhanced when later that afternoon another member from the Labour benches rose to address the House for the first time. Tom Carson cared nothing for convention and even less for keeping to tradition and made no attempt to avoid controversy in his maiden speech. He began with an attack on what he described as "the Establishment conspiracy", pointing an accusing finger as much at the ministers on his own front bench as at those opposite him, describing them all as "puppets of the capitalist system".

Members present in the Chamber restrained themselves from interrupting the scowling Liverpudlian, but the Speaker stirred several times as the accusing finger appeared to cross his path as well. He was painfully aware that the member from Liverpool Dockside was going to cause all sorts of problems if this was the way he intended to conduct himself in the House.

When Andrew left the Chamber three speeches later he went to look for Alison, but she had already left; so he took the members' lift up to the Public Gallery and invited his parents to join him for tea in the Harcourt Rooms.

"The last time I had tea here was with Ainslie Munro . . ." Sir Duncan began.

"Then it may be a very long time before you're invited again," Andrew interrupted.

"That may depend on whom we select as Tory candidate to oppose you at the next election," retorted his father.

Several members from both sides of the House came up one by one to congratulate Andrew on his speech. He thanked them all individually but kept glancing hopefully over his father's shoulder; but Alison McKenzie did not appear.

After his parents had finally left to catch the last flight back to Edinburgh Andrew returned to the Chamber to hear Alison's father summing up the debate on behalf of the Government. The Minister of State described Andrew's contribution as one of the finest maiden speeches the House had heard in years. "Maiden it may have been but virginal it was not," concluded Hugh McKenzie.

Once the debate was over and the usual ten o'clock division had been declared by the tellers Andrew left the Chamber. One final vote on a prayer detained members for a further forty-five minutes and Andrew found the tea room – the traditional haunt of the Labour party – as crowded as it had been earlier in the afternoon.

Members jostled for the remains of unappetising-looking lettuce leaves that any self-respecting rabbit would have rejected accompanied by blobs of plastic-covered sweating cheese, described optimistically on the bill board as salad. Andrew contented himself with a cup of Nescafé.

Raymond Gould sat alone, slumped in an armchair in the far corner of the tea room, apparently engrossed in a week-old copy of the *New Statesman*. He stared impassively as several of his colleagues went over to Andrew to congratulate him. His own maiden speech the previous week had not been as well received and he knew it. He believed just as passionately about war widows' pensions as Andrew did about the future of Scotland but reading from a prepared manuscript he had been unable to make members hang on his every word. He consoled himself with the thought that Andrew would have to choose the subject for his next speech very carefully as the Opposition would no longer treat him with kid gloves.

Andrew was not concerning himself with such thoughts as he slipped into one of the many internal telephone booths and after checking in his diary dialled a London number. Alison was at home, washing her hair.

"Will it be dry by the time I arrive?"

"It's very long," she reminded him.

"Then I'll have to drive slowly."

When Andrew appeared on the Chelsea doorstep he was greeted by Alison in a housecoat, her newly-dry hair falling down well below shoulder level.

"The victor come to claim his spoils?"

"No, only last night's coffee," he said.

"But won't that keep you awake?"

"I certainly hope so."

By the time Andrew left Alison's home at eight the next morning he had already decided he wanted to see a lot more of Hugh McKenzie's daughter. He returned to his own flat in

Cheyne Walk, showered and changed before making breakfast for himself and going over his mail. There were several
more messages of congratulations including one from the
Secretary of State for Scotland, while *The Times* and the
Guardian carried brief but favourable comments.

Before leaving for the Commons Andrew checked over an
amendment he wanted to move in committee that morning.
When he had reworded his efforts several times he picked up
his papers and headed off towards Westminster.

Arriving a little early for the ten-thirty committee meeting,
Andrew found time to collect his mail from the Members'
Post Office just off the Central Lobby. He set off, head
down, along the corridor towards the library, flicking
through the envelopes to see if he recognised any familiar
hand or official-looking missive that demanded to be opened
immediately.

As he turned the corner he was surprised to find the House
ticker-tape machine surrounded by Conservative members,
including the man who had agreed to be his 'pair' for voting
purposes.

Andrew stared up at the tall figure of Charles Seymour,
who, although standing on the fringe of the crowd, still found
it possible to read the tapped-out message on the telex
machine.

"What's causing so much interest?" he asked, prodding
Seymour's elbow.

"Sir Alec has just announced the timetable that'll be
followed when we select the new Tory leader."

"We all await with baited breath," said Andrew.

"As well you might," said Charles, ignoring the sarcasm,
"since the next announcement will undoubtedly be his resignation. Then the real politics will begin."

"Be sure you back the winner," said Andrew, grinning.

Charles Seymour smiled knowingly but made no comment.

CHAPTER THREE

Charles Seymour drove his Daimler from the Commons to his father's bank in the City. He still thought of Seymour's of Cheapside as his father's bank although for two generations the family had been only minority shareholders, with Charles himself in possession of a mere two per cent of the stock. Nevertheless as his brother Rupert showed no desire in representing the family interests the two per cent guaranteed Charles a place on the board and an income sufficient to ensure that his paltry parliamentary salary of £1,750 a year was adequately supplemented.

From the day Charles had first taken his place on the board of Seymour's he had no doubt that the new chairman, Derek Spencer, considered him a dangerous rival. Spencer had lobbied to have Rupert replace his father on retirement and only because of Charles's insistence had Spencer failed to move the old earl to his way of thinking.

When Charles went on to take his seat in Parliament Spencer at once raised the problem of his burdensome responsibilities at the House preventing him from carrying out his day-to-day duties for the board. However, Charles was able to convince a majority of his fellow directors of the advantages of having someone on the board at Westminster, although he knew that would cease if he was ever invited to be a minister.

As Charles left the Daimler in Seymour's courtyard it amused him to consider that his parking space was worth twenty times the value of the car. The area at the front of Seymour's was a relic of his great-grandfather's day. The twelfth Earl of Bridgwater had insisted on an entrance large enough to allow a complete sweep for his coach and four. That conveyance had long disappeared, to be replaced by twelve car spaces for Seymour directors. The bank's new management-conscious chairman, despite all his grammar school virtues, had never suggested the land be used for any other purpose.

The young girl seated at the reception desk abruptly stopped polishing her nails in time to say "Good morning, Mr Charles," as he came through the revolving doors and disappeared into a waiting lift. A few moments later Charles was seated behind a desk in his small oak-panelled office, a clean white memo pad in front of him. He pressed a button on the intercom and told his secretary that he did not want to be disturbed during the next hour.

Sixty minutes later the white pad had twelve names pencilled on it, but ten already had lines drawn through them. Only the names of Reginald Maudling and Edward Heath remained.

Charles tore off the piece of paper and the indented sheet underneath and put them both through the shredder by the side of his desk. He tried to summon up some interest in the agenda for the bank's weekly board meeting; only one item, item seven, seemed to be of any importance. Just before eleven, he gathered up his papers and headed towards the boardroom. Most of his colleagues were already seated when Derek Spencer called item number one as the boardroom clock chimed the hour.

During the ensuing predictable discussion on bank rates, the movement in metal prices, Eurobonds and client investment policy Charles's mind kept wandering back to the forthcoming leadership election and the importance of backing the winner if he were to be quickly promoted from the back benches.

By the time they reached item seven on the agenda Charles had made up his mind. Derek Spencer opened a discussion on the proposed loans to Mexico and Poland, and most of the board members agreed with him that the bank should participate in one but not risk both.

Charles's thoughts, however, were not in Mexico City or Warsaw. They were far nearer home and when the chairman called for a vote, Charles didn't register.

"Mexico or Poland, Charles. Which of the two do you favour?"

"Heath," he replied.

"I beg your pardon," said Derek Spencer.

Charles snapped back from Westminster to Cheapside to find everyone around the boardroom table staring at him. With the air of a man who had been giving the matter considerable thought Charles said firmly, "Mexico", and added, "The great difference between the two countries can best be gauged by their attitudes to repayment. Mexico might not want to repay, but Poland won't be able to, so why not limit our risks and back Mexico? If it comes to litigation I'd prefer to be against someone who won't pay rather than someone who can't." The older members round the table nodded in agreement; the right son of Bridgwater was sitting on the board.

When the meeting was over Charles joined his colleagues for lunch in the directors' dining-room. On the walls hung two Hogarths, a Brueghel, a Goya and a Rembrandt that could distract even the most indulgent gourmet: just another reminder of his great-grandfather's ability to select winners. Charles did not wait to make a decision between the Cheddar and the Stilton as he wanted to be back in the Commons for question time.

On arrival at the House he immediately made his way to the smoking room, long regarded by the Tories as their preserve. There in the deep leather armchairs and cigar-laden atmosphere the talk was entirely of who would be Sir Alec's successor.

Charles could not avoid overhearing Pimkin's high-pitched voice. "As Edward Heath is Shadow Chancellor while we debate the Finance Bill on the floor of the House, it is he who is bound to be the centre of attention."

Later that afternoon Charles returned to the Commons Chamber. He wanted to observe Heath and his Shadow team deal with the Government's amendments one by one.

He was about to leave the Chamber when Raymond Gould rose to move an amendment. Charles listened with grudging admiration as Raymond's intellectual grasp and force of argument easily compensated for his lack of oratorical skill. Although Gould was a cut above the rest of his intake on the Labour benches he didn't frighten Charles. Twelve generations of shrewd business acumen had kept large parts of Leeds in the hands of the Bridgwater family without the likes of Raymond Gould even being aware of it.

Charles took supper in the Members' Dining-room that night and sat at the large table in the centre of the room frequented by Tory back-benchers. There was only one topic of conversation and as the same two names kept emerging it was obvious that it was going to be a very close run thing.

When Charles arrived back at his Eaton Square home after the ten o'clock division Fiona was already tucked up in bed reading Philip Larkin's *The Whitsun Weddings*.

"They let you out early tonight."

"Not too bad," said Charles, and began regaling her with how he had spent his day, before disappearing into the bathroom.

If Charles imagined he was cunning, his wife, Lady Fiona, only daughter of the Duke of Falkirk, was in a different league. She and Charles had been selected for each other at an early age and neither had questioned or doubted the wisdom of the choice. Although Charles had squired numerous girl-friends before their marriage in between he had always assumed he would return to Fiona. Charles's grandfather always maintained that the aristocracy was becoming far too lax and sentimental about marriage. "Women," he declared, "are for bearing children and ensuring a continuation of the male line." The old earl became even more staid in his convictions when he was made aware that Rupert showed little interest in the opposite sex, and was rarely to be found in the company of women. Fiona would never have dreamed of disagreeing with the old man to his face as she was determined that it would be a son of hers that would inherit the earldom. But despite enthusiastic and then contrived efforts Charles seemed unable to sire an heir. Fiona was later assured by a Harley Street physician that there was no reason *she* could not bear children. The specialist had suggested that perhaps her husband pay the clinic a visit. She shook her head, knowing Charles would dismiss such an idea out of hand, and never mentioned the subject to anyone again.

Fiona spent a considerable amount of her spare time in their Sussex Downs constituency furthering Charles's political career. She had learned to live with the fact that theirs was not destined to be a romantic marriage and resigned herself to its other advantages. Although many men confessed covertly and overtly that they found the tall elegant lady desirable she either ignored their overtures or pretended not to notice them.

By the time Charles returned from the bathroom in his blue silk pyjamas Fiona had formed a plan, but first she needed some questions answered.

"Whom do you favour?"

"I'd like Sir Alec to carry on: after all, the Homes have been friends of our two families for over 400 years."

"But that's a non-starter," said Fiona. "Everyone knows Alec is on the way out."

"I agree, and that's exactly why I spent the entire afternoon observing the worthwhile candidates."

"Did you come to any serious conclusions?" Fiona asked.

"Heath and Maudling are out on their own, though to be honest I've never had a conversation with either of them that lasted for more than five minutes."

"In that case we must turn a disadvantage into an advantage."

"What do you mean, old girl?" Charles asked as he climbed into bed beside his wife.

"Think back. When you were President of Pop at Eton, could you have put a name to any of the first-year boys?"

"Certainly not," said Charles.

"Exactly. And I'd be willing to bet that neither Heath nor Maudling could put a name to twenty of the new intake on the Tory benches."

"Where are you leading me, Lady Macbeth?"

"No bloody hands will be needed for this killing. Simply, having chosen your Duncan you volunteer to organise the new intake for him. If he becomes leader, he's bound to feel it would be appropriate to select one or two new faces for his team."

"You could be right."

"Well, let's sleep on it," said Fiona, turning out the light on her side of the bed.

Charles didn't sleep on it but lay restless most of the night turning over in his mind what she had said. When Fiona awoke the next morning she carried on the conversation as if there had been no break in between. "Do you have to be rushed into a decision?"

"No, but if I let it drift I could be accused of jumping on the bandwagon and then I would have lost my chance to be seen as a leader among the new intake."

"Better still," she continued, "before the man you choose announces he is a candidate, demand that he stand on behalf of the new members."

"Clever," said Charles.

"Whom have you decided on?"

"Heath," Charles replied without hesitation.

"I'll back your political judgement," said Fiona. "Just trust me when it comes to tactics. First, we compose a letter."

In dressing-gowns, on the floor at the end of the bed, the two elegant figures drafted and redrafted a note to Edward Heath. At nine-thirty it was finally composed and sent round by hand to his rooms in Albany.

The next morning Charles was invited to the small, bachelor flat for coffee. They talked for over an hour and later, as the two men stood below a Piper landscape in the drawing-room, the deal was struck.

Charles thought Sir Alec would announce his resignation in the late summer which would give him eight to ten weeks to carry out a campaign. Fiona typed out a list of all the new members and during the next eight weeks every one of them was invited to their Eaton Square flat for drinks. Fiona was subtle enough to see that members of the Lower House were outnumbered by other guests, often from the House of Lords. Heath managed to escape from his front-bench duties on the Finance Bill to spend at least an hour with the Seymours once a week. As the day of Sir Alec Douglas-Home's resignation drew nearer Charles realised the leadership result could be almost as important to him as it would be to Heath, but he also remained confident that he had carried out his plan in a subtle and discreet way. He would have been willing to place a wager that no one other than Edward Heath had worked out how deeply he was involved.

One man who attended the second of Fiona's soirées saw exactly what was going on. While many of the guests spent their time admiring the Seymour art collection Simon Kerslake kept a wary eye on his host and hostess. Kerslake was not convinced that Edward Heath would win the forthcoming election and felt confident that Reginald Maudling would turn out to be the party's natural choice. Maudling was, after all, Shadow Foreign Secretary, a former Chancellor and far senior to Heath. More important, he was a married man. Simon doubted the Tories would ever pick a bachelor to lead them.

As soon as Kerslake had left the Seymours he jumped into a taxi and returned immediately to the Commons. He found Reginald Maudling in the Members' Dining-room seated at the table frequented only by the Shadow Cabinet. He waited until Maudling had finished his meal before asking if they could have a few moments alone. The tall shambling figure – not altogether certain of the name of the new member – leaned over and invited Simon to join him for a drink in his room.

Maudling listened intently to all the enthusiastic young man had to say and accepted the judgement of the well-informed member without question. It was agreed that Simon should try to counter the Seymour campaign and report back his results twice a week.

While Seymour could call on all the powers and influence of his Etonian background, Kerslake could rely on the knowledge and arm-twisting skills gained from his time as

President of the Oxford Union. Simon weighed up the advantages and disadvantages he possessed. He did not own a palatial home in Eaton Square in which Turners, Constables and Holbeins were not to be found in books but on the walls. He also lacked a glamorous society wife. Simon lived in a small house in Beaufort Street in Chelsea and Elizabeth was a gynaecologist at St Mary's Hospital, Paddington. Although Elizabeth gave Simon's political aspirations her full backing she still considered her own career every bit as important, an opinion with which Simon concurred. The local Coventry press had on several occasions recalled in their columns how Elizabeth had left her three-day-old child to help perform a Caesarian section on a mother in the adjoining ward and, two years later, had to be dragged off night duty just as she went into labour with their second child.

This independence of character was one of the reasons Simon had admired Elizabeth when they first met, but he realised she was no match for Lady Fiona Seymour as a hostess and he never wanted her to be. He despised pushy political wives.

Simon spent the following days trying to work out the certain Maudling and certain Heath supporters, although many members claimed they would favour both candidates, according to who asked them. These he listed as doubtfuls. When Enoch Powell threw his cap into the ring Simon could not find a single new member other than Alec Pimkin who openly supported him. That left forty members from the new intake who still had to be followed up. He estimated twelve certain Heath, eleven certain Maudling and one Powell, leaving sixteen undecided. As the day of the election drew nearer it became obvious that few of the remaining sixteen actually knew either candidate well, and were still not sure for whom they should vote.

Simon realised that he could not invite them all round to Beaufort Street between Elizabeth's ward duties, so he would have to go to them. During the last eight weeks he accompanied his chosen leader as he addressed the party faithfuls in twenty-three new members' constituencies. Simon travelled from Bodmin to Glasgow, from Penrith to Great Yarmouth, briefing Maudling studiously before every meeting.

Gradually it became obvious to everyone that Charles Seymour and Simon Kerslake were the chosen lieutenants among the new intake. Some members resented the whispered confidences at the Eaton Square cocktail parties, or the discovery that Simon Kerslake had visited their constituencies under false pretences, while others were simply envious of the reward that would inevitably be heaped on the victor.

"But why do you support Maudling?" Elizabeth had asked him one evening over dinner.

"Reggie has a great deal more experience of Government than Heath – and in any case he's more caring about those around him."

"But Heath appears to be so much more professional," Elizabeth insisted, pouring her husband a glass of wine.

"That may well be the case, but the British have always preferred good amateurs to preside over their affairs."

"If you believe all that stuff about amateurs why become so involved yourself?"

Simon considered her question for some time before answering. "Because I don't come from the type of background that automatically commands the centre of the Tory stage," he admitted.

"Neither does Heath," commented Elizabeth dryly.

Although everyone inside and outside of Parliament knew it could not be long before Sir Alec formally announced his resignation it did not become official until 22 July 1965, when he addressed the 1922 Committee of Tory back-benchers.

The date chosen for the leadership election was just five days later. During that time Simon Kerslake and Charles Seymour worked almost round the clock but, despite many national papers' commissioned polls, columns of newsprint offering statistics and opinions, no one seemed certain of the outcome, other than to predict that Powell would come third.

Charles and Simon began avoiding each other and Fiona started referring to Kerslake, first in private then in public, as "that pushy self-made man". She stopped using the expression when Alec Pimkin asked in all innocence whether she was referring to Edward Heath.

On the morning of the secret ballot Simon and Charles voted early and spent the rest of the day pacing the corridors of the Commons trying to assess the result. By lunchtime they were both outwardly exuberant, while inwardly despondent.

At two-fifteen they were seated in the large committee room to hear the chairman of the 1922 Committee make the historic announcement:

"The result of the first election for leader of the Conservative parliamentary party," said Sir William Anstruther-Gray, "is as follows:

Edward Heath	150 votes
Reginald Maudling	133 votes
Enoch Powell	15 votes."

An hour later Reginald Maudling, who had been lunching in the City, telephoned Heath to say he would be happy to serve under him as the new leader. Charles and Fiona opened a bottle of Krug while Simon took Elizabeth to the Old Vic to see *The Royal Hunt of the Sun*. He slept the entire way through Robert Stephens' brilliant performance, before Elizabeth drove him home.

"How come you didn't fall asleep? After all, you've been just as busy as I have the last few weeks," Simon asked.

Elizabeth smiled. "It was my turn to want to be involved with what was happening on the centre of the stage."

Two weeks later, on 4 August, Edward Heath announced his Shadow team. Reggie Maudling was to be deputy leader. Sir Alec accepted the Foreign Office brief while Powell went to Defence. Charles Seymour received an invitation to join the Housing and Local Government team as its junior spokesman, thus becoming the first of the new intake to be given front-bench responsibilities.

Simon Kerslake received a handwritten letter from Reggie Maudling thanking him for his valiant efforts.

BOOK TWO
1966-1974
JUNIOR OFFICE

CHAPTER FOUR

When Alison McKenzie moved into Andrew Fraser's Cheyne Walk flat everyone, including her father, the Minister of State for Scotland, assumed they would soon announce their engagement.

For the previous three months Andrew had had his head down in committee helping out with the public bills relating exclusively to Scotland which were referred to the committee from the House itself. He found much of the committee work boring, as so many members repeated the views of their colleagues, less and less articulately, and for some time only his doodling improved. Even so, Andrew's energy and charm made him a popular companion through the long summer months and he quickly gained enough confidence to suggest first minor and later major changes to amendments considered by the committee. The disparity between penalties under English and Scottish law had long worried him, and he pressed hard for changes that would bring the two systems closer together. He soon discovered that the Scottish Labour members were more traditional and clannish than even the most hide-bound of Tories.

When the session came to an end Andrew invited Alison to spend a long weekend with his parents at their country home in Stirling at the end of the recess.

"Do you expect me to sleep under the same roof as a former Conservative Lord Provost of Edinburgh?" she demanded.

"Why not? You've been sleeping with his son for the past six months."

"Well, the same roof perhaps, but there's one weekend we won't be able to sleep in the same bed."

"Why not? The Tories may be snobs but they're not hypocrites."

Alison didn't want to admit that she was actually quite nervous about spending the weekend with Andrew's father, as she had heard him continually maligned at her parents' breakfast table for over twenty years.

When she did meet 'Old Dungheap', as her father referred to the former Lord Provost, Alison liked him immediately. He reminded her so much of her own father, while Lady Fraser was not at all the snobbish little battle-axe her mother had prepared her for.

It was immediately agreed that during the weekend nobody would talk politics. Andrew and Alison spent most of the Friday afternoon walking through the heather-covered hills and discussing in detail how they saw their future. On the Saturday morning the minister telephoned Sir Duncan and invited them over to Bute House – the official residence of the Secretary of State for Scotland – for dinner.

After so many years of opposing each other both families were nervous of the social get-together, but it seemed the children were to bridge the political gap they had failed to build for themselves. The McKenzies had invited two other Edinburgh families to dinner in the hope that it would ease the tension of the occasion, a branch of the Forsyths who owned the departmental store in Princes Street, and the Menzies, who ran the largest chain of newsagents in the country.

Andrew had decided to use the gathering to make an announcement at the end of dinner, and having spent longer shopping than he originally intended was the last to arrive at Bute House.

After they had all found their place cards around the long dining-room table the fourteen guests remained silent as a lone piper played a lament before the chef entered carrying a silver salver which bore on it a large haggis for the minister's inspection. Sir Duncan's opinion was sought: "Warm – reekin rich!" he declared. It was the first occasion the two men had wholeheartedly agreed on anything.

Andrew did not eat as much as the others because he

couldn't take his eyes off the guest who had been placed opposite him. She didn't pay much attention to Andrew, but seemed always to be smiling or laughing, making those around her enjoy her company. When Andrew had last seen Louise Forsyth it had been scoring goals on a hockey pitch. She had been a dumpy little girl with long pigtails and a tendency to go for one's ankles rather than for the ball. Now the jet black hair was short and curly, while the body had become slim and graceful. After dinner Andrew mixed among the guests and it was well after one o'clock when the party broke up: he never managed a moment alone with her. Andrew was relieved to discover that Alison wanted to spend the night with her parents at Bute House while the Frasers travelled back to their home in Stirling.

"You're very silent for a Socialist," his father said, in the car on the way home.

"He's in love," said his mother fondly.

Andrew made no reply.

The next morning he rose early and travelled into Edinburgh to see his agent. The minister had caught the first flight back to London but had left a message asking if Andrew would be kind enough to see him at ten o'clock in Dover House, the London headquarters of the Scottish Office, the following day, 'on an official matter'.

Andrew was delighted but it didn't change his attitude.

Having answered his local post and dealt with some constituents' problems he left his office and made his way over to the New Club to make a private phone call. He was relieved to find her still at home. She reluctantly agreed to join him for lunch. Andrew sat alone for forty minutes, checking the grandfather clock every few moments while pretending to read the *Scotsman*. When she was eventually ushered in by the steward, Andrew knew this was the woman with whom he wanted to spend the rest of his life. He would have laughed, if he had been told – before the previous evening – that he could change his well-ordered plans on what was nothing more than a casual meeting. But then he had never met anyone like Louise before and was already convinced he never would again.

"Miss Forsyth," said the man wearing the green livery uniform of the Club. He inclined his head slightly and left them alone.

Louise smiled and Andrew guided her to a table in the corner.

"It was kind of you to come at such short notice," he said nervously.

"No," she said. "It was very stupid of me."

Over a lunch which he ordered but didn't eat Andrew learned that Louise Forsyth was engaged to an old friend of his from university days and that they planned to be married the following spring. By the end of lunch he had convinced her they should at least meet again.

Andrew caught the five-ten flight back to London and sat alone in his flat and waited. Alison returned a little after nine o'clock and asked why he hadn't travelled down from Scotland with her or at least phoned. Andrew immediately told her the truth. She burst into tears while he stood helplessly by. Within the hour she had moved all her possessions out of Andrew's flat and left.

At ten-thirty he phoned Louise again.

The next morning Andrew dropped into the Commons to collect his mail from the Members' Post Office, and to check with the Whips' office as to what time they were anticipating the votes that day.

"One at six and two at ten," shouted a junior Whip from behind his desk. "And we could lose the second so be certain you're not far away if we need you."

Andrew nodded and turned to leave.

"By the way, congratulations."

"On what?" queried Andrew.

"Oh hell, another indiscretion to start the week on. It's pencilled in on the morning sheet," said the Whip, tapping a piece of paper in front of him.

"What is?" asked Andrew impatiently.

"Your appointment as Parliamentary Private Secretary to Hugh McKenzie. For pity's sake don't let him know I told you."

"I won't," promised Andrew, breathing a sigh of relief. He

checked his watch: perfect timing to stroll over to Dover House and keep his appointment with the minister.

He whistled as he walked down Whitehall and the door-man saluted as he entered the ministry. They had obviously been briefed as well. He tried not to show too much anticipation. He was met at the top of the stone steps by the minister's secretary.

"Good morning," Andrew said, trying to sound as if he had no idea what was in store for him.

"Good morning, Mr Fraser," replied the secretary. "The minister has asked me to apologise for not being available to see you, but he has been called away to a Cabinet committee to discuss the new IMF standby credit."

"I see," said Andrew. "Has the minister rearranged my appointment?"

"Well, no, he hasn't," replied the secretary, sounding a little surprised. "He simply said that it was no longer important, and he was sorry to have wasted your time."

Charles Seymour was enjoying the challenge of his new appointment as a junior Opposition spokesman. Even if he was not actually making decisions on future policy he was listening to them, and at least he felt he was near the centre of affairs. Whenever a debate on housing took place in the Commons he was allowed to sit on the front bench along with the rest of the team. He had already caused the defeat of two amendments on the Town and Country Planning Bill in standing committee, and had added one of his own, relating to the protection of trees, during the report stage of the bill on the floor of the House. "It isn't preventing a world war," he admitted to Fiona, "but in its own way it's quite important because if we win the election I'm confident of being offered junior office and then I'll have a real chance to shape policy."

Fiona continued to play her part, hosting monthly dinner parties at their Eaton Square house. By the end of the year every member of the Shadow Cabinet had dined with the Seymours at least once and Fiona never wore the same dress twice or allowed a menu to be repeated.

When the parliamentary year began again in October

Charles was one of the names continually dropped by the political pundits. Here was someone to watch. "He makes things happen," was the sentiment that was expressed again and again. He could barely cross the Members' Lobby without a correspondent trying to solicit his views on everything from butter mountains to rape. Fiona cut out of the papers every mention of her husband and couldn't help noticing that, if any new member was receiving more press coverage than Charles, it was a young Socialist from Leeds called Raymond Gould.

Raymond's name began to disappear from political columns soon after his success on the budget debate; his colleagues assumed it was because he was busy building a career at the bar. Had they passed his room at the Temple they would have heard the continual tap of a typewriter and been unable to contact him on his off-the-hook phone.

Each night Raymond could be found in chambers writing page after page, checking then rechecking his proofs, and often referring to the piles of books that cluttered his desk. When his *Full Employment at any Cost? Reflections of a worker educated after the Thirties* was published it caused an immediate sensation. The suggestion that the unions would become impotent and the Labour party would need to be more radical to capture the young vote was never likely to endear him to the party activists. Raymond had anticipated that it would provoke a storm of abuse from union leaders, and even among some of his more left-wing colleagues. But A. J. P. Taylor suggested in *The Times* that it was the most profound and realistic look at the Labour party since Anthony Crosland's *The Future of Socialism*, and had given the country a politician of rare honesty and courage. Raymond soon became aware that his strategy and hard work was paying dividends. He found himself a regular topic of conversation at political dinner-parties in London.

Joyce thought the book a magnificent piece of scholarship and she spent a considerable time trying to convince trade unionists who had only read out-of-context quotations from it in the *Sun* or *Daily Mirror* that it in fact showed a passionate concern for the trade union movement, while at the same time realistically considering the Labour party's future in the next decade.

The Labour Chief Whip took Raymond on one side and told him, "You've caused a right stir, lad. Now keep your head down for a few months and you'll probably find every Cabinet member quoting you as if it was party policy."

Raymond took the Chief Whip's advice, but he did not have to wait months. Just three weeks after the book's publication the Prime Minister quoted a whole passage at the Durham Miners' Rally. A few weeks later Raymond received a missive from No. 10 requesting him to check over the Prime Minister's speech to the TUC conference and add any suggestions he might have.

Simon Kerslake had sulked for about twenty-four hours after Maudling's defeat for the leadership. He then decided to turn his anger and energy towards the Government benches. It hadn't taken him long to work out that there was a fifteen-minute period twice a week when someone with his skills of oratory could command notice. At the beginning of a new session each week he would carefully study the order paper and in particular the first five questions listed for the Prime Minister on the Tuesday and Thursday. Every Monday morning he would prepare a supplementary for at least three of them. These he worded, then reworded, so that they were biting and witty and always likely to embarrass the Government. Although preparation of such supplementary questions could take several hours Simon would make them sound as though they had been jotted down on the back of the order paper during question time – and in fact would even do so. Elizabeth teased him about how long he took on something she considered trivial. He reminded her of Churchill's comment after being praised for a brilliant rejoinder, "All my best off-the-cuff remarks had been worked on days before."

Even so Simon was surprised at how quickly the House took it for granted that he would be there on the attack, probing, demanding, harrying the Prime Minister's every move. Whenever he rose from his seat the party perked up in anticipation, and many of his interruptions reached the political column of the daily newspapers the following day.

Unemployment was the subject of that day's question. Simon was on his feet leaning forward jabbing a finger in the direction of the Government front bench.

"With the appointment of four extra Secretaries of State this week the Prime Minister can at least claim he has full employment – in the Cabinet."

The Prime Minister sank lower into his seat, looking forward to the recess.

CHAPTER FIVE

When the Queen opened Parliament the talk was not of the contents of her speech, which traditionally lists the aims of the Government of the day, but of how much of the legislation could possibly be carried out while the Labour party retained a majority of only four. Any contentious legislation was likely to be defeated at the committee stage and everyone knew it. The Conservatives were convinced they could win the forthcoming election whatever date the Prime Minister chose until the by-election held in Hull increased the Labour majority from 1,100 to 5,350. The Prime Minister couldn't believe the result and asked the Queen to dissolve Parliament immediately and to call a general election. The date announced from Buckingham Palace was 31 March.

Simon Kerslake began spending most of his spare time in his Coventry constituency. The local people seemed pleased with the apprenticeship of their new member, but the disinterested statisticians pointed out that a swing of less than one per cent would remove him from the House for another five years. By then his rivals would be on the second rung of the ladder.

The Tory Chief Whip advised Simon to stay put in Coventry and not to participate in any further parliamentary business. "There'll be no more three-line whips between now and the election," he assured him. "The most worthwhile thing you can do is pick up votes in Coventry, not give them in Westminster."

Elizabeth could only manage two weeks' leave of absence from St Mary's, and yet between the two of them they covered the entire constituency before election day. Simon's opponent was the former member, Alf Abbott, who became progressively confident of victory as the national swing to Labour accelerated during the campaign. The slogan 'You know Labour Government works' was sounding convincing after only eighteen months in power. The Liberals fielded a third candidate, Nigel Bainbridge, but he admitted openly that he only hoped to save his deposit.

Alf Abbott felt assured enough to challenge Simon to a public debate. Although it was usual for the sitting member to refuse to be drawn on such occasions Simon jumped at his opponent's challenge and prepared for the encounter with his usual diligence. Seven days before the election Simon and Elizabeth stood in the wings behind the stage of Coventry town hall with Alf Abbott, Nigel Bainbridge and their wives. The three men made stilted conversation while the women eyed each other's outfits critically. The political correspondent of the *Coventry Evening Telegraph*, acting as chairman, introduced each of the protagonists as they walked on to the stage, to whipped-up applause from different sections of the hall. Simon spoke first and held the attention of the large audience for over twenty minutes. Those who tried to heckle him ended up regretting having brought attention to themselves. Without once referring to his notes, he quoted figures and clauses from Government bills with an ease that impressed even Elizabeth. Abbott followed him and made a bitter attack on the Tories, accusing them of still wanting to tread down the workers at any cost, and was greeted by large cheers from his section of the audience. Bainbridge claimed that neither understood the real issues and went into an involved dissertation on the problem of the local sewers. During the questions that followed Simon once again proved to be far better informed than Abbott or Bainbridge, but he was aware that the packed hall only held 700 that cold March evening while elsewhere in Coventry were 50,000 more voters, most of them glued to 'Coronation Street'.

Although the local press proclaimed Simon the victor of a one-sided debate he remained downcast by the national dailies which were now predicting a landslide for Labour.

On election morning Simon and Elizabeth were up by six and among the first to cast their votes at the local primary school. They spent the rest of the day travelling from polling station to committee room to party checking posts, trying to keep up the morale of their supporters. Everywhere they went the committed believed in his victory but Simon knew that the national swing would be impossible to ignore. A senior Conservative back-bencher had once told him that an outstanding member could be worth a thousand personal votes and a weak opponent might sacrifice another thousand. It wasn't going to be enough.

By nine o'clock the last polling station had been locked and Simon and Elizabeth collapsed into a local pub and ordered two halves of bitter. They sat and watched the television above the bar. The commentator was saying that during the day a straw poll had been taken outside six constituencies in London and from those figures they were predicting a Labour majority of sixty to seventy seats. Up on the screen flashed the seventy seats most vulnerable to siege by Labour. Ninth on the list was Coventry Central: Simon ordered the other half.

"We should be off to watch the count soon," said Elizabeth.

"There's no hurry."

"Don't be such a wimp, Simon. And remember you're still the member," she said, surprisingly sharply. "You owe it to your supporters to remain confident after all the work they've put in."

In the town hall black boxes were being delivered by police vehicles from every ward in the constituency. Their contents were tipped on to trestle tables which made up three sides of a square on the vast cleared floor. The town clerk and his personal staff stood alone in the well made by the tables, while council workers sat around the outside carefully stacking up the votes into little piles of a hundred. These in turn were checked by party scrutineers who hovered over them, hawk-like, often demanding that a particular hundred be rechecked.

The little piles grew into large stacks which were then

placed next to each other, and as the hours passed it became obvious even to a casual observer that the outcome was going to be extremely close.

The tension on the floor mounted as each hundred, then each thousand, was handed over to the clerk. Rumours that began at one end of the room had been puffed up like *soufflés* long before they had reached the waiting crowd standing in a chill wind outside the hall. By midnight, several constituencies' results around the country had been declared. The national swing seemed to be much as predicted, around three per cent to Labour, which would give them the promised majority of seventy or over.

At twelve-twenty-one the Coventry town clerk invited all three candidates to join him in the centre of the room. He told them the result of the count.

A recount was immediately demanded. The town clerk agreed, and each pile of voting slips was returned to the tables and checked over again.

An hour later the town clerk called the three candidates together again and briefed them on the result of the recount; it had changed by only three votes.

Another recount was requested and the town clerk reluctantly acquiesced. By two o'clock in the morning Elizabeth felt she had no nails left. Another hour passed, during which Heath conceded defeat while Wilson gave an extended interview to ITN spelling out his programme for the new Parliament.

At two-twenty-seven the town clerk called the three candidates together for the last time and they all accepted the result. The town clerk walked up on to the stage accompanied by the rivals. He tapped the microphone to check the speaker was working, cleared his throat and said:

"I, the undersigned, being the acting returning officer for the constituency of Coventry Central, hereby announce the total number of votes cast for each candidate to be as follows:

Alf Abbot	19,716
Nigel Bainbridge	7,002
Simon Kerslake	19,731

I therefore declare Simon Kerslake to be the duly elected Member of Parliament for the constituency of Coventry Central."

Even though the Labour party ended up with an overall majority in the House of ninety-seven, Simon had still won by fifteen votes.

Raymond Gould increased his majority to 12,413 in line with the national swing, and Joyce was ready for a week's rest.

Andrew Fraser improved his vote by 2,468 and announced his engagement to Louise Forsyth on the night after the election.

Charles Seymour could never recall accurately the size of his majority because, as Fiona explained to the old earl the following morning, "They don't count the Conservative vote in Sussex Downs, darling, they weigh it."

CHAPTER
SIX

In most democratic countries a newly elected leader enjoys a transitional period during which he is able to announce the policies he intends to pursue and whom he has selected to implement them. In Britain MPs sit by their phones and wait for forty-eight hours immediately after the election result has been declared. If a call comes in the first twelve hours they will be asked to join the Cabinet, the second twelve given a position as a Minister of State, the third twelve made an Under-Secretary of State, and the last twelve a Parliamentary Private Secretary to a Cabinet minister. If the phone hasn't rung by then, they remain on the back benches.

Andrew Fraser had not bothered to be anywhere near a phone when the BBC midday news announced that Hugh McKenzie had been promoted from Minister of State to Secretary of State for Scotland, with a seat in the Cabinet. Andrew and Louise Forsyth decided to spend a quiet weekend at Aviemore, he to relax and climb other mountains before returning to the House, she to make plans for their forthcoming wedding.

It had taken Andrew countless trips to Edinburgh to convince Louise what had happened to him at Bute House that night had not been mere infatuation that would soon pass, but held long-term conviction. When the one weekend he couldn't travel to the Scottish capital and she came down to London he knew she no longer doubted his resolve. Andrew had found in the past that once the conquest was achieved interest soon waned. For him, though, his love for 'the wee slip of a thing', as his mother had come to describe Louise, grew and grew.

Although Louise was only five foot three she was so slim she appeared far taller, and her short black hair, blue eyes and laughing smile had many tall men bending down to take a closer look.

"You eat like a pig and look like a rake. I don't know how you manage it," grumbled Andrew over dinner one night. He played regular games of squash and swam three times a week to keep his own heavy frame in trim. He stared in admiration and not a little envy as Louise's eyes twinkled mischievously before she devoured another portion of Black Forest gâteau.

Although she had been brought up in a strict Calvinist household in which politics were never discussed Louise quickly learnt about the machinery of Government and soon found herself debating long into the night with Sir Duncan. At first he scored points off her with ease, but it was not long before he had to answer her demands with more and more reasoned arguments, and sometimes even that was not enough.

By the time the election had taken place Louise had become a total convert to Andrew's views. The squalor in some of the parts of the Edinburgh Carlton constituency, which she had never set foot in before, made her sick at heart. Like all converts, she became zealous and began by trying to reform the entire Forsyth clan. She even paid twelve shillings to join the Scottish Labour party.

"Why did you do that?" asked Andrew, trying not to show his pleasure.

"I'm against mixed marriages," she replied.

Andrew was delighted and surprised by the interest she took, and the local constituency suspicions of 'the wealthy lady' soon turned to affection.

"Your future husband will be Secretary of State for Scotland one day," many of them shouted, as she walked down the narrow cobbled streets.

"It's Downing Street, not Bute House, that I want to live in," he had once confided to her. "And in any case I've still got to become a junior minister."

"That could change in the very near future."

"Not while Hugh McKenzie is Secretary of State," he said, not under his breath.

"To hell with McKenzie," she said. "Surely one of his Cabinet colleagues has the guts to offer you the chance to be his PPS?" But despite Louise's sentiments the phone did not ring that weekend.

Raymond Gould returned from Leeds the moment the count was over, leaving Joyce to carry out the traditional 'thank you' drive around the constituency.

When he wasn't sitting by the phone the following day he was walking around it, nervously pushing his glasses back up his nose. The first call came from his mother who had rung to congratulate him.

"On what?" he asked. "Have you heard something?"

"No, love," she said, "I just rang to say how pleased I was about your increased majority."

"Oh."

"And to add how sorry we were not to see you before you left the constituency, especially as you have to pass the shop on the way to the A1."

Not again, Mother, he wanted to say.

The second call was from a colleague inquiring if Raymond had been offered a job.

"Nothing so far," he said before learning of his contemporary's promotion.

The third call was from one of Joyce's friends.

"When will she be back?" another Yorkshire accent enquired.

"I've no idea," said Raymond, desperate to get the caller off the line.

"I'll call again this afternoon, then."

"Fine," said Raymond, putting the phone down quickly.

He went into the kitchen to make himself a cheese sandwich, but there wasn't any cheese, so he ate stale bread smeared with three-week-old butter. He was half-way through a second slice when the phone rang.

"Raymond?"

He held his breath.

"Noel Brewster."

He exhaled in exasperation as he recognised the vicar's voice.

"Can you read the second lesson when you're next up in Leeds? We had rather hoped you would read it this morning – your dear wife . . ."

"Yes," he promised. "The first weekend I am back in Leeds." The phone rang again as soon as he placed it back on the receiver.

"Raymond Gould?" said an anonymous voice.

"Speaking," he said.

"The Prime Minister will be with you in one moment."

Raymond waited. The front door opened and another voice shouted, "It's only me. I don't suppose you found anything to eat, poor love." Joyce joined Raymond in the drawing-room.

Without looking at his wife he waved his hand at her to keep quiet.

"Ray," said a voice on the other end of the line.

"Good afternoon, Prime Minister," he replied, rather formally in response to the more pronounced Yorkshire accent.

"I was hoping you would feel able to join the new team as Under-Secretary for Employment?"

Raymond breathed a sigh of relief. It was exactly what he'd hoped for. "I'd be delighted, Prime Minister."

"Good, that will give the trade union leaders something new to think about." The phone went dead.

Raymond Gould, Under-Secretary of State at the Department of Employment, sat motionless on the third rung of the ladder.

As Raymond left the house the next morning he was greeted by a driver standing next to a gleaming black Austin Westminster. Unlike his second-hand Sunbeam, it glowed in the morning light. The rear door was opened and Raymond climbed in to be driven off to the department. Thank God he knows where my office is, thought Raymond as he sat alone in the back. By his side on the back seat was a red leather box the size of a very thick briefcase with gold lettering running along the edge: 'Under-Secretary of State for Employment'. Raymond turned the small key, knowing what Alice must have felt like on her way down the rabbit hole. The inside was crammed with buff files. He opened the first to see, 'A five-point plan for discussion by Cabinet on how to keep unemployment under one million'. He immediately started to read the closely-typed documents.

When Charles Seymour returned to the Commons on the Tuesday there was a note from the Whips' office waiting for him on the Members' Letter-board. One of the Housing and Local Government team had lost his seat in the general election and Charles had been promoted to number two on the Opposition bench. "No more preservation of trees. You'll be on to higher things now," chuckled the Chief Whip. "Pollution, water shortage and exhaust fumes . . ."

Charles smiled with pleasure as he walked through the Commons, acknowledging old colleagues and noticing a considerable number of new faces. He didn't stop and talk to any of the newcomers as he could not be certain if they were Labour or Conservative and, given the election result, most of them had to be Socialist. A doorkeeper in white tie and black tail-jacket handed him a message to say that a constituent was waiting to see him in the Central Lobby. He hurried off to find out what the problem was, passing some of his older colleagues who wore forlorn looks on their faces. For some it would be a considerable time before they were offered the chance of office again, while others knew they had served as ministers for the last time. As Macmillan had proclaimed, even the most glittering political career always ends in tears.

But at thirty-five Charles dismissed such thoughts as he marched towards the waiting constituent. He turned out to be a red-faced Master of Hounds who had travelled up to London to grumble about the proposed private member's bill banning hare coursing. Charles listened to a fifteen-minute monologue before assuring his constituent that any such bill was doomed through lack of parliamentary time. The Master of Hounds went away happy and Charles returned to his room to check over the constituency mail.

Fiona had reminded him of the 800 letters of thanks to the party workers that had been franked but still needed topping and tailing after every election. He groaned.

"Mrs Blenkinsop, the chairman of Sussex Ladies' Luncheon Club, wants you to be their guest speaker this year," his secretary told him once he had settled.

"Reply yes – what's the date?" asked Charles, reaching for his diary.

"16 June."

"Stupid woman, that's Ladies Day at Ascot. Tell her that I'm delivering a speech at a Housing Conference, but I'll be certain to make myself free for the function next year."

The secretary looked up anxiously.

"Don't fuss, she'll never know any better."

She moved on to the next letter. "Mr Heath wonders if you can join him for a drink on Thursday, six o'clock?"

Simon Kerslake also knew it was going to be a long slog. He was aware the Tories would not change their leader until Heath had been given a second chance at the polls, and that could take every day of five years with a Government which had a ninety-seven majority.

He began writing articles for the *Spectator* and for the *Sunday Express* centre pages, in the hope of building a reputation outside the House while at the same time supplementing his parliamentary salary of £3,400. Even with Elizabeth's income as a consultant he was finding it difficult to make ends meet, and soon their two young sons would have reached prep school age. He envied the Charles Seymours of this world who did not have to give a second thought about their next pay cheque. Simon wondered if the damn man had any problems at all. He ran a finger down his own bank account: as usual there was a figure around £500 in the right-hand margin, and as usual it was in red. Many of his Oxford contemporaries had already established themselves in the City or at the bar and on a Friday evening could be seen being driven to large houses in the country. Simon laughed whenever he read that people went into politics to make money.

He pressed on with demanding questions to the Prime Minister, and tried not to show how frustrated he was by the expectations of his colleagues whenever he rose each Tuesday and Thursday. Even after it became routine he prepared himself thoroughly, and on one occasion he even elicited praise from his normally taciturn leader. But as the weeks passed he found that his thoughts continually returned to money – or to his lack of it.

That was before he met Ronnie Nethercote.

Andrew Fraser had often read that the anger or jealousy of one man could block the advance of a political career but he still found it hard to accept that it could apply to him. What annoyed him even more was that Hugh McKenzie's tentacles seemed to have spread through every other department.

Andrew's marriage to Louise Forsyth had been expansively covered in the national papers and the absence of the Secretary of State at the wedding did not escape the notice of the *Daily Express*'s William Hickey. They even published an out-of-date photograph of Alison McKenzie looking sorrowful.

Sir Duncan reminded his son that politics was for long-distance runners, not sprinters, and that he still had a few more laps to complete yet. "An unfortunate analogy," considered Andrew as he had been a member of the Edinburgh University 4 × 110 relay team. Nevertheless he prepared himself for the marathon.

"Don't forget, Harold Macmillan spent fourteen years on the back benches before holding office," Sir Duncan added.

Louise accompanied Andrew all over the country for his speeches 'of major importance', usually to an audience of less than twenty; she only stopped travelling to Scotland every week when she discovered she was pregnant.

To Louise's surprise, Andrew turned out to be a keen anticipatory father, determined his son would not think of him only as a politician. Single-handed, he converted one of the upstairs bedrooms in Cheyne Walk into a nursery and sought her approval for a variety of blue decorative schemes.

Louise was anxious that Andrew should extend the same feelings to their unborn child, if they had a daughter.

Raymond Gould quickly gained a reputation at the Department of Employment. He was thought of as extremely bright, demanding, hard working and, not that it was ever reported to him, arrogant. His ability to cut a junior civil servant off in mid-sentence or to correct his principal Private Secretary on matters of detail did not endear him even to his closest staff, who always want to be loyal to their master.

Raymond's work load was prodigious and even the Permanent Secretary experienced Gould's unrelenting 'Don't make excuses' when he tried to trim one of the minister's private schemes. Soon senior civil servants were talking of when, not whether, he would be promoted. His Secretary of State, like all men who were expected to be in six places at once, often asked Raymond to stand in for him, but even Raymond was surprised when he was invited to represent the department as guest of honour at the annual CBI dinner.

Joyce checked to see that her husband's dinner-jacket was well brushed, his shirt spotless and his shoes shining like a guards officer's. His carefully worded speech – a combination of civil-servant draughtsmanship and a few more forceful phrases of his own to prove to the assembled capitalists that not every member of the Labour party was a 'raving commie' – was safely lodged in his inside pocket. His driver ferried him from his Lansdowne Road home towards the West End.

Raymond enjoyed the occasion; although he was nervous when he rose to represent the Government in reply to the toast of the guests. By the time he had resumed his seat he felt it had been one of his better efforts. The ovation that followed was certainly more than polite from what had to be classified as a naturally hostile audience.

"That speech was dryer than the Chablis," one guest whispered in the chairman's ear but he had to agree that, with men like Gould in high office, it was going to be a lot easier to live with the Socialists.

The man on Simon Kerslake's left was far more blunt in

voicing his opinion of Gould. "Bloody man thinks like a Tory, talks like a Tory, so why isn't he a Tory?" he demanded.

Simon grinned at the prematurely balding man who had been expressing his equally vivid views throughout dinner. Corpulent and ruddy-faced, Ronnie Nethercote looked as if he was trying to escape from every part of his bulging dinner-jacket.

"I expect," said Simon in reply, "that Gould would have found it hard to join the Young Conservatives, born in the thirties and living in Leeds."

"Balls," said Ronnie. "I managed it and I was born in the East End of London without any of his advantages. Now tell me, Mr Kerslake, what do you do when you're not wasting your time in the House of Commons?"

Raymond stayed on after dinner and chatted for some time to the captains of industry. A little after eleven he left to return to Lansdowne Road.

As his chauffeur drove slowly away from Grosvenor House down Park Lane, the Under-Secretary waved expansively back to his host. Someone else waved in reply. At first Raymond only glanced across, assuming it was another dinner guest, until he saw her legs. Standing on the corner outside the petrol station on Park Lane stood a young girl smiling at him invitingly, her white leather mini skirt so short it might have been better described as a handkerchief. Her long legs reminded him of Joyce ten years before except that they were black. Her finely curled hair and the set of her hips remained firmly implanted in Raymond's mind all the way home.

When they reached Lansdowne Road Raymond climbed out of the official car and said "Goodnight" to his driver before walking slowly towards his front door, but he did not take out his latch key. He waited until he was sure the driver had turned the corner before looking up and checking the bedroom window. All the lights were out. Joyce must be asleep.

He crept down the path and back on to the pavement, then

looked up and down the road, finally spotting the space where Joyce had parked the Sunbeam. He checked the spare key was on his key-ring and fumbled about, feeling like a car thief. It took three attempts before the car spluttered into life, and Raymond wondered if he would wake up the whole road as he moved off and headed back to Park Lane, not certain what to expect. When he reached Marble Arch he travelled slowly down in the centre stream of traffic. A few dinner guests in evening dress were still spilling out of Grosvenor House. He passed the petrol station: she hadn't moved. She smiled again and he accelerated, nearly running into the car in front of him. Raymond travelled back up to Marble Arch but, instead of turning towards home, he drove down Park Lane again, this time not as quickly and on the inside lane. He took his foot off the accelerator as he approached the petrol station and she waved again. He returned to Marble Arch before repeating his detour down Park Lane, this time even more slowly. As he passed Grosvenor House for a third time he checked to be sure that there were no stragglers still chatting on the pavement. It was clear. He touched the brakes and his car came to a stop just beyond the petrol station. He waited.

The girl looked up and down the street before strolling over to the car, opening the passenger door and taking a seat next to the Under-Secretary of State for Employment.

"Looking for business?"

"What do you mean?" asked Raymond hoarsely.

"Come on, darling. You can't imagine I was standing out there hoping to get a sun tan."

Raymond turned to look at the girl more carefully and wanted to touch her despite the aura of cheap perfume. Her black blouse had three buttons undone; a fourth would have left nothing to the imagination.

"It's ten pounds at my place."

"Where's your place?" he heard himself say.

"I use a hotel in Paddington."

"How do we get there?" he asked, putting his hand nervously through his red hair.

"Just head up to Marble Arch and I'll direct you."

Raymond pulled out and went off towards Hyde Park Corner, and drove round before travelling on up towards Marble Arch once again.

"I'm Mandy," she said, "what's your name?"

Raymond hesitated. "Malcolm."

"And what do you do, Malcolm, in these hard times?"

"I . . . I sell second-hand cars."

"Haven't picked out a very good one for yourself, have you?" She laughed.

Raymond made no comment. It didn't stop Mandy.

"What's a second-hand car salesman doing dressed up like a toff, then?"

Raymond had quite forgotten he was still in evening dress.

"I've . . . just been to a convention . . . at the . . . Hilton Hotel."

"Lucky for some," she said, and lit a cigarette. "I've been standing outside Grosvenor House all night in the hope of getting some rich feller from that posh party." Raymond's cheeks nearly turned the colour of his hair. "Slow down and take the second on the left."

He followed her instructions until they pulled up outside a small dingy hotel. "I'll get out first, then you," she said. "Just walk straight through reception and follow me up the stairs." As she got out of the car he nearly drove off and might have done so if his eye hadn't caught the sway of her hips as she walked back towards the hotel.

He obeyed her instructions and climbed several flights of narrow stairs until he reached the top floor. As he approached the landing, a large bosomy blonde passed him on the way down.

"Hi, Mandy," she shouted back at her friend.

"Hi, Sylv. Is the room free?"

"Just," said the blonde sourly.

Mandy pushed open the door and Raymond followed her in. The room was small and narrow. In one corner stood a tiny bed and a threadbare carpet. The faded yellow wallpaper was peeling in several places. There was a wash basin attached to the wall; a dripping tap had left a brown stain on the enamel.

Mandy put her hand out, and waited.

"Ah, yes, of course," said Raymond, taking out his wallet to find he only had nine pounds on him.

She scowled. "Not going to get overtime tonight, am I, darling?" she said, tucking the money carefully away in the corner of her bag before matter-of-factly taking off all her clothes.

Although the act of undressing had been totally sexless he was still amazed by the beauty of her body. Raymond felt somehow detached from the real world. He watched, eager to feel the texture of her skin, but made no move. She lay down on the bed.

"Let's get on with it, darling. I've got a living to earn."

The minister undressed quickly, keeping his back to the bed. He folded his clothes in a neat pile on the floor as there was no chair. Then he lay down on top of her. It was all over in a few minutes.

"Come quickly, don't you, darling?" said Mandy, grinning.

Raymond turned away from her and started washing himself as best he could in the little basin. He dressed hurriedly, realising he must get out of the place as rapidly as possible.

"Can you drop me back at the petrol station?" Mandy asked.

"It's exactly the opposite direction for me," he said, trying not to sound anxious as he made a bolt for the door. He passed Sylv on the stairs accompanied by a man. She stared at him more closely the second time. Raymond was back in his car a few moments later. He drove home quickly but not before unwinding the windows in an attempt to get rid of the smell of stale tobacco and cheap perfume.

Back in Lansdowne Road he had a long shower before creeping into bed next to Joyce; she stirred only slightly.

CHAPTER
SEVEN

Charles drove his wife down to Ascot early to be sure to avoid the bumper-to-bumper traffic that always developed later in the day. With his height and bearing, Charles Seymour was made for tails and a topper and Fiona wore a hat which on anyone less self-assured would have looked ridiculous. They had been invited to join the McFarlands for the afternoon and when they arrived they found Sir Robert awaiting them in his private box.

"You must have left home early," said Charles.

"About thirty minutes ago," he said, laughing. Fiona looked politely incredulous.

"I always come here by helicopter," he explained.

They lunched on lobster and strawberries accompanied by a fine vintage champagne which the waiter kept pouring and pouring. Charles might not have drunk quite as much had he not picked the winners of the first three races. He spent the fifth race slumped in a chair in the corner of the box and only the noise of the crowd kept him from nodding off.

If they hadn't waited for a farewell drink after the last race Charles might have got away with it. He had forgotten that his host was returning by helicopter.

The long tail of cars across Windsor Great Park all the way back to the M4 made Charles very short-tempered. When he eventually reached the motorway he put his Daimler into fourth gear. He didn't notice the police car until the siren sounded and he was directed to pull over.

"Do be sensible, Charles," whispered Fiona.

"Don't worry, old girl, I know exactly how to deal with the

law," he said, and wound down his window to address the policeman who stood by the car. "Do you realise who I am, officer?"

"No, sir, but I would like you to accompany me –"

"Certainly not, officer, I am a Member of . . ."

"Do be quiet," said Fiona, "and stop making such a fool of yourself."

". . . Parliament and I will not be treated . . ."

"Have you any idea how pompous you sound, Charles?"

"Perhaps you will be kind enough to accompany me to the station, sir?"

"I want to speak to my solicitor."

"Of course, sir. As soon as we reach the station."

When Charles arrived at the constabulary he proved quite incapable of walking in a straight line and refused to provide a blood sample.

"I am the Conservative MP for Sussex Downs."

Which will not help you, Fiona thought, but he was past listening and only demanded that she phone the family solicitor at Speechly, Bircham and Soames.

After Ian Kimmins had spoken first gently, then firmly to Charles his client eventually co-operated with the police.

Once Charles had completed his written statement Fiona drove him home, praying that his stupidity would pass unnoticed by the press the following day.

Andrew even bought a football but hid it from Louise.

As the months passed Louise's slight frame expanded alarmingly. Andrew would rest his head on the bulge and listen for the heartbeat. "It's a scrum-half," he declared.

"Perhaps she's a centre forward," Louise suggested, "and will want to emulate the distaff side of the family."

"If he has to be a centre forward he will play for Hearts," Andrew assured her.

"Male chauvinist pig," she called to his back as he headed off to the Commons that morning. Andrew toyed with the names of Jamie, Robert, Hector and Iain and had settled on Robert before he had reached Westminster. On arrival at

New Palace Yard he hailed the policeman on the gate and was surprised to see the familiar figure immediately rush towards him.

Andrew wound down the window. "What's the problem, officer?"

"Your wife's been taken to St Mary's, Paddington, sir. Emergency wing."

Andrew would have broken the speed limit all the way to Marble Arch if it hadn't been for the traffic. He kept praying he would be there in time, but he couldn't help remembering that Louise was only six months pregnant. When he arrived the doctor on duty would not allow him to see her.

"How is Louise?" were Andrew's first words.

The young doctor hesitated, then said, "Your wife's fine, but I'm afraid she's lost the baby."

Andrew felt his whole body go limp. "Thank God she's all right," he said.

"I'm afraid I can't let you see her until she has come out of sedation."

"Of course, Doctor," said Andrew, glancing at the lapel badge on her white coat.

"But I can see no reason why you shouldn't have more children in the future," she added gently, before he had the chance to ask the quesion.

Andrew smiled with relief and began pacing up and down the corridor, unaware of the passing of time, until the doctor returned and said it would now be all right for him to see his wife.

"I hope you're not too disappointed?" were Louise's first words when eventually he was allowed to see her.

"Don't be silly – we'll have a dozen before we're through," he said, taking her hand.

She tried to laugh. "Do you know my doctor's husband?"

"Not that I'm aware of," said Andrew.

"Simon Kerslake."

"Good heavens, yes. Very capable fellow. Look aye, lass," said Andrew, putting on a deep brogue, "you'll be a new woman after a couple of days' rest, I'll guarantee it."

"And if I'm not?"

"I'll stick with the old one. And I'll tell you what: as soon as they let you out of this place we'll go down to the South of France for the weekend."

"You don't like him because he comes from the East End," said Simon, after she had read the letter.

"That's not true," replied Elizabeth. "I don't like him because I don't trust him."

"But you've only met him twice."

"Once would have been quite enough."

"Well, I can tell you I'm impressed by the not inconsiderable empire he's built up over the last ten years, and frankly it's an offer I can't refuse," said Simon, pocketing the letter.

"I know we could do with a little more money," said Elizabeth, "but surely not at any cost."

"I won't be offered many chances like this," continued Simon, "and frankly we could use the money. The belief people have that every Tory MP has some lucrative sinecure and two or three non-executive directorships is plain baloney and you know it. Not one other serious proposition has been put to me since I've been in the House, and another £2,000 a year for a monthly board meeting would come in very handy."

"And what else?"

"What do you mean, what else?"

"What else does Mr Nethercote expect for his £2,000? Don't be naive, Simon, he's not offering you that kind of money on a plate unless he's hoping to receive some scraps back."

"Well, maybe I have a few contacts and a little influence with one or two people . . ."

"I'll bet."

"You've just taken against him, Elizabeth."

"I'm against anything that might in the long term harm your career, Simon. Struggle on but never sacrifice your integrity, as you're so fond of reminding the people of Coventry."

On Friday morning, two weeks later, Andrew and Louise set out for London airport with one suitcase between them. As Andrew locked the front door the phone rang.

"No one's in," he shouted at the door knob, "but we'll be back on Monday."

He had booked a suite at the Colombe d'Or nestled in the hills of St Paul in the south of France. He was determined to prise Louise away from London and see she had some sun and rest.

The famous old hotel was everything the brochure had promised. On the walls hung paintings by Picasso, Monet, Manet, Utrillo – all of which the patroness, Madame Reux, had accepted many years before in place of payment from artists who needed lodging and a square meal. On the way up the winding staircase Louise was nearly knocked out by a Calder mobile and a Courbet hung above the bed in their room. But it was the bed itself, a sixteenth-century four-poster, that they both coveted. They were soon to discover it possessed a mattress so comfortable that visitors always overslept.

The food was memorable and they walked through the green hills each day to be sure they could tackle another full dinner at night. Three days of no radio, no television, no papers and no telephone ensured that by Monday morning they were ready to face London. They swore they would return again soon.

Once their plane had landed at Heathrow they were made aware that the holiday was over. Twenty minutes passed before someone pushed the waiting steps up to the Vanguard's door. Then a crowded bus to the terminal that seemed miles away was followed by a route-march to customs. Despite their first-class tickets their bags were among the last off. By the time the taxi had crawled through the morning rush hour to their front door in Cheyne Walk all Louise could say was, "I need another holiday." As Andrew put his latch key in the door the telephone started ringing.

"I hope they haven't been trying all weekend," Louise said.

Andrew put the phone to his ear as it went dead.

"Just missed whoever it was," said Andrew, picking up several brown envelopes from the floor. "France already seems about a week ago." He kissed his wife. "Must get changed and be off to the House," he said, checking his watch.

"How has the nation managed to survive without you?" mocked Louise.

When the phone rang again Andrew was just stepping out of the bath.

"Can you take it, Louise?" he shouted. A moment later he heard her rushing up the stairs.

"Andrew, it's the Prime Minister's office."

He ran dripping and naked to the bedroom phone and picked up the extension.

"Andrew Fraser," he said.

"This is No. 10," said an official-sounding voice, "the Prime Minister has been wanting to contact you since Friday morning."

"I'm sorry, I took my wife to Provence for the weekend."

"Really, sir?" said the voice, not sounding at all interested. "May I tell the Prime Minister you are now free to speak to him?"

"Of course," said Andrew, frowning at his nude reflection in the mirror. He must have put on half a stone; it would have to be four games of squash this week and no more wine at lunch.

"Andrew."

"Good morning, Prime Minister."

"Sad news about Hugh McKenzie."

"Yes, sir," said Andrew, automatically.

"They warned me about his heart before the last election but he insisted he wanted to carry on. I've asked Bruce to be the new Secretary of State and Angus to take his place as minister. They both want you to be the new Under-Secretary – how do you feel about it?"

"I'd be delighted, Prime Minister," Andrew stammered, trying to take in the news.

"Good. And by the way, Andrew, when you open your first red box you won't find any tickets for Colombe d'Or, so I do hope Louise is fully recovered." The phone clicked.

They had tracked him down, but the Prime Minister had left him in peace.

The first official function Andrew Fraser attended as Her Majesty's Under-Secretary of State at the Scottish Office was Hugh McKenzie's funeral.

"Think about it, Simon," said Ronnie, as they reached the boardroom door. "Two thousand pounds a year may be helpful but if you take shares in my property company it would give you a chance to make some capital."

"What did you have in mind?" asked Simon, doing up the middle button of his blazer and trying not to sound too excited.

"Well, you've proved damned useful to me. Some of those people who you bring to lunch wouldn't have allowed me past their front doors. I'd let you buy in cheap . . . you could get hold of 50,000 shares at one pound so when we go public you'll make a killing."

"Raising £50,000 won't be that easy, Ronnie."

"When your bank manager has checked over my books he'll be only too happy to lend you the money, you see."

After the Midland Bank had studied the authorised accounts of Nethercote and Company and the area manager had interviewed Simon, they agreed to his request, on the condition that Simon lodge the shares with the bank.

How wrong Elizabeth was proving to be, Simon thought, and when Nethercote and Company went on to double their profits for the year he brought home a copy of the annual report for his wife to study.

"Looks good," she had to admit. "But that still doesn't mean I have to trust Ronnie Nethercote."

When Charles Seymour's drink-driving charge came up in front of the Reading Bench he listed himself as C. G. Seymour – no mention of MP. Under profession he entered 'Banker'.

He came sixth in the list that morning, and on behalf of his absent client Ian Kimmins apologised to the Reading magistrates and assured them it would not happen again. Charles received a fifty-pound fine and was banned from driving for six months. The whole case was over in four minutes.

When Charles was told the news by telephone later that. day he was appreciative of Kimmins's sensible advice and felt he had escaped lightly. He couldn't help remembering how many column inches George Brown, the Labour Foreign Secretary, had endured after a similar incident outside the Hilton Hotel.

Fiona kept her own counsel.

At the time Fleet Street was in the middle of 'the silly season', that period in the summer when the press are desperate for news. There had only been one cub reporter in the court when Charles's case came up, and even he was surprised by the interest the nationals took in his little scoop. The pictures of Charles taken so discreetly outside the Seymours' country home were now glaring from the pages the following morning. Headlines ranged from 'Six months' ban for drink-drive son of earl' to 'MP's Ascot binge ends in heavy fine'. Even *The Times* mentioned the case on its home news page.

By lunchtime the same day every Fleet Street newspaper had tried to contact Charles – and so had the Chief Whip. When he did track Charles down his advice was short and to the point. A junior Shadow minister can survive that sort of publicity once, not twice.

"Whatever you do, don't drive a car during the next six months and don't ever drink and drive again."

Charles concurred, and after a quiet weekend hoped he had heard the last of the case. Then he caught the headline on the front page of the *Sussex Gazette*, 'Member faces no confidence motion': Mrs Blenkinsop, the chairman of the Ladies' Luncheon Club, was proposing the motion – not for the drunken driving but for deliberately misleading her about why he had been unable to fulfil a speaking engagement at their annual luncheon.

Raymond had become so used to receiving files marked 'Strictly Private', 'Top Secret', or even 'For Your Eyes Only' in his position as a Government Under-Secretary that he didn't give a second thought to a letter marked 'Confidential and Personal' even though it was written in a scrawled hand. He opened it while Joyce was boiling his eggs.

"Four minutes and forty-five seconds, just the way you like them," she said as she returned from the kitchen and placed two eggs in front of him. "Are you all right, dear? You're white as a sheet."

Raymond recovered quickly, pushing the letter into a pocket before checking his watch. "Haven't the time for the other egg," he said. "I'm already late for Cabinet committee, I must dash."

Strange, thought Joyce, as her husband hurried to the door. Cabinet committees didn't usually meet until ten and he hadn't even cracked open his first egg. She sat down and slowly ate her husband's breakfast, wondering why he had left all his post behind.

Once he was in the back of his official car Raymond read the letter again. It didn't take long.

> Dear 'Malcolm',
>   I enjoid our little get together the other evening and five hundrud pounds would help me to forget it once and for all.
> Love, Mandy.
> PS. I'll be in touch again soon.

He read the letter once more and tried to compose his thoughts. There was no address on the top of the notebook paper. Neither letter nor envelope gave any clue as to where they had come from.

After he had arrived outside the Department of Employment Raymond remained in the back seat for several moments.

"Are you feeling all right, sir?" his driver asked.

"Fine, thank you," he replied, and jumped out of the car and ran all the way up to his office. As he passed his secretary's desk he barked at her, "No interruptions."

"You won't forget Cabinet committee at ten o'clock, will you, Minister?"

"No," replied Raymond sharply and slammed his office door. Once at his desk he tried to calm himself and recall what he would have done had he been approached by a client as a barrister at the bar: first instruct a good solicitor. Raymond considered the two most capable lawyers in England to be Arnold Goodman and Sir Roger Pelham. Goodman was getting too high a profile for Raymond's liking whereas Pelham was just as sound but virtually unknown to the general public. He called Pelham's office and made an appointment to see him that afternoon.

Raymond hardly spoke in Cabinet committee, but as most of his colleagues wanted to express their own views nobody noticed. As soon as the meeting was over Raymond hurried out and took a taxi to High Holborn.

Sir Roger Pelham rose from behind his large Victorian desk to greet the junior minister.

"I know you're a busy man, Gould," Pelham said as he fell back into his black leather chair, "so I shan't waste your time. Tell me what I can do for you."

"It was kind of you to see me at such short notice," Raymond began and without further word handed the letter over.

"Thank you," the solicitor said courteously and, pushing his half-moon spectacles higher up his nose he read the note three times before he made any comment.

"Blackmail is something we all detest," he began, "but it will be necessary for you to tell me the whole truth, and don't miss out any details. Please remember I am on your side. You'll recall only too well from your days at the bar what a disadvantage one labours under when one is in possession of only half the facts."

The tips of Pelham's fingers touched, forming a small roof in front of his nose as he listened intently to Raymond's account of what had happened that night.

"Could anyone else have seen you?" was Pelham's first question.

Raymond thought back and then nodded. "Yes," he said. "Yes, I'm afraid there was another girl who passed me on the stairs."

Pelham read the letter once more. "My immediate advice," he said, looking Raymond in the eye and speaking slowly and deliberately, "and you won't like it, is to do nothing."

"But what do I say if she contacts the press?"

"She will probably get in touch with someone from Fleet Street anyway, even if you pay the £500, or however many other £500s you can afford. Don't imagine you're the first minister to be blackmailed, Mr Gould. Every homosexual in the House lives in daily fear of it. It's a game of hide and seek. Very few people other than saints have nothing to *hide*, and the problem with public life is that a lot of busybodies want to *seek*." Raymond remained silent, trying not to show his anxiety. "Phone me on my private line immediately the next letter arrives," said Pelham, scribbling a number on a piece of paper.

"Thank you," said Raymond, at least relieved that his secret was now shared with someone else. Pelham rose from behind his desk and accompanied Raymond to the door. "You'll be glad to see Yorkshire back as county champions," said the solicitor as he walked down the long passage with the minister. Raymond did not reply. When they reached the outer door they shook hands formally. "I'll wait to hear from you," said Pelham. A pity that the man showed no interest in cricket.

Raymond left the solicitor's office feeling better, but he found it hard to concentrate on his work the rest of that day and slept only in fits and starts during the night. When he read the morning papers he was horrified to see how much space was being given to Charles Seymour's peccadillo. What a field day they would be able to have with him. When the post came, he searched anxiously for the scrawled handwriting. It was hidden under an American Express circular. He tore it open. The same hand was this time demanding that the £500 should be deposited at a newsagent in Pimlico. Sir Roger Pelham saw the minister one hour later.

Despite the renewed demand the solicitor's advice remained the same.

Andrew Fraser never stopped moving from one city to another because the Scottish Office had to show a presence in Edinburgh and Glasgow as well as in London. Louise did not complain; she had never seen her husband so happy. The only moment of light relief during his first three months as a minister came when Andrew found it necessary to send a letter to his father addressed, "Dear Sir Duncan," which went on to explain why he had to reject his offered advice on a Highlands and Islands Board project. Andrew was particularly pleased with the line, "I have for some considerable time listened to both sides of the argument."

Once he had settled in his favourite chair that night with a large whisky in his hand Louise told him she was pregnant again. "When did I find the time?" he asked, taking her in his arms.

"Maybe the half-hour between your meeting with the Norwegian Fishing Minister and the address to the Oil Conference in Aberdeen?"

When the AGM of the Sussex Downs Conservative Association came round in October Charles was pleased to learn that Mrs Blenkinsop's 'no confidence' motion had been withdrawn. The local press tried to build up the story but the nationals were full of the Aberfan coal-tip disaster, in which 116 schoolchildren had lost their lives. No editor could find space for Sussex Downs.

Charles delivered a thoughtful speech to his association which was well received. During question time he was relieved to find no embarrassing questions directed at him.

When the Seymours finally said goodnight, Charles took the chairman to one side and enquired: "How did you manage it?"

"I explained to Mrs Blenkinsop," replied the chairman, "that if her motion of no confidence was discussed at the AGM it would be awfully hard for the member to back my recommendation that she should receive an OBE in the New Year's Honours for service to the party. That shouldn't be too hard for you to pull off, should it, Charles?"

Every time the phone rang Raymond assumed it would be the press asking him if he knew someone called Mandy. Often it was a journalist, but all that was needed was a quotable remark on the latest unemployment figures, or a statement of where the minister stood on devaluation of the pound.

It was Mike Molloy, a reporter from the *Daily Mirror*, who was the first to ask Raymond what he had to say about a statement phoned in to his office by a girl with a West Indian accent called Mandy Page.

"I have nothing to say on the subject. Please speak to my solicitor, Sir Roger Pelham," was the Under-Secretary's succinct reply. The moment he put the phone down he felt queasy.

A few minutes later when the phone rang again Raymond still hadn't moved. He picked up the receiver, his hand still shaking. Pelham confirmed that Molloy had been in touch with him.

"I presume you made no comment," said Raymond.

"On the contrary," replied Pelham. "I told him the truth."

"What?" exploded Raymond.

"Be thankful she hit on a fair journalist because I expect he'll let this one go. Fleet Street are not quite the bunch of shits everyone imagines them to be," Pelham said uncharacteristically, and added, "they also detest two things, bent policemen and blackmailers. I don't think you'll see anything in the press tomorrow."

Sir Roger Pelham was wrong.

Raymond was standing outside his local newsagent the next morning when it opened at five-thirty and he surprised the proprietor by asking for a copy of the *Daily Mirror*. Raymond Gould was plastered all over page five saying, "Devaluation is not a course I can support while the unemployment figures remain so high." The photograph by the side of the article was unusually flattering.

Simon Kerslake read a more detailed account of what the minister had said on devaluation in *The Times*, and noted

Raymond Gould's firm stand against what was beginning to look like inevitable Government policy.

Simon looked up from his paper and started to consider a ploy that might trap Gould. If he could make the minister commit himself again and again on devaluation in front of the whole House he knew that when the inevitable happened Gould would be left with no choice but to resign. Simon pencilled a question on the top of the paper before returning to the political columns.

The devaluation news had caused a Tory lead in the opinion polls of eight per cent, and despite a majority of ninety-five in the Commons the Government had actually lost a vote on the floor of the House the previous day. Nevertheless, Simon still could not envisage a general election for at least another two years.

On the business front Simon had advised Ronnie Nethercote not to allow his company shares to be traded on the Stock Exchange until the Tories returned to power. "The climate," he assured Ronnie, "should be much easier then."

Charles Seymour was glad to be behind the wheel again after his driving ban had been completed, and he had the grace to smile when Fiona showed him the photograph of the happy Mrs Blenkinsop displaying her OBE outside Buckingham Palace to a reporter from the *Sussex Gazette*.

It was six months to the day of his first meeting with Sir Roger Pelham that Raymond Gould received an account from the solicitor for services rendered – £500. He sent the cheque by return of post in a parcel that also contained a copy of the recently published edition of *Wisden*.

CHAPTER
EIGHT

Andrew had been warned by his ministerial colleagues that the first day answering questions at the dispatch box would be an experience he was unlikely to forget.

Questions for the Scottish Office appear on the order paper on a Wednesday once every four or five weeks, and each minister answers on behalf of his own department between two-thirty-five and three-twenty. There are usually four or five ministers of the Crown, not including the law officer available to represent each great department of state. During the forty-minute to one-hour period the ministers would expect to reply to about twenty-five questions, but it is rarely the questions that are the problem; it is the supplementaries.

Any member can place a question through the table office to any minister, and can word it in a seemingly innocuous way. "When does the minister hope next to visit Aberdeen?" to which the minister concerned may reply anything from "next week" to "I have no plans to do so in the foreseeable future" – but when the member who put down the question rises from his seat to ask his supplementary he can change the subject completely. "Does the minister realise that Aberdeen has the highest rate of unemployment in the United Kingdom, and what new ideas does his department have to deal with this problem?" The hapless minister must then come up with a convincing reply on the spot.

In an attempt to see that a minister is adequately briefed, his department will spend the morning scrutinising each tabled question and looking for pitfalls he might encounter. A variety of possible supplementaries will be placed in his brief with appropriate answers. Ministers can, of course, always ask colleagues on their own side what they are hoping to find out from their tabled questions, but Opposition members use question time to test a minister in the hope of discovering some weakness in his armoury, thus making the Government appear incompetent.

Andrew spent a considerable time in preparation for his first encounter at the dispatch box although the more senior and experienced ministers in the Scottish Office had agreed to handle any questions that looked hostile.

He ended up having to respond to only one question from the Opposition benches, while fielding four from his own. Added to which, the timing was such that question number twenty-three from the Opposition member seemed unlikely to be reached by three-twenty, when the Solicitor General for Scotland would have to start answering questions himself.

Andrew's first four answers to questions numbers five, nine, eleven and fourteen, went smoothly enough. He opened his dark blue file and was pleased to confirm the well-prepared briefs to everything that was thrown at him. By three-fifteen, when question number nineteen was being answered, Andrew sat back on the front bench and began to relax for the first time that day.

The Solicitor General for Scotland entered a now packed Commons and, moving alongside the table in the centre of the Chamber, he crouched slightly to be sure he did not obscure the Speaker's view of the Government benches on his right. The Prime Minister had been left a place between the Chancellor and the Foreign Secretary and waited for the clock to reach three-twenty.

The Speaker called question number twenty-one but the member was not present. He called number twenty-two and once again the member was absent. Each had obviously considered that their question had little chance of being reached before three-twenty. At three-eighteen the Speaker called question twenty-three – Andrew's heart sank – which read on the order paper, "Had the minister been invited to visit the Kinross Nursing Home?"

Andrew rose, opened his folder and said, "No, sir."

"No one in the House will be surprised by the minister's reply," said George Younger, the member for Ayr, "because the nursing home has forty-nine occupants, forty-seven of whom have their own television sets and yet the minister demands forty-seven separate licence fees. If they were to congregate in one room, he would expect only one fee. Is this another example of the Labour party's 'Care for the Aged' programme that we hear so much about nowadays?"

Andrew rose to the dispatch box to cries of "Answer, answer," from the Opposition benches. He had checked his crib sheet while sitting on the edge of his seat. Andrew had a prepared answer for medical facilities, old-age pensions, supplementary benefits, food allowances, medical charges – but nothing on TV licences. As he stood stranded at the dispatch box he was aware for the first time of the pitfalls that a minister encounters when he is not fully prepared. Such a system might appear wonderfully democratic to onlookers, he thought, until you are the Christian facing the 300 hungry lions.

A handwritten note was quickly passed along the front bench to him from one of the civil servants who sit in the official box to the left behind the Speaker's chair. With no time to consider its implications Andrew crossed his fingers and read the note out to the House.

"This was a decision taken by the last administration, of which the Honourable Gentleman was a member. We have seen no reason to reverse that decision," he read, thinking how much like a parrot he sounded. He sat down to polite Government murmurs and some considerable relief.

Mr Younger rose again and was allowed a second supplementary.

"Mr Speaker, this is the sort of inaccuracy we have grown to expect from this Government. The decision he refers to was made by his Right Honourable friend, the Secretary of State, only last year, and I think the minister will find, if he does his research more fastidiously, that his party was in power at the time." The Opposition howled their delight.

Andrew rose again and gripped the sides of the dispatch box to avoid anyone seeing that he was shaking in fear.

Several members of the Government front bench had their heads bowed. The Opposition had drawn blood and were baying in triumph. Lord Attlee's words came back to Andrew. "When you are caught out by the House admit it, apologise, and sit down."

Andrew waited for the noise to subside before he replied. "The Secretary of State warned me that a new minister will never forget his first question time and I feel bound to agree with him." Andrew, who knew how the atmosphere in the House can change in a moment, felt such a moment now, and before it could turn back added, "On the question of television licences in the Kinross Nursing Home, I apologise to the Honourable Gentleman for Ayr for my mistake and I will look into the case immediately and send him a written reply within twenty-four hours." "Hear, hears" could now be heard from his own benches and the Opposition benches were quietened. Mr Younger was trying to interrupt again but as Andrew didn't give way he had to resume his seat, knowing the Speaker would not call on him again once the clock had passed three-nineteen. Andrew waited for silence before adding, "And I blame my grandmother for this who, as President of the Kinross Nursing Home and a staunch Conservative, has always believed in increasing old-age pensions rather than looking for false subsidies that can never be fair to everyone." By now the Labour members were laughing and all the heads on the front bench were looking towards the new minister, who remained at the dispatch box until the House was silent again. "My grandmother would be delighted to learn that this administration has raised that old-age pension by fifty per cent in the three years since we have taken office." The Labour back-benchers were now cheering and waving their order papers as Andrew resumed his seat, while the Opposition were silent and glum.

The hands of the clock touched three-twenty and the Speaker said, "The Solicitor General's questions."

Andrew Fraser had made a political reputation, and as the laughter echoed round the House the intense figure sitting on the end of the front bench put a hand through his red hair and wondered if he could ever match Andrew's skill at the dispatch box. On the Opposition back benches Simon Kerslake made a mental note to be cautious if he ever thought of putting a sharp question to Andrew Fraser.

As soon as the Solicitor General's questions were over Simon left the House and drove himself to Whitechapel Road. He arrived a few minutes after the four o'clock board meeting of Nethercote and Company had begun, quietly took his seat and listened to Ronnie Nethercote describing another coup.

Ronnie had signed a contract that morning to take over a major city block at a cost of fifteen million pounds with a guaranteed rental income of over 1.1 million per annum for the first seven years of a twenty-one year lease with seven-year rent reviews.

Simon formally congratulated him and asked if this made any difference to the company's timing for going public.

"Why do you ask?" said Ronnie.

"Because I still feel it might be wise to wait until we know the result of the next general election. If the Conservatives return to power, as the opinion polls forecast, that could change the whole atmosphere for launching a new company."

"If they don't, I shan't hold up going public much longer."

"I wouldn't disagree with that decision either, Mr Chairman," said Simon.

When the meeting was over he joined Nethercote in his office for a drink.

"I want to thank you," Ronnie said, "for that introduction to Harold Samuel and Louis Freedman. It made the deal go through much more smoothly."

"Does that mean you'll allow me to purchase some more shares?"

Ronnie hesitated. "Why not? You've earned them. But only another 10,000. Don't get ahead of yourself, Simon, or the other directors may become jealous."

In the car on the way to pick up Elizabeth Simon decided to take a second mortgage out on the house in Beaufort Street to raise the extra cash needed for the new shares. He thought it might be wise not to trouble her with the details. He savoured the prospect of the Conservatives winning the next election, perhaps being given office in the Government and selling his shares for a sum that would make it possible for him to stop the continual worries of how he would finance his children's education. Perhaps he could even give Elizabeth that holiday in Venice she had talked about so often.

When he drove up to the hospital Elizabeth was waiting outside the gates. "We won't be late, will we?" were her first words.

"No," said Simon, checking the clock on the dashboard as he turned the car round in the direction of Beaufort Street.

They arrived at the hall five minutes before the curtain was due to rise. The occasion was their sons' pantomime, and both Peter and Michael had assured their parents that they had major parts. It was Charles Kingsley's *The Water Babies*, and Michael turned out to be a crab, who although he never left the stage lay on his stomach throughout the entire performance and never uttered a word. Peter, who had spent the week learning his words off by heart, was an unconvincing water baby standing at the end of a row of twelve. His speaking part turned out to be one sentence: "If grown-ups go on eating all the fish in the sea there will be none left for me." King Neptune fixed his imperial eye on Peter and said, "Don't blame us, it's your father who's the MP," upon which Peter bowed his head and blushed, though not as deeply as Elizabeth when the audience in front of them turned round and smiled at Simon, who felt more embarrassed than if he had been in the centre of a raging debate in the Commons.

At coffee afterwards the headmaster admitted that the sentence had been added without the approval of the late Charles Kingsley. When Simon and Elizabeth took the children home that night they insisted on repeating Peter's one line again and again.

"If the Government did an about-turn and devalued the pound, would the Under-Secretary find it possible to remain in office?"

Raymond Gould stiffened when he heard Simon Kerslake's question. His grasp of the law and his background knowledge of the subject made all except the extremely articulate or highly experienced wary of taking him on. Nevertheless Raymond had one Achilles' heel arising from his firmly stated views in *Full Employment at any Cost?*: any suggestion that the Government would devalue. Time and again eager back-benchers would seek to tackle him on the subject but once more it was Simon Kerslake who felled his opponent.

Andrew, sitting on the front bench, composed in his mind a sharp reply about his colleagues' collective responsibility, but Raymond Gould said rather ponderously: "The policy of Her Majesty's Government is one hundred per cent against devaluation, and therefore the question does not arise."

"Wait and see," shouted Kerslake.

"Order," said the Speaker, rising from his seat and turning towards Simon as Raymond sat down. "The Honourable member knows all too well he must not address the House from a sedentary position. The Under-Secretary of State."

Raymond rose again. "This Government believes in a strong pound, which still remains our best hope for keeping unemployment figures down."

"But what would you do if Cabinet does go ahead and devalue?" Joyce asked him when she read her husband's reply to Kerslake's question reported in *The Times* the next morning.

Raymond was already facing the fact that devaluation looked more likely every day. A strong dollar causing imports to reach record levels coupled with a run of strikes during the summer of sixty-seven was causing foreign bankers to ask when, not if.

"I'd have to resign," he said in reply to Joyce's question.

"Why? No other minister will."

"I'm afraid Kerslake is right. I'm on the record and he's made sure everybody knows it. Don't worry, Harold will never devalue. He's assured me of that many times."

"He only has to change his mind once."

Pressure on the pound increased during the following weeks and Raymond began to fear that Joyce might turn out to be right.

Andrew Fraser had read *Full Employment at any Cost?* and
considered it a succinctly argued case although he did not
agree with all the small print. He personally was in favour of
devaluation but felt it should have been pushed through in
the Labour party's first week in office, so that the blame
could be left at the door of the Tories. After three years and a
second election victory any such suggestion would rightly be
considered outrageous.

As Louise's time of delivery approached she was getting
larger by the day. Andrew helped to take pressure off her as
much as he could, but this time he did not prepare so
obviously for the birth, as he felt his unbridled enthusiasm
might have contributed to her previous anxiety. He tried as
often as possible to bring the red boxes home each night, but
it remained an exception if he returned to Cheyne Walk
before eleven o'clock.

"Voting every night at ten o'clock and sometimes on
through the night into the next day is one system the rest of
the world has *not* considered worth emulating," Andrew had
told Louise after one particularly gruelling session. He
couldn't even remember what he had been voting on –
although he didn't admit that to her. "But as no Government
of whatever party has ever seriously considered the idea of
limiting the time for ending business 'the troops', as back-
benchers are known, go on charging through the lobbies day
in and day out. That's why the press refer to us as 'lobby
fodder'."

"More like a bunch of unruly children," she chided.

When Louise went into hospital one week early Elizabeth
Kerslake assured her there was nothing to be worried about,
and two days later Louise gave birth to a beautiful girl.

Andrew was in a departmental meeting discussing Glasgow's high-rise housing programme when the hospital staff
nurse rang to congratulate him. He went straight to his fridge
and took out the bottle of champagne his father had sent him
the day he joined the Scottish Office. He poured a plastic
mug of Krug for each of his team of advisers.

"Just better than drinking it out of the bottle," he suggested as he left his civil servants to go to the hospital.

On arrival at St Mary's Andrew was relieved to find Elizabeth Kerslake was on duty. She warned him that his wife was still under sedation after a particularly complicated Caesarian delivery. Elizabeth took him to see his daughter who remained under observation in an isolation unit.

"Nothing to fret about," Elizabeth assured him. "We always take this precaution after any Caesarian birth as there are a number of routine tests we still have to carry out."

She left Andrew to stare at his daughter's large blue eyes. Although he knew it might change in time the soft down on the crown of her head was already dark.

He slipped out an hour later when she had fallen asleep to return to Dover House, where he had a second celebration in the Secretary of State's office, but this time the champagne was served in crystal glasses.

When Andrew climbed into bed that night the champagne helped him fall into a deep sleep with the only problem on his mind being what they should call their daughter. Claire had always been the name Louise favoured.

The phone had rung several times before he answered it and as soon as he had replaced the receiver he dressed and drove to the hospital as quickly as possible. He parked the car and ran to the now-familiar ward. Elizabeth Kerslake was standing waiting by the door. She looked tired and dishevelled, and even with all her training and experience she found it hard to explain to Andrew what had happened.

"Your daughter died forty minutes ago when her heart stopped beating. Believe me, we tried everything."

Andrew collapsed on the bench in the corridor and didn't speak for several moments. "How's Louise?" was all he could eventually manage.

"She hasn't been told yet. She's still under sedation. Be thankful she never saw the baby."

Andrew thumped his leg until it was numb. He stopped suddenly. "I'll tell her myself," he said quietly and remained on the bench, tears coursing down his cheeks. Elizabeth sat down beside him but didn't speak. When she left it was only to check that Mrs Fraser was ready to see her husband.

Louise knew the moment Andrew walked in. It was over an hour before she managed to speak.

"I bet Alison McKenzie would have given you a dozen sons," she said, trying to make him smile.

"No doubt about that," said Andrew, "but they would have all been ugly and stupid."

"I agree with you," said Louise. "But that wouldn't have been her fault."

They both tried to laugh.

Andrew returned to Cheyne Walk a little after four o'clock, but he didn't sleep again that night.

The great orator Iain Macleod once remarked that it was the first two minutes of a speech that decided one's fate. One either grasps the House and commands it or dithers, and loses it, and once the House is lost it can rarely be brought to heel. When Charles Seymour was invited to present the winding-up speech for the Opposition during the Economic debate, he felt he had prepared himself well, and although he knew he could not expect to convert Government back-benchers to his argument he hoped the press would acknowledge the following day that he had won the argument and embarrassed the Government. The Administration was already rocking over daily rumours of devaluation and economic trouble, and Charles was confident that this was the chance to make his name.

Full parliamentary debates usually start at three-thirty, after question time, but can be delayed if there are ministerial statements to be made. The senior minister in the department concerned makes the opening speech for approximately thirty minutes and then the Opposition spokesman addresses the House for the same period of time. Between four-thirty and nine the debate is thrown open to the floor and the Speaker tries to be scrupulously fair in calling a cross-section of back-benchers who have demonstrated an interest in the subject, as well as preserving a party and regional balance. These back-bencher speeches are frowned on if they last for more than fifteen minutes. Some of the most memorable speeches delivered in the House have lasted eight or nine minutes, some of the worst over thirty.

At nine o'clock the Opposition spokesman makes his final comments, and at nine-thirty a Government minister winds up.

When Charles rose and stood at the dispatch box he intended to press home the Tory case on the Government's economic record, the fatal consequences of devaluation, the record inflation, coupled with record borrowing and a lack of confidence in Britain unknown in any member's lifetime.

He stood his full height and stared down belligerently at the Government benches.

"Mr Speaker," he began, "I can't think . . ."

"Then don't bother to speak," someone shouted from the Labour benches. Laughter broke out as Charles tried to compose himself, cursing his initial over-confidence. He began again.

"I can't imagine . . ."

"No imagination either," came another voice. "Typical Tory."

". . . why this motion was ever put before the House."

"Certainly not for you to give us a lesson in public speaking."

"Order," growled the Speaker, but it was too late.

The House was lost and Charles stumbled through thirty minutes of embarrassment until no one but the Speaker was listening to a word he said. Several members of his own front bench had their feet up on the table and their eyes closed. Back-benchers on either side sat chattering amongst themselves waiting for the ten o'clock division: the ultimate humiliation the House affords to its worst debaters. The Speaker had to call for order several times during Charles's speech, once rising to rebuke noisy members, "The House does its reputation no service by behaving in this way." But his plea fell on deaf ears as the conversations continued. At nine-thirty Charles sat down in a cold sweat. A few of his own back-benchers managed to raise an unconvincing "Hear, hear."

When the Government minister opened his speech by

describing Charles's offering as among the most pathetic he had heard in a long political career he may well have been exaggerating, but from the expressions on the Tory front benches not many Opposition members were going to disagree with him.

CHAPTER NINE

The decision was finally made by the inner Cabinet of twelve on Thursday 16 November 1967. By Friday every bank clerk in Tokyo was privy to the inner Cabinet's closest secret, and by the time the Prime Minister made the announcement official on Saturday afternoon the Bank of England had lost 600 million dollars of reserves on the foreign exchange market.

At the time of the Prime Minister's statement Raymond was in Leeds conducting one of his fortnightly constituency 'surgeries'. He was in the process of explaining the new housing bill to a young married couple when Fred Padgett, his agent, burst into the room.

"Raymond, sorry to interrupt you, but I thought you'd want to know immediately. No. 10 have just announced that the pound has been devalued from two dollars eighty to two dollars forty." The sitting member was momentarily stunned, the local housing problem driven from his mind. He stared blankly across the table at the two constituents who had come to seek his advice.

"Will you please excuse me for a moment, Mr Higginbottom," Raymond asked courteously, "but I must make a phone call." The moment turned out to be fifteen minutes, in which time Raymond had made contact with a senior civil servant from the Treasury and had all the details confirmed. He called Joyce and told her not to answer the phone until he arrived back home. It was several minutes before he felt composed enough to put his head round the office door.

"How many people are still waiting to see me, Fred?" he asked.

"After the Higginbottoms there's only the mad major, still convinced that Martians are about to land on the roof of Leeds town hall."

"Why would they want to come to Leeds first?" asked Raymond, trying to hide his anxiety with false humour.

"Once they've captured Yorkshire, the rest would be easy."

"Hard to find fault with that argument. Nevertheless, tell the major I'm deeply concerned but I need to study his claim in more detail and to seek further advice from the Ministry of Defence. Make an appointment for him to see me at the next surgery and by then I should have a strategic plan ready for him."

Fred Padgett grinned. "That will give him something to tell his friends about for at least two weeks."

Raymond returned to Mr and Mrs Higginbottom and assured them he would have their housing problem sorted out within a few days. He made a note on his file to ring the Leeds Council Housing Officer.

"What an afternoon," exclaimed Raymond after the door had closed behind them. "One wife-beating, one electricity turned off by the YEB with four children under ten in the house, one pollution of the Aire river and one appalling housing problem – never forgetting the mad major and his itinerant Martians. And on top of all of that the devaluation news."

"How can you remain so calm?" asked Fred Padgett.

"Because I can't afford to let anyone know how I really feel."

After his surgery Raymond would normally have gone round to the local pub for a pint and an obligatory natter with the locals. This always gave him the chance to catch up on what had been happening in Leeds during the past fortnight. But on this occasion he bypassed the pub and returned quickly to his parents' home.

Joyce told him that the phone had rung so often that she had finally taken it off the hook, without letting his mother know the real reason.

"Very sensible," said Raymond.

"What are you going to do?" she asked.

"I shall resign, of course."

"Why do that, Raymond? It will only harm your career."

"You may turn out to be right, but that won't stop me going."

"But you're only just beginning to get on top of your work."

"Joyce, without trying to sound pompous, I know I have many failings but I'm not a coward and I'm certainly not so self-seeking as totally to desert any principles I might have."

"You know, you just sounded like a man who is destined to become Prime Minister."

"A moment ago you said it would harm my chances. Make up your mind."

"I have," she said.

Raymond smiled wanly before retreating to his study to write a short handwritten letter.

> Saturday, 18 November 1967
>
> Dear Prime Minister,
>
> After your announcement this afternoon on devaluation and the stand I have continually taken on the issue I am left with no choice but to resign my position as Under-Secretary of State at the Department of Employment.
>
> I would like to thank you for having given me the opportunity to serve in your administration. Be assured that I shall continue to support the Government on all other issues from the back benches.
>
> Yours,
> Raymond Gould.

When the red box arrived at the house that Saturday night Raymond instructed the messenger to deliver the letter to No. 10 immediately. As he opened the box for the last time he reflected that his department was answering questions on employment in the House that Monday. He wondered who would take his place.

Because of the paraphernalia surrounding devaluation, the Prime Minister did not get round to reading Raymond's letter until late Sunday morning. The Goulds' phone was still off the hook when an anxious Fred Padgett was heard knocking on the front door later that day.

"Don't answer it," said Raymond. "It's bound to be another journalist."

"No, it's not, it's only Fred," said Joyce, peeping through an opening in the curtain.

She opened the door. "Where the hell's Raymond?" were Fred's first words.

"Right here," said Raymond, appearing from the kitchen holding the Sunday newspapers.

"The Prime Minister has been trying to contact you all morning." Raymond turned round and replaced the phone on the hook, picked it up a few seconds later and checked the tone before dialling London WHI 4433. The Prime Minister was on the line in moments. He sounded calm enough, thought Raymond.

"Have you issued any statement to the press, Ray?"

"No, I wanted to be sure you had received my letter first."

"Good. Please don't mention your resignation to anyone until we've met. Could you be at Downing Street by eight o'clock?"

"Yes, Prime Minister."

"Remember, not a word to the press."

Raymond heard the phone click.

Within the hour he was on his way to London, and arrived at his house in Lansdowne Road a little after seven. The phone was ringing again. He wanted to ignore the insistent *burr-burr* but thought it might be Downing Street.

He picked the phone up. "Hello."

"Is that Raymond Gould?" said a voice.

"Who's speaking?" asked Raymond.

"Walter Terry, *Daily Mail*."

"I am not going to say anything," said Raymond.

"Do you feel the Prime Minister was right to devalue?"

"I said nothing, Walter."

"Does that mean you are going to resign?"

"Walter, nothing."

"Is it true you have already handed in your resignation?"

Raymond hesitated.

"I thought so," said Terry.

"I said nothing," spluttered Raymond and slammed down the phone – before lifting it back off the hook.

He quickly washed and changed his shirt before leaving the house. He nearly missed the note that was lying on the doormat, and he wouldn't have stopped to open it had the envelope not been embossed with large black letters across the left-hand corner – 'Prime Minister'. Raymond ripped it open. The handwritten note from a secretary asked him on his arrival to come by the rear entrance of Downing Street and not the front door. A small map was enclosed. Raymond was becoming weary of the whole exercise.

Two more journalists were waiting by the gate and followed him to his car.

"Have you resigned, Minister?" asked the first.

"No comment."

"Are you on your way to see the Prime Minister?"

Raymond did not reply and leaped into his car. He drove off so quickly that the pursuing journalists were left with no chance of catching him.

Twelve minutes later, at five to eight, he was seated in the ante-room of No. 10 Downing Street. As eight struck he was taken through to Harold Wilson's study. He was surprised to find the Secretary of State for Employment seated in the corner of the room.

"Ray," said the Prime Minister. "How are you?"

"I'm well, thank you, Prime Minister."

"I was sorry to receive your letter and thoroughly understand the position you are in, but I hope perhaps we can work something out."

"Work something out?" Raymond repeated, puzzled.

"Well, we all realise devaluation is a problem for you after *Full Employment at any Cost?* but I felt perhaps a move to the Foreign Office as Minister of State might be a palatable way out of the dilemma. It's a promotion you've well earned."

Raymond hesitated. The Prime Minister continued. "It may interest you to know that the Chancellor of the

Exchequer has also resigned, but will be moving to the Home Office."

"I am surprised," said Raymond.

"What with the problems we are about to tackle in Rhodesia and Europe your legal skills would come in very useful."

Raymond remained silent as he listened to the Prime Minister; he knew what decision he must now make.

Monday usually gets off to a quiet start in the Commons. The Whips never plan for any contentious business to be debated, remembering that members are still arriving back from their constituencies all over the country. The House is seldom full before the early evening. But the knowledge that the Chancellor of the Exchequer would be making a statement on devaluation at three-thirty ensured that the Commons would be packed long before that hour.

The green benches, accommodating just 427 members, had deliberately been restored as they were after the Germans had bombed the Palace of Westminster on 10 May 1941. The intimate theatrical atmosphere of the House had remained intact. Sir Giles Gilbert Scott could not resist highlighting some of the Gothic décor of Barry, but he concurred with Churchill's view that to enlarge the Chamber would only destroy the packed atmosphere of great occasions.

The Commons filled up quickly, and by two-forty-five there was not a seat to be found. Members huddled up on the steps by the Speaker's canopied chair and around the legs of the chairs of the clerks at the table. One or two even perched like unfed sparrows on the empty petition bag behind the Speaker's chair. The galleries to the side and above the Chamber, which normally resembled empty benches at the Oval on a rainy day, had taken on the look of a crucial last Test match against Australia.

The chief doorkeeper checked his supply of snuff that it had been his office to keep since those days when 'unpleasant odours' wafted through London.

Raymond Gould rose to answer question number seven on

the order paper, an innocent enough inquiry concerning supplementary benefits for women. As soon as he reached the dispatch box the first cries of "Resign" came from the Tory benches. Raymond couldn't hide his embarrassment. Even those seated on the back benches could see he had gone scarlet. It didn't help that he hadn't slept the previous night following the agreement he had come to with the Prime Minister. He answered the question, but the calls for his resignation did not subside. The Opposition fell silent as he sat down, only waiting for him to rise for a further question. The next question on the order paper for Raymond to answer was from Simon Kerslake; it came a few minutes after three. "What analysis has been made by his department of the special factors contributing to increasing unemployment in the Midlands?"

Raymond checked his brief before replying. "The closure of two large factories in the area, one in the Honourable member's constituency, has exacerbated local unemployment. Both of these factories specialised in car components which have suffered from the Leyland strike."

Simon Kerslake rose slowly from his place to put his supplementary. The Opposition benches waited in eager anticipation. "But surely the minister remembers informing the House, in reply to my adjournment debate last April, that devaluation would drastically increase unemployment in the Midlands, indeed in the whole country. If the Honourable Gentleman's words are to carry any conviction, why hasn't he resigned?" Simon sat down as the Tory benches demanded, "Why, why, why?"

"My speech to the House on that occasion is being quoted out of context, and the circumstances have since changed."

"They certainly have," shouted a number of Conservatives and the benches opposite Raymond exploded with demands that he give up his office.

"Order, order," shouted the Speaker into the tide of noise.

Simon rose again, while everyone on the Conservative benches remained seated to ensure no one else was called. They were now hunting as a pack. Everyone's eyes switched back and forth between the two men, watching the dark, assured figure of Kerslake once again jabbing his forefinger at the bowed head of Raymond Gould who was now only praying for the clock to reach three-thirty.

"Mr Speaker, during the debate, which he now seems happy to orphan, the Honourable Gentleman was only echoing the views he so lucidly expressed in his book *Full Employment at any Cost?* Can those views have altered so radically in three years, or is his desire to remain a minister so great that he now realises that *his* employment can be retained at any cost?"

"This question has nothing to do with what I said to the House on that occasion," retorted Raymond angrily. His last few words were lost in Opposition shouts of "Resign, resign!"

Simon was up in a flash and the Speaker called him for a third time.

"Is the Honourable Gentleman telling the House that he has one set of moral standards when he speaks, and yet another when he writes?"

The House was now in total uproar and few members heard Raymond say, "No, sir, I try to be consistent."

The Speaker rose and the noise subsided slightly. He looked about him with an aggrieved frown. "I realise the House feels strongly on these matters, but I must ask the Honourable member for Coventry Central to withdraw his remark suggesting that the minister has behaved dishonourably."

Simon rose and retracted his statement at once, but the damage had been done. Nor did it stop members from calling "Resign" until Raymond left the Chamber a few minutes later.

Simon sat back smugly as Gould left the Chamber. Conservative members turned to nod their acknowledgement of his professional demolition of the Government's Under-Secretary of State. The Chancellor of the Exchequer rose to deliver his prepared statement on devaluation. Simon felt sick as he listened with horror to the Chancellor's opening words. "The Honourable member for Leeds North handed in his resignation to the Prime Minister on Saturday evening but graciously agreed not to make this public until I had had an opportunity to address the House."

The Chancellor went on to praise Raymond for his work in the Department of Employment, and to wish him well on the back benches.

Andrew visited Raymond in his room immediately after the Chancellor had finished answering questions. He found him slumped at his desk, a vacant look on his face. Andrew had never considered Raymond a natural friend but he wanted to express his admiration for the way he had conducted himself.

"It's kind of you," said Raymond, who was still shaking from the experience. "Particularly as you would have demolished the lot of them."

"Well, they're all demolished now," said Andrew. "Simon Kerslake must feel the biggest shit in town."

"There's no way he could have known," said Raymond. "He'd certainly done his homework and the questions were spot on. I suspect we would have approached the situation in much the same way given the circumstances."

Several other members dropped in to commiserate with Raymond after which he returned to his old department to say farewell to his team before he went home to spend a quiet evening with Joyce. There was a long silence before the Permanent Secretary ventured an opinion: "I hope, sir, it will not be long before you return to Government. You have certainly made our lives hard but for those you ultimately serve you have undoubtedly made life easier." The sincerity of the statement touched Raymond, especially as the civil servant was already serving a new master.

It felt strange to sit down and watch television, read a book, even go for a walk and not be perpetually surrounded by red boxes and ringing phones. Within forty-eight hours he missed it all.

He was to receive over a hundred letters from colleagues in the House but he kept only one.

Monday, 20 November 1967

Dear Gould,

I owe you a profound apology. We all in our political life make monumental mistakes about people and I certainly made one today.

I believe that most members of the House have a genuine desire to serve the country, and there can be no more honourable way of proving it than by resigning when one feels one's party has taken a wrong course.

I envy the respect in which the whole House now holds you.

Yours sincerely,
Simon Kerslake.

When Raymond returned to the Commons that afternoon, he was cheered by the members of both sides from the moment he entered the Chamber. The minister who had been in the middle of addressing the House at the time had no choice but to wait until Raymond had taken his seat on the back benches.

CHAPTER TEN

Simon had already left when Edward Heath called his home. It was another hour before Elizabeth was able to pass on the message that the party leader wanted to see him at two-thirty.

Charles was at the bank when the Chief Whip called, asking if they could meet at two-thirty that afternoon before Commons business began. Charles felt like a schoolboy who had been told the headmaster expected him to be in his study after lunch. The last time the Chief Whip had phoned was to ask him to make the winding-up speech and they had hardly spoken since. Charles remained apprehensive; he always preferred to be told what a problem was immediately.

He decided to skip lunch at the bank and join his colleagues in the House, to be certain he wouldn't be late for the afternoon appointment.

Charles did not enjoy eating at the House as the food, with the exception of the *hors d'oeuvres* trolley, was only a little better than Paddington station and rather worse than London airport.

He joined some of his colleagues at the large table in the centre of the Members' Dining-room and took the only seat available, next to Simon Kerslake. The two men had not really been on good terms since the Heath–Maudling leadership contest. Charles did not care much for Kerslake: he had once told Fiona that he was one of the new breed of Tories who tried a little too hard and he had not been displeased to see him embarrassed over the Gould resignation. Not that he allowed anyone other than Fiona to know his true feelings.

Simon watched Charles sit down and wondered how much longer the party could go on electing Etonian guardsmen who spent more time making money in the City and spending it at Ascot than they did working in the House – not that it was an opinion he would have expressed to anyone but his closest friend. The discussion over lunch centred on the remarkable run of by-election results the Tories had had at Acton, Meriden and Dudley. It was obvious that most of those around the table could not wait for a general election, although the Prime Minister did not have to call one for at least another three years.

Neither Charles nor Simon ordered coffee.

At two-twenty-five Charles watched the Chief Whip leave his private table in the corner of the room and turn to walk towards his office. Charles checked his watch and waited a moment before leaving his colleagues to begin a heated discussion about entry into the Common Market.

He strolled past the smoking room before turning left at the entrance to the library. Then he continued down the old Ways and Means corridor, passed through the swing doors and entered the Members' Lobby which he crossed to reach the Government Whips' office. He put his head round the secretary's door. Miss Norse OBE, the Chief's invaluable secretary, stopped typing.

"I have an appointment with the Chief Whip," said Charles.

"Yes, Mr Seymour, he is expecting you. Please go through." The typing recommenced immediately.

Charles walked on down the corridor and found the Chief Whip blocking his own doorway.

"Come on in, Charles. Can I offer you a drink?"

"No, thank you," replied Charles, not wanting to delay the news any longer.

The Chief Whip poured himself a gin and tonic before sitting down.

"I hope what I'm about to tell you will be looked upon as good news." The Chief Whip paused and took a gulp of his drink. "The leader thinks you might benefit from a spell in the Whips' office, and I must say I would be delighted if you felt able to join us . . ."

Charles wanted to protest but checked himself. "And give up my Housing and Local Government post?"

"Oh yes, and more of course, because Mr Heath expects all Whips to forgo outside commitments. Working in this office is not a part-time occupation."

Charles needed a moment to compose his thoughts. "And if I turn it down, will I keep my post at Housing and Local Government?"

"That's not for me to decide," said the Chief Whip, "but it is no secret that Ted Heath is planning several changes in the run-up to the election."

"How long do I have to consider the offer?"

"Perhaps you could let me know your decision by question time tomorrow."

"Yes, of course. Thank you," said Charles. He left the Chief Whip's office and drove to Eaton Square.

Simon arrived at two-twenty-five, five minutes before his meeting with the party leader. He had tried not to speculate as to why Heath wanted to see him, in case the meeting only resulted in disappointment. Douglas Hurd, the head of the private office, ushered him straight through to the Conservative leader.

"Simon, how would you like to join the Housing and Local Government team in the run-up to the election?" It was typical of Heath not to waste any time on small talk and the suddenness of the offer stunned Simon. He recovered quickly.

"Thank you very much," he said. "I mean er . . . yes . . . thank you."

"Good, let's see you put your back into it, and be sure the results at the dispatch box are as effective as they have been from the back benches."

The door was opened once again by the private secretary; the interview was clearly over. Simon found himself back in the corridor at two-thirty-three. It was several moments before the offer sank in. Then he suddenly felt elated and made a dash for the nearest phone. He dialled the St Mary's switchboard and asked if he could be put through to Dr Kerslake. As he spoke, his voice was almost drowned by the sound of the division bells, signalling the start of the day's business at two-thirty-five following prayers. A woman's voice came on the line.

"Is that you, darling?" asked Simon above the din.

"No, sir. It's the switchboard operator. Dr Kerslake's in the operating theatre."

"Is there any hope of getting her out?"

"Not unless you're expecting a baby, sir."

"What brings you home so early?" asked Fiona as Charles came charging through the front door.

"I need to talk to someone." Fiona could never be sure if she ought to be flattered, but she didn't express any opinion as it was all too rare these days to have his company at all.

Charles repeated to his wife as nearly verbatim as possible his conversation with the Chief Whip. Fiona remained silent when Charles had come to the end of his monologue. "Well, what's your opinion?" he asked anxiously.

"All because of one bad speech from the dispatch box," Fiona commented wryly.

"I agree," said Charles, "but nothing can be gained by tramping over that ground again."

"We'll miss the salary you earn as a director of the bank," said Fiona. "The tax on my private income has made the amount I now receive derisory."

"I know, but if I turn it down, and we win the next election . . .?"

"You'll be left out in the cold."

"More to the point, stranded on the back benches."

"Charles, politics has always been your first love," said Fiona, touching him gently on the cheek. "So I don't see that you have a choice, and if that means some sacrifices you'll never hear me complain."

Charles rose from his chair saying, "Thank you. I'd better go and see Derek Spencer immediately."

As Charles turned to leave, Fiona added, "And don't

forget, Ted Heath became leader of the party via the Whips'
office.''

Charles smiled for the first time that day.

"A quiet dinner at home tonight?'' suggested Fiona.

"Can't,'' said Charles. "I've got a late vote.''

Fiona sat alone wondering if she would spend the rest of
her life cohabiting with three-line whips.

At last they put him through.

"Let's have a celebration dinner tonight.''

"Why?'' asked Elizabeth.

"Because I've been invited to join the front-bench team to
cover Housing and Local Government.''

"Congratulations, darling, but what does Housing and
Local Government consist of?''

"Housing, urban land, transport, devolution, water, historic buildings, Stansted or Maplin airport, the Channel
tunnel, royal parks . . .''

"Have they left anything for anyone else to do?''

"That's only half of it, if it's out of doors it's mine. I'll tell
you the rest over dinner.''

"Oh, hell, I don't think I can get away until eight tonight,
and we'd still have to get a baby-sitter. Does that come under
Housing and Local Government, Simon?''

"Sure does,'' he said, laughing. "I'll fix it and book a table
at the Grange for eight-thirty.''

"Have you got a ten o'clock vote?''

"Afraid so.''

"I see, coffee with the baby-sitter,'' she said. She paused.
"Simon.''

"Yes, darling?''

"I'm very proud of you.''

Derek Spencer sat behind his massive partner's desk in
Cheapside and listened intently to what Charles had to say.

"You will be a great loss to the bank,'' were the chairman's
first words. "But no one here would want to hold up your
political career, least of all me.''

Charles noticed that Spencer could not look him in the eye as he spoke.

"Can I assume that I would be invited back on the board if for any reason my situation changed at the Commons?"

"Of course," said Spencer. "There was no need for you to ask such a question."

"That's kind of you," said Charles, genuinely relieved. He stood up, leaned forward and shook hands rather stiffly.

"Good luck, Charles," were Spencer's parting words.

"Does that mean you can no longer remain on the board?" asked Ronnie Nethercote when he heard Simon's news.

"No, not while I'm in Opposition and only a Shadow spokesman. Only the Chief Whip receives a salary and is therefore disqualified, but if we win the next election and I'm offered a job in Government I would have to resign immediately."

"So I've got your services for another three years?"

"Unless the Prime Minister goes earlier, or we lose the next election."

"No fear of the latter," said Ronnie. "I knew I'd picked a winner the day I met you, and I don't think you'll ever regret joining my board."

Over the months that followed Charles was surprised to find how much he enjoyed working in the Whips' office, although he had been unable to hide from Fiona his anger at Kerslake taking over his shadow post at Housing and Local Government. The order, discipline and *camaraderie* of the job brought back memories of his days in the Grenadier Guards. His duties were manifold and ranged from checking that members were all present in their committees to sitting on the front bench in the Commons and picking out the salient points members made in their speeches to the House. He also had to keep an eye out for any signs of dissension or rebellion on his own benches while remaining abreast of what was happening on the other side of the House. In addition he had fifty of his own members from the Midlands area to shepherd, and had to be certain that they never missed a vote unless paired, and only then when the Whips' office had been informed.

As Whips are never called on to make speeches in the House at any time Charles seemed to have discovered a role for which he was best cut out. Fiona reminded him once again that Ted Heath had a spell in the Whips' office on his way to becoming Shadow Chancellor. She was delighted to see how involved her husband had become with Commons life but still hated going to bed alone each night and regularly falling asleep before he had even arrived home.

Simon also enjoyed his new appointment from the first moment. As the junior member of the Housing and Local Government team he was given transport as his special subject. During the first year he read books, studied pamphlets, held meetings with national transport chairmen from air, sea and rail and frequently worked long into the night trying to master his new brief. Simon was one of those rare members who, after only a few weeks, looked as if he had always been on the front bench.

Both parties were surprised by the fourteen per cent swing to the Conservatives at the Louth by-election towards the end of 1969. It began to look as if the Labour party did not have enough time to recover before they had to call an election. But in March 1970 the Labour party had a surprisingly good result in the Ayrshire South by-election; it caused the press to speculate that the Prime Minister might go to the country early. The May local elections in England and Wales showed a further swing to Labour, which was contrary to every other political trend of the previous two years. Talk of a general election was suddenly in the air.

When the following month's opinion polls confirmed the swing to Labour Harold Wilson visited the Queen at Buckingham Palace and asked her to dissolve Parliament. The date of the general election was set for 18 June 1970.

The press were convinced that Wilson had got it right again, and would lead his party to victory for the third time in a row, a feat no man in political history had managed. Every

Conservative knew that would spell the end of Edward Heath's leadership of his party.

Andrew and Louise returned to Edinburgh as soon as the Queen had made the announcement. Parliament went into a limbo period while members dispersed all over the country only in order to try and return to Westminster.

Andrew found his local committee had been taken by surprise by the PM's announcement, and realised he only had a matter of days to prepare himself.

The evening he arrived back in Edinburgh he called his General Purposes Committee together and over coffee and sandwiches mapped out a demanding three-week timetable which would allow him to reach every part of the constituency not once but several times. Street cards were pinned on to an old trestle table, soon to be filled in with crayon of various colours according to the canvassing returns: a red line through a definite Labour vote, a blue line through a Conservative one, a yellow through a Liberal and a black line through the growing Scottish Nationalist party.

Andrew began each day of the campaign with a press conference at which he discussed local matters that affected his constituents, answered criticisms made by the other candidates and dealt with any national issues that had arisen during the previous twenty-four hours. He then spent the rest of the morning touring the constituency with a loudspeaker van, entreating people to "Send Fraser back to Westminster". He and Louise would fit in a pub lunch together before the dreaded door-to-door canvassing began.

"You'll enjoy this," said Andrew as they walked up to the first door on a cold Monday morning. The street list of names was on a card in his pocket. Andrew pressed the door bell, and a little jingle could be heard. A woman still in her dressing-gown answered it a few moments later.

"Good morning, Mrs Foster," he began. "My name is Andrew Fraser. I'm your Labour candidate."

"Oh, how nice to meet you. I have so much I need to discuss with you – won't you come in and have a cup of tea?"

"It's kind of you, Mrs Foster, but I have rather a lot of

ground to cover during the next few days." When the door closed, Andrew put a blue line through her name on his card.

"How can you be sure she's Conservative?" demanded Louise, "she seemed so friendly."

"The Conservatives are trained to ask all the other candidates in for tea and waste their time. Your own side will always say, 'You have my vote, don't spend your time with me,' and let you get on to those who are genuinely uncommitted."

"I always vote for Fraser," said Mrs Foster's next-door neighbour. "Labour for parliament, Tory for the local council."

"But don't you feel Sir Duncan should be removed from the council?" asked Andrew, grinning.

"Certainly not, and that's what I told him when he suggested I shouldn't vote for you."

Andrew put a red line through the name and knocked on the next door.

"My name is Andrew Fraser and I —"

"I know who you are, young man, and I'll have none of your politics, or your father's for that matter."

"May I ask who you will be voting for?" asked Andrew.

"Scottish Nationalist."

"Why?" asked Louise.

"Because the oil belongs to us, not those bloody Sassenachs."

"Surely it's better for the United Kingdom to remain as one body?" suggested Andrew. "At least that way —"

"Never. The Act of 1707 was a disgrace to our nation."

"But —" began Louise enthusiastically. Andrew put a hand on her arm. "Thank you, sir, for your time," and prodded his wife gently down the path.

"Sorry, Louise," said Andrew, when they were back on the pavement. "Once they mention the 1707 Act of Union we have no chance; some Scots have remarkably long memories."

He knocked on the next door. A fat man answered it, a dog lead in his hand.

"My name is Andrew Fraser, I —"

"Get lost, creep," came back the reply.

"Who are you calling creep?" Louise retaliated as the door was slammed in their faces. "Charming man."

"Don't be offended, darling. He was referring to me, not you."

"What will you put by his name?"

"A question mark. No way of telling who he votes for. Probably abstains."

He tried the next door.

"Hello, Andrew," said a lady before he could open his mouth. "Don't waste your time on me, I always vote for you."

"Thank you, Mrs Irvine," said Andrew, checking his house list. "What about your next-door neighbour?" he asked, pointing back.

"Ah, he's an irritable old basket, but I'll see he gets to the polls on the day and puts his cross in the right box. He'd better, or I'll stop keeping an eye on his greyhound for him when he's out."

"Thank you very much, Mrs Irvine," said Andrew, laughing.

"One more red," he told Louise as they returned to the pavement.

"And you might even pick up the greyhound vote."

They covered four streets during the next three hours, and Andrew put red lines through those names he was certain would support him on polling day.

"Why do you have to be so sure?" asked Louise.

"Because when we pick them up to vote on election day we don't want to remind the opposition, let alone arrange a lift for someone who then takes pleasure in voting Tory."

Louise laughed. "Politics is so dishonest."

"Be relieved you're not married to an American senator," said Andrew, putting a red line through the last name in the street. "At least we don't have to be millionaires to stand. Time for a quick bite before the evening meeting," he added, taking his wife's hand. On their way back to their head-quarters they came across their Conservative opponent, but Andrew didn't respond when Hector McGregor tried to engage him in conversation, again holding him up.

Louise never joined her husband again on these sessions, deciding she could be of more use working back in the Committee Rooms.

In the public meetings held each evening, Andrew made the same speech thirty-two times in twenty-four days with only slight variations to account for national developments. Louise sat loyally through every one of them, always laughing at his punch lines and starting the clapping whenever he made a telling point. Somehow she managed to remain fresh and lively even at the end of the day when she drove her husband home.

By the eve of the election all the press were predicting a clear majority for Labour, but Andrew observed the gleam in his father's eye when he passed him in the street canvassing for McGregor.

At five-thirty on the morning of the election Louise woke Andrew with a cup of tea. He didn't see another cup that day. To his relief the sun was shining when he pulled back the curtains after he had had his bath: bad weather invariably helped the Tories with their never-ending pool of cars, ferrying voters to the polling booths. He returned to the bedroom to find his wife pinning to the lapel of his jacket a vast red rosette bearing the exhortation, 'Send Fraser back to Westminster'.

He was strolling through the streets of Edinburgh shaking hands, chatting to well-wishers, trying to convince last-minute 'don't knows' when he spotted his father heading towards him. They ended up facing each other in the middle of the street.

"It's going to be a close-run thing," said Sir Duncan.

"Then I'll know who to blame if I lose by one vote," said Andrew.

Sir Duncan looked conspiratorially about him, then lowered his voice. "If you win by one vote you'll have me to thank, laddie." He marched away entreating the citizens of Edinburgh to remove the turncoat Fraser.

The next time father and son met was at the count that evening. As the little piles of votes began to grow it became

obvious that Andrew would be returned to Parliament, and
Hector McGregor was soon shaking his head in disappointment.

But when the first result was announced in Guildford and
showed a four per cent swing to the Tories all the previous
predictions of a strong Labour victory began to look unrealis-
tic. As each return was announced from town hall platforms
all over the country it became progressively more obvious
that the Tories were going to end up with a large enough
majority to govern.

"I would have thought," Sir Duncan said to his son as the
trend was confirmed across the nation, "that you'll be in for a
wee spell of Opposition."

"Wee is the important word," was all that Andrew replied.

Andrew retained his seat, keeping the swing against him
down to one per cent and his majority a safe 4,009. Scotland
wasn't as sure about Heath as the rest of the country, which
showed an average swing against Labour of 4.7 per cent.

Simon Kerslake managed a four-figure majority for the
first time when he won Coventry Central by 2,118.

When Fiona was asked by the old earl how many votes
Charles had won by, she said she couldn't be certain but she
did recall Charles telling a journalist it was more than the
other candidates put together.

Raymond Gould suffered an adverse swing of only two per
cent and was returned with a 10,416 majority. The people of
Leeds admire independence in a member, especially when it
comes to a matter of principle.

The Conservatives captured Parliament with an overall
majority of thirty. Her Majesty the Queen called for Edward
Heath and asked him to form a Government. He kissed the
hands of his sovereign and accepted her commission.

CHAPTER ELEVEN

When Simon awoke on the morning after the election he felt both exhausted and exhilarated. He lay in bed trying to imagine how those Labour ministers, who only the previous day had assumed they would be returning to their departments, would be feeling now.

Elizabeth stirred, let out a small sleep-filled sigh. Simon stared down at his wife. In the seven years of their marriage she had lost none of her attraction for him, but he still took pleasure in just looking at her sleeping form. Her long fair hair rested on her shoulders and her slim, firm figure curved gently beneath the silk nightgown. He started stroking her back and watched her slowly come out of sleep. When she finally awoke she turned over and he took her in his arms.

"I admire your energy," she said. "If you're still fit after three weeks on the trail I can hardly claim to have a headache."

He smiled, delighted to catch a moment of privacy between the seeming lunacy of electioneering and the anticipation of office. No voter was going to interrupt this rare moment of pleasure.

"Mum," said a voice, and Simon quickly turned over to see Peter standing at the door in his pyjamas. "I'm hungry."

On the way back to London in the car Elizabeth asked, "What do you think he'll offer you?"

"Daren't anticipate anything," said Simon. "But I would hope – Under-Secretary of State for Housing and Local Government."

"But you're still not certain to be offered a post?"

"Not at all. One can never know what permutations and pressures a new Prime Minister has to consider."

"Like what?" asked Elizabeth.

"Left and right wings of the party, north and south of the country – countless debts to be cleared with those people who can claim they played a role in getting him into No. 10." Simon yawned.

"Are you saying he could leave you out?"

"Oh yes. But I'll be livid if he does, and I'd certainly want to know who had been given my job – and why."

"And what could you do about it?"

"Nothing. There is absolutely nothing one can do and every back-bencher knows it. The Prime Minister's power of patronage is absolute."

"It won't matter, if you continue driving on the centre line," she said. "Are you sure you wouldn't like me to take a turn at the wheel?"

Louise let Andrew lie in on the Friday morning. She knew he had been expecting to return to a higher ministerial office and had been shattered by the election result.

By the time Andrew woke it was nearly eleven. He sat in silence in his dressing-gown, unshaven, and tapped a hard-boiled egg that refused to crack. An unopened *Times* lay by his side.

"Thank you for all your hard work," he said once the second cup of coffee had taken effect. She smiled.

An hour later, dressed in sports jacket and grey flannels, he toured the constituency in a loudspeaker van, thanking his supporters for returning him to Westminster. Louise was by his side, often able to jog his memory on names he couldn't recall.

After they had shaken the last hand they spent a quiet weekend with Sir Duncan in Stirling – who found it extremely hard to remove the smirk from his face.

Raymond was astonished by the election result. He couldn't believe that the opinion polls had been so wrong. He didn't confide in Joyce that he had hoped a Labour victory would bring him back into office after languishing on the back benches for what seemed an interminable time.

"There's nothing for it," he told her, "but to rebuild a career at the bar. We may be out of office for years."

"But surely that won't be enough to keep you fully occupied?"

"I have to be realistic about the future," he said slowly. "Although I don't intend to let Heath drag us into Europe without putting up one hell of a fight."

"Perhaps they'll ask you to Shadow someone?"

"No, there are always far fewer jobs available in Opposition, and in any case they always give the orators like Fraser the dispatch box when all you can do is to sit and make noises while we wait for another election."

Raymond wondered how he would broach what was really on his mind and tried to sound casual when he said, "Perhaps it's time we considered having our own home in the constituency."

"That seems an unnecessary expense," said Joyce, "especially as there's nothing wrong with your parents' home. And, in any case, wouldn't they be offended?"

"My first interest should be my duty to the constituents and this would be a chance to prove a long-term commitment to them. Naturally my parents will understand."

"But we can't afford the cost of two houses," said Joyce uncertainly.

"I realise that, but it's you who have always wanted to live in Leeds, and this will give you the chance to stop commuting from London every week. After I've done the rounds why don't you stay up, contact a few local estate agents and see what's on the market?"

"All right, if that's what you really want," said Joyce. "I'll start next week."

Charles and Fiona spent a quiet weekend at their cottage in Sussex. Charles tried to do some gardening while he kept one ear open for the telephone. Fiona began to realise how anxious he was when she looked through the French windows and saw her finest delphinium being taken for a weed.

Charles eventually gave the weeds a reprieve and came in and turned on the television to catch Maudling, Macleod, Thatcher and Carrington enter No. 10 Downing Street looking pensive, only to leave smiling. The senior appointments had been made: the Cabinet was taking shape. The new Prime Minister came out and waved to the crowds before being whisked away in his official car.

Would he remember who had organised the young vote for him before he was even the party leader?

"When do you want to go back to Eaton Square?" Fiona enquired from the kitchen.

"Depends," said Charles.

"On what?"

"On whether the phone rings."

Simon sat staring at the television. All those hours of work on Housing and Local Government, and the PM had offered the portfolio to someone else. He had left the set on all day but didn't learn who it was, only that the rest of the Housing and Local Government team had remained intact.

"Why do I bother?" he said out loud. "The whole thing's a farce."

"What were you saying, darling?" asked Elizabeth as she came into the room.

The phone rang again. It was the newly appointed Home Secretary, Reginald Maudling.

"Simon?"

"Reggie, many congratulations on your appointment – not that it came as a great surprise."

"That's what I'm calling about, Simon. Would you like to join me at the Home Office as Under-Secretary?"

"Like to? I'd be delighted."

"Thank heavens for that," said Maudling. "It took me a dickens of a time to convince Ted Heath that you should be released from the Housing and Local Government team."

When Andrew and Louise arrived back at Cheyne Walk after

the weekend a red box was waiting for him in the drawing-room. 'Under-Secretary of State for Scotland' was printed in gold on the side.

"They'll be round to collect that later today," he told Louise. He turned the key to find the box was empty: and then he saw the small envelope in one corner. It was addressed to 'Andrew Fraser Esquire, MP'. He tore it open. It contained a short handwritten note from the Permanent Secretary, the senior civil servant at the Scottish Office.

"In keeping with a long tradition, ministers are presented with the last red box from which they worked. *Au revoir*. No doubt we will meet again."

"I suppose it could be used as a lunch box," said Louise, standing by the door.

"Or perhaps an overnight case," offered Andrew.

"Or a very small cot," added his wife, trying to make her words casual.

Andrew looked up to see Louise looking radiant.

"I let your parents know last night, but I wasn't going to tell you until dinner this evening."

Andrew threw his arms around her.

"By the way," Louise added, "we've already decided on her name."

When Raymond arrived back at Lincoln's Inn he let his clerk know that he wanted to be flooded with work. Over lunch with Sir Nigel Hartwell, the head of chambers, he explained that he thought it unlikely that the Labour party would be in Government again for some considerable time.

"Age is on your side, Raymond. Another full Parliament and you'll be barely forty, so you can still look forward to many years in the Cabinet."

"I wonder," said Raymond, uncharacteristically hesitant.

"Well, you needn't worry about briefs. Solicitors have been calling constantly since it was known you were back on a more permanent basis."

Raymond began to relax.

Joyce phoned him after lunch with the news that she hadn't found anything suitable, but the estate agent had assured her that they were expecting a lot more on the market in the autumn.

"Well, keep looking," said Raymond.

"Don't worry, I will," said Joyce, sounding as if she was enjoying the whole exercise. "If we find something perhaps we can think of starting a family," she added tentatively.

"Perhaps," said Raymond brusquely.

Charles eventually received a call on the Monday night, not from No. 10 Downing Street but from No. 12, the office of the Chief Whip. Because the Chief Whip's is not an official post, he is paid as the Parliamentary Secretary to the Treasury and he works from No. 12. The Prime Minister and the Chancellor of the Exchequer, being the first and second Lords of the Treasury, live at Nos. 10 and 11 Downing Street respectively.

The Chief Whip had phoned to say he hoped that Charles would be willing to soldier on as a junior Whip. When he heard the disappointment in Charles's voice he added, "For the time being."

"For the time being," repeated Charles and put the phone down.

"At least you're a member of the Government. You haven't been left out in the cold," said Fiona gamely.

"True," he replied.

"People are sure to come and go during the next five years."

Charles had to agree with his wife but it didn't lessen his disappointment. Returning to the Commons as a member of the Government, however, turned out to be far more rewarding than he had expected. This time it was his party that were making the decisions.

The Queen travelled early that July morning to the House of Lords in the Irish State Coach. An escort of the Household Cavalry accompanied her, preceded by a procession of lesser state carriages in which the Imperial State Crown and other royal trappings were transported. Charles could remember watching the ceremony from the streets when he was a boy. Now he was taking part in it. When the Queen arrived at the

Upper House she was accompanied by the Lord Chancellor through the Sovereign's entrance to the robing room, where her ladies-in-waiting began to prepare her for the ceremony.

Charles always considered the State opening of Parliament a special occasion for members of both Houses. As a Whip he watched the members take their seats in the Commons and await the arrival of Black Rod. Once the Queen was seated on the throne the Lord Great Chamberlain commanded the Gentleman Usher of Black Rod to inform the Commons that: "It is Her Majesty's pleasure they attend her immediately in this House." Black Rod, wearing his black topcoat, black waistcoat, black knee-breeches, black stockings and black shoes, resembled the devil's advocate rather than the Queen's messenger. He marched alone across the great tiled floor joining the two Chambers until he reached the doors of the House of Commons which were slammed in his face when he was just two paces away from them.

He struck the door three times with the silver tip of his long thin black rod. In response a little window in the door was flicked back to check on who it was – not unlike a sleazy nightclub, Charles's father had once observed. Black Rod was then allowed admittance to the Lower House. He advanced towards the table and made three obeisances to the chair before saying, "Mr Speaker, the Queen commands this Honourable House to attend Her Majesty immediately in the House of Peers."

With that, the Serjeant-at-Arms, bearing the mace, led Mr Speaker, in full court dress, a gold embroidered gown of black satin damask, back towards the Lords. They were followed by the Clerk of the House and the Speaker's chaplain, behind whom came the Prime Minister, accompanied by the leader of the Opposition, then Government ministers with their opposite numbers, and finally as many back-benchers as could squeeze into the rear of the Lords' Chamber.

The Lords themselves were waiting in the Upper House, dressed in red capes with ermine collars, looking somewhat like benevolent Draculas, accompanied by peeresses glittering in diamond tiaras and wearing long evening dresses. The Queen was seated on the throne, in her full Monarchical robes, the Imperial State Crown on her head originally made for George IV. She waited until the procession had filled the Chamber and all was still.

The Lord Chancellor shuffled forward and, bending down on one knee, presented her with a printed document. It was the speech, written by the Government of the day, and although she had read over a copy of the script earlier that morning she had made no personal contribution to its contents, as her role on this occasion was only ceremonial. She looked up at her subjects and began to read.

Charles stood at the back of the cramped gathering, but with his height he had no trouble in following the entire proceedings. Their lordships were all in their places for the Queen's speech, with the law lords seated in their privileged position in the centre of the Chamber, an honour bestowed upon them by an Act of 1539. The Lord Chancellor stood to one side of the Woolsack, which was stuffed with wool from the days when it was the staple commodity of England. When the Lords are in session he acts much as the Speaker does for the Commons.

Charles could spot his elderly father, the Earl of Bridgwater, nodding off during the Queen's speech, which promised that Britain would make a determined effort to become a full member of the EEC. "My Government also intends to bring in a bill to enact trade union reform," she declared. Charles, along with everyone else from the Commons, was counting the likely number of bills that would be presented during the coming months and soon worked out that the Whips' office were going to be in for a busy session.

As the Queen finished her speech Charles took one more look at his father, now sound asleep. How Charles dreaded the moment when he would be standing there watching his brother Rupert in ermine. The only compensation would be if he could produce a son who would one day inherit the title, as it was now obvious Rupert would never marry.

It was not as if he and Fiona had not tried. He was

beginning to wonder if the time had not come to suggest that she visit a specialist. He dreaded finding out she was unable to bear a child.

The speech delivered, the Sovereign left the Upper House followed by Prince Philip and Prince Charles to a fanfare of trumpets. At the other end of the Chamber the procession of MPs, led again by the Speaker, made their way back in pairs from the red benches of the Lords to the green of the Commons.

The leader of the Opposition, having formed his own team, invited Andrew to cover the Home Office brief as number two. Andrew was delighted by the challenge of this new responsibility, especially when he discovered Simon Kerslake was to be his opposite number in Government.

Louise once again became very large in a short period, but Andrew tried to keep his mind off the pregnancy, as he dreaded her going through that amount of pain and sorrow for a third time. He telephoned Elizabeth Kerslake and they agreed to meet privately.

"That's a hard question to answer without ifs and buts," she told Andrew over coffee in her room the following day.

"But what would your advice be if Louise were to lose the third child?"

Elizabeth took a long time considering her reply. "If that happened I cannot believe it would be wise to put her through the same ordeal again," she said flatly. "The psychological repercussions alone might affect her for the rest of her life."

Andrew sat staring in front of him.

"Enough of this morbid talk," Elizabeth added. "I checked Louise last week and I can see no reason why this shouldn't turn out to be a routine birth."

As the first weeks of the new Tory administration took shape, Simon and Andrew became locked in battle over several issues and were soon known as 'the mongoose and the rattlesnake'. When either of the names 'Kerslake' or 'Fraser' was cranked up on the old-fashioned wall machines indicating one of them had risen to speak, members drifted back into the Chamber. Andrew found himself a constant visitor to the table office, a tiny room in the corridor behind the Speaker's chair where members tabled their questions, usually scribbled on yellow sheets, but still acceptable to the omniscient clerks had they been written on postage stamps.

The clerks often helped Andrew reword a question so that it would be acceptable to the chair, a function they carried out for any member, even Tom Carson, who had once accused them of political bias when they suggested one of his questions was out of order. When Carson was finally referred to the Speaker, he was called for and reprimanded, and his question deposited in one of the mock-Gothic waste-paper baskets in the Order office.

Once behind the Speaker's chair, Simon and Andrew would good-humouredly discuss the issues on which they were crossing swords. The opportunity to be out of sight of the Press Gallery above them was often taken by the two opposing members, but once they had both returned to the dispatch box they would tear into each other, looking for any weakness in the other's argument.

On one subject they found themselves in total accord. Ever since August 1969, when the troops had first been sent in, Parliament had been having another of its periodic bouts of trouble with Northern Ireland. In October 1970 the House devoted a full day's business to listen to members' opinions in the never-ending effort to find a solution to the growing clash between the Protestant extremists and the IRA. The motion before the House was to allow emergency powers to be renewed in the province.

Andrew rose from his seat on the front bench to deliver the opening speech for the Opposition. He said he took no side in this unhappy affair, but he felt sure the House was united in condemning violence. Yet however hard he searched for the answer he found neither faction willing to give an inch. 'Goodwill' and 'trust' were words that might as well have been left out of any dictionary printed in Ulster. It was not long before Andrew came to the conclusion that Gladstone was right when he had said, "Every time I find the solution to the Irish question, they change the question."

When Andrew had finished he surprised members by leaving the Chamber and not returning for several minutes.

Simon had been selected to wind up for the Government and had prepared his speech with meticulous care. Although both sides appeared in agreement on the main issue, the mood as always could change in a moment if an unfortunate view was expressed by a Government minister.

During the debate, much to everyone's surprise, Andrew Fraser kept leaving the Chamber. Simon left only twice between three-thirty and the ten o'clock division, once to take a call from his wife, and then again at seven-thirty for a quick supper.

When Simon came back Andrew was still absent from the Chamber, and he had not returned by the time the Shadow Home Secretary began to sum up. Andrew did eventually take his seat on the front bench but Simon had already begun his speech.

As Andrew entered the Chamber and took his place on the front bench, an elderly Conservative rose from his seat.

"On a point of order, Mr Speaker."

Simon sat down immediately and turned his head to listen to the point his colleague wanted to make.

"Is it not a tradition of this House, sir," began the elder statesman rather ponderously, "for a front-bench spokesman to have the courtesy to remain in his seat during the debate in order that he may ascertain views other than his own?"

"That is not a point of order," replied the Speaker above the cries of "Hear, hear" from the Conservative benches. Andrew scribbled a quick note and hurriedly passed it over to Simon. On it was written a single sentence.

"I accept the point my Right Honourable friend makes," Simon began, "and would have complained myself had I not known that the Honourable Gentleman, the member for Edinburgh Carlton, has spent most of the afternoon in hospital." Simon paused to let the effect sink in. "Where his wife was in labour. I am not given to accepting as necessarily accurate all the Opposition tells me," he continued, "but I am able to confirm this statement because it was my wife who delivered the baby." The House began to laugh. "I can assure my Honourable friend that my wife has spent her entire afternoon indoctrinating the infant in the value of Conservative policies as understood by his grandfather, which is why the Honourable Gentleman has found it necessary to be absent himself from so much of the debate.'' Simon waited for the laughter to subside. "For those members of the House who thrive on statistics, it's a boy and he weighs four pounds three ounces."

There are times in the House when affection is displayed on both sides, thought Andrew, who considered it was ironic that during an Irish debate an Englishman had demonstrated such affection for a Scotsman.

There was no challenge when the Speaker 'collected the voices' at ten o'clock so the matter was decided 'on the nod' and Simon joined Andrew behind the Speaker's chair.

"Just over four pounds doesn't sound very big to me. I thought I'd take a second opinion from the Minister of Health."

"I agree," said Andrew, "the little blighter is stuck in an incubator, but your wife is doing everything she can to fatten him up. I'm off to watch him now."

"Good luck," said Simon.

Andrew sat by the incubator all night, hating the drip, drip, drip of the little plastic tube that passed up the child's nose and down into his stomach. He feared that when he woke his son would be dead and continually went to the wash basin and put a damp, cold cloth over his eyes to ensure he remained awake. He finally lost the battle and dozed off in a 'dad's bed' in the corner.

When his father woke, Robert Bruce Fraser was very much alive. The crumpled father rose from his bed to admire his crumpled offspring, who was receiving milk down the plastic tube from a night nurse.

Andrew stared down at the crinkly face. The boy had inherited his square jaw, but he had his mother's nose and hair colouring. Andrew chuckled at the time Louise had wasted over girls' names. Robert it would be.

Robert Bruce Fraser travelled to Cheyne Walk with his

mother and father three weeks later, having topped the scales earlier that morning at five pounds ten ounces.

Elizabeth Kerslake had told them to be thankful: the post-natal examination had shown that it would not be possible for Louise to bear another child.

CHAPTER
TWELVE

The Chief Whip looked round at his colleagues, wondering which of them would volunteer for such a thankless task.

A hand went up, and he was pleasantly surprised.

"Thank you, Charles."

Charles had already warned Fiona that he was going to volunteer to be the Whip responsible for the issue that had most dominated the last election: Britain's entry into the EEC. Everyone in that room realised that it would be the most demanding marathon of the entire Parliament, and there was an audible sigh of relief when Charles volunteered.

"Not a job for anyone with a rocky marriage," he heard one Whip whisper. At least that's something I don't have to worry about, thought Charles, but he made a note to take home some flowers that night.

"Why was it the bill everyone wanted to avoid?" asked Fiona as she arranged the daffodils.

"Because many of our side don't necessarily back Edward Heath in his lifelong ambition to take Britain into Europe, while quite a few of the Opposition do," said Charles, accepting a large brandy. "Added to that, we have the problem of presenting a bill to curb the trade unions at the same time which may well influence many members of the Labour party from voting with us on Europe. Because of this problem, the Prime Minister requires a regular 'state of play' assessment on Europe even though legislation may not be presented on the floor of the Commons for at least another year. He'll want to know periodically how many of our side are still against entry, and how many from the Opposition we can rely on to break ranks when the crucial vote is taken."

"Perhaps I should become Member of Parliament and then at least I could spend a little more time with you."

"Especially on the European issue if you were a 'don't know'."

The 'Great Debate' was discussed by the media to the point of boredom. Members were nevertheless conscious that they were playing a part in history. And, because of the unusual spectacle of the Whips not being in absolute control of the voting procedure, the Commons sprang to life, and excitement began to build up over the weeks and months of debate.

Charles retained his normal task of watching over fifty members on all normal Government bills, but because of the priority given to the issue of entry into Europe he had been released from all other duties. He knew that this was his chance to atone for his disastrous winding-up speech on the economy which he sensed his colleagues had still not completely forgotten.

"I'm gambling everything on this one," he told Fiona. "And if we lose the final vote I will be sentenced to the back benches for life."

"And if we win?"

"It will be hard to keep me off the front bench," replied Charles.

Robert Fraser was one of those noisy children who after only a few weeks sounded as if he was on the front bench.

"Perhaps he's going to be a politician after all," concluded Louise, staring down at her son.

"What has changed your mind?" asked Andrew.

"He never stops shouting at everyone, he's totally preoccupied with himself and he falls asleep as soon as someone else offers an opinion," she replied.

"At last I think I've found it." After Raymond heard the news he took the train up to Leeds the following Friday. Joyce had selected four houses for him to consider, but he had to agree with her that the one in Chapel Allerton was exactly what they were looking for. It was also by far the most expensive.

"Can we afford it?" asked Joyce anxiously.

"Probably not, but one of the problems of seeing four houses is that you end up only wanting the best one."

"I could go on looking."

"No, you've found the right house; now I'll have to work out how we can pay for it, and I think I may have come up with an idea."

Joyce said nothing, waiting for him to continue.

"We could sell our place in Lansdowne Road."

"But where would we live when you're in London?"

"I could rent a small flat somewhere between the law courts and the Commons while you set up our real home in Leeds."

"But wouldn't you get lonely?"

"Of course I will," said Raymond, trying to sound convincing. "But almost every member north of Birmingham is parted from his wife during the week. In any case, you've always wanted to settle in Yorkshire, and this might be our best chance. If my practice continues to grow we can buy a second house in London at a later date."

Joyce looked apprehensive.

"One added bonus," said Raymond, "your being in Leeds will ensure I never lose the seat."

She smiled, as she always felt reassured whenever Raymond showed the slightest sign of needing her.

On Monday morning Raymond put in a bid for the house in Chapel Allerton before returning to London. After a little bargaining over the phone during the week, he and the owner settled on a price. By Thursday Raymond had put his Lansdowne Road house on the market and was surprised by the amount the estate agent thought it would fetch.

All Raymond had to do now was find himself a flat.

Simon sent a note to Ronnie expressing his thanks for keeping him so well informed about what was happening at Nethercote and Company. It had been eight months since he had resigned from the board because of his appointment as a minister, but Ronnie saw that the minutes of each meeting were posted to him to study in his own time. 'His own time': Simon had to laugh at the thought.

His overdraft at the bank now stood at a little over £72,000, but as Ronnie intended the shares should be offered at five pounds each when they went public Simon felt sure there was still a fair leeway, as his personal holding should realise £300,000. Elizabeth warned him not to spend a penny of the profit until the money was safely in the bank. He was thankful she didn't know the full extent of his borrowing.

Over one of their occasional lunches at the Ritz, Ronnie spelt out to Simon his plans for the future of the company.

"Now that the Tories are in I think I'll go public in eighteen months' time. This year's profits are up again and next year's look even better. So 1973 looks a perfect bet."

Simon looked apprehensive and Ronnie responded quickly. "If you're having any problem, Simon, I'll be happy to take the shares off your hands at their market value. At least that way you'd show a small profit."

"No, no," said Simon. "I'll hang in there now that I've waited this long."

"Suit yourself," said Ronnie. "Now tell me – how are you enjoying the Home Office?"

Simon put down his knife and fork. "Of the three great offices of state, it's the one most involved with people, so there's a new challenge at a personal level every day, although it can be depressing too. Locking people up in prisons, banning immigrants and deporting harmless aliens isn't my idea of fun. The Home Office never seems to want anyone to enjoy too much freedom."

"And what about Ireland?"

"What about Ireland?" said Simon, shrugging his shoulders.

"I'd give the north back to Eire," said Ronnie, "or let them go independent and give them a large cash incentive to do so. At the moment the whole exercise is money down the drain."

"We're discussing people," said Simon, "not money."

"Ninety per cent of the voters would back me," said Ronnie, lighting a cigar.

"Everyone imagines ninety per cent of the people support their views, until they stand for election," said Simon. "The issue of Ireland is far too important to be glib about. I repeat, we're discussing people, eight million people, all of whom have the same right to justice as you and I. And as long as I work in the Home Office I intend to see that they get it."

Ronnie remained silent.

"I'm sorry, Ronnie," continued Simon. "Too many people have an easy solution to Ireland. If there *was* an easy solution the problem wouldn't have lasted over two hundred years."

"Don't be sorry," said Ronnie. "I'm so stupid, I've only just worked out for the first time why you're in public office."

"You're a typical self-made Fascist," said Simon, teasing his companion once again.

"You may be right, but you won't change my mind on hanging. Your lot should bring back the rope; the streets aren't safe any longer."

"For property developers like you, hoping for a quick killing?"

Both men laughed.

"Andrew, do you want lunch?"

"In a moment, in a moment."

"That's what you said half an hour ago."

"I know, but he's nearly got it. Just give me a few more minutes." Louise waited and watched, but Robert collapsed in a heap again.

"No doubt you're expecting him to play soccer for England by the time he's two."

"No, certainly not," said Andrew, carrying his son back into the house. "Rugby for Scotland."

Louise was touched by the amount of time Andrew spent with Robert. She told her disbelieving friends that he regularly fed and bathed the baby and even changed his nappy.

"Don't you think he's good-looking?" asked Andrew, strapping his son carefully into his chair.

"Yes," said Louise, laughing.

"That's because he looks like me," said Andrew, putting his arms round his wife.

"He most certainly does not," said Louise firmly.

Crash. A bowlful of porridge had been deposited on the floor, leaving just a lump left in the spoon, which Robert was now smearing across his face and hair.

"He looks as if he has just stepped out of a concrete mixer," said Andrew.

Louise stared at her son. "Perhaps you're right. There *are* times when he looks like you."

"How do you feel about rape?" asked Raymond.

"I can't see that it's relevant," Stephanie Arnold replied.

"I think they'll go for me on it," said Raymond.

"But why?"

"They'll be able to pin me in a corner, damage my character."

"But where does it get them? They can't prove lack of consent."

"Maybe, but they will offer it as background to prove the rest of the case."

"Because you raped someone doesn't prove you murdered them."

Raymond and Stephanie Arnold, who was new to chambers, continued discussing their first case together on the way to the Old Bailey, and she left Raymond in no doubt that she was delighted to be led by him. They were to appear together to defend a labourer accused of the rape and murder of his step-daughter.

"Open and shut case unfortunately," said Raymond, "but we're going to make the Crown prove their argument beyond anyone's doubt."

When the case stretched into a second week Raymond began to believe that the jury were so gullible they might even get their client off. Stephanie was sure they would.

The day before the judge's summing up Raymond invited Stephanie to dinner at the House of Commons. That'll make them turn their heads, he thought to himself. They won't have seen anything in a white shirt and black stockings that looks like that for some time, certainly not Mr Speaker.

Stephanie seemed flattered by the invitation and sat through the stodgy meal served in the Strangers' Dining-room, obviously impressed as former Cabinet ministers flitted in and out, all of them acknowledging him.

"How's the new flat?" asked Stephanie.

"Worked out well," replied Raymond. "The Barbican is so convenient for Parliament and the law courts."

"Does your wife like it?" she asked, lighting a cigarette but not looking at him directly.

"She's not in town that much nowadays. She spends most of her time in Leeds – doesn't care much for London."

The awkward pause that followed was interrupted by a sudden clanging of bells.

"Are we on fire?" said Stephanie, quickly stubbing out her cigarette.

"No," said Raymond laughing. "Just the ten o'clock division. I have to leave you and vote. I'll be back in about fifteen minutes."

"Shall I order coffee?"

"No, don't bother," said Raymond. "It's foul. Perhaps . . . perhaps you'd like to come back to the Barbican? Then you can give a verdict on my flat."

"Maybe it's an open and shut case," she smiled.

Raymond returned the smile before joining his colleagues as they flooded out of the dining-room down the corridor towards the Commons Chamber. He didn't have time to explain to Stephanie that he had only six minutes to get into the right lobby. As Raymond had no idea what they were voting on that night he followed the surge of Labour members into the Noes lobby. The bells stopped and the doors were bolted.

Whenever the vote is called for at the end of the debate the Speaker puts the question and the moment he reaches the words, "I think the Ayes have it," the roar of "No" from those opposed to the motion ensures a vote at ten o'clock. Bells peal out over the Palace of Westminster, and in some nearby restaurants and members' homes in the division-bell area.

Members then scurry into the Ayes or Noes division lobby before the cry of "Lock the doors" is heard. Once the doors have been secured each member then files past two clerks seated at a high desk at the far end of the corridor who tick off his name. As Raymond stepped past the clerks he came towards the exit doors which were angled so as to make a funnel through which only one member at a time could pass. The Whip acting as teller shouted out the mounting vote. "Seventy-three," he called as Raymond passed him. The only particular rule relating to voting was that members could not wear a hat or overcoat while in the lobby. A clerk had once told Raymond that this dated from the days when lazy members sent their driver off in the hansom cab, hats over ears, coat buttoned up to the nose, to march through the corridors and give their masters' names. Some of them would have been a damn sight better MPs then their employers, Raymond had often thought.

While in the corridor he discovered that they were voting on a clause of the Trade Union Bill concerning the validity of closed shops. He was in no doubt that he supported his party on that subject.

When he returned to the Strangers' Dining-room after the vote he found Stephanie checking her face in a compact mirror, a small round face with green eyes and brunette hair. She was replacing the trace of lipstick. He suddenly felt conscious of being a little overweight for a man not yet forty.

"Shall we go?" he suggested, after he had signed the bill.

Once they had reached the flat Raymond put on a Charles Aznavour record and retired to the small kitchen to prepare coffee. He was totally oblivious to the fact that women were beginning to find him attractive. A little extra weight and a few grey hairs had not harmed his appearance, if anything giving him an air of authority.

"There's no doubting this is a bachelor flat," Stephanie remarked as she took in the one comfortable leather chair, the pipe stand, and the Spy cartoons of turn-of-the-century judges and politicians.

"I suppose that's because that's what it is," he mused,

setting down a tray laden with coffee and two brandy balloons generously filled with cognac.

"Don't you get lonely?" she asked.

"From time to time," he said, pouring the coffee.

"And between times?"

"Black?" he asked, not looking at her.

"Black," she said.

"Sugar?"

"For a man who has served as a minister of the Crown and who, it's rumoured, is about to become the youngest QC in the country, you're still very unsure of yourself with women."

Raymond blushed, but raised his head and stared into her eyes.

In the silence he caught Aznavour's words, "You've let yourself go . . ."

"Would my Honourable friend care to dance?" she said quietly.

Raymond could still remember the last occasion he had danced. This time he was determined it would be different. He held Stephanie so that their bodies touched and they swayed rather than danced to the music of Marcel Stellman. She didn't notice Raymond slipping off his glasses and putting them into his jacket pocket. He bent over and kissed her neck. She gave a long sigh, and when they parted, she said, "Let's hope this is between times."

Charles studied his chart of 330 Conservatives. He felt confident of 217, not sure about fifty-four and had almost given up on fifty-nine. On the Labour side the best information he could glean was that fifty Socialists were expected to defy the Whip and join the Government's ranks when the great vote took place.

"The main fly in the ointment," Charles reported to the Chief Whip, "is still the Trade Union Reform Bill. The left are trying to convince those Socialists who still support the bill that there is no cause so important for which they should enter the same lobby as those Tory trade union bashers." He went on to explain his fear that unless the Government were willing to modify the Trade Union Bill they might lose

Europe on the back of it. "Alec Pimkin doesn't help matters by trying to gather the waverers in our party round him."

"There's no chance of the Prime Minister modifying one sentence of the Trade Union Bill," said the Chief Whip, draining his gin and tonic. "He promised it in his speech at the party conference, and he intends to deliver by the time he goes to Blackpool at the end of this year. I can also tell you he isn't going to like your conclusions on Pimkin, Charles. He cares almost as passionately about trade union reform as he does about Europe." Charles was about to protest. "I'm not complaining, you've done damn well so far. Just keep working on the fifty waverers. Threaten, cajole, bully, bribe. Try anything, but get them in the right lobby come the night, Pimkin included."

"How about sex?" asked Charles.

"You've been seeing too many American films," said the Chief Whip, laughing. "In any case I don't think we've got anyone other than Miss Norse to offer them."

Charles returned to his office and went over the list once again. His forefinger stopped at the letter 'P'. Charles strolled out into the corridor and looked around; his quarry wasn't there. He checked the Chamber: no sign of him. He passed the library. No need to look in there, he thought, and moved on to the smoking room where he found his man, about to order another gin.

"Alec," said Charles expansively.

The rotund figure of Pimkin looked round.

May as well try bribery first, thought Charles. "Let me get you a drink."

"That's good of you, old fellow," said Pimkin, nervously fingering his bow tie.

"Now, Alec, what's this about your voting against the European Bill?"

Simon was horrified when he read the initial document. Its implications were all too evident.

The report of the new Boundary Commission had been left in the red box for him to study over the weekend. He had agreed at a meeting of Home Office officials that he would steer it through the House as quickly as possible so that it would make the basis for the seats to be contested at the next election. As the Secretary of State reminded him: there must be no hold-ups.

Simon had read the document carefully. In essence the changes made sense and, because of the movement of families from urban to rural areas, it would undoubtedly create more winnable seats for the Conservatives overall. No wonder the party wanted no hold-ups. But what could he do about the decision the Commission had come to on his own constituency, Coventry Central? His hands were tied. If he suggested any change from the Boundary Commission's recommendations he would rightly be accused of jerry-mandering.

Because of the city's dwindling population the Commission had recommended that the four constituencies of Coventry become three. Coventry Central was to be the one to disappear, its voters distributed among Coventry West, Coventry East and Coventry North. Simon realised this would leave one safe seat for his sitting colleague and two safe Labour seats. It had never been far from his mind how marginal a constituency he represented. Now he was on the verge of being without one at all. He would have to traipse around the country all over again looking for a new seat to fight at the next election, while at the same time taking care of his constituents in the moribund one; and at the stroke of a pen – _his_ pen – they would pass on their loyalties to someone else. If only he had remained in Housing and Local Government he could have put up a case for keeping all four seats.

Elizabeth was sympathetic when he explained the problem but told him not to concern himself too much until he had spoken to the vice-chairman of the party, who advised candidates which constituencies were likely to become available.

"It may even work out to your advantage," she added.

"What do you mean?" said Simon.

"You could get a safer seat nearer London."

"With my luck I'll end up with a marginal in Newcastle."

Elizabeth prepared his favourite meal and spent the evening trying to keep up his spirits. After three portions of shepherd's pie Simon fell asleep almost as soon as he put his head on the pillow. But she stayed awake long into the night.

The casual conversation with the head of Gynaecology at St Mary's kept running through her mind. Although she hadn't confided in Simon, she could recall her supervisor's every word.

"I notice from the roster that you've had far more days off than you are entitled to, Dr Kerslake. You must make up your mind if you want to be a doctor or the wife of an MP."

Elizabeth stirred restlessly as she considered the problem, but came to no conclusion except not to bother Simon while he had so much on his mind.

"Do these boundary changes affect you?" Louise asked, looking up from her copy of *The Times*.

Andrew was bouncing a small rubber ball on Robert's head.

"You'll give him brain damage," said Louise.

"I know, but think of the goals he'll score – and it won't be long before I can start him on rugby."

Robert started to cry when his father stopped to answer his mother's question. "No, Edinburgh isn't affected. There's such a small movement in the population that the seven city seats will remain intact. The only real changes in Scotland will be in Glasgow and the Highlands."

"That's a relief," said Louise. "I should hate to have to look for another constituency."

"Poor old Simon Kerslake is losing his seat altogether and he daren't do anything about it."

"Why not?" asked Louise.

"Because he's the minister in charge of the bill, and if he tried anything clever we would crucify him."

"So what will he do?"

"Have to shop around for a new seat, or convince an older colleague to stand down in his favour."

"But surely ministers find it easy to pick up a plum seat?"

"Not necessarily," said Andrew. "Many constituencies don't like to have someone foisted on them and want to choose their own man. And some actually prefer a local man who will never be a minister, because they feel he can devote more time to them."

"Andrew, can you revert to being some use in Opposition?"

"What are you suggesting?" asked Andrew.

"Just keep throwing that ball at your stupid son's head or he'll be crying all day."

"Take no notice of her, Robert. She'll feel differently when you score your first goal against England."

CHÁPTER THIRTEEN

At exactly the time Raymond was ready to stop the affair Stephanie began leaving a set of court clothes in the flat. Although the two had gone their separate ways at the conclusion of the case they continued to see one another a couple of evenings a week. Raymond had had a spare key made so that Stephanie didn't have to spend her life checking when he had a three-line whip.

At first he began simply to avoid her, but she would then seek him out. When he did manage to give her the slip he would often find her back in his flat when he returned from the Commons. When he suggested they should be a little more discreet she began to make threats, subtle at first, but after a time more direct.

During the period of their affair Raymond conducted three major cases for the Crown, all of which had successful conclusions and which added to his reputation. On each occasion his clerk made certain Stephanie was not assigned to be with him. Now that his residency problem had been sorted out Raymond's only worry was how to end their relationship. He quickly discovered that getting rid of Stephanie Arnold was going to prove considerably more difficult than picking her up.

Simon was on time for his appointment at Central Office. He explained his dilemma to Sir Edward Mountjoy – vice-chairman of the party responsible for candidates – in graphic detail.

"What bloody bad luck," said Sir Edward. "But perhaps I

may be able to help," he added, opening the green folder on the desk in front of him. Simon could see that he was studying a list of names. It made him feel once again like an undergraduate who needed someone to die.

"There seem to be about a dozen safe seats that will fall vacant at the next election, caused either by retirement or redistribution."

"Anywhere in particular you could recommend?"

"I fancy Littlehampton."

"Where's that?" said Simon.

"It will be a new seat, safe as houses. It's in Sussex, on the borders of Hampshire." He studied an attached map. "Runs proud to Charles Seymour's constituency which remains unchanged. Can't think you would have many rivals there," said Sir Edward. "But why don't you have a word with Charles? He's bound to know everyone involved in taking the decision."

"Anything else that looks promising?" asked Simon, only too aware that Seymour might not prove altogether co-operative.

"Let me see. Can't afford to put all your eggs in one basket, can we? Ah, yes – Redcorn, in Northumberland." Again the vice-chairman studied the map. "Three hundred and twenty miles from London and no airport within eighty miles, and their nearest main line station is forty miles. I think that one's only worth trying for if you get desperate. My advice would be to speak to Charles Seymour about Littlehampton. He must know the lay of the land in that neck of the woods."

Two clichés in one sentence, thought Simon. Thank heavens Sir Edward would never have to make a speech from the dispatch box.

"I'm sure you're right, Sir Edward," he said.

"Selection committees are being formed already," continued Sir Edward, "so you shouldn't have to wait too long."

"I appreciate your help," said Simon. "Perhaps you could let me know if anything else comes up in the meantime."

"Of course, delighted. The problem is that if one of our side were to die during the sessions you couldn't desert your present seat because that would cause two by-elections. We certainly don't want a by-election in Coventry Central with you being accused of being a carpetbagger somewhere else."

"Don't remind me," said Simon.

Charles had whittled down the fifty-nine anti-Common Market members to fifty-one, but he was now dealing with the hard kernel who seemed quite immune to future advancement or bullying. When he made his next report to the Chief Whip Charles assured him that the Conservatives who would vote against entry into Europe were outnumbered by the Socialists who had declared they would support the Government. The Chief Whip seemed pleased, but asked if Charles had made any progress with Pimkin's disciples.

"Those twelve mad right-wingers?" said Charles sharply. "They seem to be willing to follow Pimkin even into the valley of death. I've tried everything but they're still determined to vote against Europe whatever the cost."

"The maddening thing is that that bloody nuisance Pimkin has nothing to lose," said the Chief Whip. "His seat disappears at the end of this Parliament in the redistribution. I can't imagine anyone with his extreme views would find a constituency to select him, but by then he'll have done the damage." The Chief Whip paused. "If his twelve would even abstain I would feel confident of advising the PM of victory."

"The problem is to find a way of turning Pimkin into Judas and then urging him to lead the chosen twelve into our camp," said Charles.

"You achieve that, and we'd certainly win."

Charles returned to the Whips' office to find Simon Kerslake waiting by his desk.

"I dropped by on the off-chance, hoping you might be able to spare me a few moments," said Simon.

"Of course," said Charles, trying to sound welcoming. "Take a pew."

Simon sat down opposite him. "You may have heard that I lose my constituency as a result of the Boundary Commission report and Edward Mountjoy suggested I have a word with you about Littlehampton, the new seat that borders your constituency."

"It does indeed," said Charles, masking his surprise. He had not considered the problem as his own seat remained intact. He recovered quickly. "And how wise of Edward to send you to me. I'll do everything I can to help."

"Littlehampton would be ideal," said Simon. "Especially while my wife is still working in Paddington."

Charles raised his eyebrows.

"I don't think you've met Elizabeth. She's a doctor at St Mary's," Simon explained.

"Yes, I can see how convenient Littlehampton would be. Why don't I start by having a word with Alexander Dalglish, the constituency chairman, and see what I can come up with?"

"That would be extremely helpful."

"Not at all. I'll call him at home this evening and find out what stage they've reached over selection, and then I'll put you in the picture."

"I'd appreciate that."

"While I've got you, let me give you the whip for next week," said Charles, passing over a sheet of paper. Simon folded it up and put it in his pocket. "I'll call you the moment I have some news."

Simon left feeling happier and a little guilty about his past prejudice concerning Charles, whom he watched disappear into the Chamber to carry out his bench duty.

The European issue had been given six days for debate by back-benchers, the longest period of time allocated to one motion in living memory.

Charles strolled down the aisle leading to the front bench and took a seat on the end to check on another set of speeches. Usually he listened intently to see if he could spot a member wavering in his position; but on this occasion his thoughts were in Littlehampton. Andrew Fraser was on his feet, and Charles was delighted to be able to confirm the tick alongside his name before he drifted into deep thought.

"I for one shall vote for entry into Europe," Andrew was telling the House. "When my party was in power I was a pro-European, and now we are in Opposition I can see no good reason to do a volte-face. The principles that held true two years ago hold true today. Not all of us . . ."

Tom Carson leaped up and asked if his Honourable friend would give way. Andrew resumed his seat immediately.

"Would my Honourable friend really support the peasant farmers of France before the sheep farmers in New Zealand?" asked Carson.

Andrew rose and explained to his colleague that he would certainly expect safeguards for New Zealand, but the initial vote on the floor of the House was on the principle of entry. The details could and should be dealt with in committee. He went on to express the view that had his Honourable friend talked of wogs or Jews in such a context the House would have been in uproar. "Why is it therefore acceptable to the anti-marketeers to describe French farmers as peasants?"

"Perhaps it's you who is the peasant," Carson shouted back, in seven words thus ruining his case for the lamb farmers of New Zealand.

Andrew ignored the jibe and went on to tell the House that he believed in a united Europe as a further insurance against a third world war. He concluded with the words:

"Britain has for a thousand years written history, even the history of the world. Let us decide with our votes whether our children will read that history, or continue to write it." Andrew sat down to acclamation from both sides.

By the time Andrew had resumed his seat Charles had formed a plan and left the Chamber when one of his own colleagues started what promised to be a long, boring and predictable speech.

Instead of returning to the Whips' office which afforded no privacy, Charles disappeared into one of the telephone booths near the cloisters above the Members' Cloakroom. He checked the number and dialled it.

"Alexander, it's Charles. Charles Seymour."

"Good to hear from you, Charles, it's been a long time. How are you?"

"Well. And you?"

"Can't complain. What can I do for a busy man like you?"

"Wanted to chew over the new Sussex constituency with

you, Littlehampton. How's your selection of a candidate going?"

"They've left me to draw up a short list of six for final selection by the full committee in about ten days' time."

"Have you thought of standing yourself, Alexander?"

"Many times," came back the reply. "But the old lady wouldn't allow it, neither would the bank balance. Do you have any ideas?"

"Might be able to help. Why don't you come and have a quiet dinner at my place early next week?"

"That's kind of you, Charles."

"Not at all, it will be good to see you again. It's been far too long. Next Monday suit you?"

"Absolutely."

"Good, let's say eight o'clock, 27 Eaton Square."

Charles put the phone down, returned to the Whips' Office and pencilled a note in his diary.

Raymond had just finished making his contribution to the European debate when Charles returned to take a seat on a half-empty Treasury bench. Raymond had made a coherent economic case for remaining free of the other six European countries and for building stronger links with the Commonwealth and America. He doubted that Britain could take the financial burden of entering a club that had been in existence for so long. If the country had joined at its inception it might have been different, he argued, but he would have to vote against this risky, unproven venture that he suspected could only lead to higher unemployment. When Raymond sat down he did not receive the acclamation that Andrew had and, worse, what praise he did elicit came from the left wing of the party who had spent so much time in the past criticising *Full Employment at any Cost?* Charles put a cross by the name Gould.

A note was being passed along the row to Raymond from one of the House Badge messengers, dressed in white tie and black tails. It read, 'Please ring head of chambers as soon as convenient.'

Raymond left the floor of the House and went to the

nearest telephone in the corner of the Members' Lobby. He was immediately put through to Sir Nigel Hartwell.

"You wanted me to phone?"

"Yes," said Sir Nigel. "Are you free at the moment?"

"I am," said Raymond. "Why? Is it something urgent?"

"I'd rather not talk about it over the phone," said Sir Nigel ominously.

Raymond took a tube from Westminster to Temple and was in chambers fifteen minutes later. He went straight to Sir Nigel's office, sat down in the comfortable chair in the corner of the spacious club-like room, crossed his legs and watched Sir Nigel pace about in front of him. He was clearly determined to get something off his chest.

"Raymond, I have been asked by those in authority about you taking silk. I've said I think you'd make a damn good QC." A smile came over Raymond's face, but it was soon wiped off. "But I need an undertaking from you."

"An undertaking?"

"Yes," said Sir Nigel. "You must stop having this damn silly er . . . relationship with another member of chambers." He rounded on Raymond and faced him.

Raymond turned scarlet but before he could speak the head of chambers continued.

"Now I want your word on it," said Sir Nigel, "that it will end, and end immediately."

"You have my word," said Raymond quietly.

"I'm not a prig," said Sir Nigel, pulling down on his waistcoat, "but if you are going to have an affair for God's sake make it as far away from the office as possible and, if I may advise you, that should include the House of Commons and Leeds. There's still a lot of the world left over and it's full of women."

Raymond nodded his agreement: he could not fault the head of chambers' logic.

Sir Nigel continued, obviously embarrassed. "There's a nasty fraud case starting in Manchester next Monday. Our client has been accused of setting up a series of companies that specialise in life insurance but avoid paying out on the claims: I expect you remember all the publicity. Miss Arnold has been put on the case as a reserve junior. They tell me it could last several weeks."

"She'll try and get out of it," said Raymond glumly.

"She already has, but I made it quite clear that if she felt unable to take the case on she would have to find other chambers."

Raymond breathed a sigh of relief. "Thank you," he said.

"Sorry about this. I know you've earned your silk, old boy, but I can't have members of chambers going around with egg on their faces. Thank you for your co-operation: I can't pretend I enjoyed that."

"Got time for a quiet word?" asked Charles.

"You're wasting your time, dear thing, if you imagine the disciples will change their minds at this late stage," said Alec Pimkin. "All twelve of them will vote against the Government on Europe. That's final."

"I don't want to discuss Europe this time, Alec. It's far more serious, and on a personal level. Let's go and have a drink on the terrace."

Charles ordered the drinks, and the two men strolled out on to the quiet end of the terrace towards the Speaker's house. Charles stopped as soon as he was certain there was no longer anyone within earshot.

"If it's not Europe, what is it?" asked Pimkin, staring out at the Thames.

"What's this I hear about you losing your seat?"

Pimkin turned pale and touched his bow tie nervously. "It's this bloody boundary business. My constituency is swallowed up, and no one seems willing to interview me for a new one."

"What's it worth if I secure you a safe seat for the rest of your life?"

Pimkin looked suspiciously up at Charles. "Almost anything up to a pound of flesh," he added with a false laugh.

"No, I won't need to cut that deep."

The colour returned to Pimkin's cheeks. "Whatever it is, you can rely on me, old fellow."

"Can you deliver the disciples?" said Charles.

Pimkin turned pale again.

"Not on the small votes in committee," said Charles, before Pimkin could reply. "Not on the clauses even, just on the second reading, the principle itself. Standing by the party in their hour of need, no desire to cause an unnecessary general election, all that stuff – you fill in the details for the disciples. I know you can convince them, Alec."

Pimkin still didn't speak.

"I deliver a copper-bottomed seat, you deliver twelve votes. I think we can call that a fair exchange."

"What if I get them to abstain?" said Pimkin.

Charles waited, as if giving the idea considerable thought. "It's a deal," he said, never having hoped for anything more.

Alexander Dalglish arrived at Eaton Square a little after eight. Fiona met him at the door and explained that Charles had not yet returned from the Commons.

"But I expect him any moment," she added. "May I offer you a drink?"

Another thirty minutes passed before Charles hurried in.

"Sorry I'm late, Alexander," he said, grasping his guest by the hand. "Hoped I might make it just before you." He kissed his wife on the forehead.

"Not at all," said Alexander. "I couldn't have asked for more pleasant company."

"What will you have, darling?" asked Fiona.

"A strong whisky, please, and can we go straight into dinner? I've got to be back at the talkshop by ten."

Charles guided his guest towards the dining-room and seated him at the side of the table before taking his place below the Holbein portrait of the first Earl of Bridgwater, an heirloom his grandfather had left him. Fiona took a seat opposite her husband. During the meal of Beef Wellington, Charles spent a great deal of time catching up on what Alexander had been doing since they had last met. Although they had spent three years together in the Guards as brother officers they rarely saw each other outside of regimental reunions since Charles had entered the House. He made no mention of the real purpose behind the meeting until Fiona provided the opportunity when she served coffee.

"I know you two have a lot to talk about, so I'll leave you to get on with it."

"Thank you," said Alexander. He looked up at Fiona and smiled. "For a lovely dinner."

She smiled back and left them alone.

"Now, Charles," said Alexander, picking up the file he had left on the floor by his side. "I need to pick your brains."

"Go ahead, old fellow," said Charles, "only too delighted to be of assistance."

"Sir Edward Mountjoy has sent me a pretty long list for us to consider, among them a Home Office minister and one or two other Members of Parliament who'll be losing their present seats. What do you think of . . .?"

Dalglish opened the file in front of him as Charles poured him a generous glass of port and offered him a cigar from a gold case that he picked up from the sideboard.

"What a magnificent object," said Alexander, staring in awe at the crested box and the engraved C.G.S. along its top.

"A family heirloom," said Charles. "Should have been left to my brother Rupert, but I was lucky enough to have the same initials as my grandfather."

Alexander handed it back to his host before returning to his notes.

"Here's the man who impresses me," he said at last. "Kerslake, Simon Kerslake."

Charles remained silent.

"You don't have an opinion, Charles?"

"Yes."

"So what do you think of Kerslake?"

"Strictly off the record?"

Dalglish nodded, but said nothing.

Charles sipped his port. "Very good," he said.

"Kerslake?"

"No, the port. Taylor's '35. I'm afraid Kerslake is not the same vintage. Need I say more?"

"Well, no, I follow your drift but it's most disappointing. He looks so good on paper."

"On paper is one thing," said Charles, "but having him as your member for twenty years is quite another. You want a man you can rely on. And his wife – never seen in the constituency, you know." He frowned. "I'm afraid I've gone too far."

"No, no," said Alexander. "I've got the picture. Next one is Norman Lamont."

"First class but he's already been selected for Kingston, I'm afraid," said Charles.

Dalglish looked down at his file once again. "Well, what about Pimkin?"

"We were at Eton together. His looks are against him, as my grandmother used to say, but he's a sound man, and very good in the constituency, so they tell me."

"You would recommend him then?"

"I should snap him up before another constituency adopts him."

"That popular, is he?" said Alexander. "Thanks for the tip. Pity about Kerslake."

"That was strictly off the record," said Charles.

"Of course. Not a word. You can rely on me."

"Cigar to your liking?"

"Excellent," said Alexander, "but your judgement has always been so good. You only have to look at Fiona to realise that."

Charles smiled.

Most of the other names Dalglish produced were either unknown, unsuitable or easy to dismiss. When Alexander left shortly before ten Fiona asked him if the chat had been worthwhile.

"Yes, I think we've found the right man."

Raymond had the locks on his flat changed that afternoon. It turned out to be more expensive than he had bargained for, and the carpenter had insisted on cash in advance.

The carpenter grinned as he pocketed the money. "I make a fortune doing this job, Guv'nor, I can tell you. At least one gentleman a day, always cash, no receipt. Means the wife and I can spend a month in Ibiza every year, tax free."

Raymond smiled at the thought. He checked his watch; he could just catch the Thursday seven-ten from King's Cross and be in Leeds by ten o'clock for a long weekend.

Alexander Dalglish phoned Charles a week later to tell him Pimkin had made the short list, and that they hadn't considered Kerslake.

"Pimkin didn't go over very well with the committee at the first interview."

"No, he wouldn't," said Charles. "I warned you his looks were agin' him and he may come over a bit right wing at times but he's as sound as a bell and will never let you down, take my word."

"I'll have to, Charles. Because by getting rid of Kerslake we've removed his only real challenger."

Charles put the phone down and dialled the Home Office.

"Simon Kerslake, please."

"Who's calling?"

"Seymour, Whips' office." He was put straight through.

"Simon, it's Charles. I thought I ought to give you an update on Littlehampton."

"That's thoughtful of you," said Simon.

"Not good news, I'm afraid. It turns out the chairman wants the seat for himself. He's making sure the committee only interviews idiots."

"How can you be so certain?"

"I've seen the short list and Pimkin's the only sitting member they're considering."

"I can't believe it."

"No, I was pretty shocked myself. I pressed the case for you, but it fell on deaf ears. Didn't care for your views on hanging or some such words. Still, I can't believe you'll find it hard to pick up a seat."

"I hope you're right, Charles, but in any case thanks for trying."

"Any time. Let me know of any other seats you put your name in for. I have a lot of friends up and down the country."

"Thank you, Charles. Can you pair me for next Thursday?"

Two days later Alec Pimkin was invited by the Little-hampton Conservatives to attend a short-list interview for the selection of a Tory candidate for the new constituency.

"How do I begin to thank you?" he asked Charles when they met up in the bar.

"Keep your word – and I want it in writing," replied Charles.

"What do you mean?"

"A letter to the Chief Whip saying you've changed your mind on the main European vote, and you and the disciples will be abstaining on Thursday."

Pimkin looked cocky. "And if I don't play ball, dear thing?"

"You haven't got the seat yet, Alec, and I might find it necessary to phone Alexander Dalglish and tell him about that awfully nice little boy you made such a fool of yourself over when you were up at Oxford."

Three days later the Chief Whip received the letter from Pimkin. He immediately summoned his junior Whip.

"*Well done*, Charles. How did you manage to succeed where we've all failed – and the disciples as well?"

"Matter of loyalty," said Charles. "Pimkin saw that in the end."

On the final day of the Great Debate on 'the principle of entry' into Europe the Prime Minister delivered the winding-up speech. He rose at nine-thirty to cheers from both sides. At ten o'clock the House divided and voted in favour of 'the principle' by a majority of 112. Sixty-nine Labour MPs, led by Roy Jenkins, had helped to swell the Government's majority.

Raymond Gould voted against the motion in accordance with his long-held beliefs. Andrew Fraser joined Simon Kerslake and Charles Seymour in the Ayes lobby. Alec Pimkin and the twelve disciples remained in their places on the Commons benches while the vote took place.

When Charles heard the Speaker read out the final result he felt a moment of triumph, although he realised that he still had the committee stage to go through. Hundreds of clauses, any of which could go wrong and turn the bill into a farce. Nevertheless the first round belonged to him.

Ten days later Alec Pimkin defeated a keen young Conservative just down from Cambridge and a local woman councillor to be selected as prospective candidate for Littlehampton.

CHAPTER
FOURTEEN

Andrew studied the case once again and decided to make his own enquiries. Too many constituents had in the past demonstrated that they were willing to lie to him in surgery as happily as they would in the witness box to any judge.

Robert was trying to climb up on to his lap. Andrew hoisted him the remainder of the way in one tug and attempted to return to his papers. "Whose side are you on?" Andrew demanded as his son dribbled all over his freshly written notes. He stopped to pat his bottom. "Ugh," he said, putting the case file by his side on the floor. A few minutes later Robert had been changed and left with his mother.

"I'm afraid your son is not over-anxious to help me in my desire to secure the release of an innocent man," Andrew shouted over his shoulder.

He settled down to go over the papers once more, something about the case didn't ring true . . . Andrew dialled the Procurator Fiscal's number. There was one man who could cut his work in half with a sentence.

"Good morning, Mr Fraser. What can I do for you, sir?"

Andrew had to smile. Angus Sinclair was a contemporary of his father and had known Andrew all his life, but once he was in his office he treated everyone as a stranger, making no exception.

"He even calls his wife 'Mrs Sinclair' when she rings the office," Sir Duncan once told him. Andrew was willing to join in the game.

"Good morning, Mr Sinclair. I need your advice as Procurator Fiscal."

"Always happy to be of service, sir."

"I want to talk to you off the record about the Paddy O'Halloran case. Do you remember it?"

"Of course, everyone in this office remembers that case."

"Good," said Andrew. "Then you'll know what a help you can be to me in cutting through the thicket."

"Thank you, sir," the slight burr came back down the telephone.

"A group of my constituents, whom I wouldn't trust further than I could toss a caber, claim O'Halloran was framed for the Princes Street bank robbery last year. They don't deny he has criminal tendencies" – Andrew would have chuckled if he hadn't been speaking to Angus Sinclair – "but they say he never left a pub called the Sir Walter Scott the entire time the robbery was taking place. All you have to tell me, Mr Sinclair, is that you have no doubt that O'Halloran was guilty and I'll drop my enquiries. If you say nothing, I shall dig deeper."

Andrew waited, but he received no reply.

"Thank you, Mr Sinclair." Although he knew it would elicit no response, he couldn't resist adding: "No doubt I'll see you at the golf club some time over the weekend." The silence continued.

"Goodbye, Mr Sinclair."

"Good day, Mr Fraser."

Andrew settled back: it was going to be a lengthy exercise. He started by checking with all the people who had confirmed O'Halloran's alibi that night but after interviewing the first eight he came to the reluctant conclusion that none of them could be trusted as a witness. Whenever he came across another of O'Halloran's friends the expression 'anyone's for a pint' kept crossing his mind. The time had come to talk with the landlord of the Sir Walter Scott.

"I couldn't be sure, Mr Fraser, but I think he was here that evening. Trouble is, O'Halloran came almost every night. It's hard to recall."

"Do you know anyone who might remember? Someone you could trust with your cash register?"

"That'd be pushing your luck in this pub, Mr Fraser."

The landlord thought for a moment. "However, there's old Mrs Bloxham," he said at last, slapping the drying-up cloth over his shoulder. "She sits in that corner every night." He pointed to a small round table that would have been crowded had it seated more than two people. "If she says he was here, he was."

Andrew asked the landlord where Mrs Bloxham lived and then, hoping she was in, made his way to 43 Mafeking Road, neatly sidestepping a gang of young children playing football in the middle of the street. He climbed some steps that badly needed repairing and knocked on the door of number forty-three.

"Is it another general election already, Mr Fraser?" asked a disbelieving old lady as she peered through the letter-box.

"No, it's nothing to do with politics, Mrs Bloxham," said Andrew, bending down. "I came round to seek your advice on a personal matter."

"A personal matter? Better come on in out of the cold then," she said, opening the door to him. "There's a terrible draught rushes through this corridor."

Andrew followed the old lady as she shuffled down the dingy corridor in her carpet slippers to a room that he would have said was colder than it had been outside on the street. There were no ornaments in the room save a crucifix that stood on a narrow mantelpiece below a pastel print of the Virgin Mary. Mrs Bloxham beckoned Andrew to a wooden seat by a table yet unlaid. She eased her plump frame into an ancient stuffed armchair. It groaned under her weight and a strand of horsehair fell to the floor. Andrew looked more carefully at the old lady. She was wearing a black shawl over a dress she must have worn a thousand times. Once settled in her chair, she kicked off her slippers.

"Feet still giving you trouble, then?" he enquired.

"Doctor doesn't seem to be able to explain the swellings," she said, without bitterness.

Andrew leaned on the table and noticed what a fine piece of furniture it was, and how incongruous it looked in its present surroundings. He was struck by the craftsmanship of the carved Georgian legs. She noticed he was admiring it.

"My great-grandfather gave that to my great-grandmother the day they were married, Mr Fraser."

"It's magnificent," said Andrew.

She didn't seem to hear because all she said was, "What can I do for you, sir?" The second time that day he had been addressed by an elder in that way.

Andrew went over the O'Halloran story again. Mrs Bloxham listened intently, leaning forward slightly and cupping her hand round her ear to be sure she could hear every word.

"That O'Halloran's an evil one," she said, "not to be trusted. Our Blessed Lady will have to be very forgiving to allow the likes of him to enter the kingdom of heaven." Andrew smiled. "Not that I'm expecting to meet all that many politicians when I get there either," she added, giving Andrew a toothless grin.

"Could O'Halloran possibly have been there that Friday night as all his friends claim?" Andrew asked.

"He was there all right," said Mrs Bloxham. "No doubt about that – saw him with my own eyes."

"How can you be so sure?"

"Spilled his beer over my best dress, and I knew something bad would happen on the thirteenth, especially with it being a Friday. I won't forgive him for that. I still haven't been able to get the stain out despite what those washing-powder ads tell you on the telly."

"Why didn't you inform the police immediately?"

"Didn't ask," she said simply. "They've been after him for a long time for a lot of things they couldn't pin on him, but for once he was in the clear."

Andrew finished writing his notes and then rose to leave. Mrs Bloxham heaved herself out of the chair, dispensing yet more horsehair on to the floor. They walked to the door together. "I'm sorry I couldn't offer you a cup of tea but I'm right out at the moment," she said. "If you had come tomorrow it would have been all right."

Andrew paused on the doorstep.

"I get the pension tomorrow, you see," she replied to his unasked question.

It took Elizabeth some time to find a locum to cover for her so that she could travel to Redcorn for the interview. Once again the children had to be left with a baby-sitter. The local and national press had made him the hot favourite for the new seat. Elizabeth put on what she called her best Conservative outfit, a pale blue suit with a dark blue collar that hid everything on top and reached well below her knees.

The journey from King's Cross to Newcastle took three hours and twenty minutes, on what was described in the timetable as 'the express'. At least Simon was able to catch up with a great deal of the paper work that had been stuffed into his red box. Civil servants, he reflected, rarely allowed politicians time to involve themselves in politics. They wouldn't have been pleased to learn that he spent an hour of the journey reading the last four weekly copies of the *Redcorn News*.

At Newcastle they were met by the wife of the Association treasurer, who had volunteered to escort the minister and Mrs Kerslake to the constituency to be sure they were in time for the interview. "That's very thoughtful of you," said Elizabeth, as she stared at the mode of transport that had been chosen to take them the next forty miles.

The ancient Austin Mini took a further hour and a half through the winding B-roads before they reached their destination, and the treasurer's wife never drew breath once throughout the entire journey. When Simon and Elizabeth piled out of the car at the market town of Redcorn they were physically and mentally exhausted.

The treasurer's wife took them through to the constituency headquarters and introduced them both to the agent.

"Good of you to come," he said. "Hell of a journey, isn't it?"

Elizabeth felt unable to disagree with his judgement. But on this occasion she made no comment, feeling that if this was to be Simon's best chance of returning to Parliament she had already decided to give him every support possible. Nevertheless she dreaded the thought of her husband making the journey to Redcorn twice a month as she feared they would see even less of each other than they did at present, let alone the children.

"Now the form is," began the agent, "that we are interviewing six potential candidates and they'll be seeing you last." He winked knowingly.

Simon and Elizabeth smiled uncertainly.

"I'm afraid they won't be ready for you for at least another hour, so you have time for a stroll round the town."

Simon was glad of the chance to stretch his legs and take a closer look at Redcorn. He and Elizabeth walked slowly round the pretty market town, admiring the Elizabethan architecture that had somehow survived irresponsible or greedy town planners. They even climbed the hill to take a look inside the magnificent perpendicular church which dominated the surrounding area.

As he walked back past the shops in the high street Simon nodded to those locals who appeared to recognise him.

"A lot of people seem to know who you are," said Elizabeth, and then they saw the paper rack outside the local newsagent. They sat on the bench in the market square and read the lead story under a large picture of Simon.

'Redcorn's next MP?' ran the headline.

The story volunteered the fact that although Simon Kerslake had to be considered the favourite, Bill Travers, a local farmer who had been chairman of the county council the previous year, was still thought to have an outside chance.

Simon began to feel a little sick in the stomach. It reminded him of the day he had been interviewed at Coventry Central nearly eight years before. Now that he was a minister of the Crown he wasn't any less nervous.

When he and Elizabeth returned to constituency headquarters they were informed that only two more candidates had been seen and the third was still being interviewed. They walked around the town once again, even more slowly this time, watching the shopkeepers put up their coloured shutters and turn 'Open' signs to 'Closed'.

"What a pleasant market town," said Simon, trying to find out how his wife was feeling.

"And the people seem so polite after London," she added.

Simon smiled as they headed back to the party headquarters. As they passed Simon and Elizabeth they bid the strangers "Good evening," courteous people whom Simon felt he would have been proud to represent. But although they walked slowly Elizabeth and he could not make their journey last more than thirty minutes.

When they returned a third time to constituency headquarters the fourth candidate was leaving the interview room. She looked very despondent. "It shouldn't be long now," said the agent, but it was another forty minutes before they heard a ripple of applause, and a man dressed in a Harris tweed jacket and brown trousers left the room. He didn't seem happy either.

The agent ushered Simon and Elizabeth through, and as they entered everyone in the room stood. Ministers of the Crown did not visit Redcorn often.

Simon waited for Elizabeth to be seated before he took the chair in the centre of the room facing the committee. He estimated that there were about fifty people present and they were all staring at him, showing no aggression, merely curiosity. He looked around at the weather-beaten faces. Most of them, male and female, were dressed in tweed. In his dark striped London suit Simon felt out of place.

"And now," said the chairman, "we welcome the Right Honourable Simon Kerslake, MP."

Simon had to smile at the mistake so many people made in thinking that all ministers were automatically members of the Privy Council, and therefore entitled to the prefix 'Right Honourable' instead of the plain 'Honourable' accorded to all MPs – and then only when they were present in the House.

"Mr Kerslake will address us for twenty minutes, and he has kindly agreed to answer questions after that," added the chairman.

Simon felt confident he had spoken well, but even his few carefully chosen quips received no more than a smile, and his more serious comments elicited little response. This was not a group of people given to showing their emotions. When he had finished he sat down to respectful clapping and murmurs.

"Now the minister will take questions," said the chairman.

"Where do you stand on hanging?" said a scowling middle-aged woman in a grey suit seated in the front row.

Simon explained his reasons for being a convinced abolitionist. The scowl did not move from the questioner's face and Simon thought to himself how much happier she would be with Ronnie Nethercote as her member.

A man in a hacking jacket asked: "How do you feel, Mr Kerslake, about this year's farm subsidy?"

"Good on eggs, tough on beef, and disastrous for pig farmers. Or at least that's what I read on the front page of *Farmers Weekly* yesterday." Some of them laughed for the first time. "It hasn't proved necessary for me to have a great knowledge of farming in Coventry Central, but if I am lucky enough to be selected for Redcorn I shall try to learn quickly, and with your help I shall hope to master the farmers' problems." Several heads nodded their approval.

"Miss Pentecost, chairman of the Women's Advisory," announced a tall, thin spinsterish woman who had stood up to catch the chairman's eye. "May I be permitted to ask Mrs Kerslake a question? If your husband were offered this seat, would you be willing to come and live in Northumberland?"

Elizabeth had dreaded the question because she knew that if Simon was offered the constituency she would be expected to resign her post at the hospital. Simon turned and looked towards his wife.

"No," she replied directly. "I am a doctor at St Mary's Hospital, Paddington, where I practise gynaecology. I support my husband in his career but, like Margaret Thatcher, I believe a woman has the right to a good education and then the chance to use her qualifications to their best advantage."

A ripple of applause went round the room and Simon smiled at his wife.

The next question was on Europe, and Simon gave an unequivocal statement as to his reasons for backing the

Prime Minister in his desire to see Britain as part of the Common Market.

Simon continued to answer questions on subjects ranging from trade union reform to violence on television before the chairman asked, "Are there any more questions?"

There was a long silence and just as he was about to thank Simon the scowling lady in the front row, without being recognised by the chair, asked what Mr Kerslake's views were on abortion.

"Morally, I'm against it," said Simon. "At the time of the Abortion Act many of us believed it would stem the tide of divorce. We have been proved wrong: the rate of divorce has quadrupled. Nevertheless, in the cases of rape or fear of physical or mental injury arising from birth I would have to support the medical advice given at the time. Elizabeth and I have two children and my wife's job is to see that babies are safely delivered," he added.

The lips moved from a scowl to a straight line.

"Thank you," said the chairman. "It was good of you to give us so much of your time. Perhaps you and Mrs Kerslake would be kind enough to wait outside."

Simon and Elizabeth joined the other hopeful candidates, their wives and the agent in a small dingy room at the back of the building. When they saw the half-empty trestle table in front of them they both remembered they hadn't had any lunch and devoured what was left of the curling cucumber sandwiches and the cold sausage rolls.

"What happens next?" Simon asked the agent between mouthfuls.

"Nothing out of the ordinary. They'll have a discussion, allowing everyone to express their views, and then vote. It should all be over in twenty minutes."

Elizabeth checked her watch: it was seven o'clock and the last train was at nine-fifteen.

"Ought to make the train comfortably," said Simon.

An hour later when no smoke had emerged from the chimney the agent suggested to all the candidates who had a long journey ahead of them that they might like to check into the Bell Inn just over the road.

When Simon looked around the room it was clear that everyone else had done so in advance.

"You had better stay put in case you're called again," Elizabeth said. "I'll go off and book a room and at the same time call and see how the children are getting on."

"Probably eaten the poor baby-sitter by now," said Simon.

Elizabeth smiled before slipping out and making her way to the small hotel.

Simon opened his red box and tried to complete some work. The man who looked like a farmer came over and introduced himself.

"I'm Bill Travers, the chairman of the new constituency," he began. "I only wanted to say that you'll have my full support as chairman if the committee select you."

"Thank you," said Simon.

"I had hoped to represent this area, as my grandfather did. But I shall understand if Redcorn prefers to choose a man destined for the Cabinet rather than someone who would be happy to spend his life on the back benches."

Simon was touched by his opponent's goodwill, and would have liked to respond in kind but Travers quickly added, "Forgive me, I'll not waste any more of your time. I can see" – he looked down at the red box – "that you have a lot of work to catch up on."

Simon felt guilty as he watched the man walk away. A few minutes later Elizabeth returned and tried to smile. "The only room left is smaller than Peter's and it faces the main road, so it's just about as noisy."

"At least no children to say 'I'm hungry'," he said, touching her hand.

It was a little after nine when a weary chairman came out and asked all the candidates if he could have their attention. Husbands and wives all faced him. "My committee want to thank you for going through this grim procedure. It has been hard for us to decide something that we hope not to have to discuss again for twenty years." He paused. "The committee are going to invite Mr Bill Travers to fight the Redcorn seat at the next election."

In a sentence it was all over. Simon's throat went dry.

He and Elizabeth didn't get much sleep in their tiny room at the Bell Inn, and it hadn't helped that the agent told them the final vote had been twenty-five – twenty-three.

"I don't think Miss Pentecost liked me," said Elizabeth, feeling guilty. "If I had told her that I would have been willing to live in the constituency I think you'd have been offered the seat."

"I doubt it," said Simon. "In any case it's no use agreeing to their terms at the interview and then imposing your own when you have been offered the constituency. My guess is you'll find Redcorn has chosen the right man."

Elizabeth smiled at her husband, grateful for his support.

"There will be other seats," said Simon, only too aware that time was now running out. "You'll see."

Elizabeth prayed that he would prove right, and that next time the choice of a constituency would not make her have to face the dilemma she had so far managed to avoid.

When Raymond took silk, the second Tuesday after the Easter holiday, and became a Queen's Counsel, Joyce made one of her periodic trips to London. The occasion she decided warranted another visit to Harvey Nichols. She recalled her first trip to the store so many years before when she had accompanied her husband to meet the Prime Minister. Raymond had come so far since then although their relationship seemed to have progressed so little. She had given up hope of being a mother, but still wanted him to believe she was a good wife. She couldn't help thinking how much better-looking Raymond had become in middle age, and feared the same could not be said of her.

She enjoyed watching the legal ceremony as her husband was presented in court before the judges. Latin words spoken but not understood. Suddenly her husband was Raymond Gould, QC, MP.

She and Raymond arrived late in chambers for the celebration party. Everyone seemed to have turned out in her husband's honour. Raymond felt full of *bonhomie* and was chatting to the chief clerk when Sir Nigel handed him a glass of champagne. Then he saw a familiar figure by the mantelpiece and remembered that the trial in Manchester was over. He managed to circle the room speaking to everyone but Stephanie Arnold. To his horror he turned to see her introducing herself to his wife. Every time he glanced towards them they seemed deeper in conversation.

"Ladies and gentlemen," said Sir Nigel, banging a table. He waited for silence. "We are always proud in chambers when one of our members takes silk. It is a comment not only on the man but also on his chambers. And when it is the youngest silk – still under forty – it adds to that pride. All of you, of course, know that Raymond also serves in another place in which we expect him to rise to even greater glory. May I add finally how pleasant it is to have his wife Joyce among us tonight. Ladies and gentlemen," he concluded. "The toast is Raymond Gould, QC."

"Raymond Gould, QC," said everyone in chorus. Then, "Speech, speech."

"I would like to thank all those people who made this great honour possible," began Raymond. "My producer, my director, the other stars and not forgetting the criminals, without whom I would have no profession to profess. And finally," he said, "to those of you who want to see the back of me, I direct you all to work tirelessly to ensure the return of a Labour Government at the next election. Thank you."

The applause was sustained and genuine and many of his colleagues were impressed by how relaxed Raymond had become of late. As they came up to congratulate him Raymond couldn't help noticing that Stephanie and Joyce had resumed their conversation. Raymond was handed another glass of champagne just as an earnest young pupil called Patrick Montague who had recently joined them from chambers in Bristol engaged him in conversation. Although Montague had been with them for some weeks Raymond had never spoken to him at length before. He seemed to have very clear views on criminal law and the changes that were necessary. For the first time in his life Raymond felt he was no longer a young man.

Suddenly both women were at his side.

"Hello, Raymond."

"Hello, Stephanie," he said awkwardly and looked anxiously towards his wife. "Do you know Patrick Montague?" he asked, absent-mindedly.

The three of them burst out laughing.

"What's so funny?" asked Raymond.

"You do embarrass me sometimes, Raymond," said Joyce. "Surely you realise Stephanie and Patrick are engaged?"

CHAPTER
FIFTEEN

"With or without civil servants?" asked Simon as Andrew entered the minister's office.

"Without, please."

"Fine," said Simon and pressed a switch on the intercom by his desk.

"I don't want to be disturbed while I'm with Mr Fraser," he said and ushered his colleague towards a comfortable seat in the corner.

"Elizabeth was asking me this morning to find out how Robert was getting on."

"It's his second birthday next month and he's overweight for a scrum-half," replied Andrew. "And how's your search for a seat working out?"

"Not too good. The last three constituencies to come up haven't even asked to see me. I can't put a finger on why, except they all seem to have selected local men."

"It's still a long time to the next election. You're sure to find a seat before then."

"It might not be so long if the Prime Minister decides to go to the country and test his strength against the unions."

"That would be a foolish thing to do," said Andrew. "He might defeat us but he still wouldn't defeat the unions."

A young woman came into the room with two cups of coffee, put them on the low Formica table and left the two men alone.

"Have you had time to look at the file?" Andrew continued.

"Yes, I went over it last night between checking over Peter's prep and helping Michael to build a model galleon."

"And how do you feel?" Andrew asked.

"Not very good. I can't get to grips with this new maths they're now teaching, and my mast was the only one that fell off when Elizabeth launched the galleon in the bath."

Andrew laughed.

"I think you've got a case," said Simon, sounding serious.

"Good," said Andrew. "Now the reason I wanted to see you privately is because I feel there are no party political points to be made out of this case for either of us. I've no plans to try to embarrass your department, and I consider it's in the best interest of my constituents to co-operate as closely as I can with you."

"Thank you," said Simon. "So where do you want to go from here?"

"I'd like to table a planted question for your department in the hope that you would consider opening an enquiry. If the enquiry comes to the same conclusion as I have, I would expect you to order a re-trial."

Simon hesitated. "And if the enquiry goes against you will you agree to no reprisals for the Home Office?"

"You have my word on it."

"Shall I ask the civil servants to come in now?"

"Yes, please do."

Simon returned to his desk and pressed a button. A moment later three men in almost identical suits, white shirts with stiff collars and discreet ties entered the room. Between them they could have ruined any police identification parade.

"Mr Fraser," began Simon, "is asking the Home Office to consider . . ."

"Can you explain why Simon Kerslake missed a vote yesterday?"

Charles looked across the table at the Chief Whip.

"No, I can't," he said. "I've been distributing the weekly whip to him the same as every member of my group."

"What's behind it then?"

"I think the poor man has been spending a lot of his time

traipsing around the country looking for a seat to fight at the next election."

"That's no excuse," said the Chief Whip. "Duties in the House must come first, every member knows that. He missed a vote on a vital clause during the European Bill last Thursday while everyone else in your group has proved reliable. Despite our majority we seem to be in single figures for almost every clause. Perhaps I should have a word with him?"

"No, no, I'd rather you didn't," said Charles, fearing he sounded a little too insistent. "I consider it my responsibility. I'll speak to him and see that it doesn't happen again."

"All right, Charles, if that's the way you want to play it. Thank God it can't last much longer and the damn thing will soon be law, but we must remain vigilant over every clause. The Labour party know only too well that if they defeat us on certain key clauses they can still scupper the whole bill, and if I lost one of those by a single vote I would cut Kerslake's throat. Or anyone else's who was responsible."

"I'll make sure he gets the message," said Charles.

"How's Fiona reacting to all these late nights?" the Chief Whip asked, finally relaxing.

"Very well, considering. In fact now that you mention it I have never seen her looking better."

"Can't say my wife is enjoying 'the prep school antics', as she describes our continual late-night sittings. I've had to promise to take her to the West Indies this winter to make up for it. Well, I'll leave you to deal with Kerslake then. Be firm, Charles. Just remember, we can't afford to lose a vote at this late stage."

"Norman Edwards?" repeated Raymond in disbelief. "The General Secretary of the Haulage Union?"

"Yes," said Fred Padgett, getting up from behind his desk.

"But he burnt *Full Employment at any Cost?* on a public bonfire with every journalist he could lay his hands on to witness the conflagration."

"I know," said Fred, returning a letter to the filing cabinet.

"I'm only your agent, I'm not here to explain the mysteries of the universe."

"When does he want to see me?" asked Raymond.

"As soon as possible."

"Better ask him if he can come for a drink back at the house round six o'clock."

Raymond had had a heavy Saturday morning surgery and thanks to the still imminent Martians had only found time to grab a sandwich at the pub before going off to pursue his favourite pastime. This week Leeds were playing Liverpool at Elland Road. Sitting in the directors' box every other week in full view of his constituents while he supported his local football team killed 30,000 birds with one stone. Later, when talking to the lads in the dressing-room after the match, he found himself lapsing into a pronounced Yorkshire accent that bore no resemblance to the one he used to address high court judges during the week.

Leeds won three–two and after the match Raymond joined the directors for a drink in the boardroom. He became so impassioned about an off-side decision that could have lost them a point that he nearly forgot about his meeting with Norman Edwards.

Joyce was in the garden showing the union leader her early snowdrops when Raymond returned.

"Sorry I'm late," he shouted, as he hung up his yellow and blue scarf. "I've been to the match."

"Who won?" asked Edwards.

"Leeds, of course, three–two."

"Damn," said Norman, his accent leaving the other in no doubt that he had not spent many nights outside of Liverpool.

"Come on in and have a beer," said Raymond.

"I'd prefer a vodka."

The two men went into the house while Joyce continued with her gardening.

"Well," said Raymond, pouring his guest a Smirnoff. "What brings you all the way from Liverpool if it wasn't to watch the football? Perhaps you want a signed copy of my book for your next union bonfire."

"Don't give me any hassle, Ray. I came all this way because I need your help, simple as that."

"I'm all ears," said Raymond.

"We had a full meeting of the General Purposes Committee yesterday, and one of the brothers has spotted a clause in the European Bill which could put us all out of work."

Norman passed over a copy of the bill to Raymond with the relevant clause marked in red. It gave the minister power to make new haulage and lorry regulations which would come before the House as statutory instruments and thus could not be amended.

"If that gets through the House my boys are in deep trouble."

"Why?" said Raymond.

"Because those bloody Frogs know only too well that there's a Channel between us and them, and if my lads are forced by law to sleep a night each side the only people who'll end up making money on the deal will be the guest-house proprietors."

"What's behind it?" asked Raymond.

"They want us to drop the stuff our end, so they can pick it up on the other side."

"But wouldn't that also be true when they need to deliver goods to us?"

"No. Their journeys are much longer to the coast, and they have to stay overnight anyway, not to mention the fact that there are eight of them to one of us. It's diabolical. nothing less."

Raymond studied the wording in detail while Edwards helped himself to another vodka.

"The clause doesn't stop you from going over the next day."

"And how much do you think that will add to your costs?" asked Raymond.

"I'll tell you, enough to make us uncompetitive, that's how much," replied the trade-union leader.

"Point taken," said Raymond. "So what's wrong with asking your own member to put the case?"

"Don't trust him. He's pro-European at any price."

"And what about your sponsored trade union representative in the House?"

"Tom Carson? You must be joking. He's so far to the left that even his own side are suspicious when he supports a cause. We lost the 'tachograph' clause because he championed it. In any case I only put him in the House to get him off my back." Raymond laughed. "Now, all my General Purposes Committee want to know is: would you be willing to fight this clause in the House for us? Not that we can afford the sort of fees you're used to at the bar," he added.

"There would be no fee involved," said Raymond, "but I'm sure you'll be able to repay me in kind sometime in the future."

"Got the picture," said Edwards, touching the side of his nose with a forefinger. "What do I do next?"

"You go back to Liverpool and hope that I am better on an away pitch than your team."

Norman Edwards put on an old raincoat and started to button it up. He smiled at Raymond. "I may have been appalled by your book, Ray. But it doesn't mean I didn't admire it."

The Speaker looked down at the front bench. "Mr Andrew Fraser."

"Number seventeen, sir," said Andrew.

The Speaker looked down to check over the question, seeking a Home Office answer.

Simon rose to the dispatch box, opened his file and said, "Yes, sir."

"Mr Andrew Fraser," called the Speaker again.

Andrew rose from his place on the Opposition front bench to put his supplementary.

"May I thank the minister for agreeing to an enquiry so quickly, and ask him that, if he discovers an injustice has been done to my constituent Mr Paddy O'Halloran, that the Home Secretary will order a re-trial immediately?"

Simon rose again.

"Yes, sir."

"I am grateful to the Honourable Gentleman," said Andrew, half-rising from his place.

All over in less than a minute, but older members who listened to the brief exchange between Fraser and Kerslake in the House that day had no doubt that considerable preparation had gone into that minute from both sides.

"The damn man missed another three-line whip, Charles. It must be the last time. You've been protecting him for far too long."

"It won't happen again," promised Charles convincingly. "I would like to give him one more chance. Allow him that."

"You're very loyal to him," said the Chief Whip. "But next time I'm going to see Kerslake myself and get to the bottom of it."

"It won't happen again," repeated Charles.

"Hm," said the Chief Whip. "Next problem is, are there any clauses on the European Bill that we should be worried about next week?"

"Yes," replied Charles. "This haulage clause that Raymond Gould is fighting. He made a brilliant case on the floor of the House, and got all his own side and half of ours backing him."

"He's not the sponsored MP for the Haulage Union," said the Chief Whip, surprised.

"No, the unions obviously felt Tom Carson wouldn't help the cause and he's hopping mad at the slight."

"Clever of them to pick Gould. He improves as a speaker every time I hear him, and no one can fault him when it comes to a point of law."

"So we'd better face the fact that we're going to lose the clause?"

"Never. We'll redraft the damn thing so that it's acceptable and *seen* to be compassionate. It's not a bad time to be the defender of the union interests. That way we'll keep Gould from getting all the credit. I'll speak to the PM tonight – and don't forget what I said about Kerslake."

Charles returned to his office and realised that in future he would have to be more careful about telling Simon Kerslake when he was paired for the European Bill. He suspected he had carried this ploy as far as he could for now.

Simon had read the final report prepared by his department on the O'Halloran case while Elizabeth was trying to get to sleep. He only had to go over the details once to realise that he would have to order a re-trial and institute a full investigation into the past record of the police officers who had been involved in the case.

When Andrew heard the news, and that the re-trial would be held in London, he asked Raymond Gould to represent O'Halloran.

"Praise indeed," said Raymond, who still considered Andrew among the Commons' finest orators. He somehow managed to fit O'Halloran into his busy schedule.

The trial was in its third day when Mr Justice Comyns, after listening to Mrs Bloxham's evidence, stopped proceedings and instructed the jury to return a verdict of not guilty.

Andrew received praise from all quarters of the House, but he was quick to acknowledge the support given him by Simon Kerslake and the Home Office. *The Times* even wrote a leader the next day on the proper use of influence by a constituency MP.

Some months later the court awarded O'Halloran £25,000 in compensation. The only drawback Andrew's success caused was that every convict's mother north of Hadrian's wall queued to tell him about her innocent son at his fortnightly surgery. But during the year he took only one seriously and once again began to check into the details.

During the long hot summer of 1972 clause after clause of the European Bill was voted on, often through the night. On some occasions the Government managed majorities of only five or six but somehow the bill remained intact.

Charles would often arrive home at Eaton Square at three in the morning to find Fiona asleep, only to leave again before she had woken. Veterans of the House, both servants and elected, confirmed they had never experienced anything like it since the Second World War.

And, just as suddenly, the last vote was taken and the marathon was over. The European Bill was through the Commons and on its way to the Upper House to receive their lordships' approval. Charles wondered what he would do with all the hours that were suddenly left him in the day.

When the bill finally received the Royal Assent in October the Chief Whip held a celebration lunch at the Carlton Club in St James's to thank all his team. "And in particular, Charles Seymour," he said, raising his glass during an impromptu speech. When the lunch broke up the Chief Whip offered Charles a lift back to the Commons in his official car. They travelled along Piccadilly, down Haymarket, through Trafalgar Square and into Whitehall. Just as the Commons came into sight the black Rover turned into Downing Street, as Charles assumed, to drop the Chief Whip at No. 12. But as the car stopped the Chief Whip said, "The Prime Minister is expecting you in five minutes."

"What? Why?" said Charles, as he joined his colleague outside No. 10.

"Timed it rather well, didn't I?" said the Chief Whip – and headed off towards No. 12.

Charles stood alone in front of No. 10. The door was opened by a man in a long black coat. "Good afternoon, Mr Seymour."

The Prime Minister saw Charles in his study and, as ever, wasted no time on small talk.

"Thank you for all the hard work you have put in on the European Bill."

"It was a tremendous challenge," said Charles, searching for words.

"As will be your next job," said Mr Heath. "I want you to take over as one of the Ministers of State at the Department of Trade and Industry."

Charles was speechless.

"With all the problems we are going to encounter with the trade unions during the next few months, that should keep you fully occupied."

"It certainly will," said Charles.

He still hadn't been asked to sit down, but as the Prime

Minister was now rising from behind his desk it was clear that the meeting was over.

"You and Fiona must come and have dinner at No. 10 as soon as you've settled into your new department," said the Prime Minister as they walked towards the door.

"Thank you," Charles said.

As he stepped back on to Downing Street a driver opened the back door of a shiny Austin Westminster. It was several moments before Charles realised the car was his.

"The Commons, sir?"

"No, I'd like to return to Eaton Square for a few minutes," he said, sitting back and enjoying the thought of tackling his new job.

The car drove past the Commons, up Victoria Street and on to Eaton Square. He wanted to tell Fiona that all the hard work had been rewarded. He felt guilty about how little he had seen of her lately, although he could not believe it would be much better now that he was to be involved in trade union legislation. How much he still hoped for a son, perhaps even that would prove possible now. The car came to a halt outside the Georgian house. Charles ran up the steps and into the hall. He could hear his wife's voice from the first floor. He took the wide staircase in bounds of two and three at a time, and threw open the bedroom door.

"I'm the new Minister of State at the Department of Trade and Industry," he announced to Fiona, who was lying in bed.

Alexander Dalglish looked up. He showed no sign of interest in Charles's elevation.

When Andrew rang Angus Sinclair at the Procurator Fiscal's office to find that nothing was known of Ricky Hodge and that Sinclair was able to confirm that he had no criminal record, Andrew felt he had stumbled on a case with international implications.

As Ricky Hodge was in a Turkish jail any enquiries had to be made through the Foreign Office. Andrew did not have the same relationship with the Foreign Secretary as he did with Simon, so he felt the direct approach would be best and put down a question to be answered in the House. He worded

it carefully: 'What action does the Foreign Secretary intend
to take over the confiscation of a British passport from a
constituent of the Honourable member for Edinburgh Carlton, details of which have been supplied to him?"

When the question came in front of the House on the
following Wednesday the Foreign Secretary rose to answer
the question himself. He stood at the dispatch box and
peered over his half-moon spectacles and said:

"Her Majesty's Government are pursuing this matter
through the usual diplomatic channels."

Andrew was quickly on his feet. "Does the Right Honourable Gentleman realise that my constituent has been in a
Turkish prison for six months and has still not been
charged?"

"Yes, sir," replied the Foreign Secretary. "I have asked
the Turkish Embassy to supply the Foreign Office with more
details of the case."

Andrew leaped up again. "How long will my constituent
have to be forgotten in Ankara before the Foreign Secretary
does more than ask for the details of his case?"

The Foreign Secretary rose again showing no sign of
annoyance. "I will report those findings to the Honourable
member as quickly as possible."

"When? Tomorrow, next week, next year?" Andrew
shouted angrily.

"When?" joined in a chorus of Labour back-benchers, but
the Speaker called for the next question above the uproar.

Within the hour Andrew received a handwritten note from
the Foreign Office. It read: "If Mr Fraser would be kind
enough to telephone, the Foreign Secretary would be delighted to make an appointment to see him."

Andrew phoned from the Commons and was invited to
join the Foreign Secretary in Whitehall immediately.

The Foreign Office, known as 'The Palazzo' by its inmates, has an atmosphere of its own. Although Andrew had
worked in a Government department as a minister he was
still struck by its grandeur. He was met at the courtyard
entrance and guided along yards of marble corridors before
climbing a fine double staircase at the top of which he was

greeted by the Foreign Secretary's Principal Private Secretary.

"Sir Alec will see you immediately, Mr Fraser," he said, and led Andrew past the magnificent pictures and tapestries which lined the way. He was taken into a beautifully proportioned room. The Foreign Secretary stood in front of an Adam fireplace over which hung a portrait of Lord Palmerston.

"Fraser, how kind of you to come at such short notice. I do hope it has not caused you any inconvenience." Platitudes, thought Andrew. Next the silly man will be mentioning my father. "I don't think we have met before, but of course I have known your father for many years. Won't you sit down?"

"I realise you are a busy man. Can we get down to the point at issue, Foreign Secretary?" Andrew demanded.

"Of course," Sir Alec said courteously. "Forgive me for taking up so much of your time." Without a further word, he handed Andrew a file marked 'Richard M. Hodge – Confidential'. "Although Members of Parliament are not subject to the Official Secrets Act I know you will respect the fact that this file is classified."

Another bluff, thought Andrew. He flicked back the cover. It was true: exactly as he had suspected, Ricky Hodge had never been arrested or charged. He turned the page. "Rome, child prostitution; Marseilles, narcotics; Paris, blackmail." Page after page, ending in Turkey, where Hodge had been found in possession of four pounds of heroin which he had been selling in small packets on the black market. In his twenty-nine years Ricky Hodge had spent eleven of the last fourteen in foreign jails.

Andrew closed the file and could feel the sweat on his forehead. It was some moments before he spoke. "I apologise, Foreign Secretary," he said. "I have made a fool of myself."

"When I was a young man," said Sir Alec, "I made a similar mistake on behalf of a constituent. Ernie Bevin was Foreign Secretary at the time. He could have crucified me in the House with the knowledge he had. Instead he revealed everything over a drink in this room. I sometimes wish the public could see members in their quiet moments as well as in their rowdy ones."

Andrew thanked Sir Alec and walked thoughtfully back to the House. The *Evening Standard* poster outside the Commons caught his eye. 'O'Halloran arrested again.' He bought a copy, stood by the railings and began reading. Paddy O'Halloran had been detained in a Glasgow police station and charged with robbing the Bank of Scotland in Sauchiehall Street. Andrew wondered if his friends would allege it was another 'frame up' by the police until he read the next paragraph. "O'Halloran was arrested leaving the bank in possession of a shotgun and £25,000 in used notes. He said when apprehended by the police, 'I've just been clearing my account.'"

At home, Louise told him that Ricky Hodge had done him a favour.

"How's that possible?" asked Andrew.

"You won't take yourself so seriously in future," she smiled.

When Andrew conducted his next surgery in Edinburgh two weeks later he was surprised to see that Mrs Bloxham had made an appointment.

As he greeted her at the door he was even more surprised. She was wearing a bright crimplene dress and a new pair of squeaky brown leather shoes. She also looked as if 'Our Blessed Lady' might have to wait a few more years to receive her after all. Andrew motioned her to a seat.

"I came to thank you, Mr Fraser," she said, once she was settled.

"What for?" asked Andrew.

"For sending that nice young man round from Christie's. They auctioned great-grandma's table for me. I couldn't believe my luck – it fetched £1,400." Andrew smiled. "So it don't matter about the stain on the dress any more." She paused. "It even made up for having to eat off the floor for three months."

Simon steered the new Boundary Commission recommendations unspectacularly through the House as an order in
Council, and suddenly he had lost his own constituency. His
colleagues in Coventry were understanding, and nursed
those wards that would become theirs at the next election in
order that he might spend more time searching for a new
seat.

Seven seats became available during the year but Simon
was only interviewed for two of them. Both were almost on
the Scottish border and both put him in second place. He
began to appreciate what it must feel like for an Olympic
favourite to be awarded the silver medal.

Ronnie Nethercote's monthly board reports began to paint
an increasingly sombre picture, thus reflecting in real life
what the politicians were decreeing in Parliament. Ronnie
had decided to postpone going public until the climate was
more advantageous. Simon couldn't disagree with the judgement, but when he checked his special overdraft facility the
interest on his loans had pushed the figure in red to over
£90,000.

When unemployment first passed the million mark and
Ted Heath ordered a pay and prices freeze strikes broke out
all over the country.

The new parliamentary session in the autumn was dominated by the issue of a Prices and Incomes policy. Charles
Seymour became involved in putting the case for the Government. While he didn't always win every argument, he was
now so well-briefed on his subject that he no longer feared
making a fool of himself at the dispatch box. Raymond Gould
and Andrew Fraser both made passionate speeches on behalf
of the unions, but the Conservative majority beat them again
and again.

However, the Prime Minister was moving inexorably
towards a head-on clash with the unions and an early general
election.

When all three party conferences were over members
returned to the Commons aware that it was likely to be their
last session before the general election. It was openly being

said in the corridors that all the Prime Minister was waiting for was a catalyst. The miners provided it. In the middle of a bleak winter they called an all-out strike for more pay in defiance of the Government's new trade union legislation.

In a television interview the Prime Minister told the nation that with unemployment at an unprecedented 2,294,448 and the country on a three-day week he had to call an election to ensure that the rule of law be maintained. The inner Cabinet advised Heath to plump for 28 February 1974.

'Who runs the country?' became the Tory theme but seemed only to emphasise class differences, rather than uniting the country as Edward Heath had hoped.

Andrew Fraser had his doubts but he faced a different threat in his own constituency, where the Scottish National-ists were using the quarrel between the two major parties to promote their own cause. He returned to Scotland, to be warned by his father that the Scottish Nationalists were no longer a joke and that he would be facing a hard campaign against the robust local candidate, Jock McPherson.

Raymond Gould travelled back to Leeds, confident that the north-east industrial area would not tolerate Heath's high-handedness.

Charles felt sure that the people would back any party which had shown the courage to stand up to the unions, although the left wing, led vociferously by Tom Carson, made a great play of the 'two nations' issue, insisting that the Government were out to crush the Labour movement once and for all.

Charles drove down to Sussex to find his supporters glad of the chance to put those 'lazy trade unionists' in their place.

Simon, with no seat to fight, worked on in the Home Office right up to the day of the election, convinced that his career was facing only a temporary setback.

"I'll fight the first by-election that comes up," he promised Elizabeth.

"Even if it's a mining seat in South Wales?" she replied.

Many months had passed before Charles had found it possi-ble even to sustain a conversation with Fiona for any length of time. Neither wanted a divorce, both citing the ailing Earl of Bridgwater as their reason, although inconvenience and loss of face were nearer the truth. In public it would have been hard to detect the change in their relationship since they had never been given to overt affection.

Charles gradually became aware that it was possible for marriages to have been over for years without outsiders knowing it. Certainly the old earl never found out, because even on his death bed he told Fiona to hurry up and produce an heir.

"Do you think you'll ever forgive me?" Fiona once asked her husband.

"Never," he replied, with a finality that encouraged no further discourse.

During the three-week election campaign in Sussex they both went about their duties with a professionalism that masked their true feelings.

"How is your husband bearing up?" someone would enquire.

"Much enjoying the campaign and looking forward to returning to Government," was Fiona's stock reply.

"And how is dear Lady Fiona?" Charles was continuously asked.

"Never better than when she's helping in the constituency," was his.

On Sundays, at one church after another, he read the lesson with confidence while she sang 'Fight the good fight' in a clear contralto.

The demands of a rural constituency are considerably different from those of a city. Every village, however small, expects the member to visit them and to recall the local chairmen's names. Subtle changes were taking place: Fiona no longer whispered the names in Charles's ear. Charles no longer turned to her for advice.

During the campaign Charles would ring the photographer on the local paper to discover which events his editor had instructed him to cover that day. With the list of places and times in his hand Charles would arrive on each occasion a few minutes before the photographer. The Labour candidate complained officially to the local editor that Mr Seymour's photograph was never out of the paper.

"If you were present at these functions we would be only too happy to publish your photo," said the editor.

"But they never invite me," cried the Labour candidate.

They don't invite Seymour either, the editor wanted to say, but he somehow manages to be there. It was never far from the editor's mind that his proprietor was a Tory peer so he kept his mouth shut.

All the way up to election day Charles and Fiona opened bazaars, attended dinners, drew raffles and only just stopped short of kissing babies.

Once, when Fiona asked him, Charles admitted that he hoped to be moved to the Foreign Office as a Minister of State, and perhaps to be made a Privy Councillor.

On the last day of February they dressed in silence and went off to their local polling station to vote. The photographer was there on the steps to take their picture. They stood closer together than they had for some weeks, looking like a smart register office couple. Charles knew it would be the main photograph on the front page of the *Sussex Gazette* the following day, as surely as he knew the Labour candidate would be relegated to a half-column mention on the inside page not far from the obituaries.

The count in a rural seat is always taken the following morning at a more leisurely pace than is customary for its city cousins. So Charles anticipated that by the time he arrived in the town hall the Conservative majority in the House would already be assured. But it was not to be, and the result still hung in the balance that Friday morning.

Edward Heath did not concede when the newscasters predicted he would fail to be given the overall majority he required. Charles spent the day striding around the town hall with an anxious look on his face. The little piles of votes soon became larger and it was obvious that he would hold the seat with at least his usual 21,000 – or was it 22,000? – majority. He never could remember the exact figure. But as the day progressed it became more and more difficult to assess the national verdict.

The last result came in from Northern Ireland a little after four o'clock that afternoon and a BBC commentator announced –

Labour	301
Conservative	296
Liberal	14
Ulster Unionists	11
Scottish Nationalists	7
Welsh Nationalists	2
Others	4

Ted Heath invited the Liberal leader to join him at Downing Street for talks in the hope that they could form a coalition. The Liberals demanded a firm commitment to electoral reform and, in particular, to proportional representation by the next election. Heath knew he could never get his back-benchers to deliver. On the Monday morning he told the Queen in her drawing-room at Buckingham Palace that he was unable to form a Government. She called for Harold Wilson. He accepted her commission and drove back to Downing Street to enter the front door. Heath left by the back.

By the Tuesday afternoon every member, having watched the drama unfold, had returned to London. Raymond had increased his majority and now hoped that the Prime Minister had long since forgotten his resignation and would offer him a job.

Andrew had had the hard and unpleasant fight with Jock McPherson, just as his father had predicted, and held on to his seat by only 2,229.

Charles, still unsure of the exact majority by which he had won, drove back to London, resigned to Opposition. The one compensation was that he would be reinstated on the board of Seymour's where the knowledge he had gained as a minister of Trade and Industry could only be of value.

Simon left the Home Office on 1 March 1974 with little more than an empty red box to show for nine years as a parliamentarian.

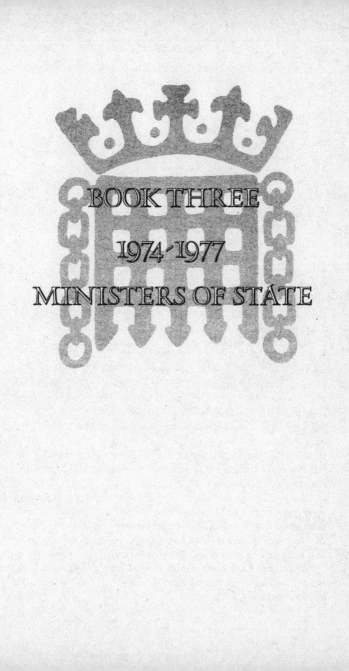

BOOK THREE

1974-1977

MINISTERS OF STATE

CHAPTER SIXTEEN

"His diary looks rather full at the moment, Mr Charles."

"Well, as soon as it's convenient," Charles replied over the phone. He held on as he heard the pages being turned.

"12 March at ten-thirty, Mr Charles?"

"But that's nearly a fortnight away," he said, irritated.

"Mr Spencer has only just returned from the States and –"

"How about a lunch, then – at my club?" Charles interrupted.

"That couldn't be until after 19 March."

"Very well, then," said Charles. "12 March, at ten-thirty."

During the fourteen-day wait Charles had ample time to become frustrated by his seemingly aimless role in Opposition. No car came to pick him up and whisk him away to an office where real work had to be done. Worse, no one sought his opinion any longer on matters that affected the nation. He was going through a sharp bout of what is known as 'ex-ministers' blues'.

He was relieved when the day for the appointment with Derek Spencer at last came round. But although he arrived on time he was kept waiting for ten minutes before the chairman's secretary took him through.

"Good to see you after so long," said Spencer, coming round his desk to greet him. "It must be nearly six years since you've visited the bank."

"Yes, I suppose it is," said Charles. "But looking around the old place it feels like yesterday. You've been fully occupied, no doubt?"

"Like a Cabinet minister, but I hope with better results."

They both laughed.

"Of course I've kept in touch with what's been happening at the bank."

"Have you?" said Spencer.

"Yes, I've read all the reports you've sent out over the past years, not to mention the *Financial Times*'s coverage."

"I hope you feel we've progressed satisfactorily in your absence."

"Oh. Yes," said Charles, still standing. "Very impressive."

"Well, now what can I do for you?" asked the chairman, returning to his seat.

"Simple enough," said Charles, finally taking an unoffered chair. "I wish to be reinstated on the board."

There was a long silence.

"Well, it's not quite that easy, Charles. I've just recently appointed two new directors and . . ."

"Of course it's that easy," said Charles, his tone changing. "You have only to propose my name at the next meeting and it will go through, especially as you haven't a member of the family on the board at the present time."

"We have, as a matter of fact. Your brother the Earl of Bridgwater has become a non-executive director."

"What? Rupert never told me," said Charles. "Neither did you."

"True, but things have changed since –"

"Nothing has changed except my estimation of the value of your word," said Charles, suddenly realising that Spencer had never intended he should return to the board. "You gave me your assurance –"

"I won't be spoken to like this in my own office."

"If you're not careful, the next place I shall do it will be in your boardroom. Now, will you honour your undertaking or not?"

"I don't have to listen to threats from you, Seymour. Get out of my office before I have you removed. I can assure you that you will never sit on the board again as long as I'm chairman."

Charles turned and marched out, slamming the door as he

left. He wasn't sure with whom to discuss the problem and returned immediately to Eaton Square to consider a plan of campaign.

"What brings you home in the middle of the afternoon?" asked Fiona.

Charles hesitated, considered the question and then joined his wife in the kitchen and told her everything that had happened at the bank. Fiona continued to grate some cheese as she listened to her husband.

"Well, one thing is certain," she said, not having spoken for several minutes but delighted that Charles had confided in her. "After that fracas, you can't both be on the board."

"So what do you think I ought to do, old girl?"

Fiona smiled; it was the first time he had called her that for nearly two years. "Every man has his secrets," she said. "I wonder what Mr Spencer's are?"

"He's such a dull middle-class fellow I doubt if —"

"I've just had a letter from Seymour's Bank," interrupted Fiona.

"What about?"

"Only a shareholder's circular. It seems Margaret Trubshaw is retiring after twelve years as the board secretary. Rumour has it she wanted to do five more years, but the chairman has someone else in mind. I think I might have lunch with her."

Charles returned his wife's smile.

Andrew's appointment as Minister of State at the Home Office came as no surprise to anyone except his three-year-old son, who quickly discovered how to empty any red boxes that were left unlocked, refilling them with marbles or sweets, and even managing to fit a football into one. As Robert didn't fully understand 'For Your Eyes Only', it didn't seem to make a lot of difference that Cabinet committee papers were sometimes found glued together with old bubble-gum.

"Can you remove that latest stain in the red box?"

"Good heavens, what caused it?" asked Louise, staring down at a jelly-like blob.

"Frog spawn," said Andrew, grinning.

"He's a brain-washed Russian spy," warned Louise, "with a mental age about the same as most of your colleagues in the House. Yes, I'll remove the stain if you sit down and write that letter."

Andrew nodded his agreement.

Among the many letters of commiseration Simon received when he did not return to the House was one from Andrew Fraser. Simon could imagine him sitting in his old office and implementing the decisions he had been involved in making just a few weeks before.

There was also a letter from Ronnie Nethercote inviting him to return to the board of Nethercote and Company at £5,000 a year, which even Elizabeth acknowledged as a generous gesture.

It was not long before Ronnie Nethercote had made Simon an executive director of the company. Simon enjoyed negotiating with the trade unions at a level he had not experienced before. Ronnie made it clear how he would have dealt with the 'Commie bastards' given half a chance. "Lock them all up until they learn to do a day's work."

"You would have lasted about a week in the House of Commons," Simon told him.

"After a week with those windbags I'd have been only too happy to return to the real world."

Simon smiled. Ronnie, he felt, was like so many others – imagining all Members of Parliament were unemployable except the one they knew.

Raymond waited until the last Government appointment was announced before he finally gave up any hope of a job. Several leading political journalists pointed out that he had been left on the back benches while lesser men had been given Government posts but it was scant comfort. Reluctantly he returned to Lincoln's Inn to continue his practice at the bar.

Harold Wilson, starting his third administration, made it

clear that he would govern as long as possible before calling an election. But as he did not have an overall majority in the House few members believed that he could hold out for more than a matter of months.

Fiona returned home after her lunch with Miss Trubshaw with a large Cheshire Cat grin on her face. It remained firmly in place during the hours she had to wait for Charles to get back from the Commons after the last division.

"You look pleased with yourself," said Charles, shaking out his umbrella before closing the front door. His wife stood in the hallway, her arms crossed.

"How has your day been?" she asked.

"So-so," said Charles, wanting to hear the news. "But what about you?"

"Oh, pleasant enough. I had coffee with your mother this morning. She seems very well. A little cold in the head, otherwise –"

"To hell with my mother. How did your lunch with Miss Trubshaw go?"

"I wondered how long it would take you to get round to that."

She continued to wait just as long as it took for them to walk into the drawing-room and sit down. "After seventeen years as secretary to your father and twelve years as secretary to the board there isn't much Miss Trubshaw doesn't know about Seymour's or its present chairman," Fiona began.

"So what did you discover?"

"Which do you want to hear about first, the name of his mistress or the number of his Swiss bank account?"

Fiona revealed everything she had learned over her two-hour lunch, explaining that Miss Trubshaw usually only drank fortified wine but on this occasion she had downed most of a vintage bottle of Pommard. Charles's smile grew wider and wider as each fact came pouring out. To Fiona he looked like a boy who has been given a box of chocolates and keeps discovering another layer underneath.

"Well done, old girl," he said when she had come to the end of her tale. "But how do I get all the proof I need?"

"I've made a deal with our Miss Trubshaw."

"You've what?"

"A deal. With Miss Trubshaw. You get the proof if she remains as secretary to the board for a further five years, and no loss of benefit to her pension."

"Is that all she wants?" said Charles, guardedly.

"And the price of another lunch at the Savoy Grill when you're invited back on the board."

Unlike many of his Labour colleagues Raymond now enjoyed dressing up in white tie and tails and mixing with London society. An invitation to the annual bankers' banquet at the Guildhall was no exception. The Prime Minister was the guest of honour and Raymond wondered if he would drop a hint as to how long he expected the parliamentary session to last before he felt he had to call an election.

At the pre-dinner drinks Raymond had a quick word with the Lord Mayor before becoming involved in a conversation with a circuit court judge on the problems of the parity of sentencing.

When dinner was announced Raymond found his seat on one of the long fingers stretching away from the top table. He checked his place card. Raymond Gould QC, MP. On his right was the chairman of Chloride, Michael Edwardes, and on his left an American banker who had just taken up an appointment in the City.

Raymond found Michael Edwardes's views on how the Prime Minister should tackle the nationalised industries fascinating, but he devoted far more of his attention to the Euro Bond manager from Chase Manhattan. She must have been thirty, Raymond decided, if only because of her elevated position at the bank and her claim to have been an undergraduate at Wellesley at the time of Kennedy's death. He would have put Kate Garthwaite at far younger and was not surprised to learn she played tennis in the summer and swam every day during the winter – to keep her weight down, she confided. She had a warm, oval face, and her dark hair was cut in what Raymond thought was a Mary Quant style. Her nose turned up slightly at the end and would have cost a lot of money for a plastic surgeon to reproduce. There was no chance of seeing her legs as they were covered by a long dress, but what he could see left Raymond more than interested.

"I see there's an 'MP' behind your name, Mr Gould. May I ask which party you represent?" she asked, in an accent heard more often in Boston.

"I'm a Socialist, Mrs Garthwaite. Where do your sympathies lie on this occasion?"

"I would have voted Labour at the last election if I had been qualified," she declared.

"Should I be surprised?" he teased.

"You certainly should. My ex-husband is a Republican congressman."

He was about to ask his next question when the toastmaster called for silence. For the first time Raymond turned his eyes to the top table and the Prime Minister. Harold Wilson's speech stuck firmly to economic problems and the role of a Labour Government in the City and gave no clue as to the timing of the next election. Nevertheless, Raymond considered it a worthwhile evening. He had made a useful contact with the chairman of a large public company. And he had acquired Kate's telephone number.

The chairman of Seymour's reluctantly agreed to see him a second time, but it was obvious from the moment Charles walked in when no hand was proffered that Derek Spencer intended it to be a short interview.

"I thought I ought to see you personally," said Charles as he settled back in the comfortable leather chair and slowly lit a cigarette, "rather than raise my query at the AGM next month."

The first sign of apprehension began to show on the chairman's face, but he said nothing.

"I'm rather keen to discover why the bank should pay out a monthly cheque of £400 to an employee called Miss Janet Darrow, whom I have never come across, although it appears she has been on the payroll for over five years. The cheques, it seems, have been going to a branch of Lloyds in Kensington."

Derek Spencer's face became flushed.

"What I am at a loss to discover," continued Charles after he had inhaled deeply, "is what services Miss Darrow has been supplying to the bank. They must be quite impressive to have earned her £25,000 over the last five years. I appreciate that this is a small amount when you consider the bank's turnover of 123 million last year, but my grandfather instilled in me at an early age the belief that if one took care of the pennies the pounds would take care of themselves."

Still Derek Spencer said nothing, although beads of sweat had appeared on his forehead. Suddenly Charles's tone changed. "If I find I am not a member of the board by the time of the Annual General Meeting I feel it will be my duty to point out this slight discrepancy in the bank's accounts to the other shareholders present."

"You're a bastard, Seymour," the chairman said quietly.

"Now that is not accurate. I am the second son of the former chairman of this bank and I bear a striking resemblance to my father, although everyone says I have my mother's eyes."

"What's the deal?"

"No deal. You will merely keep to your original agreement and see that I am reinstated on the board before the AGM. You will also cease any further payments to Miss Janet Darrow immediately."

"If I agree, will you swear never to mention this matter to anyone again?"

"I will. And, unlike you, I am in the habit of keeping my word."

Charles rose from his chair, leaned over the desk and stubbed out his cigarette in the chairman's ashtray.

Andrew Fraser was surprised when he heard that Jock McPherson wanted to see him. The two men had never been on good terms since McPherson had failed to be elected to the

Scottish Labour Party Executive Committee and had then left the party to stand against him at Edinburgh Carlton. Since McPherson had switched his allegiance they had barely been on speaking terms. However, Andrew realised it would be foolish not to see him after the SNP's sweeping successes in the election.

Andrew was even more surprised when McPherson asked if all seven SNP Members of Parliament could also attend the meeting, not in Andrew's office but somewhere private. He agreed, even more mystified.

McPherson and his band of renegade Scots arrived together at Cheyne Walk, looking as though they had already held a meeting between themselves. Andrew offered them a variety of seats, including the dining-room chairs, a pouffe and even the kitchen stool, apologising that his London flat had never been intended to accommodate nine men in the drawing-room.

While the men settled themselves Andrew remained standing by the mantelpiece, facing Jock McPherson who had obviously been chosen to act as their spokesman.

"I'll get straight to the point," McPherson began. "We want you to fight under the SNP banner at the next election."

Andrew tried not to show his disbelief, and began, "I don't feel . . ."

"Hear me out," said McPherson, raising his massive palms. "We want you to contest the Edinburgh Carlton seat not just as a Scottish Nationalist candidate but as leader of the party."

Andrew still couldn't believe what he was hearing but remained silent.

"We're convinced you'll lose your seat in any case if you stand as a Socialist," McPherson continued, "but we realise that there are many people in Scotland who, whatever their political views, admire what you have achieved in the nine years you have been in the House. After all, man, you were brought up and educated in Edinburgh. With you as leader, we believe we could capture forty to fifty of the seventy-one seats in Scotland. And I may add that your own party is moving inexorably to the left, a state of affairs that I can't believe you are altogether happy about."

Andrew still made no comment. He listened as each one of the MPs put his own view, which became predictable long before the last one had spoken. Every Scottish tone from a Highland lilt to a Glasgow growl was represented in the voices. It became clear that they had given the matter considerable thought and were obviously sincere. "I am very flattered, gentlemen," he began when the last one had said his piece. "And I assure you I will give your offer my serious consideration."

"Thank you," said McPherson. They all stood up like clan leaders in the presence of a new chief.

"We'll wait to hear from you then," said McPherson. One by one they shook hands with their host before filing out.

As soon as they had left Andrew went straight into the kitchen where Robert was still waiting impatiently to play football before going to bed.

"In a moment, in a moment," he said in response to his son's noisy demands. "I'll join you in the garden."

"And what did that lot lot want?" enquired Louise, as she continued to peel the potatoes.

Andrew went over the details of their proposition.

"And how did you respond?"

"I didn't. I shall wait a week and then decline as gracefully as possible."

"What made you decide against the offer so quickly?"

"I don't like being told by Jock McPherson, or anyone else for that matter, that I will lose my seat at the next election if I don't fall in with their plans." He headed towards the kitchen door. "I'll be back to the red box as soon as I've scored a couple of goals against MacPele." A moment later he had joined Robert in the garden.

"Now listen, clever boots, I'm going to teach you how to feint a pass so that your opponent goes one way while you go the other."

"Sounds just like politics to me," muttered Louise, watching them out of the kitchen window.

27 Eaton Square,
London, SW1
23 April 1974

Dear Derek,

Thank you for your letter of 18 April and your kind invitation to rejoin the board of Seymour's. I am delighted to accept and look forward to working with you again.

Yours sincerely,
Charles Seymour.

Fiona checked the wording and nodded. Short and to the point. "Shall I post it?"

"Yes, please," said Charles as the phone rang.

He picked it up. "730—9712. Charles Seymour speaking."

"Oh, hello, Charles. It's Simon Kerslake."

"Hello, Simon," said Charles, trying to sound pleased to hear from his former colleague. "What's it like out there in the real world?"

"Not much fun, which is exactly why I'm phoning. I've been short-listed for Pucklebridge, Sir Michael Harbour-Baker's seat. He's nearly seventy and has decided not to stand again at the next election. As his constituency touches the south border of yours, I thought you might be able to put in a word for me again."

"Delighted," said Charles. "I'll speak to the chairman tonight. You can rely on me, and good luck. It would be nice to have you back in the House."

Simon gave him his home number which Charles repeated slowly, as if he were writing it down.

"I'll be in touch," said Charles.

"I really appreciate your help."

Simon put down the phone.

Elizabeth looked up from her copy of *The Lancet*.

"I don't trust that man," she said.

"A woman's intuition again?" said Simon smiling. "You were wrong about Ronnie Nethercote."

"That's yet to be proved."

It was several days before Kate Garthwaite agreed to see Raymond again. And when she eventually joined him for dinner at the House she was not overwhelmed or flattered and she certainly didn't hang on his every word.

She was lively, fun, intelligent and well informed and they began to see each other regularly. As the months passed Raymond found himself missing her at weekends when he was in Leeds with Joyce. Kate enjoyed her independence and made none of the demands on him that Stephanie had, never once suggesting he spend more time with her or that she might leave clothes behind in the flat.

Raymond sipped his coffee. "That was a memorable meal," he said, falling back into the sofa.

"Only by the standards of the House of Commons," replied Kate.

Raymond put an arm round her shoulder before kissing her gently on the lips.

"What! Rampant sex as well as cheap Beaujolais?" she exclaimed, stretching over and pouring herself some more coffee.

"I wish you wouldn't always make a joke of our relationship," said Raymond, stroking the back of her hair.

"I have to," said Kate quietly.

"Why?" Raymond turned to face her.

"Because I'm frightened of what might happen if I take it seriously."

Raymond leant over and kissed her again. "Don't be frightened. You're the best thing that's happened to me in my whole life."

"That's what I'm worried about," said Kate, turning away.

Charles sat through the Annual General Meeting in silence. The chairman made his report for the year ending March 1974 before welcoming two new directors to the board and the return of Charles Seymour.

There were several questions from the floor which Derek Spencer had no trouble in handling. As Charles had promised, there was not even a hint of Miss Janet Darrow. Miss Trubshaw had let Fiona know that the payment had been stopped and also mentioned that she was still worried that her contract was coming to an end on 1 July.

When the chairman brought the AGM to a close Charles asked courteously if he could spare him a moment.

"Of course," said Spencer, looking relieved that the meeting had gone through without a hitch. "What can I do for you?"

"I think it might be wiser to talk in the privacy of your office."

The chairman glanced at him sharply but led him back to his room.

Charles settled himself comfortably in the leather chair once more and removed some papers from his inside pocket. Peering down at them he asked, "What does BX41207122, Bank Rombert, Zurich, mean to you?"

"You said you would never mention –"

"Miss Darrow," said Charles. "And I shall keep my word. But now, as a director of the bank, I am trying to find out what BX41207122 means to you?"

"You know damn well what it means," said the chairman, banging his clenched fist on the desk.

"I know it's your *private*" – Charles emphasised the last word – "account in Zurich."

"You could never prove anything," said Derek Spencer defiantly.

"I agree with you, but what I am able to prove," said Charles, shuffling through the papers that were resting on his lap, "is that you have been using Seymour's money to do private deals, leaving the profit in your Zurich account without informing the board."

"I've done nothing that will harm the bank, and you know it."

"I know the money has been returned with interest, and I could never prove the bank had suffered any loss. Nevertheless, the board might take a dim view of your activities remembering they pay you £40,000 a year to make profits for the bank, not for yourself."

"When they saw all the figures they would at worst rap me over the knuckles."

"I doubt if the Director of Public Prosecutions would take the same lenient attitude if he saw these documents," said Charles, holding up the papers that had been resting on his lap.

"You'd ruin the bank's name."

"And you would probably spend the next ten years in jail. If, however, you did get away with it you would be finished in the City, and by the time your legal fees had been paid there wouldn't be much left of that nest-egg in Zurich."

"So what do you want this time?" demanded Spencer, sounding exasperated.

"Your job," said Charles.

"My job?" said Spencer in disbelief. "Do you imagine because you've been a junior minister you're capable of running a successful merchant bank?" he added scornfully.

"I didn't say I would run it. I can buy a competent chief executive to do that."

"Then what will you be doing?"

"I shall be the chairman of Seymour's which will convince City institutions that we wish to continue in the traditions of generations of my family."

"You're bluffing," stammered Spencer.

"If you are still in this building in twenty-four hours' time," said Charles, "I shall send these to the DPP."

There was a long silence.

"If I agreed," said Spencer at last, "I would expect two years' salary as compensation."

"One year," said Charles. Spencer hesitated, then nodded slowly. Charles rose to his feet and put the papers resting on his lap back into his inside pocket.

They consisted of nothing more than the morning mail from Sussex Downs.

Simon felt the interview had gone well but Elizabeth was not so sure. They sat huddled in a room with five other candidates and their wives, patiently waiting.

He thought back to his answers, and to the eight men and four women on the committee.

"You must admit it's the most ideal seat I've been considered for," said Simon.

"Yes, but the chairman kept eyeing you suspiciously."

"But Millburn mentioned that he had been at Eton with Charles Seymour."

"That's what worries me," whispered Elizabeth.

"A 15,000 majority at the last election and only forty minutes from London. We could even buy a little cottage . . ."

"If they invite you to represent them."

"At least this time you were able to tell them you would be willing to live in the constituency."

"So would anyone in their right mind," said Elizabeth.

The chairman came out and asked if Mr and Mrs Kerslake would be kind enough to return once more to see the committee.

Oh, God, thought Simon. What else can they want to know?

"It's too near London to be my fault this time," chuckled Elizabeth.

The committee sat and stared at them with long faces.

"Ladies and gentlemen," said the chairman. "After our lengthy deliberations, I formally propose that Mr Simon Kerslake be invited to contest Pucklebridge at the next election. Those in favour . . .?"

All twelve hands went up.

"Those against . . .?"

"Carried unanimously," said the chairman. He then turned to Simon. "Do you wish to address your committee?"

The prospective Conservative Member of Parliament for Pucklebridge rose. They all waited expectantly.

"I don't know what to say, except that I'm very happy and honoured and I can't wait for a general election."

They all laughed and came forward and surrounded them. Elizabeth dried her eyes before anyone reached her.

About an hour later the chairman accompanied Simon and Elizabeth back to their car and bade them goodnight. Simon wound down his window.

"I knew you were the right man," Millburn said, "as soon

as Charles Seymour phoned" – Simon smiled – "and warned me to avoid you like the plague."

"Could you tell Miss Trubshaw to come in?" Charles asked his secretary.

Margaret Trubshaw arrived a few moments later and remained standing in front of his desk. She couldn't help but notice the change of furniture in the room. The modern Conran suite had been replaced by a leather club-like sofa. Only the picture of the eleventh Earl of Bridgwater remained in place.

"Miss Trubshaw," began Charles, "since Mr Spencer has felt it necessary to resign so suddenly I think it important for the bank to keep some continuity now that I'm taking over as chairman."

Miss Trubshaw stood like a Greek statue, her hands hidden in the sleeves of her dress.

"With that in mind, the board has decided to extend your contract with the bank for a further five years. Naturally, there will be no loss in your pension rights."

"Thank you, Mr Charles."

"Thank you, Miss Trubshaw."

Miss Trubshaw almost bowed as she left the room.

"And Miss Trubshaw?"

"Yes, Mr Charles," she said, holding on to the door knob.

"I believe my wife is expecting a call from you. Something about inviting you to lunch at the Savoy Grill."

CHAPTER
SEVENTEEN

"A blue shirt," said Raymond, looking at the Turnbull and Asser label with suspicion. "A *blue* shirt," he repeated.

"A fortieth-birthday present," shouted Kate from the kitchen.

I shall never wear it, he thought, and smiled to himself.

"And what's more, you'll wear it," she said, her Boston accent carrying a slight edge.

"You even know what I'm thinking," he complained as she came in from the kitchen. He always thought how elegant she looked in her tailored office suit.

"It's because you're so predictable, Carrot Top."

"Anyway, how did you know it was my birthday?"

"A massive piece of detective work," said Kate, "with the help of an outside agent and a small payment."

"An outside agent. Who?"

"The local paper shop, my darling. In the *Sunday Times* they tell you the name of every distinguished person celebrating a birthday in the following seven days. In a week during which only the mediocre were born, you made it."

Raymond had to laugh.

"Now listen, Carrot Top."

Raymond pretended to hate his new nickname. "Do you have to call me by that revolting name?"

"Yes. I can't stand Raymond."

He scowled. "In any case, carrot tops are green."

"No comment. Try on your shirt."

"Now?"

"Now."

He took off his black coat and waistcoat, removed his white shirt and eased the stud on his stiff collar, leaving a small circle above his Adam's apple. Curly red hairs stuck up all over his chest. He quickly put on the new gift. The fabric had a pleasant soft feel about it. He started to do up the buttons, but Kate walked over and undid the top two.

"You know what? You've brought a whole new meaning to the word 'uptight'."

Raymond scowled again.

"But in the right clothes you could even pass for good looking. Now. Where shall we go to celebrate your birthday?"

"The House of Commons?" suggested Raymond.

"Good God," said Kate. "I said celebrate, not hold a wake. What about Annabel's?"

"I can't afford to be seen in Annabel's."

"With me, you mean?"

"No, no, you silly woman, because I'm a Socialist."

"If members of the Labour party are not allowed to indulge in a good meal then perhaps it's time for you to change parties. In my country one only sees the Democrats in the best restaurants."

"Oh, do be serious, Kate."

"I intend to be. Now what have you been up to in the House lately?"

"Not a lot," said Raymond sheepishly. "I've been snowed under in court and . . ."

"Precisely. It's time you did something positive before your colleagues in Parliament forget you exist."

"Have you anything particular in mind?" asked Raymond, folding his arms across his chest.

"As a matter of fact, I have," said Kate. "I read in the same Sunday paper as the one in which I discovered your best-kept secret that it is proving difficult for the Labour party to repeal the Tories' trade union legislation. It appears there are long-term legal implications which the front bench are still trying to find a way round. Why don't you set that so-called 'first class' mind of yours to working out the legal niceties?"

"Not such a stupid idea." Raymond had become used to Kate's political sense, and when he had remarked on it she had only said, "Just another bad habit I picked up from my ex-husband."

"Now, where do we celebrate?" she asked.

"Compromise," said Raymond.

"I'm all ears."

"The Dorchester."

"If you insist," said Kate, not sounding over-enthusiastic.

Raymond started to change his shirt.

"No, no, no, Carrot Top, people have been known to wear blue shirts at the Dorchester."

"But I haven't got a tie to match," said Raymond triumphantly.

Kate thrust her hand into the Turnbull and Asser bag and drew out a dark blue silk tie.

"But it's got a pattern on it," said Raymond in disgust. "What will you expect next?"

"Contact lenses," said Kate.

Raymond stared at her, and blinked.

On the way out of the door Raymond's gaze fell upon the brightly wrapped package that Joyce had posted from Leeds earlier in the week. He had completely forgotten to open it.

"Damn," said Charles, putting down *The Times* and draining his coffee.

"What's the problem?" asked Fiona as she poured out another cup.

"Kerslake's been selected for Pucklebridge, which means he's back in the House for life. Obviously my chat to Archie Millburn had no effect."

"Why have you got it in for Kerslake?" asked Fiona.

Charles folded the paper and considered the question. "It's quite simple really, old girl. I think he's the only one of my contemporaries who could stop me leading the party."

"Why him in particular?"

"I first came across him when he was President of the Union at Oxford. He was damn good then, and now he's better. He had rivals, but he brushed them aside like flies.

No, despite his background, Kerslake's the one man left who frightens me."

"It's a long race yet, my darling, and he could still stumble."

"So could I, but what he doesn't realise is that I shall be putting out some of his hurdles."

Andrew worded the letter very carefully. He assured Jock McPherson and his colleagues that he had been flattered by their approach, but explained that he had decided his loyalties were still firmly based in the Labour party.

He accepted the point Jock had made about the left trying to gain control, but felt that every democratic party was bound to have a maverick element within its ranks, which was not necessarily unhealthy. He added that he considered the offer to have been confidential on both sides.

"Why add that postscript?" asked Louise when she had read the letter through.

"It's only fair to Jock," said Andrew. "If it gets around I turned him down it will have the opposite effect to the one they were trying to create."

"I'm not so sure they will act in the same magnanimous way when the next election comes round."

"Ah, Jock will make a lot of noise, but he's all right underneath . . ."

"That isn't what your father says about him," said Louise. "He's sure they'll want revenge."

"Father always sees grubs under even the greenest leaf."

"So if we're not about to celebrate your leadership of the Scottish Nationalists we'll have to be satisfied with celebrating your fortieth birthday."

"But that's not for at least –"

"– another month, a week before Robert's fourth birthday."

"How would you like to commemorate the occasion, darling?"

"I thought we might have a week in the Algarve on our own."

"Why don't we have two weeks? Then we can celebrate your fortieth birthday as well?"

"Andrew Fraser, you just lost yourself one vote in Edinburgh Carlton."

Simon listened intently to Ronnie's report at the monthly board meeting. Two tenants had not paid their quarterly rent, and another quarter date was fast approaching. Ronnie's solicitors had sent firm reminders, followed a month later by writs but this action had also failed to elicit any money.

"It only proves what I feared most," said Ronnie.

"What's that?" asked Simon.

"They just haven't got the cash."

"So we will have to replace them with new tenants."

"Simon, when you next travel from Beaufort Street to Whitechapel start counting the 'To Let' signs on office blocks along the way. When you've passed a hundred you'll find you still haven't reached the City."

"So what do you think we should do about it?"

"Try and sell one of our larger properties to secure cash flow. We can at least be thankful that even at these prices they are still worth a lot more than our borrowings. It's the companies who are the other way around that have to call in the receiver."

Simon thought about his overdraft, now approaching £100,000, and was beginning to wish he had accepted Ronnie's generous offer to buy back his shares. He accepted reluctantly that the opportunity had now passed.

When the board meeting was over he drove to St Mary's to pick up Elizabeth. It was to be one of their three-times-a-week journeys to Pucklebridge as Simon tried to get round all the villages before Wilson called an election.

Archie Millburn was turning out to be a conscientious chairman who had accompanied them on nearly every trip.

"He's been very kind to us," said Elizabeth, on their way down.

"He certainly has," said Simon. "Remember he also has to

run Millburn Electronics. But, as he reminds us so often, once he's introduced us to every village chairman we'll be on our own."

"Have you ever discovered why he and Charles Seymour didn't see eye to eye?"

"No, he hasn't mentioned his name since that night. All I know for certain is that they were at school together."

"So what do you intend to do about Seymour?"

"Not a lot I can do," said Simon. "Except keep my eyes very wide open."

"The man who has deserted Edinburgh once too often" – Andrew read the Scottish Nationalist leaflet that had been sent to him that morning by his father. It was full of half-truths and innuendoes.

"Andrew Fraser, the man who has forgotten Edinburgh, should no longer be allowed to represent a Scottish seat." It went on to declare: "He now lives far away from the problems of his constituents in a smart apartment building in fashionable Chelsea among his Tory friends. He visits the City of Edinburgh only a few times a year to make well-publicised appearances . . . Has being a minister gone to his head?"

"How dare they?" cried Louise in a rage. Andrew had never seen his wife so angry. "How dare they come to my home, offer you the leadership of their dreadful little party and then write such a pack of lies? And did you read this?" she added, pointing to the last paragraph, " 'His wife Louise, née Forsyth'," she read out aloud, " 'comes from one of the wealthiest families in Scotland. She is a close relation of the owners of Forsyth's in Princes Street.' I'm a second cousin once removed, and they don't even give me a discount in the main store."

Andrew started to laugh.

"What's so funny?"

He took her in his arms. "I always suffered under the illusion that you would inherit the Forsyth empire and I would never have to work again," he mocked. "Now we shall have to live off Robert's earnings as a star football player."

"Don't joke, Andrew. It won't seem funny when the election comes round."

"I'm far more concerned about the extreme left trying to infiltrate my General Management Committee," he said, his voice changing, "than I am by Jock McPherson's band of mad little islanders. But at this moment of time my red box is too full to worry about either of them."

Raymond made such a penetrating speech during the second reading of the new Trade Union Bill that the Whips put him on the standing committee, the perfect medium for him to display his skills as the committee debated each clause, point by point. He was able to show his colleagues where the legal pitfalls were and how to find a way round them. The rest of the committee soon learnt from Raymond the meaning of 'mastering a brief', and it was not long before trade union leaders were calling him at the House and even at his flat to learn his views on how their members should react to a host of different legal problems. Raymond showed patience with each of them and, more important, gave them excellent professional advice for the price of a phone call. He found it ironic how quickly they chose to forget that he was the author of *Full Employment at any Cost?* Snippets began to appear in the national press, ranging from laudatory comments from those involved with the bill to a pointed suggestion in the *Guardian* that, whatever had happened in the past, it would be insupportable if Raymond Gould were not made a member of the Government in the near future.

"If they were to offer you a job, would it make any difference to our relationship?" Kate asked.

"Certainly," said Raymond. "I shall have found the perfect excuse not to wear your blue shirts."

Harold Wilson held the crumbling edifice together for a further six months before finally having to call a general election. He chose 10 October 1974.

Raymond immediately returned to his constituency to fight his fifth campaign. When he met Joyce at Leeds City station he couldn't help remembering that his dumpy wife was only four years older than Kate. He kissed her on the cheek as one might a distant relative, then she drove him back to their Chapel Allerton home.

Joyce chatted away on the journey home and it became clear that the constituency was under control and that this time Fred Padgett was well prepared for a general election. "He hasn't really stopped since the last one," she said. As for Joyce, she was undoubtedly better organised than the agent and the secretary put together. What was more, Raymond thought, she enjoyed it. He glanced over at her and couldn't help thinking she even looked prettier at election time.

Unlike his colleagues in rural seats, Raymond did not have to make speech after speech in little village halls. His votes were to be found in the high street where he addressed the midday shoppers through a megaphone, and walked around supermarkets, pubs and clubs, grasping hands before repeating the whole process a few streets away.

Joyce set her husband a schedule that allowed few people in the Leeds community to escape him. Some saw him a dozen times during the three-week campaign – most of them at the football match on the Saturday afternoon before the election.

Once the game was over Raymond was back trooping round the working men's clubs, drinking pint after pint of John Smith's bitter. He accepted it was inevitable that he would put on half a stone during any election campaign. He dreaded what Kate's comments would be when she saw him. Somehow he always found a few minutes in each day to steal away and phone her. She seemed so busy and full of news it only made Raymond feel downcast; she couldn't possibly be missing him.

The local trade unionists backed Raymond to the hilt. They may have found him stuck up and distant in the past, but they knew 'where his heart was', as they confided to anyone who would listen. They banged on doors, delivered leaflets, drove cars to polling booths. They rose before he did in the morning and could still be found preaching to the converted after the pubs had thrown them out at night.

Raymond and Joyce cast their votes in the local secondary

school on the Thursday of election day, looking forward to a large Labour victory. The Labour party duly gained a working majority in the House of forty-three over the Conservatives, but only three over all the parties combined. Nevertheless Harold Wilson looked set for another five years when the Queen invited him to form his fourth administration. The count in Leeds that night gave Raymond his biggest majority ever: 12,207 votes.

He spent the whole of Friday and Saturday thanking his constituents, then set out for London on the Sunday evening.

"He must invite you to join the Government this time," said Joyce, as she walked down the platform of Leeds City station with her husband.

"I wonder," said Raymond, kissing his wife on the other cheek. He waved at her as the train pulled out of the station. She waved back enthusiastically.

"I do like your new blue shirt, it really suits you," were the last words he heard her say.

During the election campaign Charles had had to spend a lot of time at the bank because of a run on the pound. Fiona seemed to be everywhere in the constituency at once, assuring voters that her husband was just a few yards behind.

After the little slips were counted the swing against Charles to the Labour candidate didn't amount to more than one per cent in his 22,000 majority. When he heard the overall result he returned to London resigned to a long spell in Opposition. As he began to catch up with his colleagues in the House, he found many of them already saying openly that Heath had to go after two election defeats in a row.

Charles knew then that he would have to make up his mind once again on where he stood over the election of a new party leader, and that once again he must pick the right man.

Andrew Fraser returned to London after a gruelling and unhappy campaign. The Scottish Nationalists had concentrated their attack on him, Jock McPherson sailing close to libel and slander. Sir Duncan advised his son against any legal action. "Only plays into their hands," he warned. "Small parties always benefit from the publicity."

Louise wanted him to inform the press that he had been offered the leadership of the SNP but Andrew felt it would serve no purpose, and might even rebound against him: and he also reminded her that he had given his word. In the last week of the campaign he spent most of his time trying – and failing – to stop Frank Boyle, a Communist, who had recently moved from Glasgow, from being elected to his General Management Committee. On polling day he scraped home by 1,656, Jock McPherson taking second place. At least he looked secure for another five years; but it didn't help that the Scottish Nationalists had increased their overall seats in the House to eleven.

Andrew, Louise and Robert took the plane to London on the Sunday night to find the red box awaiting them and a message that the Prime Minister wanted Andrew to continue as Minister of State at the Home Office.

Simon had a glorious campaign. He and Elizabeth had started moving into their new cottage the day the election was announced, thankful that, now she had to commute, her salary at the hospital had made it possible for them to employ a nanny. A double bed and a couple of chairs sufficed as Elizabeth cooked on an old Aga from provisions still packed in tea chests. They seemed to use the same two forks for everything. During the campaign Simon covered the 200-square-mile constituency for a second time and assured his wife that she need only take the final week off from from her duties at St Mary's.

The voters of Pucklebridge sent Simon Kerslake back to Parliament with a majority of 18,419, the largest in the constituency's history. The local people had quickly come to the conclusion that they now had a member who was destined to have a Cabinet career.

Kate kept her remarks very gentle as it became obvious by the Monday night that the Prime Minister was not going to offer Raymond a job in the new administration. She cooked his favourite meal of roast beef – overdone – and Yorkshire pudding in the flat that night, but he didn't comment on it and hardly spoke.

CHAPTER EIGHTEEN

After Simon had been back at the Commons for a week he felt a sense of *déjà vu*, a feeling that most members returning to the House for a second or even third time often experience. The sense was heightened by finding everything unchanged, even the policeman who greeted him at the Members' Entrance. When Edward Heath announced his Shadow team Simon was not surprised that he wasn't included, as he never had been a known supporter of the Tory leader. He was, however, mystified but not displeased to discover Charles Seymour was not among the names to be found in the Shadow Cabinet.

"Do you regret turning him down now the full team has been published?" asked Fiona, looking up from her copy of the *Daily Mail*.

"It wasn't an easy decision but I think it'll prove right in the long run," replied Charles, buttering another piece of toast.

"What did he offer in the end?"

"Shadow Minister of Industry."

"That sounds rather interesting," said Fiona.

"Everything about it was interesting except the salary, which would have been nothing. Don't forget the bank pays me £40,000 a year while I'm chairman."

Fiona folded her paper. "But you've just appointed a full-time chief executive, so your responsibilities at the bank should be only part-time compared with when you took the chair over. So what's your real reason?"

Charles accepted that he could rarely fool Fiona. "The

truth is that I'm far from certain Ted will be leading the party at the next election."

"Then who will if he doesn't?" asked Fiona.

"Whoever's got the guts to oppose him."

"I'm not sure I understand," said Fiona, beginning to clear away the plates.

"Everyone accepts that he has to allow his name to go forward for re-election now that he's lost twice in a row."

"That's fair enough," agreed Fiona.

"But as he has appointed all possible contenders to the Cabinet or Shadow Cabinet over the last ten years, someone he has selected in the past will have to oppose him. No one of lesser stature would stand a chance."

"Is there a member of the Shadow Cabinet willing to stand?" asked Fiona, returning to her seat at the end of the table.

"One or two are considering it, but the problem is that if they lose it could easily end their political career," said Charles, folding his napkin.

"But if they win?"

"They will undoubtedly be the next Prime Minister."

"Interesting dilemma. And what are you going to do about it?"

"I'm not supporting anyone at the moment, but I've got my eyes wide open," said Charles, folding his copy of *The Times* and rising from the table.

"Is there a front runner?" asked Fiona, looking up at her husband.

"No, not really. Although Kerslake is trying to rally support for Margaret Thatcher, but that idea is doomed from the start."

"A woman leading the Tory party? Your lot haven't got the imagination to risk it," said Elizabeth, tasting the sauce. "The day that happens I shall eat my one and only Tory hat in full view of all the delegates at the party conference."

"Don't be so cynical, Elizabeth. She's the best bet we've got at the moment."

"But what are the chances of Ted Heath standing down? I

always thought the leader of the party stayed on until he was hit by the mythical bus. I don't know Heath very well, but I can never imagine him resigning."

"I agree," said Simon. "So the 1922 Committee will have to change the rules."

"You mean the back-benchers will put pressure on him to go?"

"No, but a lot of the committee in their present mood would be willing to volunteer as driver for that bus."

"If that's true, he must realise that his chances of holding on are slim?"

"I wonder if any leader ever knows that," said Simon.

"You ought to be in Blackpool next week," said Kate, resting her elbow on the pillow.

"Why Blackpool?" Raymond asked, staring up at the ceiling.

"Because, Carrot Top, that's where they are holding this year's Labour party conference."

"What do you imagine I could hope to accomplish there?"

"You'd be seen to be alive. At present you're just a rumour in trade union circles."

"But if you're not a minister or a trade union leader all you do at a party conference is spend four days eating foul food, sleeping in seedy guest houses, and applauding second-rate speeches."

"I've no interest in where you put your weary head at night but I do want you to revive your contacts with the unions during the day."

"Why?" said Raymond. "That lot can't influence my career."

"Not at the moment," said Kate. "But I predict that, like my fellow Americans at their conventions, the Labour party will one day select their leader at the party conference."

"Never," said Raymond. "That is and will always remain the prerogative of elected members of the House of Commons."

"That's the sort of crass, short-sighted, pompous statement I would expect a Republican to make," she said, before plonking a pillow over his head. Raymond feigned death, so she lifted up a corner and whispered in his ear, "Have you read any of the resolutions to be debated at this year's conference?"

"A few," came back Raymond's muffled reply.

"Then it might serve you well to note Mr Anthony Wedgwood Benn's contribution," she said, removing the pillow.

"What's he up to this year?"

"He's calling on 'conference', as he insists on describing your gathering of the brothers, to demand that the next leader be chosen by a full vote of the delegates, making up an electoral college from all the constituencies, the trade union movement and Parliament – I suspect in that order."

"Madness. But what do you expect? He's married to an American."

"Today's extremist is tomorrow's moderate," said Kate blithely.

"A typical American generalisation."

"Benjamin Disraeli, actually."

Raymond placed the pillow back over his head.

Andrew always attended the party conference, although he would never have voted for Tony Benn's resolution on the method of selecting a leader. He feared that if the trade unions were given that sort of power a leader who was totally unacceptable to his colleagues in the House of Commons could be selected. He was relieved when the motion was defeated but he noted that the majority against was far from overwhelming.

Despite being a minister Andrew could only get a small room at Blackpool in a guest house masquerading as a hotel, and that some two miles from the conference centre. Such were the problems created by 4,000 self-important people converging on a seaside resort for a week that many had to forgo the Presidential Suite.

Andrew still had to carry on his job as Minister of State, with red boxes being delivered and taken every morning and afternoon, while making his presence felt at the conference. He spent half his time on a phone in the hotel lobby putting through transfer-charge calls to the Home Office. No one in the Soviet Union would have believed it, especially if they had realised that the Minister of State for Defence, who had the room next to Andrew's, was pacing up and down the corridor waiting for the phone to be free.

Andrew had never addressed the 3,000 delegates at a party conference. Even Cabinet ministers are only allowed a maximum of ten minutes at the rostrum unless they are members of the National Executive. Over half the Labour Cabinet had failed to be elected to this body, which consisted mainly of the leaders of the larger trade unions.

As he left the morning session Andrew was surprised to find Raymond Gould roaming around looking lost. They fell on each other like sane men locked in an asylum and decided to lunch together at the River House, Andrew's favourite restaurant a few miles outside of Blackpool.

Although they had both been in the House for nearly ten years it was the first time they discovered how much they had in common. Andrew had never considered himself a close friend of Raymond's but he had always admired his stand on devaluation.

"You must have been disappointed when the PM didn't ask you to rejoin the Government," Andrew began.

Raymond stared down at the menu. "Very," he finally admitted, as a girl joined them in the bar to take their order.

"Nevertheless, you were wise to come to Blackpool. This is where your strength lies."

"You think so?"

"Come on. Everybody knows you're the trade unions' pin-up boy, and they still have a lot of influence as to who sits in the Cabinet."

"I haven't noticed," said Raymond mournfully.

"You will when they eventually choose the leader."

"That's funny, that's exactly what . . . Joyce said last week."

"Sensible girl, Joyce. I fear it will happen in our time as members."

Bill Scott, the proprietor, told them their table was ready and they went through to the small dining-room.

"Why fear?" asked Raymond, as he took his seat.

"Middle-of-the-road democrats like myself will end up as so many leaves on a bonfire."

"But I'm middle-of-the-road myself, practically right wing on some issues."

"Perhaps. But every party needs a man like you, and at this moment union leaders wouldn't mind if you were a card-carrying Fascist; they'd still back you."

"Then what makes you attend the conference?"

"Thank God it still gives one a chance to keep in touch with the grass roots, and I live in hope that the extreme left will never be much more than an unruly child that the grown-ups have to learn to live with."

"Let's hope you're right," said Raymond, "because they're never going to grow up." Andrew laughed as Raymond continued in a different mood. "I still envy you your job at the Home Office. I didn't go into politics to spend my life on the back benches."

"There may well come a day when I sit and envy you from those same back benches," said Andrew.

As he spoke, the chairman of the Boilermakers' Union shouted across as he passed their table, "Good to see you, Ray." He showed no recognition of Andrew. Raymond turned and smiled at the man and waved back as Caesar might have done to Cassius.

When they had both rejected the choice of date and walnut pudding or Pavlova, Andrew suggested a brandy.

Raymond hesitated.

"You'll see more double brandies drunk here than you will at the Conservative party conference next week. Ask any waitress."

"Have you decided how you're going to vote in the leadership battle?" asked Fiona over breakfast.

"Yes," said Charles, "and at this point in my career I can't afford to make the wrong choice."

"So who have you decided on?" asked Fiona.

"While there isn't a serious contender to oppose Ted Heath it remains in my best interest to continue backing him."

"Isn't there one Shadow Cabinet minister who has the guts to stand against him?"

"The rumour grows that Margaret Thatcher will act as whipping girl. If she gets close enough to force a second ballot the serious contenders will then join in."

"What if she won the first round?"

"Don't be silly, Fiona," said Charles, taking more interest in his scrambled egg. "The Tory party would never elect a woman to lead them. We're far too traditional. That's the sort of immature mistake the Labour party would make to prove how much they believe in equality."

Simon was still pushing Margaret Thatcher to throw her hat in the ring.

"She certainly has enough of them," said Elizabeth.

It amused Andrew and Raymond to watch the Tory party leadership struggle while they got on with their respective jobs. Raymond would have dismissed Thatcher's chances if Kate hadn't reminded him that the Tories had been the first party to choose a Jewish leader, and also the first to select a bachelor.

"So why shouldn't they be the first to elect a woman?" she demanded. He would have continued to argue with her but the damn woman had proved to be right so often in the past. "Let's wait and see," was all he said.

The 1922 Committee announced that the election for leader would take place on 4 February 1975.

At a press conference in early January at the House of Commons Margaret Thatcher announced she would allow her name to go forward to contest the leadership. Simon immediately spent his time exhorting his colleagues to support 'The Lady' and joined a small committee under Airey Neave that was formed for the purpose. Charles Seymour warned his friends that the party could never hope to win a general election with a woman leading them. As the days passed, nothing became clearer than the uncertainty of the outcome.

At four o'clock on a particularly wet and windy day the chairman of the 1922 Committee announced the figures:

> Margaret Thatcher 130
> Edward Heath   119
> Hugh Fraser   16

According to the 1922 Committee rules, the winner needed a fifteen per cent majority and so a second round was necessary. "It will be held in seven days' time," the Chief Whip announced. Three former Cabinet ministers immediately declared they were candidates, while Ted Heath, having been warned that he would get fewer votes a second time round, withdrew from the ballot.

They were the longest days in Simon's life. He did everything in his power to hold Thatcher's supporters together. Charles meanwhile decided to play the second round very low-key. When the time came to vote he put his cross on the ballot paper next to the former Secretary of State he had served under at Trade and Industry. "A man we can all trust," he told Fiona.

When the votes had been counted and confirmed the chairman of the 1922 Committee announced that Margaret Thatcher was the outright winner with a vote of 146 to 79 from her nearest challenger.

Simon was delighted while Elizabeth hoped he had forgotten about the promise to eat her hat. Charles was dumbfounded. They both wrote to their new leader immediately.

11 February 1975

Dear Margaret,

Many congratulations on your victory as the first woman leader of our party. I was proud to have played a small part in your triumph and will continue to work for your success at the next election.

Yours,
Simon.

27 Eaton Square,
London, SW1
11 February 1975

Dear Margaret,

I made no secret of backing Ted Heath in the first round of the leadership contest having had the privilege of serving in his administration. I was delighted to have supported you on the second ballot. It illustrates how progressive our party is that we have chosen a woman who will undoubtedly be Britain's next Prime Minister.

Be assured of my loyalty.

Yours,

Charles.

Margaret Thatcher answered all her colleagues' letters within the week. Simon received a handwritten letter inviting him to join the new Shadow team as number two in the Education Department. Charles received a typed note thanking him for his letter of support.

CHAPTER
NINETEEN

Seymour's Bank had weathered the Great War, the thirties' crash, and then the Second World War. Charles had no intention of being the chairman who presided over its demise in the seventies. Soon after taking over from Derek Spencer – at the board's unanimous insistence – he had discovered that being chairman wasn't quite the relaxed job he expected, and while he remained confident that the bank could ride the storm he still wasn't taking any risks. The business sections of the newspapers were full of stories of the Bank of England acting as a 'lifeboat' and having to step in to assist ailing financial institutions, along with daily reports of the collapse of yet another property company. The time when property values and rents automatically increased each year had become a thing of the past.

When he had accepted the board's offer, Charles insisted that a chief executive be appointed to carry out the day to day business while he remained the man with whom other City chairmen dealt. He interviewed several people for the position but he did not find anyone suitable. Head-hunting seemed to be the next move, the expense of which was saved when he overheard a conversation at the next table at White's that the newly appointed chief executive of the 1st Bank of America was sick of having to report to the board in Chicago every time he wanted to use a first-class stamp.

Charles immediately invited the chief executive to lunch at the House of Commons. Clive Reynolds had come from a similar background to Derek Spencer: London School of Economics, followed by the Harvard Business School and a series of successful appointments which had culminated in his becoming chief executive of the 1st Bank of America. This similarity did not worry Charles, as he made it clear to Mr Reynolds that the appointee would be the chairman's man.

When Reynolds was offered the appointment he drove a hard bargain and Charles looked forward to his doing the same on behalf of Seymour's. Reynolds ended up with £50,000 a year and enough of a profit incentive to ensure that he didn't deal for himself or encourage any other head-hunters to invite him to join their particular jungle.

"He's not the sort of fellow we could invite to dinner," Charles told Fiona, "but his appointment will enable me to sleep at night knowing the bank is in safe hands."

Charles's choice was rubber-stamped by the board at their next meeting, and as the months passed it became obvious that the 1st Bank of America had lost one of its prime assets well below the market value.

Clive Reynolds was a conservative by nature, but when he did take what Charles described as a risk – and Reynolds called a 'hunch' – over fifty per cent of them paid off. While Seymour's kept its reputation for caution and good husbandry, they managed a few quite spectacular coups thanks to their new chief executive.

Reynolds had enough sense to treat his new chairman with respect without ever showing deference while their relationship remained at all times strictly professional.

One of Reynolds's first innovations had been to suggest they check on every customer account over £250,000 and Charles had approved.

"When you've handled the account of a company for many years," Reynolds pointed out, "it sometimes is not apparent when one of your traditional customers is heading for trouble as it would be to a newcomer. If there are any 'lame ducks' let's discover them before they hit the ground" – a simile that Charles repeated at several weekend parties.

Charles enjoyed his morning meetings with Clive Reynolds as he picked up a great deal about a profession to which he had previously only brought gut feeling and common sense. In a very short time he learned enough from his new tutor to make him sound like David Rockefeller when he rose to speak in a finance debate on the floor of the House, an unexpected bonus.

Charles knew little of Reynolds's private life except what was on file. He was forty-one, unmarried and lived in Esher, wherever that was. All Charles cared about was that Reynolds arrived each morning at least an hour before him, and left after him every night, even when the House was in recess.

Charles had studied fourteen of the confidential reports on customers with loans over £250,000. Clive Reynolds had already picked out two companies with whom he felt the bank should revise their current position.

Charles still had three more reports to consider before he presented a full assessment to the board.

The quiet knock on the door, however, meant that it was ten o'clock and Reynolds had arrived to make his daily report. Rumours were circulating in the City that the bank rate would go up on Thursday, so Reynolds wanted to go short on dollars and long on gold. Charles nodded. As soon as the announcement had been made about the bank rate, Reynolds continued: "It will be wiser to return to dollars as the new round of pay negotiations with the unions is about to take place. This in turn will undoubtedly start a fresh run on the pound." Charles nodded again.

"I think the dollar is far too weak at two-ten," Reynolds added. "With the unions settling at around twelve per cent the dollar must strengthen, say, to nearer one-ninety." He added that he was not happy about the bank's large holding in Slater Walker and wanted to liquidate half the stock over the next month. He proposed to do so in small amounts over irregular periods. "We also have three other major accounts to consider before we make known our findings to the board. I'm concerned about the spending policy of one of the companies, but the other two appear stable. I think we should go over them together when you have time to consider my reports. Perhaps tomorrow morning, if you could manage that. The companies concerned are Speyward Laboratories, Blackies Limited and Nethercote and Company. It's Speyward I'm worried about."

"I'll take the files home tonight," said Charles, "and give you an opinion in the morning."

"Thank you, Chairman."

Charles had never suggested that Reynolds should call him by his first name.

Archie Millburn held a small dinner party to celebrate Simon's first anniversary as the member for Pucklebridge. Although these occasions had originally been to introduce the party hierarchy to their new member, Simon now knew more about the constituency and its flock than he did, as Archie was the first to admit.

Elizabeth, Peter and Michael had settled comfortably into their small cottage, while Simon, as a member of the Shadow Education team, had visited schools – nursery, primary, public and secondary: universities – red brick, plate glass and Oxbridge; technical colleges, art institutes and even borstals. He had read Butler, Robbins, and Plowden and listened to children and to professors of psychology alike. He felt that after a year he was beginning to understand the subject, and only longed for a general election so that he could once again turn rehearsal into performance.

"Opposition must be frustrating," observed Archie when the ladies had retired after dinner.

"Yes, but it's an excellent way to prepare yourself for Government and do some basic thinking about the subject. I never found time for such luxury as a minister."

"But it must be very different from holding office?" said Archie, clipping a cigar.

"True. In Government," said Simon, "you're surrounded by civil servants who don't allow you to lift a finger or give you a moment to ponder, while in Opposition you can think policy through even if you do often end up having to type your own letters."

Archie pushed the port down to Simon's end of the table. "I'm glad the girls are out," said Archie conspiratorially, "because I wanted you to know I've decided to give up being chairman at the end of the year."

"Why?" said Simon, taken aback.

"I've seen you elected and settled in. It's time for a younger man to have a go."

"But you're only my age."

"I can't deny that, but the truth is that I'm not giving enough time to my electronics company, and the board are continually reminding me of it. No one has to tell you that these are not easy times."

"It's sad," said Simon. "Just as you get to know someone in politics you or they always seem to move on."

"Fear not," said Archie. "I don't intend to leave the area, and I feel confident that you will be my member for at least another twenty years, by which time I will be happy to accept an invitation to dine with you in Downing Street."

"You may find that it's Charles Seymour who is residing at No. 10," said Simon, striking a match to light his cigar.

"Then I won't be getting an invitation," said Archie with a smile.

Charles couldn't sleep that night after his discovery, and his tossing and turning kept Fiona awake. He had opened the Nethercote file when he was waiting for dinner to be served. His first act with any company was to glance down the names of the directors to see if he knew anyone on the board. He recognised no one until his eye stopped at 'S. J. Kerslake, MP'. The cook felt sure that Mr Seymour had not enjoyed his dinner, because he hardly touched the main course.

On his arrival at Seymour's, only moments after Clive Reynolds, he called for his chief executive. He appeared a few minutes later without his usual armful of files, surprised to see the chairman so early. Once Reynolds was seated Charles opened the file in front of him. "What do you know about Nethercote and Company?"

"Private company. Net asset value approaching £10,000,000, running a current overdraft of £7,000,000 of which we service half. Efficiently managed with a good board of directors, will ride out the current problems in my view, and should be well oversubscribed when they eventually go public."

"How much of the company do we own?"

"Seven and a half per cent. As you know, the bank never take eight per cent of any company because then we would have to declare an interest under section twenty-three of the Finance Act. It has always been a policy of this bank to invest in a major client without becoming too involved with the running of the company."

"Who are their principal bankers?"

"The Midland."

"What would happen if we put our seven and a half per cent up for sale and did not renew the overdraft facility at the end of the quarter, but called it in instead?"

"They would have to seek finance elsewhere."

"And if they couldn't?"

"They would have to start selling their assets, which under that sort of forced-sale position would be very damaging for any company, if not impossible, in the present climate."

"And then?"

"I would have to check my file and . . ."

Charles passed over the file and Reynolds studied it carefully, frowning. "They already have a cash-flow problem because of bad debts. With a sudden increased demand they might go under. I would strongly advise against such a move, Chairman. Nethercote have proved a reliable risk over the years, and I think we stand to make a handsome profit when they are quoted on the Stock Exchange."

"For reasons I cannot disclose to you," said Charles, looking up from his chair, "I fear that remaining involved with this company may turn out to be a financial embarrassment for Seymour's." Reynolds looked at him, puzzled. "You will inform the Midland Bank that we will not be renewing this loan at the next quarter."

"Then they would have to look for support from another bank. The Midland would never agree to shoulder the entire amount on their own."

"And try to dispose of our seven and a half per cent immediately."

"But that could lead to a crisis of confidence in the company."

"So be it," said Charles, as he closed the file.

"But I do feel –"

"That will be all, Mr Reynolds."

"Yes, Chairman," said the mystified chief executive, who had never thought of his boss as an irrational man. He turned to leave. Had he looked back he would have been even more mystified by the smile that was spread across Charles Seymour's face.

"They've pulled the rug out from under our feet," said Ronnie Nethercote angrily.

"Who?" said Simon, who had just come into the room.

"The Midland Bank."

"Why would they do that?"

"An outside shareholder put all his stock on the market without warning, and the Midland got worried about their position. They wouldn't be prepared to continue such a large overdraft position on their own."

"Have you been to see the manager?" asked Simon, unable to disguise his anxiety.

"Yes, but he can't do anything. His hands are tied by a main board directive," said Ronnie, slumping deeper into his seat.

"How bad is it?"

"They've given me a month to find another bank. Otherwise I'll have to start selling some of our assets."

"What will happen if we don't manage to come up with another bank?" asked Simon desperately.

"The company could be bankrupt within weeks. Do you know any bankers who are looking for a good investment?"

"Only one, and I can assure you he wouldn't help."

Charles put the phone down satisfied. He wondered if there was anything that could still be regarded as secret. It had taken him less than an hour to find out the size of Kerslake's overdraft. "Banker to banker confidentiality," he had assured them. He was still smiling when Reynolds knocked on the door.

"The Midland weren't pleased," he immediately briefed Charles.

"They'll get over it," his chairman replied. "What's the latest on Nethercote?"

"Only a rumour, but everyone now knows they're in trouble and the chairman is searching around for a new backer," said Reynolds impassively. "His biggest problem is that no one is touching property companies at the moment."

"Once they've collapsed, what's to stop us picking up the pieces and making a killing?"

"A clause that was slipped through in the Finance Act which your Government passed three years ago. The penalties range from a heavy fine to having your banking licence taken away."

"Oh, yes, I remember," said Charles. "Pity. So how long do you expect them to last?"

"Once the month is up," said Reynolds stroking a clean-shaven chin, "if they fail to find a backer the creditors will swarm in like locusts."

"Aren't the shares worth anything?" asked Charles innocently.

"Not the paper they are written on at the moment," said Reynolds, watching his chairman carefully.

This time the chief executive couldn't miss the chairman's smile as Charles thought of Simon Kerslake and his overdraft of £108,000 now backed by worthless shares. Pucklebridge would soon be looking for a new member.

At the end of a month during which no bank came to his rescue Ronnie Nethercote caved in and agreed to call in the receiver and file a bankruptcy notice. He still hoped that he could pay off all his creditors even if the shares he and his fellow directors held remained worthless. He felt as worried for Simon and his career as he did for himself, but he knew there was nothing the receiver would allow him to do to help one individual.

When Simon told Elizabeth she didn't complain. She had always feared this could be the eventual outcome of her husband joining the board of Nethercotes.

"Can't Ronnie help?" she asked. "After all, you've supported him enough in the past."

"No, he can't," replied Simon, avoiding telling her where the real responsibility for his downfall lay.

"But do bankrupts automatically have to leave Parliament?" was Elizabeth's next question.

"No, but I shall because I could never be considered for further promotion – I'd always be rightly tainted with 'lack of judgement'."

"It seems so unfair when you weren't personally to blame."

"There are different rules for those who wish to live in the spotlight," Simon said simply.

"But in time, surely –" began Elizabeth.

"I'm not willing to remain on the back benches for another twenty years only to hear whispered in the corner of the smoking room – Would have made the Cabinet if it hadn't been for . . ."

"Does that mean the children will have to be taken away from school?"

"I'm afraid so," said Simon, his hands shaking. "As a bankrupt I can hardly expect the receiver to view the fees for my sons' education as a dire necessity even if I could find the money."

"So we'll have to get rid of the nanny, too?"

"Not necessarily, but we may both have to make sacrifices in order that she can be part-time."

"But my work at the hospital . . ." began Elizabeth but didn't complete the sentence. "What happens next?"

"I'll have to tell Archie Millburn tonight. I've already written my letter of resignation to hand to him. I shall make an appointment to see the Chief Whip on Monday to explain why I am going to apply for the Chiltern Hundreds."

"What does that mean?"

"It's one of the only ways of leaving the House in mid-session – other than dying. Officially it's a nominal office under the Crown which therefore debars you from membership of the House."

"It all sounds rather formal to me."

"I'm afraid it will cause an embarrassing by-election in Pucklebridge," Simon admitted.

"Can nobody help?"

"There aren't a lot of people around who have a spare £108,000 for a worthless bunch of shares."

"Would you like me to come with you when you go to see Archie?" Elizabeth asked, rising from her seat.

"No, darling. It's kind of you to ask, but I'm the one who made such a fool of myself."

Elizabeth leaned over and pushed back the hair that had fallen over his forehead. She couldn't help noticing some grey strands that must have appeared in the last few weeks. "We'll just have to live off my salary while you look for a job."

Simon drove slowly down to Pucklebridge to keep his impromptu appointment with the chairman. Archie Millburn, standing hands on hips in his garden, listened to the tale with a sad face. "It's been happening to a lot of good people in the City lately, but what I can't understand is: if the company owns such prime properties, why has no one made a takeover bid? Sounds as if it's an asset-stripper's dream."

"It appears to be a matter of confidence," said Simon.

"A sacred word in the City," agreed Archie, while he continued to prune his Roosevelts and Red Mistresses.

Simon handed him the prepared letter of resignation, which Millburn read over and reluctantly accepted.

"I won't mention this to anyone until you've seen the Chief Whip on Monday. I'll call a special meeting of the full committee on Tuesday evening and inform them of your decision then. You had better be prepared for an unfriendly barrage from the press on Tuesday night."

The two men shook hands. "Your misfortune is our misfortune," said Archie. "In a very short time you've gained the respect and the affection of the local people. You'll be missed."

Simon drove back to London and, although the car radio was on low, he did not take in the news flash that they kept repeating every thirty minutes.

CHAPTER
TWENTY

Raymond was among the first to hear the announcement, and was stunned by it. Harold Wilson was going to resign less than half-way through the five-year Parliament, and for no apparent reason other than that he had just passed his sixtieth birthday. He proposed to remain Prime Minister only so long as the Labour party took to select its new leader. Raymond and Kate sat glued to the television, picking up every scrap of information they could. They discussed the implications far into the night.

"Well, Carrot Top, could this mean rehabilitation for our forgotten hero?"

"Who can say?"

"Well, if you can't, who can?"

"The next leader," said Raymond.

The fight for the leadership was a straight battle between the left and right wings of the party, James Callaghan on the right and Michael Foot on the left. Andrew and Raymond both wanted the same man and it was with some relief that they saw Callaghan, despite losing the first ballot, come through to be elected leader. The Queen duly called for Callaghan and asked him to form a new administration.

As tradition demands Andrew sent his resignation to Downing Street, as did every other member of the Government, to allow the new Prime Minister to select his own team.

Raymond was in court listening to the judge's summing up when his junior passed him a note: "Please call 10 Downing Street as soon as possible." The judge took a further thirty minutes, meticulously explaining to the jury the legal definition of manslaughter, before Raymond could escape. He ran down the corridor and stopped at one of the clerks' private boxes to make the call. The plastic dial rotating back into place after each number seemed to take forever.

After he had been passed through three people a voice said, "Good afternoon, Ray": the unmistakable gravelly tones of the new Prime Minister. "I think it's time you rejoined the Government" – Raymond held his breath – "as Minister of State at the Department of Trade." Minister of State: only one place away from the Cabinet.

"You still there, Ray?"

"Yes, Prime Minister, and I'd be delighted to accept."

He put the phone down, immediately picked it up again and dialled the City office of the Chase Manhattan Bank. They put him through to the Euro Bond manager.

Andrew had left his desk at the Home Office and returned to Cheyne Walk. He stayed away from the House of Commons where the lobby correspondents were hanging about like hyenas, scampering off to phone their papers with even the rumour of a rumour. The new Cabinet had been selected, and now it was the turn of the Ministers of State. All Andrew knew for certain was that his old job at the Home Office had been given to someone else.

"Why don't you go and play football with Robert?" Louise suggested. "And stop moping around under my feet?"

"Yes, Dad, yes, Dad, yes, Dad," demanded his son, running upstairs to reappear a few minutes later dressed in the Liverpool kit that he had bought himself from eleven weeks' hard-saved pocket money.

"Go on, Andrew. I can always call you if the phone goes."

Andrew smiled, took off his jacket and put on the pair of old gym shoes Robert was holding out for him. He followed his five-year-old son into the garden to find him already dribbling up and down the thin strip between the flower beds. The little goal he had bought for Robert – or was it for himself? – at Christmas was already set up at the far end of the grass and they took turns defending it. Andrew always had to start in goal. He rubbed his hands together to keep warm as Robert dribbled towards him. He came out of the goal ready to stifle a shot, but Robert kicked the ball to the right and ran to the left, leaving his father spreadeagled on the ground before he pushed the ball gently into the goal. "That's called a feint," he shouted triumphantly, as he ran back past his prostrate father.

Andrew picked himself up. "I know what it's called," he said, laughing. "You seem to have forgotten who taught you the feint in the first place. Let's see if you can do it twice running," he added, returning to defend the goal.

Robert dribbled away from his father until he reached the end of the garden, then turned to face him again. He had begun advancing towards the goal for a second time when there was the sound of the phone ringing. Andrew looked towards the house just as Robert kicked the ball, which rising sharply, struck him in the face. He and the ball fell back into the goal mouth.

Louise opened the kitchen window and shouted, "It's only my mother."

"Wake up, Dad," demanded Robert simultaneously.

Andrew's face was still stinging from the blow. "I'm going to get you for that," he said. "Your turn to defend the goal."

Robert rushed forward to take his place between the posts, jumping up and down trying to touch the crossbar with the tips of his fingers. Andrew took his time as he moved towards his son. When he was about a yard in front of Robert he feinted to the right and ran to the left but Robert had seen the move coming and leaped on the ball shouting, "No goal."

Once again Andrew returned to the end of the garden, thinking over what move he could try next. He suddenly ran straight at Robert and kicked the ball firmly towards the right-hand corner of the goal mouth. But again Robert anticipated the move and caught the ball above his head before pulling it to his chest and shouting, "No goal, Dad, no goal!" He tossed the ball confidently back along the ground to his father's feet.

"Right, the fooling around is over," said Andrew, not quite convinced. He kicked the ball from one foot to the other, trying to look skilful.

"Come on, Dad," Robert complained.

This time Andrew advanced with a look of determination on his face. He tried a change of pace to make his son leave the goal mouth too early. Robert duly came out of the goal; Andrew kicked the ball a little harder and higher than his previous attempt. As he did so he heard the phone ring again and turned his head towards the house. He didn't see his shot cannon against the left-hand corner of the goal post and bounce away.

"It's the Prime Minister," shouted Louise from the window. Andrew turned to walk quickly back towards the house. Out of the corner of his eye he saw the ball bounce on to the path, on its way towards the gate and into the road.

Robert was already running towards the open gate. "I'll save it, Dad, I'll save it."

"No," screamed Andrew at the top of his voice and turned back to run as fast as he could after his son.

Louise froze as she stared out of the window, still holding on to the phone with her rubber gloves. She watched as Andrew turned his back and tore towards the pavement until he was only a yard behind his son. The ball bounced on into the road and Robert dived for it a split second before his father threw himself on his son.

Louise was the only one who saw the driver of the massive Shell tanker slam on its brakes and swerve – too late – to avoid them. Andrew and Robert collided with the corner of the wide metal mudguard and were thrown back together before rolling over and over several times, ending up in the gutter.

"Are you there, Andrew?" asked the Prime Minister.

Louise dropped the phone and ran out of the kitchen towards the open gate. Her husband lay motionless beside the kerb with their son in his arms, the ball still clutched against his chest. She tried to hold on to both of them as Andrew's blood poured down over Robert's red shirt and on to her rubber gloves.

She fell on to her knees by the kerb side. "Let them live, let them live," was all she said.

Robert was crying softly as he held firmly on to the ball and stared at his unconscious father. She had to lean over to hear him repeating, "No goal, Dad, no goal."

When the complete list of ministers was published in *The Times* two days later the only unfilled post left was that of Minister of State for Defence. *The Times*'s political editor, David Wood, surmised that the position was being held open for Mr Andrew Fraser, who was expected to be out of hospital by the end of the week. Wood's final paragraph read:

> Politicians from all parties joined forces in praising Mr Fraser's remarkable courage in diving in front of a moving lorry to rescue his only son, Robert, who was chasing a football. Both father and son were rushed to St Thomas's Hospital with internal injuries, where surgeons operated through the night to save Mr Fraser's life.
>
> As was reported in the final edition of yesterday's paper, his five-year-old son Robert died during the night before Mr Fraser regained consciousness.

"My God," exclaimed Elizabeth, "how dreadful."

"What's dreadful?" asked Simon, as he took his seat at the breakfast table. She passed the paper to her husband and pointed to the picture of Robert.

"Poor kid," said Simon before he had finished the article. "Certainly puts our own problems into perspective. If Peter or Michael were killed we really would have something to worry about."

Neither of them spoke for several minutes. Then Elizabeth asked, "Are you dreading it?"

"Yes, I am," said Simon. "I feel like a condemned man eating his last breakfast, and the worst part of it is that I have to drive myself to the gallows."

"I wonder if we will ever laugh about today?"

"No doubt – when I collect my parliamentary pension."

"Can we live off that?"

"Hardly. I don't get the first payment until I'm sixty-five, so we have a twenty-five-year wait to find out." He got up. "Can I give you a lift to the hospital?"

"No thanks. I intend to savour the joys of being a two-car family for at least another week. Just let's hope the new Marina holds its price as well as Sir Michael Edwardes claimed it would."

Simon laughed, kissed his wife and left for his appointment with the Chief Whip at the House of Commons. As he started the car Elizabeth rushed out. "I forgot to tell you, Ronnie phoned while you were in the bath."

"I'll call him as soon as I reach the House."

Simon made his way to the Commons. He felt sick as he passed Cheyne Walk and thought of Andrew Fraser and all he must be going through. He made a mental note to write to him immediately. At the Commons the policeman on the gate saluted as he drove in. "Good morning, sir," he said.

"Good morning," said Simon. He parked his car on the second level of the new underground car park and took the escalator up to the Members' Entrance. He couldn't help reflecting that ten years ago he would have taken the stairs. He continued through the Members' Cloakroom, up the marble staircase to the Members' Lobby. Habit made him turn left into the little post office to check whether he had any mail.

"Mr Kerslake," the man behind the counter called into an intercom, and a few seconds later a parcel and a packet of letters held together by a thick elastic band thudded into an office basket. Simon left the parcel marked 'London School of Economics' and the letters on the desk in his room and checked his watch: over forty minutes before his appointment with the Chief Whip. He went to the nearest phone and dialled Nethercote and Company. Ronnie answered the phone himself.

"Sacked the telephone operator last Friday," he explained. "Only me and my secretary left."

"You called, Ronnie," a millimetre of hope in Simon's voice.

"Yes, I wanted to express how I felt. I tried to write you a letter over the weekend but I'm not very good with words." He paused. "Nor it seems with figures. I just wanted to say how desperately sorry I am. Elizabeth told me you were going to see the Chief Whip this morning. I'll be thinking of you."

"That's kind, Ronnie, but I went into it with my eyes wide open. As an advocate of free enterprise, I can hardly complain when I turn out to be one of its victims."

"A very philosophical attitude for this time of the morning."

"How are things your end?"

"The receiver's checking the books. I still believe we can get out with all our creditors fully paid. At least that way I'll avoid the stigma of bankruptcy." There was a longer pause. "Oh Christ, that was tactless."

"Don't worry about it, Ronnie, the overdraft was my decision."

Simon already wished he had been as frank with his wife.

"Let's have lunch one day next week."

"It will have to be somewhere that takes luncheon vouchers," said Simon wryly.

"Good luck, mate," said Ronnie.

Simon decided to fill up the remaining thirty minutes at the House by going to the library and glancing over the rest of the morning press. He settled himself in a corner of the 'B' Room, next to the fireplace over which hung a notice reminding members not to have overloud or prolonged conversations. He leafed through the papers, which all carried photographs of Andrew Fraser and his wife and son. The same portrait of five-year-old Robert appeared on almost every front page. Elizabeth was right: in so many respects they were lucky.

The story of the probable break-up of Nethercote and Company was detailed on the financial pages. They quoted approvingly Ronnie's view that all creditors ought to be paid in full. Not one of the articles mentioned Simon's name, but he could already anticipate the headlines in tomorrow's paper with another picture of a young MP and his happy family. 'The Rise and Fall of Simon Kerslake.' Over ten years' work quickly forgotten: he would be old news within a week.

The library clock inched towards the hour that he could no

longer put off. Simon heaved himself out of the deep leather chair like an old man and walked slowly towards the Chief Whip's office.

Miss Norse, the Chief's ancient secretary, smiled benignly as he came in.

"Good morning, Mr Kerslake," she said brightly. "I'm afraid the Chief is still with Mrs Thatcher but I did remind him of your appointment so I don't expect him to be long. Would you care to have a seat?"

"Thank you," he said.

Alec Pimkin always claimed that Miss Norse had a set patter for every occasion. His imitation of her saying, "I hope I find you in rude health, Mr Pimkin," had brought chuckles to the Members' Dining-room on many occasions. He must have exaggerated, thought Simon.

"I hope I find you in rude health, Mr Kerslake," said Miss Norse, not looking up from her typing. Simon choked back a laugh.

"Very rude, thank you," he said, wondering how many tragic stories or tales of lost opportunities Miss Norse had had to listen to over the years. She stopped suddenly and looked at her note pad.

"I should have mentioned it to you before, Mr Kerslake, a Mr Nethercote rang."

"Thank you, I've spoken to him already."

Simon was leafing through an out-of-date copy of *Punch* when the Chief Whip strode in.

"I can spare you one minute, Simon, one and a half if you are going to resign," he said, laughing, and marched off towards his office. As Simon followed him down the corridor the phone by Miss Norse's side rang. "It's for you, Mr Kerslake," she shouted to their retreating backs.

Simon turned and said, "Can you take the number?"

"He says it's urgent."

Simon stopped, hesitating. "With you in a moment," he said to the Chief Whip, who disappeared into his office. Simon walked back and took the phone from Miss Norse's outstretched hand.

"Simon Kerslake here. Who is it?"

"It's Ronnie."

"Ronnie," said Simon flatly.

"I've just had a call from Morgan Grenfell. One of their clients has made an offer of one pound twenty-five a share for the company and they're willing to take over the current liabilities."

Simon was trying to do the sums in his head.

"Don't bother working it out," Ronnie said. "At one pound twenty-five your shares would be worth £75,000."

"It won't be enough," said Simon, as he recalled his overdraft of £108,712, a figure etched in his memory.

"Don't panic. I've told them I won't settle for anything less than one pound fifty a share and it has to be within seven days, which will give them ample time to check the books. That would bring you in £90,000 but you would still be £18,000 down the Swanee, which you'll have to learn to live with. If you sell the wife as well as the second car you should just about survive."

Simon could tell by the way his friend was speaking that Ronnie already had a cigar between his lips.

"You're a genius."

"Not me – Morgan Grenfell. And I bet they'll make a handsome profit in the long run for their unnamed client who seemed to have all the inside information. If you're still on for lunch next Tuesday, don't bring your luncheon vouchers. It's on me."

Simon put the phone down and kissed Miss Norse on the forehead. She was completely taken aback by a situation for which she had no set reply. She remained silent as the Chief Whip put his head round the door. "An orgy in the Chief Whip's office? You'll be on page three of the *Sun* next, Miss Norse." Simon laughed. "I've got a crisis on over tonight's vote. The Government are reneging on our agreement for pairing, and I have to get a delegation back from Brussels in time for the ten o'clock division. Whatever it is, can it wait, Simon?"

"Yes, of course."

"Can you come to my office, Miss Norse – if I can drag you away from James Double-O-Seven Kerslake?"

Simon left and almost bounced to the nearest phone. First he called Elizabeth and then Archie Millburn at his office. Archie didn't sound all that surprised.

"Don't you think it might be wise for us to stop seeing each other?"

"Why?" said Raymond. "Palmerston had a mistress when he was seventy, and he still beat Disraeli come the election."

"Yes, but that was before the days of a dozen national newspapers *and* investigative journalism. Frankly it wouldn't take a Woodward or Bernstein more than a few hours to discover our little secret."

"We'll be all right. I've destroyed all the tapes."

"Do be serious."

"You're always telling me I'm far too serious."

"Well, I want you to be now. Very."

Raymond turned to face Kate. "I love you, Kate, and I know I always will. Why don't we stop this charade and get married?"

She sighed. "We've been over this a hundred times. I'll want to return to America eventually, and in any case I wouldn't make a very good Prime Minister's wife."

"Three American women have in the past," said Raymond sulkily.

"To hell with your historical precedents – and what's more, I hate Leeds."

"You've never been there."

"I don't need to if it's colder than London."

"Then you'll have to be satisfied with being my mistress." Raymond took Kate in his arms. "You know, I used to think being Prime Minister was worth every sacrifice, but now I'm not so sure."

"It's still worth the sacrifice," said Kate, "as you'll discover when you live at No. 10. Come on, or my dinner will be burnt to a cinder."

"You haven't noticed these," said Raymond smugly, pointing down at his feet.

Kate stared at the fashionable new slip-ons.

"I never thought the day would come," she said. "Pity you're starting to go bald."

When Simon returned home his first words were "We'll survive."

"Thank God for that," Elizabeth said. "But what have you done about your resignation letter?"

"Archie said he would return it the day I became Prime Minister."

"If that's ever to be true I want you to promise me just one thing."

"Anything," said Simon.

"You'll never speak to Ronnie Nethercote again."

For a moment Simon hesitated before saying, "That's not completely fair, Elizabeth, because I haven't been totally straight with you from the beginning." He then sat his wife down on the sofa and told her the whole truth.

It was Elizabeth's turn to remain silent.

"Oh, hell," she said, looking up at Simon. "I do hope Ronnie can forgive me."

"What are you talking about?"

"I phoned him back soon after you had left for the Commons and I spent at least ten minutes telling him why he was the biggest two-faced bastard I'd ever come across, and I didn't want to hear from him again in my life."

It was Simon's turn to collapse on to the sofa. "How did he respond?" he asked anxiously. Elizabeth faced her husband. "That's the strange thing, he didn't even protest. He just apologised."

"Do you think she will ever speak again?"

"God knows, I hope so," said his father, staring at the picture of his grandchild on the mantelpiece. "She's still young enough to have another child."

Andrew shook his head. "No, that's out of the question. The doctor warned me a long time ago that could be dangerous."

He had returned home from hospital ten days after the accident. The first thing he and Louise did was to attend

Robert's funeral. With Andrew on crutches, Sir Duncan had to support Louise during the short service. As soon as the burial was over Andrew took his wife back to Cheyne Walk and put her to bed, before returning downstairs to join his parents.

Andrew's mother bowed her head. "Whatever happens, you must move from this place as soon as possible. Every time Louise looks out of that kitchen window she'll relive the tragedy."

"I hadn't thought of that," said Andrew. "I'll start looking for a new house immediately."

"And what do you plan to do about the Prime Minister's offer?" enquired Sir Duncan.

"I haven't finally made up my mind," he said sharply. "He's given me until Monday to come to a decision."

"You must take it, Andrew. If you don't your political career will be finished. You can't sit at home and mourn Robert's death for the rest of your life."

Andrew looked up at his father. "No goal, Dad, no goal," he murmured and left them to go and sit with Louise in the bedroom. Her eyes were open but there was no expression on her face. Little white hairs had appeared at either side of her head that he had not noticed the week before. "Feeling any better, my darling?" he asked.

There was still no reply.

He undressed and climbed into bed beside her, holding her close, but she did not respond. She felt detached and distant. He watched his tears fall on her shoulder and run down on to the pillow. He fell asleep and woke again at three in the morning. No one had closed the curtains and the moon shone in through the windows, lighting the room. He looked at his wife. She had not moved.

Charles paced up and down the room angrily.

"Give me the figures again."

"Nethercote has accepted a bid of £7,500,000, which works out at one pound fifty a share," said Clive Reynolds.

Charles stopped at his desk and scribbled the figures down on a piece of paper. £90,000, leaving a shortfall of only

£18,000. It wouldn't be enough. "Damn," he said.

"I agree," said Reynolds, "I always thought we were premature to lose our position in the company in the first place."

"An opinion you will not voice outside this room," said Charles.

Clive Reynolds did not reply.

"What's happened to Nethercote himself?" asked Charles, searching for any scrap of information he could find about Simon Kerslake.

"I'm told he's starting up again in a smaller way. Morgan Grenfell were delighted by the deal and the manner in which he handled the company during the takeover. I must say we let it fall into their laps."

"Can we get any stock in the new company?" asked Charles, ignoring his comment.

"I doubt it. It's only capitalised at one million although Morgan Grenfell are giving Nethercote a large overdraft facility as part of the deal."

"Then all that remains necessary is to see the matter is never referred to again."

Andrew spent the weekend reading over the letters of condolence sent to him and Louise. There were over a thousand, many from people he didn't even know. He selected a few to take into the bedroom and read to Louise; not that he was sure she could even hear him. The doctor had told him not to disturb her unless it was really necessary. After such a severe shock she was now suffering from acute depression and must be nursed slowly back to health. Louise had walked a few paces the previous day but needed to rest today, the doctor explained to him.

He sat by the side of their bed, and quietly read the letters from the Prime Minister, from a contrite Jock McPherson, from Simon Kerslake, from Raymond Gould and from Mrs Bloxham. There was no sign that Louise had taken in anything he had said.

"What shall I do about the PM's offer?" he asked. "Shall I accept it?"

She made no response of any kind.

"He's asked me to be the Minister of State for Defence, but I need to know how you would feel." After sitting with her for a few more minutes and eliciting no response he left her to rest.

Each night he slept with her and tried to infuse her with his love, but he only felt more alone.

On the Monday morning he called his father and told him he had decided to turn down the Prime Minister's offer. He couldn't leave Louise alone for long periods while she was still in this state.

Andrew returned to the bedroom and sat by her side.

He said in a whisper, as if to himself, "Should I have taken the job?"

Louise gave such a slight nod that Andrew nearly missed it but her fingers were moving. He placed his hand between her fingers and palm and she squeezed gently and repeated the nod, then fell asleep.

Andrew phoned the Prime Minister.

Raymond dug deeper into the red box.

"You enjoying yourself, Carrot Top?"

"It's fascinating," said Raymond. "Do you know –"

"No, I don't. You haven't spoken to me in the last three hours, and when you do it's to tell me how you spend the day with your new mistress."

"My new mistress?"

"The Secretary of State for Trade."

"Oh, him."

"Yes, him."

"What sort of day did you have at the bank?" asked Raymond, not looking up from his papers.

"I had a most fascinating day," replied Kate.

"Why, what happened?"

"One of our customers required a loan," said Kate.

"A loan," repeated Raymond, still concentrating on the file in front of him. "How much?"

"'How much do you want?' I said. 'How much have you got?' they asked. 'Four hundred and seventeen billion at the last count,' I told them. 'That will do fine to start with,' they said. 'Sign here,' I said. But I couldn't close the deal because the lady concerned was only in possession of a £50 banking card."

Raymond burst out laughing and slammed down the lid of the red box. "Do you know why I love you?"

"My taste in men's clothes?" suggested Kate.

"No, no. Just your taste in men."

"I always thought that mistresses were supposed to get fur coats, trips to the Bahamas, the odd solitaire diamond, yet all I ever get is to share you with your red box."

Raymond opened the box once more, took out a small package and handed it to Kate.

"What's this?"

"Why don't you open it and find out?"

Kate slipped off the purple Asprey paper and found inside an exquisitely made miniature, a solid gold replica of a red box on a gold chain. The neat lettering on the side of the lid read, 'For Your Eyes Only'.

"Although they don't announce the birthdays of ministers' mistresses in the *Sunday Times*, I can still remember the day we met."

Andrew made a bid for the house in Pelham Crescent the day he was shown over it, and Louise's mother came down to London immediately to organise the move.

"Let's hope this does the trick," she said.

Andrew prayed for nothing more. The move from Cheyne Walk took about a fortnight, and Louise could still walk only a few paces before she had to sit down. Louise's mother rarely left the house and Andrew began to feel guilty about how much he was enjoying his new job at the Ministry of Defence. Each night and then again in the morning he would try a few words to Louise. She nodded occasionally, touched him once in a while and even began writing notes to him, but never spoke and never cried. The doctor became even more pessimistic. "The crucial time has passed," he explained.

Andrew would sit with her for hours while he worked through the red boxes. Harrier Jump jets for the RAF,

Polaris missiles for the Royal Navy, Chieftain tanks for the Army, what should Labour's attitude be to Trident when Polaris was phased out? Should we allow Cruise to be based on British soil? There was so much to learn before he could face the civil servants on their own ground or the members from the dispatch box. As the months passed Andrew was always asking questions; a year had gone by and he was beginning to know some of the answers.

He looked up at his wife once again. She was gazing at the portrait of Robert on the mantelpiece.

On the anniversary of his son's sixth birthday Andrew stayed at Pelham Crescent all day with Louise. For the first time a tear lodged in her eye. As he held her, he kept remembering the lorry. He could see it so clearly now as if in slow motion. If only the phone hadn't gone, if only the gate had been closed, if only he had turned earlier, if only he had run a little faster. 'No goal, Dad, no goal.'

If only he had scored that goal.

CHAPTER
TWENTY ONE

Raymond entered a Washington ablaze with red, white and blue as the Americans prepared for their bicentennial. He was among the three ministers chosen to represent the United Kingdom when they presented a copy of Magna Carta to the United States Congress. He was making his first trip to America on Concorde only a few weeks after its inaugural flight. Tom Carson had complained to the House about the expense of the trip but his words had fallen upon a silent Chamber.

As the plane taxied to a halt at Dulles airport three limousines drew up. The three ministers were given a car each and motorcycle outriders rushed them to the grounds of the British Embassy on Massachusetts Avenue in less than thirty minutes.

Raymond had an immediate love affair with America, perhaps because it reminded him so much of Kate with its bubbling enthusiasm, its spirit and sense of perpetual innovation. During the ten-day visit he managed to forge several useful contacts in the Senate and House, and over the weekend became an unrepentant sightseer of the beautiful Virginia countryside. He concentrated on getting to know those contemporaries whom he felt would be on the American political stage for the next twenty years, while his more senior colleagues dealt with President Ford and his immediate entourage.

Raymond enjoyed starting each day with the *Washington Post* and the *New York Times*. He quickly learned how to reject those sections that seemed full of endless advertisements for non-essentials he couldn't believe anyone really bought.

Once he had finished reading both papers he found he had to wash his hands as they were always black with newsprint. The one occasion he kept the Outlook section of the *Washington Post* was when it did profiles on the three ministers from London. He tucked the paper away as he wanted to show Kate the paragraph that read: "The two Secretaries of State are interesting men at the end of their careers, but it is Raymond Gould we should keep our eyes on because he has the look of a future Prime Minister."

As Raymond flew out of Washington on his way back to London he presumed, like any lover, that the affair with America could be continued whenever he chose to return.

Simon was in Manchester as a guest of the Business School when he received Elizabeth's message to call her. It was most unusual for Elizabeth to phone in the middle of the day and Simon assumed the worst: something must have happened to the children. The Principal of the Business School accompanied him to his private office, then left him alone.

Dr Kerslake was not at the hospital, he was told, which made him even more anxious. He dialled the Beaufort Street number.

Elizabeth picked up the receiver so quickly that she must have been sitting by the phone waiting for him to call.

"I've been sacked," she said.

"What?" said Simon, unable to comprehend.

"I've been made redundant – isn't that the modern term meant to lessen the blow? The hospital governors have been instructed by the Department of Health and Social Security to make cutbacks and three of us in gynaecology have lost our jobs. I go at the end of the month."

"Darling, I'm sorry," he said, knowing how inadequate his words must have sounded.

"I didn't meant to bother you, but I just wanted someone to talk to," she said. "Everyone else is allowed to complain to their MP, so I thought it was my turn."

"Normally what I do in these circumstances is to put the blame on the Labour party." Simon was relieved to hear Elizabeth laugh.

"Thanks for ringing me back so quickly, darling. See you tomorrow," she said and put the phone down.

Simon returned to his group and explained that he had to leave for London immediately. He took a taxi to the airport and caught the next shuttle to Heathrow. He was back at Beaufort Street within three hours.

"I didn't mean you to come home," Elizabeth said contritely when she saw him on the doorstep.

"I've come back to celebrate," Simon said. "Let's open the bottle of champagne that Ronnie gave us when he closed the deal with Morgan Grenfell."

"Why?"

"Because Ronnie taught me one thing. You should always celebrate disasters, not successes."

Simon hung up his coat and went off in search of the champagne. When he returned with the bottle and two glasses Elizabeth asked, "What's your overdraft looking like nowadays?"

"Down to £16,000, give or take a pound."

"Well, that's another problem then, I won't be giving any pounds in the future, only taking."

"Don't be silly. Someone will snap you up," he said, embracing her.

"It won't be quite that easy," said Elizabeth.

"Why not?" asked Simon, trying to sound cheerful.

"Because I had already been warned about whether I wanted to be a politician's wife or a doctor."

Simon was stunned. "I had no idea," he said. "I'm so sorry."

"It was my choice, darling, but I will have to make one or two decisions if I want to remain in medicine, especially if you're going to become a minister."

Simon remained silent: he had always wanted Elizabeth to make this decision herself and he was determined not to try to influence her.

"If only we weren't so short of money."

"Don't worry about the money," said Simon.

"I do worry, but it may just be an excuse because I worry more about becoming bored when the children have grown up. I just wasn't cut out to be a politician's wife," she added. "You should have married someone like Fiona Seymour and you'd be Prime Minister by now."

"If that's the only way I can be sure of getting the job I'll stick with you," said Simon, taking Elizabeth in his arms. Simon couldn't help thinking of all the support his wife had given him during their marriage and even more so since his financial crisis. He knew exactly what his wife must do.

"You mustn't be allowed to give up being a doctor," he said. "It's every bit as important as wanting to be a minister. Shall I have a word with Gerry Vaughan? As Shadow spokesman for Health he might —"

"Certainly not, Simon. If I am to get another job, it'll be without anyone doing you or me a favour."

Louise was now coping on her own, and had almost returned to a normal life except she still couldn't speak. She seemed to be self-sufficient within her own world and the doctor agreed that she no longer needed a full-time nurse.

The day the nurse left Andrew decided to take Louise off for a week's holiday abroad. He wanted to return to the South of France and the Colombe d'Or, but the specialist had advised against it, explaining that any past association might trigger off a memory that in itself could cause a further relapse.

"Witch doctors' mumbo jumbo," Andrew complained but nevertheless took her to Venice, not Colombe d'Or. Once there, he was delighted by the interest Louise showed in the beautiful and ancient city. Her eyes lit up at the sight of Torcello and she appeared to revel in the trip on a gondola down the twisting waterways past irreplaceable Italian architecture. Again and again she squeezed his hand. As they sat on a piazza for an evening drink, she inclined her head and listened to a quintet playing on St Mark's Square. Andrew was confident that she could now hear everything he told her. The night before they flew back to England he woke to find her reading James Morris's *Venice* which he had left by his side of the bed. It was the first time she had opened a book since the accident. When he smiled at her she grinned back. He laughed, wanting to hear her laugh.

Andrew returned to the Ministry of Defence on Monday. On his desk there was a general directive from the Chancellor of the Exchequer, requiring the budget estimates for all the big-spending Departments of State. Andrew fought hard to keep the Polaris missile after being convinced by the Joint Chiefs of its strategic importance to the nation's defence. He was, however, continually reminded by his colleagues in the House that it was party policy to rid themselves of 'the warmongers' toy'.

When the Secretary of State returned from Cabinet he told Andrew, "We've had our way: the Cabinet were impressed by the case. But I can promise you one thing – you won't be the golden boy at this year's party conference."

"It will make a change for them even to notice me," replied Andrew.

He breathed a sigh of relief while the Joint Chiefs were delighted, but a week later he lost – by default – the same argument with his own General Purposes Committee in Edinburgh. In his absence, they passed a resolution deploring the retention of the Polaris missile and demanded that all the ministers involved should reconsider their decision. They stopped short of naming Andrew, but everyone knew whose scalp they were after. His case was not helped by Tom Carson making yet another inflammatory speech in the House, claiming that Andrew had been browbeaten by the Joint Chiefs and was nothing more than a Polaris puppet.

Andrew's trips to Edinburgh had become less frequent over the past year because of his commitments to Louise and the Defence Department. During the year three members of his General Management Committee had been replaced with a new group calling themselves 'Militant Tendency' led by Frank Boyle. It wasn't just Edinburgh Carlton that was facing the problem of a left-wing insurgence – as Andrew learned from colleague after colleague who was beginning to work out why the left were pushing a resolution at the party conference proposing that members should be re-selected for each election. Some of his more right-wing colleagues had already been replaced, and it didn't take a Wrangler to work out that once a majority of the Trotskyites had secured places on his Management Committee Andrew could be removed at their whim, whatever his past experience or record.

Whenever Andrew was in Edinburgh the local people continually assured him of their support and their confidence in him, but he could not forget, despite their avowals, that it would still take only a handful of votes to remove him. Andrew feared what the outcome would be if many other members were facing the same problem as he faced in Edinburgh.

"Dad, can I have a new cricket bat, please?"

"What's wrong with the old one?" asked Simon, as they came out of the house.

"It's too small," he said, waving it around as if it was an extension to his arm.

"It will have to do, I'm afraid."

"But Martin Henderson's dad has given him a new bat to start the season."

"I'm sorry, Peter, the truth is that Martin's father is far better off than I am."

"I'll tell you one thing," said Peter with feeling. "I'm sure not going to be an MP when I grow up." Simon smiled as his son removed an old cricket ball from his trouser pocket and tossed it over to his father. "Anyway, I bet you can't get me out even though I've only got a small bat."

"Don't forget we still have the junior size stumps left over from last year," said Simon, "so it will be just as hard to hit them."

"Stop making excuses, Dad. Just admit you're past it."

Simon burst out laughing. "We'll see," he said, with more bravado than conviction. Simon always enjoyed a few overs in the garden against his elder son although at the age of thirteen Peter was already able to play his best deliveries with a confidence that was beginning to look ominous.

It was several overs before Simon removed Peter's middle stump and took his turn at the crease.

Michael ran out of the house to join them in the field and

Simon couldn't help noticing that he was wearing a pair of jeans that were far too short and had once belonged to Peter.

"Get behind the wicket, nipper," shouted Peter at his eleven-year-old brother. "Because that's where most of the balls will be going." Michael happily obeyed without comment.

A colleague in the House had recently warned Simon that by fourteen they began to beat you and by sixteen they hoped not to show they weren't trying their hardest any longer.

Simon gritted his teeth as he watched his elder son's fastest ball safely on to the middle of the bat. The way he was going Peter wouldn't have to wait much longer before he could clean bowl him.

He managed to keep his wicket intact for a further five minutes before he was rescued by Elizabeth who came out to tell them that supper was ready.

"What, hamburgers and chips again?" said Michael as his mother put a plate in front of him.

"You're lucky to get anything," Elizabeth snapped back.

Simon cursed again at the damage his own selfish greed had brought upon his family, and marvelled at how little they all complained. He said nothing, only too aware that the previous day Elizabeth had completed her last week at the hospital and was already missing St Mary's.

"How did you all get on?" she asked cheerily.

"I'll survive," said Simon, still thinking about his overdraft.

Once the Chancellor had presented his mini budget, in November 1976, the long process of the Finance Bill, confirming all the new measures proposed, fully occupied the House. Charles, although not a member of the front-bench finance team, regularly took the lead among back-benchers on clauses on which he had specialist knowledge.

He and Clive Reynolds studied the new Finance Bill meticulously and between them picked out the seven clauses that would have an adverse effect on banking.

Reynolds guided Charles through each clause, suggesting changes, rewording, and on some occasions presenting an argument for deleting whole sections of the bill. Charles learned quickly and was soon adding his own ideas; one or two even made Clive Reynolds reconsider. After Charles had put forward amendments to the House on three of the clauses both front benches became respectfully attentive whenever he rose to present a case. One morning, after the Government's defeat on a clause relating to banking loans, he received a note of congratulation from Margaret Thatcher.

The clause Charles most wanted to see removed from the bill concerned a client's right to privacy when dealing with a merchant bank. The Shadow Chancellor was aware of Charles's specialised knowledge on this subject and invited him to oppose clause 110 from the front bench. Charles realised that if he could defeat the Government on this clause he might be invited to join the Shadow finance team in the run-up to the general election.

Judging by the chairman of Ways and Means' selection of amendments the Whips estimated that clause 110 on banking privacy would be reached some time on Thursday afternoon.

On Thursday morning Charles rehearsed his arguments thoroughly with Clive Reynolds, who only had one or two minor amendments to add before Charles set off for the House. When he arrived at the Commons there was a note on the message board asking him to phone the Shadow Chancellor urgently.

"The Government are going to accept a Liberal amendment tabled late last night," the Shadow Chancellor told him.

"Why?" said Charles.

"Minimum change is what they're really after, but it gets them off the hook and at the same time keeps the Liberal vote intact. In essence nothing of substance has changed, but you'll need to study the wording carefully. Can I leave you to handle the problem?"

"Certainly," said Charles, pleased with the responsibility with which they were now entrusting him.

He walked down the long corridor to the vote office and picked up the sheet with clause 110 on it and the proposed

Liberal amendment. He read them both through half a dozen times before he started to make notes. Parliamentary counsel, with their usual expertise, had produced an ingenious amendment. Charles ducked into a nearby phone booth and rang Clive Reynolds at the bank. Charles dictated the amendment over the phone to him and then remained silent while Reynolds considered its implications.

"Clever bunch of sharpies. It's a cosmetic job, but it won't change the power it invests in the Government one iota. Were you thinking of returning to the bank? That would give me time to work on it."

"No," said Charles. "Are you free for lunch?"

Clive Reynolds checked his diary: a Belgian banker would be lunching in the boardroom but his colleagues could handle that. "Yes, I'm free."

"Good," said Charles. "Why don't you join me at White's around one o'clock?"

"Thank you," said Reynolds. "By then I should have had enough time to come up with some credible alternatives."

Charles spent the rest of the morning rewriting his speech which he hoped would counter the Liberal argument and make them reconsider their position. If it met with Reynolds's imprimatur the day could still be his. He read through the clause once more, convinced he had found a way through the loophole the civil servants couldn't block. He placed his speech and the amended clause in his inside pocket and went down to the Members' Entrance and jumped into a waiting taxi.

As the cab drove up St James's Charles thought he saw his wife coming down the opposite side of the road. He pushed down the window to be sure but she had disappeared into Prunier's. He wondered with which of her girl friends she was lunching.

The cab travelled on up St James's and came to a halt outside White's. Charles found he was a few minutes early so he decided to walk down to Prunier's and ask Fiona if she would like to come to the House after lunch and hear him oppose the clause. Reaching the restaurant he glanced through the pane-glass window. He froze on the spot. Fiona was chatting at the bar with a man whose back was to Charles but he thought he recognised his profile although he couldn't be certain. He noticed that his wife was wearing a dress he had never seen before. He didn't move as he watched a waiter bow, then guide the pair towards a corner table where they were conveniently out of sight. Charles's first instinct was to march straight in and confront them; but he remained outside. For what seemed an interminable time he stood alone, uncertain what to do next. Finally he crossed back over St James's Street and stood in the doorway of the Economist building going over several plans. In the end he decided to do nothing but wait. He stood there so cold and so incensed that he did not consider returning for his lunch appointment with Clive Reynolds a few hundred yards up the road.

An hour and twenty minutes later the man came out of Prunier's alone and headed up St James's. Charles felt a sense of relief until he saw him turn into St James's Place. He checked his watch: Reynolds would have left by now but he would still be well in time for clause number 110. A few minutes later Fiona stepped out of the restaurant and followed in the man's footsteps. Charles crossed the road, causing a cab to swerve while another motorist slammed on her brakes. He didn't notice. He shadowed his wife, careful to keep a safe distance. When she reached the far end of the passage he watched Fiona enter the Stafford Hotel. Once she was through the swing doors Fiona stepped into an empty lift.

Charles came up to the swing doors and stared at the little numbers above the lift, watching them light up in succession until they stopped at four.

Charles marched through the swing doors and up to the reception desk.

"Can I help you, sir?" the hall porter asked.

"Er – is the dining-room in this hotel on the fourth floor?" asked Charles.

"No, sir," replied the hall porter, surprised. "The dining-room is on the ground floor to your left" – he indicated the way with a sweep of his hand — "there are only bedrooms on the fourth floor."

"Thank you," said Charles and marched back outside.

He returned slowly to the Economist building, incensed, where he waited for nearly two hours pacing up and down St James's before the man emerged from the Stafford Hotel; Alexander Dalglish hailed a taxi and disappeared in the direction of Piccadilly.

Fiona left the hotel about twenty minutes later, and took the path through to the park before setting off towards Eaton Square. On three occasions Charles had to fall back to be certain Fiona didn't spot him; once he was so close he thought he saw a smile of satisfaction come over her face.

He had followed his wife most of the way across St James's Park when he suddenly remembered. He checked his watch, then dashed back to the roadside, hailed a taxi and shouted, "The House of Commons, as fast as you can." The cabby took seven minutes and Charles passed him two pound notes before running up the steps into the Members' Lobby and through to the Chamber out of breath. He stopped by the Serjeant-at-Arms's chair.

From the table where he sat during Committee of the whole House, the Mace lowered on its supports in front of the table, the chairman of Ways and Means faced a packed House. He read from the division list.

"The Ayes to the right 294.

The Noes to the left 293.

The Ayes have it, the Ayes have it."

The Government benches cheered and the Conservatives looked distinctly glum. "What clause were they debating?" a still out of breath Charles asked the Serjeant-at-Arms.

"Clause 110, Mr Seymour."

BOOK FOUR
1977-1989
THE CABINET

CHAPTER
TWENTY TWO

Raymond's second trip to the States was at the behest of the Secretary of State for Trade: he was asked to present the country's export and import assessment to the International Monetary Fund, following up a loan granted to Britain the previous November. His civil servants went over the prepared speech with him again and again, emphasising to their minister the responsibility that had been placed on his shoulders. Even the Governor of the Bank of England's private office had been consulted.

"A chance to impress a few people beyond the boundaries of Leeds," Kate assured him.

Raymond's speech was scheduled for the Wednesday morning. He flew into Washington on the Sunday and spent Monday and Tuesday listening to the problems of other nations' trade ministers while trying to get used to the dreadful earphones and the female interpreter.

The conference was attended by most of the leading industrial nations and the British Ambassador, Sir Peter Ramsbotham, told Raymond over dinner at the Embassy that this was a real chance to convince the hard-headed international bankers that Britain cared about economic realities and was still worth their financial backing.

Raymond soon realised that convincing such a gathering required a very different technique from shouting from a soap box on a street corner in Leeds or even addressing the House from the dispatch box. He was glad he had not been scheduled to present his case on the opening day. Over leisurely lunches he re-established his existing contacts in Congress and made some new ones.

The night before he was to deliver his speech Raymond hardly slept. He continued to rehearse each crucial phrase and repeated the salient points that needed to be emphasised until he almost knew them by heart. At three o'clock in the morning he dropped his speech on the floor beside his bed and phoned Kate to have a chat before she went to work.

"I'd enjoy hearing your speech at the conference," she told him. "Although I don't suppose it would be much different from the thirty times I've listened to it in the bedroom."

Once he had said goodbye to Kate he fell into a deep sleep. He woke early that morning and went over the speech one last time before leaving for the conference centre.

All the homework and preparation proved worthwhile. By the time he turned the last page Raymond couldn't be certain how convincing his case had been, but he knew it was the best speech he had ever delivered. When he looked up the smiles all around the oval table assured him that his contribution had been well received. As the ambassador pointed out to him as he rose to leave, any signs of emotion at these gatherings were almost unknown. He felt confident that the IMF loan would be renewed.

There followed two further speeches before they broke for lunch. At the end of the afternoon session Raymond walked out into the clear Washington air and decided to make his way back to the Embassy on foot. He was exhilarated by the experience of dominating an international conference and picked up an evening paper: an article covering the conference suggested that Raymond would be Britain's next Labor Chancellor. He smiled at the spelling. Just the closing day to go, followed by the official banquet and he would be back home by the weekend.

When he reached the Embassy the guard had to double-check: they weren't used to ministers arriving on foot and without a bodyguard. Raymond was allowed to proceed down the tree-lined drive towards the massive Lutyens building. He looked up to see the British flag was flying at half mast and wondered which distinguished American had died.

"Who has died?" he asked the tail-coated butler who opened the door for him.

"The Foreign Secretary, sir."

"Anthony Crosland? I knew he had gone into hospital, but . . ." said Raymond almost to himself. He hurried into the Embassy to find it abuzz with telexes and coded messages. Raymond sat alone in his private sitting-room for several hours and later, to the horror of the security staff, slipped out for a quiet dinner at the Mayflower Hotel with Senator Hart.

Raymond returned to the conference table at nine o'clock the next morning to listen to the French Minister of Commerce put his case for renewed funds. He was savouring the thought of the official banquet at the White House to be held that evening when he was tapped on the shoulder by Sir Peter Ramsbotham, who indicated by touching his lips with his forefinger and pointing that they must have a word in private.

"The Prime Minister wants you to return on the mid-morning Concorde," said Sir Peter. "It leaves in an hour. On arrival in Britain you're to go straight to Downing Street."

"What's this all about?"

"I have no idea, that was the only instruction I received from No. 10," confided the ambassador.

Raymond returned to the conference table and made his apologies to the chairman, left the room and was driven immediately to the waiting plane. "Your bags will follow, sir," he was assured.

He was back on English soil three hours and forty-one minutes later, a little after seven-thirty. The purser ensured that he was the first to disembark. A car waiting by the side of the plane whisked him to Downing Street. He arrived just as the Prime Minister was going to dinner, accompanied by an elderly African statesman who was waving his trademark fan back and forth.

"Welcome home, Ray," said the Prime Minister, leaving the African leader. "I'd ask you to join us, but as you can see I'm entertaining the President of Malawi. Let's have a word in my study."

Once Raymond had settled into a chair Mr Callaghan wasted no time.

"Because of Tony's tragic death I have had to make a few changes which will include moving the Secretary of State for Trade. I was hoping you would be willing to take over from him."

Raymond sat up straighter. "I should be honoured, Prime Minister."

"Good. You've earned your promotion, Raymond. I also hear you did us proud in America, very proud."

"Thank you."

"You'll be appointed to the Privy Council immediately and your first Cabinet meeting will be at ten o'clock tomorrow. Now, if you'll excuse me, I must catch up with Dr Banda."

Raymond was left standing in the hall.

He asked his driver to take him back to the flat. All he wanted to do was to tell Kate the news. When he arrived the flat was empty: then he remembered she wasn't expecting him back until the next day. He phoned her home but after twenty continuous rings he resigned himself to the fact that she was out. "Damn," he said out loud, and after pacing around phoned Joyce to let her know the news. Once again there was no reply.

He went into the kitchen and checked to see what was in the fridge: a piece of curled-up bacon, some half-eaten Brie, three eggs. He couldn't help thinking about the banquet he was missing at the White House.

The Right Honourable Raymond Gould QC, MP, Her Britannic Majesty's Principal Secretary of State for Trade, sat on the kitchen stool, opened a tin of baked beans and devoured them with a fork.

Charles closed the file. It had taken him a month to gather all the proof he needed. Albert Cruddick, the private investigator Charles had selected from the Yellow Pages, had been expensive but discreet. Dates, times, places were all fully chronicled. The only name was that of Alexander Dalglish, the same rendezvous, lunch at Prunier's followed by the

Stafford Hotel. They hadn't stretched Mr Cruddick's imagination but at least the detective had spared Charles the necessity of standing in the entrance of the Economist building once, sometimes twice a week for hours on end.

Somehow he had managed to get through that month without giving himself away. He had also made his own notes of the dates and times Fiona claimed she was going to be in the constituency. He had then called his agent in Sussex Downs and, after veiled questioning, elicited answers that corroborated Mr Cruddick's findings.

Charles saw as little of Fiona as possible during this time, explaining that the Finance Bill was occupying his every moment. His lie had at least a semblance of credibility for he had worked tirelessly on the remaining clauses left for debate, and by the time the watered-down bill had become law he had just about recovered from the disaster of the Government's successful retention of clause 110.

Charles placed the file on the table by the side of his chair and waited patiently for the call. He knew exactly where she was at that moment and just the thought of it made him sick to his stomach. The phone rang.

"The subject left five minutes ago," said a voice.

"Thank you," said Charles and replaced the receiver. He knew it would take her about twenty minutes to reach home.

"Why do you think she walks home instead of taking a taxi?" he had once asked Mr Cruddick.

"Gets rid of any smells," Mr Cruddick had replied quite matter-of-factly.

Charles shuddered. "And what about him? What does he do?" He never could refer to him as Alexander, or even Dalglish; or as anything but 'him'.

"He goes to the Lansdowne Club, swims ten lengths or plays a game of squash before returning home. Swimming and squash both solve the problem," Mr Cruddick explained cheerily.

The key turned in the lock. Charles braced himself and picked up the file. Fiona came straight into the drawing-room and was visibly shaken to discover her husband sitting in an armchair with a small suitcase by his side.

She recovered quickly, walked over and kissed him on the cheek. "What brings you home so early, darling? The Socialists taken the day off?" She laughed nervously at her joke.

"This," he said, standing up and holding the file out to her.

She took off her coat and dropped it over the sofa. Then she opened the buff folder and started to read. He watched her carefully. First the colour drained from her cheeks, then her legs gave way and she collapsed on to the sofa. Finally she started to sob.

"It's not true, none of it," she protested.

"You know very well that every detail is accurate."

"Charles, it's you I love, I don't care about him, you must believe that."

"I believe nothing of the sort," said Charles. "You're no longer someone I could live with."

"Live with? I've been living on my own since the day you entered Parliament."

"Perhaps I might have come home more often if you had showed some interest in starting a family."

"And do you imagine I am to blame for that inadequacy," she said.

Charles ignored the innuendo and continued. "In a few moments I am going to my club where I shall spend the night. I expect you to be out of this house within seven days. When I return I want there to be no sign of you or any of your goods or chattels, to quote the original agreement."

"Where will I go?" she cried.

"You could try your lover first, but no doubt his wife might object. Failing that, you can camp down at your father's place."

"What if I refuse to go?" said Fiona, turning to defiance.

"Then I shall throw you out, as one should a whore, and cite Alexander Dalglish in a very messy divorce case."

"Give me another chance. I'll never look at him again," begged Fiona, starting to cry once more.

"I seem to remember your telling me that once before, and indeed I did give you another chance. The results have been all too plain to see." He pointed to the file where it had fallen to the floor.

Fiona stopped weeping when she realised that Charles remained unmoved.

"I shall not see you again. We shall be separated for at least two years, when we will carry through as quiet a divorce as possible in the circumstances. If you cause me a moment of embarrassment I shall drag you both through the mire. Believe me."

"You'll regret your decision, Charles. I promise you. I'll not be pushed aside quite that easily."

"They've done *what*?" said Joyce.

"Two Communists have put their names forward for election to the General Purposes Committee," repeated Fred Padgett.

"Over my dead body." Joyce's voice was unusually sharp.

"I thought that would be your attitude," said Fred.

Joyce searched for the pencil and paper that were normally on the table by the phone.

"When's the meeting?" she asked.

"Next Thursday."

"Have we got reliable people to stand against them?"

"Of course," said Fred. "Councillor Reg Illingworth and Jenny Simpkins from the Co-op."

"They're both sensible enough but between them they couldn't knock the skin off a rice pudding."

"Shall I phone Raymond at the House and get him to come up for the meeting?"

"No," said Joyce. "He's got enough to worry about now that he's in the Cabinet without piling up trouble for him in Leeds. Leave it to me."

She replaced the receiver and sat down to compose her thoughts. A few minutes later she went over to her desk and rummaged about for the full list of the G.P. Committee. She checked the sixteen names carefully, realising that if two Communists were to get themselves elected this time within five years they could control the committee – and then even remove Raymond. She knew how these people worked. With any luck, if they got bloody noses now they might slink off to another constituency.

She checked the sixteen names once more before putting on a pair of sensible walking shoes. During the next four days she visited several homes in the area. "I was just passing," she explained to nine of the wives who had husbands on the committee. The four men who never listened to a word their wives said were visited by Joyce after work. The three who had never cared for Raymond were left well alone.

By Thursday afternoon thirteen people knew only too well what was expected of them. Joyce sat alone hoping he would call that evening. She cooked herself a Lancashire hotpot but only picked at it, then later fell asleep in front of the television when she tried to watch the final episode of *Roots*. The phone woke her at five past eleven.

"Raymond?"

"Hope I didn't wake you," said Fred.

"No, no," said Joyce, now impatient to learn the outcome of the meeting. "What happened?"

"Reg and Jenny walked it. Those two Communist bastards only managed three votes between them."

"Well done," said Joyce.

"I did nothing," said Fred, "except count the votes. Shall I tell Raymond what's been happening?"

"No," said Joyce. "No need to let him think we've had any trouble."

Joyce fell back into the chair by the phone, kicked off her walking shoes, and went back to sleep.

She knew she had to plan the whole operation so that her husband would never find out. She sat alone in the house considering the several alternative ways in which she could deceive him. After hours of unproductive thought the idea finally came in a flash. She went over the problems and repercussions again and again until she was convinced that nothing could go wrong. She leafed through the Yellow Pages and made an appointment for the following morning.

The sales lady helped her to try on several wigs, but only one was bearable.

"I think it makes Modom look most elegant, I must say."

She knew that it didn't – it made Modom look awful – but she hoped it would serve its purpose.

She then applied the eye make-up and lipstick she had acquired at Harrods, and pulled out from the back of her cupboard a floral dress she had never liked. She stood in front of the mirror and checked herself. Surely no one would recognise her in Sussex and she prayed that if he found out he would be forgiving.

She left and drove slowly towards the outskirts of London. How would she explain herself if she was caught? Would he remain understanding when he discovered the truth? When she reached the constituency she parked the car in a side road and walked up and down the high street. No one showed any sign of recognition which gave her the confidence to go through with it. And then she saw him.

She had hoped he'd be in the City that morning. She held her breath as he walked towards her. As he passed she said, "Good morning." He turned and smiled, replying with a casual "Good morning," as he might to any constituent. Her heartbeat returned to normal and she went back to find her car.

She drove off completely reassured she could now get away with it. She went over once again what she was going to say, then all too suddenly she had arrived. She parked the car outside the house opposite, got out and bravely walked up the path.

As Raymond stood outside the Cabinet room several of his colleagues came over to congratulate him. At exactly ten o'clock the Prime Minister walked in, bade everyone "Good morning," and took his place at the centre of the oblong table, while the other twenty-one members of the Cabinet filed in behind him and took their places. The Leader of the House, Michael Foot, sat on his left, while the Foreign Secretary and Chancellor were placed opposite him. Raymond was directed to a seat at the end of the table between the Secretary of State for Wales and the Secretary of State for Education.

"I would like to start the meeting," said the Prime Minister, "by welcoming David Owen as Foreign Secretary and Raymond Gould as Secretary of State for Trade." The other nineteen Cabinet members murmured, "Hear, hear" in a discreetly conservative way. David Owen smiled slightly while Raymond could feel himself going red.

"The first item we must discuss in detail is the proposed pact with the Liberals . . ."

Raymond sat back and decided that today he would only listen.

Andrew sat in the small office and listened carefully to the specialist's opinion. Louise was restored to almost perfect health in every way except for her speech. She was reading regularly and had even begun to write short messages in reply to Andrew's questions. The specialist now felt that she needed some other outside interest to take her mind off Robert. Over a year had passed and she could still spend hours simply staring at his photograph.

"I managed to reach Dr Kerslake at home," the specialist said, "and I must concur with her opinion that it would be unwise for your wife to contemplate another pregnancy. But Dr Kerslake does accept my judgement that you should both consider adoption."

"I've already given the idea a lot of thought, even discussed it with my father," Andrew replied. "But both of us felt that Louise would never agree to it."

"It's a calculated risk in the circumstances," said the specialist. "We mustn't forget it's been a whole year. We know to our cost that Mrs Fraser loves children, and if she is set against such a course she is now well capable of letting you know."

"If Louise shows any response I'd be only too willing to give it a try. But in the end it will all depend on her."

"Good. Find out how she feels," said the specialist, "and if you both decide to go ahead I'll arrange a meeting with the local authority." He rose from behind his desk. "I'm sure it won't be hard to find you a suitable child."

"If it were possible for him to come from a Scottish orphans' home, I would appreciate it."

The specialist nodded. "I'll be in touch with you as soon as I have any news."

When Charles returned home he knew at once Fiona had left. He felt an immediate relief. After a week at his club, he was glad the charade was over, a clean, irrevocable break. He strolled into the drawing-room and stopped: something was wrong. It took him a few moments before he realised what she had done.

Fiona had removed every one of the family paintings.

No Wellington above the fireplace, no Victoria behind the sofa. Where the two Landseers and the Constable had hung there was nothing more than thin dusty outlines indicating the size of each picture she had removed. He walked to the library: the Van Dyck, the Murillo and the two small Rembrandts were also missing. Charles ran down the hall. It couldn't be possible, he thought, as he threw open the dining-room door. It was. He stared at the blank wall where only the previous week the Holbein portrait of the first Earl of Bridgwater had hung.

Charles scrabbled in the back of his pocket diary for the number and dialled it frantically. Mr Cruddick listened to the story in silence.

"Remembering how sensitive you are about publicity, Mr Seymour, there are two avenues of approach," he began in his normal level tone and sounding unperturbed. "You can grin and bear it, or the alternative is one I have used often in the past."

Because of the demands of his new job Raymond saw less of Kate and almost nothing of Joyce apart from his fortnightly visits to Leeds. He worked from eight in the morning until he fell asleep at night.

"And you love every minute of it," Kate reminded him whenever he complained. Raymond had also become aware of the subtle changes that had taken place in his life since he had become a member of the Cabinet, the way he was treated by other people, how quickly his slightest whim was granted, how flattery fell from almost every tongue. He began to enjoy the change in status although Kate reminded him that only the Queen could afford to get used to it.

At the Labour party conference that year he allowed his name to be put forward for a place on the National Executive. Although he failed to be elected he managed to finish ahead of several other Cabinet ministers and polled only a few votes less than Neil Kinnock, the darling of the constituency section.

Andrew Fraser, who now looked upon Raymond as someone he could confide in, joined Raymond for what was becoming their traditional conference lunch together on the third day. Andrew told him of his distress at the party's continued drift to the left.

"If some of those resolutions on defence are passed my life will be made impossible," he said, trying to cut into a very tough steak.

"The hotheads always put up resolutions that are never allowed more than a token discussion."

"Token discussion be damned. Some of their mad ideas are beginning to gain credence which, translated, could become party policy."

"Any particular resolution worrying you?" asked Raymond.

"Yes, Tony Benn's latest proposal that members must be re-selected before every election. His idea of democracy and accountability."

"Why should you fear that?"

"If your management committee is taken over by half a dozen Trots they can reverse a decision 50,000 voters have previously agreed on."

"You're over-reacting, Andrew."

"Raymond, if we lose the next election I can see a split in the party that will be so great we may never recover."

"They've been saying that in the Labour party since the day it was founded."

"I hope you're right, but I fear times have changed," said Andrew. "Not so long ago it was you who envied me."

"That can change again." Raymond abandoned the steak, waved his hand and asked the waitress to bring two large brandies.

Charles picked up the phone and dialled a number he had not needed to look up. The new young Portuguese maid answered.

"Is Lady Fiona at home?"

"Lady no home, sir."

"Do you know where she is?" asked Charles, speaking slowly and clearly.

"Go down to country, expect back six o'clock. Take message please?"

"No, thank you," said Charles. "I'll call this evening." He replaced the receiver.

As always the reliable Mr Cruddick was proved right about his wife's movements. Charles called him immediately. They agreed to meet as planned in twenty minutes.

He drove into the Boltons, parked on the far side of the road a few yards from his father-in-law's house and settled down to wait.

A few minutes later a large anonymous pantechnicon van came round the corner and stopped outside No. 24. Mr Cruddick jumped out from the driver's seat. He was dressed in long brown overalls and a flat cap. He was joined by a young assistant who unlocked the back of the van. Mr Cruddick nodded to Charles before proceeding up the steps to the front door.

The Portuguese maid answered when he pressed the bell.

"We have come to collect the goods for Lady Seymour."

"No understand," said the maid.

Mr Cruddick removed from an inside pocket a long typewritten letter on Lady Seymour's personal stationery. The Portuguese maid was unable to read the words of a letter her mistress had addressed to Hurlingham Croquet Club agreeing to be their Ladies' President, but she immediately recognised the letter-head and the signature. She nodded and opened the door wider. All Mr Cruddick's carefully laid plans were falling into place.

Mr Cruddick tipped his hat, the sign for Mr Seymour to join them. Charles got out of the car cautiously, checking both ways before he crossed the road. He felt uncomfortable in brown overalls and hated the cap with which Mr Cruddick had supplied him. It was a little small and Charles was acutely conscious how strange he must look but the Portuguese maid apparently didn't notice the incongruity between his aristocratic mien and the working overalls. It did not take long to discover the whereabouts of most of the pictures. Many were just stacked up in the hall, and only one or two had already been hung.

Forty minutes later the three men had located and loaded into the van all but one of them. The Holbein of the first Earl of Bridgwater was nowhere to be found.

"We ought to be on our way," suggested Mr Cruddick a little nervously, but Charles refused to give up the search. For another thirty-five minutes Mr Cruddick sat tapping the wheel of the van before Charles finally conceded that the painting must have been taken elsewhere. Mr Cruddick tipped his hat to the maid while his partner locked up the back of the van.

"A valuable picture, Mr Seymour?" he enquired.

"A family heirloom that would fetch two million at auction," said Charles matter-of-factly before returning to his car.

"Silly question, Albert Cruddick," said Mr Cruddick to himself as he pulled out from the curb and drove towards Eaton Square. When they arrived the locksmith had replaced all three locks on the front door and was waiting on the top step impatiently.

"Strictly cash, guv'nor. No receipt. Makes it possible for the missus and me to go to Ibiza each year, tax free."

By the time Fiona had returned to the Boltons from her trip to Sussex every picture was back in its place at Eaton Square with the exception of Holbein's first Earl of Bridgwater. Mr Cruddick was left clutching a large cheque and uttering the unpalatable view that Mr Seymour would probably have to grin and bear it.

"I'm delighted," said Simon, when he heard the news. "And at Pucklebridge General Hospital?"

"Yes, I answered an advertisement in *The Lancet* for the post of general consultant in the maternity section."

"But your name must have helped there?"

"Certainly not," said Elizabeth vehemently.

"How come?"

"I didn't apply as Dr Kerslake. I filled out the application form in my maiden name of Drummond."

Simon was momentarily silenced. "But they would have recognised you," he protested.

"I had the full frontal treatment from Estée Lauder to ensure they didn't. The final effect fooled even you."

"Don't exaggerate," said Simon.

"I walked straight past you in Pucklebridge High Street, and said 'Good morning,' and you returned the greeting."

Simon stared at her in disbelief. "But what will happen when they find out?"

"They already have," replied Elizabeth sheepishly. "As soon as they offered me the post I went down to see the senior consultant and told him the truth. He hasn't stopped telling everyone since."

"He wasn't cross?"

"Far from it. In fact he said I nearly failed to be offered the post because he felt I wouldn't be safe let loose on the unmarried doctors."

Andrew held Louise's hand as they approached the door of Grunechan Children's Home on the outskirts of Edinburgh. The matron was waiting on the freshly scrubbed doorstep to greet them.

"Good morning, Minister," she said. "We are honoured that you have chosen our little home."

Andrew and Louise smiled.

"Will you be kind enough to follow me?" She led them down a dimly lit corridor to her room, her starched blue uniform crackling as she walked.

"All the children are in the playground at the moment but you will be able to see them from my window." Andrew had already gone over all the orphans' histories and photographs; he couldn't help noticing how one of them bore a striking resemblance to Robert.

They both looked out of the window for several minutes but Louise showed no interest in any of the children. When the boy who resembled Robert ran towards the window, she turned away and took a seat in the corner.

Andrew shook his head. The matron's lips turned down at the corners.

Coffee and biscuits arrived and while they were eating them Andrew tried once more. "Did you want Matron to bring anyone in to meet you, darling?" Louise shook her head. Andrew cursed himself as he feared the experience might only have done her more harm.

"Have we seen everyone?" he asked, looking for an excuse to leave quickly.

"Yes, sir," said the matron, putting down her cup of coffee. "Well," she hesitated, "there was one girl we didn't bother you with."

"Why not?" asked Andrew out of curiosity.

"Well, you see, she's black."

Andrew stiffened.

"And what's more," continued the matron, "we have absolutely no idea who her parents were. She was left on the doorstep. Not at all the sort of girl to be brought up in a minister's home."

Andrew was so incensed that he quite forgot about consulting Louise who was still resting silently in the corner.

"I should like to see her," he said.

"If you insist," said the matron, a little taken aback. "I'm afraid she hasn't got her best clothes on," she added before she left the room.

Andrew paced up and down, conscious that if Louise hadn't been there he might well have lost his temper with the woman. The matron returned a few moments later with a little girl aged four, perhaps five, and so thin that her dress hung on her like a coathanger. Andrew couldn't see her face because she kept her head bowed.

"Look up, child," commanded the matron. The girl raised

her head slowly. She had the most perfect oval face and olive skin, piercing black eyes and a smile that immediately captivated Andrew.

"What's your name?" he asked quietly.

"Clarissa," she said, and dropped her head again. He wanted to help her so much, and it made him feel guilty that he had put the poor child through such a pointless ordeal.

The matron still looked affronted and with a sniff she said, "You can leave us now, child." Clarissa turned and walked towards the door. Looking at Louise the matron added, "I am sure you agree with me, Mrs Fraser, the girl's not at all suitable."

They both turned to Louise. Her face was alight, her eyes shining in a way Andrew had not seen since Robert's death. She stood up, walked quickly towards the child before she could reach the door, and stared into her black eyes.

"I think you're beautiful," Louise said, "and I do hope you will want to come and live with us."

CHAPTER
TWENTY THREE

'Order, order' had meant nothing to the British electorate until 1978 when the House passed a resolution allowing the proceedings in the Commons to be broadcast on radio. Simon had supported the motion on broadcasting, putting forward the argument that radio was a further extension of democracy as it showed the House at work and allowed the voters to know exactly what their elected representatives were up to. Simon listened carefully to a number of his supplementaries, and realised for the first time that he spoke a little too quickly when he had a minister on the run.

Raymond, on the other hand, did not support the motion as he feared that the cries of "Hear, hear" or "Shame" and the heckling of the Prime Minister would sound to listeners like schoolchildren in a playground squabble. Overhearing the words with only one's imagination to set the scene would, he believed, create a false impression about the many aspects of a member's daily duties. When one evening Raymond heard a parliamentary debate in which he had taken part he was delighted to discover his arguments carried so much conviction.

When Andrew heard his own voice on Radio Four one morning answering questions on defence issues he was suddenly aware that what he had always considered was a faint trace of a Scottish accent was in fact – when he was angry or excited – quite pronounced.

Charles found the morning programme an excellent way of catching up with any proceedings he had missed the previous day. As he now woke each morning alone, 'Yesterday in Parliament' became his constant companion. He hadn't been aware of how upper class he sounded until the occasion on which he followed Tom Carson. He had no intention of changing his voice for the radio.

When the Queen opened the new underground extension to Heathrow airport on 16 December 1977 Raymond was the minister commanded to be present. Joyce made one of her rare trips down to London as they were invited to join the Queen for lunch after the ceremony. When Joyce selected her new dress from Harvey Nichols, she stood in the little cubicle behind a drawn curtain to make sure it was possible for her to curtsey properly. "Good morning, Your Majesty," she practised with a slight wobble, to the bemusement of the shop assistant waiting patiently outside.

By the time she had returned to the flat Joyce was confident that she could carry out her part in the proceedings as well as any courtier. As she prepared for Raymond's return from the morning Cabinet meeting she hoped he would be pleased with her efforts. She had long given up hope of being a mother, but still liked to believe she could be a good wife. Raymond had forewarned her that he would have to change as soon as he arrived at the flat to be sure of being at Green Park before the Queen arrived. After they had accompanied an entourage to Heathrow on the new extension, a journey that would take thirty minutes, they were to return to Buckingham Palace for lunch. Raymond had already come in contact with his monarch on several occasions in his official capacity as a Cabinet minister, but for Joyce it was to be the first time she had been presented.

Once she had had her bath and dressed – she knew Raymond would never forgive her if she were the reason he was late – she began to lay out his clothes. Tail coat, grey pin-striped trousers, white shirt, stiff collar and a silver-grey tie, all hired that morning from Moss Bros. All that he still needed was a clean white handkerchief for his top pocket, just showing in a straight line, as the Duke of Edinburgh always wore his.

Joyce rummaged around in Raymond's chest of drawers, admiring the new shirts as she searched for a handkerchief.

When she first saw the scribbled note peaking out underneath the collar of a pink shirt lying near the bottom of the pile, she assumed it must be an old laundry bill. Then she spotted the word 'Darling'. She felt suddenly sick as she looked more closely.

> Darling Carrot Top,
>   If you ever wear this one I might even agree to marry you.
>
>   Kate.

Joyce sank on the end of the bed as the tears trickled down her face. Her perfect day was shattered. She knew at once what course of action she must take. She replaced the unworn shirt and closed the drawer, after first removing the note, and then sat alone in the drawing-room waiting for Raymond to return.

He arrived back at the flat with only a few minutes to spare and was delighted to find his wife changed and ready.

"I'm running it a bit close," he said, going straight into the bedroom.

Joyce followed and watched him don his morning dress suit. When he had straightened his tie in the mirror, she faced him.

"What do you think?" he asked, not noticing the slight paleness in her cheeks.

She hesitated. "You look fantastic, Raymond. Now come along or we'll be late, and that would never do."

When Ronnie Nethercote invited him to lunch at the Ritz, Simon knew things must be looking up again. After a drink in the lounge they were ushered to a corner table overlooking the park in the most palatial dining-room in London. Scattered around the other tables were men who were household names in Ronnie's world as well as in Simon's.

When the head waiter offered them menus Ronnie waved his hand and said, "Order the country vegetable soup, followed by beef off the trolley, take my word for it."

"Sounds like a safe bet," said Simon.

"Unlike our last little venture," Ronnie grunted. "How much are you still in hock because of the collapse of Nethercote and Company?"

"Fourteen thousand three hundred pounds when I last looked but I'm making inroads slowly. It's paying the interest before you can cut down on the capital that really hurts."

"How do you imagine I felt when we were overdrawn seven mill and then the bank decided to pull the rug from under my feet without any warning?"

"As two of the buttons on your waistcoat can no longer reach the holes they were originally tailored for, Ronnie, I must assume those problems are now a thing of the past."

"You're right." He laughed. "Which is why I invited you to lunch. The only person who ended up losing money on that deal was you. If you'd stayed on as the other directors did, at five grand a year, the company would still owe you £11,100 of earned income."

Simon groaned.

The carver wheeled the trolley of beef up to their table.

"Wait a moment, my boy, I haven't even begun. Morgan Grenfell want me to change the structure of the new company and will be injecting a large amount of cash. At the moment Whitechapel Properties – I hope you approve of the name – is still a one-hundred-pound off-the-shelf company. I own sixty per cent and the bank's got forty. Now before the new agreement is signed, I'm going to offer you –"

"Would you like it well done, as usual, Mr Nethercote?"

"Yes, Sam," said Ronnie, slipping the carver a pound note.

"I am going to offer you –"

"And your guest, sir?" the carver said, glancing at Simon.

"Medium, please."

"Yes, sir."

"I am going to offer you one per cent of the new company, in other words one share."

Simon didn't comment, feeling confident Ronnie still hadn't finished.

"Aren't you going to ask?" said Ronnie.

"Ask what?" said Simon.

"You politicians get dumber by the minute. If I am going to offer you a one-pound share, how much do you think I am going to demand in return?"

"Well, I can't believe it's going to be one pound," said Simon grinning.

"Wrong," said Ronnie. "One per cent of the company is yours for one pound."

"Will that be sufficient, sir?" said the carver, putting a plate of beef in front of Simon.

"Hold it, Sam," said Ronnie before Simon could reply. "I repeat I'm offering you one per cent of the company for one pound; now ask your question again, Sam."

"Will that be sufficient, sir?" repeated the carver.

"It's most generous," said Simon.

"Did you hear that, Sam?"

"I certainly did, sir."

"Right, Simon, you owe me a pound."

Simon laughed, removed his wallet from his inside pocket, took out a pound note and handed it over.

"Now the purpose of that little exercise," said Ronnie, turning back to the carver and pocketing the note, "was to prove that Sam here isn't the only person who could make a quid for himself this afternoon." Sam smiled, having no idea what Mr Nethercote was talking about, and placed a large plate of well-done beef in front of him.

Ronnie took out an envelope from his inside pocket and passed it to Simon.

"Do I open it now?" asked Simon.

"Yes – I want to see your reaction."

Simon opened the envelope and studied its contents. A certificate for one share in the new company with a true value of over £10,000.

"Well, well, what do you say?" said Ronnie.

"I'm speechless," said Simon.

"First politician I've known who's ever suffered from that problem."

Simon laughed. "Thank you, Ronnie. It's an incredibly generous gesture."

"No it's not. You were loyal to the old company, so why shouldn't you prosper with the new one?"

"That reminds me, does the name 'Archie Millburn' mean anything to you?" asked Simon.

Ronnie hesitated. "No, no, should it?"

"Only that I thought he might be the man who convinced Morgan Grenfell that you were worth bailing out."

"No, that name doesn't ring any bells. Mind you, Morgan Grenfell have never admitted where they obtained their information from but they knew every last detail about the old company. But if I come across the name Millburn I'll let you know. Enough of business. Fill me in on what's happening in your world. How's your lady wife?"

"Deceiving me."

"Deceiving you?"

"Yes, she's been putting on wigs and dressing up in strange clothes."

Clarissa wet her bed every night for the first month at Pelham Crescent but Louise never complained. Day by day Andrew watched as mother and daughter grew in mutual confidence. Clarissa assumed from her first meeting with Louise that she could talk as normally as any grown-up and chatted away to her night and day. Half the time Louise didn't reply, only because she couldn't get a word in.

Just when Andrew felt everything was getting back on a normal footing at home trouble erupted in Edinburgh. His General Management Committee, which now included five members of Militant Tendency, tabled a motion of no confidence in their member. Their leader, Frank Boyle, had been building up a power base with the sole intention, Andrew suspected, of ousting the member and taking over himself. He didn't discuss the problem with Louise, as the specialist had advised him to avoid any undue stress while Clarissa was settling in.

The five men who wanted Andrew removed had chosen the following Thursday to hold the meeting because they knew the annual Defence Review was due for a full debate in the House that day. If Andrew was unable to attend their meeting Frank Boyle knew they would have a better chance of winning their motion. If he did turn up to defend himself they were also aware that an embarrassing explanation would have to be made for his absence during the debate. When the Prime Minister was informed of the dilemma by the Chief Whip he had no hesitation in telling Andrew to forget the defence debate and go to Edinburgh.

Andrew took the shuttle up on Thursday afternoon and was met at the airport by his chairman, Hamish Ramsey.

"I apologise about you being put through this ordeal, Andrew," he said at once. "I can assure you it's none of my doing, but I must also warn you it's not the same Labour party that I joined over twenty years ago."

"How do you think the vote will go tonight?" asked Andrew.

"You'll win this time. The votes have been decided before the meeting takes place. There's only one waverer and he's so gutless that your very presence will stop him siding with the Trotskies."

When Andrew arrived at his Edinburgh headquarters he was left alone outside the committee room in a cold corridor for over an hour. He knew his opponents were holding things up in the hope he would become frustrated before he eventually had to face them. At last they invited him to join them and he immediately sensed what the Spanish Inquisition must have felt like: question after question from sour-faced men who had never helped him win the seat in the first place and were now alleging that he had shown scant interest in the constituency. Andrew stood his ground and became angry only when Frank Boyle referred to him as 'that son of a Tory'.

"When did you last see your father?" flashed through his mind.

"My father has done more for this city than you could ever hope to do in your lifetime," he told Boyle.

"Then why don't you join his party?" came back Boyle's retort.

Andrew was about to answer when Hamish Ramsey banged the table with his gavel and said, "Enough, enough. It's time to stop this squabbling and vote."

Andrew felt a stab of anxiety as the little slips were passed up to the chairman to be counted. The outcome was five-all and Hamish Ramsey immediately cast his vote in favour of Andrew.

"At least you'll be safe for the coming election, laddie," said Hamish as they drove to the Airport Hotel. "But I wouldn't like to account for much beyond that."

When Andrew arrived back in Pelham Crescent the next morning Louise greeted him at the door.

"Everything all right in Edinburgh?" she asked.

"Fine," said Andrew, taking her in his arms.

"Do you want to hear the good news?"

"Yes," said Andrew, smiling.

"Clarissa didn't wet her bed last night. Perhaps you should stay away more often."

Finally Charles knew he had to discuss what could be done about the stolen Holbein with his solicitor, Sir David Napley. Sir David instructed leading counsel and six weeks later Charles was told that if he sued the Holbein might eventually be returned but not before the story had been on the front page of every national paper. Charles had Albert Cruddick's opinion confirmed: "Grin and bear it."

Fiona had been out of touch for well over a year when the letter came. Charles immediately recognised her handwriting and ripped open the envelope. Only one glance at the writing was enough to make him tear up the missive and deposit the little pieces in the waste-paper basket by his desk. He left for the Commons in a rage.

All through the day he thought of the one word he had taken in from the scrawled hand. Holbein. When he returned from the Commons after the ten o'clock division Charles searched for the remains of the letter, which the daily had conscientiously deposited in the dustbin. After rummaging among potato peelings, eggshells and empty tins Charles spent over an hour Sellotaping the little pieces of paper together. Then he read the letter carefully.

24 The Boltons,
London, S W 10
11 October 1978

Dear Charles,
   Enough time has now passed for us to try and treat each
other in a civilised way. Alexander and I wish to marry
and Veronica Dalglish has agreed to an immediate divorce and has not insisted we wait the necessary two years
to establish separation.

"You'll have to wait every day of the two years, you bitch,"
he said out loud. Then he came to the one sentence for which
he was searching.

   I realise this might not immediately appeal to you but if
you felt able to fall in with our plans I would be happy to
return the Holbein immediately.
                                 Yours ever,
                                 Fiona.

He crumpled up the paper in the ball of his hand before
dropping it on the fire.

Charles remained awake into the early hours considering
his reply.

At a Thursday morning Cabinet meeting James Callaghan
informed his colleagues that the Liberal leader, David Steel,
was not willing to continue the Lib/Lab pact after the end of
the current session.

"That can only mean one thing," the Prime Minister
continued. "We must all be prepared for a general election at
any time from now on. I am confident we can hold out until
Christmas, but not for much longer after that."

Raymond was saddened by the news. He felt after two
years in the Cabinet that he was just beginning to be of some
use to the Department of Trade: the changes he was implementing were starting to take effect. But he knew he
needed considerably more time if he hoped to leave a permanent impression on his ministry.

Kate's enthusiasm spurred him on to work even longer

hours and to push through as many of his innovations before the next election as possible.

"I'm trying my damnedest," he told her. "But do remember that the speed of the bureaucratic machine makes British Rail look like Concorde."

The Labour Government struggled on through a session dubbed by the press as 'the winter of discontent': trying to push bills through the House, losing a clause here and a clause there, Raymond was only too delighted to have reached the recess in one piece.

Raymond spent a cold Christmas in Leeds with Joyce. He returned to London early in the New Year aware it could not be long before the Conservatives felt assured enough to put down a motion of no confidence. When it eventually was tabled no one in Parliament was surprised.

The debate caused a day of intense excitement, not least because a strike had caused the Commons bars to run dry and thirsty members were huddled together in the lobbies, the tea room, the smoking room and the dining-rooms. Harassed Whips rushed hither and thither checking lists, ringing up hospitals, board rooms and even great-aunts in their efforts to track down the last few elusive members.

When Mrs Thatcher rose on 6 April to address a packed House the tension was so electric that the Speaker had considerable difficulty keeping control of the over-charged conductors. She addressed the House in firm, strident tones which brought her own side to their feet when she resumed her place. The atmosphere was no different when it was the turn of the Prime Minister to reply. Both leaders made a gallant effort to rise above the petulance of their adversaries but it was the Speaker who had the last word:

"The Ayes to the right 311,
The Noes to the left 310.
The Ayes have it, the Ayes have it."

Pandemonium broke out. Opposition members waved their order papers in triumph, knowing the Prime Minister would now have to call a general election. James Callaghan immediately announced the dissolution of Parliament and after an audience with the Queen election day was set for 3 May 1979.

At the end of that momentous week those few members left at Westminster were stunned by an explosion in the Members' Car Park. Airey Neave, the Shadow spokesman on Northern Ireland, had been blown up by Irish terrorists as he was driving up the exit ramp to leave the Commons. He died on his way to hospital.

Members hurried back to their constituencies. Both Raymond and Andrew found it hard to escape from their departments at such short notice, but Charles and Simon were out in their respective high streets shaking hands with the voters by the morning following the Queen's proclamation.

For three weeks the arguments about who was competent to govern went back and forth, but on 3 May the British people elected their first woman Prime Minister and gave her party a majority of forty-three in the Commons.

Andrew's sixth election turned out to be his most unpleasant to date and he was only glad that he had left Louise and Clarissa in London. Jock McPherson, still the SNP candidate, called him every name under the sun and added one or two new ones in the evening, while the Trotskyites who had voted against him on the committee proved no help when it came to gathering in the votes on election day. But the citizens of Edinburgh, knowing nothing of the committee's opinions, sent Andrew back to Parliament with a majority of 3,738. The Scottish Nationalist vote crumbled, leaving only two members in the House – and Jock McPherson back in Scotland.

Raymond's vote in Leeds was slightly reduced, while Joyce won the office pool for predicting most accurately what her husband's majority would be. He was beginning to accept that she knew more about the constituency than he ever would.

A few days later when Raymond returned to London Kate

had never seen him so depressed and decided to hold off telling him her own news when he said, "God knows how many years it will be before I can be of some use again."

"You can spend your time in Opposition making sure the Government doesn't dismantle all your achievements."

"With a majority of forty-three they could dismantle me if they wanted to," he told her. He placed the red leather box marked 'Secretary of State for Trade' in the corner, next to the ones marked 'Minister of State at the Department of Trade' and 'Parliamentary Under-Secretary at the Department of Employment'.

"They're only your first three," Kate tried to reassure him.

Simon increased his majority at Pucklebridge to 19,461, notching up another record after which he and Elizabeth spent the weekend in their cottage with the boys waiting for Mrs Thatcher to select her team.

Simon was surprised when the Prime Minister phoned personally and asked if he could come up to see her in Downing Street: that was an honour usually afforded only to Cabinet ministers. He tried not to anticipate what she might have in mind.

He duly travelled up from the country and spent thirty minutes alone with the new Prime Minister. When he heard what Mrs Thatcher wanted him to do he was touched that she had taken the trouble to see him in person. She knew that no member ever found it easy to accede to such a request but Simon accepted without hesitation. Mrs Thatcher added that no announcement would be made until he had had time to talk his decision over with Elizabeth.

Simon thanked her and travelled back to his cottage in Pucklebridge. Elizabeth sat in silence as she listened to Simon's account of his conversation with the Prime Minister.

"Oh, my God," she said, when he had finished. "She's offered you the chance to be a Minister of State, but in return we have no certainty of peace for the rest of our lives."

"I can still say no," Simon assured her.

"That would be the act of a coward," said Elizabeth, "and you've never been that."

"Then I'll phone the Prime Minister and tell her I accept."

"I ought to congratulate you," she said. "But it never crossed my mind for one moment . . ."

Charles's was one of the few Tory seats in which the majority went down. A missing wife is hard to explain especially when it is common knowledge that she is living with the former chairman of the adjoining constituency. Charles had faced a certain degree of embarrassment with his local committee and he made sure that the one woman who couldn't keep her mouth shut was told his version of the story 'in strictest confidence'. Any talk of removing him had died when it was rumoured that Charles would stand as an independent candidate if replaced. When the vote was counted Sussex Downs still returned Charles to Westminster with a majority of 20,176. He sat alone in Eaton Square over the weekend, but no one contacted him. He read in the Monday *Telegraph* – how he missed *The Times* – the full composition of the new Tory team.

The only surprise was Simon Kerslake's appointment as Minister of State for Northern Ireland.

CHAPTER
TWENTY FOUR

"Well, say something."

"Very flattering, Kate. What reason did you give for turning the offer down?" asked Raymond, who had been surprised to find her waiting for him at the flat.

"I didn't need a reason."

"How did they feel about that?"

"You don't seem to understand. I accepted their offer."

Raymond removed his glasses and tried to take in what Kate was saying. He steadied himself by holding on to the mantelpiece.

Kate continued. "I had to, darling."

"Because the offer was too tempting?"

"No, you silly man. It had nothing to do with the offer as such, but it gives me the chance to stop letting my life drift. Can't you see it was *because* of you?"

"Because of me you're going to leave London and go back to New York."

"To work in New York and start getting my life in perspective. Raymond, don't you realise it's been five years?"

"I know how long it is and how many times I've asked you to marry me."

"We both know that isn't the answer; Joyce can't be brushed aside that easily. And it could even end up being the single reason you fail in your career."

"We can overcome that problem, given time," Raymond reasoned.

"That sounds fine now, until the party wins the next

election and lesser men than you are offered the chance to shape future policy."

"Can't I do anything to make you change your mind?"

"Nothing, my darling. I've handed Chase my resignation and begin my new job with Chemical Bank in a month."

"Only four weeks," said Raymond.

"Yes, four weeks. I had to hold off telling you until I had severed all the bonds, had resigned and could be sure of not letting you talk me out of it."

"Do you know how much I love you?"

"I hope enough to let me go, before it's too late."

Charles would not have normally accepted the invitation. Lately he had found cocktail parties to consist of nothing but silly little bits of food, never being able to get the right drink and rarely enjoying the trivial conversation. But when he glanced on his mantelpiece and saw an 'At Home' from Lady Carrington he felt it might be an amusing break from the routine he had fallen into since Fiona had left. He was also keen to discover more about the rumoured squabbles in Cabinet over expenditure cuts. He checked his tie in the mirror, removed an umbrella from the hat stand and left Eaton Square for Ovington Square.

He and Fiona had been apart for nearly two years. Charles had heard from several sources that his wife had now moved in with Dalglish on a permanent basis despite his unwillingness to co-operate over a divorce. He had remained discreetly silent on his wife's new life except for one or two selected titbits dropped selectively in the ears of well-chosen gossips. That way he had elicited for himself sympathy from every quarter while remaining the magnanimous loyal husband.

Charles had spent most of his spare time in the Commons, and his most recent budget speech had been well received both by the House and the national press. During the committee stage of the Finance Bill he had allowed himself to be burdened with a lot of the donkey work. Clive Reynolds had been able to point out discrepancies in some clauses of the bill, which Charles passed on to a grateful Chancellor.

Thus Charles received praise for saving the Government from any unnecessary embarrassment. At the same time he disassociated himself from the 'wets' as the Prime Minister referred to those of her colleagues who did not unreservedly support her monetarist policies. If he could keep up his work output he was confident he would be preferred in the first reshuffle.

By spending his mornings at the bank and afternoons and evenings in the Commons Charles managed to combine both worlds with the minimum of interruption from his almost non-existent private life.

He arrived at Lord Carrington's front door a little after six-forty-five. A maid answered his knock, and he walked straight through to a drawing-room that could have held fifty guests and very nearly did.

He even managed to be served with the right blend of whisky before joining his colleagues from both the Upper and Lower Houses. He saw her first over the top of Alec Pimkin's balding head.

"Who is she?" asked Charles, not expecting Pimkin to know.

"Amanda Wallace," said Pimkin, glancing over his shoulder. "I could tell you a thing or two . . ." but Charles had already left his colleague in mid-sentence. The sexual aura of the woman was attested to by the fact that she spent the entire evening surrounded by attentive men, like moths around a candle. If Charles had not been one of the tallest men in the room he might never have seen the flame. It took him another ten minutes to reach her side of the room where Julian Ridsdale, a colleague of Charles's in the Commons, introduced them only to find himself dragged away moments later by his wife.

Charles was left staring at a woman who would have looked beautiful in anything from a ballgown to a towel. Her slim body was encased in a white silk dress, and her fair hair touched her bare shoulders. But what struck Charles most was the translucent texture of her skin. It had been years since he had found it so hard to make conversation.

"I expect you already have a dinner engagement?"

Charles asked her in the brief intervals before the vultures closed in again.

"No," she replied and smiled encouragingly. She agreed to meet him at Walton's in an hour's time. Charles dutifully began to circulate round the room but it was not long before he found his eyes drawn back to her. Every time she smiled he found himself responding but Amanda didn't notice because she was always being flattered by someone else. When he left an hour later he smiled directly at her, and this time did win a knowing grin.

Charles sat alone at a corner table in Walton's for another hour. He was just about to admit defeat and return home when she was ushered to the table. The anger that had developed from being kept waiting was forgotten the moment she smiled and said, "Hello, Charlie."

He was not surprised to learn that his tall, elegant companion earned her living as a model. As far as Charles could see she could have modelled anything from tooth paste to stockings.

"Shall we have coffee at my place?" Charles asked after an unhurried dinner. She nodded her assent and he called for the bill, not checking the addition for the first time in many years.

He was delighted, if somewhat surprised, when she rested her head on his shoulder in the cab on the way back to Eaton Square. By the time they had been dropped off at Eaton Square most of Amanda's lipstick had been removed. The cabbie thanked Charles for his excessive tip and couldn't resist adding, "Good luck, sir."

Charles never did get round to making the coffee. When he woke in the morning, to his surprise he found her even more captivating, and for the first time in weeks quite forgot 'Yesterday in Parliament'.

Elizabeth listened carefully as the man from Special Branch explained how the safety devices worked. She tried to make Peter and Michael concentrate on not pressing the red buttons that were in every room and would bring the police at a moment's notice. The electricians had already wired the rooms in Beaufort Street and now they had nearly finished at the cottage.

At Beaufort Street a uniformed policeman stood watch by the front door night and day. In Pucklebridge, because the cottage was so isolated, they had to be surrounded by arc lamps that could be switched on at a moment's notice.

"It must be damned inconvenient," suggested Archie Millburn during dinner. After his arrival at the cottage he had been checked by security patrols with dogs before he was able to shake hands with his host.

"Inconvenient is putting it mildly," said Elizabeth. "Last week Peter broke a window with a cricket ball and we were immediately lit up like a Christmas tree."

"Do you get any privacy?" asked Archie.

"Only when we're in bed. Even then you can wake up to find you're being licked; you sigh and it turns out to be an Alsatian."

Archie laughed. "Lucky Alsatian."

Every morning when Simon was driven to work he was accompanied by two detectives, a car in front and another to the rear. He had always thought there were only two ways from Beaufort Street to Westminster. For the first twenty-one days as minister he never travelled the same route twice.

Whenever he was due to fly to Belfast he was not informed of either his departure time or from which airport he would be leaving. While the inconvenience drove Elizabeth mad the tension had the opposite effect on Simon. Despite everything, it was the first time in his life he didn't feel it was necessary to explain to anyone why he had chosen to be a politician.

Inch by inch he worked to try to bring the Catholics and Protestants together. Often after a month of inches he would lose a yard in one day, but he never displayed any anger or prejudice except perhaps, as he told Elizabeth, "a prejudice for common sense". Given time, Simon believed, a break-through would be possible – if only he could find on both sides a handful of men of goodwill.

During the all-party meetings both factions began to treat him with respect and – privately – with affection. Even the

Opposition spokesman at Westminster openly acknowledged that Simon Kerslake was turning out to be an excellent choice for the 'dangerous and thankless ministry'.

Andrew also knew he would require a handful of men of
goodwill when Hamish Ramsey resigned as chairman of
Edinburgh Carlton.

"I don't need the hassle any longer," Hamish told him.
"I'm not in politics for the same reason as that bunch of
trouble-makers." Andrew reluctantly let him go and had to
work hard to convince Hamish's deputy, David Connaught,
that he should stand in his place. When David finally agreed
to allow his name to go forward he was immediately opposed
by Frank Boyle, who had already made his opinion of the
sitting member abundantly clear. Andrew canvassed every
person on the committee during the run up to election for the
new chairman. He estimated the voting was going to be
seven-all, which would still allow Hamish to give his casting
vote in favour of Connaught.

Andrew phoned Hamish at home an hour before the
meeting was due to begin. "I'll call and leave a message for
you at the House when it's all over," Ramsey told him.
"Don't worry, you're safe this time. At least I'll leave you
with the right chairman."

Andrew left Pelham Crescent after he had tucked Clarissa
up in bed and read her another chapter of *Jacob Two Two*. He
told Louise he would return from Westminster straight after
the ten o'clock vote. He sat in the Chamber and listened to
Charles Seymour deliver a well-argued discourse on monetarist policy. Andrew didn't always agree with the logic of
Seymour's case and he had never cared much for the man
himself: but he had to admit that such talent was wasted on
the back benches.

During the speech a note was passed to Andrew by an
attendant. He unfolded the little white slip. Stuart Gray, the
lobby correspondent for *The Scotsman*, needed to speak to him
urgently. Andrew slipped from his place on the front bench,
stepping over the feet of Shadow ministers still intent on

Seymour's speech. He felt like a small boy leaving a cinema in the middle of a film in pursuit of an ice lolly. He found Gray waiting for him in the Members' Lobby.

Andrew had known Stuart since he had first entered the House, when the journalist had told him, "You and I are each other's bread and butter, so we'd better make a sandwich." Andrew had laughed, and they had had few differences of opinion in the fifteen years since. Stuart suggested that they go down to Annie's Bar for a drink. They strolled along the corridor and took the stairway near the tea room to the basement bar, named after a former barlady.

Andrew settled down on a couch at the side of a pillar while Stuart went up to the bar to order two whiskies.

"Cheers," said the journalist, putting Andrew's glass down on the table in front of him.

Andrew took a long gulp. "Now, what can I do for you?" he asked. "Is my father being tiresome again?"

"I'd call him a supporter compared with your new chairman."

"What do you mean? I've always found David Connaught to be a sound fellow myself," said Andrew, a little pompously.

"I'm not interested in your views of David Connaught," said Stuart. "I want an opinion on your new chairman, Frank Boyle." The journalist sounded very much on the record.

"What?"

"He won the vote tonight seven to six."

"But . . ." Andrew fell silent.

"Come on, Andrew. We both know the bloody man's a Commie trouble-maker, and my editor is screaming for a quote."

"I can't say anything, Stuart, not until I know all the facts."

"I've just told you all the facts: now, are you going to give me a quote?"

"Yes." Andrew paused. "I am sure Mr Boyle will continue to serve in the best traditions of the Labour party, and I look forward to working in close co-operation with him."

"Balls," said Stuart. "They will only print that in Pseuds Corner in *Private Eye*."

"It's the only quote you're going to get out of me tonight," said Andrew.

Stuart looked at his friend and could see lines on his face that he had never noticed before. "I'm sorry," he said. "I went too far. Please get in touch when the time's right. With that bastard Boyle in charge you might be in need of my help."

Andrew thanked him absent-mindedly, downed his whisky in one gulp, then walked out of Annie's Bar and along the terrace corridor to the phone booths at the foot of the stairs. He dialled Ramsey's home number.

"What in heaven's name happened?" was all he could ask.

"One of our voters didn't show," said Hamish Ramsey. "Claimed he was held up in Glasgow and couldn't get back in time. I was just about to ring you."

"Bloody irresponsible of him," said Andrew. "Why didn't you postpone the vote?"

"I tried to, but Frank Boyle produced the rule book. 'Any motion proposed fourteen days before a meeting cannot be postponed without the agreement of the proposer and seconder.' I'm sorry, Andrew: my hands were tied."

"It's not your fault, Hamish. I couldn't have had a better chairman than you. I'm only sorry you didn't leave in a blaze of glory."

Hamish chuckled. "Don't you ever forget, Andrew, the voters have the last word in a democracy. In Edinburgh you're the man who has served them for more than fifteen years and they won't forget that quickly."

"You can get dressed now, Miss Wallace," said the gynaecologist returning to her desk.

Amanda started to slip back into her latest Dior outfit – a light blue denim suit bought the previous day in Conduit Street in an attempt to cheer herself up.

"It's the third time in five years," said Elizabeth Kerslake, leafing through the confidential file and trying not to sound accusing.

"I may as well book into the same clinic as before," said Amanda, matter-of-factly.

Elizabeth was determined to make her reconsider the consequences. "Is there any chance that the father would want you to have this child?"

"I can't be certain who the father is," said Amanda, looking shame-faced for the first time. "You see, it was the end of one relationship and the beginning of another."

Elizabeth made no comment other than to say, "I estimate that you are at least eight weeks pregnant, but it could be as much as twelve." She looked back down at the file. "Have you considered giving birth to the child and then bringing it up yourself?"

"Good heavens, no," said Amanda. "I make my living as a model, not as a mother."

"So be it," Elizabeth sighed, closing the file. "I'll make all the" – she avoided saying usual – "necessary arrangements. You must see your GP immediately and ask him to sign the required clearance forms. Then phone me in about a week, rather than make the trip down to Pucklebridge again."

Amanda nodded her agreement. "Could you let me know what the clinic is going to charge this time? I'm sure they are suffering from inflation like the rest of us."

"Yes, I will look into that, Miss Wallace," said Elizabeth, just managing to keep her temper as she showed Amanda to the door. Once her patient had left Elizabeth picked up the confidential file from her desk, walked over to the cabinet and flicked through S, T, U, until she found the right slot. Perhaps she should have been sterner with her but she was convinced that it would have made little difference. She paused, wondering if having the child might change the woman's cavalier attitude to life.

Charles returned home after the debate feeling pleased with himself. He had received praise for his latest speech from every wing of the party, and the Chief Whip had made it quite clear that his efforts on the Finance Bill had not gone unnoticed.

As he drove back to Eaton Square he wound down the car

window and let the fresh air rush in and the cigarette smoke out. His smile widened at the thought of Amanda sitting at home waiting for him. It had been a glorious couple of months. At forty-eight he was experiencing realities he had never even dreamed of in fantasy. As each day passed he expected the infatuation to wear off, but instead it only grew more intense. Even the memory the day after was better than anything he had experienced in the past.

Once the Holbein had been restored to his dining-room wall Charles planned to talk to Amanda about their future; if she said "Yes" he would even be willing to grant Fiona a divorce. He parked the car and took out his latch key, but she was already there opening the front door to throw her arms around him.

"Why don't we go straight to bed?" she greeted him.

Charles would have been shocked had Fiona uttered such feelings even once in their fifteen years of married life, but Amanda made it appear quite natural. She was already lying naked on the bed before Charles could get his waistcoat off. After they had made love and she was settled in his arms Amanda told him she would have to go away for a few days.

"Why?" said Charles, puzzled.

"I'm pregnant," she said matter-of-factly. "I've already booked myself into a clinic. Don't worry. I'll be as right as rain in no time."

"But why don't we have the baby?" said a delighted Charles, looking down into her grey eyes. "I've always wanted a son."

"Don't be silly, Charlie. There's years ahead of me for that."

"But if we were married?"

"You're already married. Besides, I'm only twenty-six."

"I can get a divorce in a moment and life wouldn't be so bad with me, would it?"

"Of course not, Charlie. You're the first man I've ever really cared for."

Charles smiled hopefully. "So you'll think about the idea?"

Amanda looked into Charles's eyes anxiously. "If I *were* to have a child I do hope he'd have blue eyes like yours."

"Will you marry me?" he asked.

"I'll think about it. In any case, you may have changed your mind by morning."

Raymond drove Kate to Heathrow. He was wearing the pink shirt she had chosen for him; she was wearing the little red box. He had so much to tell her on the way to the airport that she hardly spoke at all. The last four weeks had gone by in a flash. It was the first time he had been grateful for being in Opposition.

"It's all right, Carrot Top. Don't fuss. We'll see each other whenever you come to New York."

"I've only been to America twice in my life," he said. She tried to smile.

Once she had checked her eleven bags in at the counter, a process that seemed to take forever, she was allocated a seat.

"Flight BA 107, gate number fourteen, boarding in ten minutes," she was informed.

"Thank you," she said and rejoined Raymond, who was sitting on the end of an already crowded tubular settee. He had bought two plastic cups of coffee while Kate had been checking in. They were both already cold. They sat and held hands like children who had met on a summer holiday and had now to return to separate schools.

"Promise me you won't start wearing contact lenses the moment I've gone."

"Yes, I can promise you that," said Raymond, touching the bridge of his glasses.

"I've so much I still want to tell you," she said.

He turned towards her. "Vice-presidents of banks shouldn't cry," he said, brushing a tear from her cheek. "The customers will realise you're a soft touch."

"Neither should Cabinet ministers," she replied. "All I wanted to say, is that if you really feel . . ." she began.

"Hello, Mr Gould."

They both looked up to see a broad smile spread across the face of someone whose tan proved that he had just arrived from a sunnier climate.

"I'm Bert Cox," he said, thrusting out his hand, "I don't suppose you remember me." Raymond let go of Kate's hand and shook Mr Cox's.

"We were at the same primary school in Leeds, Ray. Mind you, that was a million light years ago. You've come a long way since then."

How can I get rid of him? wondered Raymond desperately.

"This is the missus," Bert Cox continued obliviously, gesturing at the silent woman in a flowery dress by his side. She smiled but didn't speak. "She sits on some committee with Joyce, don't you, love?" he said, not waiting for her reply.

"This is the final call for Flight BA 107, now boarding at gate number fourteen."

"We always vote for you, of course," continued Bert Cox. "The missus" – he pointed to the lady in the flowered dress again – "thinks you'll be Prime Minister. I always say –"

"I must go, Raymond," said Kate, "or I'll miss my flight."

"Can you excuse me for a moment, Mr Cox?" said Raymond.

"Delighted. I'll wait. I don't often get a chance to have a word with my MP."

Raymond walked with Kate towards the barrier. "I am sorry about this. I'm afraid they're all like that in Leeds – hearts of gold, but never stop talking. What were you going to say?"

"Only that I would have been happy to live in Leeds, however cold it is. I never envied anyone in my life, but I do envy Joyce." She kissed him gently on the cheek and walked towards the barrier before he could reply. She didn't look back.

"Are you feeling all right, madam?" asked an airport official as she went through the security barrier.

"I'm fine," said Kate, brushing aside her tears. She walked slowly towards gate fourteen, happy that he had worn the pink shirt for the first time. She wondered if he had found the note she had left underneath the collar. If he had asked her just one more time . . .

Raymond stood alone and then turned to walk aimlessly towards the exit.

"An American lady, I would have guessed," said Mr Cox rejoining him. "I'm good on accents."

"Yes," said Raymond, still alone.

"A friend of yours?" he asked.

"My best friend," said Raymond.

When ten days had passed and Elizabeth had not yet heard from Miss Wallace she decided she had no choice but to contact her direct. She flicked through her personal file and noted the latest number Amanda had given.

Elizabeth picked up the phone and dialled. It was some time before anybody answered.

"730-9712. Charles Seymour speaking." There was a long silence. "Is anyone there?"

Elizabeth couldn't reply. She replaced the receiver and felt her whole body come out in a cold sweat. She closed Amanda Wallace's file and returned it to the cabinet.

CHAPTER
TWENTY FIVE

Simon had spent nearly a year preparing a White Paper entitled 'A Genuine Partnership for Ireland' for consideration by the House. The Government's aim was to bring north and south together for a period of ten years at the end of which a more permanent arrangement could be considered. During those ten years both sides would remain under the direct rule of Westminster and Dublin. Both Protestants and Catholics had contributed to 'the Charter', as the press had dubbed the complex agreement. With considerable skill, patience and fortitude Simon had convinced the political leaders of Northern Ireland to append their names to the final draft when and if it was approved by the House.

He admitted to Elizabeth that the agreement was only a piece of paper, but he felt it was a foundation stone on which the House could base an eventual settlement. On both sides of the Irish Sea politicians and journalists alike were describing the Charter as a genuine breakthrough.

The Secretary of State for Northern Ireland was to present the White Paper to the Commons when Irish business was next scheduled on the parliamentary calendar. Simon, as the architect of the Charter, had been asked to deliver the winding-up speech on behalf of the Government. He knew that if the House backed the concept of the document he might then be allowed to prepare a parliamentary bill and thus overcome a problem so many other politicians had failed to solve before him. If he succeeded Simon felt that all the sacrifices he had made in the past would prove worthwhile.

When Elizabeth sat down to read through the final draft in Simon's study that evening even she admitted for the first time that she was pleased he had accepted the Irish appointment.

"Now, embryonic statesman," she continued, "are you ready for your dinner like every normal human being at this time in the evening?"

"I certainly am." Simon moved his copy of the 129-page Charter from the dining-room table to the sideboard, planning to go over it yet again once he had finished dinner.

"Damn," he heard Elizabeth say from the kitchen.

"What is it?" he asked, not looking up from his toy, like a child studying a jigsaw and wondering where a colourless piece fitted in.

"I'm out of Bisto."

"I'll go and buy some," Simon volunteered. The two policemen on the door were chatting when the minister came out.

"Come on, my wife needs a packet of Bisto, so affairs of state must be held up for the time being."

"I'm very sorry, sir," said the sergeant. "When I was told you would be in for the rest of the evening I allowed the official car to go off duty. But Constable Barker can accompany you."

"That's no problem," said Simon. "We can take my wife's car. I'll just find out where she's parked the damn thing."

He slipped back into the house but returned a moment later. "Been in the force long?" he asked Constable Barker as they walked down the road together.

"Not that long, sir. Started on the beat just over a year ago."

"Are you married, Constable?"

"Fine chance on my salary, sir."

"Then you won't have encountered the problem of being Bisto-less."

"They've never heard of gravy in the police canteen, sir."

"You should try the House of Commons sometime," said Simon. "I don't think you'd find it any better – the food, that is, not to mention the salary."

The two men laughed as they headed off towards the car. "What does your wife think of the Mini Metro?" the constable asked as Simon put the key in the door.

Like everyone else in Beaufort Street, Elizabeth heard the explosion, but she was the first to realise what it had to be. She ran out of the front door in search of the duty policeman. She saw him running down the road and quickly followed.

The little red Metro was scattered all over the side street, the glass from its windows making the pavement look as though there had been a sudden hailstorm.

When the sergeant saw the severed head he pulled Elizabeth back. Two other bodies lay motionless in the road, one of them an old lady with the contents of her shopping bag spread around her.

Within minutes, six police cars had arrived and Special Branch officers had cordoned off the area with white ribbon. An ambulance rushed the bodies to Westminster Hospital. The job of picking up the remains of the police constable needed a very resolute man.

Elizabeth was taken to the hospital in a police car, where she learned that the old lady had died before arrival while her husband was on the critical list. When she told the surgeon in charge that she was a doctor he was more forthcoming and answered her questions candidly. Simon was suffering from multiple fractures, a dislocated hip and a severe loss of blood. The only question he was not willing to be drawn on was when she asked about his chances.

She sat alone outside the operating theatre waiting for any scrap of news. Hour after hour went by, and Elizabeth kept recalling Simon's words: "Be tolerant. Always remember there are still men of goodwill in Northern Ireland." She found it almost impossible not to scream, to think of the whole lot of them as evil murderers. Her husband had worked tirelessly on their behalf. He wasn't a Catholic or a Protestant, just a man trying to do an impossible task. Although she couldn't help thinking that it was she who had been the intended target.

Another hour passed.

A tired, grey-faced man came out into the corridor through

the flapping rubber doors. "He's still hanging on, Dr Kerslake. Your husband has the constitution of an ox; most people would have let go by now." He smiled. "Can I find you a room so that you can get some sleep?"

"No, thank you," Elizabeth replied. "I'd prefer to be near him."

She rang home to check the children were coping and her mother answered the phone. She had rushed over the moment she had heard the news and was keeping them away from the radio and television.

"How is he?" she asked.

Elizabeth told her mother all she knew, then spoke to the children.

"We're taking care of Grandmother," Peter told her.

Elizabeth couldn't hold back the tears. "Thank you, darling," she said, and quickly replaced the receiver. She returned to the bench outside the operating theatre, kicked off her shoes, curled her legs under her body and tried to snatch some sleep.

She woke with a start in the early morning. Her back hurt and her neck was stiff. She walked slowly up and down the corridor in her bare feet stretching her aching limbs, searching for anyone who could tell her some news. Finally a nurse brought her a cup of tea and assured her that her husband was still alive. But what did 'still alive' mean? She stood and watched the grim faces coming out of the operating theatre and tried not to recognise the tell-tale signs of despair. The surgeon told her she ought to go home and rest: they would have nothing to tell her for several hours. A policeman kept all journalists – who were arriving by the minute – in an ante-room off the main corridor.

Elizabeth didn't move from the corridor for another day and another night, and she didn't return home until the surgeon told her it was all over.

When she heard the news she fell on her knees and wept.

"God must want the Irish problem solved as well," he added. "Your husband will live, Dr Kerslake, but it's a miracle."

"Got time for a quick one?" asked Alexander Dalglish.

"If you press me," said Pimkin.

"Fiona," shouted Alexander. "It's Alec Pimkin, he's dropped in for a drink."

She came through to join them. She was dressed in a bright yellow frock and had allowed her hair to grow down past her shoulders.

"It suits you," said Pimkin, tapping his bald head.

"Thank you," said Fiona. "Why don't we all go through to the drawing-room?"

Pimkin happily obeyed and had soon settled himself into Alexander's favourite chair.

"What will you have?" asked Fiona, as she stood by the drinks cabinet.

"A large gin with just a rumour of tonic."

"Well, how's the constituency faring since my resignation?"

"It ticks along, trying hard to survive the biggest sex scandal since Profumo," chuckled Pimkin.

"I only hope it hasn't harmed your election chances," said Alexander.

"Not a bit of it, old fellow," said Pimkin, accepting the large Beefeaters and tonic Fiona handed him. "On the contrary, it's taken their minds off me for a change."

Alexander laughed.

"In fact," continued Pimkin, "interest in the date of your wedding has only been eclipsed by Charles and Lady Di. Gossips tell me," he continued, clearly enjoying himself, "that my Honourable friend, the member for Sussex Downs, made you wait the full two years before you could place an announcement in *The Times*."

"Yes, that's true," said Fiona. "Charles didn't even answer my letters during that period, but lately when any problem's arisen he's been almost friendly."

"Could that be because he also wants to place an announcement in *The Times*?" said Pimkin, downing his gin quickly in the hope of being offered a second.

"What do you mean?"

"The fact that he has lost his heart to another."

"Another?" said Alexander Dalglish.

"No less –" Pimkin paused as he sipped pointedly at his empty glass "– than Miss Amanda Wallace, only daughter of the late and little lamented Brigadier Boozer Wallace."

"Amanda Wallace?" said Fiona in disbelief. "Surely he's got more sense than that."

"I don't think it has a lot to do with sense," said Pimkin holding out his glass. "More to do with sex."

"But he's old enough to be her father."

"If that is the case," said Pimkin, "Charles can always adopt her."

Alexander laughed.

"But I am informed by a reliable source," continued Pimkin, "that marriage is being proposed."

"You can't be serious," said Fiona flatly.

"The subject has most certainly been broached for she is undoubtedly pregnant and Charles is hoping for a son," said Pimkin in triumph as he accepted his second double gin.

"That's not possible," said Fiona under her breath.

"And I am also informed," continued Pimkin, "that some of the more ungenerous of our brethren are already suggesting the name of several candidates for the role of father."

"Alec, you're incorrigible."

"My dear, it is common knowledge that Amanda has slept with half the Cabinet and a considerable cross section of back-benchers."

"Stop exaggerating," said Fiona.

"And what's more," continued Pimkin as if he hadn't heard her, "she has only stopped short of the Labour front bench because her mother told her they were common and she might catch something from them."

Alexander laughed again. "But surely Charles hasn't fallen for the pregnancy trick?"

"Hook, line and sinker. He's like an Irishman who's been locked into a Guinness brewery over the weekend. Dear Amanda has my Honourable friend uncorking her at every opportunity."

"But she's plain stupid," said Alexander. "The only time I

met her she assured me that Michael Parkinson was turning out to be an excellent chairman of the party."

"Stupid she may well be," said Pimkin, "but plain she is not and together, I'm told, they are updating the *Kama Sutra*."

"Enough, Alec, enough," said Fiona laughing.

"You're right," said Pimkin, aware that his glass was nearly empty once again. "A man of my impeccable reputation cannot afford to be seen associating with people living in sin. I must leave immediately, darlings," he said, rising to his feet. Pimkin put his glass down and Alexander accompanied him to the front door.

As it closed Alexander turned to Fiona. "Never short of useful information, our former member," he said.

"I agree," said Fiona. "So much gleaned for such a small investment in Beefeaters."

As Alexander walked back into the drawing-room he added, "Does it change your plans for the return of the Holbein?"

"Not in any way," said Fiona.

"So you'll still be at Sotheby's next week for their Old Masters sale?"

Fiona smiled. "Certainly. And if the price is right we won't have to worry about what we give Charles for a wedding present."

Three weeks after the bombing Simon left the Westminster Hospital on crutches, Elizabeth by his side. His right leg had been so shattered that he had been told he would never walk properly again. As he stepped out on to Horseferry Road a hundred cameras flashed to meet their editors' demand to capture the instant hero. He smiled as if there were no pain. "Don't let those murderers think they got to you," he was warned by both sides. Elizabeth's smile showed only relief that her husband was still alive.

After three weeks of complete rest Simon returned to his Irish Charter against doctor's orders, knowing the document was still due to be debated in the House in less than a fortnight. The Secretary of State and the other Minister of

State for Northern Ireland visited him at home on several occasions and it was agreed that the Minister of State would take over Simon's responsibilities temporarily and deliver the winding-up speech. During his absence the whole Northern Ireland office grew to realise just how much work Simon had put into the Charter, and no one was at all complacent about taking his place.

The attempt on Simon's life and the build up to the special debate on the Charter became of such national interest that the BBC decided to broadcast the entire proceedings on Radio Four from three-thirty to the vote at ten o'clock.

On the afternoon of the debate Simon sat up in bed listening to every word on the radio as if it were the final episode in his favourite serial and he was desperate to know the outcome. The speeches opened with a clear and concise presentation of the Charter by the Secretary of State for Northern Ireland, which left Simon feeling confident that the whole House would support him. The Opposition spokesman followed with a fair-minded speech, raising one or two queries he had over the controversial Patriots' Clause with its special rights for Protestants in the south and Catholics in the north, and also how it would affect the Catholics unwilling to register in Northern Ireland. Otherwise he reassured the House that the Opposition supported the Charter and would not be calling for a division.

Simon began to relax for the first time as the debate continued, but his mood changed as some back-bench members started to express more and more anxiety over the Patriots' Provision. One or two back-benchers were even insisting that the Charter should not be sanctioned by the House until the need for the Patriots' Provision was fully explained by the Government. Simon realised that a few narrow-minded men were simply playing for time in the hope the Charter would be held up and later forgotten. For generations such men had succeeded in stifling the hopes and aspirations of the Irish people while they allowed bigotry to undermine any real desire for peace.

Elizabeth came in and sat on the end of the bed. "How's it going?" she asked.

"Not well," said Simon, "it will all depend on the Opposition spokesman."

They both sat and listened. But no sooner had the Opposition spokesman risen than Simon realised that he too had misunderstood the real purpose of the Patriots' Provision and that what Simon had agreed to with both sides in Dublin and Belfast was not being accurately explained to the House. There was no malice in the speech and he was clearly following what had been agreed through the usual channels but Simon could sense that his lack of conviction was sowing doubts in the minds of his fellow members. He feared a division might be called after all.

After one or two members had interrupted to voice further doubts about the Patriots' Clause the Shadow minister suggested: "Perhaps we should wait until the Minister of State is fully recovered and able to report to the House himself." A few 'hear, hears' could be heard around the Chamber.

Simon felt sick. He was going to lose the Charter if it didn't get through the House tonight. All the hard work and goodwill would count for nothing. He made a decision.

"I'd love a hot cup of cocoa," he said, trying to sound casual.

"Of course, darling. I'll just go and turn the kettle on. Would you like a biscuit while I'm up?"

Simon nodded. Once the bedroom door was closed, he slipped quietly out of bed and dressed as quickly as possible. He picked up his blackthorn stick, a gift from Dr Fitzgerald, the Irish Prime Minister, which had been among the dozens of presents awaiting his return from hospital. Then he hobbled silently down the stairs and across the hall, hoping Elizabeth would not hear him. He eased the front door open. When the policeman on duty saw him Simon put a finger to his lips and closed the door very slowly behind him. He made his way laboriously up to the police car, lurched into the back and said, "Switch on the radio, please, and drive me to the House as quickly as possible."

Simon continued to listen to the Opposition spokesman as the police car weaved in and out of the traffic on a route he hadn't travelled before. They arrived at the St Stephen's entrance to the Commons at nine-twenty-five.

Visitors stood to one side as they might for royalty but Simon didn't notice. He hobbled on through the Central Lobby, oblivious to the awkwardness of his gait, turning left past the policeman and on towards the entrance of the House. He prayed he would reach the Chamber before the Government spokesman rose to deliver his winding-up speech. Simon passed an astonished chief doorkeeper and arrived at the bar of the House as the new digital clock showed nine-twenty-nine.

The Opposition spokesman was resuming his place on the front bench to muffled cries of "Hear, hear." The Speaker rose but before he had time to call upon the Minister of State to reply Simon stepped slowly forward on to the green carpet of the Commons. For a moment there was a stunned silence; then the cheering began. It had reached a crescendo by the time Simon arrived at the front bench. His blackthorn stick fell to the floor as he clutched the dispatch box. The Speaker called out his name *sotto voce*.

Simon waited for the House to come to complete silence.

"Mr Speaker, I must thank the House for its generous welcome. I return this evening because having listened to every word of the debate on the radio I feel it necessary to explain to Honourable members what was behind my thinking with the Patriots' Provision. This was not some superficial formula for solving an intractable problem, but an act of good faith to which the representatives from all sides felt able to put their names. It may not be perfect, since words can mean different things to different people – as lawyers continually demonstrate to us."

The laughter broke the tension that had been building up in the House.

"But if we allow this opportunity to pass today it will be another victory for those who revel in the mayhem of Northern Ireland whatever their reason, and a defeat for all men of goodwill."

The House was silent as Simon went on to explain in detail the thinking behind the Patriots' Provision and the effect it would have on both Protestants and Catholics in north and south. He also covered the other salient clauses in the Charter, answering the points that had been raised during the debate until, in glancing up at the clock above the Speaker's chair, he realised he had less than a minute left.

"Mr Speaker, we in this great House, who have in the past decided the fate of nations, are now given an opportunity to succeed today where our predecessors have failed. I ask you to support this Charter – not unreservedly, but to show the bombers and the murderers that here in Westminster we can cast a vote for the children of tomorrow's Ireland. Let the twenty-first century be one in which the Irish problem is only a part of history. Mr Speaker, I seek the support of the whole House."

The motion on the Charter was agreed without division.

Simon immediately returned home and on arrival silently crept upstairs. He closed the bedroom door behind him and fumbled for the switch. The light by the side of the bed went on and Elizabeth sat up.

"Your cocoa's gone cold and I've eaten all the biscuits," she said, grinning, "but thank you for leaving the radio on, at least I knew where you were."

CHAPTER
TWENTY SIX

Charles and Amanda were married at the most inconspi-
cuous register office in Hammersmith. They then departed
for a long weekend in Paris. Charles had told his bride that he
preferred her not to let anyone learn of the marriage for at
least another week. He didn't want Fiona to find yet a further
excuse for not returning the Holbein. Amanda readily
agreed, and then remembered – but surely Alec Pimkin
didn't count.

Paris turned out to be fun, even though Charles was
sensitive about Amanda's obvious pregnancy – never more
so than when they arrived on the Friday night at the Plaza
Athenée and were escorted to a suite overlooking the courtyard. Later, over dinner, Amanda astonished the waiters
with her appetite as well as the cut of her dress.

Over breakfast in bed the next day Charles read in the
Herald Tribune that Mrs Thatcher was considering a reshuffle
that very weekend. He cut the honeymoon short and returned to London on the Saturday, two days earlier than
planned. Amanda was not overjoyed. Her husband spent the
whole of Sunday at Eaton Square alongside a phone that
never rang.

That same Sunday evening the Prime Minister called for
Simon Kerslake and told him that he was to be made a Privy
Councillor and would be moved from the Northern Ireland
Office to Defence as Minister of State.

He had started to protest, but Mrs Thatcher forestalled
any discussion. "I don't want any more dead heroes,
Simon," she said sharply.

Elizabeth was relieved when she heard the news, although

it took her some time to get used to her husband being referred to as 'the Right Honourable Simon Kerslake'. For some weeks the old joke of 'rarely right and never honourable' had to be suffered by both of them from countless well-meaning constituents who imagined they were the only people who had thought of the quip.

Mrs Thatcher called Charles Seymour on the Monday morning while he was waiting in Eaton Square for the return of the Holbein. Both sides' solicitors had agreed that the first Earl of Bridgwater should be back at Charles's home by eleven that morning. Only the Queen or Mrs Thatcher could have kept Charles from being there to receive it.

The Prime Minister's call came long after he thought the reshuffle was over, but then Mrs Thatcher had been informed that Charles was in Paris on his honeymoon and wouldn't be back until the Monday morning.

Charles took a taxi to Downing Street and was quickly ushered into the Prime Minister's study. Mrs Thatcher began by complimenting him on the work he had carried out on successive Finance Bills in Opposition and in Government. She then invited him to join the front-bench team as the Financial Secretary to the Treasury.

Charles accepted gracefully, and after a short policy discussion with the Prime Minister drove back to Eaton Square to celebrate both his triumphs. Amanda met him at the door to tell him the Holbein had been returned. Fiona had kept her part of the bargain: the painting had been delivered at eleven o'clock sharp.

Charles strode confidently into his drawing-room and was delighted to find the bulky package awaiting him. He was by no means so pleased to be followed by Amanda, a cigarette in one hand and a glass of gin in the other; but this was not a day for quarrels, he decided. He told her of his appointment, but she didn't seem to take in its significance until her husband opened a bottle of champagne.

Charles poured out two glasses and handed one to his bride.

"A double celebration. What fun," she said, first draining the gin.

Charles took a quick sip of the champagne before he began to untie the knots and tear away the smart red wrapping paper that covered his masterpiece. Once the paper had been removed he pulled back the final cardboard covers. Charles stared with delight at the portrait.

The first Earl of Bridgwater was back home. Charles picked up the gold frame he knew so well to return it to its place in his study but he noticed that the picture had come a little loose. "Damn," he said.

"What's the matter?" asked Amanda still leaning against the door.

"Nothing important, only I shall have to get the frame fixed. I'll drop it into Oliver Swann on the way to the bank. I've waited nearly three years; another couple of days won't make any difference."

Now that Charles had accepted the post of Financial Secretary to the Treasury he knew there was one little arrangement he had to clear up before the appointment became public knowledge. With that in mind, he left Eaton Square and dropped the Holbein off at the framer. He then went on to the bank and summoned Clive Reynolds to his office. It was clear from Reynolds's manner that the news of Charles's ministerial appointment had not yet leaked out.

"Clive," Charles called him for the first time. "I have a proposition to put to you."

Clive Reynolds remained silent.

"The Prime Minister has offered me a post in the Government."

"Congratulations," said Reynolds, "and well deserved, if I may say so."

"Thank you," said Charles. "Now: I'm considering offering you the chance to stand in for me as chairman during my absence."

Clive Reynolds looked surprised.

"On the clear understanding that if the Conservatives were to return to Opposition or I were to lose my appointment in Government I would be reinstated as chairman immediately."

"Naturally," said Reynolds. "I should be delighted to fill the appointment for the interim period."

"Good man," said Charles. "It can't have escaped your notice what happened to the last chairman in the same situation."

"I shall make certain that will not happen again."

"Thank you," said Charles. "I shall not forget your loyalty when I return."

"And I shall also endeavour to carry on the traditions of the bank in your absence," said Reynolds, his head slightly bowed.

"I feel sure you will," said Charles.

The board accepted the recommendation that Clive Reynolds be appointed as temporary chairman and Charles vacated his office happily to take up his new post at the Treasury.

Charles considered it had been the most successful week of his life and on the Friday evening on the way back to Eaton Square he dropped into Oliver Swann's gallery to pick up the Holbein.

"I'm afraid the picture didn't quite fit the frame," said Mr Swann.

"Oh, I expect it's worked loose over the years," Charles said non-committally.

"No, Mr Seymour, this frame was put on the portrait quite recently," said Swann.

"That's not possible," said Charles. "I remember the frame as well as I remember the picture. The portrait of the first Earl of Bridgwater has been in my family for over 400 years."

"Not this picture," said Swann.

"What do you mean?" said Charles, beginning to sound anxious.

"This picture came up for sale at Sotheby's about three weeks ago."

Charles went cold as Swann continued.

"It's the school of Holbein, of course," he said, "probably painted by one of his pupils around the time of his death. I should think there are a dozen or so in existence."

"A dozen or so," repeated Charles, the blood drained from his face.

"Yes, perhaps even more. At least it's solved one mystery for me," said Swann, chuckling.

"What's that?" asked Charles, choking out the words.

"I couldn't work out why Lady Fiona was bidding for the picture, and then I remembered that your family name is Bridgwater."

"At least *this* wedding has some style," Pimkin assured Fiona between mouthfuls of sandwich at the reception after her marriage to Alexander Dalglish. Pimkin always accepted wedding invitations as it allowed him to devour mounds of smoked salmon sandwiches and consume unlimited quantities of champagne. "I particularly enjoyed that *short* service of blessing in the Guards' Chapel; and Claridges can always be relied on to understand my little proclivities." He peered round the vast room and only stopped to stare at his reflection in a chandelier.

Fiona laughed. "Did you go to Charles's wedding?"

"My darling, the only Etonians who have ever been seen in Hammersmith pass through it as quickly as possible on a boat, representing either Oxford or Cambridge."

"So you weren't invited," said Fiona.

"I'm told that only Amanda was invited, and even she nearly found she had another engagement. With her doctor, I believe."

"Well, Charles certainly can't afford another divorce."

"No, not in his present position as Her Majesty's Financial Secretary. One divorce might go unnoticed but two would be considered habit-forming, and all diligent readers of Nigel Dempster have been able to observe that consummation has taken place."

"But how long will Charles be able to tolerate her behaviour?"

"As long as he still believes she has given him a son who will inherit the family title. Not that a marriage ceremony will necessarily prove legitimacy," added Pimkin.

"Perhaps Amanda won't produce a son."

"Perhaps whatever she produces it will be obvious that it's not Charles's offspring," said Pimkin, falling into a chair that had been momentarily left by a large buxom lady.

"Even if it was I can't see Amanda as a housewife."

"No, but it suits Amanda's current circumstances to be thought of as the loving spouse."

"Time may change that too," said Fiona.

"I doubt it," said Pimkin. "Amanda is stupid, that has been proved beyond reasonable doubt, but she has a survival instinct second only to a mongoose. So while Charles is spending all the hours of the day advancing his glittering career she would be foolish to search publicly for greener pastures. Especially when she can always lie in them privately."

"You're a wicked old gossip," said Fiona.

"I cannot deny it," said Pimkin, "for it is an art at which women have never been as accomplished as men."

"Thank you for such a sensible wedding present," said Alexander, joining his wife of two hours. "You selected my favourite claret."

"Giving a dozen bottles of the finest claret serves two purposes," said Pimkin, his hands resting lightly on his stomach. "First, you can always be assured of a decent wine when you invite yourself to dine."

"And second?" asked Alexander.

"When the happy couple split up you can feel relieved that they will no longer have your present to quarrel over."

"Did you give Charles and Amanda a present?" asked Fiona.

"No," said Pimkin, deftly removing another glass of champagne from a passing waiter. "I felt your return of the bogus Earl of Bridgwater was quite enough for both of us."

"I wonder where he is now?" said Alexander.

"He no longer resides in Eaton Square," said Pimkin with the air of one who has divulged a piece of information which can only guarantee further rapt attention.

"Who would want the phoney earl?"

"We are not aware of the provenance of the buyer, as he

emanates from one of Her Majesty's former colonies, but the seller . . ."

"Stop teasing, Alec. Who?"

"None other than Mrs Amanda Seymour."

"Amanda?"

"Yes. Amanda, no less. The dear, silly creature retrieved the false earl from the cellar where Charles had buried him with full military honours."

"But she must have realised it was a fake."

"My dear Amanda wouldn't know the difference between a Holbein and an Andy Warhol but she still happily accepted £10,000 for the impersonation. I am assured that the dealer who purchased this fabricated masterpiece made what I think vulgar people in the City describe as 'a quick turn'."

"Good God," said Alexander. "I only paid £8,000 for it myself."

"Perhaps you should get Amanda to advise you on these matters in future," said Pimkin. "In exchange for my invaluable piece of information I'm bound to enquire if the real Earl of Bridgwater is to remain in hiding."

"Certainly not, Alec. He is merely awaiting the right moment to make a public appearance," said Fiona, unable to hide a smile.

"And where is Amanda now?" asked Alexander, obviously wanting to change the subject.

"In Switzerland producing a baby, which we can but hope will bear sufficient resemblance to a white Caucasian to convince one of Charles's limited imagination that he is the father."

"Where *do* you get all your information from?" asked Alexander.

Pimkin sighed dramatically. "Women have a habit of pouring their hearts out to me, Amanda included."

"Why should she do that?" asked Alexander.

"She lives safe in the knowledge that I am the one man she knows who has no interest in her body." Pimkin drew breath, but only to devour another smoked salmon sandwich.

Charles phoned Amanda every day while she was in Geneva. She kept assuring him all was well, and that the baby was expected on time. He had considered it prudent for Amanda not to remain in England advertising her pregnancy, a less than recent occurrence to even the most casual observer. She for her part did not complain. With £10,000 safely tucked away in a private Swiss account there were few little necessities she could not have brought to her, even in Geneva.

It had taken a few weeks for Charles to become accustomed to Government after such a long break. He enjoyed the challenge of the Treasury and quickly fell in with its strange traditions. He was constantly reminded that his was the department on which the Prime Minister kept the closest eye, making the challenge even greater. The civil servants, when asked their opinion of the new Financial Secretary, would reply variously: able, competent, efficient, hard-working – but without any hint of affection in their voices. When someone asked his driver, whose name Charles could never remember, the same question he proffered the view, "He's the sort of minister who always sits in the back of a car. But I'd still put a week's wages on Mr Seymour becoming Prime Minister."

Amanda produced her child in the middle of the ninth month. After a week's recuperation she was allowed to return to England. She discovered travelling with her offspring was a nuisance and by the time she arrived at Heathrow she was more than happy to turn the child over to the nanny Charles had selected.

Charles had sent a car to pick her up from the airport. He had an unavoidable conference with a delegation of Japanese businessmen, he explained, all of them busy complaining about the new Government tariffs on imports. At the first opportunity to be rid of his oriental guests he bolted back to Eaton Square.

Amanda was there to meet him at the door. Charles had almost forgotten how beautiful his wife was, and how long she had been away.

"Where's my child?" he asked, after he had given her a long kiss.

"In a nursery that's more expensively furnished than our bedroom," she replied a little sharply.

Charles ran up the wide staircase and along the passage. Amanda followed. He entered the nursery and stopped in his tracks as he stared at the future Earl of Bridgwater. The little black curls and deep brown eyes came as something of a shock.

"Good heavens," said Charles, stepping forward for a closer examination. Amanda remained by the door, her hand clutching its handle.

She had a hundred answers ready for his question.

"He's the spitting image of my great-grandfather. You skipped a couple of generations, Harry," said Charles, lifting the boy high into the air, "but there's no doubt you're a real Seymour."

Amanda sighed with inaudible relief. The hundred answers she could now keep to herself.

"It's more than a couple of generations the little bastard has skipped," said Pimkin. "It's an entire continent." He took another sip of christening champagne before continuing. "This poor creature, on the other hand," he said, staring at Fiona's firstborn, "bears a striking resemblance to Alexander. Dear little girl should have been given a kinder legacy with which to start her life."

"She's beautiful," said Fiona, picking Lucy up from the cradle to check her nappy.

"Now we know why you needed to be married so quickly," added Pimkin between gulps. "At least this child made wedlock, even if it was a close-run thing."

Fiona continued as if she had not heard his remark. "Have you actually seen Charles's son?"

"I think we should refer to young Harry as Amanda's child," said Pimkin. "We don't want to be had up under the Trade Descriptions Act."

"Come on, Alec, have you seen Harry?" she asked, refusing to fill his empty glass.

"Yes, I have. And I am afraid he also bears too striking a resemblance to his father for it to go unnoticed in later life."

"Anyone we know?" asked Fiona, probing.

"I am not a scandalmonger," said Pimkin, removing a crumb from his waistcoat. "As you well know. But a certain Brazilian *fazendeiro* who frequents Cowdray Park and Ascot during the summer months has obviously maintained his interest in English fillies."

Pimkin confidently held out his glass.

CHAPTER
TWENTY SEVEN

James Callaghan's resignation as Labour party leader in October 1980 took none of the political analysts by surprise. Unlike his predecessor he was over sixty-five, the age at which his party had recommended retirement.

Those same analysts were surprised, however, when Michael Foot, the veteran left-winger, defeated Denis Healey by 139 votes to 129 to become the new leader of the Labour party. The analysts immediately predicted a long spell of opposition for the socialists.

The Conservatives took much pleasure in watching a leadership struggle from the sidelines for a change. When Charles Seymour heard the result it amused him that the Labour party had ended up replacing a sixty-year-old with a sixty-four-year-old, who in turn was being replaced by a sixty-seven-year-old. Lord Shinwell, who at the age of ninety-six was the oldest living former Labour Cabinet minister, declared that he would be a candidate for party leadership when Foot retired.

When the election for the Shadow Cabinet came a week later Andrew decided not to submit his name. Like many of his colleagues he liked the new leader personally but had rarely been able to agree with him on domestic issues and was totally opposed to his defence and European policies. Instead he took on the chairmanship of the Select Committee on Scottish Affairs. Raymond for his part considered that Foot was destined to be no more than an interim leader and was therefore quite happy to serve under him. When the election to the Shadow Cabinet was announced Raymond came eighth. Michael Foot invited him to continue shadowing the Trade portfolio.

When Andrew entered the Commons Chamber the day after the election he walked up the gangway and took a seat on the back benches for the first time in fourteen years. He looked down at Raymond lounging on the front bench and recalled his own words: "There may well come a day when I sit and envy you from the same back benches."

Andrew was not surprised when he heard from his local committee in Edinburgh that he would once again have to submit himself to re-selection as their candidate some time during 1981. When the Labour conference the previous October had approved the mandatory re-selection of Labour MPs he had realised his biggest battle would be internal. Frank Boyle had even managed to replace another of Andrew's supporters with one of his own henchmen.

Roy Jenkins, the former deputy leader of the Labour party, was returning from Brussels as soon as his term as President of the European Commission came to an end. After delivering the Dimbleby lecture on television Jenkins made no secret of the fact that he was considering founding a new party that would take in those moderate radicals who felt the Labour party had swung too far to the left. The party conference had removed the power of selection of the leaders from Members of Parliament; for many this was the final straw, and several Labour MPs told Jenkins they were ready to defect. Andrew would have preferred to remain loyal to the party and try to change it from the inside, but he was fast coming to the conclusion that that hour had passed.

In his morning mail was a curt note from the constituency secretary informing him that Frank Boyle was going to oppose him for the nomination. Andrew flew up to Edinburgh on the day of the meeting, fearing the worst. No one met him at the airport, and at party headquarters David Connaught greeted him with a glum face.

Andrew stood in front of the committee in a cold, cheerless room and answered the same questions that had been put to him only three years before. He gave exactly the same answers: where he stood on nuclear disarmament, why he was in favour of a close association with the United States, his attitude to a wealth tax – on and on, predictable question after predictable question, but he never once allowed them to exasperate him.

He ended with the words: "I have been proud to serve the people of Edinburgh Carlton for almost twenty years as the Labour member and hope to do so for at least another twenty. If you now feel unable to re-select me I would have to consider standing as an independent candidate." For the first time, one or two members of the committee looked anxious.

"We are not intimidated by your threats, Mr Fraser," said Frank Boyle. "The Labour party has always been bigger than any individual. Now we know where Mr Fraser's real interests lie I suggest we move to a vote."

Twelve little slips of paper were passed out. 'Fraser' or 'Boyle' were scribbled on them before they were sent back to the chairman.

Frank Boyle slowly gathered up the slips, clearly relishing Andrew's discomfort. He unfolded the first slip of paper. "Boyle," he said, glancing at the others round the table.

He opened a second – "Fraser" – then a third, "Boyle", followed by "Fraser, Fraser, Fraser."

Andrew kept count in his head: four-two in his favour.

"Fraser," followed by "Boyle, Boyle, Fraser."

Six-four in Andrew's favour, with two still unopened: he only needed one more vote. "Boyle." Six-five. The chairman took some considerable time opening the last slip.

"Boyle," he announced in triumph.

He paused for effect. "Six votes all," he declared. "Under standing order forty-two of the Party Constitution," he said, as if he had learnt the words off by heart before the meeting, "in the result of a tie the chairman shall have the casting vote." He paused once again.

"Boyle," he said, lingering for a moment. "I therefore declare that Frank Boyle is selected as the official Labour party candidate for the constituency of Edinburgh Carlton at the next general election." He turned to Andrew and said,

"We shall no longer be requiring your services, Mr Fraser."

"I would like to thank those of you who supported me," Andrew said quietly and left without another word.

The next day the *Scotsman* came out with a lengthy article on the dangers of a small group of wilful people having the power to remove a member who had served his constituents honourably over a long period of time. Andrew phoned Stuart Gray to thank him. "I only wish the article had come out the day before," he said.

"It was set up for yesterday," Stuart told him, "but the announcement from Buckingham Palace of Prince Charles's engagement to Lady Diana Spencer moved everything else out – even the Rangers–Celtic report. By the way, doesn't Boyle's nomination have to be confirmed by his General Management Committee?"

"Yes, but they are putty in his hands. That would be like trying to explain to your mother-in-law about your wife's nagging."

"Then why don't you appeal to the National Executive and ask for the decision to be put to a full meeting of the constituency party?"

"Because it would take weeks to get the decision over-turned and more importantly I'm no longer certain that I want to fight the seat as a Labour candidate."

Andrew listened to the reporter's question and said, "Yes, you may quote me."

As the date for an election drew nearer Charles decided it might be wise to introduce Amanda to the constituency. He had explained to those who inquired that his wife had had rather a bad time of it after the birth, and had been told by her doctors not to participate in anything that might raise her blood pressure – though one or two constituents considered that the Sussex Downs' Conservatives would find it hard to raise the blood pressure of a ninety-year-old with a pace-maker. Charles had also decided to leave Harry at home, explaining that it was he who had chosen a public life, not his son.

The annual Garden Party held in the grounds of Lord

Cuckfield's country home seemed to Charles to be the ideal opportunity to show off Amanda and he asked her to be certain to wear something appropriate.

He was aware that designer jeans had come into fashion, and that his clothes-conscious wife never seemed to dress in the same thing twice. He also knew that liberated women didn't wear bras. But he was nevertheless shocked when he saw Amanda in a near see-through blouse and jeans so tight it looked as if she had been poured into them. Charles was genuinely horrified.

"Can't you find something a little more . . . conservative?" he suggested.

"Like the things that old frump Fiona used to wear?"

Charles couldn't think of a suitable reply. "The Garden Party will be frightfully dull," said Charles desperately. "Perhaps I should go on my own."

Amanda turned and looked him in the eye. "Are you ashamed of me, Charlie?"

He drove his wife silently down to the constituency and every time he glanced over at her he wanted to make an excuse to turn back. When they arrived at Lord Cuckfield's home his worst fears were confirmed. Neither the men nor the women could take their eyes off Amanda as she strolled around the lawns devouring strawberries. Many of them would have used the word 'hussy' if she hadn't been the member's wife.

Charles might have escaped lightly had it only been the one *risqué* joke Amanda told – to the bishop's wife – or even her curt refusals to judge the baby contest or to draw the raffle; but he was not to be so lucky. The chairman of the Women's Advisory Committee had met her match when she was introduced to the member's wife.

"Darling," said Charles. "I don't think you've met Mrs Blenkinsop."

"No, I haven't," said Amanda, ignoring Mrs Blenkinsop's outstretched hand.

"Mrs Blenkinsop," continued Charles, "was awarded the OBE for her services to the constituency."

"OBE?" Amanda asked innocently.

Mrs Blenkinsop drew herself up to her full height.

"Order of the British Empire," she said.

"I've always wondered," said Amanda, smiling. "My dad used to tell me it stood for 'other buggers' efforts'."

"Seen the Persil anywhere?" asked Louise.

"No, I stopped washing my own pants some time ago," replied Andrew.

"Ha, ha," said Louise. "But if you haven't taken them who has – two giant packets are missing?"

"The phantom Persil thief strikes again. Whatever next?" said Andrew. "The Bovril perhaps?"

"Stop making a fool of yourself and go and fish Clarissa out of the bath."

Andrew pulled himself out of the armchair, dropped *The Economist* on the carpet and ran upstairs. "Time to get out, young lady," he said even before he reached the bathroom door. First he heard the sobbing then when he opened the door he found Clarissa covered from head to toe in soap flakes. Her thick black curly hair was matted with them. Andrew burst out laughing but he stopped when he saw Clarissa's knees and shins were bleeding. She held a large scrubbing brush in one hand which was covered in a mixture of soap powder and blood.

"What's the matter, darling?" asked Andrew, kneeling on the bath mat.

"It isn't true," said Clarissa, not looking at him.

"What isn't true?" asked Andrew gently.

"Look on the box," she said pointing at the two empty packets which were standing on the end of the bath. Andrew glanced at the familiar picture on the box of a little fair-haired girl in a white party dress.

"What isn't true?" he repeated, still uncertain what Clarissa meant.

"It isn't true that Persil washes whiter and can remove even the blackest spots. Two large packets and I'm still black," she said.

Andrew had to smile which only made Clarissa cry even more. After he had washed off all the suds and gently dried her he put antiseptic ointment on the cuts and bruises.

"Why am I so black?" she asked.

"Because your mother and father were black," replied Andrew, guiding his daughter through to her bedroom.

"Why can't you be my father? Then I'd be white."

"I am your father now so you don't need to be."

"Yes, I do."

"Why?"

"Because the children at school laugh at me," Clarissa said, clutching firmly on to Andrew's hand.

"When I was at school they used to laugh at me because I was small," said Andrew. "They called me puny."

"What did you do about it?" asked Clarissa.

"I trained hard and ended up as captain of the school rugby team and that made them stop laughing."

"But by then you were big. I can't train to be white."

"No, I was still small, and you won't need to train."

"Why?" asked Clarissa, still not letting go of his hand.

"Because you're going to be beautiful, and then all those ugly white girls will be oh so jealous."

Clarissa was silent for some time before she spoke again.

"Promise, Daddy?"

"I promise," he said, remaining on the edge of the bed.

"Like Frank Boyle is jealous of you?"

Andrew was startled. "What do you know about him?"

"Only what I heard Mummy say, that he's going to be the Labour man for Edinburgh, but you'll still beat him."

Andrew was speechless.

"Is he going to be the Labour man, Daddy?" she asked.

"Yes, he is."

"And will you beat him?"

"I'll try."

"Can I help?" Clarissa asked, a tiny smile appearing on her face.

"Of course. Now off you go to sleep," said Andrew, getting up and drawing the curtains.

"Is he black?"

"Who?" asked Andrew.

"The nasty Frank Boyle."

"No," said Andrew laughing, "he's white."

"Then he ought to be made to have my skin then I could have his."

Andrew turned off the light, relieved Clarissa could no longer see his face.

Harry's second birthday party was attended by all those two-year-olds in the vicinity of Eaton Square whom his nanny considered acceptable. Charles managed to escape from a departmental meeting accompanied by a large paint board and a red tricycle. As he parked his car in Eaton Square he spotted Fiona's old Volvo driving away towards Sloane Square. He dismissed the coincidence although he still had plans for regaining the priceless Holbein. Harry naturally wanted to ride the tricycle round and round the dining-room table. Charles sat watching his son and couldn't help noticing that he was smaller than most of his friends. Then he remembered that great-grandfather had only been five feet eight inches tall.

It was the moment after the candles had been blown out, and nanny switched the light back on, that Charles was first aware that something was missing. It was like the game children play with objects on a tray: everyone shuts his eyes, nanny takes one away and then you all have to guess which piece it was.

It took Charles some time to realise that the missing object was his gold cigar box. He walked over to the sideboard and studied the empty space. He continued to stare at the spot where the small gold box left to him by his great-grandfather had been the previous night. Now all that was left in its place was the matching lighter.

He immediately asked Amanda if she knew where the heirloom was, but his wife seemed totally absorbed in lining up the children for a game of musical chairs. After checking carefully in the other rooms Charles went into his study and phoned the Chelsea police.

An inspector from the Crime Squad came round immediately and took down all the details. Charles was able to supply the police officer with a photograph of the box which carried the initials C.G.S. He stopped just short of mentioning Fiona by name. The inspector assured Charles that he would deal with the investigation personally. Charles returned to the party to find nannies arriving to gather their wards.

When the Edinburgh Carlton Labour party issued a press statement after their AGM announcing that Frank Boyle had been selected to fight the seat as their candidate, Andrew was surprised and touched by the flood of letters and calls of goodwill he received, many from people he didn't even know. Most of the messages begged him to stand at the next general election as an Independent.

Twenty Labour MPs and one Conservative had joined the newly formed Social Democratic Party and many others were expected to follow. Andrew knew he would have to make an announcement soon if he didn't want his supporters to drift away. He spent agonising hours discussing with Louise the problem of severing the final bonds with the party.

"What shall I do?" he asked, yet again.

"I can't tell you that; I just hope you make up your mind fairly quickly."

"Why quickly?"

"Because I'm going to vote for the Social Democrats at the next election, so you had better be my local candidate."

A few days later Roy Jenkins, Andrew's old chief at the Home Office, phoned to say he was fighting a by-election in Glasgow as the SDP candidate.

"I do hope you will feel able to join us," said Jenkins.

Andrew had always admired Jenkins's firm stand against the left and felt he was the one man who might break the two-party system.

"I need a little more time," he replied.

A week later Andrew made up his mind and informed the Chief Whip that he was leaving the party and would be joining the SDP. Then he packed a bag and travelled to Glasgow.

Roy Jenkins won the seat at Glasgow Hillhead with a large enough swing to worry both main parties. By Easter, a total of twenty-nine Members of Parliament had broken away to join him, while the alliance of SDP and Liberal MPs together could muster more than forty votes on the floor of the House.

With opinion polls putting them in second place, it began to look possible that the Social Democrats might hold the balance of power after the next election. The Conservatives were now running a poor third in all the national opinion polls.

Charles heard nothing for three weeks about the missing gold box and was beginning to despair when the inspector phoned to say that the family heirloom had been found.

"Excellent news," said Charles. "Are you able to bring the box round to Eaton Square?"

"It's not quite as simple as that, sir," said the policeman.

"What do you mean?"

"I would prefer not to discuss the matter over the phone. May I come and see you, sir?"

"By all means," said Charles, slightly mystified.

He waited impatiently for the inspector to arrive, although the policeman was at the front door barely ten minutes later. His first question took Charles by surprise.

"Are we alone, sir?"

"Yes," said Charles. "My wife and son are away visiting my mother-in-law in Wales. You say you've found the gold box," he continued, impatient to hear the inspector's news.

"Yes, sir."

"Well done, Inspector. I shall speak to the Commissioner personally," he added, guiding the officer towards the drawing-room.

"I'm afraid there's a complication, sir."

"How can there be when you've found the box?"

"We cannot be sure there was anything illegal about its disappearance in the first place."

"What do you mean, Inspector?"

"The gold case was offered to a dealer in Grafton Street for £2,500."

"And who was doing the selling?" asked Charles impatiently.

"That's the problem, sir. The cheque was made out to Amanda Seymour and the description fits your wife," said the inspector. Charles was speechless. "And the dealer has a receipt to prove the transaction." The inspector passed over a copy of the receipt. Charles was unable to steady his shaking hand as he recognised Amanda's signature.

"Now, as this matter has already been referred to the Director of Public Prosecutions I thought I ought to have a word with you in private, as I am sure you would not want us to prefer charges."

"Yes, no, of course, thank you for your consideration, Inspector," said Charles flatly.

"Not at all, sir. The dealer has made his position clear: he would be only too happy to return the cigar box for the exact sum he paid for it. I don't think that could be fairer."

Charles made no comment other than to thank the inspector again before showing him out.

He returned to his study, phoned Amanda at her mother's house and told her to return immediately. She started to protest, but he had already hung up.

Charles remained at home until they all arrived back at Eaton Square late that night. The nanny and Harry were immediately sent upstairs.

It took Charles about five minutes to discover that only a few hundred pounds of the money was left. When his wife burst into tears he struck her across the face with such force that she fell to the ground. "If anything else goes missing from this house," he said, "you will go with it and I will also make sure you spend a very long time in jail." Amanda ran out of the room sobbing uncontrollably.

The next day Charles advertised for a full-time governess. He also moved his own bedroom to the top floor so that he could be close to his son. Amanda made no protest.

Once the governess had settled in Amanda quickly became bored with the child and began disappearing for long periods. Charles couldn't be sure where she was most of the time, and didn't care.

After Pimkin had recounted the latest state of affairs to Alexander Dalglish in well-embroidered detail Fiona remarked to her husband, "I never thought the day would come when I would feel sorry for Charles."

On a sleepy Thursday in April 1982 Argentina attacked and occupied two small islands whose 1,800 British citizens were forced to lower the Union Jack for the first time in over a hundred years. Few members returned to their constituency that Friday and the House met unusually on a Saturday morning to debate the crisis while the nation followed every word on the radio.

The same day Mrs Thatcher immediately despatched a task force halfway around the globe to recapture the islands. Her fellow countrymen followed every scrap of news so intently that the London theatres found themselves empty at the height of the season.

Simon felt exhilarated to be a member of the Defence team at such an historic moment, and Elizabeth didn't begrudge him those days when he left before she had woken and arrived home after she had fallen asleep.

Under less public scrutiny but almost equal pressure, Charles beavered away at the Treasury addressing the economic problems that had been presented. He spent day after day in the House helping to put the Government's case. Like Simon he found he could only snatch moments to be at home but, unlike Elizabeth, his wife remained in bed until midday. When Charles did manage to slip away from the department he spent all his spare time with Harry, whose progress he followed with delighted concern.

At the time when the Union Jack was raised once again in the Falklands, the budget became an Act.

CHAPTER
TWENTY EIGHT

'PM to go in Nov' and 'Will Maggie wait till June?' were two of the headlines Andrew read on the first day of the new Parliamentary session.

Anyone who is defending a marginal seat is always on edge as the statutory five years draws to a close, and the new SDP members all treated their seats as marginal. Andrew was no exception.

He had worked hard to prove he was worth his place in the group the leader of the Social Democrats was beginning to form in the Commons. When Roy Jenkins had announced the make-up of his Shadow team Andrew was appointed Defence spokesman and enjoyed the challenge of pitting himself against the two main parties in the Commons in the run-up to the election. But once the Falklands crisis was over he knew his real problems were not going to be in Westminster but in Edinburgh, where he spent an increasing amount of his time. Hamish Ramsey phoned to ask him if there was anything he could do to help.

"Be my chairman for the election campaign," said Andrew simply.

Ramsey agreed without hesitation and within a fortnight four members of Andrew's old Labour party committee had defected to join him. Support for Andrew came from the most surprising quarters, including Jock McPherson, who pledged that the Scottish Nationalists would not be contesting the Edinburgh Carlton seat as they had no desire to see Frank Boyle in Parliament. Sir Duncan Fraser kept very quiet about what the Conservatives were up to until they announced that Jamie Lomax would be their standard-bearer.

"Lomax. Lomax," repeated Andrew. "He and I were at school together," he told his father. "He was known as Loopy Lomax. You've selected the biggest idiot of his generation."

"That's a disgraceful slur on an able man," said Sir Duncan, trying to keep a straight face. "I can assure you it took a lot of convincing the committee to make certain Lomax was selected."

"How did you fix it?"

"I must admit it wasn't easy. We had some very good applicants, but I managed to undermine every one of them and point out how blemish-free Lomax's political past was," said Sir Duncan, winking.

"Non-existent careers make for the best blemish-free pasts," said Andrew, and burst out laughing.

"Yes, I'm afraid one or two of the committee noticed that. But you must admit Lomax is a fine figure of a man," added his father.

"What's that got to do with it?" asked Andrew. "You weren't looking for a male model as candidate."

"I know, but it did help me to swing the ladies on the Women's Advisory Committee round to my way of thinking."

"You're a rogue, Father."

"No, I'm not. There isn't a Conservative in Scotland who would rather see Frank Boyle in the House than you, and as we have no chance of winning the seat, why let *him* in?"

Louise and Clarissa spent the Christmas recess in Edinburgh. Sir Duncan warned Louise that if Andrew lost this election he could never hope to return to the House of Commons again.

During 1983 Margaret Thatcher stuck firm to her monetarist policies and brought inflation below four per cent, while in parts of Scotland unemployment rose to fifteen per cent. She had gradually stifled any opposition from the 'wets' and by the end of her first administration they were totally outman-oeuvred. But it was the outcome of the Falklands crisis that had kept her ahead in the opinion polls for over a year. The press speculated on the date of the general election all through the month of April, and after the Conservatives' success in the local elections on 5 May the Prime Minister sought an audience with the Queen. Shortly afterwards Margaret Thatcher told the nation that she needed another five years to continue her policies and prove that they worked. The election date was set for 9 June.

Once the election campaign had begun in earnest Stuart Gray interviewed all three candidates on behalf of the *Scotsman* and told Andrew he had a plan to help him.

"You can't," said Andrew. "You're bound to remain neutral and give all three candidates equal column inches during the campaign."

"Agreed," said Stuart. "But on the one hand we know Frank Boyle is sharp and has the looks of an escaped convict, while Jamie Lomax looks like a film star but makes crass statements every time he opens his mouth."

"So?" said Andrew.

"So I'm going to cover the political pages with the worst shots I can find of Boyle and fill up inch after inch with the sayings of Lomax. They'll both get equal coverage while at the same time they'll lose votes."

"They'll suss it out and complain to the editor."

"I doubt it," said Stuart. "I have yet to meet a politician who complained about having his photo in the paper, or one who was angered by seeing his mad views aired to a larger audience than he could have hoped to influence in the past."

"And what do you propose to do about me?"

"That's a problem," admitted Stuart, laughing. "Perhaps I'll leave the columns blank. That's one way you can't lose votes."

Whenever Andrew carried out a door-to-door canvass he found a clear division between those who still backed him and those who thought he had been disloyal to the Labour party. As the canvass returns came in and the colours were put out on the trestle tables in the new party headquarters it became clear from even a cursory glance that it was going to be his toughest election yet.

Andrew had experienced some dirty campaigns over the years, especially when he had been up against the Scottish Nationalists, but after only a few days he had sweet memories of Jock McPherson who was Little Red Riding Hood compared with Boyle. Andrew could just about tolerate hearing that he had been thrown out of the Labour party because he was such a lazy member, even that he had left them in the lurch because he had been told he could never hope to be a minister again, but when it was repeated to him that the Boyle camp were spreading a rumour that Louise had lost her voice because, when she had her baby, it turned out to be black he was furious.

If Andrew had seen Boyle that day he would undoubtedly have hit him. Sir Duncan counselled restraint, pointing out that any other action could only harm Louise and Clarissa. Andrew took a deep breath and said nothing.

With a week to go a local opinion poll in the _Scotsman_ showed Boyle leading by thirty-five per cent to Andrew's thirty-two. The Conservatives had nineteen per cent but fourteen per cent remained undecided. Jock McPherson had kept his word: no Scottish Nationalist candidate had entered the lists.

On the Friday before the election McPherson went one better by issuing a statement advising his supporters to back Andrew Fraser.

When Andrew phoned to thank him, he said, "I'm returning a favour."

"I don't remember ever doing you a favour," said Andrew.

"You certainly did, remembering you're an Edinburgh man. One mention to the press of my offer of the leadership of the Scottish Nationalists and I'd have been sunk down the nearest pothole."

With five days to go Alliance supporters from the two Edinburgh constituencies which were not fielding an SDP candidate swarmed in to help Andrew, and he began to believe the canvass returns that were now showing he could win. With two days to go the _Scotsman_ proclaimed it was thirty-nine per cent to thirty-eight per cent in Boyle's favour, but also went on to point out that the Labour party would have a better-oiled machine to depend on when it came to polling day.

In his eve-of-poll message Andrew issued a clear statement on why his views differed from those of his opponent in the Labour party, and how he saw the future of Britain if the Alliance gained enough seats to hold the balance of power. He reminded voters that without exception the national opinion polls showed the SDP now running neck and neck with Labour.

Frank Boyle also put out an eve-of-poll message, delivered to every house in the constituency, showing a picture of Andrew holding Clarissa in his arms under the caption 'Does your member tell you the whole truth?' There was no mention of Louise or Clarissa in the text but the innuendo could not have been clearer. Andrew didn't see the sheet until the morning of polling day by which time he knew there was nothing effective he could do to refute Boyle's implied slur. Issuing a writ that could not be dealt with until weeks after the election was over could only prove impotent. He either won the day or he lost it.

To that end, he and Louise never stopped working from seven that morning until ten at night. Helpers arrived from the most unexpected places, as if to prove the *Scotsman* wrong about the Labour party machine, but Andrew couldn't help noticing that there were red rosettes everywhere he went.

Towards the end of the day even Sir Duncan joined him and began chauffeuring SDP voters to the polls in his Rolls Royce.

"We've faced the fact that our candidate has lost so now I've come to help you," he told Andrew bluntly.

As the city hall clock struck ten Andrew sat down on the steps of the last polling station. He knew there was nothing he could do now. He had done everything possible, only avoiding members of the House of Lords and lunatics – neither of which group was entitled to vote.

An old lady was coming out of the polling station with a smile on her face.

"Hello, Mrs Bloxham," said Andrew. "How are you?"

"I'm fine, Andrew," she smiled. "I nearly forgot to vote and that would never have done."

He raised his tired head.

"Now don't fret yourself, laddie," she continued, "I never failed to vote for the winner in fifty-two years and that's longer than you've lived." She chuckled and left him sitting on the steps.

Andrew somehow picked himself up and made his way through the dark cobbled streets to his election headquarters. They cheered him as he entered the room, and the chairman offered him a 'wee dram of whisky'.

"To hell with a wee dram," said Andrew. "Just keep pouring."

He tried to get round the room to thank everyone before Hamish Ramsey told him it was time to go over to the city hall for the count. A small band of supporters accompanied the Frasers to the city hall to witness the proceedings. As he entered the hall the first person he saw was Boyle, who had a big smile on his face. Andrew was not discouraged by the smile as he watched the little slips of paper pour out of the boxes. Boyle had yet to learn that the first boxes to be counted were always from the inner wards, where most of the committed Socialists lived.

As both men walked round the tables, the little piles began to be checked – first in tens, then hundreds, until they were finally placed in thousands and handed over to the Sheriff. As the night drew on Boyle's smile turned to a grin, from a grin to a poker face, and finally to a look of anxiety as the piles grew closer and closer in size.

For over three hours the process of emptying the boxes continued and the scrutineers checked each little white slip before handing in their own records. At one twenty-two in the morning the Sheriff added up the list of numbers in front of him and asked the three candidates to join him.

He told them the result.

Frank Boyle smiled once again. Andrew showed no emotion, but called for a recount.

For over an hour, he paced nervously around the room as

the scrutineers checked and double-checked each pile: a change here, a mistake there, a lost vote discovered and, on one occasion, the name on the top of a pile of one hundred votes was not the same as the ninety-nine beneath it. At last the scrutineers handed back their figures. Once again the Sheriff added up the columns of numbers and asked the candidates to join him.

This time Andrew smiled while Boyle looked surprised and demanded another recount. The Sheriff acquiesced, but said it must be the last time. Both candidates agreed in the absence of their Conservative rival, who was sleeping soundly in a corner, secure in the knowledge that no amount of recounting would alter his position in the contest.

Once again the piles were checked and double-checked and five mistakes were discovered in the 42,588 votes cast. At three-twenty a.m., with counters and checkers falling asleep at their tables, the Sheriff once more asked the two candidates to join him. They were both stunned when they heard the result and the Sheriff informed them that there would be a further recount in the morning after his staff had managed to get some sleep.

All the voting papers were then placed carefully back in the black boxes, locked and left in the safe-keeping of the local constabulary while the candidates crept away to their beds.

Andrew slept in fits and starts through the remainder of the night. Louise, pale with exhaustion but still grinning, brought him a cup of tea at eight in the morning. He took a cold shower, shaved slowly and was back at the city hall a few minutes before the count was due to recommence. As he walked up the steps he was greeted by a battery of television cameras and journalists who had heard rumours as to why the count had been held up overnight and knew they couldn't afford to be absent as the final drama unfolded.

The counters looked eager and ready when the Sheriff checked his watch and nodded. The boxes were unlocked and placed in front of the staff for the fourth time. Once again the little piles grew from tens into hundreds and then into thousands. Andrew paced around the tables, more to burn up his nervous energy than out of a desire to keep checking. He had thirty witnesses registered as his counting agents to make sure he didn't lose by sleight of hand or genuine mistake.

Once the counters and scrutineers had finished they sat in front of their piles and waited for the slips to be collected and taken to the Sheriff. When the Sheriff had added up his little columns of figures for the final time he found that no votes had changed hands.

He explained to Andrew and Frank Boyle the procedure he intended to adopt in view of the outcome. He told both candidates that he had spoken to Lord Wylie at nine that morning and the Lord Advocate had read out the relevant statute in election law that was to be followed in such circumstances. Both candidates agreed on which of the two choices they preferred.

The Sheriff walked up on to the stage with Andrew Fraser and Frank Boyle in his wake, both looking anxious.

Everyone in the room stood to be sure of a better view of the proceedings. When the pushing back of chairs, the coughing and the nervous chattering had stopped, the Sheriff began. First he tapped the microphone that stood in front of him to be sure it was working. The metallic scratch was audible throughout the silent room. Satisfied, he began to speak.

"I, the returning officer for the district of Edinburgh Carlton, hereby declare the total number of votes cast for each candidate to be as follows:

Frank Boyle	18,437
Jamie Lomax	5,714
Andrew Fraser	18,437."

The supporters of both the leading candidates erupted into a noisy frenzy. It was several minutes before the Sheriff's voice could be heard above the babble of Scottish burrs.

"In accordance with section sixteen of the Representation of the People Act 1949 and rule fifty of the Parliamentary Election Rules in the second schedule to that Act, I am

obliged to decide between tied candidates by lot," he announced. "I have spoken with the Lord Advocate of Scotland, and have confirmed that the drawing of straws or the toss of a coin may constitute decision by lot for this purpose. Both candidates have agreed to the latter course of action."

Pandemonium broke out again as Andrew and Boyle stood motionless on each side of the Sheriff waiting for their fate to be determined.

"I have borrowed from the Royal Bank of Scotland," continued the Sheriff, aware that twenty million people were watching him on television for the first and probably the last time in his life, "a golden sovereign. On one side is the head of King George III, on the other Britannia. I shall invite the sitting member, Mr Fraser, to call his preference." Boyle curtly nodded his agreement. Both men inspected the coin.

The Sheriff rested the golden sovereign on his thumb, Andrew and Boyle still standing on either side of him. He turned to Andrew and said, "You will call, Mr Fraser, while the coin is in the air."

The silence was such that they might have been the only three people in the room. Andrew could feel his heart thumping in his chest as the Sheriff spun the coin high above him.

"Tails," he said clearly when the coin was at its zenith. The sovereign hit the floor and bounced, turning over several times before settling at the feet of the Sheriff.

Andrew stared down at the lady and sighed audibly. The Sheriff cleared his throat before declaring, "Following the decision by lot, I declare the aforementioned Mr Andrew Fraser to be the duly elected Member of Parliament for Edinburgh Carlton."

Andrew's supporters charged forward and on to the stage and carried him on their shoulders out of the city hall and through the streets of Edinburgh. Andrew searched for Louise and Clarissa, but they were lost in the crush.

The Royal Bank of Scotland presented the golden sovereign to the member the next day, and the editor of the

Scotsman rang to ask if there had been any particular reason why he had selected tails.

"Naturally," Andrew replied. "George III lost America for us. I wasn't going to let him lose Edinburgh for me."

CHAPTER
TWENTY NINE

Raymond read the *Daily Mail* caption again and smiled: 'On the toss of a coin'.

It saddened Raymond that Andrew had felt it necessary to leave the Labour party, although he was delighted that he had been returned to the Commons. Raymond was only thankful that there had been no Frank Boyles in his constituency. He often wondered if it was because Joyce kept such a watchful eye on all the committees.

Margaret Thatcher's second victory had come as a bitter blow to him although he couldn't have pretended it was a surprise. Her overall majority of 144 was even larger than had been predicted, while the SDP managed only six seats – although the Alliance were only two percentage points behind Labour in actual votes cast. Raymond was enough of a realist to know that now nothing was going to stop the Tories from governing for another five-year term.

Once again Raymond returned to his practice at the bar and a new round of time-consuming briefs. When the Lord Chancellor, Lord Hailsham, offered him the chance to become a High Court judge, with a place in the House of Lords, Raymond gave the matter considerable thought before finally asking Joyce for her opinion.

"You'd be bored to tears in a week," she told him.

"No more bored than I am now."

"Your turn will come."

"Joyce, I'm nearly fifty, and all I have to show for it is the chairmanship of the Select Committee on Trade and Industry. If the party fails to win next time I may never hold office again. Don't forget that the last occasion we lost this badly we were in Opposition for thirteen years."

"Once Michael Foot has been replaced the party will take on a new look, and I bet you'll be offered one of the senior Shadow jobs."

"That'll depend on who's our next leader," said Raymond. "And I can't see a great deal of difference between Neil Kinnock who looks unbeatable, and Michael Foot – except that Kinnock's ten years younger than I am."

"Then why not stand yourself?" asked Joyce.

"It's too early for me," said Raymond.

"Then why don't you at least wait until we know who's going to be the leader of the party," said Joyce. "You can be a judge at any time – they die off just as quickly as Cabinet ministers."

When Raymond returned to his chambers the following Monday he followed Joyce's advice and let Lord Hailsham know that he was not interested in being a judge in the foreseeable future, and settled down to keep a watchful eye on Cecil Parkinson, the new Secretary of State for Trade and Industry.

Only a few days later Michael Foot announced that he would not be standing for leader when the party's annual conference took place. When he informed the Shadow Cabinet several faces lit up at the thought of the forthcoming battle at Brighton in October. Neil Kinnock and Roy Hattersley became the front runners, while during the weeks leading up to the conference several trade unionists and MPs approached Raymond and asked him to stand; but he told them all "next time".

The vote for the new leader took place on the Sunday before the conference began: as Raymond predicted Kinnock won easily and Hattersley, his closest rival, was elected as his deputy.

After the conference Raymond returned to Leeds for the weekend, still confident that he would be offered a major post in the Shadow Cabinet despite the fact he hadn't supported the winner. Having completed his morning surgery he hung around the house waiting for the new leader to call him, even missing the match against Chelsea. He didn't like being in the second division.

When Neil Kinnock eventually phoned late that evening Raymond was shocked by his offer and replied without hesitation that he was not interested. It was a short conversation.

Joyce came into the drawing-room as he sank back into his favourite armchair.

"Well, what did he offer you?" she asked, facing him.

"Transport. Virtually a demotion."

"What did you say?"

"I turned him down, of course."

"Who has he given the main jobs to?"

"I didn't ask and he didn't volunteer, but I suspect we'll only have to wait for the morning papers to find out. Not that I'm that interested," he continued, staring at the floor, "as I intend to take the first place that comes free on the bench. I've wasted too many years already."

"So have I," said Joyce quietly.

"What do you mean?" asked Raymond, looking up at his wife for the first time since she had come into the room.

"If you're going to make a complete break, I think it's time for me to do so as well."

"I don't understand," said Raymond.

"We haven't been close for a long time, Ray," said Joyce, looking straight into her husband's eyes. "If you're thinking of giving up the constituency and spending even more time in London I think we should part." She turned away.

"Is there someone else?" asked Raymond, his voice cracking.

"No one special."

"But someone?"

"There is a man who wants to marry me," said Joyce, "if that's what you mean. We were at school in Bradford together. He's an accountant now and has never married."

"But do you love him?"

Joyce considered the question. "No, I can't pretend I do. But we're good friends, he's very kind and understanding and, more important, he's there."

Raymond couldn't move.

"And the break would at least give you the chance to ask Kate Garthwaite to give up her job in New York and return to London." Raymond gasped. "Think about it and let me know what you decide." She left the room quickly so that he could not see her tears.

Raymond sat alone in the room and thought back over his years with Joyce – and Kate – and knew exactly what he wanted to do now that the whole affair was out in the open.

He caught the last train to London the same evening because he had to be in court by ten o'clock the next morning to attend a judge's summing up. In the flat that night he slept intermittently as he thought about how he would spend the rest of his new life. Before he went into court the next morning he ordered a dozen red roses via Interflora. He phoned the Attorney General. If he was going to change his life he must change it in every way.

When the summing up was over and the judge had passed sentence Raymond checked the plane schedules. Nowadays you could be there in such a short time. He booked his flight and took a taxi to Heathrow. He sat on the plane praying it wasn't too late and that too much time hadn't passed. The flight seemed endless and he took another taxi from the airport.

When he arrived at her front door she was astonished. "What are you doing here on a Monday afternoon?"

"I've come to try and win you back," said Raymond. "Christ, that sounds corny," he added.

"It's the nicest thing you've said in years," she said as he held her in his arms; over Joyce's shoulder Raymond could see the roses brightening up the drawing-room.

"Let's go and have a quiet dinner."

Over dinner Raymond told Joyce of his plans to accept the Attorney General's offer to join the bench, but only if she would agree to live in London. After a second bottle of champagne which Joyce had been reluctant to open they finally returned home.

When they arrived back a little after one the phone was

ringing. Raymond opened the door and stumbled towards it while Joyce groped for the light switch.

"Ray, I've been trying to get you all night," a lilting Welsh voice said.

"Have you now?" Raymond said thickly, trying to keep his eyes open.

"You sound as if you've been to a good party."

"I've been celebrating with my wife."

"Celebrating before you've heard the news?"

"What news?" said Raymond, collapsing into the armchair.

"I've been juggling the new team around all day and I was hoping you would agree to join the Shadow Cabinet as . . ."

Raymond sobered up very quickly and listened carefully to the new leader. "Can you hold the line?"

"Of course," said the surprised voice the other end.

"Joyce," said Raymond, as she came out of the kitchen clutching two mugs of very black coffee. "Would you agree to live with me in London if I don't become a judge?"

A broad smile spread across Joyce's face with the realisation that he was seeking her approval.

She nodded several times.

"I'd be delighted to accept," he said.

"Thank you, Raymond. Perhaps we could meet at my room in the Commons tomorrow and talk over policy in your new field."

"Yes, of course," said Raymond. "See you tomorrow." He dropped the phone on the floor and fell asleep in the chair.

Joyce replaced the phone and didn't discover until the following morning that her husband was the new Shadow Secretary of State for Social Services.

Raymond sold his flat in the Barbican, and he and Joyce moved into a small Georgian house in Cowley Street, only a few hundred yards from the House of Commons.

Raymond watched Joyce decorate his study first, then she set about the rest of the house with the energy and enthusiasm of a newly-wed. Once she had completed the guest bedroom Raymond's parents came down to spend the weekend. He burst out laughing when he greeted his father at the door clutching on to a bag, marked 'Gould, the family butcher'.

"They do have meat in London, you know," said Raymond.

"Not like mine, son," his father replied.

Over the finest beef Raymond could remember he watched Joyce and his mother chatting away. "Thank God I woke up in time," he said out loud.

"What did you say?" asked Joyce.

"Nothing, my dear, nothing."

Although Raymond spent most of his time on the overall strategy for a future Labour Government, like all politicians he had pet anomalies that particularly upset him. His had always been war widows' pensions, a preoccupation which dated back to his living with his grandmother in Leeds. He remembered the shock when he first realised shortly after leaving university that his grandmother had eked out an existence for thirty years on a weekly widow's pension that wouldn't have covered the cost of a decent meal in a London restaurant.

From the back benches, he had always pressed for the redeeming of war bonds and higher pensions for war widows. His weekly mail showed unequivocally just how major a problem war widows' pensions had become. During his years in Opposition he had worked doggedly to achieve ever-increasing, smaller rises, but he vowed that were he to become Secretary of State he would enact something more radical.

Joyce left a cutting from the *Standard* for him to read when he returned from the Commons that night. She had scribbled across it: "This could end up on the front page of every national paper."

Raymond agreed with her, and the following day he tried to press his view on to a reluctant Shadow Cabinet who seemed more concerned with the planned series of picketing by the Yorkshire miners' union than the case of Mrs Dora Benson.

Raymond researched the story carefully and discovered that the case didn't differ greatly from the many others he had looked into over the years, except for the added ingredient of a Victoria Cross. By any standards, Mrs Dora Benson highlighted Raymond's cause. She was one of the handful of surviving widows of the First World War and her husband, Private Albert Benson, had been killed at the Somme leading an attack on a German trench. Nine Germans had been killed before Albert Benson died, which was why he had been awarded the VC. His widow had continued working as a cleaner in the King's Head at Barking for over fifty years. Her only possessions of any value were her war bonds, but with no redemption date they were still passing hands at twenty-five pounds each. Mrs Benson's case might have gone unnoticed if in desperation she had not asked Sotheby's to auction her husband's medal.

Once Raymond had armed himself with all the facts he put down a question to the minister concerned asking if he would at last honour the Government's long-promised pledges in such cases. A sleepy but packed House heard Simon Kerslake, as Minister of State for Defence, reply that his department was once again considering the problem and he would make known their findings in the near future. Simon settled back on to the green benches satisfied that would pacify Gould. But Raymond's supplementary stunned him and woke up the House.

"Does the Right Honourable Gentleman realise that this eighty-four-year-old widow, whose husband was killed in action and won the Victoria Cross, has a lower income than a sixteen-year-old cadet on his first day in the armed forces?"

Simon rose once more, determined to put a stop to the issue until he had had more time to study the details of this particular case.

"I was not aware of this fact, Mr Speaker, and I can assure the Right Honourable Gentleman that I shall take into consideration all the points he has mentioned."

Simon felt confident the Speaker would now move on to the next question. But Raymond rose again, the Opposition benches spurring him on.

"Is the Right Honourable Gentleman also aware that an admiral, on an index-linked income, can hope to end his career with a pension of over £500 a week while Mrs Dora Benson's weekly income remains fixed at £47.32?"

There was a gasp even from the Conservative benches as Raymond sat down.

Simon rose again, painfully aware that he was unprepared for Gould's attack and that he had to stifle it as quickly as he could. "I was not aware of that particular comparison either, but once again I can assure the Right Honourable Gentleman I will give the case my immediate consideration."

To Simon's horror Raymond rose from the benches for yet a third time. He could see that Labour members opposite were enjoying the rare spectacle of watching him up against the ropes. "Is the Right Honourable Gentleman also aware that the annuity for a Victoria Cross is £100 with no extra pension benefits? We pay our fourth-division footballers more, while keeping Mrs Benson in the bottom league of the national income bracket."

Simon looked distinctly harassed when he in turn rose for a fourth time and made an uncharacteristic remark that he regretted the moment he said it.

"I take the Right Honourable Gentleman's point," he began, his words coming out a little too quickly. "And I am fascinated by his sudden interest in Mrs Benson. Would it be cynical of me to suggest that it has been prompted by the wide publicity this case has enjoyed in the national press?"

Raymond made no attempt to answer but sat motionless with his arms folded and his feet up on the table in front of him while his own back-benchers screamed their abuse at Simon.

The national papers the next day were covered with pictures of the arthritic Dora Benson with her bucket and mop alongside photos of her handsome young husband in private's uniform. Many of the papers went on to describe how Albert Benson had won his VC, and some of the tabloids used considerable licence. But all of them picked up Raymond's point that Mrs Benson was in the bottom one per cent of the income bracket and that the annuity for a Victoria Cross was a pathetic £100.

It was an enterprising and unusually thorough journalist from the *Guardian* who led her story on a different angle which the rest of the national press had to turn to in their second edition. It transpired that Raymond Gould had put down forty-seven questions concerning war widows' pension rights during his time in the House and spoken on the subject in three budgets and five social service debates from the back benches. He had also made the subject the thrust of his maiden speech over twenty years before. But when the journalist revealed that Raymond gave £500 a year to the Erskine Hospital for wounded soldiers every member knew that Simon Kerslake would have to retract his attack and make an apology to the House.

At three-thirty the Speaker rose from his chair and told a packed house that the Minister of State for Defence wished to make a personal statement.

Simon Kerslake rose warily from the front bench and stood nervously at the dispatch box.

"Mr Speaker," he began. "With your permission and that of the House I would like to make a personal statement. During a question put to me yesterday I impugned the integrity of the Right Honourable Gentleman, the member for Leeds North. It has since been brought to my attention that I did him a gross injustice and I offer the House my sincere apologies, and the Right Honourable Gentleman the assurances that I will not question his integrity a third time."

While younger members were puzzled by the reference, Raymond smiled to himself.

Aware of how rare personal statements were in anyone's parliamentary career, members looked on eagerly to see how he would respond.

He moved slowly to the dispatch box.

"Mr Speaker, I accept the gracious manner in which the Right Honourable Gentleman has apologised and hope that he will not lose sight of the greater issue, namely that of war widows' benefits, and in particular the plight of Mrs Dora Benson.''

Simon looked relieved and nodded courteously.

Many Opposition members told Raymond he should have gone for Simon when he had him on the run, while Tom Carson continued shouting at Simon long after the House had proceeded to the next business. *The Times* leader writer proved them wrong when he wrote the next morning: "In an age of militant demands from the left, Parliament and the Labour party have found a new Clement Attlee on their front bench. Britain need have no fear for human dignity or the rights of man should Raymond Gould ever accede to the high office which that gentleman held."

When Raymond returned home from the Commons that night he found Joyce had cut out all the press comments for him to study and had also somehow managed to make inroads into his overflowing correspondence.

Joyce turned out to have a better feel for gut politics than the entire Shadow Cabinet put together.

Alec Pimkin threw a party for all his Tory colleagues who had entered the House in 1964, "To celebrate the first twenty years in the Commons," as he described the occasion in an impromptu after-dinner speech.

Over brandy and cigars the corpulent, balding figure sat back and surveyed his fellow members. Many had fallen by the wayside over the years, but of those that were left, he believed only two men now dominated the intake.

Pimkin's eyes first settled on his old friend Charles Seymour. Despite studying him closely he was still unable to spot a grey hair on the Treasury minister's head. From time to time Pimkin still saw Amanda, who had returned to being a full-time model and was rarely to be found in England nowadays. Charles, he suspected, saw more of her on the covers of magazines than he ever did in his home at Eaton Square. Pimkin had been surprised by how much time Charles was willing to put aside for little Harry. Charles was the last man he would have suspected of ending up a doting father. Certainly there was no sign of his ambitions diminishing, and Pimkin suspected that only one man remained a worthy rival for the party leadership.

His eyes moved on to someone for whom in 1984 Orwell's big brother seemed to hold no fears. Simon Kerslake was deep in animated conversation about his work on the proposed disarmament talks between Thatcher, Gorbachov and Reagan. Pimkin studied the Defence minister intently. He considered that had *he* been graced with such looks he would not have had to fear for his dwindling majority. Rumours of some financial crisis had long since died away, and Kerslake now seemed well set for a formidable future.

The party began to break up, as one by one his contemporaries came over to thank him for such a 'splendid', 'memorable', 'worthwhile' evening. When the last one had departed and Pimkin found himself alone he drained the drop of brandy that remained in his balloon and stubbed out the dying cigar. He sighed as he speculated on the fact that he could now never hope to be made a minister. He therefore determined to become a kingmaker, for in another twenty years there would be nothing left on which to speculate.

Raymond celebrated his twenty years in the House by taking Joyce to the Guinea Restaurant off Berkeley Square for dinner. He admired the long burgundy dress his wife had chosen for the occasion and even noticed that one or two women gave it more than a casual glance throughout their meal.

He too reflected on his twenty years in the Commons, and he told Joyce over a brandy that he hoped he would spend more of the next twenty years in Government. 1984 had not turned out to be a good year for the Conservatives, and Raymond was already forming plans to make 1985 as uncomfortable for the Government as possible.

A few weeks later Tony Benn, who had lost his seat at the general election, returned to the House of Commons as the member for Chesterfield. The Conservatives came a poor third and went on to lose two more by-elections early in 1985. Even the press began to acknowledge that the Labour party was once again looking like a serious alternative Government.

The winter of 1985 brought a further rise in the unemployment figures which only increased the Labour party's lead in the polls. And then after the resignation of two cabinet ministers over a small helicopter company in the West Country and the loss of two further by-elections, the Conservatives fell into third place for the first time in five years.

A drop in the price of oil from $22 to $10 a barrel in the space of six weeks did not help the Chancellor's budget judgement. After a long, hot summer Mrs Thatcher decided on a further cabinet reshuffle bringing in those who would be formulating policy in the run-up to the general election. The average age of the cabinet fell by seven years and the press dubbed it, 'Mrs Thatcher's new lamps for old reshuffle'.

CHAPTER THIRTY

Andrew was on his way to the House of Commons when he heard the first reports on his car radio. There had been no mention of the news in the morning papers so it must have happened overnight. It began with a news flash: just the bare details. HMS *Broadsword*, one of the Navy's destroyers, had been passing through the Gulf of Surt between Tunis and Benghazi when she was boarded by a group of mercenaries, posing as coastguard officials, who took over the ship in the name of Colonel Gaddafi. The newscaster went on to say that there would be a more detailed report in their ten o'clock bulletin.

Andrew had reached his room in the House of Commons by nine-thirty, and he immediately phoned the SDP leader David Owen to discuss the political implications of the news. Once a course of action had been agreed on Andrew took a handwritten letter round to the Speaker's office before the noon deadline, requesting an emergency debate following question time that afternoon. He also sent a copy of the letter by messenger to the Foreign Secretary and the Secretary of State for Defence.

By staying near a radio most of the morning Andrew was able to learn that HMS *Broadsword* was now in the hands of over a hundred guerillas. They were demanding the freedom of all Libyan prisoners in British jails in exchange for the 217-strong crew of the *Broadsword*, who were being held hostage in the engine room.

By twelve o'clock the ticker-tape machine in the Members' Corridor was hovered over by craning necks, and the dining-rooms were so full that many members had to go without lunch.

Question time that day had been allocated to Welsh Affairs, so the Chamber itself did not start filling up until nearly three-fifteen although the Palace of Westminster was already packed and buzzing with each new snippet of information. Political correspondents waited hawk-like in the Members' Lobby seeking opinions on the crisis from any senior politicians as they passed to and from the Chamber. Few were rash enough to say anything that might be re-interpreted the next day.

When Andrew came into the Chamber he took his seat next to David Owen on the Opposition front bench below the gangway. Since Andrew had the overall responsibility for the Alliance Defence portfolio he was expected to represent the other twenty-two Alliance members. At three-twenty-seven the Prime Minister, followed by the Foreign Secretary and the Secretary of State for Defence, filed into the House and took their places on the Treasury bench. All three looked suitably sombre. The last two questions on Welsh Affairs had the largest audience of members since the Aberfan disaster of 1966.

At three-thirty Mr Speaker Weatherill rose and called for order.

"Statements to the House," he announced in his crisp, military style. "There will be two statements on HMS *Broadsword* before the House debates Welsh Affairs." The Speaker then called the Secretary of State for Defence.

Simon Kerslake rose from the front bench and placed a prepared statement on the dispatch box in front of him.

"Mr Speaker, with your permission and that of the House, I would like to make a statement concerning Her Majesty's frigate *Broadsword*. At seven-forty GMT this morning HMS *Broadsword* was passing through the Gulf of Surt between Tunis and Benghazi when a group of guerillas, posing as official coastguards, boarded the ship and seized the officer in command, Captain Lawrence Packard, and placed the crew under arrest. The captain and his company did everything possible to resist but were outnumbered three to one. The guerillas, claiming to represent the People's Liberation Army, have since placed Captain Packard and the crew in the engine room of the ship. As far as it is possible to ascertain from our Embassy in Tripoli no lives have been lost, although Captain Packard sustained severe injuries during the battle, and we cannot be certain of his fate. There is no suggestion that *Broadsword* was doing anything other than going about her lawful business. This barbaric act must be looked upon as piracy under the 1958 Geneva Convention on the High Seas. The guerillas are demanding the release of all Libyan prisoners in British prisons in exchange for the return of HMS *Broadsword* and her crew. My Right Honourable friend, the Home Secretary, informs me there are only nine known Libyans in British jails at the present time, two of whom have been sentenced to three months for persistent shoplifting, two who were convicted on more serious drug charges, and the five who tried to hijack a British Airways 747 last year. Her Majesty's Government cannot and will not interfere with the due process of law and has no intention of releasing any of these men."

Loud "Hear, hears," came from all sections of the House.

"My Right Honourable friend, the Foreign Secretary, has made Her Majesty's Government's position clear to the Libyan Ambassador, in particular that Her Majesty's Government cannot be expected to tolerate this sort of treatment of British subjects or of British property. We have demanded and expect immediate action from the Libyan Government."

Simon sat down to loud and prolonged cheers before the leader of the Opposition rose from his place to say that he would wish it to be known that the Opposition gave the Government their full backing. He asked if any plans had been formulated at this early stage for the recovery of *Broadsword*.

Simon rose again. "We are, Mr Speaker, at present seeking a diplomatic solution, but I have already chaired a meeting of the Joint Chiefs and I anticipate making a further statement to the House tomorrow."

"Mr Andrew Fraser," said the Speaker.

Andrew rose from his place. "May I inform the Right

Honourable Gentleman that we in the Alliance also concur with his views that this is an act of piracy. But can he tell the House how long he will allow negotiations to continue when it is well known throughout the diplomatic world that Gaddafi is a master of procrastination, especially if we were to rely on the United Nations to adjudicate on this issue?" From the noise that greeted Andrew's question it seemed that his views were shared by the majority of the House.

Simon rose to answer the question. "I accept the point the Honourable Gentleman is making but he will know, having been a Minister of State for Defence himself, that I am not in a position to divulge any information which might imperil the safety of *Broadsword*."

Question after question came at Simon. He handled them with such confidence that visitors to the Strangers' Gallery would have found it hard to believe that he had been invited to join the Cabinet only five weeks before.

At four-fifteen, after Simon had answered the last question the Speaker was going to allow, he sank back on the front bench to listen to the statement from the Foreign Office. The House fell silent once again as the Foreign Secretary rose from his place and checked the large double-spaced sheets in front of him. All eyes were now on the tall, elegant man who was making his first official statement since his appointment.

"Mr Speaker, with your permission and that of the House, I too would like to make a statement concerning HMS *Broadsword*. Once news had reached the Foreign Office this morning of the plight of Her Majesty's ship *Broadsword* my office immediately issued a strongly worded statement to the Government of Libya. The Libyan Ambassador has been called to the Foreign Office and I shall be seeing him again immediately this statement and the questions arising from it has been completed."

Raymond looked up at the Strangers' Gallery from his place on the Opposition front bench. It was one of the ironies of modern diplomacy that the Libyan Ambassador was sitting in the gallery making notes while the Foreign Secretary delivered his statement. He couldn't imagine Colonel Gaddafi inviting the British Ambassador to take notes while he sat in his tent addressing his followers. Raymond was pleased to see an attendant ask the ambassador to stop writing; the prohibition dated from the time when the House had jealously guarded its privacy. Raymond's eyes dropped back to the front bench, and he continued to listen to Charles Seymour.

"Our ambassador to the United Nations has tabled a resolution to be debated by the General Assembly this afternoon, asking representatives to back Britain against this flagrant violation of the 1958 Geneva Convention on the High Seas. I confidently expect the support of the free world over this act of piracy against Her Majesty's ship *Broadsword*. Her Majesty's Government will do everything in its power to ensure a diplomatic solution bearing in mind that the lives of 217 British servicemen are still at risk."

The leader of the Opposition rose for a second time and asked at what point the Foreign Secretary would consider once again breaking off diplomatic relations with Libya.

"I naturally hope it will not come to that, Mr Speaker, and I expect the Libyan Government to deal quickly with their own mercenaries."

Charles continued to answer questions from all sections of the House but could only repeat that there was little new intelligence to offer the House at the present time. Raymond watched his two contemporaries as they displayed over twenty years of parliamentary skill in presenting their case. He wondered if this episode would make one of them Mrs Thatcher's obvious successor.

At four-thirty, the Speaker, realising nothing original had been said for some time, announced that he would allow one further question from each side before returning to the business of the day. He shrewdly called Alec Pimkin who sounded to Raymond like 'the very model of a modern major-general' and then Tom Carson who suggested that Colonel Gaddafi was often grossly misrepresented by the British press. Once Carson had sat down, Mr Speaker found it easy to move on to other business.

The Speaker rose again and thanked the Honourable Gentleman, the member for Edinburgh Carlton, for his courtesy in informing him that he would be making an application under standing order number ten for an emergency debate. The Speaker said he had given the matter careful thought but he reminded the House that, under the terms of the standing order, he did not need to divulge the reasons for his decision, merely decide whether the matter should have precedence over the orders of the day. He ruled that the matter was not proper for discussion within the terms of standing order number ten.

Andrew rose to protest but as the Speaker remained standing he had to resume his seat.

"This does not mean, however," continued Mr Speaker, "that I would not reconsider such a request at a later date."

Andrew realised that Charles Seymour and Simon Kerslake must have pleaded for more time, but he was only going to allow them twenty-four hours. The clerk at the table rose and bellowed above the noise of members leaving the Chamber, "Adjournment." The Speaker called the Secretary of State for Wales to move the adjournment motion on the problems facing the Welsh mining industry. The Chamber emptied of all but the thirty-eight Welsh MPs who had been waiting weeks for a full debate on the Principality's affairs.

Andrew went straight to his office and tried to piece together the latest information from news bulletins before preparing himself for a full debate the following day. Simon made his way back to the Ministry of Defence to continue discussions with the Joint Chiefs of Staff, while Charles was driven quickly to the Foreign Office.

When Charles reached his room, he was told by the Permanent Under-Secretary that the Libyan Ambassador awaited him.

"Does he have anything new to tell us?" asked Charles.

"Frankly, nothing; it seems that we're not the only people who are unable to make any contact with Colonel Gaddafi."

"Send him in then."

Charles stubbed out his cigarette and stood by the mantelpiece below a portrait of Palmerston. Charles had never met the ambassador before, largely because he had taken over at the Foreign Office only five weeks previously.

When Mr Kadir, the five-foot-one, dark-haired, immaculately dressed Ambassador for Libya entered the room, the office resembled nothing so much as a study in which a headmaster was about to tick off an unruly boy from the lower fifth.

Charles was momentarily taken aback when he noticed the ambassador's old Etonian tie. He recovered quickly.

"Foreign Secretary?" began Mr Kadir.

"Her Majesty's Government wishes to make it abundantly clear to your Government," began Charles, not allowing the ambassador to complete his sentiments, "that we consider the act of boarding and holding Her Majesty's ship *Broadsword* against her will as one of piracy on the high seas."

"May I say –?" began Mr Kadir.

"No, you may not," said Charles, "and until our ship has been released, we shall do everything in our power to bring pressure, both diplomatic and economic, on your Government."

"But may I just say –?" Mr Kadir tried again.

"My Prime Minister also wants you to know that she wishes to speak to your Head of State at the soonest possible opportunity, so I shall expect to hear back from you within the hour."

"Yes, Foreign Secretary, but may I –"

"And you may further report that we will reserve our right to take any action we deem appropriate if you fail to secure the release into safe custody of HMS *Broadsword* and her crew by twelve noon tomorrow, GMT. Do I make myself clear?"

"Yes, Foreign Secretary, but I would like to ask –"

"Good day, Mr Kadir."

After the Libyan Ambassador was shown out Charles couldn't help wondering what it was he had wanted to know.

"What do we do now?" he asked when the Permanent Under-Secretary returned, having deposited Mr Kadir in the lift.

"We act out the oldest diplomatic game in the world."

"What do you mean?" said Charles.

"Our sit-and-wait policy. We're awfully good at it," said

the Permanent Under-Secretary, "but then we've been at it for nearly a thousand years."

"Well, while we sit let's at least make some phone calls. I'll start with Secretary of State Kirkpatrick in Washington and then I'd like to speak to Gromyko in Moscow."

When Simon arrived back at the Ministry of Defence from the Commons he was told that the Joint Chiefs were assembled in his office waiting for him to chair the next strategy meeting. As he entered the room to take his place at the head of the table the Joint Chiefs rose.

"Good afternoon, gentlemen," Simon said. "Please be seated. Can you bring me up to date on the latest situation, Sir John?"

Admiral Sir John Fieldhouse, Chief of the Defence Staff, pushed up the half-moon glasses from the end of his nose and checked the notes in front of him.

"Very little has changed in the last hour, sir," he began. "The Prime Minister's office has still had no success in contacting Colonel Gaddafi. I fear we must now treat the capture of *Broadsword* as a blatant act of terrorism, rather similar to the occupation seven years ago of the American Embassy in Iran by students who backed the late Ayatollah Khomeini. In such circumstances we can either 'jaw-jaw or war-war', to quote Churchill. With that in mind, this committee will have formed a detailed plan by the early evening for the recapture of HMS *Broadsword*, as we assume the Foreign Office are better qualified to prepare for jaw-jaw." Sir John replaced his glasses and looked towards his minister.

"Are you in a position to give me a provisional plan which I could place in front of the Cabinet for their consideration?"

"Certainly, Minister," said Sir John, removing his glasses again before opening a large blue file in front of him.

Simon listened intently as Sir John went over his provisional strategy. Around the table sat eight of the senior-ranking staff officers of the Army, Navy and Air Force, and even the first draft plan bore the stamp of their 300 years of military experience. He couldn't help remembering that his call-up status was still that of a Second Lieutenant. For an hour he asked the Joint Chiefs questions that ranged from the elementary to ones that demonstrated a clear insight into their problems. By the time Simon left the room to attend the Cabinet meeting at No. 10 the Joint Chiefs were already up-dating their plan.

Simon walked slowly across Whitehall from the Department of Defence to Downing Street, his private detective by his side. Downing Street was thronged with people curious to see the comings and goings of ministers involved in the crisis. Simon was touched that the crowd applauded him all the way to the front door of No. 10, where the journalists and TV crews awaited each arrival. The great television arc lights were switched on as he reached the door and a microphone was thrust in front of him, but he made no comment. Simon was surprised by how many of the normally cynical journalists called out, "Good luck" and "Bring our boys home."

The front door opened and he went straight through to the corridor outside the Cabinet room, where twenty-two of his colleagues were already waiting. A moment later the Prime Minister walked into the Cabinet room and took her seat in the centre of the table with Charles and Simon opposite her.

Mrs Thatcher began by telling her colleagues that she had been unable to make any contact with Colonel Gaddafi and that they must therefore decide on a course of action that did not involve his acquiescence. She invited the Foreign Secretary to brief the Cabinet first.

Charles went over the actions in which the Foreign Office was involved at the diplomatic level. He reported his meeting with Ambassador Kadir, and the resolution which had been tabled at the UN and was already being debated at an emergency session of the General Assembly. The purpose of asking the United Nations to back Britain on Resolution 12/40, he said, was to gain the diplomatic initiative and virtually guarantee international sympathy. Charles went on to tell the Cabinet that he expected a vote to take place in the General Assembly in New York that evening which would demonstrate overwhelming support for the United Kingdom's resolution, and which would be regarded as a moral victory by the whole world. He was delighted to be able to report to the Cabinet that the Foreign Ministers of both the United States and Russia had agreed to back the UK in her diplomatic endeavours as long as she launched no retaliatory action. Charles ended by reminding his colleagues of the importance of treating the whole affair as an act of piracy, rather than an injury at the hands of the Libyan Government itself.

A legal nicety, thought Simon as he watched the faces of his colleagues round the table. They were obviously impressed that Charles had brought the two super powers together in support of Britain. The Prime Minister's face remained inscrutable. She called upon Simon to air his views.

He was able to report that *Broadsword* had, since the last meeting of the Cabinet, been towed into the Bay of Surt and moored; there was no hope of boarding her except by sea. Captain Packard and his crew of 216 remained under close arrest in the engine room on the lower deck of the ship. From confirmed reports Simon had received in the last hour it appeared that the ship's company were bound, gagged and that the ventilation systems had been turned off. "Captain Packard," he informed the House, "had refused to co-operate with the guerillas in any way, and we remain unsure of his fate." He paused. "I therefore suggest," Simon continued, "that we have no choice but to mount a rescue operation in order to avoid a protracted negotiation that can only end in grave loss of morale for the entire armed forces. The longer we put off such a decision the harder our task will become. The Joint Chiefs are putting the final touches to a plan code-named 'Shoplifter' which they feel must be carried out in the next forty-eight hours, if the men and the ship are to be saved." Simon added that he hoped diplomatic channels would be kept open while the operation was being worked out, in order that the rescue team could be assured of the greatest element of surprise.

"But what if your plan fails?" interrupted Charles. "We would risk losing not only *Broadsword* and her crew but also the goodwill of the free world."

"There is no serving officer in the British Navy who will

thank us for leaving *Broadsword* in Libyan waters while we negotiate a settlement in which, at best, our ship will be returned when it suits the guerillas – to say nothing of the humiliation of our Navy. Gaddafi can laugh at the United Nations while he has captured not only one of our most modern frigates but also the headlines of the world's press. As Ayatollah Khomeini did, he will want to keep them both for as long as he can. These headlines can only demoralise our countrymen and invite the sort of election defeat Carter suffered at the hands of the American people after the Iranian Embassy débâcle."

"We would be foolish to take such an unnecessary risk while we have world opinion on our side," protested Charles. "Let us at least wait a few more days."

"I fear that if we wait," said Simon, "the crew will be transferred from the ship to a military prison, which would only result in our having two targets to concentrate on, and then Gaddafi can sit around in the desert taking whatever amount of time suits him."

Simon and Charles weighed argument against counter-argument while the Prime Minister listened, taking note of the views of her other colleagues round the table to see if she had a majority for one course or the other. Three hours later, when everyone had given his opinion, she had 'fourteen-nine' written on the pad in front of her.

"I think we have exhausted the arguments, gentlemen," she said, "and having listened to the collective views around this table I feel we must on balance allow the Secretary of State for Defence to proceed with Operation Shoplifter. I therefore propose that the Foreign Secretary, the Defence Secretary, the Attorney General and myself make up a sub-committee, backed up by a professional staff, to consider the Joint Chiefs' plan. The utmost secrecy will be required from us at all times, so the subject will not be raised again until the plan is ready for presentation to a full meeting of the Cabinet. Therefore, with the exception of the sub-committee, all ministers will return to their departments and carry on with their normal duties. We must not lose sight of the fact that the country still has to be governed. Thank you, gentlemen." The Prime Minister asked Charles and Simon to join her in the study.

As soon as the door was closed she said to Charles, "Please let me know the moment you hear the result of the vote in the General Assembly. Now that the Cabinet has favoured a military initiative, it is important that you are seen to be pressing for a diplomatic solution."

"Yes, Prime Minister," said Charles without emotion.

Mrs Thatcher then turned to Simon. "When can I have a run-down on the details of the Joint Chiefs' plan?"

"We anticipate working on the strategy through the night, Prime Minister, and I should be able to make a full presentation to you by ten tomorrow."

"No later, Simon," said the Prime Minister. "Now our next problem is tomorrow's proposed emergency debate. Andrew Fraser will undoubtedly put in a second request for a full debate under standing order number ten and the Speaker gave a clear hint today he will allow it. Anyway, we can't avoid making a policy statement without an outcry from the Opposition benches – and I suspect our own – so I've decided that we will grasp the nettle and no doubt get stung."

The two men looked at each other, exasperated at the thought of having to waste precious hours in the Commons.

"Charles, you must be prepared to open the debate for the Government, and Simon, you will wind up. At least the debate will be on Thursday afternoon; that way some of our colleagues may have gone home for the weekend, though frankly I doubt it. But with any luck we will have secured a moral victory at the United Nations, and we can keep the Opposition minds concentrating on that. When you sum up, Simon, just answer the questions put during the debate without offering any new initiative."

She then added, "Report any news you hear direct to me. I shan't be sleeping tonight."

Charles walked back to the Foreign Office, at least thankful that Amanda was somewhere in South America.

Simon returned to the Joint Chiefs to find a large map of Libyan territorial waters pinned to a blackboard. Generals, admirals and air marshals were studying the contours and ocean depths like children preparing for a geography test.

They all stood again when Simon entered the room. They looked at him in anticipation, men of action who were suspicious of talk. When Simon told them the Cabinet's decision was to back the Ministry of Defence the suggestion of a smile came over the face of Sir John. "Perhaps that battle will turn out to be our hardest," he said, just loud enough for everyone to hear.

"Take me through the plan again," said Simon, ignoring Sir John's comment. "I have to present it to the Prime Minister by ten o'clock tomorrow."

Sir John placed the tip of a long wooden pointer on a model of HMS *Broadsword* in the middle of a stretch of water in a well-protected bay.

When Charles reached his office the international telegrams and telexes of support for a diplomatic solution were piled high on his desk. The Permanent Under-Secretary reported that the debate in the United Nations had been so one-sided that he anticipated an overwhelming majority when they came to vote. Charles feared his hands were tied; he had to be seen to go through the motions, even by his own staff, although he had not yet given up hopes of undermining Simon's plan. He intended the whole episode to end up as a triumph for the Foreign Office and not for 'those warmongers' at the Ministry of Defence. After consulting the Permanent Under-Secretary Charles appointed a small Libyan task force consisting of some older Foreign Office mandarins with experience of Gaddafi and four of the department's most promising high fliers.

Mr Oliver Miles, the former Ambassador to Libya, had his leave cancelled and was deposited in a tiny room in the upper reaches of the Foreign Office so that Charles could call on his local knowledge at any time, day or night, throughout the crisis.

Charles asked the Permanent Under-Secretary to link him up with Britain's ambassador at the United Nations.

"And keep trying to raise Gaddafi."

Simon listened to Sir John go over the latest version of Operation Shoplifter. Thirty-seven men from the crack Special Boat Service, the Marine equivalent of the SAS regiment which had been involved in the St James's Square siege in April 1984, were now in Rosyth on the Scottish coast, preparing to board HMS *Brilliant*, the sister ship to *Broadsword*.

The men were to be dropped from a submarine a mile outside Rosyth harbour and to swim the last mile and a half under water until they reached the ship. They would then board *Brilliant* and expect to recapture her from a mock Libyan crew in an estimated twelve minutes. *Brilliant* would then be sailed to a distance of one nautical mile off the Scottish coast. The operation was to be completed in sixty-five minutes. The SBS planned to rehearse the procedure on *Brilliant* three times before first light the following morning, when they hoped to have the entire exercise down to one hour.

Simon had already confirmed the order to send two submarines from the Mediterranean full steam in the direction of the Libyan coast. The rest of the fleet was to be seen to be conspicuously going about its normal business while the Foreign Office appeared to be searching for a diplomatic solution.

Simon's request to the Joint Chiefs came as no surprise and was granted immediately. He phoned Elizabeth to explain why he wouldn't be home that night. An hour later the Secretary of State for Defence was strapped into a helicopter and on his way to Rosyth.

Charles followed the proceedings at the United Nations live in his office on a satellite link-up. At the end of a brief debate a vote was called for. The Secretary General announced 147–3 in Great Britain's favour, with twenty-two abstentions. Charles wondered if such an overwhelming vote would be enough to get the Prime Minister to change her mind over Kerslake's plan. He checked over the voting list carefully. The Russians, along with the Warsaw Pact countries and the Americans, had kept their word and voted with the UK.

Only Libya, South Yemen and Djibouti had voted against. Charles was put through to Downing Street and passed on the news. The Prime Minister, although delighted with the diplomatic triumph, refused to change course until she had heard from Gaddafi. Charles put the phone down and asked his Permanent Under-Secretary to call Ambassador Kadir to the Foreign Office once more.

"But it's two o'clock in the morning, Foreign Secretary."

"I am quite aware what time it is but I can see no reason why, when we are all awake, he should be having a peaceful night's sleep."

When Mr Kadir was shown into his room it annoyed Charles to see the little man still looking fresh and dapper. It was obvious that he had just shaved and put on a clean shirt.

"You called for me, Foreign Secretary?" asked Mr Kadir politely, as if he had been invited to afternoon tea.

"Yes," said Charles. "We wished to be certain that you are aware of the vote taken at the United Nations an hour ago supporting the United Kingdom's Resolution 12/40."

"Yes, Foreign Secretary."

"In which your Government was condemned by the leaders of ninety per cent of the people on the globe" – a fact the Permanent Under-Secretary had fed to Charles a few minutes before Mr Kadir had arrived.

"Yes, Foreign Secretary."

"My Prime Minister is still waiting to hear from your Head of State."

"Yes, Foreign Secretary."

"Have you yet made contact with Colonel Gaddafi?"

"No, Foreign Secretary."

"But you have a direct telephone link to his head-quarters."

"Then you will be only too aware, Foreign Secretary, that I have been unable to speak to him," said Mr Kadir with a wry smile.

Charles saw the Permanent Under-Secretary lower his eyes. "I shall speak to you on the hour every hour, Mr Kadir, but do not press my country's hospitality too far."

"No, Foreign Secretary."

"Good night, Ambassador," said Charles.

"Good night, Foreign Secretary."

Kadir turned and left the Foreign Office to be driven back to his Embassy. He cursed the Right Honourable Charles Seymour. Didn't the man realise that he hadn't been back to Libya, except to visit his mother, since the age of four? Colonel Gaddafi was ignoring his ambassador every bit as much as he was the British Prime Minister. He checked his watch: it was two forty-four.

Simon's helicopter landed in Scotland at two forty-five. He and Sir John were immediately driven to the dockside, then ferried out to HMS *Brilliant* through the misty night.

"The first Secretary of State not to be piped on board in living memory," said Sir John as Simon made his way with difficulty, his blackthorn stick tapping up the gangplank. The captain of the *Brilliant* couldn't disguise his surprise when he saw his uninvited guests and took them quickly to the bridge. Sir John whispered something in the captain's ear which Simon missed.

"When is the next raid due?" asked Simon, staring out from the bridge but unable to see more than a few yards in front of him.

"They leave the sub at 0300, sir," said the captain, "and should reach *Brilliant* at approximately three-twenty. They hope to have taken command of the ship in eleven minutes and be a mile beyond territorial waters in under the hour."

Simon checked his watch: it was five to three. He thought of the SBS preparing for their task, unaware that the Secretary of State and the Chief of the Defence Staff were on board *Brilliant* waiting for them. He pulled his coat collar up.

Suddenly he was thrown to the deck, a black and oily hand clamped over his mouth before he could protest. He felt his arms whipped up and tied behind his back as his eyes were blindfolded and he was gagged. He tried to retaliate and received a sharp elbow in the ribs. Then he was dragged down a narrow staircase and dumped on to a wooden floor. He lay trussed up like a chicken for what he thought was about ten minutes before he heard the ship's engines revving up and felt the movement of the ship below him. The Secretary of State could not move for another fifteen minutes.

"Release them," Simon heard a voice say in distinctly Oxford English. The rope around his arms was untied and the blindfold and gag removed. Standing over the Secretary of State was an SBS frogman, black from head to toe, his white teeth gleaming. Simon was still slightly stunned as he turned to see the Services Chief also being untied.

"I must apologise, Minister," said Sir John, as soon as his gag was removed, "but I told the captain not to inform the submarine commander we were on board. If I am going to risk 217 of my men's lives I wanted to be sure this rabble from the SBS knew what they were up to." Simon backed away from the six-foot-two giant who towered over him, still grinning.

"Good thing we didn't bring the Prime Minister along for the ride," said Sir John.

"I agree," said Simon, looking up at the SBS commando. "She would have broken his neck." Everyone laughed except the frogman who pursed his lips.

"What's wrong with him?" said Simon.

"If he utters the slightest sound during the first sixty minutes he has no hope of being selected for the final team."

"The Conservative party could do with some back-bench Members of Parliament like that," said Simon, "especially when I have to address the House tomorrow and explain why I'm doing nothing."

By three-forty-nine *Brilliant* was a mile beyond territorial waters. The newspaper headlines that morning ranged from 'Diplomatic Victory' in *The Times* to 'Gaddafi the Pirate' in the *Mirror*.

At a meeting of the inner Cabinet held at ten in the morning Simon reported his first-hand experience of Shoplifter to the Prime Minister. Charles was quick to follow him. "But after the overwhelming vote in our favour at the UN it must be sensible for us to postpone anything that might be construed as an outright act of aggression."

"If the SBS don't go tomorrow morning we will have to

wait another month, Prime Minister," said Simon, interrupting him. All eyes at the meeting of the inner Cabinet turned to Kerslake.

"Why?" asked Mrs Thatcher.

"Because Ramadan, when Moslems fast and cannot take drink during daylight hours, will be coming to an end tomorrow. Traditionally the heaviest eating and drinking takes place the following day, which means tomorrow night will be our best chance to catch the guerillas off guard. I have been over the entire operation in Rosyth and by now the SBS are well on their way to the submarines and preparing for the assault. It's all so finely tuned, Prime Minister, that obviously we can't throw away such a strategic advantage."

"That's good reasoning," she concurred. "With the weekend ahead of us we must pray that this mess will be all over by Monday morning. Let's put on our negotiating faces for the Commons this afternoon. I expect a very convincing performance from you, Charles."

When Andrew rose at three-thirty that Thursday afternoon to ask for a second time for an emergency debate under standing order number ten the Speaker granted his request, directing that the urgency of the matter warranted a debate to commence at seven o'clock that evening.

The Chamber emptied quickly as the members scuttled off to prepare their speeches, although they all knew that less than two per cent of them could hope to be called. The Speaker departed the Chamber and did not return until five to seven when he took over the chair from his deputy.

By seven o'clock, when Charles and Simon had entered the House, all thirty-seven SBS men were aboard Her Majesty's submarine *Conqueror*, lying on the ocean bed about sixty nautical miles off the Libyan coast. A second submarine, *Courageous*, was ten miles to her rear. Neither had broken radio silence for the past twelve hours.

The Prime Minister had still not heard from Colonel Gaddafi and they were now only eight hours away from Operation Shoplifter. Simon looked around him. The atmosphere resembled Budget Day and an eerie silence fell as the Speaker called Andrew Fraser to address the House.

He began by explaining, under standing order number ten, why the matter he had raised was specific, important and needed urgent consideration. He quickly moved on to demand that the Foreign Secretary confirm that if negotiations with Gaddafi failed or dragged on the Secretary of State for Defence would not hesitate to take the necessary action to recover HMS *Broadsword*. Simon sat on the front bench looking glum and shaking his head.

"Gaddafi's nothing more than a pirate," said Andrew. "Why talk of diplomatic solutions?"

The House cheered as each well-rehearsed phrase rolled off Andrew's tongue. When he sat down the cheers came from all parts of the Chamber and it was several minutes before the Speaker could bring the House back to order. Mr Kadir sat in the distinguished Strangers' Gallery staring impassively down, trying to memorise the salient points that had been made and the House's reaction to them, so that – if he were ever given the chance – he could pass them on to Colonel Gaddafi.

"The Foreign Secretary," called the Speaker and Charles rose from his place on the Treasury bench. He placed his speech on the dispatch box in front of him and waited. Once again the House fell silent.

Charles opened his case by emphasising the significance of the United Nations' vote as the foundation for a genuine negotiated settlement. He went on to say that his first priority was to secure the lives of the 217 men on board HMS *Broadsword* and that he intended to work tirelessly to that end. The Secretary General was hoping to contact Gaddafi personally and brief him on the strong feelings of his colleagues in the General Assembly. Charles stressed that taking any other course at the present time could only lose the support and goodwill of the free world. When Charles sat down he realised that the rowdy House was not convinced.

The contribution from the back benches confirmed the Prime Minister's and Simon's beliefs that they had gauged the feelings of the nation correctly, but neither of them allowed the slightest show of emotion to cross their faces and give hope to those who were demanding military action.

By the time Simon rose to wind up for the Government at nine-thirty that night he had spent two and a half hours in the Chamber listening to men and women tell him to get on with exactly what he was already doing. Blandly, he backed the Foreign Secretary in his pursuit of a diplomatic solution. The House became restive, and when the clock reached ten Simon sat down to cries of "Resign" from some of his own colleagues and the more right-wing of the Labour benches.

Andrew watched carefully as Kerslake and Seymour left the Chamber. He wondered what was really going on in his old department.

He arrived home after the debate. Louise congratulated him on his speech and added, "But it didn't evoke much of a response from Simon Kerslake."

"He's up to something," said Andrew. "I only wish I was sitting in his office tonight and could find out what it is."

When Simon arrived in that office he phoned Elizabeth and explained that he would be spending another night at the ministry.

"Some women do lose their men to the strangest mistresses," said Elizabeth. "By the way, your younger son wants to know if you will have time to watch him play hockey in his cuppers' match at Oxford on Saturday."

"What's today?"

"It's still Thursday," she said, "and you're the one in charge of the nation's defences."

Simon knew the rescue attempt would be all over one way or the other by lunchtime the next day. Why shouldn't he watch his son play hockey?

"Tell him I'll be there," he said.

Although nothing could be achieved between midnight and six o'clock now the submarines were in place, none of the Joint Chiefs left the operations room. Radio silence was not broken once through the night as Simon tried to occupy himself with the bulging red boxes containing other pressing matters which still demanded his attention. He took advantage of the presence of the Joint Chiefs and had a hundred queries answered in minutes that would normally have taken him a month.

At midnight the first editions of the morning papers were brought to him. Simon pinned up the *Telegraph*'s headline on the operations board. 'Kerslake's in his Hammock till the great Armada comes.' The article demanded to know how the hero of Northern Ireland could be so indecisive while our sailors lay bound and gagged in foreign waters, and ended with the words 'Captain, art thou sleeping there below?' "Not a wink," muttered Simon. 'Resign' was the single-word headline in the *Daily Express*. Sir John looked over the minister's shoulder and read the opening paragraph.

"I shall never understand why anyone wants to be a politician," he said before reporting: "We have just heard from reconnaissance in the area that both submarines *Conqueror* and *Courageous* have moved up into place."

Simon picked up his stick from the side of his desk and left the Joint Chiefs to go to Downing Street. He took the private lift to the basement and then walked through the tunnel which runs under Whitehall direct to the Cabinet room, thus avoiding the press and any curious onlookers.

He found the Prime Minister sitting alone in the Cabinet room.

Simon went over the final plan with her in great detail, explaining that everything was ready and would be over by the time most people were having their breakfasts.

"Let me know the moment you hear anything, however trivial," she concluded, before returning to the latest gloomy study of the economy from the Wynne Godley team, who were suggesting the pound and the dollar would be on an equal parity by 1988. "One day you may have all these problems on *your* shoulders," she said.

Simon smiled and left her to walk back through the private tunnel to his office on the other side of Whitehall.

He took the lift back up to his room on the sixth floor and joined the Joint Chiefs. Although it was past midnight none of them looked tired despite their all having shared the lonely vigil with their comrades 2,000 miles away. They told stories

of Suez and the Falklands, and there was frequently laughter. But it was never long before their eyes returned to the clock.

As Big Ben struck two chimes, Simon thought: four o'clock in Libya. He could visualise the men falling backwards over the side of the boat and deep into the water before starting the long, slow swim towards *Broadsword*.

When the phone rang, breaking the eerie silence like a fire alarm, Simon picked it up to hear Charles Seymour's voice.

"Simon," he began, "I've finally got through to Gaddafi and he wants to negotiate." Simon looked at his watch; the SBS men could only be a few hundred yards from *Broadsword*.

"It's too late," he said. "I can't stop them now."

"Don't be such a bloody fool – order them to turn back. Don't you understand we've won a diplomatic coup?"

"Gaddafi could negotiate for months and still end up humiliating us. No, I won't turn back."

"We shall see how the Prime Minister reacts to your arrogance," said Charles and slammed down the receiver.

Simon sat at his desk and waited for the telephone to ring. He wondered if he could get away with taking the damn thing off the hook – the modern equivalent of Nelson placing the telescope to his blind eye, he considered. He needed a few minutes, but the phone rang again only seconds later. He picked it up and heard Margaret Thatcher's unmistakable voice.

"Can you stop them if I order you to, Simon?"

He considered lying. "Yes, Prime Minister," he said.

"But you would still like to carry it through, wouldn't you?"

"I only need a few minutes, Prime Minister."

"Do you understand the consequences if you fail, with Charles already claiming a diplomatic victory?"

"You would have my resignation within the hour."

"I suspect mine would have to go with it," she said. "In which case Charles would undoubtedly be Prime Minister by this time tomorrow." There was a moment's pause before she continued. "Gaddafi is on the other line and I am going to tell him that I *am* willing to negotiate." Simon felt defeated.

"Perhaps that will give you enough time, and let's hope it's Gaddafi who has to worry about resignations at breakfast."

Simon nearly cheered.

"Do you know the hardest thing I have had to do in this entire operation?"

"No, Prime Minister."

"When Gaddafi rang in the middle of the night, I had to pretend to be asleep so that he didn't know I was sitting by the phone."

He laughed.

"Good luck, Simon. I'll phone and explain my decision to Charles."

The clock read three-thirty.

On his return the bevy of admirals were variously clenching their fists, tapping the table or walking around it, and Simon began to sense what the Israelis must have felt like as they waited for news from Entebbe.

The phone rang again. He knew it couldn't be the Prime Minister this time as she was the one woman in England who never changed her mind. It was Charles Seymour.

"I want it clearly understood, Simon, that I gave you the news concerning Gaddafi's desire to negotiate at three-twenty. That is on the record, so there will be only one minister handing in his resignation later this morning."

"I know exactly where you stand, Charles, and I feel confident that whatever happens you'll come through your own mound of manure smelling of roses." He slammed down the phone just as four o'clock struck. For no fathomable reason everyone in the room stood up, but as the minutes passed again one by one they sat back down.

At seven minutes past four radio silence was broken with the five words, "Shoplifter apprehended, repeat Shoplifter apprehended."

Simon watched the Joint Chiefs cheer like schoolchildren reacting to the winning goal at a football match. *Broadsword* was on the high seas in neutral waters. He sat down at his desk and asked to be put through to No. 10. The Prime Minister came on the line. "Shoplifter apprehended," he told her.

"Congratulations, continue as agreed," was all she said.

The next move was to be sure that all the Libyan prisoners who had been taken aboard *Broadsword* would be discharged at Malta and sent home unharmed. Simon waited impatiently for radio silence to be broken again, as agreed, at five o'clock.

Captain Lawrence Packard came on the line as Big Ben struck five. He gave Simon a full report on the operation: one Libyan guerilla had been killed and eleven injured. There had been no, repeat no, British deaths and only a few minor injuries sustained. The thirty-seven SBS men were back on board the submarines *Conqueror* and *Courageous*. HMS *Broadsword* had two engines out of action and currently resembled an Arab bazaar, but was sailing the high seas on her way home. God Save the Queen.

"Congratulations, Captain," said Simon. He returned to Downing Street, no longer bothering to use the secret tunnel. As he limped up the road journalists with no idea of the news that was about to be announced were already gathering outside No. 10. Once again he answered none of their shouted questions. When he was shown into the Cabinet room he found Charles already there with the Prime Minister. He told them both the latest news.

"Well done, Simon," said Mrs Thatcher.

Charles made no comment.

It was agreed that the Prime Minister would make a statement to the House at three-thirty that afternoon.

"I must admit that my opinion of Charles Seymour has gone up," said Elizabeth in the car on the way to Oxford to watch Peter play in his hockey match.

"What do you mean?" asked Simon.

"He's just been interviewed on television. He said he had backed your judgement all along while having to pretend to carry out pointless negotiations. He had a very good line to the effect that it was the first time in his life that he had felt honourable about lying."

"Smelling like roses," Simon said sharply. Elizabeth didn't understand her husband's response.

He went on to tell his wife everything that had gone on between them during the last few hours.

"Why didn't you say something?"

"And admit that the Foreign Secretary and I were quarrelling throughout the entire operation? It would only show up the Government in a bad light and give the Opposition something to latch on to."

"I'll never understand politics," said Elizabeth resignedly.

It amused Simon to watch his son massacred in the mud while he stood on the touchline in the rain only hours after he had feared Gaddafi might have done the same to him. "It's a walkover," he told the Principal when Peter's college were four goals down by half-time.

"Perhaps he'll be like you and surprise us all in the second half," came back the reply.

At eight o'clock on the following Saturday morning Simon sat in his office and heard the news that *Broadsword* had all engines on full speed and was expected to reach Portsmouth by three o'clock, exactly one week after his son had lost his college match eight—nil: they hadn't had a good second half. Simon had tried to console his downcast son but it didn't help that he had been the goalkeeper.

He was smiling when his secretary interrupted his thoughts to remind him that he was due in Portsmouth in an hour. As Simon reached the door the phone rang. "Explain to whoever it is I'm already late," he said.

His secretary replied, "I don't think I can, sir."

Simon turned round, puzzled. "Who is it?" he asked.

"Her Majesty the Queen."

Simon returned to his desk, picked up the receiver and listened to the sovereign. When she had finished Simon thanked her and said he would pass on her message to Captain Packard as soon as he reached Portsmouth. During the flight down Simon looked out of the helicopter and stared at a traffic jam that stretched from the coast to London with people who were going to welcome *Broadsword* home. The helicopter landed an hour later.

The Secretary of State for Defence stood on the pier and was able to pick out the destroyer through a pair of binoculars. She was about an hour away but was already so surrounded by a flotilla of small craft that it was hard to identify her.

Sir John told him that Captain Packard had signalled to ask if the Secretary of State wished to join him on the bridge as they sailed into port. "No, thank you," said Simon. "It's his day, not mine."

"Good thing the Foreign Secretary isn't with us," said Sir John. A squad of Tornadoes flew over, drowning Simon's reply. As *Broadsword* sailed into port, the ship's company were all on deck standing to attention in full dress uniform. The ship itself shone like a Rolls-Royce that had just come off the production line.

By the time the captain descended the gangplank a crowd of some 500,000 were cheering so loudly that Simon could not hear himself speak. Captain Packard saluted as the Secretary of State leaned forward and whispered the Queen's message in his ear:

"Welcome home, Rear-Admiral Sir Lawrence Packard."

CHÁPTER
THIRTY ONE

The *Broadsword* factor remained in the memories of the electorate for a far shorter time than had the Falklands victory and the Conservative cause was not helped by the breakdown in Geneva of the disarmament talks between Reagan, Gorbachov and Thatcher.

The Russians put the blame for the breakdown on Mrs Thatcher's 'aggressive stance' over *Broadsword* after they had backed her for a diplomatic solution at the UN. Within six months the Conservative lead in the opinion polls had dropped to three per cent.

"The truth is," noted Raymond at a Shadow Cabinet meeting, "Mrs Thatcher has had nearly eight years at No. 10 and no Prime Minister has served two full terms in succession – let alone three – since Lord Liverpool in 1812."

At that time of the year when referees leave the field to be replaced by umpires Raymond watched his predictions become history. Once the Christmas recess had ended he felt sure the Prime Minister would go to the country in late May or some time in June rather than face another winter. When the Conservatives held on to the marginal seat in Birmingham and fared better than expected at the local elections in May no one believed the Prime Minister would delay the announcement much longer.

Margaret Thatcher seemed to care nothing for Lord Liverpool or historical precedent, because she called an election for late June, believing that the month that had been a winner for her in the past would prove to be good for her again.

"It's time to let the nation choose who is to govern for the next five years," she declared on *Panorama*.

"Of course, it's got nothing to do with the fact she's regained a slight lead in the opinion polls," said Joyce tartly.

"A lead that could well disappear during the next few weeks," Raymond added.

He returned to Yorkshire for only three days of the campaign. As one of the party's leading spokesmen he had to travel around the country addressing meeting after meeting in marginal seats. Many journalists went as far as to suggest that were Raymond leading the party they would be in a far stronger position to win the election. On the few occasions he was back in Leeds he enjoyed the electioneering and felt completely relaxed with his constituents for the first time in his life. He also felt his age when he discovered that the new Tory candidate for Leeds North had been born in 1964, the year he had first entered Parliament. When they met the only insult Raymond suffered at his young rival's hands was being called 'sir'.

"Please call me by my Christian name," said Raymond.

"Raymond —" began the young man.

"No, Ray will do just fine."

Charles and Simon also saw little of their constituencies as they too toured the marginal seats, adding more and more to their schedules as the polling day became closer. Half-way through the campaign the Conservatives mounted a massive attack on the Alliance, as opinion polls were continuing to show that they were making considerable inroads into the Conservative vote, while traditional Labour supporters were returning to their old allegiance.

Andrew had to remain in Edinburgh for the entire campaign, to face Frank Boyle once again. But this time, as Stuart Gray informed the constituents of Edinburgh Carlton through his columns in the *Scotsman*, it was a Frank Boyle without teeth. Andrew felt what was left of those teeth a few times during the final three weeks but at least the Royal Bank of Scotland did not find it necessary to part with a second golden sovereign in their 300-year history. Andrew retained his seat by over 2,000 votes, to be returned to Parliament for the eighth time. Louise claimed that her husband's majority were the 2,000 people who had fallen in love with the thirteen-year-old coltish Clarissa, who was already fulfilling her father's prophecy as gauche fifteen-year-old Scots blushed in her presence.

The final result of the election did not become clear until four o'clock on the Friday afternoon as several recounts took place up and down the country.

"It will be a hung Parliament," David Dimbleby told the viewers tuned into the BBC 'Election Special' programme that afternoon. He repeated the detailed figures for those people still returning from work:

Conservative	313
Labour	285
Liberal/SDP Alliance	31
Irish/Ulster Unionist	17
Speaker and others	4

Dimbleby went on to point out that there was no necessity for Mrs Thatcher to resign as she was still the leader of the largest party in the Commons. But one thing was apparent, the SDP might well hold the balance at the next election.

The Prime Minister made very few changes to her frontbench team as she clearly wished to leave an impression of unity despite her small majority. The press dubbed it 'The cosmetic Cabinet'. Charles moved to the Home Office while Simon became Foreign Secretary.

Everyone at Westminster was thankful when a few weeks later Parliament broke up for the summer recess and politicians returned home for a rest.

That rest was to last a complete week before Tony Benn rolled a thundercloud across the clear blue summer sky by announcing he would contest the leadership of the Labour party at the October conference.

Benn claimed that Kinnock's naivety and gauche approach as leader had been the single reason that the Labour party had not been returned to power. There were many Socialists who agreed with this judgement, but they also felt they would have fared considerably worse under Benn.

What his announcement did, however, was to make respectable the claim of any other candidates who wished their names to be put forward. Roy Hattersley and John Smith joined Benn and Kinnock for the first ballot. Many Members of Parliament, trade-union leaders and constituency activists pressed Raymond to stand for the leadership.

"If you don't stand now," Joyce told him, "you'll have no chance in the future."

"It's the future I'm thinking about," replied Raymond.

"What do you mean?" she asked.

"I want to stand for deputy leader against Michael Meacher and John Cunningham, and that will secure me a power base in the party which would afford me a better chance next time."

Raymond waited another week before he launched his candidacy. On the following Monday, at a packed press conference, he announced he would be standing for deputy leader.

With four candidates in the field for the leadership no clear favourite emerged although most prophets accepted Benn would lead after the first ballot. Hattersley came to an agreement with Smith that whichever one of them captured the most votes in the first round the other would drop out and support the leader of the right in the final ballot.

When the vote had been counted Benn, as predicted, topped the first ballot, with Kinnock in third place. To everyone's surprise when Kinnock dropped out he advised his supporters not to back Benn as he felt it could only spell a further prolonged period of Opposition for the Labour party.

A few hours later the party chairman announced that Tony Benn had been soundly beaten. The Labour party had a new moderate leader.

The vote then took place for the deputy leadership and although the new leader made clear his preference for Raymond everyone still expected it to be close. Joyce spent the last hour running from delegate to delegate while

Raymond tried to appear calm. At eleven o'clock that Sunday night the chairman of the Labour party's National Executive announced that by a mere three per cent Raymond Gould was the newly elected deputy leader of the Labour party.

The new leader immediately appointed Raymond Shadow Chancellor of the Exchequer.

Among the many letters and telegrams Raymond received was one from Kate, which read: Congratulations. But have you read standing order no. 5(4) of the party constitution? Raymond replied: Hadn't. Have now. Let's hope it's an omen.

In their first twelve months the new Labour team looked fresh and innovative as Mrs Thatcher began to look tired and out of touch. She was not helped in her cause by the election of Gary Hart to the White House in November 1988. President Hart's avowed intention to lower unemployment and spend more of the nation's wealth to help 'genuine Democrats' left Britain with a handful of new problems. The pound strengthened against the dollar overnight, and large export orders sat gathering dust in dockside warehouses.

But what threw her economic forecasts into total disarray was the decision of the recently elected Governments of Brazil and Argentina to refuse to repay any of the loans negotiated by their former military rulers leaving the Bank of England with what could only be described as an overdraft.

During the long cold winter of 1988 the Conservatives lost several votes on the floor of the House and many more upstairs in committee. The Prime Minister seemed somewhat relieved to find herself spending Christmas at Chequers.

The relief did not last long as two elderly Conservative members died before the House convened in January. The press dubbed the Government the 'lame drake' administration.

Both of the pending by-elections were held in May: the Conservatives fared far better than might have been expected, holding on to one and just losing the other. For a third time Mrs Thatcher plumped for a June election.

After a decade of the lady from Grantham Raymond sensed the mood was for change. The monthly unemployment, inflation and import/export figures announced at regular intervals during the campaign all augured badly for the Conservatives.

The Prime Minister's reiterated plea that a Government shouldn't be judged on one month's figures now sounded unconvincing, and by the final week the only point of contention was whether the Labour party would end up with a decent working majority.

Raymond woke up on the Friday morning after the election to be told by Joyce that the computer predictions indicated an overall majority of four seats. Together they toured the constituency that morning before joining Raymond's parents for a late lunch. When they left the little butcher's shop that afternoon there was a crowd of well-wishers awaiting them on the pavement who cheered them all the way to their car. Raymond and Joyce travelled down to London and were back in Cowley Street in time to watch the first Labour Prime Minister since 1979 emerge from Buckingham Palace with the television cameras following him all the way back until he took up residence at 10 Downing Street.

This time Raymond did not have long to wait for a telephone call because the first appointment the new Prime Minister confirmed was his Chancellor. Raymond and Joyce travelled to No. 11 later that afternoon, instructing estate agents to lease their Cowley Street house on a six-month let that might or might not be renewable. Joyce spent hours checking over her new home and replacing some of the objects she had inherited from Diana Brittan while Raymond called his team over from Transport House to prepare the Labour party's first budget, and replace even more of what Leon Brittan had left behind.

After Raymond's advisers returned to Transport House that night he started to go over the hundreds of letters and telegrams of congratulations that had been flooding in throughout the day. One from America made him particularly happy, and he returned his own best wishes to Mrs Kate Wilberhoff.

Andrew had defeated Frank Boyle for a third time and the left-winger announced that he would not be standing again.

Andrew had also spent a weekend thanking all his helpers. When he returned to the Commons on the Monday morning he found a note awaiting him on the Members' Letter-board.

Over lunch in the Members' Dining-room David Owen informed him privately that he would not be seeking re-election as leader of the SDP: seven years had been quite enough. Although the party had slightly improved their position in the House he accepted that they now faced a five-year Parliament, and he wanted Andrew to take over.

As soon as Owen had issued an official press statement Geoffrey Parkhouse of the *Glasgow Herald* was the first to phone and ask Andrew, "When will you be announcing your bid for the SDP leadership?"

Leaving the Home Office came as a great blow to Charles. His period of time there had been so short that he felt he had achieved very little. The civil servants had procrastinated over all major decisions as they waited for another general election and a clear mandate. He informed Amanda over breakfast on the Monday after the election that he would be returning to Seymour's Bank and that his salary would once again be sufficient for her allowance to remain constant – so long as she kept to her part of the bargain. Amanda nodded and left the breakfast table without comment just as Harry came in.

It was an important morning for Harry as he was to be taken to his first day of prep school at Hill House to begin the academic course mapped out for him by his father. Charles tried to convince him that it would be the start of a wonderful future, but Harry looked apprehensive. Once he had deposited a tearful eight-year-old with his first headmaster Charles continued on to the City, cheerful at the prospect of returning to the world of banking.

When he arrived at Seymour's, he was met by Clive Reynolds's secretary who immediately took him through to the boardroom and asked him if he would like a coffee.

"Thank you," said Charles, taking off his gloves, placing

his umbrella in the stand and settling himself in the chairman's seat at the head of the table. "And would you tell Mr Reynolds I'm in?"

"Certainly," said the secretary.

Clive Reynolds joined him a few moments later.

"Good morning, Mr Seymour. How nice to see you again after such a long time," he said, shaking Charles by the hand.

"Good morning, Clive. It's nice to see you too. First I must congratulate you on the manner in which you have conducted the bank's affairs in my absence."

"It's kind of you to say so, Mr Seymour."

"I was particularly impressed by the Distillers takeover; that certainly took the City by surprise."

"Yes, quite a coup, wasn't it?" said Reynolds, smiling. "And there's another one in the pipeline."

"I shall look forward to hearing the details."

"Well, I'm afraid it remains confidential at the moment," said Clive, taking the seat beside him.

"Of course, but now I have returned I had better be briefed fairly soon."

"I'm afraid shareholders cannot be briefed until we are certain the deals have been concluded. We can't afford any rumours harming our chances, can we?"

"But I'm not an ordinary shareholder," said Charles sharply. "I am returning as chairman of the bank."

"No, Mr Seymour," said Reynolds quietly. "I am chairman of this bank."

"Do you realise whom you are addressing?" said Charles.

"Yes, I think so. A former Foreign Secretary, a former Home Secretary, a former chairman of the bank and a two per cent shareholder."

"But you are fully aware that the board agreed to have me back as chairman when the Conservatives went into Opposition," Charles reminded him.

"The composition of the board has changed considerably since those days," said Reynolds. "Perhaps you've been too busy running the rest of the world to notice minor comings and goings in Cheapside."

"I shall call a board meeting."

"You don't have the authority."

"Then I shall demand an Extraordinary General Meeting," said Charles.

"And tell the shareholders what? That you had a standing order to return as Chairman when you felt like it? That won't sound like a former Foreign Secretary."

"I'll have you out of this office in twenty-four hours," Charles continued, his voice suddenly rising.

"I don't think so, Mr Seymour. Miss Trubshaw has completed her five years and left us on a full pension, and it won't take you long to discover that I don't possess a Swiss bank account or a well-compensated mistress."

Charles went red in the face. "I'll get you removed. You don't begin to understand how far my influence stretches."

"I hope I'm not removed, for your sake," said Reynolds calmly.

"Are you threatening me?"

"Certainly not, Mr Seymour, but I would hate to have to explain how Seymour's lost over £500,000 on the Nethercote account because of your personal wish to ruin Simon Kerslake's career. It may interest you to know that the only thing the bank gained from that fiasco was goodwill, and we only managed that because I recommended that Morgan Grenfell pick up the pieces."

Charles couldn't resist a smile. "When I make that public it will finish you," he said triumphantly.

"Perhaps," said Reynolds calmly, "but it would also stop you from becoming Prime Minister."

Charles turned, picked up his umbrella, put on his gloves and walked away. As he reached the door, a secretary walked in holding two cups of coffee. Charles passed her without a word and slammed the door.

"I'll only be needing one, Miss Bristow."

During the first week after the Queen's Speech Andrew was pleased to discover that a majority of his colleagues wrote to say that they would support him if he put his name forward for the leadership of the SDP.

At their weekly parliamentary meeting the party Whip asked that names for the post of party leader be submitted to his office within seven days. Each candidate had to be proposed and seconded by Members of Parliament.

For the next week the popular press tried to suggest, conjure up or even invent a rival for Andrew. Louise, who believed almost everything she read in the papers, took to perusing the *Morning Star*, the only paper which showed no interest in the outcome. But by five o'clock on the seventh day it had become obvious that Andrew was to be the sole nomination.

At the next parliamentary meeting of the SDP he was not so much elected as anointed. On the following Saturday, having been made a Privy Councillor the day before, Andrew addressed the party faithful at a packed Albert Hall. After a well-received speech, the press unanimously predicted – yet again – an SDP-Liberal revival. One or two journalists were quick to point out that if the balance of power did ever rest in his hands the Right Honourable Andrew Fraser might not know which way to jump: with on the one hand a father who was a distinguished Tory, while on the other having been a member of the Labour party himself for twenty years, which party would he consider the lesser of the two evils? Andrew always told the press that he would worry about that when the problem arose, because the SDP might not even be able to come to an agreement with the Liberals.

Numerous articles on the new SDP leader appeared in newspapers and magazines across the country. They all reported the stories of his attempt to save his son's life, the gradual recovery of his wife after Robert's death, the successful adoption of Clarissa and his re-election to Parliament on the toss of a golden sovereign.

All the publicity made Clarissa feel like a film star, she told her father. She was the most popular girl in school, she added, so he had better become Prime Minister. He laughed but proceeded to lead his party with a determination and energy that caused him to be talked of in the same breath as the leaders of the two main parties.

No sooner had the publicity over Andrew's election died

down than the press started speculating as to whether Mrs
Thatcher would now make way for a younger man.

"Don't you know any other restaurant?"

"Yes, but they don't know me," replied Ronnie Nethercote, as the two men strolled into the Ritz for the first time in
a couple of years. Heads turned as people leaned forward and
whispered Simon's name to their guests.

"What are you up to nowadays? I can't believe Opposition
fully occupies you," Ronnie said as they took their seats.

"Not really. I might also be described as one of the four
million unemployed," replied Simon.

"That's what we're here to talk about," said Ronnie, "but
first I recommend the country vegetable soup and the . . ."

"Beef off the trolley," interjected Simon.

"You remembered."

"It's the one thing you've always been right about."

Ronnie laughed more loudly than people normally did in
the Ritz before saying, "Now you no longer have the entire
armed forces at your disposal or ambassadors to call you
Your Eminence or whatever they call you now, why don't
you join the board of my new company?"

"It's kind of you to ask, Ronnie, but the answer has to be
no."

They both broke off their conversation to allow the head
waiter to take their orders.

"There's a salary of £20,000 a year that goes with it."

"I can't deny that Elizabeth and I could do with the
money. With Peter staying up at Oxford to do a D.Phil. and
Michael bent on being an actor I wonder if my bank account
will ever be in credit."

"Then why not come in with us?" asked Ronnie.

"Because I'm a committed politician," said Simon, "and I
no longer want to involve myself in any commercial activities."

"That might stop you becoming Prime Minister?"

Simon hesitated at the bluntness of Ronnie's question then
said, "Frankly, yes. I've got a better than outside chance and

I'd be foolish to lengthen the odds by becoming involved in anything else right now."

"But everyone knows that as soon as Margaret announces she's going to pack up you'll be the next leader. It's as simple as that."

"No, Ronnie, it's never as simple as that."

"Then tell me, who could beat you?"

"Charles Seymour, for one."

"Seymour? He's a toffee-nosed git," said Ronnie.

"He has a lot of friends in the party, and his patrician background still counts for something with the Tories. Sir Alec remains the best loved of our most recent Prime Ministers."

"Yes, but he was given the leadership by the magic circle," said Ronnie. "You'd kill Seymour with every elected member of the party having a vote."

"Time will tell," said Simon, bored with a conversation he had had with so many people lately. "But what have you been up to?" he asked, deliberately changing the subject.

"I've been working my backside off in preparation for going public in about a year's time, which is why I wanted you on the board."

"You never give up."

"No, and I hope you haven't given up your one per cent of the company."

"Elizabeth has it locked away somewhere."

"Then you had better find the key."

"Why?" asked Simon.

"Because when I put out ten million shares on the market at three quid a time, your one original share will be exchanged for 100,000 shares of common stock. I know you weren't ever Chancellor but that's £300,000 of anyone's money."

Simon was speechless.

"Well, say something," said Ronnie.

"Frankly I'd forgotten the share existed," Simon finally managed.

"Well, I think I can safely say," said Ronnie, parodying

one of Mrs Thatcher's favourite phrases, "that's not a bad investment for a pound, and one you will never regret."

As the budget debate drew nearer Raymond found twenty-four hours each day were not enough, even without sleep. He discussed the changes he required with the Treasury mandarins, but it became more obvious as each week passed that he would have to make sacrifices. He was sick of being told that there would always be next year, feeling he had waited far too long already. He often went over to Transport House to discuss with his party researchers those promises in the manifesto which they considered the top priorities. Raymond had been pleased by the party's decision to leave Walworth Road and return to Transport House as the party headquarters soon after their victory at the polls.

As the weeks passed, compromises were reached and cut-backs agreed but Raymond managed to cling to the changes about which he felt most passionate. By the Friday morning before the budget the mandarins had handed him his speech. It ran to 143 pages and they estimated it would keep him at the dispatch box for two and a half hours.

On the Tuesday morning of Budget Day he spelt out his tax changes to the Cabinet, who traditionally did not hear the full details until a few hours before the budget was presented to the House.

Budget Day in the House of Commons is a traditional affair. Ambassadors, diplomats, bankers and members of the House of Lords rub shoulders with the general public in the tiny Strangers' Gallery. The queue for seats often stretches for a quarter of a mile from St Stephen's to Westminster Bridge, but only half a dozen people at the front of the line actually hear the Chancellor's speech, because every other place has been allocated even before the queue has begun to form. The Chamber itself is usually packed by two-thirty although the Chancellor does not rise until an hour later. The Press Gallery is equally overcrowded with correspondents ready to run to the nearest phone as soon as any change in taxation is announced. Back-benchers, who because of the size of the Chamber cannot be guaranteed their normal places, are mostly seated by two-twenty-five. Conservatives can reserve their seats by filling in a small prayer card during the morning and leaving it on the place they wish to occupy. Socialists, who consider the system undemocratic, refuse to use the prayer cards and make a mad rush for places at two-thirty. The atheists on both sides wait for the chaplain to finish prayers before they charge in, hoping to find their usual places free.

Budget Day is also traditionally one for eccentric dress. A few top hats can be observed on the Conservative benches and the odd miner's helmet rests on a Labour head. Tom Carson arrived in a boiler suit with a Liverpool scarf around his neck, while Alec Pimkin satisfied himself with a red silk waistcoat and a white carnation in the buttonhole of his morning coat.

The green leather of the two front benches begins to disappear long before three o'clock, and by then any straggling back-bencher will be relegated to the floor or to the upstairs galleries, known as the 'Members' Side Galleries', which lack the atmosphere of the House and from which members traditionally do not rise to interrupt or make a speech.

At ten past three Raymond stepped out of No. 11 and held the famous battered budget box, first used by Gladstone, high above his head, so that the press photographers could take the traditional picture before he was driven off to the Commons.

By three-fifteen, when the Prime Minister rose to answer questions, the Chamber had taken on the look of an opening night in the West End, for what members were about to experience was pure theatre.

At three-twenty-five Raymond entered the Chamber to be greeted by cheers from his own side. Every place in the Commons except his had been filled. He looked up to see Joyce in the Strangers' Gallery, and smiled. At three-thirty, when the Prime Minister had finished answering questions, the chairman of Ways and Means – who traditionally takes the Speaker's place for a budget debate as the Speaker, being 'the King's man', does not preside over money matters – rose from his chair and called:

"Budget statement, Mr Chancellor of the Exchequer."

Raymond rose and placed his speech in front of him. He began with a review of the world economic position and went on to inform the House of the philosophy behind his first budget, namely to bring down unemployment without driving up inflation. He spoke for the first hour and a half without divulging to the House any of the fiscal changes that he would be making, so abiding by the tradition that no irreversible decisions could be considered until the Stock Exchange had closed, but also giving him the opportunity to tease the House with the odd hint or suggestion.

Raymond took a sip from the glass of water by his side when he had turned page seventy-eight. He had finished with the theory and was now ready to start on the practice.

"Old-age pensions will be raised to a record level," he declared, "as will allowances for single-parent families and disablement grants." Raymond paused and taking a faded sheet from his inside pocket read from the first speech he had ever delivered in public. "No woman whose husband has sacrificed his life for his country shall be allowed to suffer because of an ungrateful nation. War widows' pensions will go up by fifty per cent and war bonds will be honoured at their full face value." The cheering after this statement lasted for some considerable time. Once the House had settled again he continued. "The tax on beer, cigarettes, petrol and perfume will go up by five per cent. Taxes on salaries of more than £30,000 a year will be raised to eighty-five per cent and capital gains tax to fifty per cent." Several Conservatives looked glum. The Chancellor went on to announce an expansion programme in the regions to stimulate employment. He detailed his plan region by region, to cheers from different sections of the House.

He ended his speech by saying, "My purpose as the first Labour Chancellor for ten years is not to rob the rich and give to the poor, but rather to make those who live in comparative ease pay taxes that will alleviate the plight of those in genuine need. Let me tell those Honourable members who sit on the benches opposite that this is only a fifth of what I intend to achieve in the lifetime of this Parliament, and by then Britain can hope to be a more equal and just society. We intend to create a generation in which class is as outdated as the debtors' prison, in which talent, hard work and honesty are their own reward, a Socialist society that is the envy of the East as well as the West. This budget, Mr Speaker, is nothing more than the architect's plan for that dream. I look forward to being given enough time to build the reality."

When Raymond resumed his seat after two hours and twenty minutes, the length of time it takes to run a world-class marathon, he was greeted by cheers and the waving of order papers from the benches behind him.

The leader of the Opposition was faced with the almost impossible task of an immediate response, and couldn't hope to do more than pick up one or two weaknesses in the Chancellor's philosophy. The House did not hang on her every word.

BOOK FIVE

1989-1991

PARTY LEADERS

CHAPTER
THIRTY TWO

After the success of Raymond's first budget the leader of the Opposition made changes to her Shadow Cabinet as quickly as was diplomatic. She moved the former Chancellor to cover the Foreign Office, Simon to tackle Home Affairs and Charles to counter the formidable problems now raised by Raymond Gould at the Treasury.

Raymond soon discovered his task of pushing legislation through became that much harder when Charles had added the enthusiasm of his new young team to his own considerable experience of financial matters.

Raymond's success continued, however, even if it was at a slower pace than that for which he would have hoped. Labour won the first two by-elections occasioned by members' deaths, which in itself was remarkable in Government. The by-election results only started a fresh round of rumours that Denis Thatcher was pressing his wife to retire.

Charles Seymour knew that when such moves were finally made they could happen so suddenly that everyone seemed unprepared and uncertain what to do next. By the time Mrs Thatcher announced her resignation he had been building up a loyal team around him for several months.

The former Prime Minister sent a letter to Sir Cranley Onslow, the new chairman of the 1922 Committee, letting him know that she would not be putting her name forward for re-election. She explained that she would be over sixty-five at the next election and had already led the party for fourteen years, the longest period for any Conservative since Churchill, and that she now felt she was ready to pass the leadership on to new blood.

The moment everyone in the party had said the usual phrases about the retiring leader being the greatest Prime Minister since Churchill, they proceeded to look for the new Churchill.

Within hours of Mrs Thatcher's resignation both Charles Seymour and Simon Kerslake had received calls and messages from about fifty or sixty supporters, and been contacted by all the leading political journalists. Charles went about his campaign in the thorough manner in which he approached everything, appointing lieutenants to cover each intake of new members since 1964. Simon had invited Bill Travers to organise his back-up team. Travers, like any farmer, rose early each morning to gather in his harvest.

Both Simon and Charles were nominated within twenty-four hours of the necessary seven days, and by the weekend none of the rumoured third candidates had appeared in the lists which convinced the press it would be a two-horse race.

The *Financial Times* went one better than its rivals. Its political editor, Peter Riddell, spent the whole week trying to contact the 289 Tory members. He succeeded in reaching 228 of them and was able to report to his readers that 101 had said they would vote for Simon Kerslake, ninety-eight for Charles Seymour, while twenty-nine had refused to give any opinion. The article's headline read 'Narrow lead for Kerslake', and went on to point out that although the two men were polite about each other in public no one pretended they were friends.

'King Kerslake' ran the banner headline in the Monday editions of the *Sun*, and its political editor predicted Simon would win by 116 to 112: Simon suspected that they had done little more than divide the *Financial Times*'s don't-knows down the middle. With eight days to go he was being quoted at two–one on with Charles eleven–eight against by the veteran ex-Labour MP Lord Mikardo, who had run a book on the last fourteen leadership contests irrespective of party. When Elizabeth told him the odds Simon remained sceptical, as he knew from bitter experience that it never paid to underestimate the Right Honourable member for Sussex

Downs. Elizabeth agreed and then pointed to a small paragraph in the paper which he had overlooked. Ronnie's new company was going public, and the shares looked certain to be well over-subscribed.

"That's one prediction that's turned out to be accurate," said Simon, smiling.

With twelve hours to go to the close of nominations a new candidate appeared in the lists, which came as a shock to everyone because until that moment the general public were entirely unaware of Alec Pimkin. Some of his colleagues even expressed surprise that he had been able to find a proposer and a seconder. As it had been assumed that Pimkin's supporters were all men who would have backed Charles it was considered a blow to his cause, although most political pundits doubted if Pimkin could scrape together more than seven or eight out of the 289 votes to be cast.

Charles pleaded with Pimkin to withdraw but he stubbornly refused, admitting to Fiona that he was thoroughly enjoying his brief moment of glory. He held a press conference in the Commons, gave endless interviews to television, radio and the national press, and found he was receiving considerable political attention for the first time in his life since the Common Market debate. He even enjoyed the cartoon that appeared in the *Daily Telegraph* of the three candidates in the 100 metres which had Charles portrayed as a string bean, Simon as a jumping bean and Alec as a has-bean waddling in a long way behind the other two. But Alexander Dalglish remained puzzled as to what had made Pimkin place his name in the lists in the first place.

"My majority in Littlehampton had plummeted from over 12,000 to 3,200 since I was first elected, and frankly the Social Democrats have been getting a little too close for comfort. That tiresome fellow Andrew Fraser is in Sussex once a month making speeches on behalf of his candidate and there are still over four years to go until the election."

"But how many votes can you hope to pick up?" asked Fiona.

"Many more than those drunken scribblers realise. I have

nine votes already pledged, not including my own, and I could well end up with as many as fifteen."

"Why so many?" asked Fiona, immediately realising how tactless the question must have sounded.

"Dear, simple creature," Pimkin replied. "There are some members of our party who do not care to be led either by a middle-class pushy minor public schoolboy or an aristocratic, arrogant snob. By voting for me they can lodge their protest very clearly."

"But isn't that irresponsible of you?" asked Fiona, annoyed by the 'simple' quip.

"Irresponsible it may be, but you can't begin to imagine the invitations I have been receiving during the last few days. They should continue for at least a year after the election is over."

Bombshells occur in the House of Commons only on rare occasions, mainly because the elements of bad luck and timing have to come together. Something that will create a headline one week may be hardly worthy of a mention the next. On the Thursday before the leadership election the House was packed for questions to the Chancellor. Raymond and Charles were having their usual verbal battles across the dispatch box, Charles coming out slightly on top. As the Treasury wasn't his portfolio, all Simon could do was sit with his legs up on the table and listen while his rival scored points.

Tom Carson seemed extremely anxious to get in a supplementary on almost any question that was down on the order paper. Between two-thirty and five past three he had leaped up from his place no less than a dozen times. The digital clock above the Speaker's chair had reached three-twelve when, out of exasperation, the Speaker called him on a seemingly innocuous question on windfall profits.

With Prime Minister's questions just about to begin Carson faced a packed House and a full press gallery. He paused for a moment before putting his question.

"What would be my Right Honourable friend's attitude to a man who invests one pound in a company and, five years later, receives a cheque for £300,000 despite not being on the board or appearing to be involved in any way with that company?"

Raymond was puzzled as he had no idea what Carson was talking about. He did not notice that Simon Kerslake had turned white.

Raymond rose to the dispatch box. "I would remind my Honourable friend that I put capital gains tax up to fifty per cent which might dampen his ardour a little," he said. It was about the only attempt at humour Raymond had made at the dispatch box that year, which may have been the reason so few members laughed. As Carson rose a second time Simon slipped a note across to Raymond which he hurriedly skimmed.

"But does the Chancellor consider that such a person would be fit to be Prime Minister or even leader of the Opposition?"

Members started talking amongst themselves, trying to work out at whom the question was directed while the Speaker stirred restlessly in his seat, anxious to bring a halt to such disorderly supplementaries. Raymond returned to the dispatch box and told Carson that the question was not worthy of an answer. There the matter might have rested had Charles not risen to the dispatch box.

"Mr Speaker, is the Chancellor aware that this personal attack is aimed at my Right Honourable friend, the member for Pucklebridge, and is a disgraceful slur on his character and reputation? The Honourable member for Liverpool Dockside should withdraw his allegation immediately."

The Conservatives cheered their colleague's magnanimity while Simon remained silent, knowing that Charles had successfully put the story on the front page of every national paper.

Simon read the papers over breakfast on the Friday morning, and was not surprised by the coverage of Charles's bogus supplementary. The details of his transaction with Ronnie Nethercote were chronicled in the fullest extent, and it did not read well that he had received £300,000 from a 'property speculator' for a one pound investment. Some of the papers felt 'bound to ask' what Nethercote hoped to gain out of the transaction. No one seemed to realise that Simon had been on the previous company's board for five years, had invested £60,000 of his own money in that company and had only recently finished paying off the overdraft.

By the Sunday Simon had made a full press statement to put the record straight, and most of the papers had given him a fair hearing. However, Sir Peter McKay, the editor of the *Sunday Express*, didn't help matters with a comment in his widely-read PM column on the centre page.

> I would not suggest for one moment that Simon Kerslake has done anything that might be described as dishonest, but with the spotlight turned so fiercely on him there may be some Members of Parliament who feel they cannot risk going into a general election with an accident-prone leader. Mr Seymour, on the other hand, has made his position abundantly clear. He did not seek to return to his family bank in Opposition while he was still hoping to hold public office.

The Monday papers were reassessing the outcome of the ballot to take place the next day and were predicting that Seymour now had the edge. Some journalists went so far as to suggest that Alec Pimkin might profit from the incident as members waited to see if there would be a second chance to give their final verdict.

Simon had received several letters of sympathy during the week, including one from Raymond Gould. Raymond assured Simon that he had not been prepared for the Carson supplementary and apologised for any embarrassment his first answer might have caused.

"It never crossed my mind that he had," said Simon, as he passed Raymond's letter over to Elizabeth.

"*The Times* was right," she said a few moments later. "He is a very fair man."

A moment later Simon passed his wife another letter.

Seymour's Bank,   15 May 1989
202 Cheapside,
London, EC1

Dear Mr Kerslake,

I write to correct one fact to which the press have
continually referred. Mr Charles Seymour, the former
chairman of this bank, did seek to return to Seymour's
after the Conservatives went into Opposition. He hoped
to continue as chairman on a salary of £40,000 a year.

The board of Seymour's did not fall in with his wishes.

Yours sincerely,
Clive Reynolds.

"Will you use it?" asked Elizabeth, when she had finished
reading the letter through.

"No. It will only draw more attention to the issue."

Elizabeth looked at her husband as he continued to read
the letters, and remembered the file that she still possessed on
Amanda Wallace. She would never reveal its contents to
Simon; but perhaps the time had come to make Charles
Seymour sweat a little.

On the Monday evening Simon sat on the front bench
listening to the Financial Secretary moving those clauses of
the short Finance Bill which were being taken in committee
on the floor of the House. Charles never let any of Raymond
Gould's team get away with a phrase or even a comma if he
could see a weakness in their case, and the Opposition were
enjoying every moment. Simon sat and watched the votes
slipping away, knowing he could do nothing to stop the
process.

Of the three candidates only Pimkin slept well the night
before the election.

Voting began promptly at nine o'clock the next day in the
Grand Committee room of the House of Commons, the party
Whips acting as tellers. By three-ten all but one of those
entitled to vote had done so. John Cope, the Chief Whip,
stood guard over the large black tin box until Big Ben struck
four, when it became apparent that Mrs Thatcher had
decided to remain neutral.

At four o'clock the box was removed to the Chief Whip's

office and the little slips were tipped out and checked twice in less than fifteen minutes. As John Cope left his room he was followed, Pied Piper-like, by lobby correspondents hoping to learn the result, but he had no intention of divulging anything before he reached the 1922 Committee who were keenly awaiting him.

Committee room fourteen was filled to overflowing, with some 280 of the 289 Conservative Members of Parliament present. Their chairman, Sir Cranley Onslow, welcomed the Chief Whip and asked him to join him on the small raised platform. He did so and passed over a folded piece of paper. The chairman of the 1922 Committee rose, faced the committee, unfolded the piece of paper and pushed up his glasses. He hesitated as he took in the figures.

"The result of the ballot carried out to select the leader of the parliamentary party is as follows:

Charles Seymour	138
Simon Kerslake	135
Alec Pimkin	15"

There was a gasp followed by prolonged chatter, which lasted until members noticed that the chairman remained standing as he waited for some semblance of order to return among his colleagues.

"There being no outright winner," Sir Cranley continued, "a second ballot will take place next Tuesday without Mr Pimkin."

The national press surrounded Pimkin as he left the Commons that afternoon, wanting to know whom he would advise his supporters to vote for in the second ballot. Pimkin, obviously relishing every moment, declared a little pompously that he intended to interview both candidates in the near future and ask them one or two apposite questions. He was at once dubbed 'Kingmaker' by the press, and the phones at his home and office never stopped ringing. Whatever their private thoughts, both Simon and Charles agreed to see Pimkin before he told his supporters how he intended to cast his vote.

Elizabeth sat alone at her desk willing herself to go through with it. She glanced down at the faded file that she had not looked at for so many years. She sipped the brandy from the tumbler by her side, both of which she had discovered in the medicine cabinet a few minutes before. All her years of training and commitment to the Hippocratic oath went against what she felt she must now do. While Simon had slept soundly she had lain awake considering the consequences, then made the final decision. Simon's career came first. She picked up the receiver, dialled the number and waited. She nearly replaced it at once when she heard his voice.

"730–9712. Charles Seymour speaking."

"It's Elizabeth Kerslake," she said, trying to sound confident. There was a long silence in which neither of them spoke.

Once Elizabeth had taken another sip of brandy she added, "Don't hang up, Mr Seymour, because I feel confident you'll be interested in what I have to say."

Charles still didn't speak.

"Having watched you from a distance over the years I am sure that your reaction to Carson's question in the Commons last week was not spontaneous."

Charles cleared his throat but still didn't speak.

"And if anything else happens this week that could cause my husband to lose the election, be assured I shall not sit by and watch."

There was still no reply.

"I have a file in front of me marked 'Miss Amanda Wallace', and if you wish all its contents to remain confidential I would advise you to avoid any repercussion of your antics. It's packed with names *Private Eye* would wallow in for months."

Charles said nothing.

Elizabeth's confidence was growing. "You needn't bother to inform me that such an action would get me struck off the medical register. That would be a small penalty for watching you have to suffer the way my husband has this week." She paused. "Good day, Mr Seymour."

Charles still didn't speak.

Elizabeth put the phone down and swallowed the remainder of the brandy. She prayed that she had sounded convincing because she knew she could never carry out such a threat.

Charles took Pimkin to dinner at White's – where Alec had always wanted to be a member – and was escorted to a private room on the first floor.

Charles didn't wait long to ask, "Why are you going through with this charade? Don't you realise I would have won it in the first round, if you hadn't stood?"

Pimkin bridled. "No doubt, but I haven't had so much fun in years."

"Who the hell got you your seat in the first place?"

"I well remember," said Pimkin. "And I also remember the price you exacted for it. But now it's my turn to call the tune, and this time I require something quite different."

"What are you hoping for? Chancellor of the Exchequer in my first administration?" said Charles, barely able to keep the sarcasm from his voice.

"No, no," said Pimkin, "I know my worth; I am not a complete fool."

"So what do you want? Membership of White's? Perhaps I could fix that."

"Nothing as mundane. In return for putting you into Downing Street I expect to be translated to the House of Lords."

Charles hesitated. He could always give Pimkin his word; and who other than Pimkin would notice if in three years' time he didn't carry it through?

"If you and your fifteen men vote for me next Tuesday I'll put you in the Lords," said Charles. "You have my word on it."

"Good," said Pimkin. "But one small thing, old chum," he added as he closely folded his napkin.

"Christ – what do you want now?" asked Charles, exasperated.

"Like you, I want the agreement in writing."

Charles hesitated again, but this time he knew he was beaten. "I agree," he said.

"Good, then it's a deal," said Pimkin. Looking round for a waiter he added, "I rather think champagne is called for."

When Pimkin put the same proposition two days later Simon Kerslake took some time before he answered. Then he said, "That's a question I would have to consider on its merits at the time, if and when I became Prime Minister."

"So bourgeois," said Pimkin as he left Simon's room. "I offer him the keys to No. 10 and he treats me like a locksmith."

Charles left the Commons that night having spent his time going round a large cross-section of his supporters, and he was reassured to discover they were standing firm. Wherever he went in the long Gothic corridors members singly or in groups came up to pledge their support. It was true that Kerslake's windfall of £300,000 was fast becoming yesterday's news, but Charles still felt enough blood had been let from that wound to ensure his final victory, even though he still cursed Pimkin for holding up the result. One anonymous note, with all the necessary details, sent to the right Labour member, had certainly proved most effective. Charles cursed as he realised Elizabeth Kerslake had successfully stopped any further covert attacks on his rival.

When he arrived home he was appalled to find Amanda waiting for him in the drawing-room.

"I thought I told you to stay away until the middle of next week?"

"I changed my mind, Charlie," said Amanda.

"Why?" he asked suspiciously.

"I think I've earned a little reward for being such a good girl."

"What do you have in mind?" he asked as he stood by the mantelpiece.

"Fair exchange."

"For what?"

"For the world rights to my life story."

"Your *what*?" said Charles in disbelief. "Who is going to be the slightest bit interested in you?"

"It's not me they're interested in, Charlie, it's you. The *News of the World* have offered me £100,000 for the unexpurgated story of life with Charles Seymour." She added dramatically, "Or what it's like to live with the second son of an earl who will go to any lengths to become Prime Minister."

"You can't be serious," said Charles.

"Deadly serious. I've made quite a few notes over the years. How you got rid of Derek Spencer but failed to pull the same trick on Clive Reynolds. The extremes you went to trying to keep Simon Kerslake out of the House. How your first wife swapped the famous Holbein picture of the first Earl of Bridgwater. But the story which will cause the most interest is the one in which the real father of young Harry Seymour is revealed because his dad's life story was serialised in the *People* a couple of years ago, and that seems to be one episode they missed out."

"You bitch. You know Harry is my son," said Charles, advancing towards her. But Amanda stood her ground.

"And perhaps I should include a chapter on how you assault your wife behind the closed doors of your peaceful Eaton Square mansion."

Charles came to a halt. "What's the deal?"

"I keep quiet for the rest of my life and you present me with £50,000 now and a further £50,000 when you become leader."

"You've gone mad."

"Not me, Charlie, I've always been sane. You see, I don't have a paranoia to work out on dear harmless brother Rupert. The *News of the World* will love that part now that he's the fifteenth Earl. I can just see the picture of him wearing his coronet and decked out in his ermine robes."

"They wouldn't print it."

"They would when they learn that he's as queer as a two-pound note, and therefore our only son will collect the earldom when he's not entitled to it."

"No one would believe it, and by the time they print the story it will be too late," said Charles.

"Not a bit," said Amanda. "I am assured by my agent that the true reason behind the resignation of the leader of the

Conservative party would be an even bigger scoop than that of a one-time contestant."

Charles sank down in the nearest armchair.

"Twenty-five thousand," he said.

"Fifty thousand," replied his wife. "It's only fair. After all, it's a double deal: no story to the press and you become leader of the Conservative party."

"All right," whispered Charles, rising to leave the room.

"Wait a minute, Charlie. Don't forget I've dealt with you in the past."

"What else are you hoping for?" said Charles, swinging round.

"Just the autograph of the next Tory leader," she replied producing a cheque.

"Where the hell did you get hold of that?" asked Charles, pointing to the slip of paper.

"From your cheque book," said Amanda innocently.

"Don't play games with me."

"From the top drawer of your desk."

Charles snatched it from her and nearly changed his mind. Then he thought of his brother in the House of Lords, his only son not inheriting the title and having to give up the leadership. He took out his pen and scribbled his name on the cheque before leaving his wife in the drawing-room holding £50,000. She was checking the date and the signature carefully.

Simon and Elizabeth spent a quiet weekend in their country cottage while the photographers pitched camp in Eaton Square. They had received a leak from an 'authoritative' source that Pimkin would come out in support of his old school chum.

"A brilliant move," said Elizabeth over breakfast on the Sunday morning admiring the picture on the front page of the *Observer*.

"Another photo of Seymour telling us what he will do when he's Prime Minister?" said Simon, not looking up from the *Sunday Times*.

"No," said Elizabeth, and passed her paper across the

table. Simon stared at the Holbein portrait of the first Earl of Bridgwater under the headline 'A gift to the nation'.

"Good God," said Simon. Are there no depths he will not sink to, to win this election?"

"My dear, by any standards you have delivered the *coup de grâce*," said Pimkin to Fiona over lunch that Sunday.

"I thought you would appreciate it," said Fiona, pouring him another glass of his own wine.

"I certainly did and I particularly enjoyed the director of the National Gallery's comments – 'that Charles's gesture of presenting the priceless painting to the nation was the act of a selfless man'."

"Of course, once the story had been leaked to the press Charles was left with no choice," said Alexander Dalglish.

"I realise that," said Pimkin, leaning back, "and I would have given a dozen bottles of my finest claret to have seen Charles's face the moment he realised the first Earl of Bridgwater had escaped his clutches for ever. If he had denied giving the earl to the nation the publicity that would have followed would have certainly ensured defeat in the election on Tuesday."

"Win or lose next week, he daren't then suggest it was all done without his approval," said Alexander.

"I love it, I love it," said Pimkin. "I am told that Princess Diana will be unveiling the portrait on behalf of the nation – and rest assured that when she performs the official ceremony, I shall be there to bear witness."

"Ah, but will Charles?" asked Fiona.

On Monday morning Charles's brother phoned from Somerset to ask why he had not been consulted about donating the Holbein to the nation.

"It was my picture to dispose of as I pleased," Charles reminded him and slammed down the phone.

By nine o'clock on Tuesday morning, when the voting took place for the last time, the two contestants had spoken to nearly every member twice. Charles joined his colleagues in the Members' Dining-room for lunch while Simon took Elizabeth to Locketts in Marsham Street. She showed him some coloured brochures of a holiday on the Orient Express which would be the most perfect way to see Venice. She hoped that they wouldn't have time to go on the trip. Simon hardly mentioned the vote that was simultaneously taking place in the Commons but it never was far from either of their minds.

The voting ended at three-fifty but once again the Chief Whip did not remove the black box until four o'clock. By four-fifteen he knew the winner but did not reveal his name until the 1922 Committee had assembled at five o'clock. He informed their chairman at one minute to five.

Once again, Sir Cranley Onslow stood on the small raised platform in the committee room fourteen to declare the result. There was no need to ask if the people at the back could hear.

"Ladies and gentlemen," he said, his words echoing round the room, "the result of the second ballot for the leadership of the Tory Party is as follows:

> Charles Seymour   130
> Simon Kerslake   158."

Just over half the members present rose and cheered while Bill Travers ran all the way to Simon's room to be the first to report the news. When he arrived Simon swung round and faced the open door.

"You look and sound as though you'd run a marathon."

"Like Pheidippides, I bring great news of victory."

"I hope that doesn't mean you're going to drop down dead," said Simon, grinning.

The new leader of the Conservative party said nothing more for a few moments. It was obvious that Pimkin had come out in favour of him. Later that night, one or two other members also admitted that they had changed their minds during the second week because they hadn't liked the blatant opportunism of Charles presenting a priceless portrait to the nation only a few days before the final vote.

The following morning Fiona phoned Pimkin to ask him

why he had acted as he did. "My dear Fiona," he replied, "like Sidney Carton I considered it would be good to go to my grave knowing I had done one honourable thing in my life."

It took only a week for Simon's little house in Beaufort Street to be transformed. He could not as much as turn his head without facing a camera. Everywhere he went he was followed by a platoon of press men. He was surprised how quickly the experience became part of his daily routine, although Elizabeth never found it an edifying experience. She was, however, as booked up as Simon and once again they seemed only to meet in the evenings. He spent his first two weeks selecting the Shadow Cabinet he wanted to take into the next general election. He was able to announce the composition of his new team to the press fourteen days after his election as leader of the Conservative party. He made one sentimental appointment: that of Bill Travers as Shadow Minister of Agriculture.

When asked at a press conference why his defeated rival would not be serving in the team Simon explained that he had offered Charles Seymour the deputy leadership and any portfolio of his choice, but Charles had turned the offer down, saying he preferred to return to the back benches for the present time.

Charles had left for Scotland the same morning for a few days' rest by the river Spey, taking his son with him. Although he spent much of their short holiday feeling depressed about the final outcome of the leadership struggle, Harry's original efforts at fishing helped deaden some of the pain. Harry even ended up with the biggest fish.

Amanda, on the other hand, realising how slim her chances were of coaxing any more cash out of her husband, re-opened negotiations over her life story with the *News of the World*.

When Nick Lloyd, the editor, read through Amanda's notes he decided on two things. She would require a ghost writer and the paper would have to halve their original offer.

"Why?" demanded Amanda.

"Because we daren't print the better half of your story."

"Why not?"

"No one would believe it."

"But every word is true," she insisted.

"I'm not doubting the veracity of the facts," said Lloyd, "only readers' ability to swallow them."

"They accepted that a man climbed the walls of Buckingham Palace and found his way into the Queen's bedroom."

"Agreed," replied Lloyd, "but only after the Queen had confirmed the story. I'm not so sure that Charles Seymour will be quite as co-operative."

Amanda remained silent long enough for her agent to close the deal.

The watered-down version of 'My Life with Charles Seymour' appeared a few months later to coincide with Charles's much-publicised divorce, but it made no more than a faint ripple in political circles. Now that Charles had no prospect of leading his party it was very much yesterday's news.

Amanda came out of the divorce settlement with another £50,000 but lost custody of Harry, which was all Charles really cared about. He prayed her irresponsible remarks reported in the papers concerning the boy's claim to the title had been quickly forgotten.

Then Rupert phoned from Somerset and asked to see him privately.

A week later they sat facing each other in Charles's drawing-room at Eaton Square.

"I am sorry to broach such an embarrassing subject," said Rupert, "but I feel it is my duty to do so."

"Duty, poppycock," said Charles, stubbing out his cigarette. "I tell you Harry is my son, and as such will inherit the title. He's the spitting image of great-grandfather and that ought to be enough proof for anyone."

"In normal circumstances I would agree with you, but the recent publicity in the *News of the World* has been brought to my notice and I feel . . ."

"That sensationalist tabloid," said Charles sarcastically, his voice rising. "Surely you don't take their word before mine?"

"Certainly not," said Rupert, "but if Amanda is to be believed Harry is not your son."

"How am I meant to prove he is?" asked Charles, trying to control his temper. "I didn't keep a diary of the dates when I slept with my wife."

"But it seems Amanda did so I have had to take legal advice on the matter," continued Rupert, "and am informed that a blood test is all that will prove necessary to verify Harry's claim to the title. We both share a rare blood group as did our father and grandfather, and if Harry is of that group I shall never mention the subject again. If not, then the title will eventually be inherited by our second cousin in Australia."

"And if I don't agree to put my son through this ridiculous test?"

"Then the matter must be placed in the hands of our family solicitors," said Rupert, sounding unusually in control. "And they must take whatever course they consider fit."

CHAPTER
THIRTY THREE

Simon's first year as leader was one of unbounded energy and ideas which bore fruit as the Conservatives picked up three seats at by-elections and whittled away the Government's majority. The press were already predicting that the Socialists wouldn't be able to complete their full five-year term, which moved Simon to goad Central Office into a perpetual state of readiness for an election.

Raymond continued to gain respect at the Treasury as his policies began to show results. He had to cut back on some of the more ambitious projects as his gloomy predictions about American interest rates and the drop in the production of North Sea oil proved daily more accurate. After his second budget the financial press felt he had done all that was possible, given the world situation. When unemployment fell below two million and strikes to their lowest level since the Second World War some members hailed Raymond as the unions' Messiah, while others noted that he had been shrewd enough to steal some of the Opposition's co-inflation clothes in the absence of Charles Seymour.

As Raymond entered his third year as Chancellor the opinion polls showed the two main parties neck and neck again, with a surprising proportion of people saying that they would vote for the Alliance for the first time.

The Liberals still held sixteen seats in the Commons but, as in the past three elections, they had decided to fight under the collective banner as the Social Democrats during the general election campaign.

As the time for election drew near both small parties knew they would have to declare their choice for overall leader if a combination of Liberals and Social Democrats ever held the balance of power in Parliament. When the pollsters dug a little deeper it transpired that Andrew Fraser had become the most popular political leader in the country despite the fact he only led forty-two members in the Commons.

Andrew spent a lot of his time addressing meetings all over the country trying to convince the voters that at the next election the political balance would change. He said it so often he began to believe it himself, and two good by-election victories early in 1990 helped his supporters feel it was possible too. The press began to take such claims seriously when at the local election in May the Alliance captured 102 council seats at the expense of both the major parties.

"Daddy, Daddy, open my school report."

Charles left the morning mail unopened as he held Harry in his arms. He knew nothing could ever part them now but he dreaded Harry finding out that he might not be his real father.

"Please open it," pleaded Harry, wriggling free.

The school doctor had been asked to take a sample of Harry's blood along with six other boys from his form so that he would not consider the request unusual. Even the doctor hadn't been told the full significance of the action.

Harry extracted the envelope from the pile by Charles's side – the one with the school crest in the top left-hand corner – and held it out for his father to open. He looked excited and seemed hardly able to contain himself. Charles had promised he would phone his brother as soon as the result of the blood test was confirmed. He had wanted to phone the doctor a hundred times during the past week but had always stopped himself, knowing it would only add to the man's curiosity.

"Come on, Dad, read the report and you'll see it's true."

Charles tore open the letter and removed the little book which would reveal the result of all Harry's efforts during the term. He flicked through the pages – Latin, English, History, Geography, Art, Divinity, Games, Form master, Head-master. He reached the last page, a small yellow sheet headed: 'Term medical report'. It started: Harry Seymour, age eleven, height four feet nine inches – he's suddenly sprung up, thought Charles – weight five stone four pounds. He glanced up at Harry who looked as if he was about to burst.

"It is true, Dad, isn't it?"

Charles read on without answering the boy's question. At the foot of the page was a typewritten note signed by the school doctor. Charles read it twice before he understood its full significance and then a third time. "As requested I took a sample of Harry's blood and analysed it. The result shows that Harry shares a rare blood group . . ."

"Is it true, Dad?" asked Harry yet again.

"Yes, my son, it's true."

"I told you, Dad – I knew I'd be top in the class. That means I'll be captain of the school next term. Just like you."

"Just like me," said his father, as he picked up the phone by his side and began to dial his brother's number in Somerset.

When the Prime Minister went into hospital for a minor operation the press immediately started to speculate on his resignation. Ten days later when he walked out looking better than ever the rumours ceased immediately. In the Prime Minister's absence as deputy leader Raymond chaired Cabinet meetings and stood in for him during questions in the Commons. This gave the lobby correspondents a chance to proclaim, like Caesarian soothsayers plucking at entrails, that Raymond was *primus inter pares*.

Raymond enjoyed presiding over the Cabinet, but was surprised that the civil servants expected him to spend his entire Tuesday and Thursday mornings preparing for Prime Minister's questions.

Both Simon Kerslake and Andrew Fraser had gained formidable reputations during Prime Minister's questions, and Raymond found the fifteen-minute encounter more demanding than a full winding-up speech in a major debate;

in retrospect, he was relieved that he had prepared so thoroughly. The lobby correspondents seemed to be in agreement that Raymond had held his own on both occasions and that, if anything, Simon Kerslake had underestimated him.

The Prime Minister returned to Downing Street the following week and assured Raymond that the operation had been a success and the likelihood of any recurrence of the trouble was, in the surgeon's opinion, minimal. He admitted to Raymond that he hoped to lead the party to a second victory at the polls, by which time he would be within a few years of his seventieth birthday and ready to bow out quietly. He told Raymond bluntly that he hoped he would be his successor. But Raymond couldn't help remembering that Neil Kinnock was eight years younger than he was.

Raymond returned to the Treasury to prepare for what looked like his final budget before the general election. His stewardship had made it possible to loosen the reins slightly with an election in mind. He described the loosening to the Cabinet as no more than a percentage point or two; he had no intention, he assured them, of letting three years' hard work be sacrificed at the altar of vote-catching. Some of his colleagues round the Cabinet table wished he were not quite so unbending at times.

Whenever Raymond spoke around the country more and more people approached him about standing for the leadership. He always thanked them courteously but maintained his loyalty to the Prime Minister, which loyalty, he added, would remain constant until he chose to resign.

Simon and Andrew also spent every weekend in planes, cars or trains fulfilling speaking engagements right up until the party conferences in October.

Andrew, in his summing-up speech to the SDP conference at Weston-super-Mare, told the delegates that they should expect to hold the balance of power between the two major parties after the next election. For the first time, he told them, they would have the chance to participate in a national Government. He sent the delegates home warning them to prepare for an election within the coming twelve months, by which time they would be able to welcome SDP Members of

Parliament who would already be playing a major role in the running of the nation. Andrew's supporters left the West Country keyed up for battle.

The Labour party conference followed a week later at Brighton and Raymond delivered a keynote speech on the state of the nation's finances. He pressed the unions to continue supporting their Government by keeping the twin evils of inflation and unemployment at acceptable levels. "Let us not pass on three years of achievement to be squandered by a Conservative Government," he told the cheering delegates. "Brothers, I look forward to presenting five more Labour budgets that will make it impossible for the Tories to imagine a future victory at the polls."

Raymond received one of the rare standing ovations to be given to any Cabinet minister at a Labour party conference. The delegates had never doubted his ability, but over the years they had grown to respect his sincerity as well as his judgement.

Seven more days passed before Simon addressed the Tory faithful at the Conservative party conference in Blackpool. By tradition, the leader always receives a four-to-six-minute standing ovation after he completes his speech on the final day. "He'd still get four minutes," said Pimkin to a colleague, "if he read them *Das Kapital*."

Simon had spent six weeks preparing for the occasion since, like Andrew, he was convinced this would be the last conference before the election. He was pleasantly surprised to find Charles Seymour coming forward with new ideas on tax reform which he hoped might be considered for inclusion in the leader's speech to the conference.

Charles had recently been making useful contributions in the House during finance debates, and Simon hoped that it would not be long before he would be willing to return to the front bench. His main preoccupation in the House had been as a member of the Chairmen's Panel from which committee chairmen were recruited for each bill. Charles had mellowed considerably during his time on the back benches and many of his friends feared he had lost his ambition for high office and might not even stand at the next election. Simon hoped this wasn't the case as he desperately needed someone of Charles's ability to counter Raymond Gould at the Treasury. Simon included Charles's suggestions in the final draft of his speech and dropped him a handwritten note of thanks.

On that Friday morning in Blackpool, in front of 2,000 delegates and millions more watching on television, Simon presented a complete and detailed plan of what he hoped to achieve when the Conservatives were returned to Government.

"Power is what we want and *power* is what we seek," he told a mesmerised audience. "For without *power* we cannot serve."

After the peroration the delegates duly rose for a genuine six-minute ovation. When the noise had died down Pimkin was heard to remark, "I think I made the right decision."

The conference season over, members made their way back from the three seasides to Westminster. Sadness overcame the House in their first week back when the ageing Mr Speaker Weatherill suffered a minor heart attack and retired to the Lords. The Government's overall majority was only two at the time and the Labour party Chief Whip feared that if they supplied the new Speaker from their own ranks and the Conservatives were to retain the old Speaker's safe seat the Government majority would cease to exist.

Simon reluctantly agreed that the Speaker should come from his own benches and asked his Chief Whip to suggest a suitable candidate.

When Charles Seymour asked to be granted a private interview with the leader Simon agreed immediately.

Charles arrived at the Opposition leader's office the following morning. It was the first time they had talked alone since the leadership battle. A head of white hair had grown from the roots of Charles's once Odyssean locks, and the deeper lines in Charles's face gave him a more gentle look. Simon couldn't help noticing a slight stoop had replaced his ramrod bearing. Looking at them now no one would have suggested they were contemporaries. Charles's request came as a shock to Simon for he had never once considered his great rival as a candidate for that particular job.

"But I want you to return to the front bench and be my Chancellor," said Simon. "You must know I would be delighted to have you back in the team."

"That's considerate of you," said Charles. "But I would prefer the more restful life of being an arbitrator rather than an antagonist. I've lost that desire always to be on the attack. For over twenty years you've had the advantage of Elizabeth and two sons to keep your feet on the ground. It's only quite recently that Harry has done the same for me."

All men are thought to have one great moment in their careers in the House, and for Alec Pimkin it was to be that day. The election of a Speaker in the Commons is a quaint affair. By ancient tradition no one must appear to want the honour, and it is rare for more than one person to be proposed for the post. During Henry VI's reign three Speakers were beheaded within a year, although in modern times it has been more the heavy burden of duties that has often led to an early grave. This tradition of reluctance has carried on through the ages, and for that reason a future Speaker frequently does not know who has sponsored him. Dressed in a smart blue suit, sporting a red carnation and his favourite pink-spotted bow tie, Alec Pimkin rose from his seat on the back benches to move that 'the Right Honourable Charles Seymour does take the chair of this House as Speaker'. His speech was serious yet witty, informed but personal. Pimkin held the House in his grasp for nine minutes and never once let it go. "He's done his old friend proud," one member muttered to another across the gangway when Pimkin sat down, and indeed the look on Charles's face left no doubt that he felt the same way, whatever had taken place in the past.

After Charles had been seconded the tradition of dragging the Speaker-elect to the chair was observed. This normally humorous affair, usually greeted with hoots of laughter and cheering, became even more of a farce with the sight of the small, portly Pimkin and his Labour seconder dragging the six-foot-four former Guards' officer from the third row of the back benches all the way to the chair.

Charles surveyed the Commons from his new vantage point. He began by expressing his grateful thanks for the high honour the House had bestowed on him. From the moment he rose and stood his full height, every member knew they had selected the right man to guide them through the parliamentary calendar. The sharpness of his tongue may have gone but there remained a firm delivery and natural authority that left none of his colleagues in any doubt that Mr Speaker Seymour intended to keep 'order' for many years to come.

The Conservatives held the Croydon North-East seat comfortably at the by-election, and captured a marginal six weeks later. The press pointed out that it only needed the Tories and the SDP/Liberal Alliance to join together for the Government and Opposition to be in equal numbers, leaving the seventeen Irish members to decide the fate of the Parliament. Raymond was determined that the Government should hold on for another few weeks so that he could deliver his third budget, which he was convinced would act as a launching pad on which to fight the election.

Andrew had realised that Raymond's next budget might help Labour's chances at the polls, and he sought an official meeting with the leader of the Opposition to discuss the possibility of a 'no confidence' motion.

Simon agreed with Andrew's suggestion and thought that they should time the debate for the end of March. If they won that would ensure an election before the budget.

Raymond had accepted an invitation to address a large Labour rally in Cardiff the weekend before the vote of 'no confidence'. He boarded the train at Paddington, settled into his compartment and began to check over his speech. As the train pulled into Swindon a railway official stepped on board and, having discovered where the Chancellor of the Exchequer was seated, asked if he could speak to him privately for a few minutes. Raymond listened carefully to what the man had to say, replaced the speech in his brief case, got off the train, crossed the platform and returned by the first available train to London.

On the journey back he tried to work out all the consequences of the news he had just been told. As soon as he arrived at Paddington he made his way through the waiting photographers and journalists, answering no questions. A car took him straight to Westminster Hospital. Raymond was shown into a private room, to find the Prime Minister sitting upright in bed.

"Now don't panic," he said before Raymond could speak. "I'm in fine shape considering I'm over sixty and with all the pressure we've been under this last year."

"What's wrong with you?" asked Raymond, taking a chair next to the bed.

"Recurrence of the old trouble, only this time they say it will take major surgery. I'll be out of this place in a month, six weeks at the most, and then I'll live as long as Harold Macmillan, they tell me. Now, to more important matters. I want you to take over for me again, which will mean you will have to speak in my place during the 'no confidence' debate on Wednesday. If we lose the vote, I shall resign as leader."

Raymond tried to protest as he had already worked out the implications the moment he had heard his leader was ill again. The Prime Minister held up his hand and continued talking. "No party can fight an election with its leader laid up in bed for six weeks, however well he might be when they release him. If there is to be an election, the voters have the right to know who is going to lead the party in Parliament, and of course in such an emergency under standing order number five (four) of the Labour party's constitution," continued the Prime Minister, "the National Executive would meet and automatically select you to take over as party leader."

Raymond raised his head. "Yes. The importance of that particular standing order has already been pointed out to me."

The Prime Minister smiled. "Joyce, no doubt."

"Her name was Kate, actually."

The Prime Minister looked puzzled and then continued. "I think you must get used to the idea, Raymond, that you may well be running for Prime Minister in three weeks' time. Because if we lose the 'no confidence' vote on Wednesday I am given no choice but to advise the Queen to call an immediate general election."

Raymond remained silent.

"I can assure you," continued the Prime Minister, "the National Executive will not want an internal blood bath three weeks before a general election. Nothing could be more certain to guarantee a Tory victory. If, however, we do win the 'no confidence' vote then it's a different matter altogether because I'll be back and running the ship long before the Easter recess is over. That will give us enough time to call the election after you've delivered your third budget. So make sure you win on Wednesday."

"I am unable to express how much we will all miss your leadership," said Raymond, without guile.

"As every member of the House except the Irish will know which lobby they'll be voting in long before the debate begins, my leadership may turn out to be less important than any single vote. And don't forget it will be the first occasion at which they've allowed television on the floor of the Commons, so make sure Joyce picks out one of those smart shirts you sometimes wear."

Raymond spent the final few days before the 'no confidence' vote preparing his speech. He cancelled all the engagements in his diary except for the Speaker's dinner to celebrate the Queen's sixty-fifth birthday, at which he would be standing in for the Prime Minister.

The Government and Opposition Whips spent Monday and Tuesday checking that every member would be present in the House by ten o'clock on Wednesday night. The political journalists pointed out that, if the vote were a tie, Mr Speaker Seymour had already made it clear that he would abide by the ancient tradition of giving his casting vote to the Government of the day. Charles was armed with precedents from Speaker Addington in the eighteenth century to Speaker Denison in the nineteenth. Charles pointed out that, in line with the principle, he must vote in such a manner as not to make the decision of the chair final.

Simon was to open the debate for the Opposition while Andrew was being allowed to wind up, the only concession Simon had granted the SDP/Liberal Alliance for ensuring their support in the lobbies. Neil Kinnock was to open for the Government with Raymond winding up.

When Raymond read his speech out to Joyce on the Tuesday night the entire rehearsal took only twenty-four minutes, but he explained to her that with the noise and interruptions that would occur in the Chamber he would be on his feet the full thirty minutes. In fact he might have to cut short some lines on the night.

The following day members began arriving hours before the debate was due to begin. The Strangers' Gallery had been booked days in advance, with many senior ambassadors and even some Privy Councillors unable to be guaranteed a seat. The Press Gallery was filled and editors were sitting at the feet of their political journalists' desks. The Commons itself was like a stand at a cup final where twice as many tickets had been sold as there were seats. The only difference from a Budget Day was that the House was taken up with lighting equipment that had been tested a dozen times that morning.

Between two-thirty and three-thirty Mr Speaker Seymour had been unable to stop members chattering during questions to Mr Meacher, the Secretary of State for Education, but at three-thirty he duly shouted for "Order" and did not have to wait long for silence before calling: "The leader of the Opposition."

Simon rose from his place on the front bench to be greeted with cheers from his own side. He was momentarily surprised by the brightness of the arc lights which he had been assured he would hardly notice, but soon he was into his stride. Without a note in front of him he addressed the House for fifty minutes, tearing into the Government one moment, then switching to the policies he would implement the next. He ended his peroration by describing the Labour party as "the party of wasted opportunity" then added – jabbing his finger at Raymond – "but you will be replaced by a party of ideas and ideals."

He sat down to the cheers of his back-benchers who thought they had already won the vote – if not the next election as well. The noise continued for some time before Charles could bring the House back to order and call the next speaker.

Neil Kinnock had always revelled in his Welsh ancestry and had often been compared by older members to Aneurin Bevan. The *bête noire* of the Tories set in to the Opposition leader with a vengeance, expounding his beliefs and rousing his own side to cheers when he said that the Tories would be routed and would regret this no confidence 'trick' for a decade. "The Right Honourable Gentleman," he said, pointing at Simon, "has the nerve to call us the party of wasted opportunities. For the past two years it is he who has led the party of opportunists, and who will be the leader of the Opposition until it is time for him to be replaced." When Kinnock sat down the television producers couldn't be blamed for thinking that they were covering a lions *v* Christians slaughter. Again it took the Speaker several minutes to bring the House back to order.

The back-benchers also rose to the occasion with speeches from past ministers quoting precedent and from young turks demanding change, which helped confirm old and established new reputations. The House remained packed that night right up until nine o'clock when the Speaker called Andrew Fraser to wind up for the Opposition.

Andrew delivered a 'plague on both your houses' speech and shouted above the protests from the two main parties. "When the time comes you will both need to call on an honest broker." At nine-thirty when he resumed his seat Andrew was cheered as loudly as forty-two members in unison could manage.

When it came to Raymond's turn to wind up, members wondered how he would make himself heard above the noise that greeted him. He rose to the dispatch box and, looking grave, with head bowed, almost whispered his first words, "Mr Speaker, I know the whole House would wish me to open my speech by saying how sad we all are that the Prime Minister is unable to be present tonight. I am sure all Honourable members will want to join me in sending him, his wife and family our best wishes as he prepares for his operation."

Suddenly the House was silent and, having caught its mood Raymond raised his head and delivered for the eleventh time the speech he had prepared so assiduously. When he had seen Simon give his apparently impromptu speech Raymond had torn up his notes. He spelt out the achievements of the Government during the past two and a half years and assured the House that he was only half-way through his time as Chancellor. "I have not been able to achieve equality in three years, but of one thing I am certain: I look forward to delivering my next budget whatever the outcome of the vote tonight. We shall not see the opportunist Government of the Conservatives or the Alliance's so-called 'honest broker'. Indeed, looking at the Alliance I can say there is no one less honest and no one more broke. We, Mr Speaker, will see the return of a Labour Government for another full Parliament." Raymond sat down as the clock reached ten. He found, like the speakers before him, that he was drenched in sweat from the heat sent out by the powerful arc lights.

The Speaker rose and his first words were lost as he put the question:

"This House has no confidence in Her Majesty's Government. As many as are of that opinion say Aye, to the contrary, No. I think the Ayes have it."

"No," hollered back the voices from the Government benches.

"Clear the lobbies," called the Speaker above the cheers for Raymond Gould. Members departed to the lobbies to cast their votes. The Irish members surprised no one by dividing among themselves. Fourteen minutes later the tellers returned to a noisy Chamber to give the result of the division to the clerk at the table who then entered the figures on a division paper. The four tellers lined up and advanced towards the table from the bar of the House. They came to a

halt and bowed for a third time. One of the Opposition
Whips read out: "Ayes to the right 323, Noes to the left 322"
and passed the piece of paper to the Speaker who tried to
repeat it above the bedlam. Few members heard him say:

"The Ayes have it, the Ayes have it."

Raymond sat on the front bench and watched the delighted Tories bobbing up and down like children on a carousel.
He reflected that if the Prime Minister had been present to
register his vote the Government would have saved the day.

Her Majesty the Queen visited her Prime Minister in hospital twenty-four hours after his successful operation. He
advised the monarch to dissolve Parliament immediately
and asked that the general election be set for 9 May. He
explained to the Queen that he intended to resign as leader of
his party that morning and would relinquish the office of
Prime Minister as soon as the outcome of the election was
clear.

Before she left the Westminster Hospital the Queen spent
some time discussing a private constitutional issue with the
Prime Minister. He suggested that when the Labour party
had confirmed their new leader he must be the man to offer
her advice on such a personal matter.

The National Executive of the Labour party met behind the
closed doors of Transport House in Smith Square at ten
o'clock the following morning to select their new leader.

Three hours and twenty minutes later the committee
issued a one-line press statement: "Mr Raymond Gould has
been invited to lead the party at the forthcoming general
election."

Although no one was in any doubt about the fierce arguments that must have taken place during the meeting the
press were met by a unified voice once the committee finally
broke up.

As Lord Broadstairs, the former Prime Minister, wrote in
the centre page of the *Sunday Express* that weekend, "The
Labour party in selecting their leader resembled nothing less
than the old-fashioned magic circle of Lord Rosebery in their

determination to prove unity." The only leak he had managed to gather from the meeting was that Raymond Gould's acceptance speech had impressed every one present.

But Lord Broadstairs went on to point out that if the Labour party should lose the general election Raymond Gould could be the shortest serving leader in the Labour party's history, as under standing order five (four) of the constitution his appointment had to be confirmed by the delegates at the next party conference in October.

It had been two hours before Raymond was able to leave Transport House and escape the press. When he eventually got away he went straight to Westminster Hospital to visit the Prime Minister. The operation had visibly aged him. He was in good spirits, but admitted that he was glad not to be facing a gruelling election campaign. After he had congratulated Raymond on his new post he went on to say: "You're dining with the Queen tonight?"

"Yes, to celebrate her sixty-fifth birthday," said Raymond.

"There's more to it than that," said the Prime Minister gravely and he then revealed the private conversation that he had had with the monarch the previous day.

"And will her decision depend on the four people in that room?"

"I suspect it will."

"And what's your attitude?"

"That's no longer relevant because I shall resign as Prime Minister the day after the election, so it's more important the new Prime Minister considers what is best for the country."

For the first time Raymond felt like the leader of the party.

CHAPTER
THIRTY FOUR

Elizabeth straightened Simon's white tie and took a pace back to look at him.

"Well, at least you *look* like a Prime Minister," she said, smiling.

Her husband checked his watch. Still a few minutes to spare before he needed to be at the Speaker's private apartments – not that he was willing to risk being late for this particular birthday celebration. Elizabeth helped him on with his overcoat and after a search realised he had lost another pair of gloves.

"I do hope you can take care of the nation's belongings a little better than you do your own," she sighed.

"I'm sure I'll find it hard to lose a whole country," said Simon.

"Do remember that Raymond Gould will be trying to help you," said Elizabeth.

"Yes, that's true. I only wish I was fighting Kinnock."

"Why?" she asked.

"Because Gould was born into the wrong party," said Simon as he kissed his wife and walked towards the front door, "and a lot of the electorate have already reached the same conclusion."

The policeman on the gates of New Palace Yard saluted as Simon was driven into the courtyard and dropped at the Members' Entrance. He glanced at his watch again: ten minutes to spare. He never could resist checking how many people were in the Chamber or what the latest news was on the ticker-tape machine.

He put his head round the door of the smoking room. A few members were scattered around, mainly from safe seats they felt did not need nursing. Pimkin, surrounded by his usual cronies, hailed him. His face lit up when he saw Simon formally dressed. "I say, waiter, mine's a double gin and tonic." His companions duly laughed. Simon responded by asking the barman to give Mr Pimkin a large gin and tonic and to charge it to his account.

He spent a few minutes moving from group to group chatting to members about how the election might go in their constituencies. Pimkin assured Simon that the Tories would return in triumph. "I wish everyone was as confident as you are," Simon told him before leaving for the Speaker's private apartments as Pimkin ordered another gin.

He strolled along the library corridor, lined from floor to ceiling with venerable old journals of the House, until he reached the Speaker's office, which is the route members take to the Speaker's private rooms. When Simon reached the Grand Stairway dominated by Speaker Addington's portrait he was met by the Speaker's train-bearer clad in white tie and black tails.

"Good evening, Mr Kerslake," he said and led Simon down the corridor into the antechamber where a relaxed Charles Seymour stood ready to receive his guests. Charles shook Simon's hand warmly. Simon thought how well his colleague looked compared with their meeting of a few months before.

Andrew Fraser had already arrived and soon the three men were deep into a discussion about the course the election would take when another guest walked in.

"The Right Honourable Raymond Gould," announced the train-bearer. Charles went over to greet his guest.

"Many congratulations on your election as leader," were his first words. "You've had one hell of a week; you must be exhausted."

"Exhilarated, to be honest," replied Raymond.

He moved towards Simon, who in turn offered his congratulations. The two men shook hands and for a moment resembled medieval knights who had lowered their visors before the final joust. The unnatural silence that followed was broken by Andrew.

"Well, I hope it's going to be a clean fight," he said. Both men laughed.

The train-bearer came to the Speaker's side to inform him that Her Majesty had left Buckingham Palace a few moments earlier.

Charles excused himself while the three leaders continued their conversation.

"Has either of you been told the real reason why we are bidden here this evening?" asked Raymond.

"Isn't the Queen's sixty-fifth birthday enough?" said Simon.

"No, that's just an excuse for us to meet without suspicion. I think it might be helpful for you both to know that Her Majesty has a highly sensitive question to put to us."

Simon and Andrew listened as Raymond revealed the substance of his discussion with the Prime Minister.

Charles waited in the entrance of the courtyard of the Speaker's House to welcome the Queen.

It was only a few minutes before he spotted two police outriders entering the gates of New Palace Yard followed by the familiar maroon Rolls Royce, which displayed no numberplate. A tiny white light on the centre of the roof blinked in the evening dusk. As soon as the car had come to a halt a footman leaped down and opened the back door.

The Queen stepped out, to be greeted by the commoner history had judged to be the monarch's man. She was dressed in a simple cocktail dress. The only jewellery she wore was a string of pearls and a small diamond brooch. Charles bowed before shaking hands and taking his guest up the carpeted staircase to his private apartments. Her three party leaders stood in line waiting to greet her. She shook hands first with the new leader of the Labour party and congratulated him on his election that afternoon before enquiring how the Prime Minister was faring. Then she shook hands with her leader of the Opposition and asked how his wife was coping at Pucklebridge General Hospital after the new National

Health cutbacks. Simon was always amazed by how much the Queen could recall from her past conversations, few of which could ever last more than a few moments. She then moved on to Andrew whom she teased about his father's recent speech in Edinburgh on the Social Democrats' greatest weakness being their lack of leadership.

"He's very old, ma'am," insisted Andrew.

"Not as old as Gladstone when he formed his last administration," she replied.

She removed the gin and tonic offered to her on a silver tray and looked around the magnificent room. "My husband and I are great admirers of the Gothic revival in architecture, though being infrequent visitors to Westminster we are, however, usually forced to view the better examples from the outside of railway stations or from the inside of cathedrals."

The four men smiled and a few minutes later Charles suggested they adjourn to the State dining-room where five places were set out round an oval table covered with silver which glittered in the candlelight. The four men waited until the Queen was seated at the head of the table.

Charles had placed Raymond on the Queen's right and Simon on her left while he and Andrew filled the other two places.

When the champagne was served Charles and his colleagues rose and toasted the Queen's health. She reminded them that her birthday was not for another two weeks and remarked that she had twenty-four official birthday engagements during the month, which didn't include the family's private celebrations. "I would happily weaken but the Queen Mother attended more functions for her ninetieth birthday last year than I have planned for my sixty-fifth. I can't imagine where she gets the energy."

"Perhaps she would like to take my place in the election campaign," said Raymond.

"Don't suggest it," the Queen replied. "She would leap at the opportunity without a second thought."

The chef had prepared a simple dinner of smoked salmon followed by lamb in red wine and aspic. His only flamboyant gesture was a birthday cake in the shape of a crown resting on a portcullis of sponge. No candles were evident.

After the meal had been cleared away and the cognac served the servants left them alone. The four men remained in a light mood until the Queen without warning put to them a delicate question that surprised only Charles. She waited for an answer.

No one spoke.

"Perhaps I should ask you first," said the Queen, turning to Raymond, "as you are standing in for the Prime Minister."

Raymond didn't hesitate. "I am in favour, ma'am," he said quietly.

She next turned to Simon.

"I would also support such a decision, Your Majesty," he replied.

"Thank you," said the Queen, and turned to Andrew.

"At heart I am a traditionalist, Your Majesty, but I confess to having given the subject a great deal of thought over the last few years and I have come round to supporting what I think is described as the 'modern approach'."

"Thank you," she repeated, her eyes finally resting on Charles Seymour.

"Against, ma'am," he said without hesitation, "but then I have never been a modern man."

"That is no bad thing in Mr Speaker," she said, and paused before adding: "Some years ago I asked a former Lord Chancellor to draw up the necessary papers. He assured me then that if none of my parliamentary leaders was against the principle the legislation could be carried through while both Houses were still in session."

"That is correct, ma'am," said Charles. "It would require two or three days at most if all the preparations have already been completed. It's only a matter of proclamation to both Houses of Parliament: your decision requires no vote."

"Excellent, Mr Speaker. Then the matter is settled."

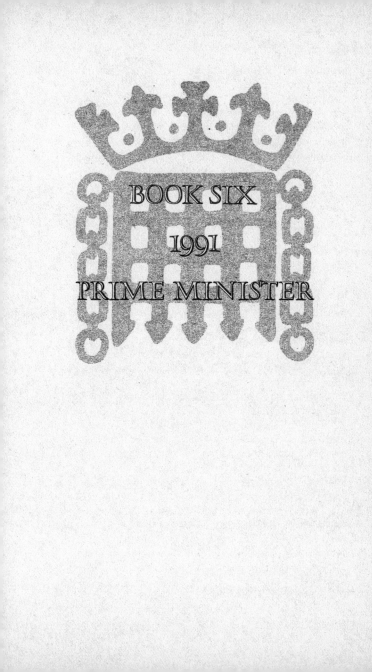

BOOK SIX

1991

PRIME MINISTER

CHAPTER
THIRTY FIVE

Her Majesty's proclamation passed through the Lords and Commons without a division.

Once the initial shock had been absorbed by the nation the election campaign took over. The first polls gave the Tories a two-point lead. The press attributed this to the public's unfamiliarity with the new Labour leader, but by the end of the first week the Tories had slipped a point while the press had decided that Raymond Gould had begun his steward-ship well.

"A week is a long time in politics," he quoted.

"And there are still two to go," Joyce reminded him.

The pundits put forward the theory that Raymond had increased his popularity during the first week because of the extra coverage he had received as the new leader of the Labour party. He warned the press department at Transport House that it might well be the shortest honeymoon on record, and they certainly couldn't expect him to be treated like a bridegroom for the entire three weeks. The first signs of a broken marriage came when the Department of Employ-ment announced that inflation had taken an upturn for the first time in nine months.

"And who has been Chancellor for the last three years?" demanded Simon in that night's speech in Manchester.

Raymond tried to dismiss the figures as a one-off monthly hiccup but the next day Simon was insistent that there was more bad news just around the corner.

When the Department of Trade announced the worst deficit in the balance of payments for fourteen months Simon took on the mantle of a prophet and the Tories edged back into a healthy lead, but with the Social Democrats stealing a point from both of them.

"Honeymoon, broken marriage and divorce, all in a period of fourteen days," said Raymond wryly. "What can happen in the last seven?"

"Reconciliation, perhaps?" suggested Joyce.

During the campaign all three leaders managed to visit most of the one hundred marginal seats in which the outcome of any general election is decided. None of them could afford to spend too much time worrying about those 550 of the 650 seats that could not change hands without a swing of at least eight per cent.

Andrew was willing to make one exception to the eight per cent rule in the case of Alec Pimkin's seat in Littlehampton, which he had considered vulnerable for some time. The Social Democrats had selected an able young candidate who had nursed the constituency assiduously over the past three years and couldn't wait to take on Pimkin.

Alec Pimkin eventually made an appearance in Little-hampton – only after the local chairman had tracked him down to his London flat to say they were becoming desperate. The Alliance yellow lines were almost as abundant on the canvass returns as the Conservative blue ones, he warned.

"Don't you realise that I have had grave responsibilities in the Commons?" Pimkin declared. "No one could have anticipated that members would have been called back for a special declaration by the monarch."

"Everyone knows about that," said the chairman. "But the bill commanded by the Queen went through all its three readings last week without a division."

Pimkin inwardly cursed the day they allowed television into the House. "Don't fuss," he soothed. "Come the hour, cometh the man and the voters will remember that I have had a long and distinguished parliamentary career. Damn it, old thing, have you forgotten that I was a candidate for the leadership of the Tory party?"

No, and how many votes did you receive on that occasion, the chairman wanted to say, but he took a deep breath and repeated his urgent request that the member visit the constituency as soon as possible.

Pimkin arrived seven days before the election and, as in past campaigns, settled himself in the private bar of the Swan Arms – the only decent pub in the constituency, he assured those people who took the trouble to come over and seek his opinion.

"But the Alliance candidate has visited every pub in the division," wailed the chairman.

"More fool he. We can say that he's looking for any excuse for a pub crawl," said Pimkin, roaring with laughter.

From time to time Pimkin did stroll over to his local committee headquarters to find a few loyal workers, licking envelopes and folding election messages. On the one occasion on which he ventured into the high street he was appalled to discover Andrew Fraser standing on an upturned box extolling the virtues of the Alliance candidate to a large crowd. Pimkin wandered over to listen to what Andrew had to say and was not pleased to find that hardly anyone in the crowd recognised him.

"Humbug," said Pimkin at the top of his voice. Andrew waved back. "Littlehampton needs a member who lives in the constituency," declared Andrew genially, and went on with his speech. Pimkin turned to retreat to the warmth of the fireside at the Swan Arms. After all, as the landlord had assured him, put up a donkey with a blue ribbon as the Conservative candidate in Littlehampton and they would elect it. Pimkin had not been overwhelmed by the analogy.

With six days to go Andrew held a meeting with the Liberals to discuss tactics. The Alliance began to record over twenty-two per cent in some polls while the Labour and Conservative vote remained neck and neck with thirty-eight per cent each. Andrew's continual claim that he would hold the balance of power in the next Parliament was analysed seriously by the *Observer* and *Sunday Times* over the last weekend of the campaign, and few political pundits were now disagreeing with him. Both the BBC and ITV were already trying to book him for the first interview after the election. Andrew made no commitment.

He travelled up from Liverpool to Glasgow on the Monday before the election and then trekked across Scotland, pursued by a pack of journalists, until he reached Edinburgh on the Wednesday night.

The same evening Simon returned to Pucklebridge to deliver his last speech of the campaign in the local village hall. Four hundred and eighteen sat inside to hear his speech. Four thousand more stood outside in the cold listening to his words being relayed by loudspeaker. Simon's final message to his supporters all over the country was, "Be sure you go to the polls tomorrow. Every vote will be vital."

The statement turned out to be the most accurate any of the three leaders had made during the entire three-week campaign.

Raymond had returned to Leeds on the evening and was met on the platform of Leeds City station by the Lord Mayor and over half the Corporation. He was driven to the town hall to deliver his last appeal to the electorate before an audience of 2,000 people. Somehow he raised himself to give one more speech, and the cheers that greeted his arrival at the town hall made him forget he hadn't had more than four hours' sleep a night during the last month. Introducing the Labour leader the Mayor said, "Ray has come home."

Raymond stood up and delivered his speech as vigorously as if it were the opening day of the campaign. When he sat down forty minutes later he felt his legs give way. As soon as the hall was cleared Joyce and Fred Padgett took the exhausted candidate home. He fell asleep in the car on the way back so the two of them helped him upstairs, undressed him and let him sleep on until six the next morning.

All three leaders were up by six preparing for interviews on both breakfast television channels followed by the obligatory photo of each arriving at a polling station accompanied by his wife to cast their votes.

Andrew enjoyed being back in Edinburgh where for a few hours he was allowed to recall the days of recounts and catch up with the many old friends who had made it possible for him to remain in Parliament. Once again he ended up on the steps of the final polling station as the city hall clock struck ten. No Mrs Bloxham was there to remind him that she only voted for winners; she had died the previous year. Andrew, Louise and Clarissa walked back to the local SDP head-quarters arm in arm to join their supporters and watch the results as they came in on television.

Raymond and Joyce remained in Leeds overnight while Simon and Elizabeth returned to London to follow the outcome at Central Office in Smith Square. Raymond couldn't remember when he had last watched television for three hours without a break. The first result came from Guildford at eleven-twenty-one, and showed a two per cent swing to the Conservatives.

"Not enough," said Simon from the party chairman's room at Central Office.

"It may not be enough," said Raymond when the next two seats delivered their verdict, and the swing remained the same. The first shock came a few minutes after midnight when the Social Democrats captured the Labour seat of Rugby, and less than thirty minutes later followed it by taking Billericay from the Conservatives. When the first hundred seats had been declared the pundits were certain of only one thing: they were uncertain what the final outcome would be. Opinions, expert and amateur, were still fluid at one o'clock that morning, by which time 200 results were in, and remained so at two o'clock when over 300 constituencies had selected their member.

Raymond went to bed with a lead of 236–191 over Simon, knowing it would be offset by the county shires the next day. Andrew had gained four seats and lost one, to give the Alliance thirty-two seats overnight.

The next morning pundits were back on radio and television by six o'clock, all agreeing with the *Daily Mail*'s headline 'Stalemate'. Raymond and Joyce returned to London on the early morning train while the rural seats were proving their traditional loyalty to the Conservatives. Simon travelled down to Pucklebridge to acknowledge a record majority. He wished he could have sacrificed a couple of thousand for the marginals that weren't going his way. By twelve-thirty-three when Raymond had reached No. 11 Downing Street, the

Labour lead had fallen to 287–276 while the Alliance had captured forty-four seats.

At twelve o'clock that Friday morning, the cameras from all four channels swung over to Edinburgh where the Sheriff was declaring that Andrew Fraser had been returned to the House with a majority of over 7,000. The cameras moved on to show the victor, hands high above his head. The number on the SDP chart flicked up to forty-five. By one o'clock the Social Democrats had notched up their forty-sixth victory by a mere seventy-two votes, a result which saddened Simon.

"The House won't be quite the same without Alec Pimkin," he told Elizabeth.

At two-twenty-three that Friday afternoon both the major parties had 292 seats with only two safe Tory-held seats still to be declared. Simon retained the first but Andrew picked up the last after three re-counts.

At four o'clock Lord Day of Langham announced from the BBC studios the final result of the 1991 election:

Conservative	293
Labour	292
SDP/Liberal	47
Irish	17
Speaker	1

Lord Day went on to point out that the popular vote made the outcome even more finely balanced with Labour taking 12,246,341 (35.2 per cent), Conservatives 12,211,907 (35.1 per cent) and the Alliance 8,649,881 (25.4 per cent). He told viewers that he had never experienced a result like it in his thirty-six years as a political journalist. He apologised for his failure to get an interview with Andrew Fraser who now held the key as to who would form the next Government.

Andrew phoned Simon first, then Raymond. He listened intently to both men and what they were willing to offer before telling them that he intended to hold a meeting of his members in London on Sunday and relay their comments. He would report back with their decision in the hope that a Government could be formed by Monday.

Andrew and Louise flew down from Edinburgh on the

Saturday morning together with a planeload of journalists but by the time Andrew disappeared outside Terminal One into a waiting car the press had nothing new to report.

Sir Duncan had already told the *Scotsman* that his son would naturally back the Conservatives, while the former Prime Minister announced from his bedside that Andrew had always been a good Socialist at heart and would have nothing to do with the capitalist cause.

On the Saturday Andrew held several informal meetings in Pelham Crescent with senior members of the Alliance to ascertain the views of his colleagues, old and new. By the time he went to bed he still had no clear mandate and when a newscaster said no one was sure how the SDP/Liberal Alliance would vote the following day in their private meeting Andrew added out loud, "Me included." Even so he had decided after much deliberation on the qualities of the two men and what they stood for and that helped him make up his mind which party he thought should form the next Government.

At the Commons the next morning he and every other SDP and Liberal member had to run the gauntlet of journalists and photographers on the way to a closely guarded committee room on the third floor. The Whip had deliberately selected one of the less accessible rooms and had asked the Serjeant-at-Arms to be certain the recording machines were disconnected.

Andrew opened the meeting by congratulating his colleagues on their election to the House of Commons. "But it is important to remember," he continued, "that the nation will never forgive us if we are irresponsible with our new power. We cannot afford to say we will support one party, then change our minds after only a few weeks, causing another general election. We must be seen to be responsible. Or you can be sure that when the next election comes every one of us will forfeit our seats."

He went on to describe in detail how both the major party leaders had accepted the general direction in which he felt the new Government should be moving. He reported that they had both accepted that two members of the Alliance should have seats in the Cabinet. Both had also agreed to back a motion in the Commons for a referendum on proportional representation. For three hours the SDP/Liberal members gave their views, but by the end of that time Andrew was still unable to steer them to a consensus and had to call for a ballot. Andrew did not vote himself and left the SDP Liberal and Chief Whips to count the votes and announce the result.

Twenty-three votes each was the decision of his members.

The Chief Whip informed the parliamentary party that they would have to allow their elected leader to make the final decision. He, after all, was the biggest single reason they had been returned to the House in such relatively large numbers. After twenty-seven years in the Commons he must have the clearest view of which man and which party was most capable of governing the country.

When the Chief Whip sat down, the word "Agreed" came over clearly from the lips of the members sitting round the long table, and the meeting broke up.

Andrew returned to Pelham Crescent and told Louise which man he had decided to support. She seemed surprised. Later that night he left for a quiet dinner at the Atheneum with the sovereign's private secretary. The equerry returned to Buckingham Palace a little after eleven o'clock and briefed the monarch on the salient points of their discussion.

"Mr Fraser," the private secretary said, "is not in favour of another quick election and has made it quite clear which party the Social Democrats are willing to support in the Commons."

The monarch nodded thoughtfully, thanked his private secretary and retired to bed.

CHAPTER
THIRTY SIX

King Charles III made the final decision.

As Big Ben struck ten o'clock on that Saturday morning, a private secretary to the Royal household phoned the Right Honourable Simon Kerslake and asked if he would be kind enough to attend His Majesty at the palace.

Simon stepped out of the Conservative party headquarters on the corner of Smith Square and into the clear morning sunlight to be greeted by crowds of wellwishers, television cameras and journalists. He only smiled and waved as this was not the occasion to make a statement. He slipped quickly through the police cordon and into the back of his black Rover. Motor cycle outriders guided the chauffeur-driven car through the dense crowds slowly past Transport House. Simon wondered what would be going through Raymond Gould's mind at that moment as he considered the decision Andrew Fraser must have made.

The chauffeur drove on to Millbank past the House of Commons, round Parliament Square and left into Birdcage Walk before reaching the Mall.

Scotland Yard had been briefed as to which party leader had been called to see the King and the car never stopped once on its journey to the palace.

The chauffeur then swung into the Mall and Buckingham Palace loomed in front of Simon's eyes. At every junction a policeman held up the traffic and then saluted. Suddenly it was all worthwhile: Simon went back over the years and then considered the future. His first thoughts were of Elizabeth and the children. How he wished they could be with him now. He recalled his selection at Coventry, the loss of his seat and the continual rejections before Pucklebridge. The financial crisis, the resignation letter that Archie Millburn had promised to return the day he became Prime Minister. The Irish Charter, *Broadsword*, and his final battle with Charles Seymour.

The Rover reached the end of the Mall and circled the statue of Queen Victoria before arriving at the vast wrought-iron gates outside Buckingham Palace. A sentry in the scarlet uniform of the Grenadier Guards presented arms. The huge crowds that had been waiting round the gates from the early hours craned their necks in an effort to see who had been chosen to lead them. Simon smiled and waved. In response some of them waved back and cheered more loudly while others looked sulky and downcast.

The Rover continued on its way past the sentry and across the courtyard through the archway and into the quadrangle before coming to a halt on the gravel by a side entrance. Simon stepped out of the car to be met by the King's private secretary. The silent equerry led Simon up a semicircular staircase, past the Alan Ramsey portrait of George III and down a long corridor before entering the audience chamber. He bowed and left Simon alone with his new sovereign.

Simon could feel his pulse quicken as he took three paces forward, bowed and waited for the King to speak.

The forty-three-year-old monarch showed no sign of nervousness in carrying out his first official duty, despite its unusual delicacy.

"Mr Kerslake," he began, "I wanted to see you first as I thought it would be courteous to explain to you in detail why I shall be inviting Mr Raymond Gould to be my first Prime Minister."

The End

CAT O' NINE TALES

And Other Stories

For Elizabeth

Contents

Foreword

While I was incarcerated for two years, in five different prisons, I picked up several stories that were not appropriate to include in the day-to-day journals of a prison diary. These tales are marked in the contents with an asterisk.

Although all nine stories have been embellished, each is rooted in fact. In all but one, the prisoner concerned has asked me not to reveal his real name.

The other three stories included in this volume are also true, but I came across them after being released from prison: in Athens – 'A Greek Tragedy', in London – 'The Wisdom of Solomon', and in Rome my favourite – 'In the Eye of the Beholder'.

The Man Who Robbed His Own Post Office

The Beginning

MR JUSTICE GRAY STARED down at the two defendants in the dock. Chris and Sue Haskins had pleaded guilty to the theft of £250,000, being the property of the Post Office, and to falsifying four passports.

Mr and Mrs Haskins looked about the same age, which was hardly surprising as they had been at school together some forty years before. You could have passed them in the street without giving either of them a second look. Chris was about five foot nine, his dark wavy hair turning grey, and he was at least a stone overweight. He stood upright in the dock, and although his suit was well worn, his shirt was clean and his striped tie suggested that he was a member of a club. His black shoes looked as if they had been spit-and-polished every morning. His wife Sue stood by his side. Her neat floral dress and sensible shoes hinted at an organized and tidy woman, but then they were both wearing the clothes that they would normally have worn to church. After all, they considered the law to be nothing less than an extension of the Almighty.

Mr Justice Gray turned his attention to Mr and Mrs Haskins's barrister, a young man who had been selected on the grounds of cost, rather than experience.

'No doubt you wish to suggest there are mitigating circumstances in this case, Mr Rodgers,' prompted the judge helpfully.

'Yes, m'lord,' admitted the newly qualified barrister as

he rose from his place. He would like to have told his lordship that this was only his second case, but he felt his lordship would be unlikely to consider that a mitigating circumstance.

Mr Justice Gray settled back as he prepared to listen to how poor Mr Haskins had been thrashed by a ruthless step-father, night after night, and Mrs Haskins had been raped by an evil uncle at an impressionable age, but no; Mr Rodgers assured the court that the Haskins came from happy, well-balanced backgrounds and had in fact been at school together. Their only child, Tracey, a graduate of Bristol University, was now working as an estate agent in Ashford. A model family.

Mr Rodgers glanced down at his brief before going on to explain how the Haskins had ended up in the dock that morning. Mr Justice Gray became more and more intrigued by their tale, and by the time the barrister had resumed his place the judge felt he needed a little more time to consider the length of the sentence. He ordered the two defendants to appear before him the following Monday at ten o'clock in the forenoon, by which time he would have come to a decision.

Mr Rodgers rose a second time.

'You were no doubt hoping that I would grant your clients bail, Mr Rodgers?' enquired the judge, raising an eyebrow, and before the surprised young barrister could respond Mr Justice Gray said, 'Granted.'

Jasper Gray told his wife about the plight of Mr and Mrs Haskins over lunch on Sunday. Long before the judge had devoured his rack of lamb, Vanessa Gray had offered her opinion.

'Sentence them both to an hour of community service, and then issue a court order instructing the Post Office to return their original investment in full,' she declared, revealing a common sense not always bestowed on the male of the species. To do him justice, the judge agreed with his spouse, although he told her that he would never get away with it.

'Why not?' she asked.

'Because of the four passports.'

Mr Justice Gray was not surprised to find Mr and Mrs Haskins standing dutifully in the dock at ten o'clock the following morning. After all, they were not criminals.

The judge raised his head, stared down at them and tried to look grave. 'You have both pleaded guilty to the crimes of theft from a post office and of falsifying four passports.' He didn't bother to add any adjectives such as evil, heinous or even disgraceful, as he didn't consider them appropriate on this occasion. 'You have therefore left me with no choice,' he continued, 'but to send you both to prison.' The judge turned his attention to Chris Haskins. 'You were obviously the instigator of this crime, and with that in mind, I sentence you to three years' imprisonment.' Chris Haskins was unable to hide his surprise: his barrister had warned him to expect at least five years. Chris had to stop himself from saying, thank you, my lord.

The judge then looked across at Mrs Haskins. 'I accept that your part in this conspiracy was possibly no more than an act of loyalty to your husband. However, you are well aware of the difference between right and wrong, and therefore I shall send you to prison for one year.'

'My lord,' protested Chris Haskins.

Mr Justice Gray frowned for the first time. He was not in the habit of being interrupted while passing sentence. 'Mr Haskins, if it is your intention to appeal against my judgement—'

'Certainly not, my lord,' said Chris Haskins, interrupting the judge for a second time. 'I was just wondering if you would allow me to serve my wife's sentence.'

Mr Justice Gray was so taken aback by the request that he couldn't think of a suitable reply to a question he had never been asked before. He banged his hammer, stood up and quickly left the courtroom. An usher hurriedly shouted, 'All rise.'

Chris and Sue first met in the playground of their local primary school in Cleethorpes, a seaside town on the east coast of England. Chris was standing in a queue waiting for his third of a pint of milk – government regulation for all schoolchildren under the age of sixteen. Sue was the milk monitor. Her job was to make sure everyone received their correct allocation. As she handed over the little bottle to Chris, neither of them gave the other a second look. Sue was in the class above Chris, so they rarely came across each other during the day, except when Chris was standing in the milk queue. At the end of the year Sue passed her eleven-plus and took up a place at the local grammar school. Chris was appointed the new milk monitor. The following September he also passed his eleven-plus, and joined Sue at Cleethorpes Grammar.

They remained oblivious to each other throughout their school days until Sue became head girl. After that, Chris couldn't help but notice her because at the end of morning assembly she would read out the school notices for the day. Bossy was the adjective most often trotted out by the lads whenever Sue's name came up in conversation (strange how women in positions of authority so often acquire the sobriquet *bossy*, while a man holding the same rank is somehow invested with qualities of leadership).

When Sue left at the end of the year Chris once again forgot all about her. He did not follow in her illustrious footsteps and become head boy, although he had a successful – by his standards – if somewhat uneventful year. He played for the school's second eleven cricket team, came fifth in the cross-country match against Grimsby Grammar, and did well enough in his final exams for them to be unworthy of mention either way.

No sooner had Chris left school than he received a letter from the Ministry of Defence, instructing him to report to his local recruiting office to sign up for a spell of National Service – a two-year compulsory period for all boys at the age of eighteen, when they had to serve in the armed forces. Chris's only choice in the matter was between the Army, the Royal Navy or the Royal Air Force.

He selected the RAF, and even spent a fleeting moment wondering what it might be like to be a jet pilot. Once Chris had passed his medical and filled in all the necessary forms at the local recruiting office, the duty sergeant handed him a rail pass to somewhere called Mablethorpe; he was to report to the guardhouse by eight o'clock on the first of the month.

Chris spent the next twelve weeks being put through basic training, along with a hundred and twenty other raw recruits. He quickly discovered that only one applicant in a thousand was selected to be a pilot. Chris was not one in a thousand. At the end of the twelve weeks he was given the choice of working in the canteen, the officers' mess, the quartermaster's stores or flight operations. He opted for flight operations, and was allocated a job in the stores.

It was when he reported for duty the following Monday that he once again met up with Sue, or to be more accurate Corporal Sue Smart. She was inevitably standing at the head of the line; this time giving out job instructions. Chris didn't immediately recognize her, dressed in her smart blue uniform with her hair almost hidden under a cap. In any case, he was admiring her shapely legs when she said, 'Haskins, report to the quartermaster's stores.' Chris raised his head. It was that voice he could never forget.

'Sue?' he ventured tentatively. Corporal Smart looked up from her clipboard and glared at the recruit who dared to address her by her first name. She recognized the face, but couldn't place him.

'Chris Haskins,' he volunteered.

8

'Ah, yes, Haskins,' she said, and hesitated before adding, 'report to Sergeant Travis in the stores, and he'll brief you on your duties.'

'Yes, Corp,' Chris replied and quickly disappeared off in the direction of the quartermaster's stores. As he walked away, Chris didn't notice that Sue was taking a second look.

Chris didn't come across Corporal Smart again until his first weekend leave. He spotted her sitting at the other end of a railway carriage on the journey back to Cleethorpes. He made no attempt to join her, even pretending not to see her. However, he did find himself looking up from time to time, admiring her slim figure – he didn't remember her being as pretty as that.

When the train pulled into Cleethorpes station, Chris spotted his mother chatting to another woman. He knew immediately who she must be – the same red hair, the same trim figure, the same . . .

'Hello, Chris,' Mrs Smart greeted him as he joined his mother on the platform. 'Was Sue on the train with you?'

'I didn't notice,' said Chris, as Sue walked up to join them.

'I expect you see a lot of each other now you're based at the same camp,' suggested Chris's mother.

'No, not really,' said Sue, trying to sound disinterested.

'Well, we'd better be off,' said Mrs Haskins. 'I have to give Chris and his dad dinner before they go off to watch the football,' she explained.

'Do you remember him?' asked Mrs Smart as Chris and his mother walked along the platform towards the exit.

'Snotty Haskins?' Sue hesitated. 'Can't say I do.'

'Oh, you like him that much, do you?' said Sue's mother with a smile.

✵ ✵ ✵

When Chris boarded the train that Sunday evening, Sue was already sitting in her place at the end of the carriage. Chris was about to walk straight past her and find a seat in the next carriage, when he heard her say, 'Hi, Chris, did you have a nice weekend?'

'Not bad, Corp,' said Chris, stopping to look down at her. 'Grimsby beat Lincoln three–one, and I'd forgotten how good the fish and chips are in Cleethorpes compared to camp.'

Sue smiled. 'Why don't you join me?' she said, patting the seat beside her. 'And I think it will be all right to call me Sue when we're not in barracks.'

On the journey back to Mablethorpe, Sue did most of the talking, partly because Chris was so smitten with her – could this be the same skinny little girl who had handed out the milk each morning? – and partly because he realized the bubble would burst the moment they set foot back in camp. Non-commissioned officers just don't fraternize with the ranks.

The two of them parted at the camp gates and went their separate ways. Chris walked back to the barracks, while Sue headed off for the NCO quarters. When Chris strolled into his Nissen hut to join his fellow conscripts, one of them was bragging about the WRAF he'd had it off with. He even went into graphic detail, describing what RAF knickers look like. 'A dark shade of blue held up by thick elastic,' he assured the mesmerized onlookers. Chris lay on his bed and stopped listening to the unlikely tale, as his thoughts returned to Sue. He wondered how long it would be before he saw her again.

Not as long as he feared because when Chris went to the canteen for lunch the following day he spotted Sue sitting in the corner with a group of girls from the ops room. He wanted to stroll across to her table and, like David Niven, casually ask her out on a date. There was a Doris Day film showing at the Odeon that he thought she might enjoy, but he'd sooner have walked across a minefield than interrupt her while his mates were watching.

Chris selected his lunch from the counter – a bowl of vegetable soup, sausage and chips, and custard pie. He carried his tray across to a table on the other side of the room and joined a group of his fellow conscripts. He was tucking into the custard pie, while discussing Grimsby's chances against Blackpool, when he felt a hand touch his shoulder. He looked round to see Sue smiling down at him. Everyone else at the table stopped talking. Chris turned a bright shade of red.

'Doing anything on Saturday night?' Sue asked. The red deepened to crimson as he shook his head. 'I was thinking of going to see *Calamity Jane*.' She paused. 'Care to join me?' Chris nodded. 'Why don't we meet outside the camp gates at six?' Another nod. Sue smiled. 'See you then.' Chris turned back to find his friends staring at him in awe.

Chris didn't remember much about the film because he spent most of his time trying to summon up enough courage to put his arm round Sue's shoulder. He didn't even manage it when Howard Keel kissed Doris Day. However, after they left the cinema and walked back towards the waiting bus, Sue took his hand.

'What are you going to do once you've finished your National Service?' Sue asked as the last bus took them back to camp.

'Join my dad on the buses, I suppose,' said Chris. 'How about you?'

'Once I've served three years, I have to decide if I want to become an officer, and make the RAF my career.'

'I hope you come back and work in Cleethorpes,' Chris blurted out.

Chris and Sue Haskins were married a year later in St Aidan's parish church.

After the wedding, the bride and groom set off for Newhaven in a hired car, intending to spend their honeymoon on the south coast of Portugal. After only a few days on the Algarve, they ran out of money. Chris drove them back to Cleethorpes, but vowed that they would return to Albufeira just as soon as he could afford it.

Chris and Sue began married life by renting three rooms on the ground floor of a semi-detached in Jubilee Road. The two milk monitors were unable to hide their contentment from anyone who came into contact with them.

Chris joined his father on the buses and became a conductor with the Green Line Municipal Coach Company, while Sue was employed as a trainee with a local insurance company. A year later Sue gave birth to Tracey and left her job to bring up their daughter. This spurred Chris on to work even harder and seek promotion. With the occasional prod from Sue, Chris began to study for the company's promotion exam. Four years later Chris was appointed an inspector. All boded well in the Haskins household.

When Tracey informed her father that she wanted a pony for Christmas, he had to point out that they didn't have enough room. Chris compromised, and on Tracey's seventh birthday presented her with a Labrador puppy, which they christened Corp. The Haskins family wanted for nothing, and that might have been the end of this tale if Chris hadn't got the sack. It happened thus.

The Green Line Municipal Coach Company was taken over by the Hull Carriage Bus Company. With the merger of the two firms, job losses became inevitable, and Chris was among those offered a redundancy package. The only alternative the new management came up with was the reinstatement of Chris as a conductor. Chris turned his nose up at the offer. He felt confident of finding another job, and therefore accepted the settlement.

It wasn't long before the redundancy money ran out, and despite Ted Heath's promise of a brave new world, Chris quickly discovered that alternative employment wasn't that easy to find in Cleethorpes. Sue never once complained and, now that Tracey was going to school, took on a part-time job at Parsons', a local fish-and-chip shop. Not only did this bring in a weekly wage, supplemented by the occasional tip, but it also allowed Chris to enjoy a large plate of cod and chips every lunchtime.

Chris continued to try and find a job. He visited the employment exchange every morning, except on Friday, when he stood in a long line, waiting to collect his meagre unemployment benefit. After twelve months of failed interviews, and sorry-you-don't-seem-to-have-the-necessary-qualifications, Chris became anxious enough to seriously consider returning to his old job as a bus conductor. Sue assured him that it wouldn't be long before he was once again promoted to inspector.

Meanwhile, Sue took on more responsibility at the fish-and-chip shop and a year later was made assistant manager. Once again, this tale might have reached its natural conclusion, except this time it was Sue who was given her notice.

She warned Chris over a fish supper that Mr and Mrs Parsons were considering early retirement and planning to put the shop up for sale.

'How much are they expecting it to fetch?'

'I heard Mr Parsons mention the figure of five thousand pounds.'

'Then let's hope the new owners know a good thing when they see it,' said Chris, forking another chip.

'The new owners are far more likely to come with their own staff. Don't forget what happened to you when the bus company was taken over.'

Chris thought about it.

At eight thirty the following morning, Sue left the house to take Tracey to school, before going on to work. Once the two of them had departed, Chris and Corp set out for their morning constitutional. The dog was puzzled when his master didn't head for the beach, where he could enjoy his usual frolic in the waves, but instead marched off in the opposite direction, towards the centre of the town. Corp loyally bounded after him, and ended up being tied to a railing outside the Midland Bank in the High Street.

The manager of the bank could not hide his surprise

when Mr Haskins requested an interview to discuss a business venture. He quickly checked Mr and Mrs Haskins' joint bank account, to find that they were seventeen pounds and twelve shillings in credit. He was pleased to note that they had never run up an overdraft, despite Mr Haskins being out of work for over a year.

The manager listened sympathetically to his client's proposal, but sadly shook his head even before Chris had come to the end of his well-rehearsed presentation.

'The bank couldn't consider such a risk,' the manager explained, 'at least not while you have so little security to offer as collateral. You don't even own your own home,' the banker pointed out. Chris thanked him, shook him by the hand and left undaunted.

He crossed the High Street, tied Corp to another railing and entered Martins Bank. Chris had to wait for quite some time before the manager was able to see him. He was greeted with the same response, but at least on this occasion the manager recommended that Chris should approach Britannia Finance, who, he explained, were a new company specializing in start-up loans for small businesses. Chris thanked him, left the bank, untied Corp and jogged back to Jubilee Road, arriving only moments before Sue returned home with his lunch: cod and chips.

After lunch, Chris left the house and headed for the nearest phone box. He put four pennies in the box and pressed button A. The conversation lasted for less than a minute. He then returned home, but didn't tell Sue who he had an appointment with the following day.

The next day Chris waited for Sue to take Tracey off to school before he slipped back upstairs to their bedroom. He took off his jeans and sweater, and replaced them with the suit he'd worn at his wedding, a cream shirt he only put on for church on Sundays, and a tie his mother-in-law had given him for Christmas, which he thought he'd never wear. He then shone his shoes until even his old drill sergeant would have agreed that they passed muster. He checked himself in the mirror, hoping he looked like the potential manager of a new business venture. He left the dog in the back garden, and headed into town.

Chris was fifteen minutes early for his meeting with a Mr Tremaine, the loans manager with Britannia Finance Company. He was asked to take a seat in the waiting room. Chris picked up a copy of the *Financial Times* for the first time in his life. He couldn't find the sports pages. Fifteen minutes later a secretary ushered him through to Mr Tremaine's office.

The loans executive listened with sympathy to Chris's ambitious proposal, and then enquired, just as the two bank managers had, 'What security do you have to offer?'

'Nothing,' replied Chris without guile, 'other than the fact that my wife and I will work all the hours we're awake, and she already knows the business backwards.' Chris waited to hear the many reasons why Britannia couldn't consider his request.

Instead Mr Tremaine asked, 'As your wife would constitute half of our investment, what does she think about this whole enterprise?'

'I haven't even discussed it with her yet,' Chris blurted out.

'Then I suggest you do so,' said Mr Tremaine, 'and fairly quickly, because before we would consider investing in Mr and Mrs Haskins, we will need to meet Mrs Haskins in order to find out if she's half as good as you claim.'

Chris broke the news to his wife over supper that evening. Sue was speechless. A problem Chris had not come up against all that often in the past.

Once Mr Tremaine had met Mrs Haskins, it was only a matter of filling in countless forms before Britannia Finance advanced them a loan of £5,000. A month later Mr and Mrs Haskins moved from their three rooms in Jubilee Road to a fish-and-chip shop on Beach Street.

The Middle

Chris and Sue spent their first Sunday scraping the name *PARSONS* off the front of the shop, and painting in *HASKINS: under new management*. Sue quickly set about teaching Chris how to prepare the right ingredients to make the finest batter. If it was that easy, she kept reminding him, there wouldn't be a queue outside one chippy while a rival a few yards up the road remained empty. It was some weeks before Chris could guarantee his chips were always crisp and not hard or, worse, soggy. While he became the front-of-house manager, wrapping up the fish and dispensing the salt and vinegar, Sue took her place behind the till and collected the takings. In the evening, Sue always brought the books up to date, but she didn't go upstairs to join Chris in their little self-contained flat until the shop was spotless and you could see your face in the counter-top.

Sue was always the last to finish, but then Chris was the first to rise in the morning. He would be up by four o'clock, pull on an old tracksuit and head off for the docks with Corp.

He returned a couple of hours later, having selected the finest cod, hake, skate and plaice, moments after the trawlers had docked with their morning catch.

Although Cleethorpes has several fish-and-chip shops, it was not long before a queue began to form outside Haskins, sometimes even before Sue had turned the closed sign round to allow the first customer to enter the shop. The queue never slackened between the hours of eleven a.m. and three p.m., or from five to nine in the evening, when the sign would finally be turned back round – but not until the last customer had been served.

At the end of their first year the Haskins declared a profit of just over £900. As the queues lengthened, the debt to Britannia Finance diminished, so they were able to return the loan in full, with interest, eight months before the five-year agreement ended.

During the next decade, the Haskins' reputation grew on land, as well as sea, which resulted in Chris being invited to join the Cleethorpes Rotary Club, and Sue becoming deputy chairman of the Mothers' Union.

On their twentieth wedding anniversary Sue and Chris returned to Portugal for a second honeymoon. They stayed in a four-star hotel for a fortnight and this time they didn't have to come home early. Mr and Mrs Haskins returned to Albufeira every summer for the next ten years. Creatures of habit, the Haskins.

Tracey left Cleethorpes Grammar School to attend Bristol University, where she studied business management. The only sadness in the Haskins' life was when Corp died. But then he was fourteen years old.

✵ ✵ ✵

Chris was enjoying a drink with some fellow Rotarians when Dave Quenton, the manager of the town's most prestigious post office, told him that he was moving to the Lake District and planning to sell his interest in the business.

This time Chris did discuss his latest proposal with his wife. Sue was once again taken by surprise and, when she recovered, needed several questions answered before she agreed to pay a return visit to Britannia Finance.

'How much do you have on deposit with the Midland Bank?' asked Mr Tremaine, recently promoted to loans manager.

Sue checked her ledger. 'Thirty-seven thousand, four hundred and eight pounds,' she replied.

'And what value have you put on the fish-and-chip shop?' was his next question.

'We will be considering offers over one hundred thousand,' said Sue confidently.

'And how much has the post office been valued at, remembering that it's in such a prime location?'

'Mr Quenton says that the Post Office is looking for two hundred and seventy thousand, but he assures me they would settle for a quarter of a million, if they can find a suitable applicant.'

'So you're likely to be a little over one hundred thousand short of your target,' said the analyst, not having to refer to a ledger. He paused. 'What was the post office's turnover last year?'

'Two hundred and thirty thousand pounds,' replied Sue.

'Profit?'

Once again, Sue needed to check her figures. 'Twenty-six thousand, four hundred, but that doesn't include the added bonus of spacious living accommodation, with rates and taxes covered in the annual return.' She paused. 'And this time we would own the property.'

'If all those figures can be confirmed by our accountants,' said Mr Tremaine, 'and you are able to sell the fish-and-chip shop for around a hundred thousand, it certainly appears to be a sound investment. But . . .' The two would-be clients looked apprehensive. 'And there always is a but, when it comes to lending money. The loan would, of course, be subject to the post office maintaining its category A status. Property in that area is currently trading at around twenty thousand, so the real value of the post office is as a business, and only then if, I repeat, if, it continues to have category A status.'

'But it's been a category A post office for the past thirty years,' said Chris. 'Why should that change in the future?'

'If I could predict the future, Mr Haskins,' replied the analyst, 'I would never make a bad investment, but as I can't I have to take the occasional risk. Britannia invests in people, and on that front you have nothing to prove.' He smiled. 'We would, as with our first investment, expect any loan to be repaid in quarterly instalments, over a period of five years, and on this occasion, as such a large sum is involved, we would want to take a charge over the property.'

'At what percentage?' demanded Chris.

'Eight and a half per cent, with added penalties should increments not be paid on time.'

'We'll need to consider your offer carefully,' said Sue, 'and we'll let you know once we've made our decision.'

Mr Tremaine stifled a smile.

✳ ✳ ✳

'What was all that about category A status?' asked Sue as they walked quickly back towards the seafront, still hoping to open the shop in time for their first customer.

'Category A is where all the profits are,' said Chris. 'Savings accounts, pensions, postal orders, vehicle road tax and even premium bonds all guarantee you a handsome profit. Without them, you have to rely on TV licences, stamps, electricity bills, and perhaps a little extra income if they allow you to run a shop on the side. If that was all Mr Quenton had to offer, we'd be better off continuing to run the fish-and-chip shop.'

'And is there any risk of us losing our category A status?' asked Sue.

'None whatsoever,' said Chris, 'or that's what the area manager assured me, and he's a fellow member of Rotary. He told me that the matter has never even come up for discussion at headquarters, and you can be pretty confident that Britannia will also have checked that out long before they would be willing to part with a hundred thousand.'

'So you still think we should go ahead?'

'With a few refinements to their terms,' said Chris.

'Like what?'

'Well, to start with, I've no doubt that Mr Tremaine will come down to eight per cent, now that the High Street banks have also begun investing in business ventures, and don't forget, this time he will have a charge over the property.'

The Haskins sold their fish-and-chip shop for £112,000 and were able to add a further £38,000 from their credit account. Britannia topped it up with a loan of £100,000 at 8 per cent. A cheque for £250,000 was sent to Post Office headquarters in London.

'Time to celebrate,' declared Chris.

'What do you have in mind?' asked Sue. 'Because we can't afford to spend any more money.'

'Let's drive down to Ashford and spend the weekend with our daughter –' he paused – 'and on the way back . . .'

'And on the way back?' repeated Sue.

'Let's drop into Battersea Dogs' Home.'

A month later, Mr and Mrs Haskins and Stamps, another Labrador, this time black, moved from their fish-and-chip shop on Beach Street to a category A post office in Victoria Crescent.

Chris and Sue quickly returned to working hours that they hadn't experienced since they first opened the fish-and-chip shop. For the next five years they cut down on any little extras, and even went without holidays, although they often thought about another trip to Portugal, but that had to be put on hold until they completed their quarterly payments to Britannia. Chris continued to carry out his Rotary Club duties, while Sue became chairman of the Cleethorpes branch of the Mothers' Union. Tracey was promoted to sites manager, and Stamps ate more food than the three of them put together.

In their fourth year, Mr and Mrs Haskins won the 'Area Post Office of the Year' award, and nine months later paid off the final instalment to Britannia.

The board of Britannia invited Chris and Sue to join them for lunch at the Royal Hotel to celebrate the fact that they now owned the post office without a penny of debt to their name.

'We still have to earn back our original investment,' Chris reminded them. 'A mere matter of two hundred and fifty thousand pounds.'

'If you keep going at your present rate,' suggested the chairman of Britannia, 'it should only take you another five years to achieve and then you could be sitting on a business worth over a million.'

'Does that mean I'm a millionaire?' asked Chris.

'No, it does not,' butted in Sue. 'Our current account is showing a credit of a little over ten thousand pounds. You're a ten thousandaire.'

The chairman laughed, and invited the board to raise their glasses to Chris and Sue Haskins.

'My spies tell me, Chris,' added the chairman, 'that you are likely to be the next president of our local Rotary.'

'Many a slip,' said Chris as he lowered his glass, 'and certainly not before Sue takes her place on the area committee of the Mothers' Union. Don't be surprised if she ends up as national chairman,' he added, with considerable pride.

'So what do you plan to do next?' asked the chairman.

'Take a month's holiday in Portugal,' said Chris without hesitation. 'After five years of having to make do with the beach at Cleethorpes and a plate of fish and chips, I think we've earned it.'

That also would have made a satisfactory conclusion to this tale, had officialdom not stepped in once again; this time with a letter addressed to Mr and Mrs Hoskins from the finance director of the Post Office. They found it waiting for them on the mat when they returned from Albufeira.

Post Office Headquarters,
148 Old Street, London EC1V 9HQ

Dear Mr and Mrs Hoskins,
The Post Office is in the process of re-evaluating its

property portfolio, and to that end, will be making some changes to the status of some of its older establishments.

I therefore have to inform you that the board has come to the reluctant conclusion that we will no longer require two category A status facilities in the Cleethorpes area. While the new High Street branch will continue as a category A post office, Victoria Crescent will be downgraded to category B. In order that you can make the necessary adjustments, we do not propose to bring in these changes until the New Year.

We look forward to continuing our relationship with you.

Yours sincerely,

Finance Director

'Does that mean what I think it means?' said Sue after she had read the letter a second time.

'In simple terms, love,' said Chris, 'we can never hope to earn back our original investment of two hundred and fifty thousand, even if we go on working for the rest of our lives.'

'Then we'll have to put the post office up for sale.'

'But who will want to buy it at that price,' asked Chris, 'once they discover that the business no longer has category A status?'

'The man from Britannia assured us that once we'd paid off the debt it would be worth a million.'

'Only while the business has a turnover of five hundred thousand and generates a profit of around eighty thousand a year,' said Chris.

'We should take legal advice.'

Chris reluctantly agreed, although he wasn't in much doubt what his solicitor's opinion would be. The law, their advocate dutifully advised them, was not on their side, and therefore he wouldn't recommend them to sue the Post Office, as he couldn't guarantee the outcome. 'You might well win a moral victory,' he said, 'but that won't assist your bank balance.'

The next decision Chris and Sue made was to put the post office on the market as they wanted to find out if anyone would show an interest. Once again Chris's judgement turned out to be correct: only three couples even bothered to look over the property, and none of them returned for a second viewing once they discovered it was no longer category A status.

'My bet,' said Sue, 'is that those officials back at headquarters knew only too well they were going to change our status long before they pocketed our money, but it suited them not to tell us.'

'You may well be right,' said Chris, 'but you can be sure of one thing – they won't have put anything in writing at the time, so we would never be able to prove it.'

'And neither did we.'

'What are you getting at, love?'

'How much have they stolen from us?' demanded Sue.

'Well, if by that you mean our original investment—'

'Our life savings, every penny we've earned over the past thirty years, not to mention our pension.'

Chris paused and raised his head, while he made some calculations. 'Not including any profit we might have hoped for, once we'd seen our capital returned—'

'Yes, only what they've stolen from us,' Sue repeated.

'A little over two hundred and fifty thousand, if you don't include interest,' said Chris.

'And we have no hope of seeing a penny of that original investment back, even if we were to work for the rest of our lives?'

'That's about the sum of it, love.'

'Then it's my intention to retire on January the first.'

'And what are you expecting to live off for the rest of your life?' asked Chris.

'Our original investment.'

'And how do you intend to go about that?'

'By taking advantage of our spotless reputation.'

The End

Chris and Sue rose early the following morning: after all, they had a lot of work to do during the next three months if they hoped to accumulate enough capital to retire by 1 January. Sue warned Chris that meticulous preparation would be needed if her plan was to succeed. He didn't disagree. They both knew that they couldn't risk pressing the button until the second Friday in November, when they would have a six-week window of opportunity – Chris's expression – before 'those people back in London' worked out what they were really up to. But that didn't mean there wasn't a lot of preliminary work to be done in the meantime. To start with, they needed to plan their getaway, even before they set about retrieving any stolen money.

Neither considered what they were about to embark on as theft.

Sue unfolded a map of Europe and spread it across the post office counter. They discussed the different alternatives for several days and finally settled on Portugal, which they both considered would be ideal for early retirement. On their many visits to the Algarve they had always returned to Albufeira, the town where they had spent their shortened honeymoon, and revisited on their tenth, twentieth, and many more wedding anniversaries. They had even promised themselves that was where they would retire if they won the lottery.

The next day Sue purchased a tape of *Portuguese for Beginners* which they played before breakfast every morning, and then spent an hour in the evening, testing out their new skills. They were pleased to discover that over the years they had both picked up more of the language than they realized. Although not fluent, they were certainly not beginners. The two of them quickly moved on to the advanced tapes.

'We won't be able to use our own passports,' Chris pointed out to his wife while shaving one morning. 'We'll have to consider a change of identity, otherwise the authorities would be on to us in no time.'

'I've already thought about that,' said Sue, 'and we should take advantage of working in our own post office.'

Chris stopped shaving, and turned to listen to his wife.

'Don't forget, we already supply all the necessary forms for customers who want to obtain passports.'

Chris didn't interrupt as Sue went over how she planned to make sure that they could safely leave the country under assumed names.

Chris chuckled. 'Perhaps I'll grow a beard,' he said, putting his razor down.

Over the years, Chris and Sue had made friends with several customers who regularly shopped at the post office. The two of them wrote down on separate sheets of paper the names of all their customers who fulfilled the criteria Sue was looking for. They ended up with a list of two dozen candidates: thirteen women and eleven men. From that moment on, whenever one of the unsuspecting regulars entered the shop, Sue or Chris would strike up a conversation that had only one purpose.

'Going away for Christmas this year, are we, Mrs Brewer?'

'No, Mrs Haskins, my son and his wife will be joining us on Christmas Eve so that we can get to know our new granddaughter.'

'How nice for you, Mrs Brewer,' replied Sue. 'Chris and I are thinking of spending Christmas in the States.'

'How exciting,' said Mrs Brewer. 'I've never even been abroad,' she admitted, 'let alone America.'

Mrs Brewer had reached the second round, but would not be questioned again until her next visit.

By the end of September, seven other names had joined Mrs Brewer on the shortlist – four women and three men, all between the ages of fifty-one and fifty-seven, who had only one thing in common: they had never travelled abroad.

The next problem the Haskins faced was filling in an application for a birth certificate. This required far more detailed questioning, and both Sue and Chris quickly backed off whenever one of the shortlisted candidates showed the slightest sign of suspicion. By the beginning of October they were down to the names of four customers who had unwittingly supplied their date of birth, place of birth, mother's maiden name and father's first name.

The Haskins' next visit was to Boots the chemist in St Peter's Avenue, where they took turns to sit in a little cubicle and have several strips of photographs taken at £2.50 a time. Sue then set about completing the necessary application forms for a passport, on behalf of four of her unsuspecting customers. She filled in all the relevant details, while enclosing photographs of herself and Chris, along with a postal order for £42. As the postmaster, Chris was only too happy to pen his real signature on the bottom of each form Sue filled in.

The four application forms were posted to the passport office at Petty France in London on the Monday, Thursday, Friday and Saturday of the last week in October.

On Wednesday, 11 November the first passport arrived back at Victoria Crescent, addressed to Mr Reg Appleyard. Two days later, a second appeared, for Mrs Audrey

Ramsbottom. The following day Mrs Betty Brewer's turned up, and finally, a week later, Mr Stan Gerrard's.

Sue had already pointed out to Chris that they would have to leave the country using one set of passports, which they would then need to discard, before they switched to the second pair, but not until they had found somewhere to live in Albufeira.

Chris and Sue continued to practise their Portuguese whenever they were alone in the shop, while informing any regulars that they would be away over the Christmas period as they were planning a trip to America. The inquisitive were rewarded with such details as a week in San Francisco, followed by a few days in Seattle.

By the second week in November, everything was in place to press the button for Operation Money Back Guaranteed.

⚬⚬⚬⟫⟫⟫✦⟪⟪⟪⚬⚬⚬

At nine o'clock on Friday morning Sue made her weekly phone call to headquarters. She entered her personal code before being transferred to forward finance. The only difference this time was that she could hear her heart beating. Sue repeated her code before informing the credit officer how much cash she would require for the following week – an amount large enough to allow her to cover withdrawals for any post office savings accounts, pensions and cashed postal orders. Although an accountant from headquarters always checked the books at the end of every month, considerable leeway was allowed in the run-up to Christmas. A demanding audit was then carried out in January to make sure the books balanced, but neither Chris nor Sue had any intention of being around in January. For the past six years

30

Sue's books had always balanced, and she was considered by headquarters to be a model manager.

Sue had to check the records to remind herself of the amount she had requested in the same week of the previous year – £40,000, which had turned out to be £800 more than she needed. This year she asked for £60,000, and waited for some comment from the credit officer, but the voice from headquarters sounded neither surprised nor concerned. The full amount was delivered by a security van the following Monday.

During the week Chris and Sue fulfilled all their customers' obligations; after all, it had never been their intention to short-change any of their regulars, but they still found themselves with a surplus of £21,000 at the end of week one. They left the cash – used notes only – locked up in the safe, just in case some fastidious official from headquarters decided to carry out a spot-check.

Once Sue had closed the front door at six o'clock and pulled down the blinds, the two of them would only converse in Portuguese, while they spent the rest of the evening filling in postal orders, rubbing out scratch cards and entering lottery numbers, often falling asleep as they worked.

Every morning Chris would rise early and climb into his ageing Rover, with Stamps as his only companion. He travelled north, east, south and west – Monday Lincoln, Tuesday Louth, Wednesday Skegness, Thursday Hull and Friday Immingham, where he would cash several postal orders, and also collect his winnings on the scratch cards and lottery tickets, enabling him to supplement their newly acquired savings with an extra few hundred pounds each day.

On the last Friday in November, week two, Sue applied

for £70,000 from head office, so that by the following Saturday they were able to add a further £32,000 to their invisible earnings.

On the first Friday in December, Sue raised the stakes to £80,000, and was surprised to discover that there were still no questions back at headquarters: after all, hadn't Sue Haskins been manager of the year, with a special commendation from the board? A security van dutifully delivered the full amount in cash early on the Monday morning.

Another week of increased profits allowed Sue Haskins to add a further £39,000 to the pot without any of the other players round the table demanding to see her hand. They were now showing a surplus of well over £100,000, which was stacked up in neat little piles of used notes, resting on top of the four passports buried at the bottom of the safe.

Chris hardly slept at night as he continued to sign countless postal orders, rub out piles of scratch cards and, before going to bed, fill in numerous lottery tickets with endless combinations. By day he visited every post office within a fifty-mile radius, gathering his spoils, but, despite his dedication, by the second week in December Mr and Mrs Haskins had only collected just over half the amount required to retrieve the £250,000 they had originally invested.

Sue warned Chris that they would have to take an even bigger risk if they still hoped to acquire the full amount by Christmas Eve.

On the second Friday in December, week four, Sue called the issuing manager at headquarters, and made a request for £115,000.

'You're having a busy Christmas,' suggested a voice on the other end of the line. First sign of any suspicion, thought Sue, but she had her script well prepared.

'Run off my feet,' Sue told him, 'but don't forget, more people retire to Cleethorpes than any other seaside town in Britain.'

'You learn something new every day,' came back the voice on the other end of the line, before adding, 'Don't worry, the cash will be with you on Monday. Keep up the good work.'

'I will,' promised Sue, and, emboldened by the exchange, requested £140,000 for the final week before Christmas, aware that any sum above £150,000 was always referred back to head office in London.

When Sue pulled down the blinds at six o'clock on Christmas Eve, both of them were exhausted.

Sue was the first to recover. 'We haven't a moment to waste,' she reminded her husband as she walked across to the bulging safe. She entered the code, pulled open the door and withdrew everything from their current account. She then placed the money on the counter in neat bundles – fifties, twenties, tens and fives – before they set about counting their spoils.

Chris checked the final figure and confirmed that they were £267,300 in credit. They put £17,300 back in the safe, and locked the door. After all, they had never intended to make a profit – that would be stealing. Sue began to put elastic bands around each thousand, while Chris transferred the two hundred and fifty bundles carefully into an old RAF duffel bag. By eight o'clock they were ready to leave. Chris set the alarm, slipped quietly out of the back door and placed the duffel bag in the boot of their Rover, on top of four other cases his wife had packed earlier that morning. Sue joined him in the front of the car, as Chris turned on the ignition.

'We've forgotten something,' said Sue as she pulled the door closed.

'Stamps,' they said in unison. Chris turned off the ignition, got out of the car and returned to the post office. He re-entered the code, switched off the alarm and opened the back door in search of Stamps. He found him fast asleep in the kitchen, reluctant to be enticed out of his warm basket and into the back seat of the car. Didn't they realize it was Christmas Eve?

Chris reset the alarm and locked the door for a second time.

At eight nineteen p.m. Mr and Mrs Haskins set out on the journey for Ashford in Kent. Sue worked out that they had four clear days before anyone would be aware of their absence. Christmas Day, Boxing Day, Sunday, Monday (a bank holiday), back in theory on Tuesday morning, by which time they would be viewing properties in the Algarve.

The two of them hardly spoke a word on the long journey to Kent, not even in Portuguese. Sue couldn't believe they'd gone through with it, and Chris was even more surprised that they'd got away with it.

'We haven't yet,' Sue reminded him, 'not until we drive into Albufeira, and don't forget, Mr Appleyard, we no longer have the same names.'

'Living in sin after all these years are we, Mrs Brewer?'

Chris brought the car to a halt outside their daughter's home just after midnight. Tracey opened the front door to greet her mother, while Chris removed one of the suitcases and the duffel bag from the boot. Tracey had never seen her parents looking so exhausted, and felt they had aged since she'd last seen them in the summer. Perhaps it was just the long journey. Tracey took them through to the kitchen, sat them both down and made them a cup of tea. They hardly spoke, and when Tracey eventually bundled them off to bed, her father wouldn't allow her to carry the old duffel bag up to the guest bedroom.

Sue woke every time she heard a car come to a halt in the street outside, wondering if it was marked with the bold fluorescent lettering POLICE. Chris waited for the front-door bell to ring before someone came bounding up the stairs to drag the duffel bag from under the bed, arrest them and escort them both to the nearest police station.

After a sleepless night they joined Tracey in the kitchen for breakfast.

'Happy Christmas,' said Tracey, before kissing them both on the cheek. Neither of them responded. Had they forgotten it was Christmas Day? They both looked embarrassed as they stared at the two wrapped boxes that their daughter had placed on the table. They hadn't remembered to buy Tracey a Christmas present and resorted to giving her cash, something they hadn't done since she was a teenager. Tracey hoped that it was nothing more than the Christmas rush, and excitement at the thought of their visit to the States, which had caused such uncharacteristic behaviour.

Boxing Day turned out to be a little better. Sue and Chris appeared more relaxed, although they often lapsed into long silences. After lunch Tracy suggested that they take Stamps for a run across the Downs and get some fresh air. During the long walk one of them would begin a sentence and then fall silent. A few minutes later the other would finish it.

By Sunday morning Tracey felt that they both looked a lot better, even chatting away about their trip to America.

But two things puzzled her. When she saw her parents coming down the stairs carrying the duffel bag with Stamps in their wake, she could have sworn they were speaking Portuguese. And why bother to take Stamps to America, when she had already offered to take care of the dog while they were away?

The next surprise came when they set off for Heathrow after breakfast. When her father packed the duffel bag and their suitcase into the boot of the car, she was surprised to see three large bags already in the boot. Why bother with so much luggage when they were only going away for a fortnight?

Tracey stood on the pavement and waved goodbye, as her parents' car trundled off down the road. When the old Rover reached the end of the street it swung right, instead of left, which took them in the opposite direction to Heathrow. Something was wrong. Tracey dismissed the mistake, aware that they could correct their error long before they reached the motorway.

Once Chris and Sue had joined the motorway, they followed the signs for Dover. The two of them became more and more nervous as each minute passed, aware that there was now no turning back. Only Stamps seemed to be enjoying the adventure as he stared out of the back window wagging his tail.

Once again, Mr Appleyard and Mrs Brewer went over their plan. When they reached the docks, Sue would jump out of the car and join the queue of foot passengers waiting to board, while Chris drove the Rover up the car ramp and on to the ferry. They agreed not to meet again until the boat had docked in Calais and Chris had driven on to the dockside.

Sue stood at the bottom of the gangway and waited nervously at the back of the queue as she watched their Rover edge towards the entrance of the hold. Her heart raced when she saw a customs officer double-check Chris's passport, and invite him to step out of the car and stand to one side. She had to stop herself from running across so she could overhear their conversation – she couldn't risk it now they were no longer married.

'Good morning, Mr Appleyard,' said the customs officer, and then added after looking in the back of the car, 'were you hoping to take the dog abroad with you?'

'Oh yes,' replied Chris. 'We never travel anywhere without Stamps.'

The customs official studied Mr Appleyard's passport more carefully. 'But you don't have the necessary documents to take a dog abroad with you.'

Chris felt beads of sweat running down his forehead. Stamps's papers were still attached to the passport of Mr Haskins, which he had left in the safe back at Cleethorpes.

'Oh hell,' said Chris. 'I must have left them at home.'

'Bad luck, sir. I hope you don't have far to travel because there isn't another ferry until this time tomorrow.'

Chris glanced helplessly across at his wife, before climbing back into the car. He looked down at Stamps, who was sleeping soundly on the back seat, oblivious to the problem he was causing. Chris swung the car round and joined an overwrought Sue, who was waiting impatiently to find out why he hadn't been allowed to board. Once Chris had explained the problem, all she said was, 'We can't risk returning to Cleethorpes.'

'I agree,' said Chris, 'we'll have to go back to Ashford, and hope we can find a vet that's open on a bank holiday.'

'That wasn't part of our plan,' said Sue.

'I know,' said Chris, 'but I'm not willing to leave Stamps behind.' Sue nodded in agreement.

Chris swung the Rover onto the main road, and began the journey back to Ashford. Mr and Mrs Haskins arrived just in time to join their daughter for lunch. Tracey was delighted that her parents were able to spend a couple more days with her, but she still couldn't understand why they weren't willing to leave Stamps with her; after all, it wasn't as if they were going away for the rest of their lives.

Chris and Sue spent another uncommunicative day and a further sleepless night in Ashford. A duffel bag containing a quarter of a million pounds was tucked under the bed.

On Monday a local vet kindly agreed to give Stamps all the necessary injections. He then attached a certificate to Mr Appleyard's passport, but not in time for them to catch the last ferry.

The Haskins didn't sleep a wink on the Monday night, and by the time the street lights went out the following morning, they both knew they could no longer go through with it. They lay awake, preparing a new plan – in English.

Chris and Sue finally left their daughter after breakfast the following morning. They drove to the end of the road and this time, to Tracey's relief, turned left, not right, and headed back in the direction of Cleethorpes. By the time they'd swept past the Heathrow exit, their revised plan was in place.

'The moment we arrive home,' said Sue, 'we'll put all the money back in the safe.'

'How will we explain having that amount of cash, when the Post Office accountant carries out his annual audit next month?' asked Chris.

'By the time they get around to checking what's left in the safe, as long as we don't apply for any more money, we should have been able to dispose of most of the cash simply by carrying out our regular transactions.'

'What about the postal orders that we've already cashed?'

'There's still enough cash left in the safe to cover them,' Sue reminded her husband.

'But the scratch cards and the lottery tickets?'

'We'll have to make up the difference from our own money – that way they'll end up none the wiser.'

'I agree,' said Chris, sounding relieved for the first time in days, and then he remembered the passports.

'We'll destroy them,' said Sue, 'as soon as we get home.'

By the time the Haskins had crossed the Lincolnshire border, they had made up their minds to continue running the post office, despite its diminished status. Sue had already come up with several ideas for extra items they could sell over the counter, while making the best of what was left of their franchise.

A smile settled on Sue's lips when Chris finally turned into Victoria Crescent, a smile that was quickly removed when she saw the flashing blue lights. When the old Rover came to a halt, a dozen policemen surrounded the car.

'Oh shit,' said Sue. Extreme language for the chairman of the Mothers' Union, thought Chris, but on balance, he had to agree with her.

Mr and Mrs Haskins were arrested on the evening of 29 December. They were driven to Cleethorpes police station and placed in separate interview rooms. There was no need for the local police to conduct a good cop, bad cop routine, as both of them confessed immediately. They spent the night in separate cells, and the following morning they were charged with the theft of £250,000, being the property of the Post Office, and obtaining, by deception, four passports.

They pleaded guilty to both charges.

Sue Haskins was released from Moreton Hall after serving four months of her sentence. Chris joined her a year later.

While he was in prison Chris worked on another plan. However, when he was released Britannia Finance didn't feel able to back him. To be fair, Mr Tremaine had retired.

Mr and Mrs Haskins sold their property on Victoria Crescent for £100,000. A week later they climbed into their ancient Rover and drove off to Dover, where they boarded the ferry after presenting the correct passports. Once they had found a suitable location on the seafront in Albufeira, they opened a fish-and-chip shop. Haskins' hasn't caught on with the locals yet, but with a hundred thousand Brits visiting the Algarve every year, there's proved to be no shortage of customers.

I was among those who risked a small investment in the new enterprise, and I am happy to report that I have recouped every penny with interest. Funny old world. But then as Mr Justice Gray observed, Mr and Mrs Haskins were not criminals.

Only one footnote. Stamps died while Sue and Chris were in prison.

Maestro

THE ITALIANS ARE THE ONLY RACE I know who have the ability to serve without appearing subservient. The French will happily spill sauce all over your favourite tie, with no hint of an apology, at the same time cursing you in their native tongue. The Chinese don't speak to you at all, and the Greeks think nothing of leaving you alone for an hour before they even offer you a menu. The Americans are at pains to let you know that they aren't really waiters at all, but out-of-work actors, who then proceed to recite the specials on the menu as if performing for an audition. The English are quite likely to engage you in a long conversation, leaving an impression that you ought to be having dinner with them, rather than your guest, and as for the Germans . . . well, when did you last eat at a German restaurant?

So it is left to the Italians to sweep the board and gather up the crumbs. They combine the charm of the Irish, the culinary expertise of the French and the thoroughness of the Swiss, and despite their ability to produce a bill that never seems to add up, we allow them to go on fleecing us.

This was certainly true of Mario Gambotti.

Mario came from a long line of Florentines who could not sing, paint or play football, so he happily joined his fellow exiles in London, where he began an apprenticeship in the restaurant business.

Whenever I go to his fashionable little restaurant in

Fulham for lunch, he somehow manages to hide his disapproval when I order minestrone soup, spaghetti Bolognese and a bottle of Chianti classico.

'What an excellent choice, maestro,' he declares, not bothering to scribble down my order on his pad. Please note 'maestro': not my lord, which would be sycophantic, not sir, which would be ridiculous after twenty years of friendship, but maestro, a particularly flattering sobriquet, as I have it on good authority (his wife) that he has never read one of my books.

When I was in attendance at North Sea Camp open prison, Mario wrote to the governor and suggested that he might be allowed to come down one Friday and cook lunch for me. The governor was amused by the request, and wrote a formal reply, explaining that should he grant the boon, it would not only break several penal regulations, but undoubtedly stir the tabloids into a frenzy of headlines. When the governor showed me a copy of his reply, I was surprised to see that he had signed the letter, *yours ever, Michael*.

'Are you also a customer of Mario's?' I enquired.

'No,' replied the governor, 'but he has been a customer of mine.'

Mario's can be found on the Fulham Road in Chelsea, and the restaurant's popularity is due in no small part to his wife, Teresa, who runs the kitchen. Mario always remains front of house. I regularly have lunch there on a Friday, often accompanied by my two sons and their latest girlfriends, who used to change more often than the menu.

Over the years I have become aware that many of the customers are regulars, which leaves an impression that we are all part of an exclusive club, in which it's almost impossible to book a table unless you are a member. However, the real proof of Mario's popularity is that the restaurant does not accept credit cards – cheques, cash and account-paying customers are all welcome, but **NO CREDIT CARDS** is printed in bold letters at the foot of every menu.

During the month of August the establishment is closed, in order for the Gambotti family to return to their native Florence and reunite with all the other Gambottis.

Mario is quintessentially Italian. His red Ferrari can be seen parked outside the restaurant, his yacht – my son James assures me – is moored in Monte Carlo, and his children, Tony, Maria and Roberto, are being educated at St Paul's, Cheltenham and Summer Fields respectively. After all, it is important that they mix with the sort of people they will be expected to fleece at some time in the future. And whenever I see them at the opera – Verdi and Puccini, never Wagner or Weber – they are always seated in their own box.

So, I hear you ask, how did such a shrewd and intelligent man end up serving at Her Majesty's pleasure? Was he involved in some fracas following a football match between Arsenal and Fiorentina? Did he drive over the speed limit once too often in that Ferrari of his? Perhaps he forgot to pay his poll tax? None of the above. He broke an English law with an action that in the land of his forefathers would be considered no more than an acceptable part of everyday life.

Enter Mr Dennis Cartwright, who worked for another of Her Majesty's establishments.

Mr Cartwright was an inspector with the Inland Revenue. He rarely ate out at a restaurant, and certainly not one as exclusive as Mario's. Whenever he and his wife Doris 'went Italian', it was normally Pizza Express. However, he took a great interest in Mr Gambotti, and in how he could possibly maintain such a lifestyle on the amount he was declaring to his local tax office. After all, the restaurant was showing a profit of a mere £172,000, on a turnover of just over two million. So, after tax, Mr Gambotti was only taking home – Dennis carefully checked the figures – just over £100,000. With a home in Chelsea, three children at private schools and a Ferrari to maintain, not to mention the yacht moored in Monte Carlo, and heaven knows what else in Florence, how did he manage it? Mr Cartwright, a determined man, was determined to find out.

The tax inspector checked all the figures in Mario's books, and he had to admit they balanced and, what's more,

Mr Gambotti always paid his taxes on time. However, Mr Cartwright wasn't in any doubt that Mr Gambotti had to be siphoning off large sums of cash, but how? He must have missed something. Cartwright leapt up in the middle of the night and shouted out loud, '*No credit cards.*' He woke his wife.

The next morning, Cartwright went over the books yet again; he was right. There were no credit-card entries. Although all the cheques were properly accounted for, and all the customers' accounts tallied, when you considered that there were no credit-card entries, the small amount of cash declared seemed completely out of proportion to the over-all takings.

Mr Cartwright didn't need to be told that his masters would not allow him to waste much time dining at Mario's in order to resolve the mystery of how Mr Gambotti was salting away such large sums of money. Mr Buchanan, his supervisor, reluctantly agreed to allow Dennis an advance of £200 to try to discover what was happening on the inside – every penny was to be accounted for – and he only agreed to this after Dennis had pointed out that if he was able to gather enough evidence to put Mr Gambotti behind bars, imagine just how many other restaurateurs might feel obliged to start declaring their true incomes.

Mr Cartwright was surprised that it took him a month to book a table at Mario's, and it was only after several calls, always made from home, that he finally was able to secure a reservation. He asked his wife Doris to join him, hoping it would appear less suspicious than if he was sitting on his own, compiling notes. His supervisor agreed with the ploy, but told Dennis that he would have to cover his wife's half of the bill, at his own expense.

'It never crossed my mind to do otherwise,' Dennis assured his supervisor.

During a meal of Tuscan bean soup and gnocchi – he was hoping to pay more than one visit to Mario's – Dennis kept a wary eye on his host as he circled the different tables, making small talk and attending to his customers' slightest whims. His wife couldn't help but notice that Dennis seemed distracted, but she decided not to comment, as it was a rare occurrence for her husband to invite her out for a meal, other than on her birthday.

Mr Cartwright began committing to memory that there were thirty-nine tables dotted around the restaurant (he double-checked) and roughly a hundred and twenty covers. He also observed, by taking time over his coffee, that Mario managed two sittings on several of the tables. He was impressed by how quickly three waiters could clear a table, replace the cloth and napkins, and moments later make it appear as if no one had ever been sitting there.

When Mario presented Mr Cartwright with his bill, he paid in cash and insisted on a receipt. When they left the restaurant, Doris drove them both home, which allowed Dennis to write down all the relevant figures in his little book while they still remained fresh in his memory.

'What a lovely meal,' commented his wife on their journey back to Romford. 'I do hope that we'll be able to go there again some time.'

'We will, Doris,' he promised her, 'next week.' He paused. 'If I can get a table.'

Mr and Mrs Cartwright visited the restaurant again three weeks later, this time for dinner. Dennis was impressed that Mario not only remembered his name, but even seated him at the same table. On this occasion, Mr Cartwright observed that Mario was able to fit in a pre-theatre booking – almost full; an evening sitting – packed out; and a post-theatre sitting – half full; while last orders were not taken until eleven o'clock.

Mr Cartwright estimated that nearly three hundred and fifty customers passed through the restaurant during the evening, and if you added that to the lunchtime clientele, the total came to just over five hundred a day. He also calculated that around half of them were paying cash, but he still had no way of proving it.

Dennis's dinner bill came to £75 (it's fascinating how restaurants appear to charge more in the evening than they do for lunch, even when they serve exactly the same food). Mr Cartwright estimated that each customer was being charged between £25 and £40, and that was probably on the conservative side. So in any given week, Mario had to be serving at least three thousand customers, returning him an income of around £90,000 a week, which was in excess of four million pounds a year, even if you discounted the month of August.

When Mr Cartwright returned to his office the following morning, he once again went over the restaurant's books. Mr Gambotti was declaring a turnover of £2,120,000, and showing, after outgoings, a profit of £172,000. So what was happening to the other two million?

Mr Cartwright remained baffled. He took the ledgers home in the evening, and continued to study the figures long into the night.

'Eureka,' he declared just before putting on his pyjamas. One of the outgoings didn't add up. The following morning he made an appointment to see his supervisor. 'I'll need to get my hands on the details of these particular weekly numbers,' Dennis told Mr Buchanan, as he placed a forefinger on one of the items listed under outgoings, 'and more important,' he added, 'without Mr Gambotti realizing what I'm up to.' Mr Buchanan sanctioned a request for him to be out of the office, as long as it didn't require any further visits to Mario's.

Mr Cartwright spent most of the weekend refining his plan, aware that just the slightest hint of what he was up to would allow Mr Gambotti enough time to cover his tracks.

On Monday Mr Cartwright rose early and drove to Fulham, not bothering to check in at the office. He parked his Skoda down a side street that allowed him a clear view of the entrance to Mario's restaurant. He removed a notebook from an inside pocket and began to write down the names of every tradesman who visited the premises that morning.

The first van to arrive and park on the double yellow line outside the restaurant's front door was a well-known purveyor of vegetables, followed a few minutes later by a master butcher. Next to unload her wares was a fashionable florist, followed by a wine merchant, a fishmonger and finally the one vehicle Mr Cartwright had been waiting for – a laundry van. Once the driver had unloaded three large crates, dumped them inside the restaurant and come back out, lugging three more crates, he drove away. Mr Cartwright didn't need to follow the van as the company's name, address and telephone number were emblazoned across both sides of the vehicle.

Mr Cartwright returned to the office, and was seated behind his desk just before midday. He reported immediately to his supervisor, and sought his authority to make a spot-check on the company concerned. Mr Buchanan again sanctioned his request, but on this occasion recommended caution. He advised Cartwright to carry out a routine enquiry, so that the company concerned would not work out what he was really looking for. 'It may take a little longer,' Buchanan added, 'but it will give us a far better chance of success in the long run. I'll drop them a line today, and then you can fix up a meeting, at their convenience.'

Dennis went along with his supervisor's suggestion, which meant that he didn't turn up at the offices of the Marco Polo laundry company for another three weeks. On arrival at the laundry, by appointment, he made it clear to the manager that his visit was nothing more than a routine check, and he wasn't expecting to find any irregularities.

Dennis spent the rest of the day checking through every one of their customers' accounts, only stopping to make detailed notes whenever he came across an entry for Mario's restaurant. By midday he had gathered all the evidence he needed, but he didn't leave Marco Polo's offices until five, so that no one would become suspicious. When Dennis departed for the day, he assured the manager that he was well satisfied with their bookkeeping, and there would be no follow-up. What he didn't tell him was that one of their most important customers would be followed up.

Mr Cartwright was seated at his desk by eight o'clock the following morning, making sure his report was completed before his boss appeared.

When Mr Buchanan walked in at five to nine, Dennis leapt up from behind his desk, a look of triumph on his face. He was just about to pass on his news, when the supervisor placed a finger to his lips and indicated that he should follow him through to his office. Once the door was closed, Dennis placed the report on the table and took his boss through the details of his enquiries. He waited patiently while Mr Buchanan studied the documents and considered their implications. He finally looked up, to indicate that Dennis could now speak.

'This shows,' Dennis began, 'that every day for the past twelve months Mr Gambotti has sent out two hundred tablecloths and over five hundred napkins to the Marco Polo laundry. If you then look at this particular entry,' he added, pointing to an open ledger on the other side of the desk, 'you will observe that Gambotti is only declaring a hundred and twenty bookings a day, for around three hundred customers.' Dennis paused before delivering his accountant's coup de grâce. 'Why would you need a further three thousand table-cloths and forty-five thousand napkins to be laundered every year, unless you had another forty-five thousand customers?' he asked. He paused once again. 'Because he's laundering money,' said Dennis, clearly pleased with his little pun.

'Well done, Dennis,' said the head of department. 'Prepare a full report and I'll see that it ends up on the desk of our fraud department.'

Try as he might, Mario could not explain away 3,000 tablecloths and 45,000 napkins to Mr Gerald Henderson, his cynical solicitor. The lawyer only had one piece of advice for his client, 'Plead guilty, and I'll see if I can make a deal.'

The Inland Revenue successfully claimed back two million pounds in taxes from Mario's restaurant, and the judge sent Mario Gambotti to prison for six months. He ended up only having to serve a four-week sentence – three months off for good behaviour and, as it was his first offence, he was put on a tag for two months.

Mr Henderson, an astute lawyer, even managed to get the trial set in the court calendar for the last week in July.

He explained to the presiding judge that it was the only time Mr Gambotti's eminent QC would be available to appear before his lordship. The date of 30 July was agreed by all parties.

After a week spent in Belmarsh high-security prison in south London, Mario was transferred to North Sea Camp open prison in Lincolnshire, where he completed his sentence. Mario's lawyer had selected the prison on the grounds that he was unlikely to meet up with many of his old customers deep in the fens of Lincolnshire.

Meanwhile, the rest of the Gambotti family flew off to Florence for the month of August, not able fully to explain to the grandmothers why Mario couldn't be with them on this occasion.

Mario was released from North Sea Camp at nine o'clock on Monday, 1 September.

As he walked out of the front gate, he found Tony seated behind the wheel of his Ferrari, waiting to pick his father up. Three hours later Mario was standing at the front door of his restaurant to greet the first customer. Several regulars commented on the fact that he appeared to have lost a few pounds while he'd been away on holiday, while others remarked on how tanned and fit he looked.

Six months after Mario had been released, a newly promoted deputy supervisor decided to carry out another spot-check on Marco Polo's laundry. This time Dennis turned up unannounced. He ran a practised eye over the books, to find that Mario's was now sending only 120 tablecloths to the laundry each day, along with 300 napkins, despite the fact that the restaurant appeared to be just as popular. How was he managing to get away with it this time?

The following morning Dennis parked his Skoda down a side street off the Fulham Road once again, allowing him an uninterrupted view of Mario's front door. He felt confident that Mr Gambotti must now be using more than one laundry service, but to his disappointment the only van to appear and deposit and collect any laundry that day was Marco Polo's.

Mr Cartwright drove back to Romford at eight that evening, completely baffled. Had he hung around until just after midnight, Dennis would have seen several waiters leaving the restaurant, carrying bulging sports bags with squash racquets poking out of the top. Do you know any Italian waiters who play squash?

Mario's staff were delighted that their wives could earn some extra cash by taking in a little laundry each day, especially as Mr Gambotti had supplied each of them with a brand-new washing machine.

I booked a table for lunch at Mario's on the Friday after I had been released from prison. He was standing on the doorstep, waiting to greet me, and I was immediately ushered through to my usual table in the corner of the room by the window, as if I had never been away.

Mario didn't bother to offer me a menu because his wife appeared out of the kitchen carrying a large plate of spaghetti, which she placed on the table in front of me. Mario's son Tony followed close behind with a steaming bowl of Bolognese sauce, and his daughter Maria with a large chunk of Parmesan cheese and a grater.

'A bottle of Chianti classico?' suggested Mario, as he removed the cork. 'On the house,' he insisted.

'Thank you, Mario,' I said, and whispered, 'by the way, the governor of North Sea Camp asked me to pass on his best wishes.'

'Poor Michael,' Mario sighed, 'what a sad existence. Can you begin to imagine a lifetime spent eating toad-in-the-hole, followed by semolina pudding?' He smiled as he poured me a glass of wine. 'Still, maestro, you must have felt quite at home.'

Don't Drink The Water

'IF YOU WANT TO murder someone,' said Karl, 'don't do it in England.'

'Why not?' I asked innocently.

'The odds are against you getting away with it,' my fellow inmate warned me, as we continued to walk round the exercise yard. 'You've got a much better chance in Russia.'

'I'll try to remember that,' I assured him.

'Mind you,' added Karl, 'I knew a countryman of yours who did get away with murder, but at some cost.'

It was Association, that welcome 45-minute break when you're released from your cell. You can either spend your time on the ground floor, which is about the size of a basketball court, sitting around chatting, playing table tennis or watching television, or you can go out into the fresh air and stroll around the perimeter of the yard – about the size of a football pitch. Despite being surrounded by a twenty-foot-high concrete wall topped with razor wire, and with only the sky to look up at, this was, for me, the highlight of the day.

While I was incarcerated at Belmarsh, a category A high-security prison in south-east London, I was locked in my cell for twenty-three hours a day (think about it). You are let out only to go to the canteen to pick up your lunch (five minutes), which you then eat in your cell. Five hours later you collect your supper (five more minutes), when they also hand you tomorrow's breakfast in a plastic bag so that they don't have to let you out again before lunch the following day. The only other blessed release is Association, and even that can be cancelled if the prison is short-staffed (which happens about twice a week).

I always used the 45-minute escape to power-walk, for two reasons: one, I needed the exercise because on the outside I attend a local gym five days a week, and, two, not many prisoners bothered to try and keep up with me. Karl was the exception.

Karl was a Russian by birth who hailed from that beautiful city of St Petersburg. He was a contract killer who had just begun a 22-year sentence for disposing of a fellow countryman who was proving tiresome to one of the Mafia gangs back home. He cut his victims up into small pieces, and put what was left of them into an incinerator. Incidentally, his fee – should you want someone disposed of – was five thousand pounds.

Karl was a bear of a man, six foot two and built like a weightlifter. He was covered in tattoos and never stopped talking. On balance, I didn't consider it wise to interrupt his flow. Like so many prisoners, Karl didn't talk about his own crime, and the golden rule – should you ever end up inside – is never ask what a prisoner is in for, unless they raise the subject. However, Karl did tell me a tale about an Englishman he'd come across in St Petersburg, which he claimed to have witnessed in the days when he'd been a driver for a government minister.

Although Karl and I were resident on different blocks, we met up regularly for Association. But it still took several perambulations of the yard before I squeezed out of him the story of Richard Barnsley.

✳ ✳ ✳

DON'T DRINK THE WATER. Richard Barnsley stared at the little plastic card that had been placed on the washbasin in his bathroom. Not the kind of warning you expect to find when you're staying in a five-star hotel, unless, of course, you're in St Petersburg. By the side of the notice stood two bottles of Evian water. When Dick strolled back into his spacious bedroom, he found two more bottles had been placed on each side of the double bed, and another two on a table by the window. The management weren't taking any chances.

Dick had flown into St Petersburg to close a deal with the Russians. His company had been selected to build a pipeline that would stretch from the Urals to the Red Sea, a project that several other, more established, companies had tendered for. Dick's firm had been awarded the contract, against considerable odds, but those odds had shortened once he guaranteed Anatol Chenkov, the Minister for Energy and close personal friend of the President, two million dollars a year for the rest of his life – the only currencies the Russians trade in are dollars and death – especially when the money is going to be deposited in a numbered account.

Before Dick had started up his own company, Barnsley Construction, he had learnt his trade working in Nigeria for Bechtel, in Brazil for McAlpine and in Saudi Arabia for Hanover, so along the way he had picked up a trick or two about bribery. Most international companies treat the practice simply as another form of tax, and make the necessary provision for it whenever they present their tender. The secret is always to know how much to offer the minister, and how little to dispose of among his acolytes.

Anatol Chenkov, a Putin appointee, was a tough negotiator, but then under a former regime he had been a major in the KGB. However, when it came to setting up a bank account in Switzerland, the minister was clearly a novice. Dick took full advantage of this; after all, Chenkov had never travelled beyond the Russian border before he was appointed to the Politburo. Dick flew him to Geneva for the weekend, while he was on an official visit to London for trade talks. He opened a numbered account for him with Picket & Co, and deposited $100,000 – seed money – but more than Chenkov had been paid in his lifetime. This sweetener was to ensure that the umbilical cord would last for the necessary nine months until the contract was signed; a contract that would allow Dick to retire – on far more than two million a year.

Dick returned to the hotel that morning after his final meeting with the minister, having seen him every day for the past week, sometimes publicly, more often privately. It was no different when Chenkov visited London. Neither man trusted the other, but then Dick never felt at ease with anyone who was willing to take a bribe because there was always someone else happy to offer him another percentage point. However, Dick felt more confident this time, as both of them seemed to have signed up for the same retirement policy.

Dick also helped to cement the relationship with a few added extras that Chenkov quickly became accustomed to. A Rolls-Royce would always pick him up at Heathrow and drive him to the Savoy Hotel. On arrival, he would be shown to his usual riverside suite, and women appeared every evening as regularly as the morning papers. He preferred two of both, one broadsheet, one tabloid.

When Dick checked out of the St Petersburg hotel half

an hour later, the minister's BMW was parked outside the front door waiting to take him to the airport. As he climbed into the back seat, he was surprised to find Chenkov waiting for him. They had parted after their morning meeting just an hour before.

'Is there a problem, Anatol?' he asked anxiously.

'On the contrary,' said Chenkov. 'I have just had a call from the Kremlin which I didn't feel we should discuss over the phone, or even in my office. The President will be visiting St Petersburg on the sixteenth of May and has made it clear that he wishes to preside over the signing ceremony.'

'But that gives us less than three weeks to complete the contract,' said Dick.

'You assured me at our meeting this morning,' Chenkov reminded him, 'that there were only a few *i*s to dot and *t*s to cross – an expression I'd not come across before – before you'd be able to finalize the contract.' The minister paused and lit his first cigar of the day before adding, 'With that in mind, my dear friend, I look forward to seeing you back in St Petersburg in three weeks' time.' Chenkov's statement sounded casual, whereas, in truth, it had taken almost three years for the two men to reach this stage, and now it would only be another three weeks before the deal was finally sealed.

Dick didn't respond as he was already thinking about what needed to be done the moment his plane touched down at Heathrow.

'What's the first thing you'll do after the deal has been signed?' asked Chenkov, breaking into his thoughts.

'Put in a tender for the sanitation contract in this city, because whoever gets it would surely make an even larger fortune.'

The minister looked round sharply. 'Never raise that subject in public,' he said gravely. 'It's a very sensitive issue.'

Dick remained silent.

'And take my advice, don't drink the water. Last year we lost countless numbers of our citizens who contracted . . .' the minister hesitated, unwilling to add credence to a story that had been splashed across the front pages of every Western paper.

'How many is countless?' enquired Dick.

'None,' replied the minister. 'Or at least that's the official statistic released by the Ministry of Tourism,' he added as the car came to a halt on a double red line outside the entrance of Pulkovo II airport. He leant forward. 'Karl, take Mr Barnsley's bags to check-in, while I wait here.'

Dick leant across and shook hands with the minister for the second time that morning. 'Thank you, Anatol, for everything,' he said. 'See you in three weeks' time.'

'Long life and happiness, my friend,' said Chenkov as Dick stepped out of the car.

Dick checked in at the departure desk an hour before boarding was scheduled for his flight to London.

'This is the last call for Flight 902 to London Heathrow,' came crackling over the tannoy.

'Is there another flight going to London right now?' asked Dick.

'Yes,' replied the man behind the check-in desk. 'Flight 902 has been delayed, but they're just about to close the gate.'

'Can you get me on it?' asked Dick, as he slid a thousand-rouble note across the counter.

Dick's plane touched down at Heathrow three and a half hours later. Once he'd retrieved his case from the carousel, he pushed his trolley through the Nothing to Declare channel and emerged into the arrivals hall.

Stan, his driver, was already waiting among a group of chauffeurs, most of whom were holding up name cards. As soon as Stan spotted his boss, he walked quickly across and relieved him of his suitcase and overnight bag.

'Home or the office?' Stan asked as they walked towards the short-stay carpark.

Dick checked his watch: just after four. 'Home,' he said. 'I'll work in the back of the car.'

Once Dick's Jaguar had emerged from the carpark to begin the journey to Virginia Water, Dick immediately called his office.

'Richard Barnsley's office,' said a voice.

'Hi, Jill, it's me. I managed to catch an earlier flight, and I'm on my way home. Is there anything I should be worrying about?'

'No, everything's running smoothly this end,' Jill replied. 'We're all just waiting to find out how things went in St Petersburg.'

'Couldn't have gone better. The minister wants me back on May sixteenth to sign the contract.'

'But that's less than three weeks away.'

'Which means we'll all have to get a move on. So set up a board meeting for early next week, and then make an appointment for me to see Sam Cohen first thing tomorrow morning. I can't afford any slip-ups at this stage.'

'Can I come to St Petersburg with you?'

'Not this time, Jill, but once the contract has been signed

block out ten days in the diary. Then I'll take you somewhere a little warmer than St Petersburg.'

Dick sat silently in the back of the car, going over everything that needed to be covered before he returned to St Petersburg. By the time Stan drove through the wrought-iron gates and came to a halt outside the neo-Georgian mansion, Dick knew what had to be done. He jumped out of the car and ran into the house. He left Stan to unload the bags, and his housekeeper to unpack them. Dick was surprised not to find his wife standing on the top step, waiting to greet him, but then he remembered that he'd caught an earlier flight, and Maureen wouldn't be expecting him back for at least another couple of hours.

Dick ran upstairs to his bedroom, and quickly stripped off his clothes, dropping them in a pile on the floor. He went into the bathroom and turned on the shower, allowing the warm jets of water to slowly remove the grime of St Petersburg and Aeroflot.

After he'd put on some casual clothes, Dick checked his appearance in the mirror. At fifty-three, his hair was turning prematurely grey, and although he tried to hold his stomach in, he knew he ought to lose a few pounds, just a couple of notches on his belt – once the deal was signed and he had a little more time, he promised himself.

He left the bedroom and went down to the kitchen. He asked the cook to prepare him a salad, and then strolled into the drawing room, picked up *The Times,* and glanced at the headlines. A new leader of the Tory Party, a new leader of the Liberal Democrats, and now Gordon Brown had been elected leader of the Labour Party. None of the major political parties would be fighting the next election under the same leader.

Dick looked up when the phone began to ring. He walked across to his wife's writing desk and picked up the receiver, to hear Jill's voice on the other end of the line.

'The board meeting is fixed for next Thursday at ten o'clock, and I've also arranged for you to see Sam Cohen in his office at eight tomorrow morning.' Dick removed a pen from an inside pocket of his blazer. 'I've emailed every member of the board to warn them that it's a priority,' she added.

'What time did you say my meeting was with Sam?'

'Eight o'clock at his office. He has to be in court by ten for another client.'

'Fine.' Dick opened his wife's drawer and grabbed the first piece of paper available. He wrote down, *Sam, office, 8, Thur board mtg, 10.* 'Well done, Jill,' he added. 'Better book me back into the Grand Palace Hotel, and email the minister to warn him what time I'll be arriving.'

'I already have,' Jill replied, 'and I've also booked you on a flight to St Petersburg on the Friday afternoon.'

'Well done. See you around ten tomorrow.' Dick put the phone down, and strolled through to his study, with a large smile on his face. Everything was going to plan.

When he reached his desk, Dick transferred the details of his appointments to his diary. He was just about to drop the piece of paper into a wastepaper basket when he decided just to check and see if it contained anything important. He unfolded a letter, which he began to read. His smile turned to a frown, long before he'd reached the final paragraph. He started to read the letter, marked private and personal, a second time.

Dear Mrs Barnsley,

This is to confirm your appointment at our office on
Friday, 30 April, when we will continue our discussions
on the matter you raised with me last Tuesday.
Remembering the full implications of your decision,
I have asked my senior partner to join us on this occasion.
We both look forward to seeing you on the 30th.

Yours sincerely,

Andrew Symonds

Dick immediately picked up the phone on his desk, and
dialled Sam Cohen's number, hoping he hadn't already left
for the day. When Sam pick up his private line, all Dick
said was, 'Have you come across a lawyer called Andrew
Symonds?'

'Only by reputation,' said Sam, 'but then I don't
specialize in divorce.'

'Divorce?' said Dick, as he heard a car coming up the
gravel driveway. He glanced out of the window to see a
Volkswagen swing round the circle and come to a halt
outside the front door. Dick watched as his wife climbed out
of her car. 'I'll see you at eight tomorrow, Sam, and the
Russian contract won't be the only thing on the agenda.'

Dick's driver dropped him outside Sam Cohen's office in
Lincoln's Inn Field a few minutes before eight the following
morning. The senior partner rose to greet his client as he
entered the room. He gestured to a comfortable chair on the
other side of the desk.

Dick had opened his briefcase even before he'd sat

down. He took out the letter and passed it across to Sam. The lawyer read it slowly, before placing it on the desk in front of him.

'I've thought about the problem overnight,' said Sam, 'and I've also had a word with Anna Rentoul, our divorce partner. She's confirmed that Symonds only handles matrimonial disputes, and with that in mind, I'm sorry to say that I'll have to ask you some fairly personal questions.'

Dick nodded without comment.

'Have you ever discussed divorce with Maureen?'

'No,' said Dick firmly. 'We've had rows from time to time, but then what couples who've been together for over twenty years haven't?'

'No more than that?'

'She once threatened to leave me, but I thought that was all in the past.' Dick paused. 'I'm only surprised that she hasn't raised the subject with me, before consulting a lawyer.'

'That's all too common,' said Sam. 'Over half the husbands who are served with a divorce petition claim they never saw it coming.'

'I certainly fall into that category,' admitted Dick. 'So what do I do next?'

'Not a lot you can do before she serves the writ, and I can't see that there's anything to be gained by raising the subject yourself. After all, nothing may come of it. However, that doesn't mean we shouldn't prepare ourselves. Now, what grounds could she have for divorce?'

'None that I can think of.'

'Are you having an affair?'

'No. Well, yes, a fling with my secretary – but it's not going anywhere. She thinks it's serious, but I plan to replace her once the pipeline contract is signed.'

'So the deal is still on course?' said Sam.

'Yes, that's originally why I needed to see you so urgently,' replied Dick. 'I have to be back in St Petersburg for May the sixteenth, when both sides will be signing the contract.' He paused. 'And it's going to be witnessed by President Putin.'

'Congratulations,' said Sam. 'How much will that be worth to you?'

'Why do you ask?'

'I'm wondering if you're not the only person who's hoping that the deal will go through.'

'Around sixty million –' Dick hesitated – 'for the company.'

'And do you still own fifty-one per cent of the shares?'

'Yes, but I could always hide—'

'Don't even think about it,' said Sam. 'You won't be able to hide anything if Symonds is on the case. He'll sniff out every last penny, like a pig hunting for truffles. And if the court were to discover that you attempted to deceive them, it would only make the judge more sympathetic to your wife.' The senior partner paused, looked directly at his client, and repeated, 'Don't even think about it.'

'So what should I do?'

'Nothing that will arouse suspicion; go about your business as usual, as if you have no idea what she's up to. Meanwhile, I'll fix a consultation with counsel, so at least we'll be better prepared than Mr Symonds will be anticipating. And one more thing,' said Sam, once again looking directly at his client, 'no more extra-marital activities until this problem has been resolved. That's an order.'

Dick kept a close eye on his wife during the next few days, but she gave no sign of there being anything untoward. If anything, she showed an unusual interest in how the trip to St Petersburg had gone, and over dinner on Thursday evening even asked if the board had come to a decision.

'They most certainly have,' Dick replied emphatically. 'Once Sam had taken the directors through each clause, gone over every detail, and answered all of their questions, they virtually rubber-stamped the contract.' Dick poured himself a second cup of coffee. He was taken by surprise by his wife's next question.

'Why don't I join you when you go to St Petersburg? We could fly out on the Friday,' she added, 'and spend the weekend visiting the Hermitage and the Summer Palace. We might even find enough time to see Catherine's amber collection – something I've always wanted to do.'

Dick didn't reply immediately, aware that this was not a casual suggestion as it had been years since Maureen had accompanied him on a business trip. Dick's first reaction was to wonder what she was up to. 'Let me think about it,' he eventually responded, leaving his coffee to go cold.

Dick rang Sam Cohen within minutes of arriving at his office and reported the conversation to his lawyer.

'Symonds must have advised her to witness the signing of the contract,' suggested Cohen.

'But why?'

'So that Maureen will be able to claim that over the years she has played a leading role in your business success, always being there to support you at those critical moments in your career . . .'

'Balls,' said Dick, 'she's never taken any interest in how I make my money, only in how she can spend it.'

' . . . and therefore she must be entitled to fifty per cent of your assets.'

'But that could amount to over thirty million pounds,' Dick protested.

'Symonds has obviously done his homework.'

'Then I'll simply tell her that she can't come on the trip. It's not appropriate.'

'Which will allow Mr Symonds to change tack. He'll then portray you as a heartless man, who, the moment you became a success, cut his client out of your life, often travelling abroad, accompanied by a secretary who—'

'OK, OK, I get the picture. So allowing her to come to St Petersburg might well prove to be the lesser of two evils.'

'On the one hand . . . ' counselled Sam.

'Bloody lawyers,' said Dick before he could finish the sentence.

'Funny how you only need us when you're in trouble,' Sam rejoined. 'So let's make sure that this time we anticipate her next move.'

'And what's that likely to be?'

'Once she's got you to St Petersburg, she'll want to have sex.'

'We haven't had sex for years.'

'And not because I haven't wanted to, m'lord.'

'Oh, hell,' said Dick, 'I can't win.'

'You can as long as you don't follow Lady Longford's advice – when asked if she had ever considered divorcing Lord Longford, she replied, "Divorce, never, murder, often."'

Mr and Mrs Richard Barnsley checked into the Grand Palace Hotel in St Petersburg a fortnight later. A porter placed their bags on a trolley, and then accompanied them to the Tolstoy Suite on the ninth floor.

'Must go to the loo before I burst,' said Dick as he rushed into the room ahead of his wife. While her husband disappeared into the bathroom, Maureen looked out of the window and admired the golden domes of St Nicholas's Cathedral.

Once he'd locked the door, Dick removed the DON'T DRINK THE WATER sign that was perched on the wash-basin and tucked it into the back pocket of his trousers. Next he unscrewed the tops of the two Evian bottles and poured the contents down the sink. He then refilled both bottles with tap water, before screwing the tops firmly back on and returning them to their place on the corner of the basin. He unlocked the door and strolled out of the bathroom.

Dick started to unpack his suitcase, but stopped the moment Maureen disappeared into the bathroom. First, he transferred the DON'T DRINK THE WATER sign from his back pocket into the side flap of his suitcase. He zipped up the flap, before checking around the room. There was a small bottle of Evian water on each side of the bed, and two large bottles on the table by the window. He grabbed the bottle by his wife's side of the bed and retreated into the kitchenette at the far end of the room. Dick poured the contents down the sink, and refilled the bottle with tap water. He then returned it to Maureen's side of the bed. Next, he took the two large bottles from the table by the window and repeated the process.

By the time his wife had come out of the bathroom, Dick had almost finished unpacking. While Maureen continued to unpack her suitcase, Dick strolled across to his side of the bed and dialled a number he didn't need to look up. As he waited for the phone to be answered, he opened the bottle of Evian water on his side of the bed, and took a gulp.

'Hi, Anatol, it's Dick Barnsley. I thought I'd let you know that we've just checked in to the Grand Palace.'

'Welcome back to St Petersburg,' said a friendly voice. 'And is your wife with you on this occasion?'

'She most certainly is,' replied Dick, 'and very much looking forward to meeting you.'

'Me too,' said the minister, 'so make sure that you have a relaxed weekend because everything is set up for Monday morning. The President is due to fly in tomorrow night so he'll be present when the contract is signed.'

'Ten o'clock at the Winter Palace?'

'Ten o'clock,' repeated Chenkov. 'I'll pick you up from your hotel at nine. It's only a thirty-minute drive, but we can't afford to be late for this one.'

'I'll be waiting for you in the lobby,' said Dick. 'See you then.' He put the phone down and turned to his wife. 'Why don't we go down to dinner, my darling? We've got a long day ahead of us tomorrow.' He adjusted his watch by three hours and added, 'So perhaps it would be wise to have an early night.'

Maureen placed a long silk nightdress on her side of the bed and smiled in agreement. As she turned to place her empty case in the wardrobe, Dick slipped an Evian bottle from the bedside table into his jacket pocket. He then accompanied his wife down to the dining room.

The head waiter guided them to a quiet table in the corner and, once they were seated, offered his two guests menus. Maureen disappeared behind the large leather cover while she considered the table d'hôte, which allowed Dick enough time to remove the bottle of Evian from his pocket, undo the cap and fill his wife's glass.

Once they had both selected their meals, Maureen went over her proposed itinerary for the next two days. 'I think we should begin with the Hermitage, first thing in the morning,' she suggested, 'take a break for lunch, and then spend the rest of the afternoon at the Summer Palace.'

'What about the amber collection?' asked Dick, as he topped up her water glass. 'I thought that was a no-miss.'

'I'd already scheduled in the amber collection and the Russian Museum for Sunday.'

'Sounds as if you have everything well organized,' said Dick, as a waiter placed a bowl of borscht in front of his wife.

Maureen spent the rest of the meal telling Dick about some of the treasures that they would see when they visited the Hermitage. By the time Dick had signed the bill, Maureen had drunk the bottle of water.

Dick slipped the empty bottle back in his pocket. Once they had returned to their room, he filled it with tap water and left it in the bathroom.

By the time Dick had undressed and climbed into bed, Maureen was still studying her guidebook.

'I feel exhausted,' Dick said. 'It must be the time change.' He turned his back on her, hoping she wouldn't work out that it was just after eight p.m. in England.

Dick woke the following morning feeling very thirsty. He looked at the empty bottle of Evian on his side of the bed and remembered just in time. He climbed out of bed, walked across to the fridge and selected a bottle of orange juice.

'Will you be going to the gym this morning?' he asked a half-awake Maureen.

'Do I have time?'

'Sure, the Hermitage doesn't open until ten, and one of the reasons I always stay here is because of the hotel's gym.'

'So what about you?'

'I still have to make some phone calls if everything is to be set up for Monday.'

Maureen slipped out of bed and disappeared into the bathroom, which allowed Dick enough time to top up her glass and replace the empty bottle of Evian on her side of the bed.

When Maureen emerged a few minutes later, she checked her watch before slipping on her gym kit. 'I should be back in about forty minutes,' she said, after tying up her trainers.

'Don't forget to take some water with you,' said Dick, handing her one of the bottles from the table by the window. 'They may not have one in the gym.'

'Thank you,' she said.

Dick wondered, from the expression on her face, if he was being just a little too solicitous.

While Maureen was in the gym, Dick took a shower. When he walked back into the bedroom, he was pleased to see that the sun was shining. He put on a blazer and slacks, but only after he'd checked that none of the bottles had been replaced by the hotel staff while he'd been in the bathroom.

Dick ordered breakfast for both of them, which arrived moments after Maureen returned from the gym, clutching the half-empty Evian bottle.

'How did your training go?' Dick asked.

'Not great,' Maureen replied. 'I felt a bit listless.'

'Probably just jetlag,' suggested Dick as he took his place on the far side of the table. He poured his wife a glass of water, and himself another orange juice. Dick opened a copy of the *Herald Tribune*, which he began to read while he waited for his wife to dress. Hillary Clinton said she wouldn't be running for president, which only convinced Dick that she would, especially as she made the announcement standing by her husband's side.

Maureen came out of the bathroom wearing a hotel dressing gown. She took the seat opposite her husband and sipped the water.

'Better take a bottle of Evian with us when we visit the Hermitage,' said Maureen. Dick looked up from behind his paper. 'The girl in the gym warned me not, under any circumstances, to drink the local water.'

'Oh yes, I should have warned you,' said Dick, as Maureen took a bottle from the table by the window and put it in her bag. 'Can't be too careful.'

Dick and Maureen strolled through the front gates of the Hermitage a few minutes before ten, to find themselves at the back of a long queue. The crocodile of visitors progressed slowly forward along an unshaded cobbled path. Maureen took several sips of water between turning the pages of the guidebook. It was ten forty before they reached the ticket booth. Once inside, Maureen continued to study her guidebook. 'Whatever we do, we must be sure to see Michelangelo's *Crouching Boy*, Raphael's *Virgin*, and Leonardo's *Madonna Benois*.'

Dick smiled his agreement, but knew he wouldn't be concerning himself with the masters.

As they climbed the wide marble staircase, they passed several magnificent statues nestled in alcoves. Dick was surprised to discover just how vast the Hermitage was. Despite visiting St Petersburg several times during the past three years, he had only ever seen the building from the outside.

'Housed on three floors, Tsar Peter's collection displays treasures in over two hundred rooms,' Maureen told him, reading from the guidebook. 'So let's get started.'

By eleven thirty they had only covered the Dutch and Italian schools on the first floor, by which time Maureen had finished the large bottle of Evian.

Dick volunteered to go and buy another bottle. He left his wife admiring Caravaggio's *The Lute Player*, while he slipped into the nearest rest room. He refilled the empty Evian bottle with tap water before rejoining his wife. If

Maureen had spent a little time studying one of the many drinks counters situated on each floor, she would have discovered that the Hermitage doesn't stock Evian, because it has an exclusive contract with Volvic.

By twelve thirty they had all but covered the sixteen rooms devoted to the Renaissance artists, and agreed it was time for lunch. They left the building and strolled back into the midday sun. The two of them walked for a while along the bank of the Moika River, stopping only to take a photograph of a bride and groom posing on the Blue Bridge in front of the Mariinsky Palace.

'A local tradition,' said Maureen, turning another page of her guidebook.

After walking another block, they came to a halt outside a small pizzeria. Its sensible square tables with neat red-and-white check tablecloths and smartly dressed waiters tempted them inside.

'I must go to the loo,' said Maureen. 'I'm feeling a little queasy. It must be the heat.' She added, 'Just order me a salad and a glass of water.'

Dick smiled, removed the Evian bottle from her bag and filled up the glass on her side of the table. When the waiter appeared, Dick ordered a salad for his wife, and ravioli plus a large diet Coke for himself. He was desperate for something to drink.

Once she'd eaten her salad, Maureen perked up a little, and even began to tell Dick what they should look out for when they visited the Summer Palace.

On the long taxi ride through the north of the city, she continued to read extracts from her guidebook. 'Peter the Great built the Summer Palace after he had visited Versailles, and on returning to Russia employed the finest landscape

gardeners and most gifted craftsmen in the land to reproduce the French masterpiece. He intended the finished work
to be a homage to the French, whom he greatly admired as
the leaders of style throughout Europe.'

The taxi driver interrupted her flow with a snippet of
information of his own. 'We are just passing the recently
constructed Winter Palace, which is where President Putin
stays whenever he's in St Petersburg.' The driver paused.
'And, as the national flag is flying, he must be in town.'

'He's flown down from Moscow especially to see me,'
said Dick.

The taxi driver dutifully laughed.

The taxi drove through the gates of the Summer Palace half
an hour later and the driver dropped his passengers off in a
crowded carpark, bustling with sightseers and traders, who
were standing behind their makeshift stalls plying their
cheap souvenirs.

'Let's go and see the real thing,' suggested Maureen.

'I wait for you here,' said the taxi driver. 'No extra charge.
How long?' he added.

'I should think we'd be a couple of hours,' said Dick. 'No
more.'

'I wait for you here,' he repeated.

The two of them strolled around the magnificent gardens,
and Dick could see why it was described in the guidebooks
as a 'can't afford to miss', with five stars. Maureen continued to brief him between sips of water. 'The grounds
surrounding the palace cover over a hundred acres, with
more than twenty fountains, as well as eleven other palatial
residences.' Although the sun was no longer burning down,

the sky was still clear and Maureen continued to take regular gulps of water, but however many times she offered the bottle to Dick, he always replied, 'No thanks.'

When they finally climbed the steps of the palace, they were greeted by another long queue, and Maureen admitted that she was feeling a little tired.

'Pity to have travelled this far,' said Dick, 'and not take a look inside.'

His wife reluctantly agreed.

When they reached the front of the queue, Dick purchased two entrance tickets and, for a small extra charge, selected an English-speaking guide to show them around.

'I don't feel too good,' said Maureen as they entered the Empress Catherine's bedroom. She clung onto the four-poster bed.

'You must drink lots of water on such a hot day,' suggested the tour guide helpfully. By the time they had reached Tsar Nicholas IV's study, Maureen warned her husband that she thought she was going to faint. Dick apologized to their guide, put an arm around his wife's shoulder and assisted her out of the palace on an unsteady journey back to the carpark. They found their taxi driver standing by his car waiting for them.

'We must return to the Grand Palace Hotel immediately,' said Dick, as his wife fell into the back seat of the car like a drunk who has been thrown out of a pub on a Saturday night.

On the long drive back to St Petersburg, Maureen was violently sick in the back of the taxi, but the driver didn't comment, just maintained a steady speed as he continued along the highway. Forty minutes later, he came to a halt outside the Grand Palace Hotel. Dick handed over a wodge of notes and apologized.

'Hope madam better soon,' he said.

'Yes, let's hope so,' replied Dick.

Dick helped his wife out of the back of the car, and guided her up the steps into the hotel lobby and quickly towards the lifts, not wishing to draw attention to himself. He had her safely back in their suite moments later. Maureen immediately disappeared into the bathroom, and even with the door closed Dick could hear her retching. He searched around the room. In their absence, all the bottles of Evian had been replaced. He only bothered to empty the one by Maureen's bedside, which he refilled with tap water from the kitchenette.

Maureen finally emerged from the bathroom, and collapsed onto the bed. 'I feel awful,' she said.

'Perhaps you ought to take a couple of aspirin, and try to get some sleep?'

Maureen nodded weakly. 'Could you fetch them for me? They're in my wash bag.'

'Of course, my darling.' Once he'd found the pills, he filled a glass with tap water, before returning to his wife's side. She had taken off her dress, but not her slip. Dick helped her to sit up and became aware for the first time that she was soaked in sweat. She swilled down the two aspirins with the glass of water Dick offered her. He lowered her gently down onto the pillow before drawing the curtains. He then strolled across to the bedroom door, opened it, and placed the *Do Not Disturb* sign on the door knob. The last thing he needed was for a solicitous maid to come barging in and find his wife in her present state. Once Dick was certain she was asleep, he went down to dinner.

'Will madam be joining you this evening?' enquired the head waiter, once Dick was seated.

'No, sadly not,' replied Dick, 'she has a slight migraine. Too much sun I fear, but I'm sure she'll be fine by the morning.'

'Let's hope so, sir. What can I interest you in tonight?'

Dick took his time perusing the menu, before he eventually said, 'I think I'll start with the foie gras, followed by a rump steak –' he paused – 'medium rare.'

'Excellent choice, sir.'

Dick poured himself a glass of water from the bottle on the table and quickly gulped it down, before filling his glass a second time. He didn't hurry his meal, and when he returned to his suite just after ten, he was delighted to find his wife was fast asleep. He picked up her glass, took it to the bathroom and refilled it with tap water. He then put it back on her side of the bed. Dick took his time undressing, before finally slipping under the covers to settle down next to his wife. He turned out the bedside light and slept soundly.

When Dick woke the following morning, he found that he too was covered in sweat. The sheets were also soaked, and when he turned over to look at his wife all the colour had drained from her cheeks.

Dick eased himself out of bed, slipped into the bathroom and took a long shower. Once he had dried himself, he put on one of the hotel's towelling dressing gowns and returned to the bedroom. He crept over to his wife's side of the bed and once again refilled her empty glass with tap water. She had clearly woken during the night, but not disturbed him.

He drew the curtains before checking that the *Do Not Disturb* sign was still on the door. He returned to his wife's side of the bed, pulled up a chair and began to read the *Herald Tribune*. He had reached the sports pages by the time she woke. Her words were slurred. She managed, 'I feel awful.' A long pause followed before she added, 'Don't you think I ought to see a doctor?'

'He's already been to examine you, my dear,' said Dick. 'I called for him last night. Don't you remember? He told you that you'd caught a fever, and you'll just have to sweat it out.'

'Did he leave any pills?' asked Maureen plaintively.

'No, my darling. He just said you weren't to eat anything, but to try and drink as much water as possible.' He held the glass up to her lips and she attempted to gulp some more down. She even managed, 'Thank you,' before collapsing back onto the pillow.

'Don't worry, my darling,' said Dick. 'You're going to be just fine, and I promise you I won't leave your side, even for a moment.' He leant over and kissed her on the forehead. She fell asleep again.

The only time Dick left Maureen's side that day was to assure the housekeeper that his wife did not wish to have the sheets changed, to refill the glass of water on her bed-side table, and late in the afternoon to take a call from the minister.

'The President flew in yesterday,' were Chenkov's opening words. 'He's staying at the Winter Palace, where I've just left him. He wanted me to let you know how much he is looking forward to meeting you and your wife.'

'How kind of him,' said Dick, 'but I have a problem.'

'A problem?' said a man who didn't like problems, especially when the President was in town.

'It's just that Maureen seems to have caught a fever. We were out in the sun all day yesterday, and I'm not sure that she will have fully recovered in time to join us for the signing ceremony, so I may be on my own.'

'I'm sorry to hear that,' said Chenkov, 'and how are you?'

'Never felt better,' said Dick.

'That's good,' said Chenkov, sounding relieved. 'So I'll pick you up at nine o'clock, as agreed. I don't want to keep the President waiting.'

'Neither do I, Anatol,' Dick assured him. 'You'll find me standing in the lobby long before nine.'

There was a knock on the door. Dick quickly put the phone down and rushed across to open it before anyone was given a chance to barge in. A maid was standing in the corridor next to a trolley laden with sheets, towels, bars of soap, shampoo bottles and cases of Evian water.

'You want the bed turned down, sir?' she asked, giving him a smile.

'No, thank you,' said Dick. 'My wife is not feeling well.' He pointed to the *Do Not Disturb* sign.

'More water, perhaps?' she suggested, holding up a large bottle of Evian.

'No,' he repeated firmly and closed the door.

The only other call that evening came from the hotel manager. He asked politely if madam would like to see the hotel doctor.

'No, thank you,' said Dick. 'She just caught a little sun but she's on the mend, and I feel sure she will have fully recovered by the morning.'

'Just give me a call,' said the manager, 'should she change her mind. The doctor can be with you in minutes.'

'That's very considerate of you,' said Dick, 'but it won't be necessary,' he added before putting the phone down. He returned to his wife's side. Her skin was now pallid and blotchy. He leant forward until he was almost touching her lips – she was still breathing. He walked across to the fridge, opened it and took out all the unopened bottles of Evian water. He placed two of them in the bathroom, and one each side of the bed. His final action, before undressing, was to take the DON'T DRINK THE WATER sign out of his suitcase and replace it on the side of the washbasin.

Chenkov's car pulled up outside the Grand Palace Hotel a few minutes before nine the following morning. Karl jumped out to open the back door for the minister.

Chenkov walked quickly up the steps and into the hotel, expecting to find Dick waiting for him in the lobby. He looked up and down the crowded corridor, but there was no sign of his business partner. He marched across to the reception desk and asked if Mr Barnsley had left a message for him.

'No, Minister,' replied the concierge. 'Would you like me to call his room?' The minister nodded briskly. They both waited for some time, before the concierge added, 'No one is answering the phone, Minister, so perhaps Mr Barnsley is on his way down.'

Chenkov nodded again, and began pacing up and down the lobby, continually glancing towards the elevator, before checking his watch. At ten past nine, the minister became even more anxious, as he had no desire to keep the President waiting. He returned to the reception desk.

'Try again,' he demanded.

The concierge immediately dialled Mr Barnsley's room number, but could only report that there was still no reply.

'Send for the manager,' barked the minister. The concierge nodded, picked up the phone once again and dialled a single number. A few moments later, a tall, elegantly dressed man in a dark suit was standing by Chenkov's side.

'How may I assist you, Minister?' he asked.

'I need to go up to Mr Barnsley's room.'

'Of course, Minister, please follow me.'

When the three men arrived on the ninth floor, they quickly made their way to the Tolstoy Suite, where they found the *Do Not Disturb* sign hanging from the door knob. The minister banged loudly on the door, but there was no response.

'Open the door,' he demanded. The concierge obeyed without hesitation.

The minister marched into the room, followed by the

manager and the concierge. Chenkov came to an abrupt halt when he saw two motionless bodies lying in bed. The concierge didn't need to be told to call for a doctor.

Sadly, the doctor had attended three such cases in the past month, but with a difference – they had all been locals. He studied his two patients for some time before he passed a judgement.

'The Siberian disease,' he confirmed, almost in a whisper. He paused and, looking up at the minister, added, 'The lady undoubtedly died during the night, whereas the gentleman has passed away within the last hour.'

The minister made no comment.

'My initial conclusion,' continued the doctor, 'is that she probably caught the disease from drinking too much of the local water –' he paused as he looked down at Dick's lifeless body – 'while her husband must have contracted the virus from his wife, probably during the night. Not an uncommon occurrence among married couples,' he added. 'Like so many of our countrymen, he clearly wasn't aware that –' he hesitated before uttering the word in front of the minister – '*Siberius* is one of those rare diseases that is not only infectious but highly contagious.'

'But I called him last night,' protested the manager, 'and asked if he'd like to see a doctor, and he said it wasn't necessary, as his wife was on the mend and he was confident that she would be fully recovered by the morning.'

'How sad,' said the doctor, before adding, 'if only he'd said yes. It would have been too late to revive his wife, but I still might have saved him.'

It Can't Be October Already

PATRICK O'FLYNN STOOD in front of H. Samuel, the jeweller's, holding a brick in his right hand. He was staring intently at the window. He smiled, raised his arm and hurled the brick at the glass pane. The window shattered like a spider's web, but remained firmly in place. An alarm was immediately set off, which in the still of a clear, cold October night could be heard half a mile away. More important to Pat, the alarm was directly connected to the local police station.

Pat didn't move as he continued to stare at his handiwork. He only had to wait ninety seconds before he heard the sound of a siren in the distance. He bent down and retrieved the brick from the pavement, as the whining noise grew louder and louder. When the police car came to a screeching halt by the kerbside, Pat raised the brick above his head and leant back, like an Olympic javelin thrower intent on a gold medal. Two policemen leapt out of the car. The older one ignored Pat, who remained poised, arm above his head with the brick in his hand, and walked across to the window to check the damage. Although the pane was shattered, it was still firmly in place. In any case, an iron security grille had descended behind the window, something Pat knew full well would happen. But when the sergeant returned to the station, he would still have to phone the manager, get him out of bed and ask him to come down to the shop and turn off the alarm.

The sergeant turned round to find Pat still standing with the brick high above his head.

'OK, Pat, hand it over and get in,' said the sergeant, as he held open the back door of the police car.

Pat smiled, passed the brick to the fresh-faced constable and said, 'You'll need this as evidence.'

The young constable was speechless.

'Thank you, Sergeant,' said Pat as he climbed into the back of the car, and, smiling at the young constable, who took his place behind the wheel, asked, 'Have I ever told you about the time I tried to get a job on a building site in Liverpool?'

'Many times,' interjected the sergeant, as he took his place next to Pat and pulled the back door closed.

'No handcuffs?' queried Pat.

'I don't want to be handcuffed to you,' said the sergeant, 'I want to be rid of you. Why don't you just go back to Ireland?'

'An altogether inferior class of prison,' Pat explained, 'and in any case, they don't treat me with the same degree of respect as you do, Sergeant,' he added, as the car moved away from the kerb and headed back towards the police station.

'Can you tell me your name?' Pat asked, leaning forward to address the young constable.

'Constable Cooper.'

'Are you by any chance related to Chief Inspector Cooper?'

'He's my father.'

'A gentleman,' said Pat. 'We've had many a cup of tea and biscuits together. I hope he's in fine fettle.'

'He's just retired,' said Constable Cooper.

'I'm sorry to hear that,' said Pat. 'Will you tell him that Pat O'Flynn asked after him? And please send him, and your dear mother, my best wishes.'

'Stop taking the piss, Pat,' said the sergeant. 'The boy's only been out of Peel House for a few weeks,' he added, as the car came to a halt outside the police station. The sergeant climbed out of the back and held the door open for Pat.

'Thank you, Sergeant,' said Pat, as if he was addressing the doorman at the Ritz. The constable grinned as the sergeant accompanied Pat up the stairs and into the police station.

'Ah, and a very good evening to you, Mr Baker,' said Pat when he saw who it was standing behind the desk.

'Oh, Christ,' said the duty sergeant. 'It can't be October already.'

'I'm afraid so, Sergeant,' said Pat. 'I was wondering if my usual cell is available. I'll only be staying overnight, you understand.'

'I'm afraid not,' said the desk sergeant, 'it's already

occupied by a real criminal. You'll have to be satisfied with cell number two.'

'But I've always had cell number one in the past,' protested Pat.

The desk sergeant looked up and raised an eyebrow.

'No, I'm to blame,' admitted Pat. 'I should have asked my secretary to call and book in advance. Do you need to take an imprint of my credit card?'

'No, I have all your details on file,' the desk sergeant assured him.

'How about fingerprints?'

'Unless you've found a way of removing your old ones, Pat, I don't think we need another set. But I suppose you'd better sign the charge sheet.'

Pat took the proffered biro and signed on the bottom line with a flourish.

'Take him down to cell number two, Constable.'

'Thank you, Sergeant,' said Pat as he was led away. He stopped, turned around and said, 'I wonder, Sergeant, if you could give me a wake-up call around seven, a cup of tea, Earl Grey preferably, and a copy of the *Irish Times*.'

'Piss off, Pat,' said the desk sergeant, as the constable tried to stifle a laugh.

'Which reminds me,' said Pat, 'have I told you about the time I tried to get a job on a building site in Liverpool, and the foreman—'

'Get him out of my sight, Constable, if you don't want to spend the rest of the month on traffic duty.'

The constable grabbed Pat by the elbow and hurried him downstairs.

'No need to come with me,' said Pat. 'I can find my own way.' This time the constable did laugh as he placed a key in the lock of cell number two. The young policeman unlocked the cell and pulled open the heavy door, allowing Pat to stroll in.

'Thank you, Constable Cooper,' said Pat. 'I look forward to seeing you in the morning.'

'I'll be off duty,' said Constable Cooper.

'Then I'll see you this time next year,' said Pat without explanation, 'and don't forget to pass on my best wishes to your father,' he added as the four-inch-thick iron door was slammed shut.

Pat studied the cell for a few moments: a steel washbasin, a bog and a bed, one sheet, one blanket and one pillow. Pat was reassured by the fact that nothing had changed since last year. He fell on the horsehair mattress, placed his head on the rock-hard pillow and slept all night – for the first time in weeks.

Pat was woken from a deep sleep at seven the following morning, when the cell-door flap was flicked open and two black eyes stared in.

'Good morning, Pat,' said a friendly voice.

'Good morning, Wesley,' said Pat, not even opening his eyes. 'And how are you?'

'I'm well,' replied Wesley, 'but sorry to see you back.' He paused. 'I suppose it must be October.'

'It certainly is,' said Pat climbing off the bed, 'and it's important that I look my best for this morning's show trial.'

'Anything you need in particular?'

'A cup of tea would be most acceptable, but what I really require is a razor, a bar of soap, a toothbrush and some toothpaste. I don't have to remind you, Wesley, that a defendant is entitled to this simple request before he makes an appearance in court.'

'I'll see you get them,' said Wesley, 'and would you like to read my copy of the *Sun*?'

'That's kind of you, Wesley, but if the chief superintendent has finished with yesterday's *Times*, I'd prefer that.' A West Indian chuckle was followed by the closing of the shutter on the cell door.

Pat didn't have to wait long before he heard a key turn in the lock. The heavy door was pulled open to reveal the smiling face of Wesley Pickett, a tray in one hand, which he placed on the end of the bed.

'Thank you, Wesley,' said Pat as he stared down at the bowl of cornflakes, small carton of skimmed milk, two slices of burnt toast and a boiled egg. 'I do hope Molly remembered,' added Pat, 'that I like my eggs lightly boiled, for two and a half minutes.'

'Molly left last year,' said Wesley. 'I think you'll find the egg was boiled last night by the desk sergeant.'

'You can't get the staff nowadays,' said Pat. 'I blame it on the Irish, myself. They're no longer committed to domestic service,' he added as he tapped the top of his egg with a plastic spoon. 'Wesley, have I told you about the time I tried to get a labouring job on a building site in Liverpool, and the foreman, a bloody Englishman—' Pat looked up and sighed as he heard the door slam and the key turn in the lock. 'I suppose I must have told him the story before,' he muttered to himself.

After Pat had finished breakfast, he cleaned his teeth with a toothbrush and a tube of toothpaste that were even smaller than the ones they'd supplied on his only experience of an Aer Lingus flight to Dublin. Next, he turned on the hot tap in the tiny steel washbasin. The slow trickle of water took some time to turn from cold to lukewarm. He rubbed the mean piece of soap between his fingers until he'd whipped up enough cream to produce a lather, which he then smeared all over his stubbled face. Next he picked up the plastic Bic razor, and began the slow process of removing a four-day-old stubble. He finally dabbed his face with a rough green hand towel, not much larger than a flannel.

Pat sat on the end of the bed and, while he waited, read Wesley's *Sun* from cover to cover in four minutes. Only an article by their political editor Trevor Kavanagh – he must surely be an Irishman, thought Pat – was worthy of his attention. Pat's thoughts were interrupted when the heavy metal door was pulled open once again.

'Let's be 'avin you, Pat,' said Sergeant Webster. 'You're first on this morning.'

Pat accompanied the officer back up the stairs, and when he saw the desk sergeant, asked, 'Could I have my valuables back, Mr Baker? You'll find them in the safe.'

'Like what?' said the desk sergeant, looking up.

'My pearl cufflinks, the Cartier Tank watch and a silver-topped cane engraved with my family crest.'

'I flogged 'em all off last night, Pat,' said the desk sergeant.

'Probably for the best,' remarked Pat. 'I won't be needing them where I'm going,' he added, before following Sergeant Webster out of the front door and onto the pavement.

'Jump in the front,' said the sergeant, as he climbed behind the wheel of a panda car.

'But I'm entitled to two officers to escort me to court,' insisted Pat. 'It's a Home Office regulation.'

'It may well be a Home Office regulation,' the sergeant replied, 'but we're short-staffed this morning, two off sick, and one away on a training course.'

'But what if I tried to escape?'

'A blessed release,' said Sergeant Webster, as he pulled away from the kerb, 'because that would save us all a lot of trouble.'

'And what would you do if I decided to punch you?'

'I'd punch you back,' said an exasperated sergeant.

'That's not very friendly,' suggested Pat.

'Sorry, Pat,' said the sergeant. 'It's just that I promised my wife that I'd be off duty by ten this morning, so we could go shopping.' He paused. 'So she won't be best pleased with me – or you for that matter.'

'I apologize, Sergeant Webster,' said Pat. 'Next October I'll try to find out which shift you're on, so I can be sure to avoid it. Perhaps you'd pass on my apologies to Mrs Webster.'

The sergeant would have laughed, if it had been anyone else, but he knew Pat meant it.

'Any idea who I'll be up in front of this morning?' asked Pat as the car came to a halt at a set of traffic lights.

'Thursday,' said the sergeant, as the lights turned green and he pushed the gear lever back into first. 'It must be Perkins.'

'Councillor Arnold Perkins OBE, oh good,' said Pat. 'He's got a very short fuse. So if he doesn't give me a long enough sentence, I'll just have to light it,' he added as the car swung into the private carpark at the back of Marylebone Road Magistrates' Court. A court officer was heading towards the police car just as Pat stepped out.

'Good morning, Mr Adams,' said Pat.

'When I looked at the list of defendants this morning, Pat, and saw your name,' said Mr Adams, 'I assumed it must be that time of the year when you make your annual appearance. Follow me, Pat, and let's get this over with as quickly as possible.'

Pat accompanied Mr Adams through the back door of the courthouse and on down the long corridor to a holding cell.

'Thank you, Mr Adams,' said Pat as he took a seat on a thin wooden bench that was cemented to a wall along one side of the large oblong room. 'If you'd be kind enough to just leave me for a few moments,' Pat added, 'so that I can compose myself before the curtain goes up.'

Mr Adams smiled, and turned to leave.

'By the way,' said Pat, as Mr Adams touched the handle of the door, 'did I tell you about the time I tried to get a labouring job on a building site in Liverpool, but the foreman, a bloody Englishman, had the nerve to ask me—'

'Sorry, Pat, some of us have got a job to do, and in any case, you told me that story last October.' He paused. 'And, come to think of it, the October before.'

Pat sat silently on the bench and, as he had nothing else to read, considered the graffiti on the wall. *Perkins is a prat.* He felt able to agree with that sentiment. *Man U are the champions.* Someone had crossed out *Man U* and replaced it with *Chelsea.* Pat wondered if he should cross out Chelsea, and write in Cork, whom neither team had ever defeated. As there was no clock on the wall, Pat couldn't be sure how much time had passed before Mr Adams finally returned to escort him up to the courtroom. Adams was now dressed in a long black gown, looking like Pat's old headmaster.

'Follow me,' Mr Adams intoned solemnly.

Pat remained unusually silent as they proceeded down the yellow brick road, as the old lags call the last few yards before you climb the steps and enter the back door of the court. Pat ended up standing in the dock, with a bailiff by his side.

Pat stared up at the bench and looked at the three magistrates who made up this morning's panel. Something was wrong. He had been expecting to see Mr Perkins, who had been bald this time last year, almost Pickwickian. Now, suddenly, he seemed to have sprouted a head of fair hair. On his right was Councillor Steadman, a liberal, who was much too lenient for Pat's liking. On the chairman's left sat a middle-aged lady whom Pat had never seen before; her thin lips and piggy eyes gave Pat a little confidence that the liberal could be outvoted two to one, especially if he played his cards right. Miss Piggy looked as if she would have happily supported capital punishment for shoplifters.

Sergeant Webster stepped into the witness box and took the oath.

'What can you tell us about this case, Sergeant?' Mr Perkins asked, once the oath had been administered.

'May I refer to my notes, your honour?' asked Sergeant Webster, turning to face the chairman of the panel. Mr Perkins nodded, and the sergeant turned over the cover of his notepad.

'I apprehended the defendant at two o'clock this morning, after he had thrown a brick at the window of H. Samuel, the jeweller's, on Mason Street.'

'Did you see him throw the brick, Sergeant?'

'No, I did not,' admitted Webster, 'but he was standing on the pavement with the brick in his hand when I apprehended him.'

'And had he managed to gain entry?' asked Perkins.

'No, sir,' said the sergeant, 'but he was about to throw the brick again when I arrested him.'

'The same brick?'

'I think so.'

'And had he done any damage?'

'He had shattered the glass, but a security grille prevented him from removing anything.'

'How valuable were the goods in the window?' asked Mr Perkins.

'There were no goods in the window,' replied the sergeant, 'because the manager always locks them up in the safe, before going home at night.'

Mr Perkins looked puzzled and, glancing down at the charge sheet, said, 'I see you have charged O'Flynn with attempting to break and enter.'

'That is correct, sir,' said Sergeant Webster, returning his notebook to a back pocket of his trousers.

Mr Perkins turned his attention to Pat. 'I note that you have entered a plea of guilty on the charge sheet, O'Flynn.'

'Yes, m'lord.'

'Then I'll have to sentence you to three months, unless you can offer some explanation.' He paused and looked down at Pat over the top of his half-moon spectacles. 'Do you wish to make a statement?' he asked.

'Three months is not enough, m'lord.'

'I am not a lord,' said Mr Perkins firmly.

'Oh, aren't you?' said Pat. 'It's just that I thought as you were wearing a wig, which you didn't have this time last year, you must be a lord.'

'Watch your tongue,' said Mr Perkins, 'or I may have to consider putting your sentence up to six months.'

'That's more like it, m'lord,' said Pat.

'If that's more like it,' said Mr Perkins, barely able to control his temper, 'then I sentence you to six months. Take the prisoner down.'

'Thank you, m'lord,' said Pat, and added under his breath, 'see you this time next year.'

The bailiff hustled Pat out of the dock and quickly down the stairs to the basement.

'Nice one, Pat,' he said before locking him back up in a holding cell.

Pat remained in the holding cell while he waited for all the necessary forms to be filled in. Several hours passed before the cell door was finally opened and he was escorted out of the courthouse to his waiting transport; not on this occasion a panda car driven by Sergeant Webster, but a long blue-and-white van with a dozen tiny cubicles inside, known as the sweat box.

'Where are they taking me this time?' Pat asked a not very communicative officer whom he'd never seen before.

'You'll find out when you get there, Paddy,' was all he got in reply.

'Have I ever told you about the time I tried to get a job on a building site in Liverpool?'

'No,' replied the officer, 'and I don't want to 'ear—'

'—and the foreman, a bloody Englishman, had the nerve to ask me if I knew the difference between a—' Pat was shoved up the steps of the van and pushed into a little cubicle that resembled a lavatory on a plane. He fell onto the plastic seat as the door was slammed behind him.

Pat stared out of the tiny square window, and when the vehicle turned south onto Baker Street, realized it had to be Belmarsh. Pat sighed. At least they've got a half-decent library, he thought, and I may even be able to get back my old job in the kitchen.

When the Black Maria pulled up outside the prison gates, his guess was confirmed. A large green board attached to the prison gate announced BELMARSH, and some wag had replaced BEL with HELL. The van proceeded through one set of double-barred gates, and then another, before finally coming to a halt in a barren yard.

Twelve prisoners were herded out of the van and marched up the steps to an induction area, where they waited in line. Pat smiled when he reached the front of the queue and saw who was behind the desk, checking them all in.

'And how are we this fine pleasant evening, Mr Jenkins?' Pat asked.

The Senior Officer looked up from behind his desk and said, 'It can't be October already.'

'It most certainly is, Mr Jenkins,' Pat confirmed, 'and may I offer my commiserations on your recent loss.'

'My recent loss,' repeated Mr Jenkins. 'What are you talking about, Pat?'

'Those fifteen Welshmen who appeared in Dublin earlier this year, passing themselves off as a rugby team.'

'Don't push your luck, Pat.'

'Would I, Mr Jenkins, when I was hoping that you would allocate me my old cell?'

The SO ran his finger down the list of available cells. ''Fraid not, Pat,' he said with an exaggerated sigh, 'it's already double-booked. But I've got just the person for you to spend your first night with,' he added, before turning to the night officer. 'Why don't you escort O'Flynn to cell one nineteen.'

The night officer looked uncertain, but after a further look from Mr Jenkins, all he said was, 'Follow me, Pat.'

'So who has Mr Jenkins selected to be my pad mate on this occasion?' enquired Pat, as the night officer accompanied him down the long, grey-brick corridor before coming to a halt at the first set of double-barred gates. 'Is it to be Jack the Ripper, or Michael Jackson?'

'You'll find out soon enough,' responded the night officer as the second of the barred gates slid open.

'Have I ever told you,' asked Pat, as they walked out on to the ground floor of B block, 'about the time I tried to get a job on a building site in Liverpool, and the foreman, a bloody Englishman, had the nerve to ask me if I knew the difference between a joist and a girder?'

Pat waited for the officer to respond, as they came to a halt outside cell number 119. He placed a large key in the lock.

'No, Pat, you haven't,' the night officer said as he pulled open the heavy door. 'So what is the difference between a joist and a girder?' he demanded.

Pat was about to reply, but when he looked into the cell was momentarily silenced.

'Good evening, m'lord,' said Pat, for the second time that day. The night officer didn't wait for a reply. He slammed the door closed, and turned the key in the lock.

Pat spent the rest of the evening telling me, in graphic detail, all that had taken place since two o'clock that morning. When he had finally come to the end of his tale, I simply asked, 'Why October?'

'Once the clocks go back,' said Pat, 'I prefer to be inside, where I'm guaranteed three meals a day and a cell with central heating. Sleeping rough is all very well in the summer, but it's not so clever during an English winter.'

'But what would you have done if Mr Perkins had sentenced you to a year?' I asked.

'I'd have been on my best behaviour from day one,' said Pat, 'and they would have released me in six months. They have a real problem with overcrowding at the moment,' he explained.

'But if Mr Perkins had stuck to his original sentence of

just three months, you would have been released in January, mid-winter.'

'Not a hope,' said Pat. 'Just before I was due to be let out, I would have been found with a bottle of Guinness in my cell. A misdemeanour for which the governor is obliged to automatically add a further three months to your sentence, and that would have taken me comfortably through to April.'

I laughed. 'And is that how you intend to spend the rest of your life?' I asked.

'I don't think that far ahead,' admitted Pat. 'Six months is quite enough to be going on with,' he added, as he climbed on to the top bunk and switched off the light.

'Goodnight, Pat,' I said, as I rested my head on the pillow.

'Have I ever told you about the time I tried to get a job on a building site in Liverpool?' asked Pat, just as I was falling asleep.

'No, you haven't,' I replied.

'Well, the foreman, a bloody Englishman, no offence intended –' I smiled – 'had the nerve to ask me if I knew the difference between a joist and a girder.'

'And do you?' I asked.

'I most certainly do. Joyce wrote *Ulysses*, and Goethe wrote *Faust*.'

Patrick O'Flynn died of hypothermia on 23 November 2005, while sleeping under the arches on Victoria Embankment in central London.

His body was discovered by a young constable, just a hundred yards away from the Savoy Hotel.

The Red King

'THEY CHARGED ME with the wrong offence, and sentenced me for the wrong crime,' Max said as he lay in the bunk below me, rolling another cigarette.

While I was in prison, I heard this claim voiced by inmates on several occasions, but in the case of Max Glover it turned out to be true.

Max was serving a three-year sentence for obtaining money by false pretences. Not his game. Max's speciality was removing small items from large homes. He once told me, with considerable professional pride, that it could be years before an owner became aware that a family heirloom has gone missing, especially, Max added, if you take one small, but valuable, object from a cluttered room.

'Mind you,' continued Max, 'I'm not complaining, because if they had charged me with the crime I did commit, I would have ended up with a much longer sentence –' he paused – 'and nothing to look forward to once I'm released.'

Max knew he had aroused my curiosity, and as I had nowhere to go for the next three hours before the cell door would be opened for Association – that glorious forty-five minutes when prisoners are allowed out of their cell for a stroll around the yard – I picked up my pen, and said, 'OK, Max, I'm hooked. So tell me how you came to be sentenced for the wrong crime.'

Max struck a match, lit his hand-rolled cigarette and inhaled deeply before he began. In prison, every action is exaggerated, as no one is in a hurry. I lay on the bunk above and waited patiently.

'Does the Kennington Set mean anything to you?' Max began.

'No,' I replied, assuming he must be referring to a group of red-coated gentlemen on horseback, glass of port in one hand, whip in the other, surrounded by a pack of hounds with intent to spend their Saturday morning in pursuit of a furry animal with a bushy tail. I was wrong. The Kennington Set, as Max went on to explain, was in fact a chess set.

'But no ordinary chess set,' he assured me. I became more interested. The pieces were probably crafted by Lu Ping (1469–1540), a master craftsman of the Ming Dynasty (1368–1644). All thirty-two ivory pieces were exquisitely carved and then delicately painted in red and white. The details have been faithfully recorded in several historic documents, though it has never been conclusively established exactly how many sets Lu Ping was responsible for producing in his lifetime.

'Three complete sets were known to be in existence,' continued Max as smoke spiralled up from the lower bunk. 'The first is displayed in the throne room of the People's Palace in Peking; the second in the Mellon Collection in Washington, and the third at the British Museum. Many collectors scoured the great continent of China in search of the fabled fourth set, and although such efforts always ended in failure, several individual pieces appeared on the market from time to time.'

Max stubbed out the smallest cigarette butt I have ever seen. 'I was at the time,' continued Max, 'carrying out some research into the smaller objects of Kennington Hall in Yorkshire.'

'How did you manage that?' I asked.

'*Country Life* commissioned Lord Kennington to write a coffee-table book for Christmas, in which he detailed the treasures of Kennington Hall,' Max said, before rolling a second cigarette. 'Most considerate of him,' he added.

'Among the peer's ancestors was one James Kennington (1552–1618), a true adventurer, buccaneer, and loyal servant of Queen Elizabeth I. James rescued the first set in 1588, only moments before he sunk the *Isabella*. On returning to Plymouth, following a seventeen–four victory in the match against the Spanish, Captain Kennington lavished treasure plundered from the sinking ship on his monarch. Her Majesty always showed a great deal of interest in anything solid, especially if she could wear it – gold, silver, pearls or rare gems – and rewarded Captain Kennington with a knighthood. Elizabeth had no use for the chess set, so Sir James was stuck with it. Unlike Sir Francis or Sir Walter, Sir James continued to plunder the high seas. He was so successful that, a decade later, his monarch elevated him to the House of Lords, with the title the first Lord Kennington, for services rendered to the Crown.' Max paused before adding, 'The only difference between a pirate and a peer is who you divide the spoils with.'

The second Lord Kennington, like his monarch, showed no interest in chess, so the set was left to gather dust in one of the ninety-two rooms in Kennington Hall. As there were few historical incidents worthy of mention during the uneventful lives of the third, fourth, fifth or sixth Lords Kennington, we can only assume that the remarkable chess set remained in situ, its pieces never moved in anger. The seventh Lord Kennington served as a colonel in the 12th Light Dragoons at the time of Waterloo. The colonel played the occasional game of chess, so the set was dusted down and returned to the Long Gallery.

The eighth Lord Kennington was slaughtered during the Charge of the Light Brigade, the ninth in the Boer War, and the tenth at Ypres. The eleventh, a playboy, led a more peaceful life, but eventually found it necessary, for pecuniary reasons – Kennington Hall required a new roof – to open his home to the public. They turned up every weekend in countless numbers, and for a small sum were allowed to stroll around the Hall; when they ventured into the Long Gallery they came across the Chinese masterpiece on its stand, surrounded by a red rope.

With mounting debts, which the public's entrance fees could not offset, the eleventh Lord Kennington was forced to sell off several of the family heirlooms, including the Kennington Set.

Christie's placed an estimate of £100,000 on the masterpiece, but the auctioneer's hammer finally fell at £230,000.

'When you next visit Washington,' added Max between puffs, 'you can view the original Kennington Set, as it's now part of the Mellon Collection. This would have been the end of my tale,' continued Max, 'if the eleventh Lord Kennington hadn't married an American striptease artiste, who gave birth to a son. This child displayed a quality that the Kennington lineage had not troubled themselves with for several generations – brains.

'The Hon. Harry Kennington became, much to the disapproval of his father, a hedge-fund manager, and thus the natural heir to the first Lord Kennington. He was a man who took as easily to the currency market as his pirate ancestor had to the high seas. By the age of twenty-seven, Harry had plundered his first million as an asset stripper, much to his mother's amusement, who suggested that stripping was clearly a hereditary trait. By the time Harry inherited the title he was chairman of Kennington's Bank. The first thing he did with his new-found wealth was to set about restoring Kennington Hall to its former glory. He certainly did not allow members of the public to pay five pounds to park their cars on his front lawn.

'The twelfth Lord Kennington, like his father, also married a remarkable woman. Elsie Trumpshaw was the offspring of a Yorkshire cotton mill proprietor, and the product of a Cheltenham Ladies' College education. Like any self-respecting Yorkshire lass, Elsie considered the saying, *If you take care of the pennies, the pounds will take care of themselves* to be a creed, not a cliché.

'While her husband was away making money, Elsie was unquestionably the mistress of Kennington Hall. Having spent her formative years wearing her elder sister's hand-me-downs, carrying her thumbed books to school and later borrowing her lipstick, whatever the colour, Elsie was well qualified to be the guardian of a hereditary pile. With consummate skill, diligence and good housekeeping, she set about the maintenance and upkeep of the newly restored Hall. Although she had no interest in the game of chess, she was irritated by the empty display cabinet in the Long Gallery. She finally solved the problem while strolling around a local car-boot sale,' said Max, 'and at the same time changed the fortunes of so many people, myself included.' Max stubbed out his second cigarette and I was relieved that he didn't immediately roll another, as our little cell was fast coming to resemble Paddington Station in the era of the steam engine.

❋ ❋ ❋

Elsie was trudging around a car-boot sale in Pudsey on a rainy Sunday morning – she only ever attended such events when it was raining, as that ensured fewer customers and it was therefore easier for her to strike a bargain. She was rummaging through some clothes when she came across the chessboard. The red and white squares brought back memories of a photograph she had seen in the old Christie's catalogue, dating from when the original set had been sold. Elsie bargained for some time with the man standing at the back of an ancient Jaguar, and ended up having to part with £23 for the ivory chessboard.

When Elsie returned to the Hall, she placed the newly acquired board in the empty display cabinet and was delighted to discover that it was a perfect fit. She thought nothing more of the coincidence, until her uncle Bertie advised her to have it valued – for insurance purposes, he explained.

Unconvinced, but unwilling to slight her uncle, Elsie took the board up to London on one of her monthly trips to visit her aunt Gertrude. Lady Kennington – she was always Lady Kennington in London – dropped into Sotheby's on her way to Fortnum & Mason. A young assistant in the Chinese department asked if her ladyship would be kind enough to come back later that afternoon, by which time their expert would have placed a value on the board.

Elsie returned to Sotheby's after a leisurely lunch with Aunt Gertrude. She was greeted by a Mr Sencill, the head of the Chinese department, who offered the opinion that the piece was unquestionably Ming Dynasty.

'And are you able to place a value on it –' she paused – 'for insurance purposes?'

'Two thousand, two thousand five hundred, m'lady,' said

Mr Sencill. 'Ming chessboards are fairly common,' he explained. 'It is the individual pieces that are rare, and a complete set . . .' He raised the palms of his hands and placed them together, as if praying to the unseen God of auctioneers. 'Are you perhaps considering selling the board?' he enquired.

'No,' replied Elsie firmly. 'On the contrary, I'm thinking of adding to it.'

The expert smiled. After all, Sotheby's is nothing more than a glorified pawn shop, with each generation of the aristocracy either buying or selling.

On arriving back at Kennington Hall, Elsie returned the board to its position of honour in the drawing room.

Aunt Gertrude set the ball rolling. On Christmas Day she presented her niece with a white pawn. Elsie placed the single piece on the empty board. It looked lonely.

'And now, my dear, you must see if you can complete the set in your lifetime,' the old lady challenged, unaware of the chain of events she was about to set in motion. What had begun as a whim, while attending a car-boot sale in Pudsey, turned into an obsession, as Elsie began to search the globe for the missing pieces. The first Lord Kennington would have been proud of her.

When Lady Kennington gave birth to their first son, Edward, a grateful husband presented his wife with a white queen. A magnificently sculptured ivory lady adorned in a long, intricately carved royal gown. Her Majesty stared down with disdain on the single pawn.

The next acquisition was another white pawn, acquired by Uncle Bertie from a dealer in New York. This allowed the white queen to reign over two of her subjects.

The birth of a second son, James, was rewarded with a

red bishop, resplendent in a flowing surplice and carrying a shepherd's crook. The queen and her two subjects were now able to celebrate Holy Communion, even if they had to travel to the other side of the board to do so. Soon the whole family began to join in the search for the missing pieces. A red pawn was the next acquisition, when it came under the auctioneer's hammer at Bonham's. He took up his place on the far side of the board, waiting to be taken. By now, everyone in the trade was only too aware of Lady Kennington's lifetime mission.

Next to find its place on the board was a white castle, which Aunt Gertrude left Elsie in her will.

In 1991 the twelfth Lord Kennington passed away, by which time the white set was lacking only two pawns and a knight, while the red set was short of four pawns, one rook and a king.

On 11 May 1992, a dealer in possession of three red pawns and a white knight knocked on the door of Kennington Hall. He had recently returned from a journey through the outer regions of China. A long and arduous trek, he told her ladyship. But, he assured her, he had not returned empty-handed.

Although her ladyship was in her declining years, she still held out for several days, before the dealer finally settled his bill at the Kennington Arms and left clutching a cheque for £26,000.

Despite following up rumours from Hong Kong, flying to Boston, contacting dealers as far afield as Moscow and Mexico, rumour rarely became reality in Lady Kennington's unremitting search for the last of the missing pieces.

During the next few years, Edward, the thirteenth Lord

Kennington, came across the last red pawn and a red rook in the home of a penniless peer, who had been on the same staircase as Eddie at Eton. His brother James, not to be out-done, acquired two white pawns from a dealer in Bangkok.

This left only the red king to be unearthed.

The family had for some time been paying well over the odds for any missing pieces, since every dealer across the globe was well aware that if Lady Kennington was able to complete the set it would be worth a fortune.

When Elsie entered her ninth decade, she informed her

sons that on her demise she planned to divide the estate equally between the two of them, with one proviso. She intended to bequeath the chess set to whichever one of them found the missing red king.

Elsie died at the age of eighty-three, without her king.

Edward had already acquired the title – something you can't dispose of in a will – and now, after death duties, also inherited the Hall and a further £857,000. James moved into the Cadogan Square apartment, and also received the sum of £857,000. The Kennington Set remained in its display case for all to admire, one square still unoccupied, ownership unresolved. Enter Max Glover.

Max had one undisputed gift, his ability to wield a willow. Educated at one of England's minor public schools, his talent as a stylish left-handed batsman allowed him to mix with the very people that he would later rob. After all, a chap who can score an effortless half century is obviously somebody one can trust.

Away fixtures suited Max best, as they allowed him the opportunity to meet eleven potential new victims. Kennington Village XI was no exception. By the time his lordship had joined the two teams for tea in the pavilion, Max had wormed out of the local umpire the history of the Kennington Set, including the provision in the will that whichever son came up with the missing red king would automatically inherit the complete set.

Max boldly asked his lordship, while devouring a portion of Victoria sponge, if he might be allowed to view the Kennington Set, as he was fascinated by the game of chess. Lord Kennington was only too happy to invite a man with such an effortless cover drive into his drawing room.

The moment Max spotted the empty square, a plan began to form in his mind. A few well-planted questions were indiscreetly answered by his host. Max avoided making any reference to his lordship's brother, or the clause in the will. He then spent the rest of the afternoon at square leg, refining his plan. He dropped two catches.

When the match was over, Max declined an invitation to join the rest of the team at the village pub, explaining that he had urgent business in London.

Moments after arriving back at his flat in Hammersmith, Max phoned an old lag he'd shared a pad with when he'd been locked up in a previous establishment. The former inmate assured Max that he could deliver, but it would take him about a month and 'would cost 'im'.

Max chose a Sunday afternoon to return to Kennington Hall and continue his research. He left his ancient MG – soon to become a collector's item, he tried to convince himself – in the visitors' carpark. He followed signs to the front door, where he handed over five pounds in exchange for an entrance ticket. Maintenance and running costs had once again made it necessary for the Hall to be opened to the public at weekends.

Max walked purposefully down a long corridor adorned with ancestral portraits painted by such luminaries as Romney, Gainsborough, Lely and Stubbs. Each would have fetched a fortune on the open market, but Max's eyes were set on a far smaller object, currently residing in the Long Gallery.

When Max entered the room that displayed the Kennington Set, he found the masterpiece surrounded by an attentive group of visitors who were being addressed by a tour guide. Max stood at the back of the crowd and listened to a tale he knew only too well. He waited patiently for the group to move on to the dining room and admire the family silver.

'Several pieces were captured at the time of the Armada,' the tour guide intoned as the group followed him into an adjoining room.

Max looked back down the corridor to check that the next group was not about to descend upon him. He placed a hand in his pocket and withdrew the red king. Other than the colour, the intricately carved piece was identical in every detail to the white king standing on the opposite side of the board. Max knew the counterfeit would not pass a carbon-dating test, but he was satisfied that he was in possession of a perfect copy. He left Kennington Hall a few minutes later, and drove back to London.

Max's next problem was to decide which city would have the most relaxed security to carry out his coup: London, Washington or Peking. The People's Palace in Peking won by a short head. However, when it came to considering the cost of the whole exercise, the British Museum was the only horse left in the race. But what finally tipped the balance for Max was the thought of spending the next five years locked up in a Chinese jail, an American penitentiary, or residing at an open prison in the east of England. England won in a canter.

The following morning Max visited the British Museum for the first time in his life. The lady seated behind the information desk directed him to the back of the ground floor, where the Chinese collection is housed.

Max discovered that hundreds of Chinese artefacts occupied the fifteen rooms, and it took him the best part of an hour to locate the chess set. He had considered seeking guidance from one of the uniformed guards, but as he had no desire to draw attention to himself, and also doubted that they would be able to answer his question, he thought better of it.

Max had to hang around for some time before he was left alone in the room. He could not afford a member of the public or, worse, a guard, to witness his little subterfuge. Max noted that the security guard covered four rooms every thirty minutes. He would therefore have to wait until the guard had departed for the Islam room, while at the same time being sure that no other visitors were in sight, before he could make his move.

It was another hour before Max felt confident enough to take the bastard out of his pocket and compare the piece with the legitimate king, standing proudly on its red square in the display cabinet. The two kings stared at each other, identical twins, except that one was an impostor. Max glanced around – the room was still empty. After all, it was eleven o'clock on a Tuesday morning, half term, and the sun was shining.

Max waited until the guard had moved on to Islamic artefacts before he carried out his well-rehearsed move. With the help of a Swiss Army knife, he carefully prised open the lid of the display cabinet that covered the Chinese master-piece. A raucous alarm immediately sounded, but long before the first guard appeared, Max had switched the two kings, replaced the cover of the case, opened a window and strolled casually into the next room. He was studying the costume of a samurai when two guards rushed into the adjoining room. One cursed when he spotted the open win-dow, while the other checked to see if anything was missing.

'Now, you'll want to know,' suggested Max, clearly enjoying himself, 'how I trapped both brothers into a fool's mate.' I nodded, but he didn't speak again until he'd rolled another cigarette. 'To start with,' continued Max, 'never rush a transaction when you're in possession of something *two* buyers want, and in this case, *desperately* want. My next visit –' he paused to light his cigarette – 'was to a shop in the Charing Cross Road. This had not required a great deal of research, because they advertised themselves in the *Yellow Pages* under Chess, as Marlowe's, *the people who serve the masters and advise the beginners.*'

Max stepped into the musty old shop, to be greeted by an elderly gentleman who resembled one of life's pawns: some-one who took the occasional move forward, but still looked as if he must eventually be taken – certainly not the type who reached the other side of the board to become a king. Max asked the old man about a chess set that he had spotted in the window. There then followed a series of well-rehearsed questions, which casually led to the value of a red king in the Kennington Set.

'Were such a piece ever to come onto the market,' the elderly assistant mused, 'the price could be in excess of fifty thousand pounds, as everyone knows there are two certain bidders.'

It was this piece of information that caused Max to make a few adjustments to his plan. His next problem was that he knew his bank account wouldn't stretch to a visit to New York. He ended up having to 'acquire' several small objects from large houses, which could be disposed of quickly, so he could visit the States with enough capital to put his plan into effect. Luckily it was in the middle of the cricket season.

When Max landed at JFK, he didn't bother to visit Sotheby's or Christie's, but instead instructed the yellow cab to drive him to Phillips Auctioneers on East 79th Street. He was relieved to find that, when he produced the delicate carving stolen from the British Museum, the young assistant didn't show a great deal of interest in the piece.

'Are you aware of its provenance?' asked the assistant.

'No,' replied Max, 'it's been in my family for years.'

Six weeks later a sales catalogue was published. Max was delighted to find that Lot 23 was listed as being of no known provenance, with a high value of $300. As it was not one of the items graced with a photograph, Max felt confident that few, if any, would take much interest in the red king, and it would therefore be unlikely to come to the attention of either Edward or James Kennington. That is, until he made them aware of it.

A week before the sale was due to take place, Max rang Phillips in New York. He had only one question for the young assistant, who replied that although the catalogue had been available for over a month, no one had shown any particular interest in his red king. Max feigned disappointment.

The next call Max made was to Kennington Hall. He tempted his lordship with several ifs, buts and even a maybe, which elicited an invitation to join Lord Kennington for lunch at White's.

Lord Kennington explained to his guest over a bowl of brown Windsor soup that Max could not produce any papers over lunch as it was against the club rules. Max nodded, placed the Phillips catalogue under his chair, and began an elaborate tale of how by sheer accident, while viewing the figure of a mandarin on behalf of a client, he had come across the red king.

'I would have missed it myself,' said Max, 'if you hadn't acquainted me with its history.'

Lord Kennington did not bother with pudding (bread and butter), cheese (Cheddar) or biscuits (water), but suggested they took coffee in the library, where you are allowed to discuss business.

Max opened the Phillips catalogue to reveal Lot 23, along with several loose photographs he had not shown the auctioneer. When Lord Kennington saw the estimate of three hundred dollars, his next question was, 'Do you think Phillips might have told my brother about the sale?'

'There is no reason to believe so,' replied Max. 'I've been assured by one of the assistants working on the sale that the public have shown little interest in lot twenty-three.'

'But how can you be so sure of its provenance?'

'That's what I do for a living,' said Max with confidence. 'But you can always have the piece carbon-dated, and if I'm proved wrong, you won't have to pay for it.'

'Can't ask for more than that,' said Lord Kennington, 'so

I suppose I'll have to fly to America and bid for the piece myself,' he added, thumping the arm of the leather chair. A cloud of elderly dust rose into the air.

'I wonder if that would be wise, my lord,' said Max, 'after all—'

'And why not?' demanded Kennington.

'It's just that, if you were to fly to the States without explanation, it might arouse unnecessary curiosity among certain members of your family,' Max paused, 'and if you were then spotted in an auction house . . . '

'I take your point,' said Kennington, and looking across at Max added, 'so what do you advise, old boy?'

'I would be only too happy to represent your lordship's interests,' said Max.

'And what would you charge for such a service?' Lord Kennington enquired.

'One thousand pounds plus expenses,' said Max, 'against two and a half per cent of the hammer price, which I can assure you is standard practice.'

Lord Kennington removed his chequebook from an inside pocket and wrote out the figure £1,000. 'How much do you estimate the piece might fetch?' he asked casually.

Max was pleased that Lord Kennington had raised the subject of price, as it would have been his next question. 'That will depend on whether anyone else is privy to our little secret,' said Max. 'However, I would suggest that you place an upper limit of fifty thousand dollars on the piece.'

'Fifty thousand?' spluttered Kennington in disbelief.

'Hardly excessive,' suggested Max, 'remembering that a complete set could fetch more than a million –' he paused – 'or nothing, were your brother to acquire the red king.'

'I take your point,' repeated Kennington. 'But you still might be able to pick it up for a few hundred dollars.'

'Let's hope so,' said Max.

Max Glover left White's Club a few minutes after three, explaining to his host that he had another appointment that afternoon, which indeed he did.

Max checked his watch and decided he still had enough time to stroll through Green Park and not be late for his next meeting.

Max arrived in Sloane Square a few minutes before four, and took a seat on a bench opposite the statue of Sir Francis Drake. He began to rehearse his new script. When he heard the clock on a nearby tower chime four times, he leapt up and walked briskly across to Cadogan Square. He stopped at No 16, climbed the steps, and rang the doorbell.

James Kennington opened the door and greeted his guest with a smile.

'I rang earlier this morning,' explained Max. 'My name's Glover.'

James Kennington ushered him through to the drawing room and offered Max a seat by an unlit fire. The younger brother took the seat opposite him.

Although the apartment was spacious, even grand, there were one or two clear outlines on the walls to suggest where pictures had once hung. Max suspected that they were not being cleaned or reframed. Gossip columns regularly referred to the Hon. James's drinking habits and hinted at several unpaid gambling debts.

When Max came to the end of his tale, he was well prepared for the Hon. James's first question.

'How much do you imagine the piece will fetch, Mr Glover?'

'A few hundred dollars,' Max replied. 'That's assuming your brother doesn't find out about the auction.' He paused, sipped his tea, and added, 'In excess of fifty thousand, if he does.'

'But I don't have fifty thousand,' said James, something else Max was well aware of. 'And if my brother were to find out,' James continued, 'there would be nothing I could do about it. The terms of the will couldn't be clearer – whoever finds the red king inherits the set.'

'I'd be willing to put up the necessary capital to secure the piece,' said Max, not missing a beat, 'if in turn you would then agree to sell me the set.'

'And how much would you be willing to pay?' asked James.

'Half a million,' said Max.

'But Sotheby's have already valued a complete set at over a million,' protested James.

'That may well be the case,' said Max, 'but half a million is surely better than nothing, which would be the outcome if your brother were to learn of the red king's existence.'

'But you said that the red king might sell for a few hundred—'

'In which case, I would require only a thousand pounds in advance, against two and a half per cent of the hammer price,' said Max for the second time that afternoon.

'That's a risk I am quite willing to take,' said James with the smile of someone who believes he has gained the upper hand. 'If the red king should sell for less than fifty thousand,' he continued, 'I'd be able to raise the money myself. If it goes for more than fifty thousand, you can purchase the piece and I'll sell you the set for half a million.' James sipped his tea, before adding, 'I can't lose either way.'

Neither can I, thought Max, as he extracted a contract from an inside pocket. James read the document slowly. He looked up and said, 'You obviously felt confident that I would fall in with your plan, Mr Glover.'

'If you hadn't,' said Max, 'my next visit would have been to your brother, which would have left you with nothing. At least now, to quote you, you can't lose either way.'

'Presumably I will have to travel to New York,' said James.

'Not necessary,' replied Max. 'You can bid for the piece by phone, which has the added advantage that no one else will know who's on the other end of the line.'

'But how do I go about that?' asked James.

'It couldn't be easier,' Max assured him. 'The New York sale begins at two in the afternoon, which will be seven o'clock in the evening in London. The red king is lot twenty-three, so I'll arrange for Phillips to place a call through to you once they reach lot twenty-one. Just be sure you're sitting by the phone, with no one else blocking the line.'

'And you'll take over, if it goes above fifty thousand?'

'You have my word,' said Max, looking him straight in the eye.

Max flew to New York the weekend before the sale was due to take place. He booked himself into a small hotel on the East Side and settled for a room not much larger than our cell, but then he only had enough money left over to cover the endgame.

Max rose early on the Monday morning. He hadn't been able to sleep because of an orchestra of New York traffic and police sirens. He used the time to go over and over the different permutations that might occur once the sale began.

He would be on centre stage for less than two minutes and, if he failed, would be back on the next plane to Heathrow, with nothing to show for his efforts other than an overdrawn bank account.

He grabbed a bagel on the corner of Third and 66th, before walking another few blocks to Phillips. He spent the rest of the morning at a manuscript sale that was being held in the room where the Chinese auction would take place. He sat silently at the back of the room, watching how the Americans conduct an auction, so that he wouldn't be wrong-footed later that afternoon.

Max didn't eat any lunch, and not just because his meagre funds were already stretched to their limit. Instead, he used the time to make two overseas calls; the first to Lord Kennington, to confirm that he still had his authority to take the bidding for the red king up to fifty thousand dollars. Max assured him that, the moment the hammer fell, he would call to let him know what sum the piece had sold for. A few minutes later Max made a second call, this time to the Hon. James Kennington at his home in Cadogan Square. James picked up the phone after one ring, clearly relieved to hear Max's voice on the other end of the line. Max made the Hon. James Kennington exactly the same promise.

Max replaced the phone and made his way across to the bidding counter, where he gave an assistant the details of James Kennington's telephone number in London and told her of his intention to bid for Lot 23.

'Leave it to us, sir,' the assistant replied. 'I'll make sure we're in touch with him well in time.'

Max thanked the assistant, made his way back to the sale-room and took his favoured place on the end of the eighth row, just to the right of the auctioneer. He began to turn the pages of the catalogue, checking on items in which he had no interest. While he sat around, impatiently waiting for the auctioneer to invite bids for lot number one, he tried to work out who were the dealers, who the serious bidders and who the simply curious.

By the time the auctioneer climbed the steps of the rostrum at five minutes to two, the saleroom was full of expectant faces. At two o'clock the auctioneer smiled down at his clientele.

'Lot number one,' he declared, 'a delicately crafted ivory fisherman.'

The piece sold for $850, giving no hint of the drama that was about to follow.

Lot 2 reached $1,000, but it wasn't until Lot 17, the figure of a mandarin bent over a desk reading a ledger, that the $5,000 mark was achieved.

One or two dealers whose only interest was clearly in later lots began to drift into the room, while a couple of others left, having failed or succeeded in acquiring the items they'd been after. Max could hear his heart pounding, although it would still be some time before the auctioneer reached Lot 23.

He turned his attention to the row of phones on a long table by the side of the room. Only three were manned. When the auctioneer called Lot 21, an assistant started to dial. A few moments later, she cupped a hand over the mouthpiece and began to whisper. When Lot 22 was offered, she spoke briefly to her client again. Max assumed that she must be warning James Kennington that the red king would be the next item to come under the hammer.

'Lot twenty-three,' declared the auctioneer glancing down

at his notes. 'An exquisitely carved red king, provenance unknown. Do I have an opening bid of three hundred dollars?'

Max raised his catalogue.

'Five hundred?' enquired the auctioneer turning to face the assistant on the phone. She whispered into the mouthpiece and then nodded firmly. The auctioneer turned his attention back to Max, who had raised his catalogue even before a price had been suggested.

'I have a bid of a thousand dollars,' said the auctioneer, returning to face the telephone bidder. 'Two thousand,' he ventured, surprised to see the assistant nod so quickly.

'Three thousand?' he suggested as he looked back at Max. The catalogue shot up again, and several dealers at the back of the room began chatting among themselves.

'Four thousand?' enquired the auctioneer, staring in disbelief at the assistant on the phone. $5,000, $6,000, $7,000, $8,000, $9,000 and $10,000 were overtaken in less than a minute. The auctioneer tried desperately to look as if this was exactly what he had anticipated as the murmurs in the room grew louder and louder. Everyone seemed to have an opinion. One or two dealers abandoned their favoured places and quickly walked to the back of the room, hoping to find an explanation for the bidding frenzy. Some were already beginning to make assumptions, but were in no position to bid under such pressure, especially as the amounts were now going up in leaps of $5,000.

Max raised his catalogue in response to the auctioneer's enquiry, 'Forty-five thousand? Are you bidding fifty thousand?' he enquired of the lady on the telephone. Everyone in the room turned to see how she would respond. For the first time she hesitated. The auctioneer repeated,

'Fifty thousand.' She whispered the figure into the phone and, after a long pause, nodded, but not quite so enthusiastically.

When Max was offered the piece for $55,000, he also hesitated, taking his time before he finally raised his catalogue.

'Sixty thousand?' suggested the auctioneer to the assistant on the phone. Max waited nervously as she cupped her hand over the mouthpiece and repeated the figure. Beads of sweat began to appear on Max's forehead, as he wondered if James Kennington had managed to raise more than $50,000, in which case he would just about clear his expenses on the whole exercise. After what seemed like an eternity, but was, in fact, only twenty seconds, the assistant shook her head. She put the phone down.

When the auctioneer smiled in Max's direction and said, 'Sold to the gentleman on my left, for fifty-five thousand dollars,' Max felt sick, triumphant, dazed and relieved all at the same time.

Max remained in his place, as he waited for the furore to die down. After a dozen more lots had been disposed of, he slipped quietly out of the room, unaware of the suspicious stares from dealers, who wondered who he was. He strolled across the thick green carpet and stopped at the purchasing counter.

'I wish to leave a deposit on lot twenty-three.'

The clerk looked down at her list. 'A red king,' she said, and double-checked the price. 'Fifty-five thousand dollars,' she added, and looked up at Max for confirmation.

He nodded as the assistant began to fill in the little boxes on the purchasing document. A few moments later she swivelled the form round for Max to sign.

'That will be five thousand, five hundred dollars deposit,' she said, 'and the full amount must be settled within twenty-eight days.' Max nodded nonchalantly, as if this was a procedure he was well familiar with. He signed the agreement and then wrote out a cheque for $5,500, aware that it would empty his account. He pushed it across the counter. The assistant handed him back the top copy of the agreement and retained the duplicate. When she checked the signature, she hesitated. It might have been a coincidence: after all, Glover was a common enough name. She didn't want to insult a customer, but she knew she would have to report the anomaly to their compliance department, before they could consider cashing the cheque.

Max left the auction house and headed north to Park Avenue. He strode confidently into Sotheby Parke Bernet and approached the reception desk. He asked if he could have a word with the Head of the Oriental Department. He was kept waiting for only a few minutes.

On this occasion, Max didn't waste time with any preliminary questions that would have only been a smoke-screen to disguise his true intent. After all, as the sales clerk at Phillips had pointed out, he only had twenty-eight days to complete the transaction.

'Should the Kennington Chess Set come onto the market, what would you expect it to fetch?' Max asked.

The expert looked incredulous, although he had already been briefed on the sale of the red king at Phillips, and on the price the piece had fetched. 'Seven hundred and fifty thousand, possibly as much as a million,' came back the reply.

'And if I was able to deliver the Kennington Set, and you were in a position to authenticate it, what amount would Sotheby's be willing to advance against a future sale?'

'Four hundred thousand, possibly five, if the family were able to confirm that it was the Kennington Set.'

'I'll be in touch,' promised Max, all his immediate and long-term problems solved.

✵ ❀ ✵

Max checked out of his little hotel on the East Side later that evening, and took a taxi to Kennedy Airport. Once the plane had taken off, he slept soundly for the first time in days.

The 727 touched down at Heathrow just as the sun was rising over the Thames. Having nothing to declare, Max took the Heathrow Express to Paddington, and was back in his flat in time for breakfast. He began to fantasize about what it would be like to dine regularly at his favourite restaurant and always hail a taxi, rather than having to wait for the next bus.

Once he'd finished breakfast, Max put the plates in the sink and settled down in the one comfortable chair. He began to consider his next move, confident that now the red king had found its place on the board, the game must end in checkmate.

At eleven o'clock – a proper hour to phone a peer of the realm – Max put a call through to Kennington Hall. When the butler transferred the call to Lord Kennington, his first words were, 'Did we get it?'

'Unfortunately not, my lord,' replied Max. 'We were outbid by an unknown party. I carried out your instructions to the letter, and stopped bidding at fifty thousand dollars.' He paused. 'The hammer price was fifty-five thousand.'

There was a long silence. 'Do you think the other bidder could have been my brother?'

'I've no way of knowing,' replied Max. 'All I can tell you is that they were bidding by phone, no doubt wishing to ensure their anonymity.'

'I'll find out soon enough,' responded Kennington, before hanging up.

'You certainly will,' agreed Max as he began to dial a number in Chelsea.

'Congratulations,' said Max the moment he heard the Hon. James's plummy voice. 'I've purchased the piece, so you're now in a position to claim your inheritance, under the terms of the will.'

'Well done, Glover,' said James Kennington.

'And the moment you deliver the rest of the set, my

lawyers have been instructed to hand over a cheque for four hundred and forty-five thousand dollars,' said Max.

'But we agreed on half a million,' snapped James.

'Minus the fifty-five thousand I had to pay for the red king.' Max paused. 'You'll find it's all spelled out in the contract.'

'But—' James began to protest.

'Would you prefer me to call your brother?' Max asked, as the front door bell rang. 'Because I'm still in possession of the piece.' James didn't immediately reply. 'Think about it,' added Max, 'while I answer the front door.' Max placed the receiver on the side table, and strolled out into the hall, almost rubbing his hands. He released the chain, undid the Yale lock, and pulled the door open a couple of inches. Two tall men wearing identical trench coats stood in front of him.

'Max Victor Glover?' enquired one of them.

'Who wants to know?' asked Max.

'I'm Detective Inspector Armitage of the Fraud Squad, and this is Detective Sergeant Willis.' They both produced warrant cards, with which Max was only too familiar. 'May we come in, sir?'

Once the police had taken down Max's statement, which consisted of little more than, 'I'll need to speak to my solicitor,' the two men departed. They then drove up to Yorkshire for a meeting with Lord Kennington. Having obtained a detailed statement from his lordship, they returned to London to interview his brother James. The police found him just as cooperative.

A week later Max was arrested for fraud. The judge took into account his past blemished record, and did not grant bail.

'But how did they find out that you'd stolen the red king?' I asked.

'They didn't,' Max replied as he stubbed out his cigarette.

I put my pen down. 'I'm not sure I understand,' I murmured from the upper bunk.

'And neither did I,' admitted Max, 'at least not until they charged me.' I remained silent, as my pad mate began to roll his next cigarette. 'When they read out the charge sheet,' he continued, ' no one was more surprised than me.

'"Max Victor Glover, you are charged with attempting to obtain money by false pretences. Namely that on October seventeenth, two thousand, you bid fifty-five thousand dollars for a red king, lot twenty-three at Phillips auctioneers in New York, while enticing other interested parties to bid against you, without informing them that you were the owner of the piece."'

A heavy key turned in the lock and our cell door cranked open.

'Visits,' bellowed the wing officer.

'So you see,' said Max as he swung his legs off the bunk, 'I was charged with the wrong offence, and sentenced for the wrong crime.'

'But why go through such an elaborate charade, when you could have sold the red king to either of the brothers?'

'Because then I would have had to show them how I got hold of the piece in the first place, and if I had been caught . . .'

'But you were caught.'

'But not charged with theft,' Max reminded me.

'So what happened to the red king?' I demanded, as we stepped out into the corridor and made our way across to the visits centre.

'It was returned to my solicitor after the trial,' said Max, 'and locked up in his safe, where it will remain until I'm released.'

'But that means—' I began.

'Have you ever met Lord Kennington?' Max asked casually.

'No, I haven't,' I replied.

'Then I'll introduce you, old boy,' he mimicked, 'because he's coming to visit me this afternoon.' Max paused. 'I have a feeling that his lordship is about to make me an offer for the red king.'

'And will you accept his offer?' I asked.

'Steady on, Jeff,' Max replied as we entered the visits room. 'I won't be able to answer that question until next week, when I've had a visit from his brother James.'

The Wisdom Of Solomon

'MIND YOUR OWN business,' was Carol's advice.

'But it is my business,' I reminded my wife as I climbed into bed. 'Bob and I have been friends for over twenty years.'

'All the more reason to keep your own counsel,' she insisted.

'But I don't like her,' I replied tartly.

'You made that abundantly clear during dinner,' Carol reminded me as she switched off her bedside light.

'But surely you can see that it's going to end in tears.'

'Then you'll just have to buy a large box of Kleenex.'

'She's only after his money,' I muttered.

'He hasn't got any,' replied Carol. 'Bob's practice is quite successful, but hardly puts him in the Abramovich league.'

'That may well be the case, but it's still my duty, as a friend, to warn him not to marry her.'

'He doesn't want to hear that at the moment,' said Carol, 'so don't even think about it.'

'Explain to me, O wise one,' I said as I plumped up my pillow, 'why not.'

Carol ignored my sarcasm. 'If it should end up in the divorce courts, you'll just look smug. If the marriage turns out to be wedded bliss, he'll never forgive you – and neither will she.'

'I wasn't planning to tell her.'

'She already knows exactly how you feel about her,' said Carol. 'Believe me.'

'It won't last a year,' I predicted, just as the phone rang

on my side of the bed. I picked it up, praying it wasn't a patient.

'I've only got one question for you,' said a voice that needed no introduction.

'And what's that, Bob?' I asked.

'Will you be my best man?'

Bob Radford and I first met at St Thomas' Hospital when we were both house officers. To be more accurate, we had first come into contact with each other on the rugby field, when he tackled me just as I thought I was about to score the winning try. In those days we were on opposite sides.

After we were appointed senior house officers at Guy's, we started playing for the same rugby team and regularly had a mid-week game of squash – which he invariably won. In our final year we ended up sharing digs in Lambeth. We didn't need to look far for female companionship as St Thomas' had over three thousand nurses, most of whom wanted sex and for some unfathomable reason considered doctors a safe bet. Both of us looked forward to taking advantage of our new status. And then I fell in love.

Carol was also a house officer at Guy's, and on our first date made it abundantly clear that she wasn't looking for a long-term relationship. However, she underestimated my one talent, persistence. She finally gave in after I'd proposed for the ninth time. Carol and I were married a few months after she'd qualified.

Bob headed off in the opposite direction. Whenever we invited him to dinner, he would turn up escorted by a new companion. I sometimes got their names muddled up, a mistake Carol never made. However, as the years passed, even Bob's appetite to taste some new delicacy from the table d'hôte became less hearty than it had been during his student days; after all, we had both recently celebrated our fortieth birthdays. It didn't help when Bob was named in the student rag as the most eligible bachelor in the hospital, not least because he had built up one of the most successful private practices in London. He had a set of rooms in Harley Street, with none of the expenses associated with marital bliss. But now that finally seemed to be coming to an end.

When Bob invited Carol and me to join him for dinner so that he could introduce us to Fiona, whom he described as the woman he was going to spend the rest of his life with, we were both surprised and delighted. We were also a little perplexed as we couldn't recall the name of his last girlfriend. We were fairly confident it wasn't Fiona.

When we arrived at the restaurant, we saw the two of them seated in the far corner of the room, holding hands. Bob rose to greet us and immediately introduced Fiona as the most wonderful girl in the world. To be fair to the woman, no red-blooded male could have denied Fiona's physical attributes. She must have been about five foot nine, made up of thirty inches of leg, attached to a figure honed in the gym and no doubt perfected on a diet of lettuce leaves and water.

Our conversation during the meal was fairly limited, partly because Bob spent most of the time staring at Fiona in a way that should be reserved for one of Donatello's nudes. By the end of the meal, I had come to the conclusion that Fiona would end up costing about as much, and it wasn't just because she read the wine list from the bottom upwards, ordered caviar as a starter and asked, with a sweet smile, for her pasta to be covered in truffles.

Frankly, Fiona was the type of long-legged blonde whom you hope to bump into, while perched on a stool in a hotel bar, late at night and preferably on another continent. I am unable to tell you how old she was, but I did learn during dinner that she had been married three times before she met Bob. However, she assured us that, this time, she had found the right man.

I was only too happy to escape that night and, as you have already discovered, I didn't waste much time making my wife aware of my views on Fiona.

The marriage took place some three months later at the Chelsea Register Office in the King's Road. The ceremony was attended by several of Bob's friends from St Thomas' and Guy's – some of whom I hadn't set eyes on since our rugby days. I felt it unwise to point out to Carol that Fiona didn't seem to have any friends, or at least none who were willing to attend her latest nuptials.

I stood silently by Bob's side as the registrar intoned the words, 'If anyone can show lawful reason why these two should not be joined in matrimony, then they should declare that reason to me now.'

I wanted to offer an opinion, but Carol was too close at hand to risk it. I must confess that Fiona did look radiant on that occasion, not unlike a python about to devour a lamb – whole.

The reception was held at Lucio's on the Fulham Road. The best man's speech might have been more coherent if I hadn't consumed quite so much champagne, or if I'd believed a word I was uttering.

When I sat down to indulgent applause, Carol didn't lean across to congratulate me. I avoided her until we all joined the bride and groom on the pavement outside the restaurant. Bob and Fiona waved goodbye before stepping into a white stretch limousine that would take them to Heathrow. From there, they were to board a plane to Acapulco, where they would spend a three-week honeymoon. Neither the transport to Heathrow, which incidentally could have accommodated the entire wedding party, nor the final destination for the honeymoon, had been Bob's first choice. A piece of information I didn't pass on to Carol, as she would undoubtedly have accused me of being prejudiced – and she would have been right.

I can't pretend that I saw a lot of Fiona during their first year of marriage, although Bob called from time to time, but only from his practice in Harley Street. We even managed the occasional lunch, but he no longer seemed to be able to fit in a game of squash in the evening.

Over lunch Bob never failed to expound the virtues of his remarkable wife, as if only too aware of my attitude to his spouse – although I never at any time expressed my true feelings. I could only assume that this was the reason Carol and I were never invited to dinner at their home, and whenever we asked them to join us for supper, Bob made some unconvincing excuse about having to visit a patient, or being out of town on that particular evening.

The change was subtle to begin with, almost imperceptible. Our lunches became more regular, even the occasional game of squash was fitted in, and perhaps more relevant, there were fewer and fewer references to Fiona's pending sainthood.

It was soon after the death of Bob's aunt, a Miss Muriel Pembleton, that the change became far less subtle. To be honest, I didn't even realize that Bob had an aunt, let alone one who was the sole heir to Pembleton Electronics.

The Times revealed that Miss Pembleton had left a little over seven million pounds in shares and property, as well as a considerable art collection. With the exception of a few minor bequests to charitable organizations, her nephew turned out to be the sole beneficiary. God bless the man, because coming into an unexpected fortune didn't change Bob in any way; but the same couldn't be said of Fiona.

When I called Bob to congratulate him on his good fortune, he sounded very low. He asked if I could possibly join him for lunch, as he needed to seek my advice on a personal matter.

We met a couple of hours later, at a gastro pub just off Devonshire Place. Bob didn't talk about anything consequential until after the waiter had taken our order, but once the first course had been served, Fiona was the only other dish on the menu. He had received a letter that morning from Abbott Crombie & Co, Solicitors, stating, in unambiguous terms, that his wife was filing for divorce.

'Can't fault her timing,' I said tactlessly.

'And I didn't even spot it,' said Bob.

'Spot it?' I repeated. 'Spot what?'

'How Fiona's attitude to me changed not long after she'd met my aunt Muriel. In fact, that same night, she literally charmed the pants off me.'

I reminded Bob of what Woody Allen had said on the subject. Mr Allen could not understand why God had given man a penis and a brain, but not enough blood to connect the two. Bob laughed for the first time that day, but it was only moments before he lapsed back into a maudlin silence.

'Is there anything I can do to help?' I asked.

'Only if you know the name of a first-class divorce lawyer,' Bob replied, 'because I'm told that Mrs Abbott has a reputation for extracting the last drop of blood on behalf of her clients, especially following the latest law lords' ruling in favour of spouses.'

'Can't say I do,' I responded. 'Having been happily married for sixteen years, I fear I'm the wrong man to advise you. Why don't you have a word with Peter Mitchell? After all, with four ex-wives, he ought to be able to tell you who's the best advocate available.'

'I called Peter first thing this morning,' admitted Bob. 'He's always been represented by Mrs Abbott – told me that he keeps her on a permanent retainer.'

During the next few weeks, Bob and I returned to the squash court regularly, and I started beating him for the first time. He would then join Carol and me for dinner afterwards. We tried to steer clear of any talk about Fiona. However, he did let slip that she was refusing to leave the stage gracefully, even after he had offered her half of Aunt Muriel's bequest.

As the weeks turned into months, Bob began losing

weight and his golden locks were turning prematurely grey. Fiona, on the other hand, seemed to go from strength to strength, taking each new hurdle like a seasoned thoroughbred. When it came to tactics, Fiona clearly understood the long game, but then she had the advantage of having experienced three away victories, and was clearly looking forward to a fourth.

It must have been about a year later that Fiona finally agreed to a settlement. All of Bob's assets were to be divided equally between them, while he would also cover her legal costs. A date was set for a formal signing in chambers. I agreed to act as a witness and give Bob, as Carol described it, much-needed moral support.

I never even took the top off my pen because Fiona burst into tears long before Mrs Abbott had read out the terms, declaring that she was being cruelly treated and Bob was causing her to have a nervous breakdown. She then flounced out of the office without another word. I must confess that I had never seen Fiona looking less nervous. Even Mrs Abbott couldn't hide her exasperation.

Harry Dexter, whom Bob had selected as his solicitor, warned him that this was likely to end up in a lengthy and expensive courtroom battle if he couldn't agree to a settlement. Mr Dexter added, for good measure, that judges often instruct the defending party to shoulder the injured party's costs. Bob shrugged his shoulders, not even bothering to respond.

Once both sides had accepted that an out-of-court settlement could not be reached, a day was fixed in the judge's calendar for a hearing.

Mr Dexter was determined to counter Fiona's outrageous demands with equally fierce resistance, and to begin with Bob went along with all his recommendations. But with each new demand from the other side, Bob's resolve began to weaken until, like a punch-drunk boxer, he was ready to throw in the towel. He became more and more depressed as the day of the hearing drew nearer, and even began saying, 'Why don't I just give her everything because that's the only way she'll ever be satisfied?' Carol and I tried to lift his spirits, but with little success, and even Mr Dexter was finding it harder and harder to convince his client to hang in there.

We both assured Bob that we would be in court to support him on the day of the hearing.

Carol and I took our places in the gallery of court number three, matrimonial division, on the last Thursday in June, and waited for proceedings to begin. By ten to ten the court officials began to drift in and take their places. A few minutes later Mrs Abbott arrived, with Fiona by her side. I stared down at the plaintiff, who was wearing no jewellery and a black suit that would have been more appropriate for a funeral – Bob's.

A moment later Mr Dexter appeared with Bob in his wake. They took their places at a table on the other side of the courtroom.

As ten o'clock struck, my worst fears were realized. The judge entered the courtroom – a woman who immediately brought back memories of my old school matron – a martinet who didn't believe that the punishment should fit the crime. The judge took her place on the bench and smiled down at Mrs Abbott. They'd probably been at university together. Mrs Abbott rose from her place and returned the judge's smile. She then proceeded to do battle for every jot and tittle in Bob's possession, even arguing over who should end up with his college cufflinks, saying that it had been agreed that all Mr Radford's assets should be divided equally, so that if he had one cufflink, her client must be entitled to the other.

As each hour passed, Fiona's demands expanded. After all, Mrs Abbot explained, hadn't her client given up a rewarding and happy lifestyle in America, which included a thriving family business – something I'd never heard mentioned before – to devote herself to her husband? Only to discover that he rarely arrived home in the evening before eight, and then only after he'd been out with his friends to play squash, and when he eventually turned up – Mrs Abbott paused – drunk, he didn't want to eat the meal she had spent hours preparing for him – she paused again – and when they later went to bed, he quickly fell into a drunken slumber. I rose from my place in the gallery to protest, only to be told by an usher to sit down or I would be asked to leave the court. Carol tugged firmly on my jacket.

Finally, Mrs Abbot reached the end of her demands, with the suggestion that her client should be given their home in the country (Aunt Muriel's), while Bob would be allowed to keep his London apartment; she should have the villa in Cannes (Aunt Muriel's), while he kept his rooms at Harley Street (rented). Mrs Abbott finally turned her attention to Aunt Muriel's art collection, which she also felt should be divided equally; her client should have the Monet, while he kept the Manguin. She should have the Picasso, he the Pasmore, she the Bacon, etc. When Mrs Abbott finally sat down, Mrs Justice Butler suggested that perhaps they should take a break for lunch.

During a lunch, not eaten, Mr Dexter, Carol and I tried valiantly to convince Bob that he should fight back. But he wouldn't hear of it.

'If I can hold on to everything I had before my aunt died,' Bob insisted, 'that will be quite enough for me.'

Mr Dexter felt certain he could do far better than that, but Bob showed little interest in putting up a fight.

'Just get it over with,' he instructed. 'Try not to forget who's paying her costs.'

When we returned to the courtroom at two o'clock that afternoon, the judge turned her attention to Bob's solicitor.

'And what do you have to say about all this, Mr Dexter?' asked Mrs Justice Butler.

'We are happy to go along with the division of my client's assets as suggested by Mrs Abbott,' he replied with an exaggerated sigh.

'You're happy to go along with Mrs Abbott's recommendations, Mr Dexter?' repeated the judge in disbelief.

Once again Mr Dexter looked at Bob, who simply nodded, like a dog on the back shelf of a car.

'So be it,' said Mrs Justice Butler, unable to mask her surprise.

She was just about to pass judgement, when Fiona broke down and burst into tears. She leant across and whispered into Mrs Abbott's ear.

'Mrs Abbott,' said Mrs Justice Butler, ignoring the plaintiff's sobs, 'am I to sanction this agreement?'

'It seems not,' said Mrs Abbott, rising from her place and looking somewhat embarrassed. 'It appears that my client still feels that such a settlement favours the defendant.'

'Does she indeed?' said Mrs Justice Butler and turned to face Fiona. Mrs Abbott touched her client on the shoulder and whispered in her ear. Fiona immediately rose, and kept her head bowed while the judge spoke.

'Mrs Radford,' she began, looking down at Fiona, 'am I to understand that you are no longer happy with the settlement your solicitor has secured for you?'

Fiona nodded demurely.

'Then may I suggest a solution, that I hope will bring this case to a speedy conclusion.' Fiona looked up and smiled sweetly at the judge, while Bob sank lower into his seat.

'Perhaps it would be easier, Mrs Radford, if *you* were to draw up two lists for the court's consideration, that *you* believe to be a fair and equitable division of your husband's assets?'

'I'd be happy to do that, your honour,' said Fiona meekly.

'Does this meet with your approval, Mr Dexter?' asked Mrs Justice Butler, turning back to Bob's solicitor.

'Yes, m'lady,' said Mr Dexter, trying not to sound exasperated.

'Can I take it that those are your client's instructions?'

Mr Dexter glanced down at Bob, who didn't even bother to offer an opinion.

'And Mrs Abbott,' she said, turning her attention back to Fiona's solicitor, 'I want your word that your client will not back down from such a settlement.'

'I can assure you, m'lady, that she will comply with your ruling,' replied Fiona's solicitor.

'So be it,' said Mrs Justice Butler. 'We will adjourn until tomorrow morning at ten o'clock, when I will look forward to considering Mrs Radford's two lists.'

✼ ✼ ✼

Carol and I took Bob out for dinner that night – a pointless exercise. He rarely opened his mouth to either eat or speak.

'Let her have everything,' he finally ventured over coffee, 'because that's the only way I'm ever going to be rid of the woman.'

'But your aunt wouldn't have left you her fortune if she'd known this would have been the eventual outcome.'

'Neither Aunt Muriel nor I worked that one out,' Bob replied with resignation. 'And you can't fault Fiona's timing. She only needed another month after meeting my dear aunt before she accepted my proposal.' Bob turned and stared at me, an accusing look in his eyes. 'Why didn't you warn me not to marry her?' he demanded.

When the judge entered the courtroom the following morning all the officials were already in place. The two adversaries were seated next to their solicitors. All those in the well of the court rose and bowed as Mrs Justice Butler resumed her place, leaving only Mrs Abbott on her feet.

'Has your client had enough time to prepare her two lists?' enquired the judge, as she stared down at Fiona's counsel.

'She has indeed, m'lady,' said Mrs Abbott, 'and both are ready for your consideration.'

The judge nodded to the clerk of the court. He walked slowly across to Mrs Abbott, who handed over the two lists. The clerk then walked slowly back to the bench and passed them up to the judge for her consideration.

Mrs Justice Butler took her time studying the two inventories, occasionally nodding, even adding the odd 'Um', while Mrs Abbott remained on her feet. Once the judge had reached the last items on the lists, she turned her attention back to counsel's bench.

'Am I to understand,' enquired Mrs Justice Butler, 'that both parties consider this to be a fair and equitable distribution of all the assets in question?'

'Yes, m'lady,' said Mrs Abbott firmly, on behalf of her client.

'I see,' said the judge and, turning to Mr Dexter, asked, 'Does this also meet with your client's approval?'

Mr Dexter hesitated. 'Yes, m'lady,' he eventually managed, unable to mask the irony in his voice.

'So be it.' Fiona smiled for the first time since the case had opened. The judge returned her smile. 'However, before I pass judgement,' she continued, 'I still have one question for Mr Radford.' Bob glanced at his solicitor before rising nervously from his seat. He looked up at the judge.

What more can she want? was my only thought as I sat staring down from the gallery.

'Mr Radford,' began the judge, 'we have all heard your wife tell the court that she considers these two lists to be a fair and equitable division of all your assets.'

Bob bowed his head and remained silent.

'However, before I pass judgement, I need to be sure that you agree with that assessment.'

Bob raised his head. He seemed to hesitate a moment, but then said, 'I do, m'lady.'

'Then I am left with no choice in this matter,' declared Mrs Justice Butler. She paused, and stared directly down at Fiona, who was still smiling. 'As I allowed Mrs Radford the opportunity to prepare these two lists,' continued the judge, 'which in her judgement are an equitable and fair division of your assets –' Mrs Justice Butler was pleased to see Fiona nodding her agreement – 'then it must also be fair and equitable,' the judge added, turning her attention back to Bob, 'to allow Mr Radford the opportunity to select which of the two lists he would prefer.'

Know What
I Mean

'IF YOU WANNA FIND out what's goin' on in this nick, I'm the man to 'ave a word with,' said Doug. 'Know what I mean?'

Every prison has one. At North Sea Camp his name was Doug Haslett. Doug was half an inch under six foot, with thick, black, wavy hair that was going grey at the temples, and a stomach that hung out over his trousers. Doug's idea of exercise was the walk from the library, where he was the prison orderly, to the canteen a hundred yards away, three times a day. I think he exercised his mind at about the same pace.

It didn't take me long to discover that he was bright, cunning, manipulative and lazy – traits that are common among recidivists. Within days of arriving at a new prison, Doug could be guaranteed to have procured fresh clothes, the best cell, the highest-paid job, and to have worked out which prisoners, and – more important – which officers he needed to get on the right side of.

As I spent a lot of my free time in the library – and it was rarely overcrowded, despite the prison accommodating over four hundred inmates – Doug quickly made me aware of his case history. Some prisoners, when they discover that you're a writer, clam up. Others can't stop talking. Despite the silence notices displayed all around the library, Doug fell into the latter category.

When Doug left school at the age of seventeen, the only exam he passed was his driving test – first time. Four years later he added a heavy goods licence to his qualifications, and at the same time landed his first job as a lorry driver.

Doug quickly became disillusioned with how little he could earn, traipsing backwards and forwards to the south of France with a load of Brussels sprouts and peas, often returning to Sleaford with an empty lorry and therefore no bonus. He regularly fouled up (his words) when it came to EU regulations, and took the view that somehow he was exempt from having to pay tax. He blamed the French for too much unnecessary red tape and a Labour government for punitive taxes. When the courts finally served a debt order on him, everyone was to blame except Doug.

The bailiff took away all his possessions – except the lorry, which Doug was still paying for on a hire-purchase agreement.

Doug was just about to pack in being a lorry driver and join the dole queue – almost as remunerative, and you don't have to get up in the morning – when he was approached by a man he'd never come across before, while on a stopover in Marseilles. Doug was having breakfast at a dockside cafe when the man slid on to the stool next to him. The stranger

didn't waste any time with introductions, he came straight to the point. Doug listened with interest; after all, he had already dumped his cargo of sprouts and peas on the dockside, and had been expecting to return home with an empty lorry. All Doug had to do, the stranger assured him, was to deliver a consignment of bananas to Lincolnshire once a week.

I feel I should point out that Doug did have some scruples. He made it clear to his new employer that he would never be willing to transport drugs, and wouldn't even discuss illegal immigrants. Doug, like so many of my fellow inmates, was very right wing.

When Doug arrived at the drop-off point, a derelict barn deep in the Lincolnshire countryside, he was handed a thick brown envelope containing £25,000 in cash. They didn't even expect him to help unload the produce.

Overnight, Doug's lifestyle changed.

After a couple of trips, Doug began to work part-time, making the single journey to Marseilles and back once a week. Despite this, he was now earning more in a week than he was declaring on his tax return for a year.

Doug decided that one of the things he'd do with his new-found wealth was to move out of his basement flat on the Hinton Road and invest in the property market.

Over the next month he was shown around several properties in Sleaford, accompanied by a young lady from one of the local estate agents. Sally McKenzie was puzzled how a lorry driver could possibly afford the type of properties she was offering him.

Doug eventually settled on a little cottage on the outskirts of Sleaford. Sally was even more surprised when he put down the deposit in cash, and shocked when he asked her out on a date.

Six months later Sally moved in with Doug, although it still worried her that she couldn't work out where all the money was coming from.

Doug's sudden wealth created other problems that he hadn't anticipated. What do you do with £25,000 in cash each week, when you can't open a bank account, or pay a monthly cheque into a building society? The basement flat on Hinton Road had been replaced with a cottage in the country. The second-hand fork-lift truck had been traded in for a sixteen-wheel Mercedes lorry. The annual holiday at a bed and breakfast in Blackpool had been upgraded to a rented villa in the Algarve. The Portuguese seemed quite happy to accept cash, whatever the currency.

On their second visit to the Algarve a year later, Doug fell on one knee, proposed to Sally and presented her with a diamond engagement ring the size of an acorn: traditional sort of chap, Doug.

Several people, not least his young wife, remained puzzled as to how Doug could possibly afford such a lifestyle while only earning £25,000 a year. 'Cash bonuses for overtime,' was all he came up with whenever Sally asked. This surprised Mrs Haslett because she knew that her husband only worked a couple of days a week. And she might never have found out the truth if someone else hadn't taken an interest.

Mark Cainen, an ambitious young assistant officer with HM Customs, decided the time had come to check exactly what Doug was importing, after a nark tipped him off it might not just be bananas.

When Doug was returning from one of his weekly trips to Marseilles, Mr Cainen asked him to pull over and park his lorry in the customs shed. Doug climbed down from the cab and handed over his worksheet to the officer. Bananas were the only entry on the manifest: fifty crates of them. The young customs official set about opening the crates one by one, and by the time he'd reached the thirty-sixth, was beginning to wonder if he had been given a bum steer; that opinion changed when he opened the forty-first crate, which was packed tightly with cigarettes – Marlboro, Benson & Hedges, Silk Cut and Players. By the time Mr Cainen had opened the fiftieth crate, he had placed an estimated street value on the contraband of over £200,000.

'I had no idea what was in those crates,' Doug assured his wife, and she believed him. He repeated the same story to his defence team, who wanted to believe him, and for a third time, to the jury, who didn't. Doug's defence silk reminded his lordship that this was Mr Haslett's first offence and his wife was expecting a baby. The judge listened in stony silence, and sent Doug down for four years.

Doug spent his first week in Lincoln high-security prison, but once he'd completed an induction form and was able to place a tick in all the right boxes – no drugs, no violence, no previous offences – he was quickly transferred to an open prison.

At North Sea Camp, Doug, as I've already explained, opted to work in the library. The alternatives were the pig farm, the kitchen, the stores or cleaning out the lavatories. Doug quickly discovered that despite there being over four hundred residents in the prison, as librarian he was on to a cushy number. His income fell from £25,000 a week to £12.50, of which he spent £10 on phone cards so that he could keep in touch with his pregnant wife.

Doug rang Sally twice a week – you can only phone out when you're in prison, no one can call you – to promise his wife repeatedly that once he was released, he would never get into trouble with the law again. Sally was reassured by this news.

In Doug's absence, and despite being heavily pregnant, Sally was still holding down her job at the estate agent's, and had even managed to hire out Doug's lorry for the period of time he would be away. However, Doug wasn't telling his wife the whole story. While other prisoners were being sent in *Playboy*, *Readers' Wives* and the *Sun*, Doug was receiving *Haulage Weekly* and *Exchange & Mart* for his bedside reading.

He was browsing through *Haulage Weekly* when he found exactly what he was looking for: a second-hand, left-hand-drive, forty-ton, American Peterbilt lorry, which was being offered for sale at a knock-down price. Doug took a long time – but then he had a long time – considering the vehicle's added extras. While he sat alone in the library, he began to draw diagrams on the back of the magazine. He then used a ruler to measure the exact size of a box of Marlboro. He realized that the cash return might be smaller this time, but at least he wouldn't be caught.

Among the problems of earning £25,000 a week, and not having to pay tax, is that after being released from prison you are expected to settle for a job that only offers you £25,000 a year before tax; a common enough dilemma for most criminals, especially drug dealers.

With less than a month of his sentence to serve, Doug phoned his wife and asked her to sell his top-of-the-range Mercedes truck, in part exchange for the massive second-hand eighteen-wheel Peterbilt lorry that he'd seen advertised in *Haulage Weekly*.

When Sally first saw the truck, she couldn't understand why her husband wanted to exchange his magnificent vehicle for such a monstrosity. She accepted his explanation that he would be able to drive from Sleaford to Marseilles without having to stop for refuelling.

'But it's a left-hand drive.'

'Don't forget,' Doug reminded her, 'the longest section of the journey is from Calais to Marseilles.'

Doug turned out to be a model prisoner, so ended up serving only half of his four-year sentence.

On the day of his release, his wife and eighteen-month-old daughter Kelly were waiting for him at the prison gates. Sally drove them back to Sleaford in her old Vauxhall. On arrival, Doug was pleased to find the second-hand pantech-nicon parked in the field next to their little cottage.

'But why haven't you sold my old Merc?' he asked.

'Haven't had a decent offer,' Sally admitted, 'so I hired it out for another year. At least that way it's showing us a small return.' Doug nodded. He was pleased to find that both vehicles were spotless, and after an inspection of the engines, discovered they were also in good nick.

Doug went back to work the following morning. He repeatedly assured Sally that he would never make the same mistake twice. He filled up his lorry with sprouts and peas from a local farmer, before setting out on his journey to Marseilles. He then returned to England with a full load of bananas. A suspicious, recently promoted Mark Cainen regularly pulled Doug over so that he could carry out a spot-check to find out what he was bringing back from Marseilles. But however many crates he prised open, they were always filled with bananas. The officer remained unconvinced, but couldn't work out what Doug was up to.

'Give me a break,' said Doug, when Mr Cainen pulled him over yet again in Dover. 'Can't you see that I've turned over a new leaf?' The customs officer didn't give him a break because he was convinced it was a tobacco leaf, even if he couldn't prove it.

Doug's new system was working like a dream, and although he was now only clearing £10,000 a week, at least this time he couldn't be caught. Sally kept all the books up to date for both lorries so that Doug's tax returns were always filled in correctly and paid on time, and any new EU regulations were complied with. However, Doug didn't brief his wife on the details of his new untaxed benefit scheme.

One Thursday afternoon, just after Doug had cleared customs in Dover, he drove into the nearest petrol station to refuel before continuing his journey north to Sleaford. An Audi followed him onto the forecourt, and the driver began to curse about how long he was going to have to wait before the massive pantechnicon would be filled up. To his surprise, the lorry driver only took a couple of minutes before he replaced the nozzle in its holder. As Doug drove out onto the road, the car behind moved up to take his place. When Mr Cainen saw the name on the side of the lorry, his curiosity was aroused. He checked the pump, to find that Doug had only spent £33. He stared at the massive eighteen-wheeler as it trundled off down the highway, aware that with that amount of petrol Doug could only hope to cover a few more miles before he would have to fill up again.

It took Mr Cainen only a few minutes to catch up with Doug's truck. He then followed the lorry at a safe distance for the next twenty miles before Doug pulled into another petrol station. Once Doug was back on the road a few minutes later, Mr Cainen checked the pump – £34 – only enough to cover another twenty miles. As Doug continued on his journey to Sleaford, the officer returned to Dover with a smile on his face.

When Doug was driving back from Marseilles the following week, he showed no concern when Mr Cainen asked him to pull over and park his lorry in the customs shed. He knew that every crate on board was, as the manifest stated, full of bananas. However, the customs officer didn't ask Doug to unlock the back door of the truck. He simply walked around the outside of the vehicle clutching a spanner as if it were a tuning fork while he tapped the massive fuel tanks. The officer was not surprised that the eighth tank rang out with a completely different timbre to the other seven. Doug sat around for hours while customs mechanics removed all eight fuel tanks from both sides of the lorry. Only one was half full of diesel, while the other seven contained over £100,000 worth of cigarettes.

On this occasion the judge was less lenient, and Doug was sent down for six years, even after his barrister pleaded that a second child was on the way.

Sally was horrified to discover that Doug had broken his word, and sceptical when he promised her never, ever, again. The moment her husband was locked up, she rented out the second vehicle and returned to her job as an estate agent.

A year later Sally was able to declare an increased income of just over £3,000, on top of her earnings as an estate agent.

Sally's accountant advised her to buy the field next door to the cottage, where the lorries were always parked at night, as she could claim it against tax. 'A carpark,' he explained, 'would be a legitimate business expense.'

As Doug had just begun a six-year sentence and was back to earning £12.50 a week as the prison librarian, he was hardly in a position to offer an opinion. However, even he was impressed when, the following year, Sally declared an income of £37,000, which included her added sales bonuses. This time, the accountant advised her to purchase a third lorry.

Doug was eventually released from prison having only served half his sentence (three years). Sally was parked outside the prison gates in her Vauxhall, waiting to drive her husband home. His nine-year-old daughter, Kelly, was strapped into the back, next to her three-year-old sister Sam. Sally had not allowed either of the children to visit their father in prison, so when Doug took the little girl in his arms for the first time, Sam burst into tears. Sally explained to her that the strange man was her father.

Over a welcome breakfast of bacon and eggs, Sally was able to report that she had been advised by her accountant to form a limited company. Haslett Haulage had declared a profit of £21,600 in its first year, and she had added two more lorries to their growing fleet. Sally told her husband that she was thinking of giving up her job at the estate agent's to become full-time chair of the new company.

'Chair?' said Doug. 'What's that?'

Doug was only too pleased to leave Sally to run the company, as long as he was allowed to take his place behind the wheel as one of her drivers. This state of affairs would have continued quite happily, if Doug had not once again been approached by the man from Marseilles – who never seemed to end up in jail – with what he confidently assured him was a fool-proof plan with no risks attached and, more important, this time his wife need never find out.

Doug resisted the Frenchman's advances for several months, but after losing a rather large sum in a poker game, finally succumbed. Just one trip, he promised himself. The man from Marseilles smiled, as he handed over an envelope containing £12,500 in cash.

Under Sally's chairmanship, the Haslett Haulage Company continued to grow, in both reputation and below the bottom line. Meanwhile, Doug once again became used to having cash in hand; money which did not rely on a balance sheet, and was not subject to a tax return.

Someone else was continuing to keep a close eye on the Haslett Haulage Company, and Doug in particular. Regular as clockwork, Doug could be seen driving his lorry through the Dover terminal, with a full load of sprouts and peas, destined for Marseilles. But Mark Cainen, now an anti-smuggling officer working as part of the Law Enforcement Unit, never once saw Doug make the return journey. This worried him.

The officer checked his records, to find that Haslett Haulage was now running nine lorries a week to different parts of Europe. Their chairman, Sally Haslett, had a spotless reputation – not unlike her vehicles – with everyone she dealt with, from customs to customers. But Mr Cainen was still curious to find out why Doug was no longer driving back through his port. He took it personally.

A few discreet enquiries revealed that Doug could still be seen in Marseilles unloading his sprouts and peas, and later loading up with crates of bananas. However, there was one slight variation. He was now driving back via Newhaven, which Cainen estimated must have added at least a couple of hours to Doug's journey.

All customs officers have the option of serving one month a year at another port of entry, to further their promotion prospects. The previous year Mr Cainen had selected Heathrow airport; that year he opted for a month in Newhaven.

Officer Cainen waited patiently for Doug's lorry to appear on the dockside, but it wasn't until the end of his second week that he spotted his old adversary waiting in line to disembark from an Olsen's ferry. The moment Doug's lorry drove onto the dock, Mr Cainen disappeared upstairs into the staffroom and poured himself a cup of coffee. He walked across to the window and watched Doug's vehicle came to a halt at the front of the line. He was waved quickly through by the two officers on duty. Mr Cainen made no attempt to intervene as Doug drove out onto the road to continue his journey back to Sleaford. He had to wait another ten days before Doug's lorry reappeared, and this time he noted that only one thing hadn't changed. Mr Cainen didn't think it was a coincidence.

When Doug returned via Newhaven five days later, the same two officers gave his vehicle no more than a cursory glance, before waving him through. The officer now knew that it wasn't a coincidence. Mr Cainen reported his observations to his boss in Newhaven and, as his month was up, made his way back to Dover.

Doug completed three more journeys from Marseilles via Newhaven before the two customs officers were arrested. When Doug saw five officers heading towards his truck, he knew that his new impossible-to-be-caught system had been sussed.

Doug didn't waste the court's time pleading not guilty, because one of the customs officers with whom he had been splitting the take had made a deal to have his sentence reduced if he named names. He named Douglas Arthur Haslett.

The judge sent Doug down for eight years, with no remission for good behaviour, unless he agreed to pay a fine of £750,000. Doug didn't have £750,000 and begged Sally to help out, as he couldn't face the thought of another eight years behind bars. Sally had to sell everything, including the cottage, the carpark, nine lorries and even her engagement ring, so that her husband could comply with the court order.

After serving a year at Wayland Category C prison in Norfolk, Doug was transferred back to North Sea Camp. Once again, he was appointed as librarian, which was where I first met him.

I was impressed that Sally and his two – now grown-up – daughters came to visit Doug every weekend. He told me that they didn't discuss business, even though he'd sworn on his mother's grave never, ever again.

'Don't even think about it,' Sally had warned him. 'I've already sent your lorry to the scrapyard.'

'Can't blame the woman, after all I've put her through,' said Doug when I next visited the library. 'But if they won't let me get behind a wheel once I'm released, what am I going to do for the rest of my life?'

I was released a couple of years before Doug, and if I hadn't been addressing a literary festival in Lincoln some years later, I might never have discovered what had become of the chief librarian.

As I stared down into the audience during questions, I thought I recognized three vaguely familiar faces looking up at me from the third row. I racked that part of my brain that is meant to store names, but it didn't respond. That was, until I had a question about the difficulties of writing while in prison. Then it all came flooding back. I had last seen Sally some three years before, when she was visiting Doug accompanied by her two daughters, Kelly and, and . . . Sam.

After I'd taken the final question, we broke for coffee, and the three of them came across to join me.

'Hi, Sally. How's Doug?' I asked even before they could introduce themselves. An old political ploy, and they looked suitably impressed.

'Retired,' said Sally without explanation.

'But he was younger than me,' I protested, 'and never stopped telling everyone what he planned to do once he was released.'

'No doubt,' said Sally, 'but I can assure you he's retired. Haslett Haulage is now run by me and my two daughters, with a backroom staff of twenty-one, not including the drivers.'

'So you're obviously doing well,' I said, fishing.

'You clearly don't read the financial pages,' she teased.

'I'm like the Japanese,' I countered, 'I always read my papers from back to front. So what have I missed?'

'We went public last year,' chipped in Kelly. 'Mum's chair, I'm in charge of new accounts and Sam is responsible for the drivers.'

'And if I remember correctly, you had about nine lorries?'

'We now have forty-one,' said Sally, 'and our turnover last year was just under five million.'

'And Doug doesn't play any role?'

'Doug plays golf,' said Sally, 'which doesn't require him to travel through Dover, or,' she added with a sigh, as her husband appeared in the doorway, 'back via Newhaven.'

Doug remained still, as his eyes searched the room for his family. I waved and caught his attention. Doug waved back and wandered slowly across to join us.

'We still allow him to drive us home from time to time,' whispered Sam with a grin, just as Doug appeared by my side.

I shook hands with my former inmate, and when Sally and the girls had finished their coffee, I accompanied them all back to their car, which gave me the chance to have a word with Doug.

'I'm delighted to hear that Haslett Haulage is doing so well,' I volunteered.

'Put it all down to experience,' said Doug. 'Don't forget I taught them everything they know.'

'And since we last met, Kelly tells me that the company's gone public.'

'All part of my long-term plan,' said Doug as his wife climbed into the back of the car. He turned and gave me a knowing look. 'A lot of people sniffing around at the moment, Jeff, so don't be surprised if there's a takeover bid in the near future.' Just as he reached the driver's side of the car, he added, 'Chance for you to make a few bob while the shares are still at their present price. Know what I mean?'

Charity Begins At Home

HENRY PRESTON, HARRY to his friends – and they didn't number many – wasn't the sort of person you'd bump into at the local pub, meet at a football match or invite home for a barbecue. Frankly, if there was a club for introverts, Henry would be elected chairman – reluctantly.

At school, the only subject in which he excelled was mathematics, and his mother, the one person who adored him, was determined that Henry would have a profession. His father had been a postman. With one A level in maths, the field was fairly limited – banking or accountancy. His mother chose accountancy.

Henry was articled to Pearson, Clutterbuck & Reynolds, and when he first joined the firm as a clerk he dreamt of the headed notepaper reading *Pearson, Clutterbuck, Reynolds & Preston*. But as the years went by, and younger and younger men found their names embossed on the left-hand side of the company notepaper, the dream faded.

Some men, aware of their limitations, find solace in another form – sex, drugs or a hectic social life. It's quite difficult to conduct a hectic social life on your own. Drugs? Henry didn't even smoke, although he allowed himself the occasional gin and tonic, but only on Saturday. And as for sex, he felt confident he wasn't gay, but his success rate with the opposite sex, 'hits' as some of his younger colleagues described them, hovered around zero. Henry didn't even have a hobby.

There comes a point in every man's life when he realizes *I'm going to live forever* is a fallacy. It came all too soon for Henry, as he progressed quickly through middle age and suddenly began to think about early retirement. When Mr Pearson, the senior partner, retired, a large party was held in his honour in a private room at a five-star hotel. Mr Pearson, after a long and distinguished career, told his colleagues that he would be retiring to a cottage in the Cotswolds to tend the roses and try to lower his golf handicap. Much laughter and applause followed. The only thing Henry recalled of that occasion was Atkins, the firm's latest recruit, saying to him as he left for the evening, 'I suppose it won't be that long, old chap, before we're doing the same sort of thing for you.'

Henry mulled over young Atkins's words as he walked towards the bus stop. He was fifty-four years old, so in six years' time, unless he made partner, in which case his tenure would be extended to sixty-five, they would be holding a farewell party for him. In truth, Henry had long ago given up any thought of becoming a partner, and he had already accepted that his party would not be held in the private room of a five-star hotel. He certainly wouldn't be retiring to a cottage in the Cotswolds to tend his roses, and he already had enough handicaps, without thinking about golf.

Henry was well aware that his colleagues considered him to be reliable, competent and thorough, which only added to his sense of failure. The highest praise he ever received was, 'You can always depend on Henry. He's a safe pair of hands.'

But all of that changed the day he met Angela.

Angela Forster's company, Events Unlimited, was neither large enough to be assigned to one of the partners, nor small enough to be handled by an articled clerk, which is how her file ended up on Henry's desk. He studied the details carefully.

Ms Forster was the sole proprietor of a small business that specialized in organizing events – anything from the local Conservative Association's annual dinner to a regional Hunt Ball. Angela was a born organizer and after her husband left her for a younger woman – when a man leaves his wife for a younger woman, it's a short story, when a woman leaves her husband for a younger man, it's a novel (I digress) – Angela made the decision not to sit at home and feel sorry for herself but, following our Lord's advice in the parable of the talents, opted to use her one gift, so that she could fully occupy her time while making a little pin money on the side. The problem was that Angela had become a little more successful than she'd anticipated, which is how she ended up having an appointment with Henry.

Before Henry finalized Ms Forster's accounts, he took her slowly through the figures, column by column, showing his new client how she was entitled to claim for certain items against tax, such as her car, travel and even her clothes. He pointed out that she ought to be dressed appropriately when she attended one of her functions. Henry managed to save Ms Forster a few hundred pounds on her tax bill; after all, he considered it a matter of professional pride that, having heeded his advice, all his clients left the office better off. That was even after they'd settled his company's fees, which, he pointed out, could also be claimed against tax.

Henry always ended every meeting with the words, 'I can assure you that your accounts are in apple-pie order, and the tax man will not be troubling you.' Henry was only too aware that very few of his clients were likely to interest the tax man, let alone be troubled by him. He would then accompany his client to the door with the words, 'See you next year.' When he opened the door for Ms Forster, she smiled, and said, 'Why don't you come along to one of my functions, Mr Preston? Then you can see what I get up to most evenings.'

Henry couldn't recall when he'd last been invited to anything. He hesitated, not quite sure how to respond. Angela filled the silence. 'I'm organizing a ball for African famine relief on Saturday evening. It's at the town hall. Why don't you join me?'

Henry heard himself saying, 'Yes, thank you, how nice. I'll look forward to it,' and regretted the decision the moment he had closed the door. After all, on Saturday nights he always watched film of the week on Sky, while enjoying a Chinese takeaway and a gin and tonic. In any case, he needed to be in bed by ten because on Sunday morning he was responsible for checking the church collection. He was also their accountant. Honorary, he assured his mother.

Henry spent most of Saturday morning trying to come up with an excuse: a headache, an emergency meeting, a previous engagement he'd forgotten about, so that he could ring Ms Forster and call the whole thing off. Then he realized that he didn't have her home number.

At six o'clock that evening Henry put on the dinner jacket his mother had given him on his twenty-first birthday, which didn't always have an annual outing. He looked at himself in the mirror, nervous that his attire must surely be out of date – wide lapels and flared trousers – unaware that this look was actually back in fashion. He was among the last to arrive at the town hall, and had already made up his mind that he would be among the first to leave.

Angela had placed Henry on the end of the top table, from where he was able to observe proceedings, while only occasionally having to respond to the lady seated on his left.

Once the speeches were over, and the band had struck up, Henry felt he could safely slip away. He looked around for Ms Forster. He had earlier spotted her dashing all over the place, organizing everything from the raffle and the heads-and-tails competition to the ten-pound-note draw and even the auction. When he looked at her more closely, dressed in her long red ball gown, her fair hair falling to her shoulders, he had to admit . . . Henry stood up and was about to leave, when Angela appeared by his side. 'Hope you've enjoyed yourself,' she said, touching his arm. Henry couldn't remember the last time a woman had touched him. He prayed she wasn't going to ask him to dance.

'I've had a wonderful time,' Henry assured her. 'How about you?'

'Run off my feet,' Angela replied, 'but I feel confident that we'll raise a record amount this year.'

'So how much do you expect to make?' asked Henry, relieved to find himself on safer ground.

Angela checked her little notebook. 'Twelve thousand, six hundred in pledges, thirty-nine thousand, four hundred and fifty in cheques, and just over twenty thousand in cash.' She handed over her notebook for Henry to inspect. He expertly ran a finger down the list of figures, relaxing for the first time that evening.

'What do you do with the cash?' Henry asked.

'I always drop it off on my way home at the nearest bank that has an overnight safe. If you'd like to accompany me, you'll have experienced the whole cycle from beginning to end.' Henry nodded. 'Just give me a few minutes,' she said. 'I have to pay the band, as well as my helpers – and they always insist on cash.'

That was probably when Henry first had the idea. Just a passing thought to begin with, which he quickly dismissed. He headed towards the exit and waited for Angela.

'If I remember correctly,' said Henry as they walked down the steps of the town hall together, 'your turnover last year was just under five million, of which over a million was in cash.'

'What a good memory you have, Mr Preston,' Angela said as they headed towards the High Street, 'but I'm hoping to raise over five million this year,' she added, 'and I'm already ahead of my target for March.'

'That may well be the case,' said Henry, 'but you still only paid yourself forty-two thousand last year,' he continued, 'which is less than one per cent of your turnover.'

'I'm sure you're right,' said Angela, 'but I enjoy the work, and it keeps me occupied.'

'But don't you consider you deserve a better return for your efforts?'

'Possibly, but I only charge my clients five per cent of the profits, and every time I suggest putting my fee up, they always remind me that they are a charity.'

'But you're not,' said Henry. 'You're a professional, and should be recompensed accordingly.'

'I know you're right,' said Angela as they stopped outside the Nat West bank and she dropped the cash into the night safe, 'but most of my clients have been with me for years.'

'And have taken advantage of you for years,' insisted Henry.

'That may well be so,' said Angela, 'but what can I do about it?'

The thought returned to Henry's mind, but he said nothing other than, 'Thank you for a most interesting evening, Ms Forster. I haven't enjoyed myself so much in years.' Henry thrust out his right hand, as he always did at the end of every meeting, and had to stop himself saying, 'See you next year.'

Angela laughed, leant forward and kissed him on the cheek. Henry certainly couldn't remember when that had last occurred. 'Goodnight, Henry,' she said as she turned and began to walk away.

'I don't suppose . . .' he hesitated.

'Yes, Henry?' she said, turning back to face him.

'That you'd consider having dinner with me some time?'

'I'd like that very much,' said Angela. 'When would suit you?'

'Tomorrow,' said Henry, suddenly emboldened.

Angela removed a diary from her handbag and began to flick through the pages. 'I know I can't do tomorrow,' she said. 'I have a feeling it's Greenpeace.'

'Monday?' said Henry, not having to check his diary.

'Sorry, it's the Blue Cross Ball,' said Angela, turning another page of her diary.

'Tuesday?' said Henry trying not to sound desperate.

'Amnesty International,' said Angela, flicking over another page.

'Wednesday,' said Henry, wondering if she had changed her mind.

'Looks good,' said Angela, staring at a blank page. 'Where would you like to meet?'

'How about La Bacha?' said Henry, remembering that it was the restaurant where the partners always took their most important clients to lunch. 'Eight o'clock suit you?'

'Suits me fine.'

Henry arrived at the restaurant twenty minutes early and read the menu from cover to cover – several times. During his lunch break, he'd purchased a new shirt and a silk tie. He was already regretting that he hadn't tried on the blazer that was displayed in the window.

Angela strolled into La Bacha just after eight. She was wearing a pale green floral dress that fell just below the knee. Henry liked the way she'd done her hair, but knew that he wouldn't have the courage to tell her. He also approved of the fact that she wore so little make-up and her only jewellery was a modest string of pearls. Henry rose from his place as she reached the table. Angela couldn't remember the last person who'd bothered to do that.

Henry had feared that they wouldn't be able to find anything to talk about – small talk had never been his forte – but Angela made it all so easy that he found himself ordering a second bottle of wine, long before the meal was over – another first.

Over coffee, Henry said, 'I think I've come up with a way of supplementing your income.'

'Oh, don't let's talk business,' said Angela, touching his hand.

'It's not business,' Henry assured her.

When Angela woke the following morning, she smiled as she remembered what a pleasant evening she'd spent with Henry. All she could recall him saying as they parted was, 'Don't forget that any winnings made from gambling are tax-free.' What was all that about?

Henry, on the other hand, could recall every detail of the advice he'd given Angela. He rose early on the following Sunday and began preparing an outline plan, which included opening several bank accounts, preparing spread-sheets and working on a long-term investment programme. He nearly missed matins.

The following evening Henry made his way to the Hilton Hotel on Park Lane, arriving a few minutes after midnight. He was carrying an empty Gladstone bag in one hand and an umbrella in the other. After all, he had to look the part.

The Westminster and City Conservative Association's annual ball was coming to an end. As Henry entered the ballroom, party-goers were beginning to burst balloons and drain the last drops of champagne from any remaining bottles. He spotted Angela seated at a table in the far corner, sorting out pledges, cheques and cash before placing them in three separate piles. She looked up and couldn't mask her surprise when she saw him. Angela had spent the day convincing herself that he didn't mean it and, if he did turn up, she wouldn't go through with it.

'How much cash?' he asked matter-of-factly, even before she could say hello.

'Twenty-two thousand three hundred and seventy pounds,' she heard herself saying.

Henry took his time. He double-checked the notes before placing the cash in his battered bag. Angela's calculation had proved to be accurate. He handed her a receipt for £19,400.

'See you later,' he said, just as the band struck up 'Jerusalem'. Henry left the ballroom as the words 'Bring me my bow of burning gold' were rendered lustily and out of tune. Angela remained transfixed as she watched Henry walk away. She knew that if she didn't chase after him and stop the man before he reached the bank, there could be no turning back.

'Congratulations on another well-organized event, Angela,' said Councillor Pickering, interrupting her thoughts. 'I don't know how we'd manage without you.'

'Thank you,' said Angela, turning to face the chairman of the ball committee.

Henry pushed his way through the hotel's swing doors and out onto the street, feeling for the first time that his anonymity was no longer a weakness but a strength. He could hear his heart beating as he headed towards the local branch of HSBC, the nearest bank with an overnight safe deposit. Henry dropped £19,400 into the safe, leaving £2,970 of the cash in his bag. He then hailed a taxi – another departure from his usual routine – and gave the cabby an address in the West End.

The taxi drew up outside an establishment that Henry had never entered before, although he had kept their accounts for over twenty years.

The night manager of the Black Ace Casino tried not to look surprised when Mr Preston walked onto the floor. Had he come to make a spot-check? It seemed unlikely, as the company accountant didn't acknowledge him but headed straight for the roulette table.

Henry knew the odds only too well because he signed off the casino's end-of-year balance sheet every April, and despite rent, rates, staff wages, security and even free meals and drinks for favoured customers, his client still managed to declare a handsome profit. But it wasn't Henry's intention to make a profit, or, for that matter, a loss.

Henry took a seat at the roulette table and saw red. He opened his Gladstone bag, extracted ten ten-pound notes and handed them across to the croupier, who in turn counted them slowly before he gave Henry ten little blue and white chips in return.

There were a number of gamblers already seated at the table, placing bets of different denominations, five, ten, twenty, fifty and even the occasional hundred-pound golden chip. Only one punter had a stack of golden chips in front of him, which he was spreading randomly around the different numbers. Henry was pleased to see that he held the attention of most of the onlookers standing round the table.

While the man on the far side of the table continued to litter the green baize with golden chips, Henry placed one of his ten-pound chips on red. The wheel spun and the little white ball revolved in the opposite direction until it finally settled in red 19. The croupier returned one ten-pound chip to Henry, while he raked in over a thousand pounds' worth of golden chips from the gambler on the other side of the table.

While the croupier prepared for the next spin of the wheel, Henry slipped his single chip in the left-hand pocket of his jacket, while leaving his original stake on red.

The croupier spun the wheel again and this time the little white ball came to a halt in black 4, and Henry's chip was raked in by the croupier. Two bets, and Henry had broken even. He placed another ten-pound chip on red. Henry had already accepted that if he was to exchange all the cash for chips, it would be a long and arduous process. But then Henry, unlike most gamblers, was a patient man, whose only purpose was to break even. He placed another ten pounds on red.

Three hours later, by which time he had managed to exchange all £2,970 of cash for chips without anyone becoming suspicious, Henry left the table and headed for the bar. If any one had been following closely what Henry had been up to, they would have observed that he had just about broken even. But then that was his intention. He only ever meant to exchange all the surplus cash for chips before he could execute the second part of his plan.

When Henry reached the bar, his Gladstone bag empty and his pockets bulging with chips, he took a seat next to a woman who appeared to be on her own. He didn't speak to her and she showed no interest in him. When Angela ordered another drink, Henry bent down and deposited all of his chips into the open handbag she had left on the floor beside her. He was already walking towards the exit before the barman could take his order.

The manager pulled open the front door for him.

'I hope it won't be too long before we see you again, sir.'

Henry nodded, but didn't bother to explain that the whole exercise was about to become part of a nightly routine. Once Henry was back outside on the pavement, he walked towards the nearest tube station, but didn't start whistling until he'd turned the corner.

Angela bent down and closed her bag, but not before she'd finished her drink. Two men had propositioned her earlier in the evening and she'd felt quite flattered. She slipped off her stool and walked across to join a short queue of punters at the cashier's window. When she reached the front, Angela pushed the pile of ten-pound chips under the steel grille and waited.

'Cash or cheque, madam?' enquired the teller, once he'd counted her chips.

'A cheque please,' Angela replied.

'What name should the cheque be made out to?' was the teller's next question.

After a moment's hesitation, Angela said, 'Mrs Ruth Richards.'

The cashier wrote out the name Ruth Richards, and the figure, £2,930, before slipping the cheque under the grille. Angela checked the figure. Henry had lost £40. She smiled, remembering that he had assured her that over a year it would even out. After all, as he had explained often enough, he wasn't playing the odds, but simply exchanging any traceable cash for chips, so that she would end up with a cheque which no one would later be able to trace.

Angela slipped out of the casino when she saw the manager chatting to another customer who had clearly lost a large sum of money. Henry had warned her that the management keeps a much closer eye on winners than losers, and that as she was about to embark on a long and profitable run she shouldn't draw attention to herself.

One of Henry's stipulations was that there should not be any contact between the two of them, other than when he came to collect the takings, and then again for that brief moment when he deposited the chips into her open bag. He didn't want anyone to think that they might be an item. Angela reluctantly agreed with his reasoning. Henry's only other piece of advice was that she should not be seen collecting the cash herself during any function.

'Leave that to the volunteers,' he said, 'so that if anything goes wrong, no one will suspect you.'

There are one hundred and twelve casinos located across central London, so Henry and Angela didn't find it necessary to return to any particular establishment more than once a year.

For the next three years, Henry and Angela took their holidays at the same time, but never in the same place, and always in August. Angela explained that not many organizations hold their annual events in that particular month. During the season Henry had to make sure that he was never out of town because from September to December Sunday was the only night Angela could guarantee not to be working, and in the run-up to Christmas she often had a lunchtime event, followed by a couple more functions in the evening.

Although Henry had written the rulebook, Angela had insisted on adding a subclause. Nothing would be deducted from any organization which failed to reach the previous year's total. Despite this addendum, which incidentally Henry heartily agreed with, he rarely left a function with his Gladstone bag empty.

The two of them still met once a year at Mr Preston's office to go over Ms Forster's annual accounts, which was followed by a dinner a week later at La Bacha. Neither of them ever alluded to the fact that she had siphoned off £267,900, £311,150 and £364,610 during the past three years, and after each function deposited the latest cheque in different bank accounts right across London, always in the name of Mrs Ruth Richards. Henry's other responsibility was to ensure that their new-found wealth was invested shrewdly, remembering that he wasn't a gambler. However, one of the advantages of preparing other companies' accounts is that it isn't too difficult to predict who is likely to have a good year. As the cheques were never made out in his or her name, any subsequent profits couldn't be traced back to either of them.

After they had banked the first million, Henry felt that they could risk a celebration dinner. Angela wanted to go to Mosimann's in West Halkin Street, but Henry vetoed the idea. He booked a table for two at La Bacha. No need to draw attention to their new-found wealth, he reminded her.

Henry made two other suggestions during dinner. Angela was quite happy to go along with the first, but didn't want to talk about the second. Henry had advised her to transfer the first million to an offshore account in the Cook Islands, while he carried on with the same investment policy; he also recommended that in future whenever they cleared another hundred thousand, Angela would immediately transfer the sum to the same account.

Angela raised her glass. 'Agreed,' she said, 'but what is the second item on the agenda, Mr Chairman?' she asked, teasing him. Henry took her through the details of a contingency plan she didn't even want to think about.

Henry finally raised his glass. For the first time in his life, he was looking forward to retirement, and joining all his colleagues for a farewell party on his sixtieth birthday.

Six months later, the chairman of Pearson, Clutterbuck & Reynolds sent out invitations to all the firm's employees, asking them to join the partners for drinks at a local three-star hotel to celebrate the retirement of Henry Preston and to thank him for forty years of dedicated service to the company.

Henry was unable to attend his own farewell party, as he ended up celebrating his sixtieth birthday behind bars, and all for a mere £820.

※ ―◁O▷― ※

Miss Florence Blenkinsopp double-checked the figures. She'd been right the first time. They were £820 short of the amount she had calculated before the uninvited guest dressed in a pinstriped suit had walked into the ballroom with his little bag and disappeared with all the cash. It couldn't be Angela who was responsible; after all, she had been one of her pupils at St Catherine's Convent. Miss Blenkinsopp dismissed the discrepancy as her mistake, especially as the takings were comfortably up on the previous year's total.

The following year would be the convent's one-hundredth anniversary, and Miss Blenkinsopp was already planning a centenary ball. She told her committee that she expected them to pull their socks up if they hoped to set records during the centenary year. Although Miss Blenkinsopp had retired as headmistress of St Catherine's some seven years before, she continued to treat her committee of old gals as if they were still adolescent pupils.

The centenary ball could not have been a greater success, and Miss Blenkinsopp was the first to single out Angela for particular praise. She made it clear that in her opinion, Ms Forster had certainly pulled her socks up.

However, Miss Blenkinsopp felt it necessary to triple-check the cash they had collected that night, before the little man turned up with his Gladstone bag and took it all away. When she went over the figures later in the week, although their previous record had been broken by a considerable amount, the cash entry was over two thousand short of the figure she had scribbled on the back of her place card.

Miss Blenkinsopp felt she had no choice but to point out the discrepancy (two years running) to her president, Lady Travington, who in turn sought the advice of her husband, who was chairman of the local watch committee. Sir David promised, before putting the light out that night, that he would have a word with the chief constable in the morning.

When the chief constable was informed of the misappropriation, he passed on the details to his chief superintendent. He sent it further down the line to a chief inspector, who would like to have told his boss that he was in the middle of a murder hunt and also staking out a shipment of heroin with a street value of over ten million. The fact that St Catherine's Convent had mislaid – he checked his notes – just over £2,000, wasn't likely to be placed at the top of his priority list. He stopped the next person walking down the corridor and passed her the file. 'See you have a full report on my desk, Sergeant, before the watch committee meet next month.'

Detective Sergeant Janet Seaton set about her task as if she was stalking Jack the Ripper.

First, she interviewed Miss Blenkinsopp, who was most cooperative, but insisted that none of her gals could possibly have been involved with such an unpleasant incident, and therefore they were not to be interviewed.

Ten days later, DS Seaton purchased a ticket for the Bebbington Hunt Ball, despite the fact that she had never mounted a horse in her life.

DS Seaton arrived at Bebbington Hall just before the gong was struck and the toastmaster bellowed out, 'Dinner is served.' She quickly identified Angela Forster, even before she had located her table. Although DS Seaton had to engage in polite conversation with the men on either side of her, she was still able to keep a roving eye on Ms Forster. By the time cheese and coffee were served, the detective had come to the conclusion that she was dealing with a consummate professional. Not only could Ms Forster handle the regular outbursts of Lady Bebbington, the Master of Hounds' wife, but she also found time to organize the band, the kitchen, the waiters, the cabaret and the voluntary staff without once breaking into a gallop. But, more interesting, she seemed to have nothing to do with the collecting of any money. That was carried out by a group of ladies, who performed the task without appearing to consult Angela.

When the band struck up its opening number, several young men asked the detective sergeant for a dance. She turned them all down, one somewhat reluctantly.

It was a few minutes before one, when the evening was drawing to a close, that the detective sergeant spotted the man she had been waiting for. Among the red and black jackets, he would have been easier to identify than a fox on the run. He also fitted the exact description Miss Blenkinsopp had provided: a short, rotund, bald-headed man of around sixty who would be more appropriately dressed for an accountant's office than a Hunt Ball. She never took her eyes off him as he progressed unobtrusively around the outside of the dance floor to disappear behind the bandstand. The detective quickly left her table and walked to the other side of the ballroom, coming to a halt only when she had a perfect sighting of the two of them. The man was seated next to Angela counting the cash, unaware that an extra pair of eyes was watching him. The detective sergeant stared at Angela, as the man carefully placed the cheques, the pledges and the cash in separate piles. Not a word passed between them.

Once Henry had double-checked the amount of cash, he didn't even give Angela a second look. He placed the notes in his bag and handed her a receipt. With no more than a slight bow of the head, he retraced his steps round the outside of the dance floor and quickly left the ballroom. The whole operation had taken him less than seven minutes. Henry didn't notice that one of the revellers was only a few paces behind him, and, more important, her eyes never left him.

DS Seaton watched as the unidentified man made his way down the long drive, through the wrought-iron gates and on towards the village.

Since it was a clear night and the streets were empty, it was not difficult for DS Seaton to follow the progress of the man with the bag without being spotted. He must have been supremely confident because he never once looked back. She only had to slip into the shadows on one occasion, when her quarry came to a halt outside a local branch of the Nat West Bank. He opened his bag, removed a package and dropped it into the overnight safe. He then continued on his way, hardly breaking his stride. Where was he going?

The young detective had to make an instant decision. Should she follow the stranger, or return to Bebbington

Hall and see what Ms Forster was up to? Follow the money, she had always been instructed by her supervisor at Peel House. When Henry reached the station, the detective sergeant cursed. She had left her car in the grounds of the hall, and if she was to continue pursuing the bag man, she would have to abandon the vehicle and pick it up first thing in the morning.

The last train to Waterloo that night trundled into Bebbington Halt a few minutes later. It was becoming clear that the man with the bag had everything timed to the minute. The detective remained out of sight until her suspect had boarded the train. She then took a seat in the next carriage.

When they reached Waterloo, the man stepped off the train and made his way quickly across to the nearest taxi rank. The detective stood to one side and watched as he progressed to the front of the queue. The moment he climbed into a cab, the detective walked briskly to the top of the queue, produced her warrant card and apologized to the person who was about to step into a cab. She jumped in the taxi and instructed the driver to follow the one that had just moved off the rank.

When the driver pulled up outside the Black Ace Casino, the detective remained in the back of her cab until the man had disappeared inside.

She took her time paying the cab driver before she climbed out and followed her quarry into the casino. She filled in a temporary membership form, as she didn't want anyone to realize that she was on duty.

DS Seaton strolled onto the floor and glanced around the gaming tables. It only took her a few moments before she spotted her man seated next to one of the roulette wheels.

She took a step closer and joined a group of onlookers who formed a horseshoe around the table. The detective sergeant made sure that she remained some distance away from her quarry because, dressed in a long blue silk gown more appropriate for a ball, he might spot her and even wonder if she had followed him from Bebbington Hall.

For the next hour she watched the man remove wads of cash from his bag at regular intervals, then exchange them for chips. An hour later the bag was clearly empty because he left the table with a glum look on his face, and made his way towards the bar.

DS Seaton had cracked it. The anonymous man was siphoning off money from the evening events in order to finance his gambling habit, but she still couldn't be sure if Angela was involved.

The detective slipped behind a marble pillar as the man climbed onto a stool next to a lady in a blue suit with a short skirt.

Did he have enough money over to pay for a prostitute? The detective stepped out from behind the pillar to take a closer look, and nearly bumped into Henry as he began walking back towards the exit. Later, much later, DS Seaton thought it strange that he had left the bar without having a drink. Perhaps the woman on the stool had rejected him.

Henry stepped out onto the pavement and hailed a taxi. The detective grabbed the next one. She followed his cab as it made its way across Putney Bridge and continued its journey along the south side of the river. The taxi finally came to a halt outside a block of flats in Wandsworth. DS Seaton made a note of the address and decided that she had earned a taxi ride home.

The following morning, DS Seaton placed her report on the chief inspector's desk. He read it, smiled, left his office and walked down the corridor to brief the chief superintendent, who in turn phoned the chief constable. The chief decided not to mention it to the chairman of the watch committee until after an arrest had been made, as he wanted to present Sir David with an open-and-shut case, one that a jury could not fail to convict on.

Henry deposited the cash from the Butterfly Ball in the overnight vault of Lloyds TSB just a couple of hundred yards away from the hotel where the Masons were holding their annual dinner. He must have walked about another thirty yards before a police car drew up beside him. There wouldn't have been much point in making a dash for it, as Henry wasn't built for a change of gear. And in any case he had already planned for this moment, right down to the last detail. Henry was arrested and charged two days before the watch committee was due to meet.

Henry selected Mr Clifton-Smyth to represent him, a solicitor whose accounts he had handled for the past twenty years.

Mr Clifton-Smyth listened carefully to his client's defence, making copious notes, but when Henry finally came to the end of his tale, the lawyer only had one piece of advice to offer him: plead guilty.

'I will of course,' added the lawyer, 'brief counsel of any mitigating circumstances.'

Henry accepted his solicitor's advice; after all, Mr Clifton-Smyth had never once, in the past two decades, questioned *his* judgement.

Henry made no attempt to contact Angela during the run-up to the trial, and although the police felt fairly confident that she was playing Bonnie to his Clyde, they quickly worked out that they shouldn't have arrested him until he'd gone to the casino a second time. Who was the woman seated at the bar? Had she been waiting for him? The Special Crime Unit spent weeks collecting bank stubs from casinos right across London, but they couldn't find a single cheque made out to a Ms Angela Forster, and even more puzzling, they didn't come up with one for a Mr Henry Preston. Did he always lose?

When they checked Angela's events book, they discovered that Henry had always taken responsibility for counting the cash, and signed the receipt. Her bank account was then picked over by a bunch of treasury vultures, and found to be only £11,318 in credit, a sum that had showed very little movement either way for the past five years. When DS Seaton reported back to Miss Blenkinsopp, she seemed quite content to believe that the right man had been apprehended. After all, she told the detective, a St Catherine's gal couldn't possibly be involved in that sort of thing.

With the murder hunt still in progress, and the drugs stash not yet unearthed, the chief superintendent sent down an instruction to close the St Catherine's file. They'd made an arrest, and that was all that would matter when they reported their annual crime statistics.

Once the Treasury solicitors had accepted that they couldn't trace any of the missing money, Henry's solicitor managed to broker a deal with the CPS. If he pleaded guilty to the theft of £130,000, and was willing to return the full amount to the injured parties concerned, they would recommend a reduced sentence.

'And no doubt there are mitigating circumstances in this case that you wish to bring to my attention, Mr Cameron?' suggested the judge as he stared down from the bench at Henry's Silk.

'There most certainly are, m'lord,' replied Mr Alex Cameron QC as he rose slowly from his place. 'My client,' he began, 'makes no secret of his unfortunate addiction to gambling, which has been the cause of his tragic downfall. However,' Mr Cameron continued, 'I feel confident that your lordship will take into account that this is my client's first offence, and until this sad lapse of judgement he had been a pillar of the community with an unblemished reputation. Indeed, my client has given years of selfless service to his local church as its honorary treasurer, to which you will recall, m'lord, the vicar bore witness.'

Mr Cameron cleared his throat before continuing. 'M'lord, you see before you a broken and penniless man, who has nothing to look forward to except long lonely years of retirement. He has even,' added Mr Cameron, tugging at his lapels, 'had to sell his flat in Wandsworth in order to repay his creditors.' He paused. 'Perhaps you might feel, in the circumstances, m'lord, that my client has suffered quite enough and should therefore be treated leniently.' Mr Cameron smiled hopefully at the judge, and resumed his seat.

The judge looked down at Henry's advocate, and returned his smile. 'Not quite enough, Mr Cameron. Try not to forget that Mr Preston was a professional man who violated a position of trust. But first let me remind your client,' said the judge, turning his attention to Henry, 'that gambling is a sickness, and the defendant should seek some help for his malady the moment he is released from prison.' Henry braced himself as he waited to learn how long his sentence would be.

The judge paused for what seemed an eternity, as he continued to stare at Henry. 'I sentence you to three years,' he said, before adding, 'take the prisoner down.'

Henry was shipped off to Ford open prison. No one noticed him come and no one noticed him go. He led just as anonymous an existence on the inside as he had outside. He received no mail, made no phone calls and entertained no visitors. When they released him eighteen months later,

having completed half his sentence, there was no one waiting at the barrier to greet him.

Henry Preston accepted his £45 discharge pay, and was
last seen heading towards the local railway station, carrying
a Gladstone bag containing only his personal belongings.

Mr and Mrs Graham Richards enjoy a pleasant, if somewhat
uneventful retirement on the island of Majorca. They
have a small, front-line villa overlooking the Bay of Palma,
and both of them are proving to be popular with the local
community.

The chairman of the Royal Overseas Club in Palma
reported to the AGM that he considered he'd pulled off
quite a coup, convincing the former finance director of the
Nigerian National Oil Company to become the club's
honorary treasurer. Nods, hear-hears and a sprinkling of
applause followed. The chairman went on to suggest that the
secretary should record a note in the minutes, that since Mr
Richards had taken over the responsibility as treasurer, the
club's accounts had been in apple-pie order.

'And by the way,' he added, 'his wife Ruth has kindly
agreed to organize our annual ball.'

The Alibi

'HE GOT AWAY WITH murder, didn't he?' said Mick.

'How did he manage that?' I asked.

'Because if two screws say that's what happened, then that's what happened,' said Mick, 'and no con will be able to tell you any different. Understood?'

'No, I don't understand,' I admitted.

'Then I'll have to explain it to you, won't I?' said Mick. 'There's a golden rule among cons – never have sex with a mate's tart while he's banged up. It's all part of the code.'

'That might be a bit rough on a young girl whose boyfriend has just been given a lengthy sentence because then you'd be sentencing her to the same number of years without sex.'

'That's not the point,' said Mick, 'because Pete made it clear to Karen that he'd wait for her.'

'But he wasn't going anywhere for the next six years,' I suggested.

'You're missing the point, Jeff. It's the code and, to be fair to the tart, by all accounts Karen was as good as gold for the first six months and then she came off the rails. Truth is,' said Mick, 'Pete's best mate Brian had already had sex with Karen, but that was before she became Pete's girl, on account of the fact that they'd all been at secondary modern together. But that didn't count because Karen stopped whoring around once she'd moved in with Pete. Understood?'

'I think so,' I said.

'Mind you, the rule doesn't apply to Pete on account of the fact that he's a man. It's only logic, isn't it, because men are different. We're lions, they're lambs.' Lionesses would have seemed more appropriate. However, I confess I didn't voice my opinion at the time. 'Still,' Mick continued, 'the code is clear. You don't have sex with a mate's tart while he's banged up.'

I put my pen down and continued to listen to the Gospel according to St Mick – another burglar who was in and out of prison as if the building had revolving doors. I decided to abandon any attempt to write my daily diary. It was clear Mick was on a roll and nothing was going to stop him – certainly not me. And as the door was locked and I couldn't escape, I decided to take down his words. But first a little background.

Mick Boyle was my cell mate at Lincoln, and serving his ninth sentence during the past seventeen years, all for burglary. 'I may be a tea-leaf,' he proclaimed, 'but I can't be doing with violence. Don't approve,' he added, clearly attempting to capture the moral high ground. He told me that he had six children that he knew of, by five different women, but had had little or no contact with any of them since. I must have looked surprised, because he added, 'Don't worry yourself, Jeff, they're all taken care of by the Social.'

'If you want pussy,' Mick continued, 'there's quite enough going spare without having sex with your best mate's tart; after all, most of us are in and out, in and out,' he repeated, laughing at his own joke.

Mick's friend Pete Bailey – the hero or the villain in this tale, according to your viewpoint – had been charged with aggravated robbery, which covers a multitude of sins, especially if you ask the court – after you've been found guilty – to take into consideration one hundred and twelve similar offences.

'Result? Pete gets six years in the slammer.' Mick paused to draw breath. 'Mind you, he still killed his best mate while he was inside and got away with it, didn't he?'

'Did he?' I asked, showing a little more interest.

'Yeah, he sure did. Mind you, he knew he'd only have to serve three years on account of the fact that he was always on his best behaviour, whenever he was inside,' said Mick. 'Logic, isn't it? So after fifteen months in Wakefield – awful nick – they sent him off to Hollesley Bay open prison in Suffolk, didn't they, to finish off his sentence. Bloody holiday camp. See, the theory is,' continued Mick, 'an open prison is meant to prepare you for returning to society. Some hope. All Pete did was spend his time in the prison library reading through back copies of *Country Life*, supplied by some do-gooder, so he could work out in advance which houses he was going to rob the moment he got out. Now another rule in an open prison,' continued Mick, 'is that you're entitled to a visit once a week, not like the once a month you get in closed conditions; that is as long as you're enhanced, and not been put on report for at least a month.'

'Enhanced?' I ventured.

'That's when a con's been on good behaviour for at least three months. When he's enhanced he gets all sorts of privileges, like more time out of his cell, better job, even more pay in some nicks.'

'And how do you get put on report?'

'That's easy enough. Swear at a screw, turn up late for work, fail a drugs test. I was once put on report for nicking an orange from the kitchen. Diabolical liberty.'

'So was your friend Pete ever put on report?' I asked.

'Never,' Mick replied. 'Good as gold, wasn't he, because he wanted a visit from his tart. Well, he does his three months, works in the stores, keeps his nose clean, and Bob's your uncle, he's enhanced. Following Saturday his tart turns up at the nick to pay him a visit.

'In open prisons, visits are held in the biggest room available, usually the gym or the canteen. And you have to remember, security isn't like a closed nick, with sniffer dogs and CCTV cameras following your every move, so you can behave natural when you're with your tart.' He paused. 'Well, within limits. I mean you can't have sex like they do in Swedish prisons. You know – what do they call it?'

'Conjugal visits?'

'Well, whatever, it's sex, and we don't allow it. Mind you, a screw will turn a blind eye – when a con puts his hand up a tart's skirt, but then I remember in one prison—'

'Pete,' I reminded him.

'Oh, yeah, Pete. Well, Karen came to visit Pete the following Saturday. All's going well until Pete asks about his best mate, Brian. Karen clams up, doesn't say a word does she, then turns bright red. Pete susses straight away what she's been up to: tart, having it off with his best mate while he's inside. She lit his short fuse, didn't she? So Pete jumps up and puts one on her. Karen goes arse over tits, and lands up flat on the floor. The alarm goes off and screws come running through every door. They had to pull him off Karen and drag him away to segregation. Ever been to segregation, Jeff?'

'No, can't say I have.'

'Well, don't bother. Diabolical liberty. Bare cell, mattress on the floor, steel basin screwed into the wall and a steel bog what don't flush. Next day Pete's put on report, and comes up in front of the governor, who, you have to remember, is God Almighty. He don't need no judge or jury to help him decide if you're guilty – Home Office regulations are quite enough.'

'So what happened to Pete?'

'Sent back to closed conditions, wasn't he? Shipped off to Lincoln prison the same day, with another three months added to his sentence. Some cons, when they're sent back to a closed nick, lose their rag, start breaking the place up, taking drugs, setting their cell on fire, so they never get out. I was banged up with a muppet in Liverpool once. Started off with a three-year sentence and he's still there – eleven years later. Last time he came up in front of the governor for—'

'Pete,' I said, trying not to sound exasperated.

'Oh, yeah, Pete. Well, Pete goes the other way.'

'The other way?'

'Good as gold all the time he's banged up at Lincoln. Three months later he's back enhanced, with all his privileges restored. Gets a job in the kitchen, works like a slave, six months later he puts in a request for a visit and it's granted, with the exception of one Karen Slater. But he never wanted to see that whore again anyway. No, this time Pete applied for a visit from one of his old mates who was on the out at the time. Now this mate confirms that Brian is not only having it off with Karen, but now that Pete's safely banged up in Lincoln she's moved in with him. What a diabolical liberty,' said Mick. 'Pete's mate even asked if he wanted Brian done over. "No, don't go down that road," Pete told him. "I'll be taking care of him myself, all in good time." He never went into no detail of what he had in mind, on account of the fact that in the end someone always opens their mouth. Must be the same in politics, Jeff.'

'Pete.'

'Well, Pete goes on being as good as gold. Cleanest pad, working all hours, never swearing at no screws, never on report. Result? Twelve months later he's back at Hollesley Bay open prison, with only nine months left to serve.'

'And once he was back at Hollesley Bay, did he try to contact Karen?'

'No, didn't put in a request for a visit. In fact, never even mentioned her name.'

'So what was his game?' I asked, slipping into the prison jargon.

'He only had one game all along, Jeff: he wanted to get himself transferred to the enhancement block, on the other side of the prison, didn't he.'

'I've lost you,' I admitted.

'All part of his master plan, wasn't it? When you first arrive at Hollesley Bay, which, don't forget, is an open nick, you're allocated a room in one of the two main blocks.'

'Are you?'

'Yeah, north and south block. But if you get enhanced – another three more months of behaving like a saint – then they move you across to the enhancement block, which gives you even more privileges.'

'Like what?'

'You can have a visit from a mate every Saturday. Pete wasn't interested. You can go home once a month on a Sunday – he's still not interested. You can apply for a job outside of the prison during the week – still no interest, even though it would of given him a chance to pick up an extra bob or two before he's released.'

'Then why bother to earn all those privileges if you don't plan to take advantage of them?' I asked.

'Weren't part of Pete's master plan, was it? Trouble with you, Jeff, is that you don't think like a criminal.'

'So why was Pete so keen to get himself transferred to the enhancement block?'

'Good question at last, Jeff, but for that you'll need a little background. Pete 'ad already worked out that over on the enhancement block they 'ad five screws on duty during the day, but only two at night, on account of the fact that if a prisoner reaches enhanced status he can be trusted, not to mention how short-staffed the prison service is. And don't forget that, in an open nick, there are no cells, no bars, no keys and no perimeter walls, so anyone can abscond.'

'So why don't they?' I asked.

'Because not many cons who've made it to an open prison are that interested in escaping.'

'Why not?'

'Logic, isn't it? They're coming to the end of their sentence, and if they're caught, and nine out of ten of the morons are, you're sent straight back to a closed nick, with extra time added to your sentence. So forget it, it's just not worth it. I remember a con called Dale. What a muppet he was. He only had three weeks left to serve, when he—'

'Pete,' I tried again.

'You're such an impatient bastard, Jeff, and it's not as if you're going anywhere. So where was I?'

'Only two officers on duty in the enhancement block at night,' I said, checking my notes.

'Oh, yeah. But even on the enhancement block you have to report to the front office at seven in the morning, and then again at nine each night. Now Pete, as I told you, 'ad a job in the prison stores, handing out clothes to the new cons, and supplying laundry once a week for the regulars, so the screws always knew where he was, which was also part of Pete's plan. But if he hadn't reported to the front office at seven in the morning and then again at nine at night, he would have been put on report, which would have meant he'd be sent back to north block with all his privileges removed. So Pete never once misses a roll call, his cell was always spick and span, and his light is always out long before eleven.'

'All part of Pete's master plan?'

'You catch on fast,' said Mick. 'But then Pete came up against an obstacle – that the right word, Jeff?' I nodded, not wishing to interrupt his flow. 'During the night, one of the screws would walk round the block at one o'clock and then return again at four in the morning, to check that every con was in bed and asleep. All the screw has to do is pull back the curtain on the outside of the door, look through the glass panel and shine his torch on the bed to make sure the con is snoring away. Have I ever told you about the con who was caught in his room, with a—'

'Pete,' I said, not even looking up at Mick.

'Pete would lay awake at night until the first screw came round at one o'clock to make sure he was in his room. The screw lifts the curtain, shines the torch on his bed and then disappears. Pete would then go back to sleep, but he always set his alarm for ten to four when he'd carry out the same routine. A different screw always turns up at four to check you're still in bed. It took Pete just over a month to work out that there were two screws, Mr Chambers and Mr Davis, who didn't bother to make the nightly rounds and check everyone was in bed. Chambers used to fall asleep and Davis couldn't be dragged away from the TV. After that, all Pete had to do was wait until the two of them were on duty the same night.'

With only about six weeks to go before Pete was due to be released, he returned to the enhancement block after work to find that Chambers and Davis were the duty officers that night. When Pete signed the roll-call sheet at nine, Mr Chambers was already watching a football match on TV, and Mr Davis had his feet up on the table drinking a Coke and reading the sports pages of the *Sun*. Pete went up to his room, watched TV till just after ten, and then turned off his light. He got into bed and pulled the blanket over him, but kept on his tracksuit and trainers. He waited until a few minutes after one before he crept out into the corridor and checked to make sure no one was around – not a sign of Chambers or Davis. He then went to the end of the corridor, opened the fire-escape door, and disappeared down the back stairs, leaving a wedge of paper in the door, before he set off on an eight-mile run into Woodbridge.

No one can be sure when Pete got back that night, but he reported into the office as usual at seven the next morning. Mr Chambers ticked off his name. When Pete glanced down at the screw's clipboard, all four of his roll-call columns – nine, one, four and seven – had a tick in every box. Pete had breakfast in the canteen before reporting to the stores for work.

'So he got away with it?'

'Not quite,' said Mick. 'Later that morning the cops turn up in numbers and begin crawling all over the place, but they're only looking for one man. They end up in the stores, arrest Pete and haul him off to Woodbridge nick for questioning. They interrogate him for hours about the deaths of Brian Powell and Karen Slater, both found strangled in their bed. Rumour has it that they were having it off at the time. Pete stuck to the same line: "Can't have been me, guv. I was banged up in prison at the time. You only have to ask Mr Chambers and Mr Davis, the officers who were on duty that night." The copper in charge of the case visited the enhancement block and checked the roll-call sheet. Brian and the tart were strangled some time between three and five, according to the police doctor, so if Chambers saw Pete asleep in bed at four, he couldn't have been in Woodbridge at the same time, could he? Logic, isn't it?

'An independent inquiry was set up by the Home Office. Chambers and Davis both confirmed that they'd checked every prisoner at one o'clock and then again at four, and on both occasions Pete had been asleep in his room. Several of the other cons were only too happy to appear in front of the inquiry and confirm they'd been woken by the flashlight, when Chambers and Davis did their rounds. This only strengthened Pete's defence. So the inquiry concluded that Pete must have been in his bed at one o'clock and four o'clock on the night in question, so he couldn't have committed the murders.'

'So he got away with it,' I repeated.

'Depends on how you describe got away with it,' said Mick, 'because although the police never charged Pete, the copper in charge of the case later made a statement saying that they'd closed their inquiries, as there was no one else they wanted to interview – hint, hint. That wasn't what you call a good career move for Chambers and Davis, so they set about stitching Pete up.'

'But Pete only had six weeks to serve before he was due to be released,' I reminded Mick, 'and he was always as good as gold.'

'True, but another screw, a mate of Davis's, reported Pete for stealing a pair of jeans from the stores just a few days before he was due for release. Pete was carted off to segregation and the governor had him transported back to Lincoln nick even before they'd served up tea that night, with another three months added to his sentence.'

'So he ended up having to serve another three months?'

'That was six years ago,' said Mick. 'And Pete's still banged up in Lincoln.'

'So how do they manage that?'

'The screws just come up with a new charge every few weeks, so that whenever Pete comes up on report the governor adds another three months to his sentence. My bet is Pete's stuck in Lincoln for the rest of his life. What a liberty.'

'But how do they get away with it?' I asked.

'Haven't you been listening to anything I've been saying,

Jeff? If two screws say that's what happened, then that's what happened,' repeated Mick, 'and no con will be able to tell you any different. Understood?'

'Understood,' I replied.

On 12 September 2002 Prison Service Instruction No. 47/2002 stated that the judgement of the European Court of Human Rights in the case of Ezeh & Connors ruled that, where an offence was so extreme as to result in a punishment of additional days, the protections inherent in Article 6 of the European Convention of Human Rights applied. A hearing must be conducted by an independent and impartial tribunal, and prisoners are entitled to legal assistance at such hearings.

Pete Bailey was released from Lincoln prison on 19 October 2002.

A Greek Tragedy

ΤΙ ΦΡΙΚΗ !

ΑΓΩΝΙΑ

GEORGE TSAKIRIS IS NOT ONE of those Greeks you need to beware of when he is bearing gifts.

George is fortunate enough to spend half his life in London and the other half in his native Athens. He and his two younger brothers, Nicholas and Andrew, run between them a highly successful salvage company, which they inherited from their father.

George and I first met many years ago during a charity function in aid of the Red Cross. His wife Christina was a member of the organizing committee, and she had invited me to be the auctioneer.

At almost every charity auction I have conducted over the years, there has been one item for which you just can't find a buyer, and that night was no exception. On this occasion, another member of the committee had donated a landscape painting that had been daubed by their daughter and would have been orphaned at a village fete. I felt, long before I climbed up onto the rostrum and searched around the room for an opening bid, that I was going to be left stranded once again.

However, I had not taken George's generosity into consideration.

'Do I have an opening bid of one thousand pounds?' I enquired hopefully, but no one came to my rescue. 'One thousand?' I repeated, trying not to sound desperate, and just as I was about to give up, out of a sea of black dinner jackets a hand was raised. It was George's.

'Two thousand,' I suggested, but no one was interested

in my suggestion. 'Three thousand,' I said looking directly at George. Once again his hand shot up. 'Four thousand,' I declared confidently, but my confidence was short-lived, so I returned my attention to George. 'Five thousand,' I demanded, and once again he obliged. Despite his wife being on the committee, I felt enough was enough. 'Sold for five thousand pounds, to Mr George Tsakiris,' I announced to loud applause, and a look of relief on Christina's face.

Since then poor George, or to be more accurate rich George, has regularly come to my rescue at such functions, often purchasing ridiculous items, for which I had no hope of arousing even an opening bid. Heaven knows how much I've prised out of the man over the years, all in the name of charity.

Last year, after I'd sold him a trip to Uzbekistan, plus two economy tickets courtesy of Aeroflot, I made my way across to his table to thank him for his generosity.

'No need to thank me,' George said as I sat down beside him. 'Not a day goes by without me realizing how fortunate I've been, even how lucky I am to be alive.'

'Lucky to be alive?' I said, smelling a story.

Let me say at this point that the tired old cliché, that there's a book in every one of us, is a fallacy. However, I have come to accept over the years that most people have experienced a single incident in their life that is unique to them, and well worthy of a short story. George was no exception.

'Lucky to be alive,' I repeated.

George and his two brothers divide their business responsibilities equally: George runs the London office, while Nicholas remains in Athens, which allows Andrew to roam around the globe whenever one of their sinking clients needs to be kept afloat.

Although George maintains establishments in London, New York and Saint-Paul-de-Vence, he still regularly returns to the home of the gods, so that he can keep in touch with his large family. Have you noticed how wealthy people always seem to have large families?

At a recent Red Cross Ball, held at the Dorchester, no one came to my rescue when I offered a British Lions' rugby shirt – following their tour of New Zealand – that had been signed by the entire losing team. George was nowhere to be seen, as he'd returned to his native land to attend the wedding of a favourite niece. If it hadn't been for an incident that took place at that wedding, I would never have seen George again. Incidentally, I failed to get even an opening bid for the British Lions' shirt.

George's niece, Isabella, was a native of Cephalonia, one of the most beautiful of the Greek islands, set like a magnificent jewel in the Ionian Sea. Isabella had fallen in love with the son of a local wine grower, and as her father was no longer alive, George had offered to host the wedding reception, which was to be held at the bridegroom's home.

In England it is the custom to invite family and friends to attend the wedding service, followed by a reception, which is often held in a marquee on the lawn of the home of the daughter's parents. When the lawn is not large enough, the festivities are moved to the village hall. After the formal speeches have been delivered, and a reasonable period of time has elapsed, the bride and groom depart for their honeymoon, and fairly soon afterwards the guests make their way home.

Leaving a party before midnight is not a tradition the Greeks have come to terms with. They assume that any festivities after a wedding will continue long into the early hours of the following morning, especially when the bridegroom owns a vineyard. Whenever two natives are married on a Greek island, an invitation is automatically extended to the locals so that they can share in a glass of wine and toast the bride's health. Wedding crasher is not an expression that the Greeks are familiar with. The bride's mother doesn't bother sending out gold-embossed cards with RSVP in the lower left-hand corner for one simple reason: no one would bother to reply, but everyone would still turn up.

Another difference between our two great nations is that it is quite unnecessary to hire a marquee or rent the village hall for the festivities, as the Greeks are unlikely to encounter the occasional downpour, especially in the middle of summer – about ten months. Anyone can be a weather forecaster in Greece.

The night before the wedding was due to take place, Christina suggested to her husband that, as host, it might be wise for him to remain sober. Someone, she added, should keep an eye on the proceedings, bearing in mind the bridegroom's occupation. George reluctantly agreed.

The marriage service was held in the island's small church, and the pews were packed with invited, and uninvited, guests long before vespers were chanted. George accepted with his usual grace that he was about to host a rather large gathering. He looked on with pride as his favourite niece and her lover were joined together in holy matrimony. Although Isabella was hidden behind a veil of white lace, her beauty had long been acknowledged by the young men of the island. Her fiancé, Alexis Kulukundis, was tall and slim, and his waistline did not yet bear testament to the fact that he was heir to a vineyard.

And so to the service. Here, for a moment, the English and the Greeks come together, but not for long. The ceremony was conducted by bearded priests attired in long golden surplices and tall black hats. The sweet smell of incense from swinging burners wafted throughout the church, as the priest in the most ornately embroidered gown, who also boasted the longest beard, presided over the marriage, to the accompaniment of murmured psalms and prayers.

George and Christina were among the first to leave the church once the service was over, as they wanted to be back at the house in good time to welcome their guests.

The bridegroom's rambling old farmhouse nestled on the slopes of a hill above the plains of the vineyard. The spacious garden, surrounded by terraced olive groves, was full of chattering well-wishers long before the bride and bridegroom made their entrance. George must have shaken over two hundred hands, before the appearance of Mr and Mrs Kulukundis was announced by a large group of the bridegroom's rowdy friends who were firing pistols into the air in celebration; a Greek tradition which I suspect would not go down well on an English country lawn, and certainly not in the village hall.

With the exception of the immediate family and those guests selected to sit on the long top table by the side of the dance floor, there were, in fact, very few people George had ever set eyes on before.

George took his place at the centre of the top table, with Isabella on his right and Alexis on his left. Once they were all seated, course after course of overladen dishes was set before his guests, and the wine flowed as if it were a Bacchanalian orgy rather than a small island wedding. But then Bacchus – the god of wine – was a Greek.

When, in the distance, the cathedral clock chimed eleven times, George hinted to the best man that perhaps the time had come for him to make his speech. Unlike George, he *was* drunk, and certainly wouldn't be able to recall his words the following morning. The groom followed, and when he tried to express how fortunate he was to have married such a wonderful girl, once again his young friends leapt onto the dance floor and fired their pistols in the air.

George was the final speaker. Aware of the late hour, the pleading look in his guests' eyes, and the half-empty bottles littering the tables around him, he satisfied himself with wishing the bride and groom a blessed life, a euphemism for lots of children. He then invited those who still could to rise and toast the health of the bride and groom. Isabella and Alexis, they all cried, if not in unison.

Once the applause had died down, the band struck up. The groom immediately rose from his place, and, turning to his bride, asked her for the first dance. The newly married couple stepped onto the dance floor, accompanied by another volley of gunfire. The groom's parents followed next, and a few minutes later George and Christina joined them.

Once George had danced with his wife, the bride and the groom's mother, he made his way back to his place in the centre seat of the top table, shaking hands along the way with the many guests who wished to thank him.

George was pouring himself a glass of red wine – after all, he had performed all his official duties – when the old man appeared.

George leapt to his feet the moment he saw him standing alone at the entrance to the garden. He placed his glass back on the table and walked quickly across the lawn to welcome the unexpected guest.

Andreas Nikolaides leant heavily on his two walking sticks. George didn't like to think how long it must have taken the old man to climb up the path from his little cottage, halfway down the mountain. George bowed low and greeted a man who was a legend on the island of Cephalonia as well as in the streets of Athens, despite the fact that he had never once left his native soil. Whenever Andreas was asked why, he simply replied, 'Why would anyone leave Paradise?'

In 1942, when the island of Cephalonia had been overrun by the Germans, Andreas Nikolaides escaped to the hills and, at the age of twenty-three, became the leader of the resistance movement. He never left those hills during the long occupation of his homeland and, despite a handsome bounty being placed on his head, did not return to his people until, like Alexander, he had driven the intruders back into the sea.

Once peace was declared in 1945, Andreas returned in triumph. He was elected mayor of Cephalonia, a position which he held, unopposed, for the next thirty years. Now that he was well into his eighties, there wasn't a family on

Cephalonia who did not feel in debt to him, and few who didn't claim to be a relative.

'Good evening, sir,' said George stepping forward to greet the old man. 'We are honoured by your presence at my niece's wedding.'

'It is I who should be honoured,' replied Andreas, returning the bow. 'Your niece's grandfather fought and died by my side. In any case,' he added with a wink, 'it's an old man's prerogative to kiss every new bride on the island.'

George guided his distinguished guest slowly round the outside of the dance floor and on towards the top table. Guests stopped dancing and applauded as the old man passed by. George insisted that Andreas take his place in the centre of the top table, so that he could be seated between the bride and groom. Andreas reluctantly took his host's place of honour. When Isabella turned to see who had been placed next to her, she burst into tears and threw her arms around the old man. 'Your presence has made the wedding complete,' she said.

Andreas smiled and, looking up at George, whispered, 'I only wish I'd had that effect on women when I was younger.'

George left Andreas seated in his place at the centre of the top table, chatting happily to the bride and groom. He picked up a plate and walked slowly down a table laden with food. George took his time selecting only the most delicate morsels that he felt the old man would find easy to digest. Finally he chose a bottle of vintage wine from a case that his own father had presented to him on the day of his wedding. George turned back to take the offering to his honoured guest just as the chimes on the cathedral clock struck twelve, hailing the dawn of a new day.

Once more, the young men of the island charged onto the dance floor and fired their pistols into the air, to the cheers of the assembled guests. George frowned, but then for a moment recalled his own youth. Carrying the plate in one hand and a bottle of wine in the other, he continued walking back towards his place in the centre of the table, now occupied by Andreas Nikolaides.

Suddenly, without warning, one of the young bandoliers, who'd had a little too much to drink, ran forward and tripped on the edge of the dance floor, just as he was discharging his last shot. George froze in horror when he saw the old man slump forward in his chair, his head falling onto the table. George dropped the bottle of wine and the plate of food onto the grass as the bride screamed. He ran quickly to the centre of the table, but it was too late. Andreas Nikolaides was already dead.

The large, exuberant gathering was suddenly in turmoil, some screaming, some weeping, while others fell to their knees, but the majority were hushed into a shocked, sombre silence, unable to grasp what had taken place.

George bent down over the body and lifted the old man into his arms. He carried him slowly across the lawn, the guests forming a corridor of bowed heads, as he walked towards the house.

George had just bid five thousand pounds for two seats at a West End musical that had already closed when he told me the story of Andreas Nikolaides.

'They say of Andreas that he saved the life of everyone on that island,' George remarked as he raised his glass in memory of the old man. He paused before adding, 'Mine included.'

The Commissioner

'WHY DOES HE WANT to see me?' asked the Commissioner.

'He says it's a personal matter.'

'How long has he been out of prison?'

The Commissioner's secretary glanced down at Raj Malik's file. 'He was released six weeks ago.'

Naresh Kumar stood up, pushed back his chair and began pacing around the room; something he always did whenever he needed to think a problem through. He had convinced himself – well, almost – that by regularly walking round the office he was carrying out some form of exercise. Long gone were the days when he could play a game of hockey in the afternoon, three games of squash the same evening and then jog back to police headquarters. With each new promotion, more silver braid had been sewn on his epaulet and more inches appeared around his waist.

'Once I've retired and have more time, I'll start training again,' he told his number two, Anil Khan. Neither of them believed it.

The Commissioner stopped to stare out of the window and look down on the teeming streets of Mumbai some fourteen floors below him: ten million inhabitants who ranged from some of the poorest to some of the wealthiest people on earth. From beggars to billionaires, and it was his responsibility to police all of them. His predecessor had left him with the words: 'At best, you can hope to keep the lid on the kettle.' In less than a year, when he passed on the responsibility to his deputy, he would be proffering the same advice.

Naresh Kumar had been a policeman all his life, like his

father before him, and what he most enjoyed about the job was its sheer unpredictability. Today was no different, although a great deal had changed since the time when you could clip a child across the ear if you caught him stealing a mango. If you tried that today, the parents would sue you for assault and the child would claim he needed coun-selling. But, fortunately, his deputy Anil Khan had come to accept that guns on the street, drug dealers and the war against terrorism were all part of a modern policeman's lot.

The Commissioner's thoughts returned to Raj Malik, a man he'd been responsible for sending to prison on three occasions in the past thirty years. Why did the old con want to see him? There was only one way he was going to find out. He turned to face his secretary. 'Make an appointment for me to see Malik, but only allocate him fifteen minutes.'

The Commissioner had forgotten that he'd agreed to see Malik until his secretary placed the file on his desk a few minutes before he was due to arrive.

'If he's one minute late,' said the Commissioner, 'cancel the appointment.'

'He's already waiting in the lobby, sir,' she replied.

Kumar frowned, and flicked open the file. He began to familiarize himself with Malik's criminal record, most of which he was able to recall because on two occasions – one when he had been a detective sergeant, and the second, a newly promoted inspector – he had been the arresting officer.

Malik was a white-collar criminal who was well capable of holding down a serious job. However, as a young man he had quickly discovered that he possessed enough charm and native cunning to con naive people, particularly old ladies, out of large sums of money, without having to exert a great deal of effort.

His first scam was not unique to Mumbai. All he required was a small printing press, some headed notepaper and a list of widows. Once he'd obtained the latter – on a daily basis from the obituary column of the *Mumbai Times* – he was in business. He specialized in selling shares in overseas companies that didn't exist. This provided him with a regular income, until he tried to sell some stock to the widow of another conman.

When Malik was charged, he admitted to having made over a million rupees, but the Commissioner suspected that it was a far larger sum; after all, how many widows were willing to admit they had been taken in by Malik's charms? Malik was sentenced to five years in Pune jail and Kumar lost touch with him for nearly a decade.

Malik was back inside again after he'd been arrested for selling flats in a high-rise apartment block on land that turned out to be a swamp. This time the judge sent him down for seven years. Another decade passed.

Malik's third offence was even more ingenious, and resulted in an even longer sentence. He appointed himself a life-assurance broker. Unfortunately the annuities never matured – except for Malik.

His barrister suggested to the presiding judge that his client had cleared around twelve million rupees, but as little of the money was available to be given back to those who were still living, the judge felt that twelve years would be a fair return on this particular policy.

By the time the Commissioner had turned the last page, he was still puzzled as to why Malik could possibly want to see him. He pressed a button under the desk to alert his secretary that he was ready for his next appointment.

Commissioner Kumar glanced up as the door opened. He stared at a man he barely recognized. Malik must have been ten years younger than he was, but they would have passed for contemporaries. Although Malik's file stated that he was five foot nine and weighed a hundred and seventy pounds, the man who walked into his office did not fit that description.

The old con's skin was lined and parched, and his back was hunched, making him appear small and shrunken. Half a life spent in jail had taken its toll. He wore a white shirt that was frayed at the collar and cuffs, and a baggy suit that might at some time in the past have been tailored for him. This was not the self-confident man the Commissioner had first arrested over thirty years ago, a man who always had an answer for everything.

Malik gave the Commissioner a weak smile as he came to a halt in front of him.

'Thank you for agreeing to see me, sir,' he said quietly. Even his voice had shrunk.

The Commissioner nodded, waved him to the chair on the other side of his desk and said, 'I have a busy morning ahead of me, Malik, so perhaps you could get straight to the point.'

'Of course, sir,' Malik replied, even before he'd sat down. 'It's simply that I am looking for a job.'

The Commissioner had considered many reasons why Malik might want to see him, but seeking employment had not been among them.

'Before you laugh,' continued Malik, 'please allow me to put my case.'

The Commissioner leant back in his chair and placed the tips of his fingers together, as if in silent prayer.

'I have spent too much of my life in jail,' said Malik. He paused. 'I've recently reached the age of fifty, and can assure you that I have no desire to go back inside again.'

The Commissioner nodded, but didn't express an opinion.

'Last week, Commissioner,' continued Malik, 'you addressed the annual general meeting of the Mumbai Chamber of Commerce. I read your speech in the *Times* with great interest. You expressed the view to the leading businessmen of this city that they should consider employing people who had served a prison sentence – give them a second chance, you said, or they will simply take the easy option and return to a life of crime. A sentiment I was able to agree with.'

'But I also pointed out,' interrupted the Commissioner, 'that I was only referring to first offenders.'

'Exactly my point,' countered Malik. 'If you consider there is a problem for first offenders, just imagine what I come up against, when I apply for a job.' Malik paused and straightened his tie before he continued. 'If your speech was sincere and not just delivered for public consumption, then perhaps you should heed your own advice, and lead by example.'

'And what did you have in mind?' asked the Commissioner. 'Because you certainly do not possess the ideal qualifications for police work.'

Malik ignored the Commissioner's sarcasm and ploughed boldly on. 'In the same paper in which your speech was reported, there was an advertisement for a filing clerk in your records department. I began life as a clerk for the P & O Shipping Company, right here in this city. I think that you will find, were you to check the records, that I carried out that job with enthusiasm and efficiency, and on that occasion left with an unblemished record.'

'But that was over thirty years ago,' said the Commissioner, not needing to refer to the file in front of him.

'Then I will have to end my career as I began it,' replied Malik, 'as a filing clerk.'

The Commissioner didn't speak for some time while he considered Malik's proposition. He finally leant forward, placed his hands on the desk, and said, 'I will give some thought to your request, Malik. Does my secretary know how to get in touch with you?'

'Yes, she does, sir,' Malik replied as he rose from his place. 'Every night I can be found at the YMCA hostel on Victoria Street.' He paused. 'I have no plans to move in the near future.'

Over lunch in the officers' dining room, Commissioner Kumar briefed his deputy on the meeting with Malik.

Anil Khan burst out laughing. 'Hoist with your own petard, Chief,' he said with considerable feeling.

'True enough,' replied the Commissioner as he helped himself to another spoonful of rice, 'and when you take over from me next year, this little episode will serve to remind you of the consequences of your words, especially when they are delivered in public.'

'Does that mean that you are seriously considering employing the man?' asked Khan, as he stared across the table at his boss.

'Possibly,' replied Kumar. 'Why, are you against the idea?'

'You are in your last year as Commissioner,' Khan reminded him, 'with an enviable reputation for probity and competence. Why take a risk that might jeopardize such a fine record?'

'I feel that's a little over-dramatic,' said the Commissioner. 'Malik's a broken man, which you would have seen for yourself had you been present at the meeting.'

'Once a conman, always a conman,' replied Khan. 'So I repeat, why take the risk?'

'Perhaps because it's the correct course of action, given the circumstances,' replied the Commissioner. 'If I turn Malik down, why should anyone bother to listen to my opinion ever again?'

'But a filing clerk's job is particularly sensitive,' remonstrated Khan. 'Malik would have access to information that should only be seen by those whose discretion is not in question.'

'I've already considered that,' said the Commissioner. 'We have two filing departments: one in this building, which is, as you rightly point out, highly sensitive, and another based on the outskirts of the city that deals only with dead cases, which have either been solved or are no longer being followed up.'

'I still wouldn't risk it,' said Khan as he placed his knife and fork back on the plate.

'I've cut down the risk even more,' responded the Commissioner. 'I'm going to place Malik on a month's trial. A supervisor will keep a close eye on him, and then report directly back to me. Should Malik put so much as a toe over the line, he'll be back on the street the same day.'

'I still wouldn't risk it,' repeated Khan.

On the first of the month, Raj Malik reported for work at the police records department on 47 Mahatma Drive, on the outskirts of the city. His hours were eight a.m. to six p.m. six days a week, with a salary of nine hundred rupees a month. Malik's daily responsibility was to visit every police station in the outer district, on his bicycle, and collect any dead files. He would then pass them over to his supervisor, who would file them away in the basement, rarely to be referred to again.

At the end of his first month, Malik's supervisor reported back to the Commissioner as instructed. 'I wish I had a dozen Maliks,' he told the chief. 'Unlike today's young, he's always on time, doesn't take extended breaks, and never complains when you ask him to do something not covered by his job description. With your permission,' the supervisor added, 'I would like to put his pay up to one thousand rupees a month.'

The supervisor's second report was even more glowing. 'I lost a member of staff through illness last week, and Malik took over several of his responsibilities and somehow still managed to cover both jobs.'

The supervisor's report at the end of Malik's third month was so flattering that when the Commissioner addressed the annual dinner of the Mumbai Rotary Club, not only did he appeal to its members to reach out their hands to ex-offenders, but he went on to assure his audience that he had heeded his own advice and been able to prove one of his long-held theories. If you give former prisoners a real chance, they won't reoffend.

The following day, the *Mumbai Times* ran the headline:
COMMISSIONER LEADS BY EXAMPLE

Kumar's sentiments were reported in great detail, alongside a photo of Raj Malik, with the caption, *a reformed character*. The Commissioner placed the article on his deputy's desk.

Malik waited until his supervisor had left for his lunch break. He always drove home just after twelve and spent an hour with his wife. Malik watched as his boss's car disappeared out of sight before he slipped back down to the basement. He placed a stack of papers that needed to be filed on the corner of the counter, just in case someone came in unannounced and asked what he was up to.

He then walked across to the old wooden cabinets that were stacked one on top of the other. He bent down and pulled open one of the files. After nine months he had reached the letter P and still hadn't come across the ideal candidate. He had already thumbed through dozens of Patels during the previous week, dismissing most of them as either irrelevant or inconsequential for what he had in mind. That was until he reached one with the first initials H.H.

Malik removed the thick file from the cabinet, placed it on the counter-top and slowly began to turn the pages. He didn't need to read the details a second time to know that he'd hit the jackpot.

He scribbled down the name, address and telephone numbers neatly on a slip of paper, and then returned the file to its place in the cabinet. He smiled. During his tea break, Malik would call and make an appointment to see Mr H.H. Patel.

With only a few weeks to go before his retirement, Commissioner Kumar had quite forgotten about his prodigy. That was until he received a call from Mr H.H. Patel, one of the city's leading bankers. Mr Patel was requesting an urgent meeting with the Commissioner – to discuss a personal matter.

Commissioner Kumar looked upon H.H. not only as a friend, but as a man of integrity, and certainly not someone who would use the word urgent without good reason.

Kumar rose from behind his desk as Mr Patel entered the room. He ushered his old friend to a comfortable chair in the corner of the room and pressed a button under his desk. Moments later his secretary appeared with a pot of tea and a plate of Bath Oliver biscuits. The Deputy Commissioner followed in her wake.

'I thought it might be wise to have Anil Khan present for this meeting, H.H., as he will be taking over from me in a few weeks' time.'

'I know of your reputation, of course,' said Mr Patel, shaking Khan warmly by the hand, 'and I am delighted that you are able to join us.'

Once the secretary had served the three men with tea, she left the room. The moment the door was closed, Commissioner Kumar dispensed with any more small talk. 'You asked to see me urgently, H.H., concerning a personal matter.'

'Yes,' replied Patel. 'I thought you ought to know that I had a visit yesterday from someone who claims to work for you.'

The Commissioner raised an eyebrow.

'A Mr Raj Malik.'

'He is a junior filing clerk in the—'

'In a private capacity, he was at pains to emphasize.'

The Commissioner began tapping the armrest of his chair with the palm of his right hand, as Patel continued. 'Malik said that you were in possession of a file that showed that I was under investigation for money laundering.'

'You were, H.H.,' said the Commissioner, with his usual candour. 'Following nine/eleven, the Minister of Internal Affairs instructed me to investigate any organization which dealt in large sums of cash. That included casinos, racetracks and, in your case, the Bank of Mumbai. A member of my team interviewed your chief teller and advised him about what he should be on the lookout for, and I personally signed the clearance certificate for your company.'

'I remember, you briefed me at the time,' said Patel, 'but your fellow, Malik –'

'He's not my fellow.'

'– said that he could arrange to have my file destroyed.' He paused. 'For a small consideration.'

'He said what?' said Kumar almost exploding out of his chair.

'How small?' asked Deputy Commissioner Khan calmly.

'Ten million rupees,' replied Patel.

'H.H., I don't know what to say,' said the Commissioner.

'You don't have to say anything,' said Patel, 'because it never crossed my mind, even for a moment, that you could be involved in anything quite so stupid, and I told Malik as much.'

'I am grateful,' said the Commissioner.

'No need to be,' said Patel, 'but I did think that perhaps others, less charitable . . .' He paused. 'Especially as Malik's visit came so close to your retirement . . .' He hesitated again. 'And were the press to get hold of the story, it might so easily be misunderstood.'

'I am grateful for your concern, and the speed with which you have acted,' said Kumar. 'I will remain eternally in your debt.'

'I want nothing more than to be sure that this city rightly remains eternally in your debt,' said Patel, 'so that when you leave office it will be in a blaze of glory, rather than with question marks hanging over your head, which, as we both know, would linger on long after your retirement.'

The Deputy Commissioner nodded his agreement as Patel rose from his place.

'You know, Naresh,' Patel said, turning to face the Commissioner, 'I would never have agreed to see the damn man, if you had not spoken so highly of him in your speech to the Rotary Club last month. He even produced the article in the *Mumbai Times*. I therefore assumed that the fellow had come with your blessing.' Mr Patel turned to face Khan. 'May I wish you luck when you take over as Commissioner,' he added, shaking hands with the deputy. 'I don't envy you having to follow such a fine man.' Kumar smiled for the first time that morning.

'I'll be back in a moment,' the Commissioner said to his deputy as he left his office to accompany Patel to the front door.

The Deputy Commissioner stared out of the window as he waited for the Chief to return. He munched on a biscuit as he mulled over several possible alternatives. By the time the Commissioner walked back into the room, Khan knew exactly what had to be done. But would he be able to convince his boss this time?

'I'll have Malik arrested and behind bars within the hour,' said the Commissioner as he picked up the phone on his desk.

'I wonder, sir,' said Deputy Khan quietly, 'if that's the best course of action – given the circumstances?'

'I don't have much choice,' said the Commissioner as he began dialling.

'You may be right,' said Khan, 'but before you make such an irrevocable decision, perhaps we should consider how this is all going to play –' he paused – 'with the press.'

'They'll have a field day,' said Kumar as he replaced the

phone and began pacing around the room. 'They won't be able to make up their minds if I should be hanged as a crook who's willing to accept bribes, or dismissed as the most naive fool ever to hold the office of Commissioner. Neither scenario bears thinking about.'

'But we have to think about it,' insisted Deputy Khan, 'because your enemies – and even good men have enemies – will happily settle for someone who's willing to take kickbacks, while your friends will not be able to deny the lesser charge of naivety.'

'But surely after forty years of service, people will believe . . .'

'People will believe whatever they want to believe,' said Khan, confirming the Commissioner's worst fears, 'and certainly you won't be able to send Malik back to prison until he's been given the chance to appear in a witness box and tell the world his side of the story.'

'But who would believe that old—'

'No smoke without fire, they'll be whispering in the corridors of the law courts, and that will be tame compared with the headlines in the morning papers once Malik has spent a couple of days in the witness box being questioned by a friendly barrister who sees you as nothing more than a stepping stone in his career.'

Kumar continued to pace around the room, but didn't respond.

'Let me try and second-guess the headlines that would follow such a cross-examination.' Khan paused before saying, '"Commissioner accepts bribes to destroy friends' files" might be the headline in the *Times*, while the tabloids will surely be a little more colourful – "Bung money left in Commissioner's office by delivery boy", or perhaps

"Commissioner Kumar employs ex-con to carry out his dirty work"?'

'I think I've got the picture,' said the Commissioner, as he sank back into the chair next to Khan. 'So what the hell am I supposed to do about it?'

'What you've always done in the past,' Khan replied. 'Play it by the book.'

The Commissioner looked across at his deputy quizzically. 'What do you have in mind?'

'Malik,' shouted the supervisor at the top of his voice, even before he'd put the phone down. 'Commissioner Kumar wants to see you, immediately.'

'Did he say why?' asked Malik nervously.

'No, he's not in the habit of confiding in me,' replied the supervisor, 'but don't hang about because he's not a man who likes to be kept waiting.'

'Yes, sir,' Malik replied. He closed the file he'd been working on and placed it back on the supervisor's desk. He walked across to his locker, removed his bicycle clips and left the building without another word. It wasn't until he was outside on the pavement that he began to shake. Had they caught on to his latest scam? Not that it had proved that successful. He unlocked the chain that was attached to the railings and began to consider his options. Should he make a run for it, or simply try to brazen it out? He hadn't been left with a lot of choice. After all, where would he run to? And even if he did decide to run, it would only be a matter of days, perhaps hours, before they caught up with him.

Malik slipped on his bicycle clips, mounted his third-hand Raleigh Lenton and began to pedal slowly towards the city centre. The dusty brown roads were teeming with other bicycles, cars and countless numbers of people, all heading in different directions. The incessant honking of horns, the multitude of different smells, the beating down of the sun and the bustle of everyday life ensured that Mumbai was like no other city on earth. Street traders thrust out their arms as Malik passed, trying to sell him their wares, while beggars with no arms ran by his side, not assisting his progress. Should he come clean and admit what he'd been up to?

He cycled for a few more yards. No, never admit to anything, a golden rule that he'd learnt after long years in prison. He swerved to avoid a cow and nearly fell off.

Assume they know nothing until you're cornered. Even then, deny everything. As he rounded the next corner, police headquarters loomed up in front of him. If he was going to make a dash for it, it would have to be now or never. He pedalled on, until he was only a few yards away from the steps leading up to the front entrance. He tugged firmly on the tired brake handles until his bike came to a slow, unsteady halt. He climbed off, and padlocked his one asset to the nearest railing. He walked slowly up the steps to police headquarters, pushed his way through the swing doors and headed nervously towards the reception desk. He told the duty officer his name. Perhaps there had been a mistake.

'I have an appointment with—'

'Ah, yes,' the duty officer replied ominously, without needing to consult his roster. 'The Commissioner is waiting to see you. You'll find his office is on the fourteenth floor.'

Malik turned and began walking towards the lifts, aware that the duty officer's eyes never left him. Malik glanced at the front door. This would be his last chance to escape, he thought, as the doors of one of the lifts slid open. He stepped into a crowded elevator, which made several stops on its slow interrupted journey to the fourteenth floor. By the time Malik reached the top floor, he was sweating profusely, and it wasn't just the crowded space and lack of air conditioning that caused his unease.

When the doors finally parted, he was on his own. Malik stepped out onto the only thickly carpeted corridor in the building. He looked around and then recalled his last visit. He began to walk slowly towards an office at the far end of the corridor. The word Commissioner was printed in bold stencilled letters on the door.

Malik knocked quietly – perhaps something more important had arisen, causing the Commissioner to leave the office without warning. He heard a female voice invite him to enter. He opened the door to find the Commissioner's secretary seated behind her desk, tapping away furiously. She stopped typing the moment she saw Malik.

'The Commissioner is expecting you,' was all she offered. She didn't smile and she didn't frown as she rose from her place. Perhaps she was unaware of his fate. The secretary disappeared through another door and returned almost immediately. 'The Commissioner will see you now, Mr Malik,' she said, and held the door open for him.

Malik walked into the Commissioner's office, to find him seated at his desk, eyes down, studying an open file. He raised his head, looked directly at him and said, 'Have a seat, Malik.' Not Raj, not Mr, just Malik.

Malik slipped into the chair opposite the Commissioner. He sat in silence, trying not to appear nervous as he watched the second hand of the clock on the wall behind the desk complete a full minute.

'Malik,' the Commissioner eventually said as he looked up from the papers on his desk, 'I've just been reading your supervisor's annual report.'

Malik remained silent, although he could feel a bead of sweat trickling down his nose.

The Commissioner looked back down again. 'He's very complimentary about your work,' said Kumar, 'full of praise. Far better than I could have hoped for when you sat in that chair just a year ago.' The Commissioner looked up and smiled. 'In fact, he's recommending that you should be promoted.'

'Promoted?' said Malik in disbelief.

'Yes, though it may not prove that easy, as there are not too many appropriate jobs available at the present time. However, I do believe I have come across a position that is ideally suited for your particular talents.'

'Oh, thank you, sir,' said Malik, relaxing for the first time.

'There is a vacancy –' the Commissioner opened another file and smiled – 'for an assistant in the city morgue.' He extracted a single sheet of paper and began reading from it.

'It would be your responsibility to scrub the blood off the slabs and clean the floor immediately after the bodies have been dissected and stored away. I'm told the stench is not all that pleasant, but a face mask is supplied, and I have no doubt that, in time, one gets used to it.' He continued to smile at Malik. 'The appointment comes with the rank of sub-supervisor, along with a corresponding rise in salary. It also has other perks, not least that you would have your own room directly above the morgue, so you wouldn't have to bed down any longer at the YMCA.' The Commissioner paused. 'And, should you continue to hold the post until your sixtieth birthday, you would also be entitled to a modest pension.' The Commissioner closed Malik's file and looked directly at him. 'Any questions?' he asked.

'Only one, sir,' said Malik. 'Is there any alternative?'

'Oh, yes,' replied the Commissioner. 'You can spend the rest of your life in jail.'

In The Eye Of The Beholder

OTHER THAN THE FACT that they had been to school together, the two of them had little in common.

Gian Lorenzo Venici had been a diligent child since his first roll call at the age of five, whereas Paolo Castelli somehow managed always to be late, even for his first roll call.

Gian Lorenzo felt at home in the classroom with books, essays and exams, where he outshone his contemporaries. Paolo achieved the same results on the football field, with a change of pace, a deceptive turn and a shot at goal which beguiled his own team as well as the opposition. Both young men progressed to St Cecilia's, the most prestigious high school in Rome, where they were able to display their talents to a wider audience.

When their school days were over, they both graduated to Roma: Gian Lorenzo to the nation's oldest university as a scholar, Paolo to the nation's oldest football club as a striker. Although they didn't mix in the same circles, they were both well aware of the other's achievements. While Gian Lorenzo collected honours in one field, Paolo won them on another, both achieving their goals.

After leaving university, Gian Lorenzo joined his father at the Venici Gallery. He immediately set about converting those years of study into something more practical, as he wished to emulate his father and become the most respected art dealer in Italy.

By the time Gian Lorenzo had began his apprenticeship, Paolo had been appointed captain of Roma. With the cheers and adulation of the fans ringing in his ears, he led them to championship and European glory. Gian Lorenzo only had to turn to the back pages of any newspaper, on an almost daily basis, to follow the exploits of his former classmate, and to the gossip columns to discover who was the latest beauty to be found dangling from his arm: another difference between them.

Gian Lorenzo quickly discovered that in his chosen profession long-term reputation would be built not on the occasional inspired goal, but on hours of dedicated research, combined with good judgement. He had inherited from his father the two most important gifts in any art dealer's armoury – a good eye and a good nose. Antonio Venici also taught his son not only how to look, but *where* to look, when searching for a masterpiece. The old man only dealt in the finest examples of Renaissance painting and sculpture, which would never appear on the open market. Unless a piece was exclusive, Antonio didn't venture out of his gallery. His son followed in his footsteps. The gallery bought and sold only three, perhaps four, paintings a year, but those masters changed hands at around the same price as one of Roma's strikers. After forty years in the business, Gian Lorenzo's father knew not only who possessed the great collections, but more important, who might be willing or, better still, needed to part with the occasional masterpiece.

Gian Lorenzo became so engrossed in his work that he missed the injury Paolo Castelli sustained while playing for Italy against Spain in the European Cup. This personal setback placed Paolo on the sidelines of the football field, as well as the newspapers, especially when it became clear that he had reached his sell-by date.

Paolo left the world stage just as Gian Lorenzo strode onto it. He began to travel around Europe representing the gallery in an endless quest to seek out only the rarest examples of genius, and, having acquired a masterpiece, to find someone who could afford to purchase it.

Gian Lorenzo often wondered what had become of Paolo since he'd stopped playing football and the press no longer reported his every move. He was to discover overnight when Paolo announced his engagement.

Paolo's choice of marriage partner ensured that his exploits were transferred from the back pages to the front.

Angelina Porcelli was the only daughter of Massimo Porcelli, president of Roma Football Club and chairman of Ulitox, the largest pharmaceutical company in Italy. *A marriage of two heavyweights*, declared the banner headline in one of the tabloids.

Gian Lorenzo turned to page three to discover what merited such a comment. Paolo's bride-to-be was six foot two – an advantage for a model, I hear you say – but there the comparison ended, because the other vital statistic the reporters latched on to was Angelina's weight. This seemed to vary between three hundred and three hundred and fifty pounds, according to whether it was reported by a broadsheet or a tabloid.

A picture is worth a thousand words. Gian Lorenzo studied several photographs of Angelina, and concluded that only Rubens would have considered her as a model. In every picture of Paolo's future bride, no amount of skill displayed by the couturiers of Milan, the stylists of Paris, the jewellers of London, not to mention the legions of personal trainers, dietitians and masseurs, was able to transform her image from sugar plum fairy to prima ballerina. Whichever angle the photographers took, however considerate they tried to be, and some didn't, they only emphasized the transparent difference between her and her fiancé, especially when she stood alongside Roma's former hero. The Italian press, clearly obsessed by Angelina's size, reported nothing else about her of any interest.

Gian Lorenzo turned to the arts pages, and had quite forgotten about Paolo and his future bride when he strode into the gallery later that morning. As he opened the door to his office, he was greeted by his secretary, who thrust a large, gold-embossed card into his hand. Gian Lorenzo glanced down at the invitation.

> *Signor Massimo Porcelli*
> *has pleasure in inviting*
>
> *Gian Lorenzo Venici*
>
> *to the marriage of his daughter,*
> *Angelina,*
> *to Signor Paolo Castelli*
> *at the Villa Borghese.*

Six weeks later Gian Lorenzo joined a thousand guests in the grounds of the Villa Borghese. It soon became clear that Signor Porcelli was determined his only child would enjoy a wedding that not only she, but everyone else present, would never forget.

The setting in the Borghese Gardens, perched on one of the seven hills overlooking Rome, with its imposing terracotta and cream villa in the background, was the stuff of fairytales. Gian Lorenzo strolled around the grounds, admiring the sculptures and fountains while catching up with old friends and contemporaries, some of whom he had not seen since his school days. Some twenty minutes before the ceremony was due to take place, a dozen liveried ushers, in long blue coats trimmed with gold braid and wearing white wigs, moved among the throng. They invited the guests to take their seats in the rose garden as the wedding ceremony was about to commence.

Gian Lorenzo joined a large crowd as they made their way towards a recently constructed stand with an elevated semi-circle of seats surrounding a raised stage with an altar as its centrepiece; not unlike a football ground where a different form of worship takes place on a Saturday afternoon. His connoisseur's eye took in the magnificent view over Rome, a scene made even more dazzling by the number of beautiful women, dressed in clothes that he suspected had never been worn before, and in some cases would never be worn again. They were complemented by elegantly dressed men in tailcoats and white shirts, with only different coloured ties and cravats to suggest the peacock in them. Gian Lorenzo looked around to find that he was surrounded by leading politicians, captains of industry, actors, socialites, as well as many of Paolo's old team-mates.

The next actor to take his place on the stage was Paolo himself, accompanied by his best man. Gian Lorenzo knew he was a well-known footballer, but couldn't recall his name. As Paolo strode down the grass path and onto the pitch, Gian Lorenzo understood only too well why women could not take their eyes off the man. Paolo walked up onto the stage, took his place on the right of the altar and waited to be joined by his bride.

A forty-piece string orchestra, almost hidden among the trees behind the altar, struck up the opening chords of Mendelssohn's Wedding March. A thousand guests rose from their seats and turned to see the bride as she progressed slowly up the thick grass carpet on the arm of her proud father.

'What a beautiful dress,' said the lady standing in front of Gian Lorenzo. He nodded his agreement and, staring at the yards of Persian silk that formed a magnificent train behind Angelina, didn't express the one thought that must have been on everyone's mind. Nevertheless, the look on

Angelina's face was that of a bride displaying total content-ment with her lot. She was walking towards the man she adored, aware that many of the women present would have been only too happy to take her place.

As Angelina climbed the steps up onto the stage, the boards creaked. Her future husband smiled as he took a pace forward to join his bride. They both turned to face Cardinal Montagni, the Archbishop of Naples. One or two guests failed to stifle a smile when the cardinal turned to Paolo and enquired, 'Do you take this woman to be your lawful wedded wife, for better for worse, for richer for poorer . . .'

Once bride and groom had been joined together in holy matrimony, Gian Lorenzo made his way to the Long Garden, to join a thousand other guests for dinner. A feast followed that began with champagne and truffle risotto, and ended with chocolate soufflé and a Chateau d'Yquem. Gian Lorenzo could barely move by the time Paolo rose to reply to his best man's speech.

'I am the happiest man on earth,' he declared, as he turned to face his beaming bride. 'I have found the ideal woman for me, and I am only too aware that I must be the envy of every bachelor present.' A sentiment which Gian Lorenzo could not quite agree with, but he quickly banished the ungracious thought from his mind. Paolo continued, 'You know, I was the first suitor to win Angelina's heart. No longer will I have to search for the perfect woman because I have found her. Please rise and join me in a toast to Angelina, my little angel.' The gathering rose as one and toasted, 'Angelina.' One or two even managed 'his little angel'.

After the speeches were over, the dancing began to yet another band – this time one that had been flown in from

New Orleans. Gian Lorenzo overheard that Angelina had once mentioned to Papa that she liked jazz.

As the band struck up and the champagne continued to flow, the newlyweds moved among their guests, which gave Gian Lorenzo a fleeting moment to thank Paolo and his bride for including him in such an unforgettable occasion. 'Medici would have swooned,' he told her, as he kissed her hand. She gave him a warm, gentle smile, but didn't respond.

'Let's keep in touch,' suggested Paolo as the two of them drifted away. 'Angelina is fascinated by art, you know, and is thinking of starting her own collection,' were the last words Gian Lorenzo heard, before Paolo moved on to another guest.

Just before the sun rose and breakfast was about to be served, Signor and Signora Castelli set off for the airport, with a thousand hands waving their farewells. They drove out of the grounds of the Borghese with Paolo at the wheel of his latest Ferrari – not the ideal car for his bride. When they reached the airport, Paolo drove out onto a private airstrip and brought the car to a halt by the side of a Lear jet that was waiting for two passengers. The newlyweds left the Ferrari parked on the runway, climbed the steps and disappeared inside Papa's aircraft. Within minutes of fastening their seatbelts, the jet took off for Acapulco, the first stop on their three-month honeymoon.

Despite Paolo's parting words, when the Castellis returned from their honeymoon they made no attempt to keep in touch with Gian Lorenzo. However, he was able to follow their exploits on an almost daily basis in the gossip columns of the national press.

A year later he read that they would be moving to Venice, where they had purchased the type of villa that makes the covers, not the inside pages, of glossy magazines. Gian Lorenzo assumed that he and his old friend were unlikely to bump into each other again.

When Antonio Venici retired, he happily handed over the responsibility for the family business to his son. As the new owner of the Venici Gallery, Gian Lorenzo spent half his time travelling around Europe in search of that elusive painting which makes collectors gasp, while not insulting the dealer with any suggestion of bargaining.

One such journey was to Venice, to view a Canaletto owned by the Contessa di Palma – a lady who, having divorced her third husband and sadly no longer possessing the looks to guarantee a fourth, had decided she would have to part with one or two of her treasures. The Contessa's only stipulation was that no one must discover that she was facing temporary financial difficulties. Every leading dealer in Italy knew of her mounting debts and unpaid creditors. Gian Lorenzo was only thankful that the Contessa had chosen him to share her confidences with.

Gian Lorenzo took some time to study the Contessa's considerable collection and concluded that she had an eye not only for rich men. After he had agreed a price for the Canaletto, he expressed the hope that this might be the beginning of a long and fruitful relationship.

'Let's start with dinner at Harry's Bar, my darling,' said the Contessa, once she had Gian Lorenzo's cheque in her hand.

Gian Lorenzo was making up his mind between an affogato or an espresso when Paolo and Angelina strolled into Harry's Bar. Everyone in the room followed their progress, as the maître d' ushered them unctuously to a corner table.

'Now there's someone who can afford to buy my *entire* collection,' whispered the Contessa.

'Without a doubt,' agreed Gian Lorenzo, 'but unfortunately Paolo only collects rare cars.'

'And even rarer women,' interjected the Contessa.

'And I'm not altogether sure what Angelina collects.'

'A few extra pounds each year,' suggested the Contessa. 'She once came to tea with my second husband and literally ate us out of house and home. By the time she left we were down to the water biscuits.'

'Well, let's try and make up for that tonight,' said Gian Lorenzo. 'I'm told the zabaglione is their signature dish?'

The Contessa showed no interest in the zabaglione, but simply sailed on, ignoring her companion's unsubtle hint. 'Can you imagine what those two get up to, when they're in bed?'

Gian Lorenzo was surprised that the Contessa was willing to voice a question he had often thought about but never felt able to express. And there was worse to come as the Contessa went on to describe things that hadn't, until then, even crossed Gian Lorenzo's mind.

'Do you think he climbs on top of her?' Gian Lorenzo didn't offer an opinion. 'A feat in itself,' she continued, 'because if they did it the other way round, surely she'd suffocate him.'

Gian Lorenzo didn't care to think about the image, so he tried once again to change the subject. 'We went to the same school, you know – one hell of an athlete.'

'You'd have to be, to satisfy her.'

'I even attended their wedding,' he added. 'A truly memorable occasion, though I doubt after all this time that he would even remember I was among the guests.'

'Would you really be willing to spend the rest of your life with such a creature, however much money she had to offer?' asked the Contessa, not paying attention to her host's words.

'He claims to adore her,' said Gian Lorenzo, 'calls her his little angel.'

'In that case, I wouldn't want to meet up with his idea of a big angel.'

'But if he felt otherwise,' suggested Gian Lorenzo, 'he could always divorce her.'

'Not a chance,' said the Contessa. 'You clearly haven't been told about their pre-nuptial agreement.'

'No, I haven't,' admitted Gian Lorenzo, trying not to sound interested.

'Her father had much the same opinion of that clapped-out footballer as I do. Old man Porcelli made him sign an agreement which spelt out that if Paolo ever divorced his daughter he would end up with nothing. Paolo was also forced to sign a second document stating that he would never reveal the contents of the pre-nuptial to anyone, including Angelina.'

'Then how do you know about it?' prompted Gian Lorenzo.

'When you've signed as many pre-nuptials as I have, darling, you hear things.'

Gian Lorenzo laughed and called for the bill.

The maître d' smiled. 'It's already been taken care of, signor,' he said, nodding in the direction of Paolo, 'by your old school friend.'

'How kind of him,' said Gian Lorenzo.

'No, her,' the Contessa reminded him.

'Please excuse me for a moment,' said Gian Lorenzo.

'I must just thank them before we leave.' He rose from his place, and made his way slowly across the crowded room.

'How are you?' said Paolo, who was on his feet long before Gian Lorenzo had reached their table. 'You know my little angel, of course,' he said, turning to smile at his wife, 'but then how could you ever forget?'

Gian Lorenzo took Angelina's hand and kissed it gently. 'And I will also never forget your magnificent wedding.'

'Medici would have swooned,' said Angelina.

Gian Lorenzo gave a slight bow in acknowledgement.

'Is that the Contessa di Palma you are dining with?' asked Paolo. 'Because if it is, she has something my little angel desires.' Gian Lorenzo made no comment. 'I do hope, Gian Lorenzo, that she's a client, not a friend, because if my little angel wants something, then I will stop at nothing to ensure she gets it.' Gian Lorenzo still considered it wise to remain silent. Never forget, his father had once told him, only restaurateurs close deals in restaurants – when they hand you the bill. 'And as it's a field I know little about,' continued Paolo, 'and you are acknowledged as one of the nation's leading authorities, perhaps you would be kind enough to represent Angelina on this occasion?'

'I would be delighted to do so,' said Gian Lorenzo, as the head waiter placed a chocolate trifle in front of Paolo's wife, with a bowl of crème fraîche on the side.

'Excellent,' said Paolo, 'let's keep in touch.'

Gian Lorenzo smiled and shook his old friend by the hand. He well remembered the last occasion Paolo had made such an offer. But then some people consider such suggestions nothing more than polite conversation. Gian Lorenzo turned to Angelina and bowed low before walking back across the restaurant to rejoin the Contessa.

'Time for us to leave, I fear,' said Gian Lorenzo, glancing at his watch, 'especially if I'm to catch the first plane to Rome in the morning.'

'Did you manage to sell my Canaletto to your friend?' asked the Contessa, as she rose from her place.

'No,' replied Gian Lorenzo, as he waved in the direction of Paolo's table, 'but he did suggest that we keep in touch.'

'And will you?'

'That might be quite difficult,' admitted Gian Lorenzo, 'as he didn't give me his number, and I have a feeling Signor and Signora Castelli may not be listed.'

Gian Lorenzo took the first flight back to Rome the following morning. The Canaletto was to follow him at a more leisurely pace. No sooner had he set foot in the gallery than his secretary rushed out of the office, spilling out the words, 'Paolo Castelli has already called twice this morning. He apologized for not giving you his number,' she added, 'and wondered if you would be kind enough to phone him, just as soon as you get in.'

Gian Lorenzo walked calmly into his office, sat down at his desk and composed himself. He then tapped out the number his secretary had placed in front of him. The call was first answered by a butler, who transferred him to a secretary, before he was finally connected to Paolo.

'After you left last night, my little angel spoke of nothing else,' began Paolo. 'She has never forgotten her visit to the Contessa's home, where she first saw her magnificent art collection. She wondered if the reason you were meeting with the Contessa was—'

'I don't think it would be wise to discuss this matter over the phone,' said Gian Lorenzo, whose father had also taught him that deals are rarely made on the telephone, but almost always face to face. One needs the client to view the picture, and then you allow them to hang it on a wall in their home for several days. There is a crucial moment when the buyer considers the painting already belongs to them. Not until then do you start to negotiate the price.

'Then you'll have to return to Venice,' said Paolo matter-of-factly. 'I'll send the private jet.'

Gian Lorenzo flew to Venice the following Friday. A Rolls-Royce was parked on the runway, waiting to take him to the Villa Rosa.

A butler greeted Gian Lorenzo at the front door before escorting him up a large marble staircase to a suite of private rooms that exhibited barren walls – an art dealer's fantasy. Gian Lorenzo was reminded of the collection that his father had put together for Agnelli over a period of thirty years, now considered to be one of the finest in private hands.

Gian Lorenzo spent most of the Saturday – between meals – being escorted round the one hundred and forty-two rooms of the Villa Rosa by Angelina. He quickly discovered that there was far more to his hostess than he had anticipated.

Angelina showed a genuine interest in wanting to start her own art collection, and had clearly visited all the great galleries round the world. Gian Lorenzo concluded that she only lacked the courage of her own convictions – a not uncommon problem for the only child of a self-made man – although she didn't lack knowledge or, to Gian Lorenzo's surprise, taste. He felt guilty for making assumptions based only on comments he had read in the press. Gian Lorenzo found himself enjoying Angelina's company, and even began to wonder what this shy, thoughtful young woman could possibly see in Paolo.

Over dinner that night, Gian Lorenzo could not miss the adoration in her eyes whenever Angelina looked at her husband, even though she rarely interrupted him.

Over breakfast the following morning, Angelina hardly uttered a word. It was not until Paolo suggested that his wife show their guest round the grounds that his little angel once again came alive.

Angelina escorted Gian Lorenzo round a sixty-acre garden that possessed no immovable objects, or even havens where they might rest to cool their brows. Whenever Gian Lorenzo made a suggestion, she responded with enthusiasm, clearly willing to be led, if only he would take her by the hand.

Over dinner that night, it was Paolo who confirmed that it was his little angel's desire to build a great collection in memory of her late father.

'But where to begin?' asked Paolo, stretching a hand across the table to take his wife's hand.

'Canaletto, perhaps?' suggested Gian Lorenzo.

Gian Lorenzo spent the next five years commuting between Rome and Venice as he continued to coax pictures out of the Contessa, before rehanging them in the Villa Rosa. But as each new gem appeared, Angelina's appetite only became more voracious. Gian Lorenzo found himself having to travel as far afield as America, Russia and even Colombia, so that he could keep Paolo's 'little angel' satisfied. She seemed determined to outdo Catherine the Great.

Angelina became more and more captivated by each new masterpiece Gian Lorenzo put before her – Canaletto, Caravaggio, Tintoretto, Bellini and Da Vinci were among the natives. Not only did Gian Lorenzo begin to fill up the few remaining places on the walls of the villa, but he also had statues crated and sent from every quarter of the globe to be sited alongside other immigrants on the vast lawn – Moore, Brancusi, Epstein, Miró, Giacometti and, Angelina's favourite, Botero.

With every new purchase she made, Gian Lorenzo presented her with a book about the artist. Angelina would devour them in one sitting and immediately demand more. Gian Lorenzo had to acknowledge that she had become not only the gallery's most important client but also his most ardent student – what had begun as a flirtation with Canaletto was fast turning into a promiscuous affair with almost all the great masters of Europe. And it was

Gian Lorenzo who was expected to continually supply new lovers. Something else Angelina had in common with Catherine the Great.

Gian Lorenzo was visiting a client in Barcelona, who for tax reasons had to dispose of a Murillo, *The Birth of Christ*, when he heard the news. He considered that the asking price for the painting was too high, even though he knew that Angelina would be willing to pay it. He was in the middle of haggling when his secretary called. Gian Lorenzo took the next available flight back to Rome.

Every paper reported, some in great detail, the death of Angelina Castelli. A massive heart attack while she was in her garden trying to move one of the statues.

The tabloids, unwilling to mourn the lady for a single day, went on to inform their readers in the second paragraph that she had left her entire fortune to her husband. A photograph of a smiling Paolo – taken long before her death – ran alongside the story.

Four days later Gian Lorenzo flew to Venice to attend the funeral.

The little chapel in the grounds of the Villa Rosa was packed with Angelina's family and friends, some of whom Gian Lorenzo hadn't seen since the wedding celebration, a generation before.

When the six pallbearers carried the coffin into the chapel, and lowered it gently on a bier in front of the altar, Paolo broke down and sobbed. After the service was over, Gian Lorenzo offered his condolences, and Paolo assured him that he had enriched Angelina's life beyond recompense. He went on to say that he intended to continue building the collection in her memory. 'It is no more than my little angel would have wanted,' he explained, 'so it must be done.'

Paolo didn't get in touch with him again.

Gian Lorenzo was about to dip a spoon into a pot of Oxford marmalade – another habit he had acquired from his father – when he saw the headline. The spoon remained lodged in the marmalade while he read the words a second time. He wanted to be sure that he hadn't misunderstood the headline. Paolo was back on the front page, declaring it was 'love at first sight – turn to page 22 for details'.

Gian Lorenzo quickly flicked through the pages to a column he rarely troubled himself with. '*Gossip Roma*, we give you the truth behind the stories.' Paolo Castelli, former captain of Roma, and the ninth richest man in Italy, is to marry again, only four years after the death of his little angel. 'There's more to her than meets the eye,' declared the headline. The paper went on to assure its readers that there couldn't be a bigger contrast between his first wife, Angelina, a billionairess, and Gina, a twenty-four-year-old waitress from Naples, and the daughter of a tax inspector.

Gian Lorenzo chuckled when he saw Gina's photograph, aware that many of Paolo's friends wouldn't be able to resist teasing him.

Every morning Gian Lorenzo found himself turning to *Gossip Roma*, in the hope of learning some new titbit about the forthcoming marriage. The wedding, it seemed, would be held in the chapel of the Villa Rosa, which only had enough space to seat a mere two hundred, so the guests would be restricted to close family and friends. The bride could no longer leave her little home without being pursued by a legion of paparazzi. The groom, they informed their readers, had returned to the gym, in the hope of losing a few pounds before the ceremony took place. But the biggest surprise for Gian Lorenzo came when *Gossip Roma* claimed – in an exclusive – that Signor Gian Lorenzo Venici, Roma's leading art dealer, and old school chum of Paolo, would be among the fortunate guests.

An invitation arrived in the morning post the following day.

Gian Lorenzo flew into Venice on the evening before the ceremony and checked into the Hotel Cipriani. He decided a light meal and an early night might perhaps be wise when he thought about the previous wedding.

Gian Lorenzo rose early the following morning and took some time dressing for the occasion. Despite this, he still arrived at the Villa Rosa long before the service was due to commence. He wished to stroll among the statues that littered the lawn and become reacquainted with some old friends. Donatello smiled down on him. Moore looked regal. Miró made him laugh, and Giacometti stood tall and thin, but his favourite remained the fountain which graced the centre of the lawn. Ten years before he had removed each piece of the fountain, stone by stone, statue by statue, from a courtyard in Milan. Bellini's *The Escaping Hunter* looked even more magnificent in its new surroundings. It gave Gian Lorenzo particular pleasure to see how many other guests had also arrived early, clearly with the same thought in mind.

A single usher in a smart dark suit walked among the guests suggesting that they might like to make their way to the chapel as the ceremony was about to begin. Gian Lorenzo was one of the first to heed his advice, as he wanted to be well placed to watch the bride make her entrance.

Gian Lorenzo found a vacant seat on the aisle about halfway back that would allow him an uninterrupted view of the proceedings. He could see the little choir in their stalls, already singing vespers accompanied by a string quartet.

At five minutes to three Paolo and his best man entered the chapel and walked slowly down the aisle. Gian Lorenzo knew he'd been a well-known footballer, but he still couldn't remember his name. They both took their places by the side of the altar, while Paolo waited for his young bride to appear. Paolo looked fit, tanned and trim, and Gian Lorenzo noted that women still stared at him with adoring eyes. Paolo didn't notice them and a grin that would have excited comment from Lewis Carroll never left the bride-groom's face.

There was a buzz of expectation as the string quartet

struck up the opening chords of the Wedding March, to herald the entrance of the bride. The young woman walked slowly down the aisle on the arm of her father, and drew intakes of breath as she passed each new row.

Gian Lorenzo could hear her approaching, so he turned to look at Gina for the first time. How would he respond, when asked to describe the bride, to someone who hadn't been invited to the ceremony? Should he emphasize her beautiful long, thick, raven hair, or possibly comment on the smooth olive texture of her skin, or even add some remark about the magnificent wedding dress that he remembered so well? Or would Gian Lorenzo simply tell all those who enquired that it had become immediately clear to him why Paolo had declared that it was love at first sight. The same shy smile as Angelina, the same bright enthusiastic twinkle in her eyes, the same gentleness that was clear for all to see, or was it, as Gian Lorenzo suspected, that the journalists would only report that she fitted snugly into Angelina's old wedding dress – the yards and yards of silk forming a magnificent train behind the bride as she walked slowly towards her lover.

The End